THE BEST OF
ARCHIE COMICS

STARRING

Betty &
Veronica

BOOK TWO

WRITTEN BY:

Dan DeCarlo, Angelo DeCesare, Frank Doyle, George Frese,
Ed Goggin, George Gladir, Michael Grassi, Adam Hughes,
Sam Kujava, Dick Malmgren, Al McLean, Dan Parent, Mike Pellowski,
Adam Philips, Jamie Lee Rotante, Barbara Slate, Bill Vigoda,
Mark Waid, Kathleen Webb

ART BY:

Bob Bolling, Eva Cabrera, Doug Crane, Dan DeCarlo, Dan DeCarlo Jr.,
Jim DeCarlo, Vincent DeCarlo, Rachel Deering, Joe Eisma, Alison Flood,
George Frese, Ed Goggin, Victor Gorelick, Barry Grossman, Clem Harrison,
Adam Hughes, Rich Koslowski, Rudy Lapick, Harry Lucey, Al Milgrom,
Jack Morelli, Dan Parent, Rosario "Tito" Peña, Harry Sahle, Henry Scarpelli,
Samm Schwartz, Jeff Shultz, Pen Shumaker, Bob Smith, Fiona Staples,
Terry Szenics, Andre Szymanowicz, Elaina Unger, Janice Valleau,
Jen Vaughn, Bill Vigoda, José Villarrubia, Glenn Whitmore, John Workman,
Vickie Williams, Bill Yoshida

Published by Archie Comic Publications, Inc. 629 Fifth Avenue, Suite 100, Pelham, NY
10803-1242

Publisher / Co-CEO: **Jon Goldwater**

Co-CEO: **Nancy Silberkleit**

Co-President / Editor-In-Chief: **Victor Gorelick**

Co-President: **Mike Pellerito**

Co-President: **Alex Segura**

Chief Creative Officer: **Roberto Aguirre-Sacasa**

Chief Operating Officer: **William Mooar**

Chief Financial Officer: **Robert Wintle**

Director of Book Sales & Operations: **Jonathan Betancourt**

Production Manager: **Stephen Oswald**

Lead Designer: **Kari McLachlan**

Associate Editor: **Carlos Antunes**

Production: **Rosario "Tito" Peña**

Assistant Editor / Proofreader: **Jamie Lee Rotante**

ArchieComics.com

WELCOME TO THE BEST OF ARCHIE COMICS
STARRING BETTY & VERONICA

Name a more iconic duo than Betty and Veronica—it's nearly impossible! The two BFFs/occasional frenemies have permeated pop culture in such a significant way that people have been comparing themselves to the notable blonde and brunette ladies for decades! Stemming from the early days of Archie Comics, girl-next-door Betty Cooper and wealthy socialite Veronica Lodge have continued to gain recognition over the years—be it through not only comics but also, especially recently, fashion and television. Not only can you read their stories in comics and digests, but you can even dress like Betty and Veronica and watch their adventures together on the smash hit CW TV series *Riverdale*.

Though the two young women have become household names in America and beyond, their roots are still directly tied to comics. In this collection, you'll find over 400 pages of hilarious, entertaining, dramatic, action-packed and fun stories that shine the spotlight on the two best friends. From the girls trying their hands flying airplanes to becoming super spies to leading a motorcycle gang— these ladies have done it all! As an added bonus, you'll also get some insight from some of the wonderful artists, writers and editors who have helped to bring these characters to life. As you read along, we hope you'll encounter some memorable Betty and Veronica stories—or maybe even find some new favorites!

THE BEST OF ARCHIE COMICS STARRING

BETTY & VERONICA

1940s

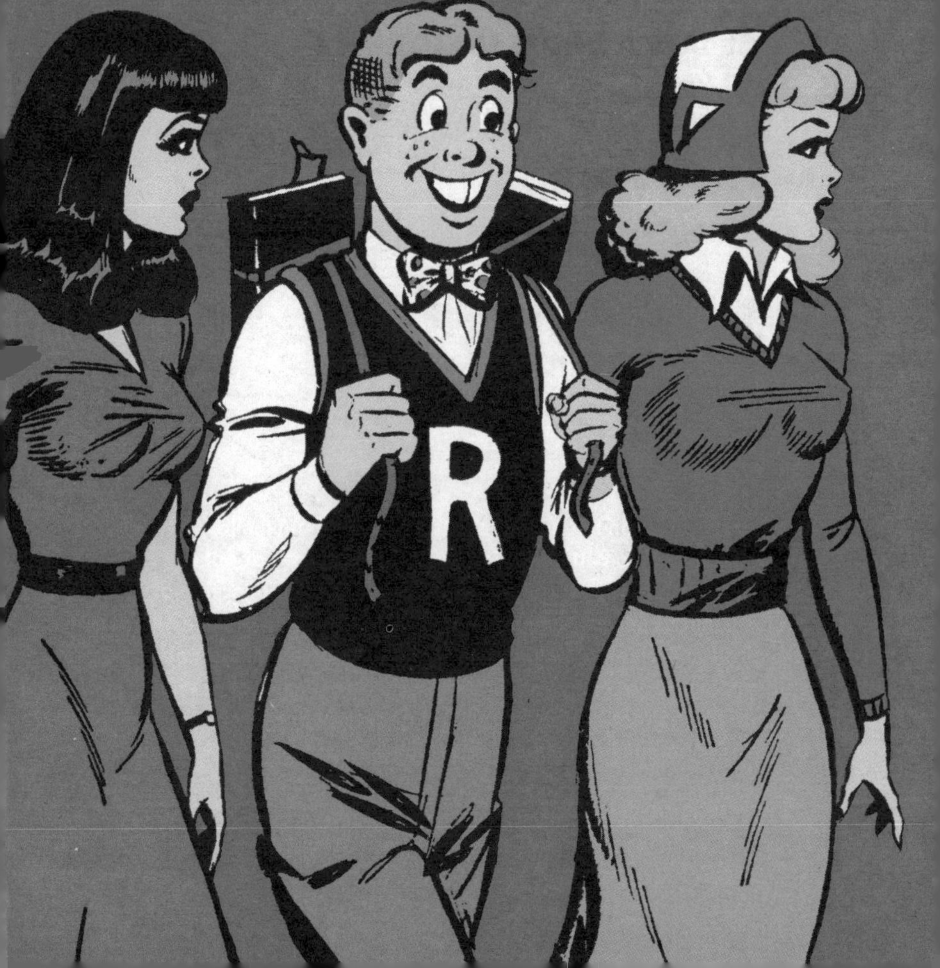
R

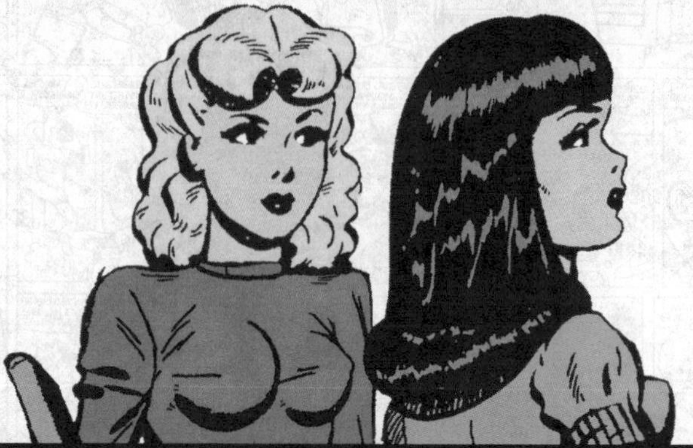

NOMINATE A DRUM MAJORETTE
ARCHIE #6, 1944
Ed Goggin, Harry Sahle, Clem Harrison

AND NOW GIRLS
ARCHIE #9, 1944
Ed Goggin, Janice Valleau

WHY LOOK, NEW NEIGHBORS
ARCHIE #10, 1944
Bill Vigoda

My first introduction to geometry was learning about the love triangle made up of Archie, Betty and Veronica. In fact, that's about as far as I got in Geometry. This triangle has been the foundation of Archie comics since issue number one. The competition between these two girls for Archie's affections is the basis for some funniest and entertaining stories ever written. Now you have a chance to enjoy some of these great stories. So put that geometry book back in your backpack and have some fun reading the best of Betty and Veronica.

- VICTOR GORELICK *Editor-In-Chief, Archie Comics*

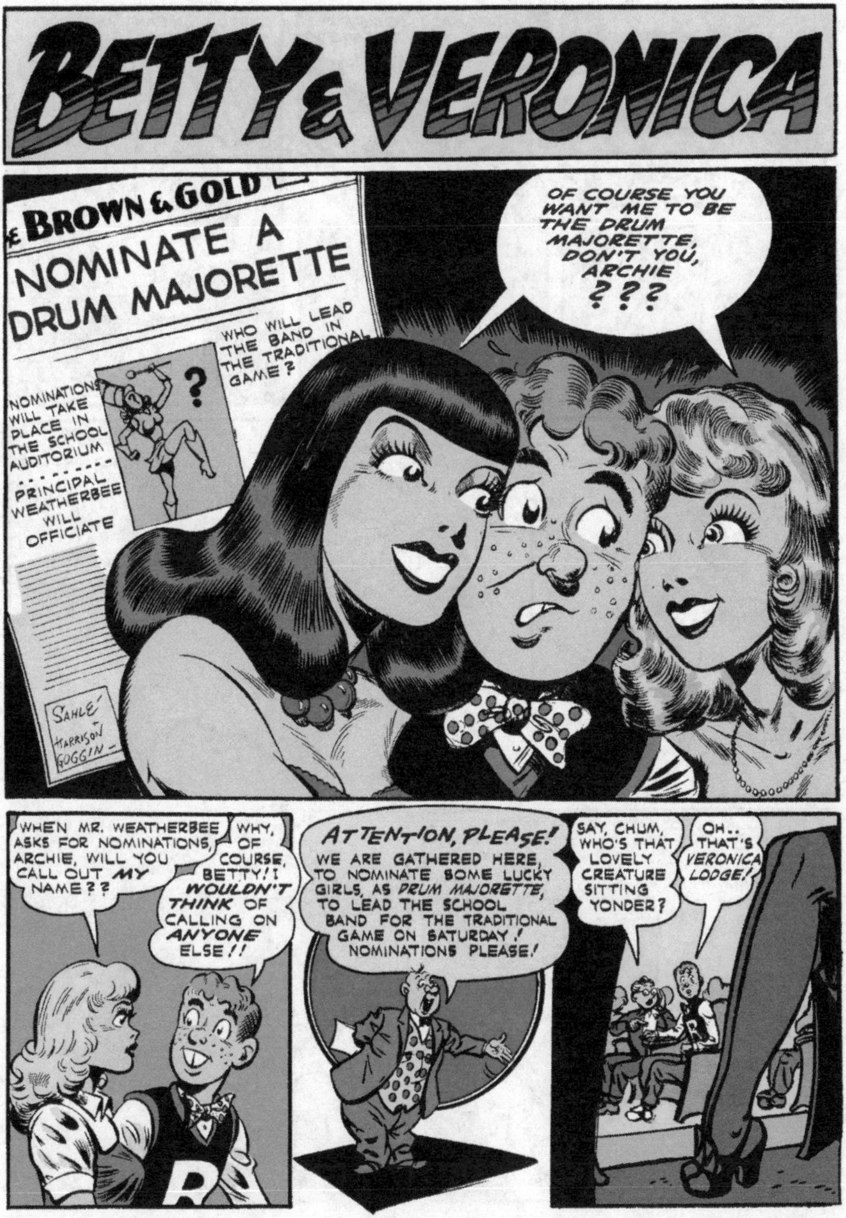
BETTY & VERONICA
BROWN & GOLD
NOMINATE A DRUM MAJORETTE
WHO WILL LEAD THE BAND IN THE TRADITIONAL GAME?
NOMINATIONS WILL TAKE PLACE IN THE SCHOOL AUDITORIUM
PRINCIPAL WEATHERBEE WILL OFFICIATE
?
OF COURSE YOU WANT ME TO BE THE DRUM MAJORETTE, DON'T YOU, ARCHIE ???
SAHLE' + HARRISON GOGGIN
WHEN MR. WEATHERBEE ASKS FOR NOMINATIONS, ARCHIE, WILL YOU CALL OUT MY NAME??
WHY, OF COURSE, BETTY! I WOULDN'T THINK OF CALLING ON ANYONE ELSE!!
ATTENTION, PLEASE! WE ARE GATHERED HERE, TO NOMINATE SOME LUCKY GIRLS, AS DRUM MAJORETTE, TO LEAD THE SCHOOL BAND FOR THE TRADITIONAL GAME ON SATURDAY! NOMINATIONS PLEASE!
SAY, CHUM, WHO'S THAT LOVELY CREATURE SITTING YONDER?
OH.. THAT'S VERONICA LODGE!

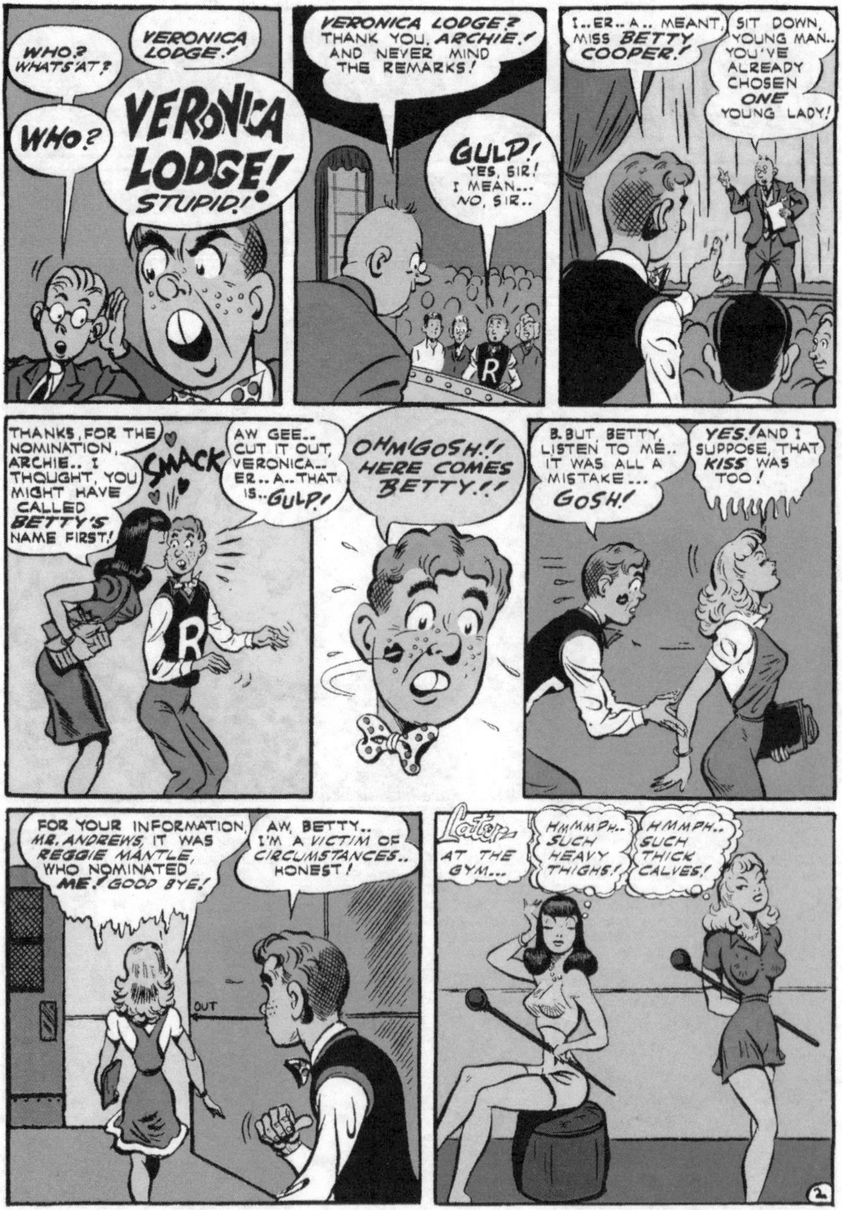
WHO? WHAT'S'AT?
VERONICA LODGE!
WHO?
VERONICA LODGE! STUPID!
VERONICA LODGE? THANK YOU, ARCHIE! AND NEVER MIND THE REMARKS!
GULP! YES, SIR! I MEAN... NO, SIR..
I..ER..A.. MEANT, MISS BETTY COOPER!
SIT DOWN, YOUNG MAN.. YOU'VE ALREADY CHOSEN ONE YOUNG LADY!
THANKS, FOR THE NOMINATION, ARCHIE.. I THOUGHT, YOU MIGHT HAVE CALLED BETTY'S NAME FIRST!
SMACK
AW GEE.. CUT IT OUT, VERONICA... ER.. A.. THAT IS.. GULP!
OHM'GOSH!! HERE COMES BETTY!!
B. BUT, BETTY, LISTEN TO ME.. IT WAS ALL A MISTAKE... GOSH!
YES! AND I SUPPOSE, THAT KISS WAS TOO!
FOR YOUR INFORMATION, MR. ANDREWS, IT WAS REGGIE MANTLE, WHO NOMINATED ME! GOOD BYE!
AW, BETTY.. I'M A VICTIM OF CIRCUMSTANCES.. HONEST!
OUT
Later AT THE GYM...
HMMMPH.. SUCH HEAVY THIGHS!
HMMPH.. SUCH THICK CALVES!
2

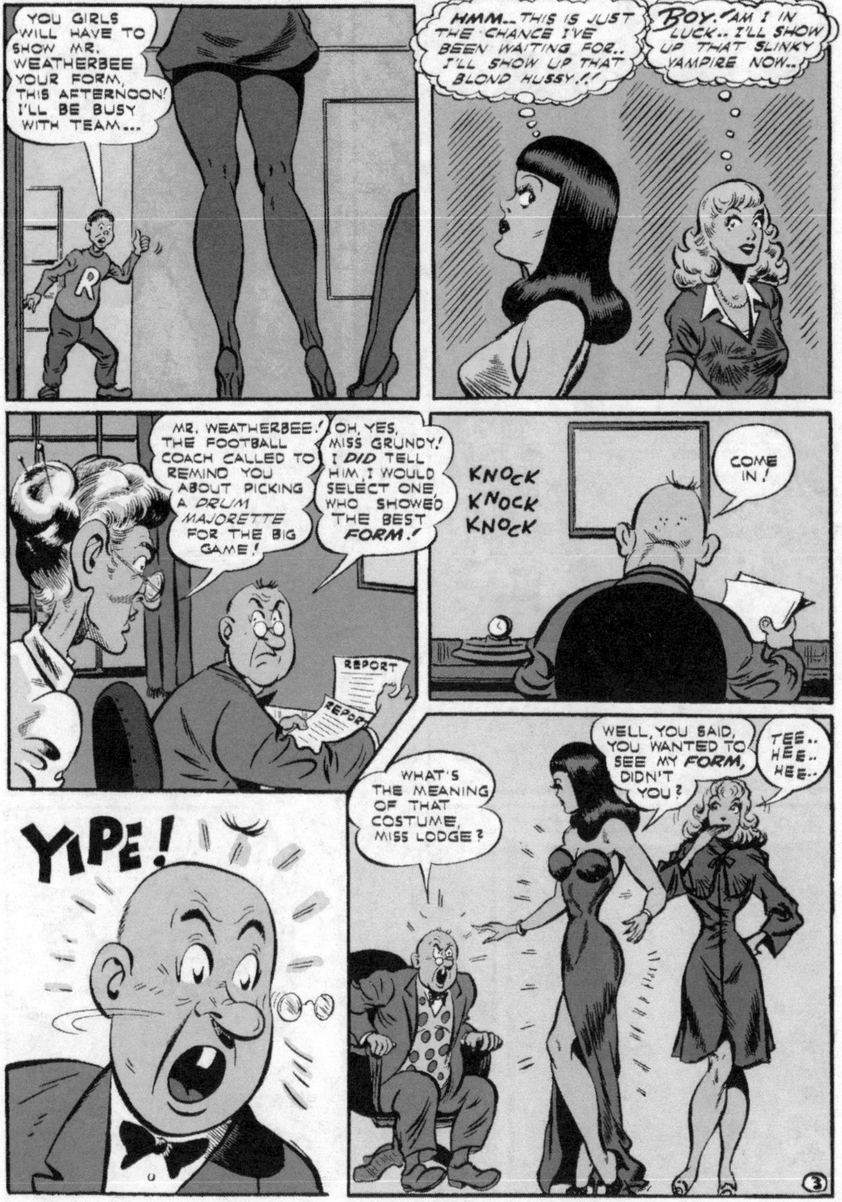

YOU GIRLS WILL HAVE TO SHOW MR. WEATHERBEE YOUR FORM, THIS AFTERNOON! I'LL BE BUSY WITH TEAM...
HMM.. THIS IS JUST THE CHANCE I'VE BEEN WAITING FOR.. I'LL SHOW UP THAT BLOND HUSSY!!
BOY! AM I IN LUCK.. I'LL SHOW UP THAT SLINKY VAMPIRE NOW..
MR. WEATHERBEE! THE FOOTBALL COACH CALLED TO REMIND YOU ABOUT PICKING A DRUM MAJORETTE FOR THE BIG GAME!
OH, YES, MISS GRUNDY! I DID TELL HIM, I WOULD SELECT ONE, WHO SHOWED THE BEST FORM!
REPORT
REPORT
KNOCK KNOCK KNOCK
COME IN!
YIPE!
WHAT'S THE MEANING OF THAT COSTUME, MISS LODGE?
WELL, YOU SAID, YOU WANTED TO SEE MY FORM, DIDN'T YOU?
TEE.. HEE.. HEE..
3

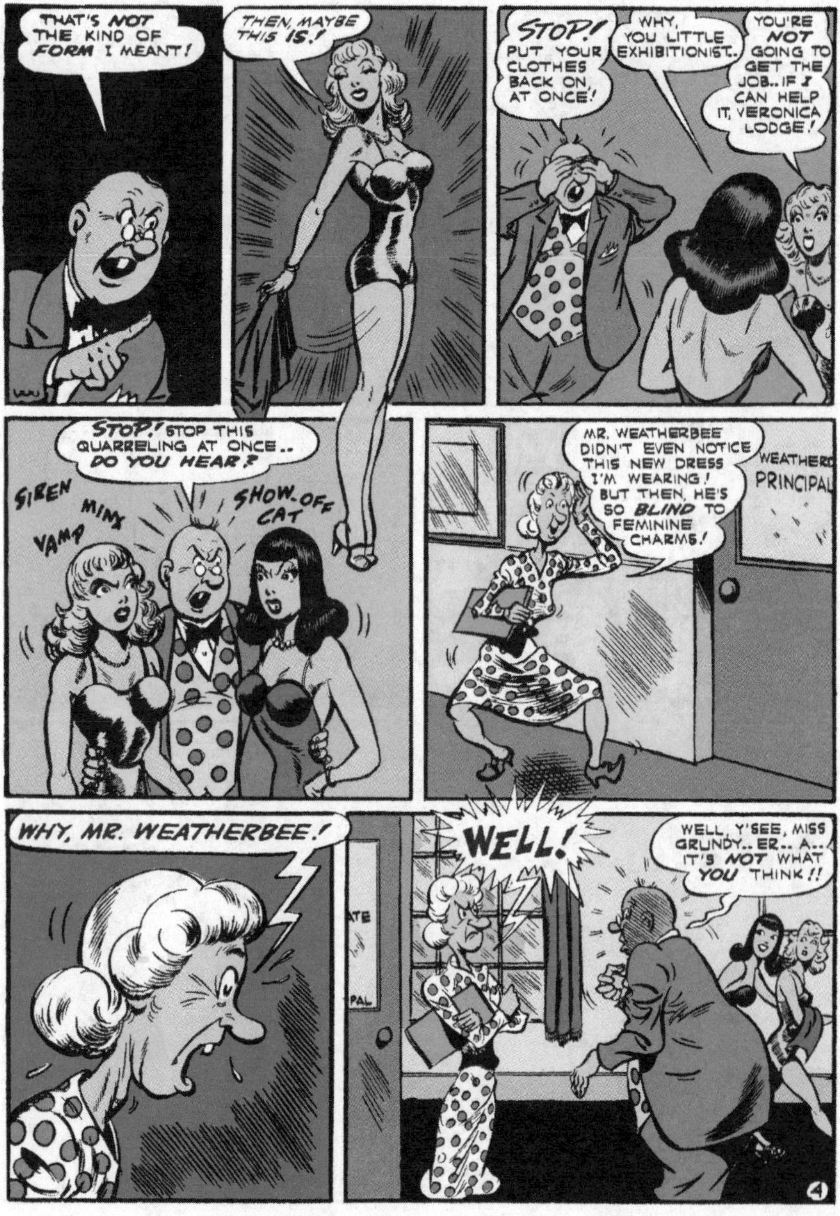

THAT'S NOT THE KIND OF FORM I MEANT!
THEN, MAYBE THIS IS!
STOP! PUT YOUR CLOTHES BACK ON, AT ONCE!
WHY, YOU LITTLE EXHIBITIONIST..
YOU'RE NOT GOING TO GET THE JOB.. IF I CAN HELP IT, VERONICA LODGE!
STOP! STOP THIS QUARRELING AT ONCE.. DO YOU HEAR?
SIREN
MINX
VAMP
SHOW-OFF
CAT
MR. WEATHERBEE DIDN'T EVEN NOTICE THIS NEW DRESS I'M WEARING! BUT THEN, HE'S SO BLIND TO FEMININE CHARMS!
WEATHERB
PRINCIPAL
WHY, MR. WEATHERBEE!
WELL!
WELL, Y'SEE, MISS GRUNDY.. ER.. A.. IT'S NOT WHAT YOU THINK!!
4

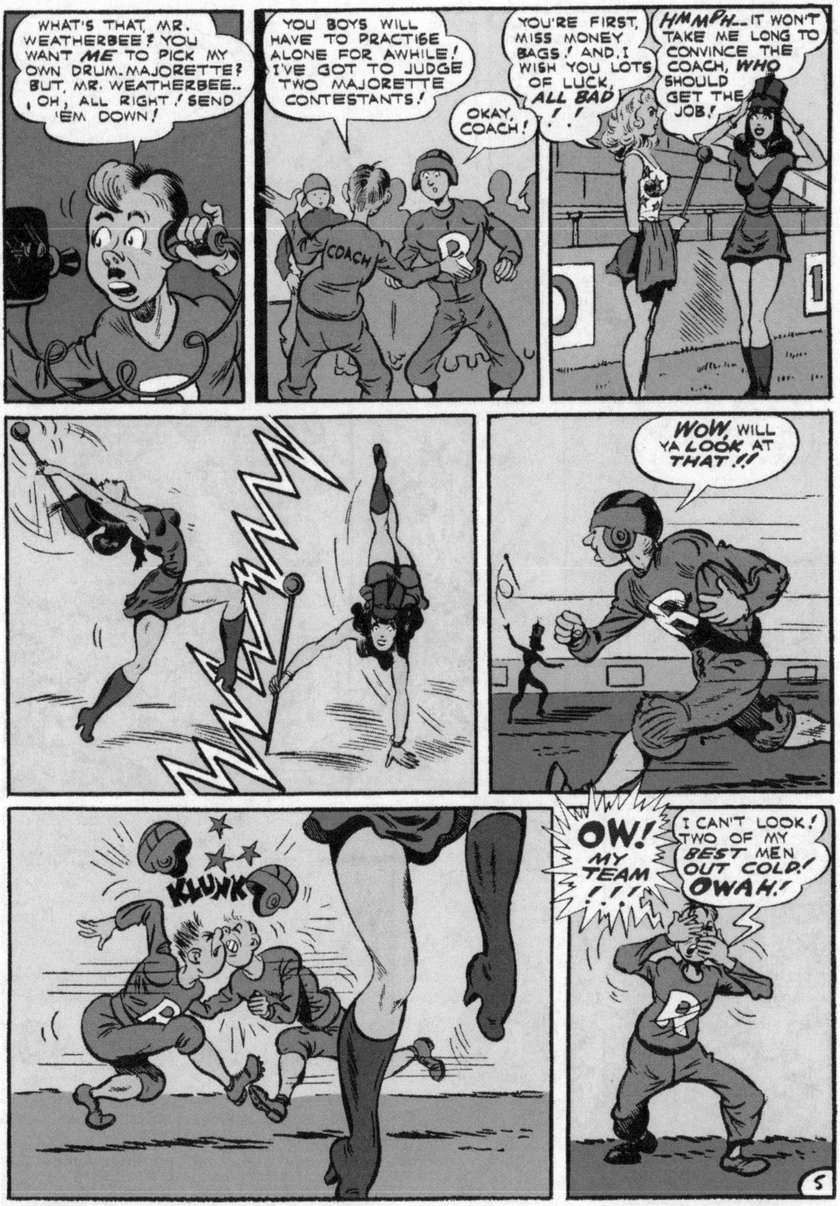
WHAT'S THAT, MR. WEATHERBEE? YOU WANT ME TO PICK MY OWN DRUM-MAJORETTE? BUT, MR. WEATHERBEE.. , OH, ALL RIGHT! SEND 'EM DOWN!
YOU BOYS WILL HAVE TO PRACTISE ALONE FOR AWHILE! I'VE GOT TO JUDGE TWO MAJORETTE CONTESTANTS!
OKAY, COACH!
COACH
YOU'RE FIRST, MISS MONEY BAGS! AND, I WISH YOU LOTS OF LUCK, ALL BAD!!
HMMPH-- IT WON'T TAKE ME LONG TO CONVINCE THE COACH, WHO SHOULD GET THE JOB!
WOW, WILL YA LOOK AT THAT!!
KLUNK
OW! MY TEAM!!!
I CAN'T LOOK! TWO OF MY BEST MEN OUT COLD! OWAH!
5

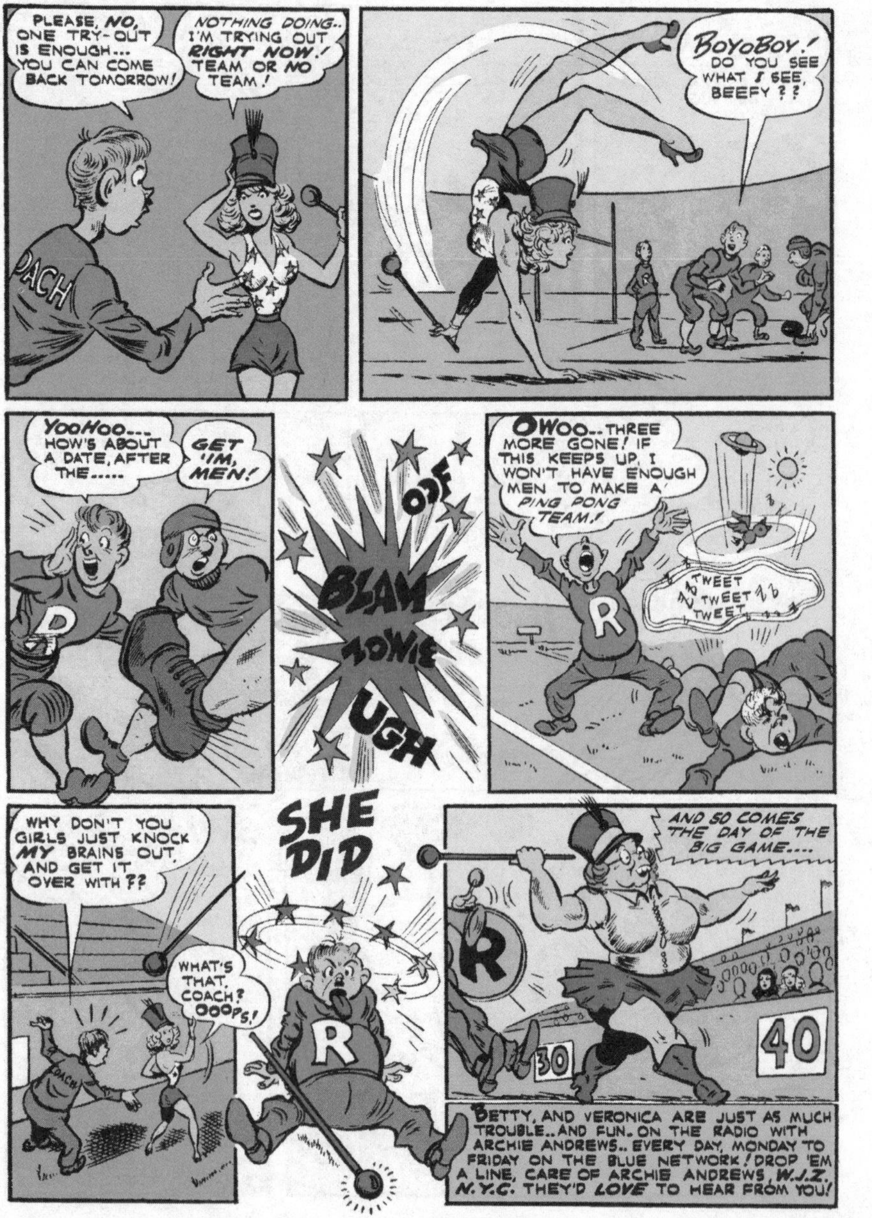
PLEASE, NO, ONE TRY-OUT IS ENOUGH... YOU CAN COME BACK TOMORROW!
NOTHING DOING.. I'M TRYING OUT RIGHT NOW! TEAM OR NO TEAM!
COACH
BOYOBOY! DO YOU SEE WHAT I SEE, BEEFY??
YOOHOO.... HOW'S ABOUT A DATE, AFTER THE.....
GET 'IM, MEN!
OOF
BLAM
ZOWIE
UGH
OWOO-- THREE MORE GONE! IF THIS KEEPS UP, I WON'T HAVE ENOUGH MEN TO MAKE A PING PONG TEAM!
TWEET TWEET TWEET
WHY DON'T YOU GIRLS JUST KNOCK MY BRAINS OUT, AND GET IT OVER WITH??
SHE DID
WHAT'S THAT, COACH? OOOPS!
COACH
AND SO COMES THE DAY OF THE BIG GAME....
30
40
BETTY, AND VERONICA ARE JUST AS MUCH TROUBLE..AND FUN..ON THE RADIO WITH ARCHIE ANDREWS.. EVERY DAY, MONDAY TO FRIDAY ON THE BLUE NETWORK! DROP 'EM A LINE, CARE OF ARCHIE ANDREWS, W.J.Z. N.Y.C. THEY'D LOVE TO HEAR FROM YOU!

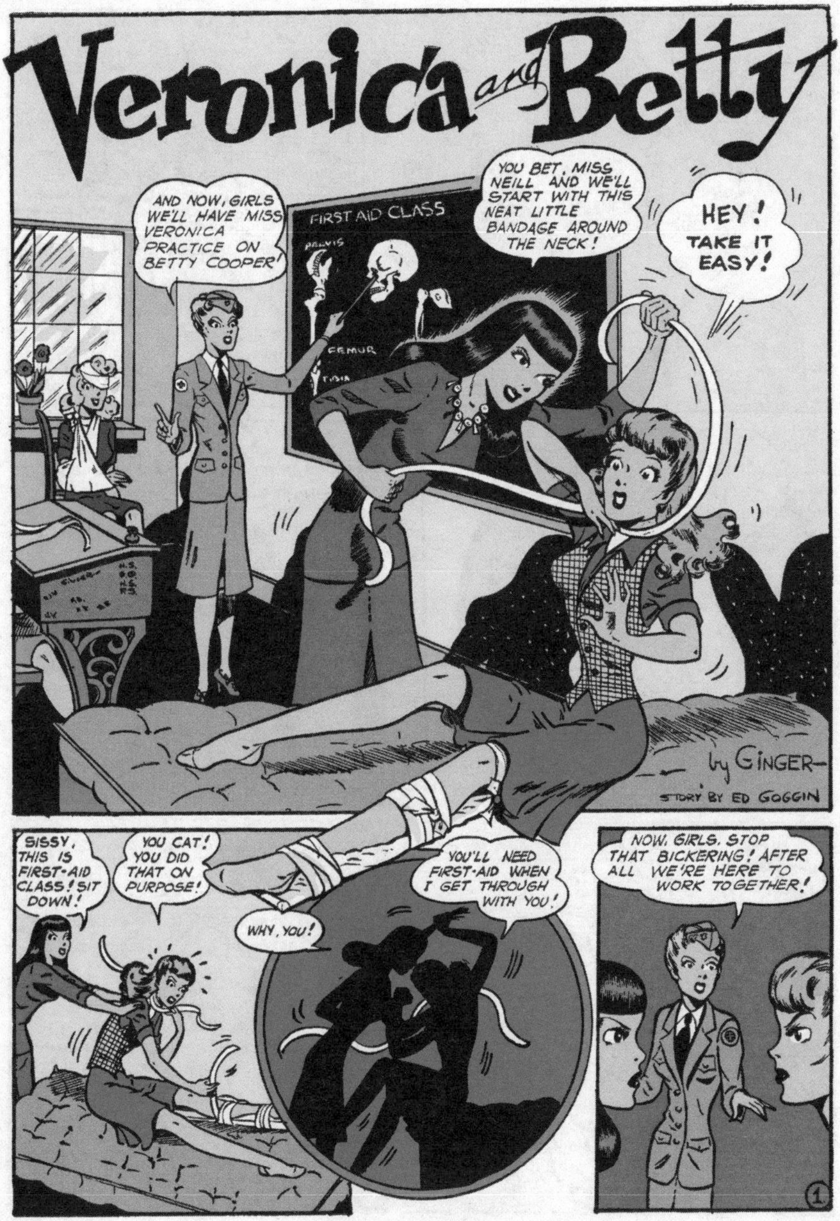
Veronica and Betty
AND NOW, GIRLS WE'LL HAVE MISS VERONICA PRACTICE ON BETTY COOPER!
FIRST AID CLASS
PELVIS
FEMUR
TIBIA
YOU BET, MISS NEILL AND WE'LL START WITH THIS NEAT LITTLE BANDAGE AROUND THE NECK!
HEY! TAKE IT EASY!
by GINGER
STORY BY ED GOGGIN
SISSY, THIS IS FIRST-AID CLASS! SIT DOWN!
YOU CAT! YOU DID THAT ON PURPOSE!
YOU'LL NEED FIRST-AID WHEN I GET THROUGH WITH YOU!
WHY, YOU!
NOW, GIRLS, STOP THAT BICKERING! AFTER ALL WE'RE HERE TO WORK TOGETHER!
1

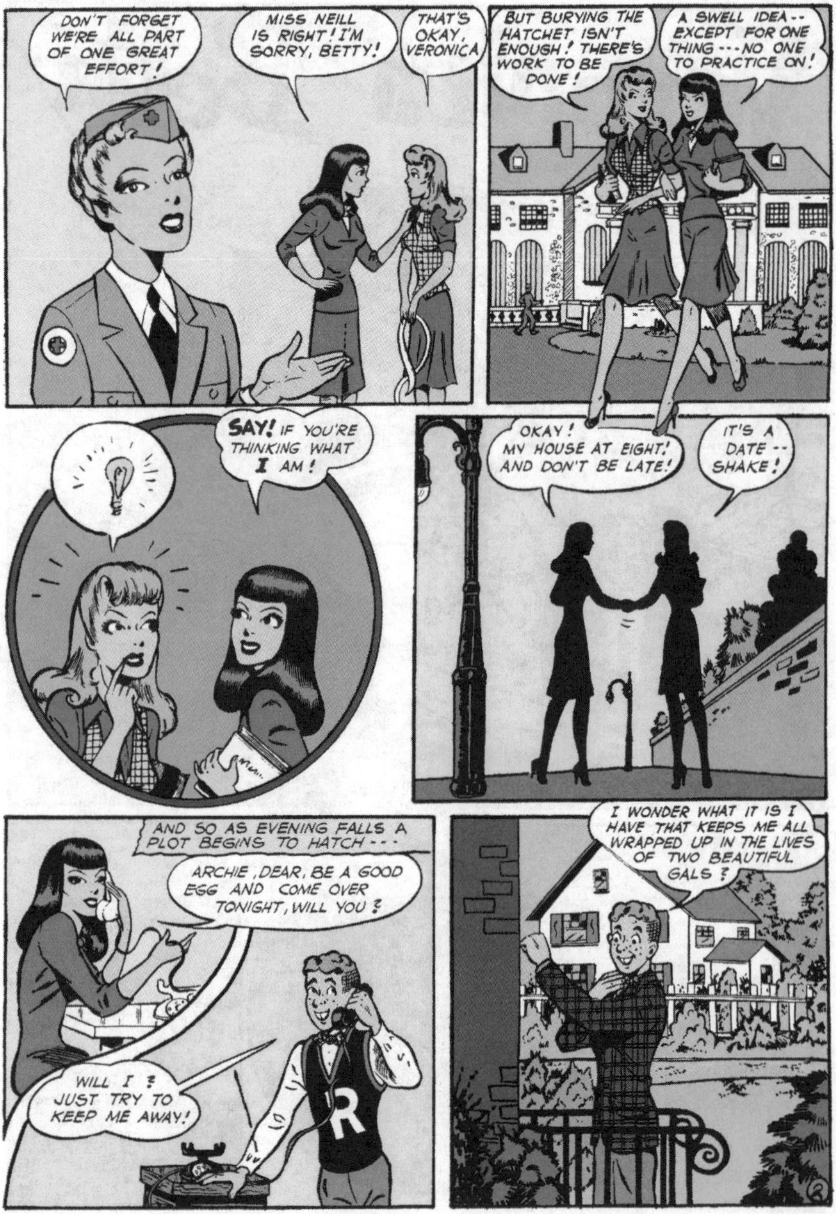
DON'T FORGET WE'RE ALL PART OF ONE GREAT EFFORT!
MISS NEILL IS RIGHT! I'M SORRY, BETTY!
THAT'S OKAY, VERONICA
BUT BURYING THE HATCHET ISN'T ENOUGH! THERE'S WORK TO BE DONE!
A SWELL IDEA -- EXCEPT FOR ONE THING --- NO ONE TO PRACTICE ON!
SAY! IF YOU'RE THINKING WHAT I AM!
OKAY! MY HOUSE AT EIGHT! AND DON'T BE LATE!
IT'S A DATE -- SHAKE!
AND SO AS EVENING FALLS A PLOT BEGINS TO HATCH ---
ARCHIE, DEAR, BE A GOOD EGG AND COME OVER TONIGHT, WILL YOU?
WILL I? JUST TRY TO KEEP ME AWAY!
I WONDER WHAT IT IS I HAVE THAT KEEPS ME ALL WRAPPED UP IN THE LIVES OF TWO BEAUTIFUL GALS?

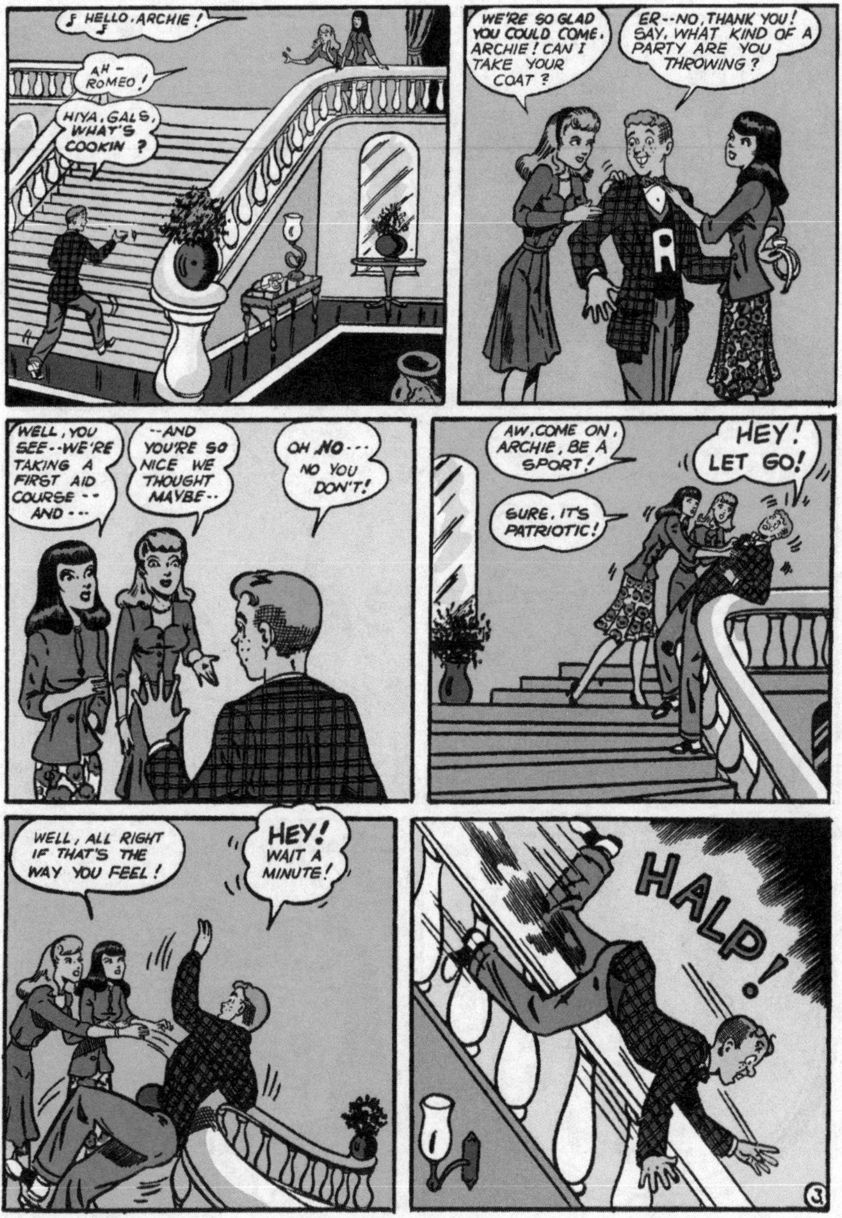
HELLO, ARCHIE!
AH - ROMEO!
HIYA, GALS, WHAT'S COOKIN ?
WE'RE SO GLAD YOU COULD COME, ARCHIE! CAN I TAKE YOUR COAT ?
ER--NO, THANK YOU! SAY, WHAT KIND OF A PARTY ARE YOU THROWING ?
WELL, YOU SEE--WE'RE TAKING A FIRST AID COURSE -- AND ---
--AND YOU'RE SO NICE WE THOUGHT MAYBE--
OH NO--- NO YOU DON'T!
AW, COME ON, ARCHIE, BE A SPORT!
HEY! LET GO!
SURE, IT'S PATRIOTIC!
WELL, ALL RIGHT IF THAT'S THE WAY YOU FEEL!
HEY! WAIT A MINUTE!
HALP!
3

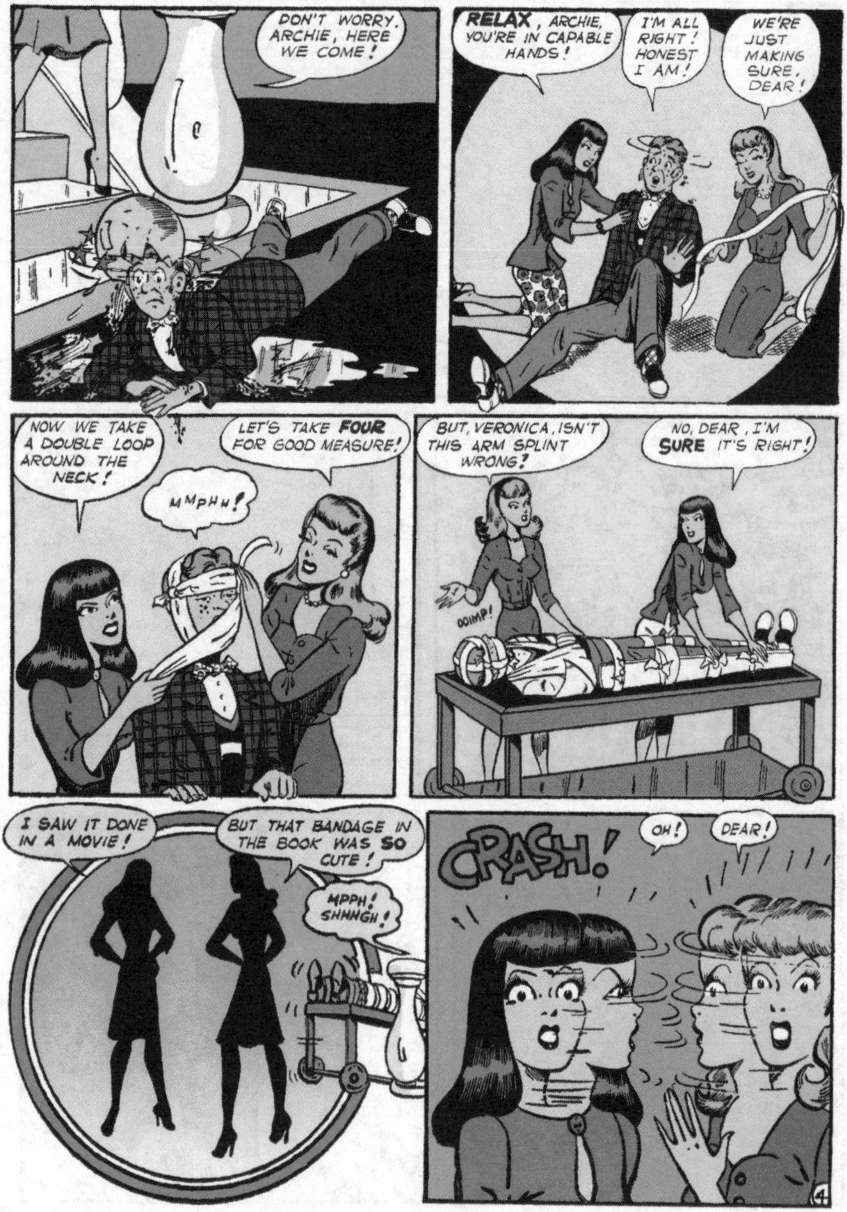
DON'T WORRY, ARCHIE, HERE WE COME!
RELAX, ARCHIE, YOU'RE IN CAPABLE HANDS!
I'M ALL RIGHT! HONEST I AM!
WE'RE JUST MAKING SURE, DEAR!
NOW WE TAKE A DOUBLE LOOP AROUND THE NECK!
LET'S TAKE FOUR FOR GOOD MEASURE!
MMPHH!
BUT, VERONICA, ISN'T THIS ARM SPLINT WRONG?
NO, DEAR, I'M SURE IT'S RIGHT!
OOIMP!
I SAW IT DONE IN A MOVIE!
BUT THAT BANDAGE IN THE BOOK WAS SO CUTE!
MPPH! SHNNGH!
CRASH!
OH!
DEAR!
4

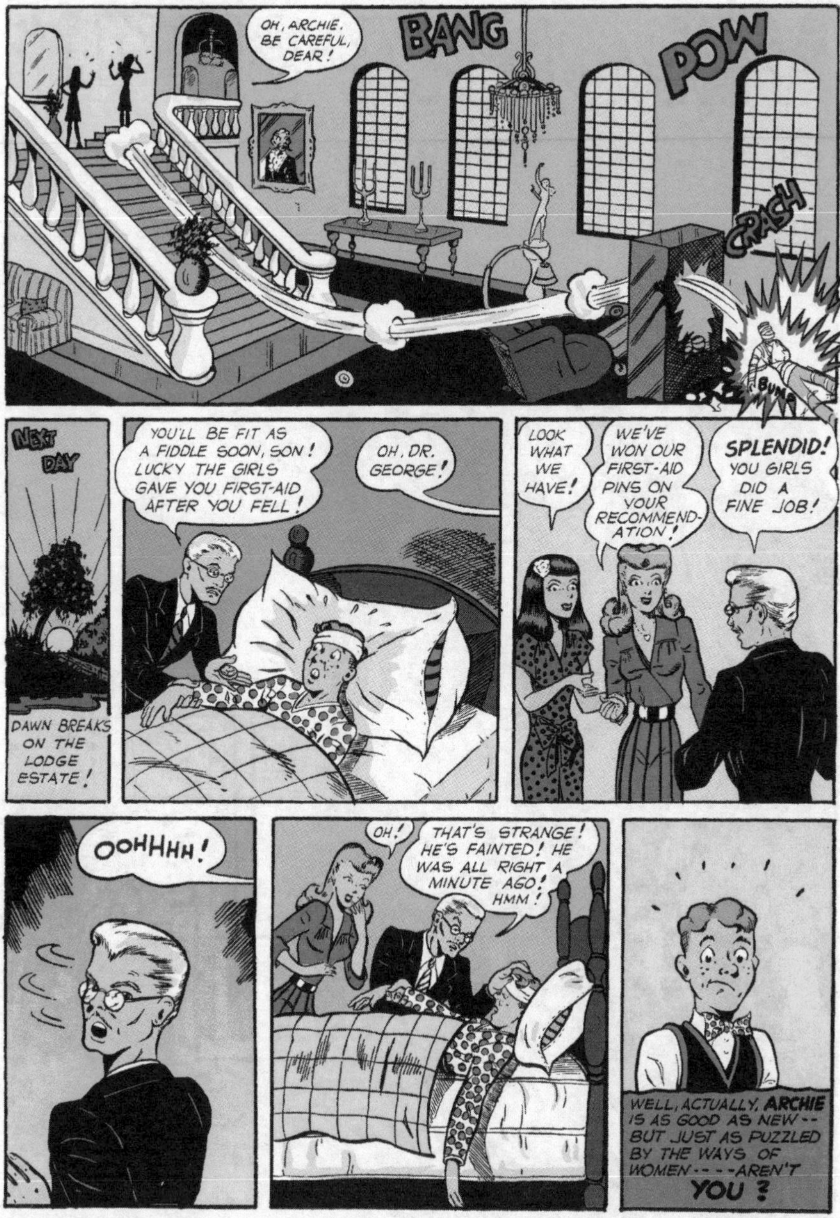
OH, ARCHIE. BE CAREFUL, DEAR!
BANG
POW
CRASH
BUMP
NEXT DAY
DAWN BREAKS ON THE LODGE ESTATE!
YOU'LL BE FIT AS A FIDDLE SOON, SON! LUCKY THE GIRLS GAVE YOU FIRST-AID AFTER YOU FELL!
OH, DR. GEORGE!
LOOK WHAT WE HAVE!
WE'VE WON OUR FIRST-AID PINS ON YOUR RECOMMENDATION!
SPLENDID! YOU GIRLS DID A FINE JOB!
OOHHHH!
OH!
THAT'S STRANGE! HE'S FAINTED! HE WAS ALL RIGHT A MINUTE AGO! HMM!
WELL, ACTUALLY, ARCHIE IS AS GOOD AS NEW -- BUT JUST AS PUZZLED BY THE WAYS OF WOMEN ---- AREN'T YOU?

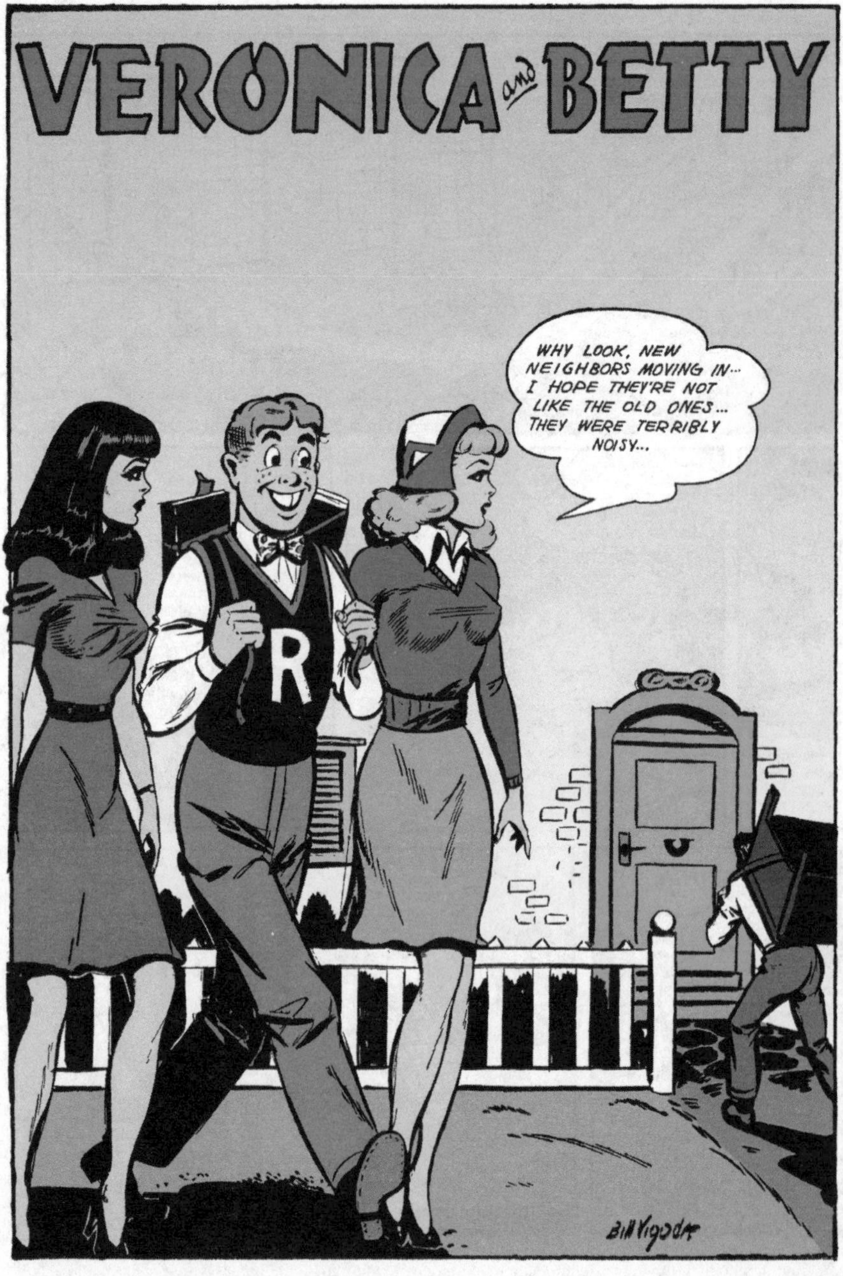
VERONICA and BETTY
WHY LOOK, NEW NEIGHBORS MOVING IN... I HOPE THEY'RE NOT LIKE THE OLD ONES... THEY WERE TERRIBLY NOISY...
R
Bill Vigoda

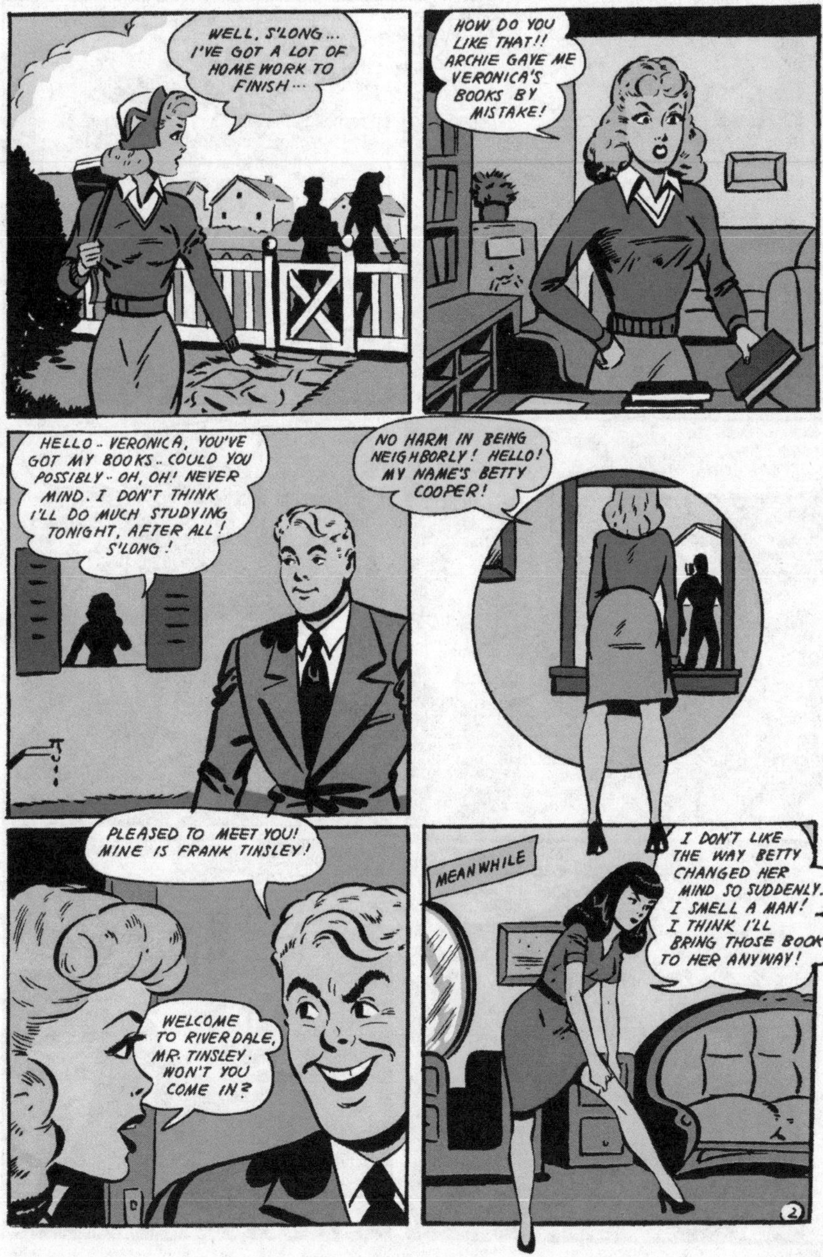
WELL, S'LONG... I'VE GOT A LOT OF HOME WORK TO FINISH...
HOW DO YOU LIKE THAT!! ARCHIE GAVE ME VERONICA'S BOOKS BY MISTAKE!
HELLO - VERONICA, YOU'VE GOT MY BOOKS.. COULD YOU POSSIBLY - OH, OH! NEVER MIND. I DON'T THINK I'LL DO MUCH STUDYING TONIGHT, AFTER ALL! S'LONG!
NO HARM IN BEING NEIGHBORLY! HELLO! MY NAME'S BETTY COOPER!
PLEASED TO MEET YOU! MINE IS FRANK TINSLEY!
WELCOME TO RIVERDALE, MR. TINSLEY. WON'T YOU COME IN?
MEANWHILE
I DON'T LIKE THE WAY BETTY CHANGED HER MIND SO SUDDENLY. I SMELL A MAN! I THINK I'LL BRING THOSE BOOKS TO HER ANYWAY!
2

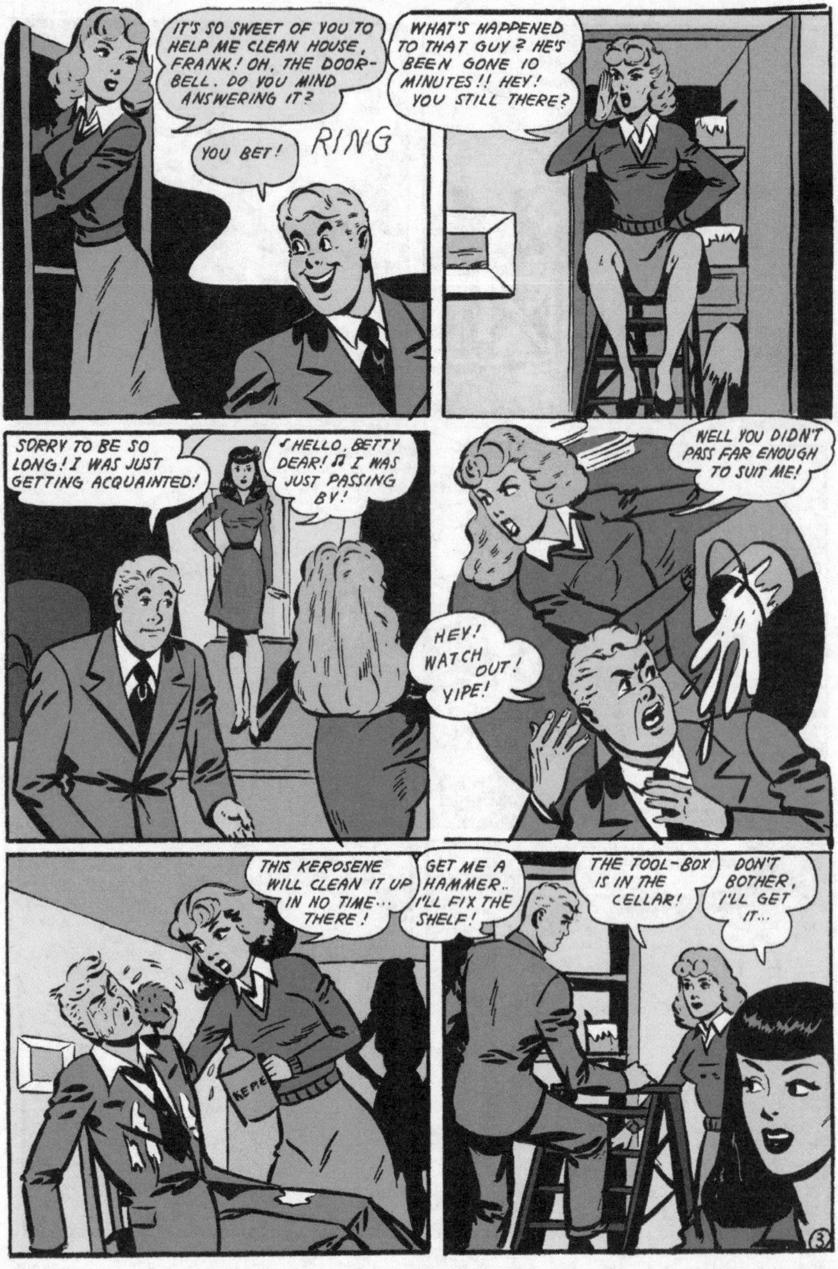
IT'S SO SWEET OF YOU TO HELP ME CLEAN HOUSE, FRANK! OH, THE DOOR-BELL. DO YOU MIND ANSWERING IT?
YOU BET!
RING
WHAT'S HAPPENED TO THAT GUY? HE'S BEEN GONE 10 MINUTES!! HEY! YOU STILL THERE?
SORRY TO BE SO LONG! I WAS JUST GETTING ACQUAINTED!
♪ HELLO, BETTY DEAR! ♫ I WAS JUST PASSING BY!
WELL YOU DIDN'T PASS FAR ENOUGH TO SUIT ME!
HEY! WATCH OUT! YIPE!
THIS KEROSENE WILL CLEAN IT UP IN NO TIME... THERE!
GET ME A HAMMER.. I'LL FIX THE SHELF!
THE TOOL-BOX IS IN THE CELLAR!
DON'T BOTHER, I'LL GET IT...
3

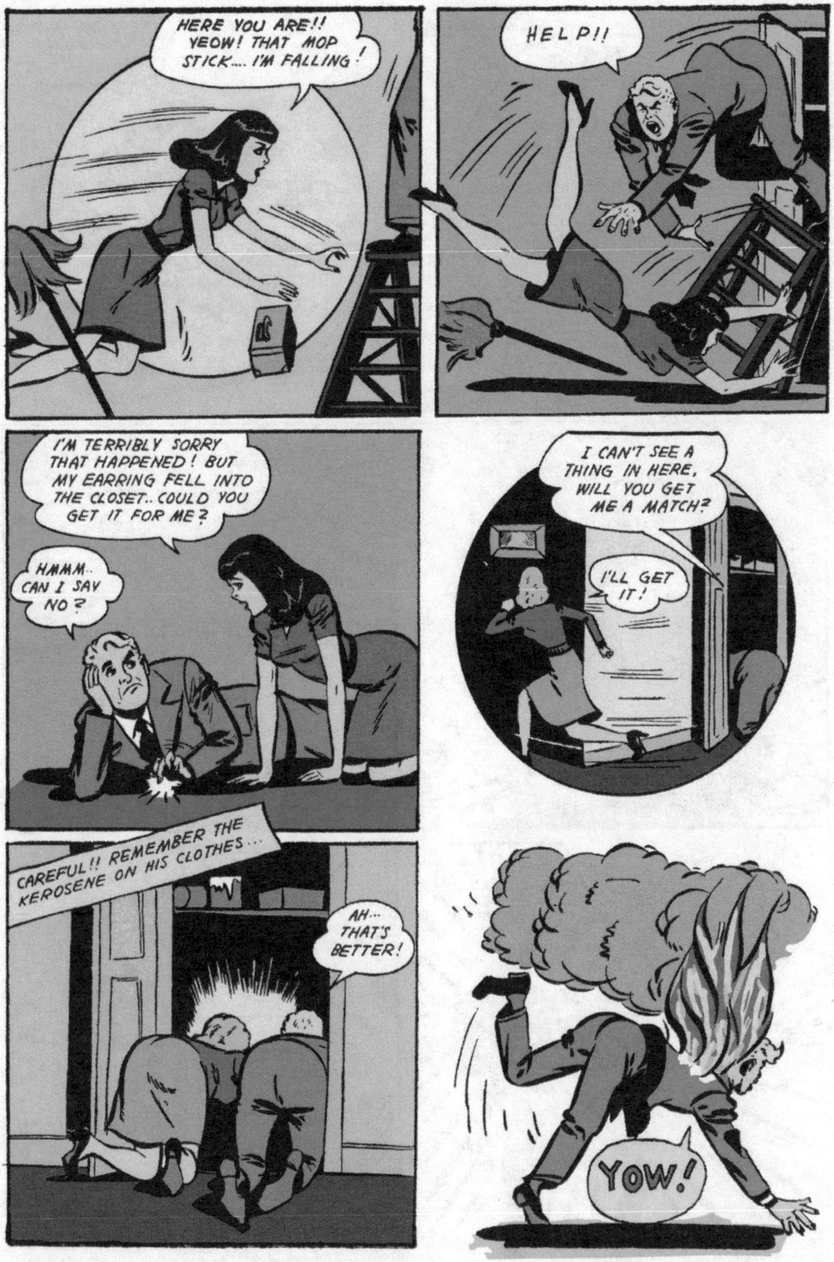
HERE YOU ARE!! YEOW! THAT MOP STICK.... I'M FALLING!
HELP!!
I'M TERRIBLY SORRY THAT HAPPENED! BUT MY EARRING FELL INTO THE CLOSET.. COULD YOU GET IT FOR ME?
HMMM.. CAN I SAY NO?
I CAN'T SEE A THING IN HERE, WILL YOU GET ME A MATCH?
I'LL GET IT!
CAREFUL!! REMEMBER THE KEROSENE ON HIS CLOTHES...
AH... THAT'S BETTER!
YOW!

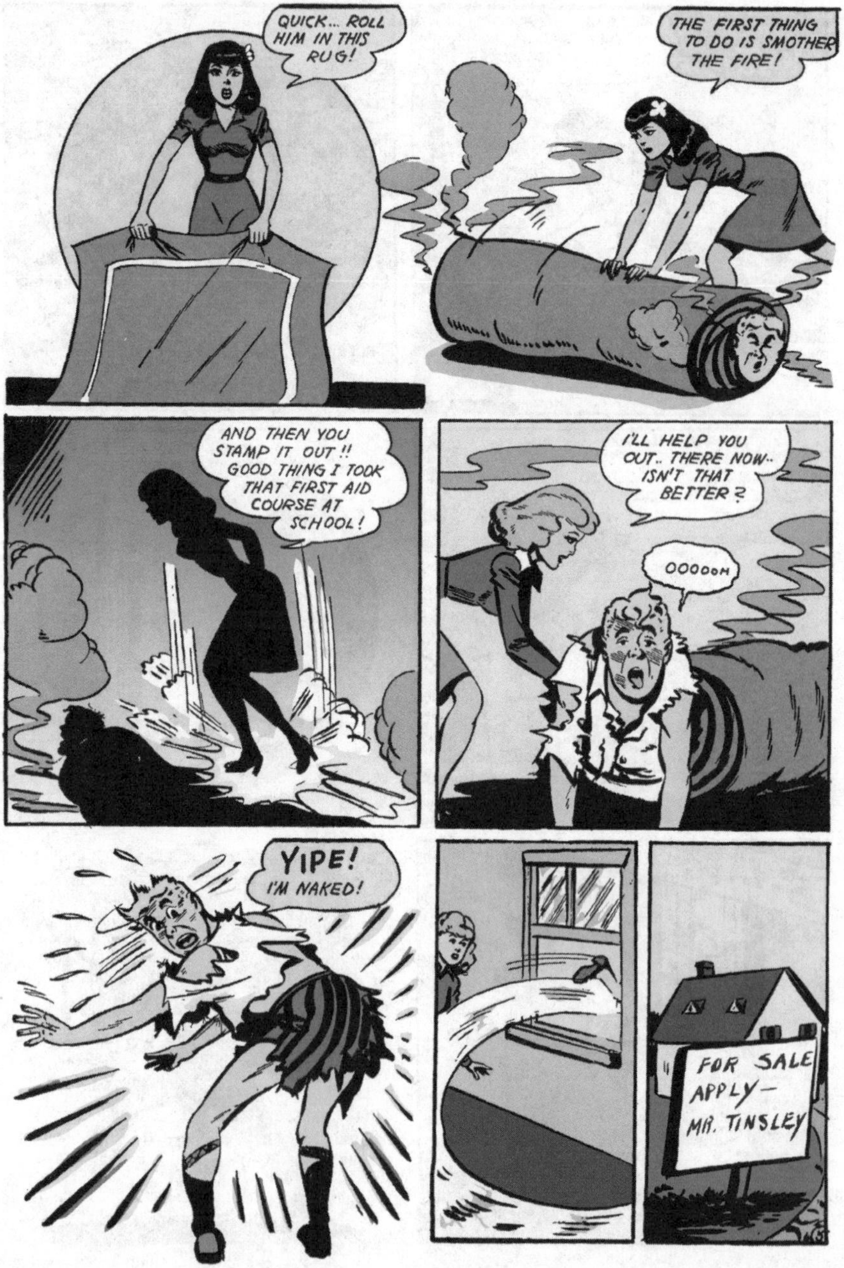
QUICK... ROLL HIM IN THIS RUG!
THE FIRST THING TO DO IS SMOTHER THE FIRE!
AND THEN YOU STAMP IT OUT!! GOOD THING I TOOK THAT FIRST AID COURSE AT SCHOOL!
I'LL HELP YOU OUT.. THERE NOW.. ISN'T THAT BETTER?
OOOOOM
YIPE! I'M NAKED!
FOR SALE
APPLY—
MR. TINSLEY

NOTICE
ARCHIE #14, 1945
Bill Vigoda, Terry Szenics

AVIATION TRAINING
ARCHIE #19, 1946
Bill Vigoda, Pen Shumaker

'RAY!
ARCHIE #20, 1946
Al McLean, Bill Vigoda

My earliest memories of reading comics were stocking up on *Betty and Veronica* comics and double-digests during shopping trips with my mom and grandma. I'd pick up every new issue and read them during the drive home, finishing the comics before we even made it back to our apartment. I always envied the kids who had their fan art featured and wished I could contribute something creative—unfortunately my drawing skills were, let's just say, subpar. But still, I dreamed of having my name appear in print on those pages.

- JAMIE LEE ROTANTE *Writer/Editor, Archie Comics*

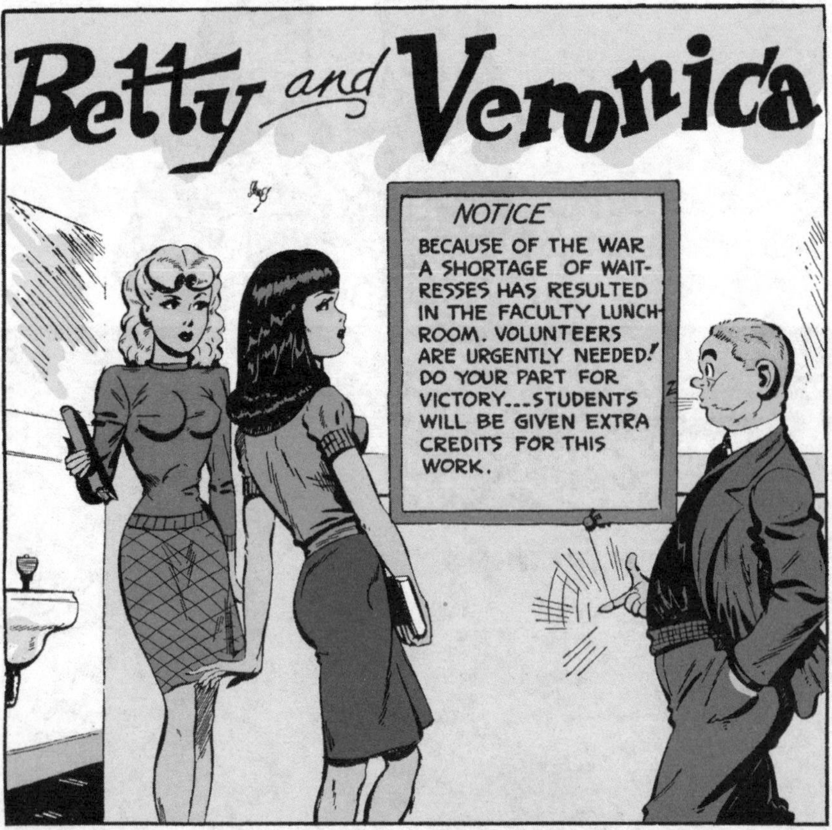
Betty and Veronica
NOTICE
BECAUSE OF THE WAR A SHORTAGE OF WAIT-RESSES HAS RESULTED IN THE FACULTY LUNCH-ROOM. VOLUNTEERS ARE URGENTLY NEEDED! DO YOUR PART FOR VICTORY... STUDENTS WILL BE GIVEN EXTRA CREDITS FOR THIS WORK.

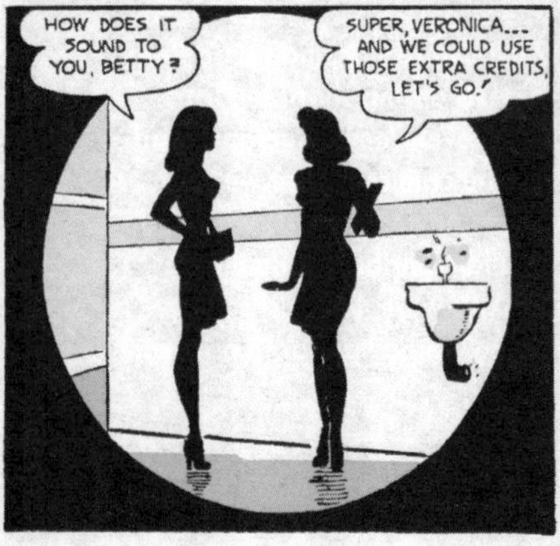
HOW DOES IT SOUND TO YOU, BETTY?
SUPER, VERONICA... AND WE COULD USE THOSE EXTRA CREDITS, LET'S GO!

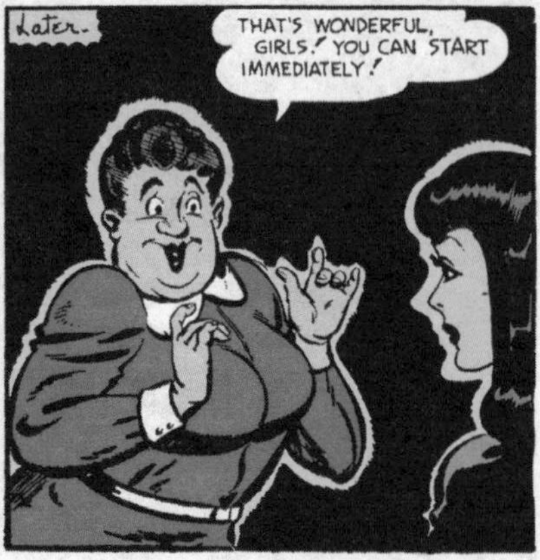
Later.
THAT'S WONDERFUL, GIRLS! YOU CAN START IMMEDIATELY!

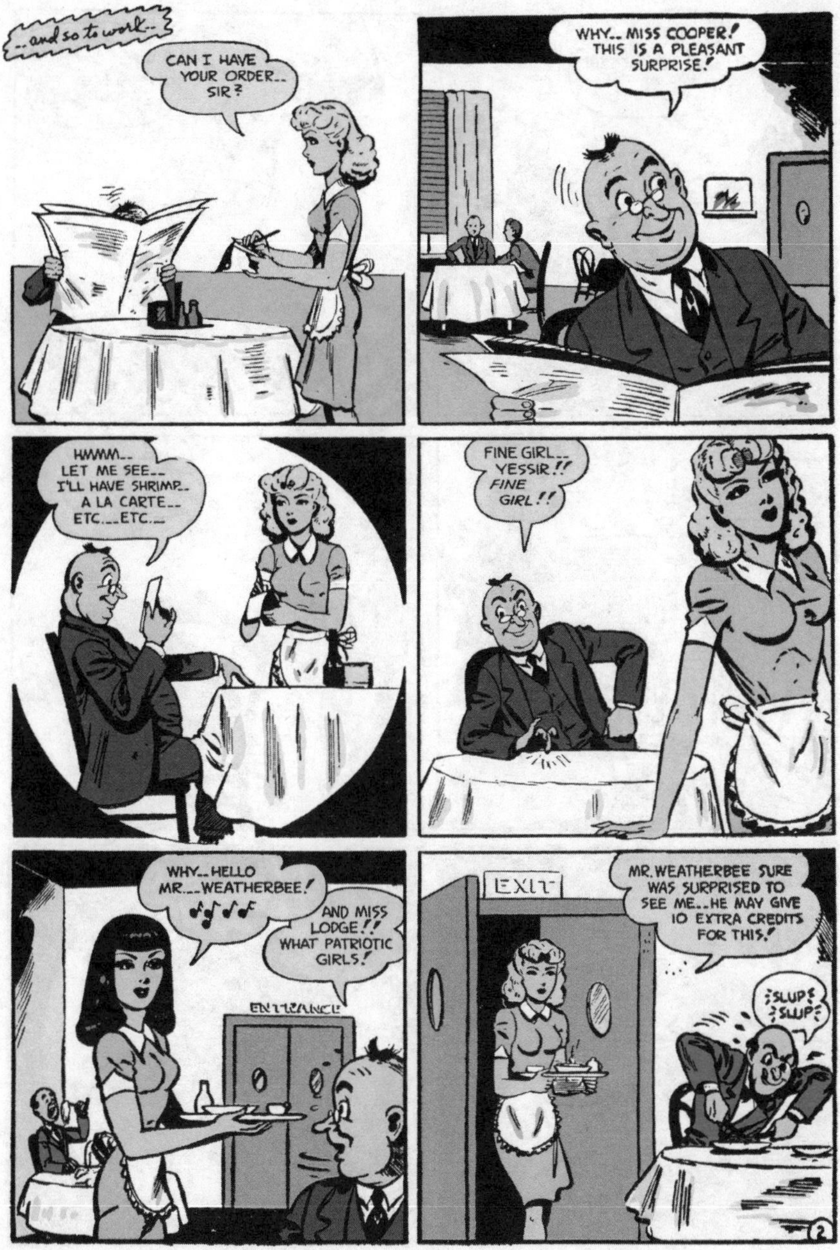
...and so to work...
CAN I HAVE YOUR ORDER... SIR?
WHY... MISS COOPER! THIS IS A PLEASANT SURPRISE!
HMMM... LET ME SEE... I'LL HAVE SHRIMP... A LA CARTE... ETC....ETC....
FINE GIRL... YESSIR!! FINE GIRL!!
WHY... HELLO MR.... WEATHERBEE!
AND MISS LODGE!! WHAT PATRIOTIC GIRLS!
ENTRANCE
EXIT
MR. WEATHERBEE SURE WAS SURPRISED TO SEE ME... HE MAY GIVE 10 EXTRA CREDITS FOR THIS!
SLUP SLUP
2

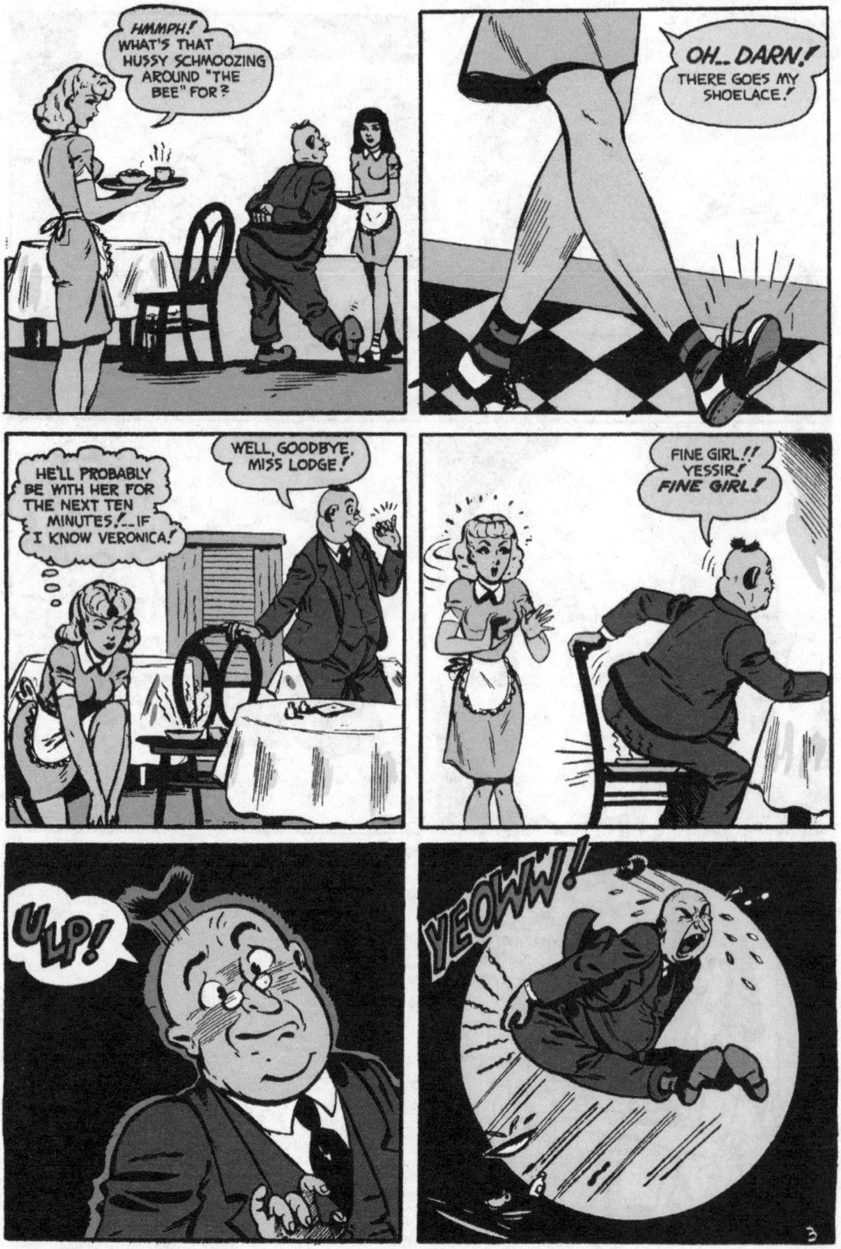
HMMPH! WHAT'S THAT HUSSY SCHMOOZING AROUND "THE BEE" FOR?
OH... DARN! THERE GOES MY SHOELACE!
HE'LL PROBABLY BE WITH HER FOR THE NEXT TEN MINUTES!--IF I KNOW VERONICA!
WELL, GOODBYE, MISS LODGE!
FINE GIRL!! YESSIR! FINE GIRL!
ULP!
YEOWW!
3

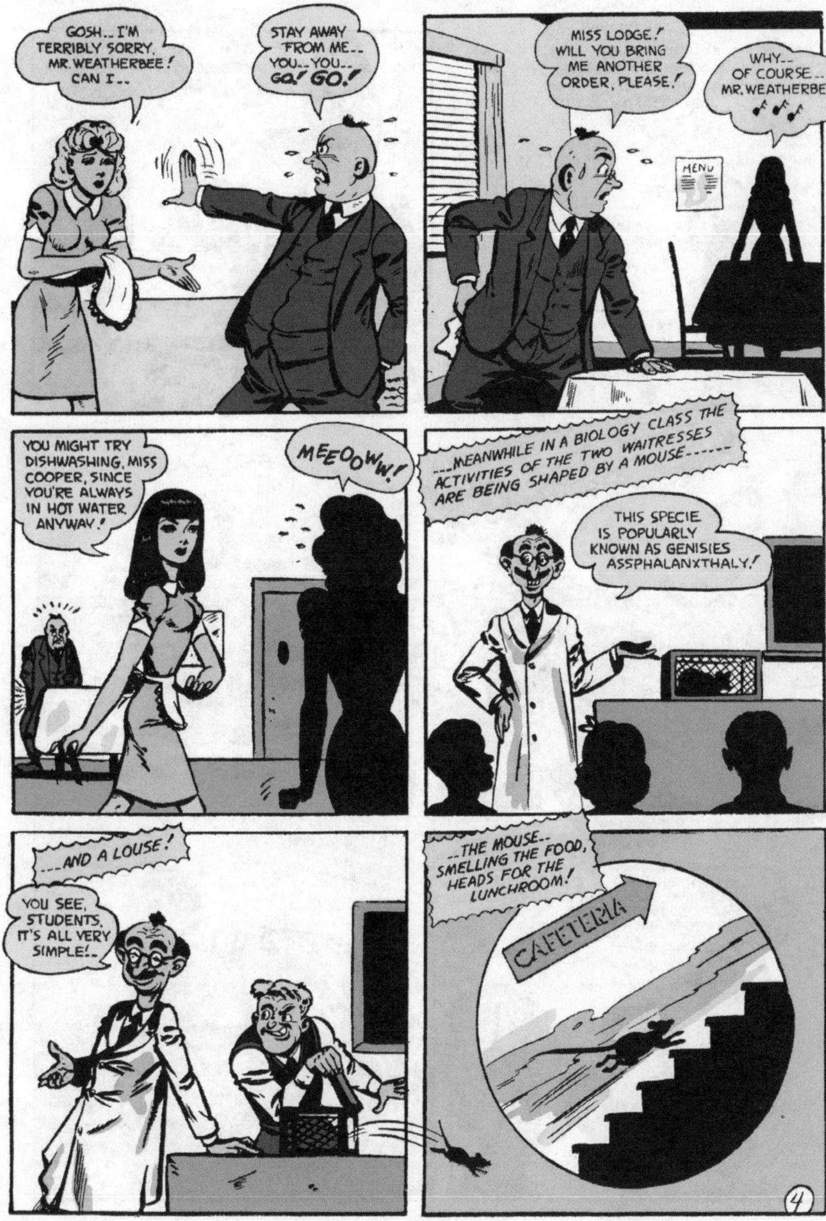

GOSH.. I'M TERRIBLY SORRY, MR. WEATHERBEE! CAN I..
STAY AWAY FROM ME.. YOU..YOU.. GO! GO!
MISS LODGE! WILL YOU BRING ME ANOTHER ORDER, PLEASE!
WHY-- OF COURSE.. MR. WEATHERBEE
MENU
YOU MIGHT TRY DISHWASHING, MISS COOPER, SINCE YOU'RE ALWAYS IN HOT WATER ANYWAY!
MEEOOWW!
...MEANWHILE IN A BIOLOGY CLASS THE ACTIVITIES OF THE TWO WAITRESSES ARE BEING SHAPED BY A MOUSE......
THIS SPECIE IS POPULARLY KNOWN AS GENISIES ASSPHALANXTHALY!
...AND A LOUSE!
YOU SEE, STUDENTS, IT'S ALL VERY SIMPLE!..
..THE MOUSE.. SMELLING THE FOOD, HEADS FOR THE LUNCHROOM!
CAFETERIA
4

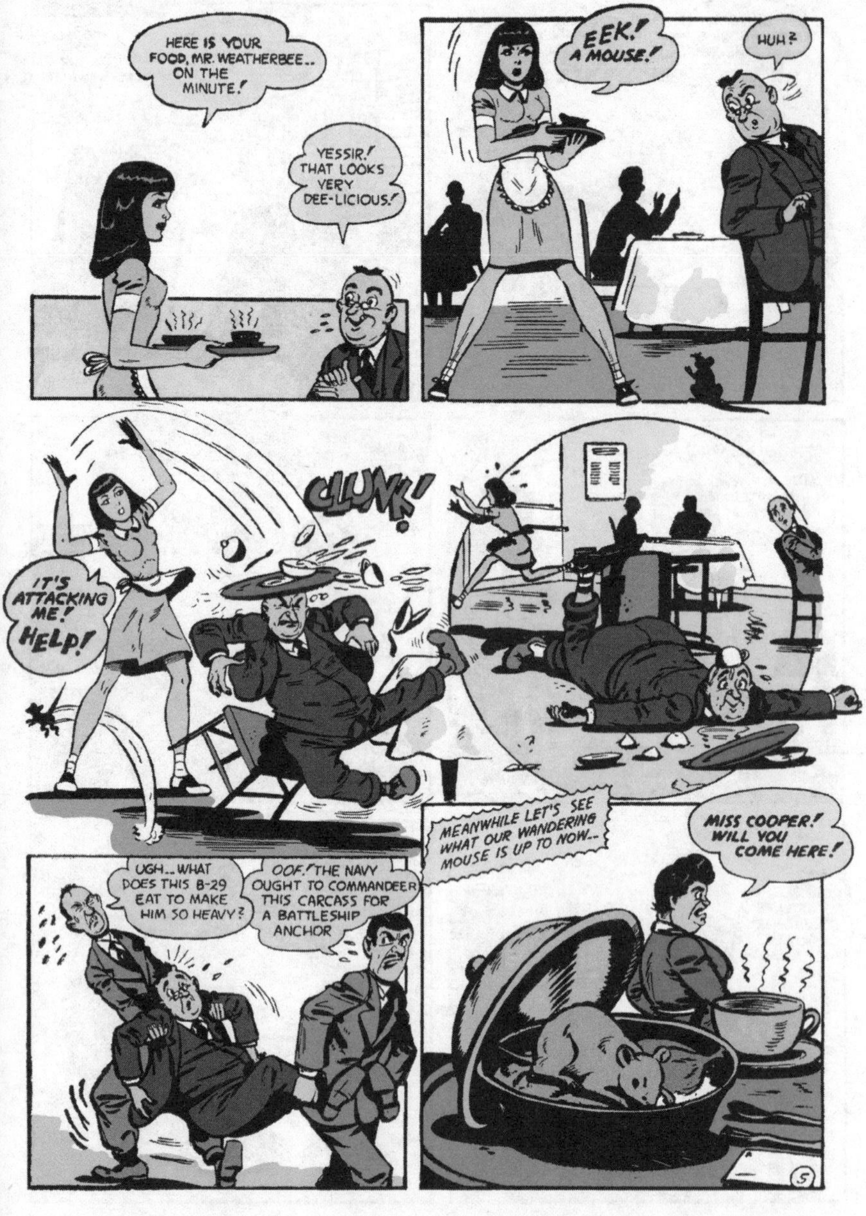
HERE IS YOUR FOOD, MR. WEATHERBEE.. ON THE MINUTE!
YESSIR! THAT LOOKS VERY DEE-LICIOUS!
EEK! A MOUSE!
HUH?
CLUNK!
IT'S ATTACKING ME! HELP!
MEANWHILE LET'S SEE WHAT OUR WANDERING MOUSE IS UP TO NOW...
UGH... WHAT DOES THIS B-29 EAT TO MAKE HIM SO HEAVY?
OOF! THE NAVY OUGHT TO COMMANDEER THIS CARCASS FOR A BATTLESHIP ANCHOR
MISS COOPER! WILL YOU COME HERE!
5

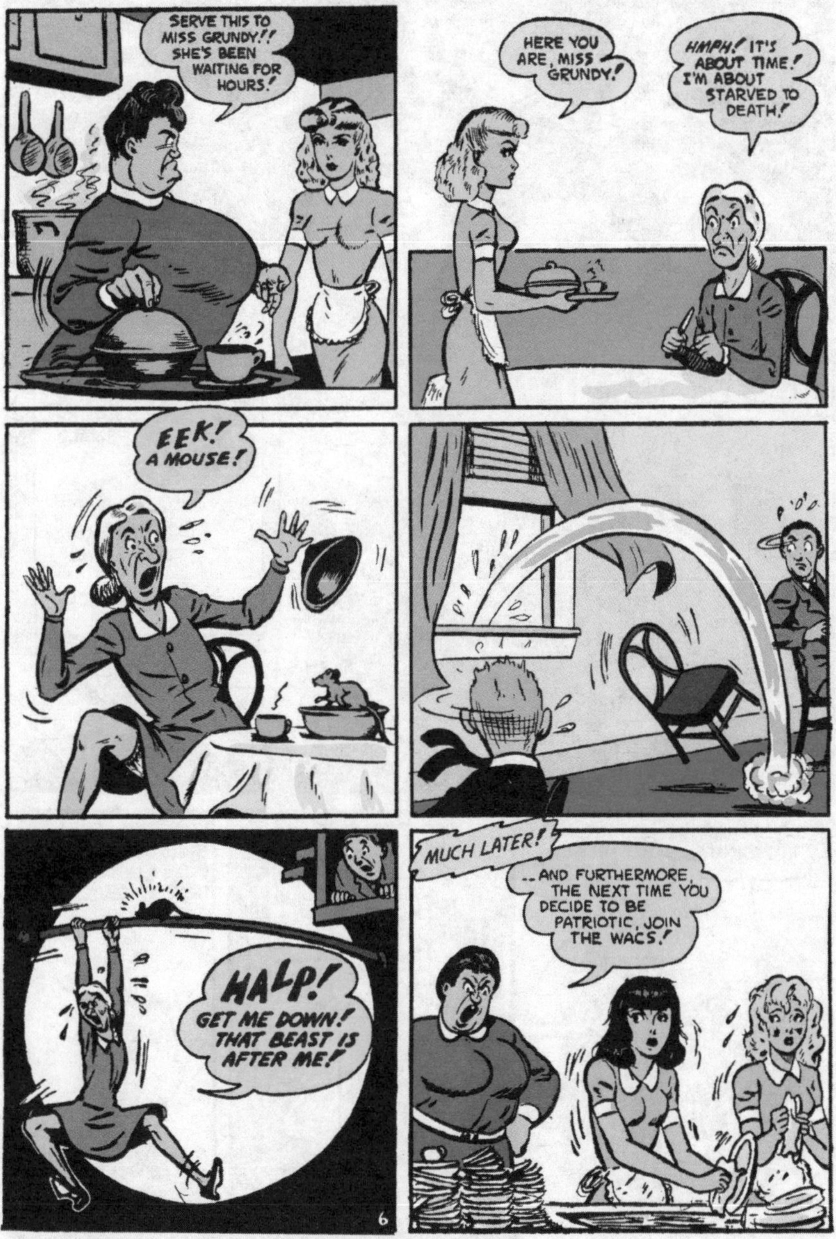
SERVE THIS TO MISS GRUNDY!! SHE'S BEEN WAITING FOR HOURS!
HERE YOU ARE, MISS GRUNDY!
HMPH! IT'S ABOUT TIME! I'M ABOUT STARVED TO DEATH!
EEK! A MOUSE!
HALP! GET ME DOWN! THAT BEAST IS AFTER ME!
MUCH LATER!
..AND FURTHERMORE, THE NEXT TIME YOU DECIDE TO BE PATRIOTIC, JOIN THE WACS!
6

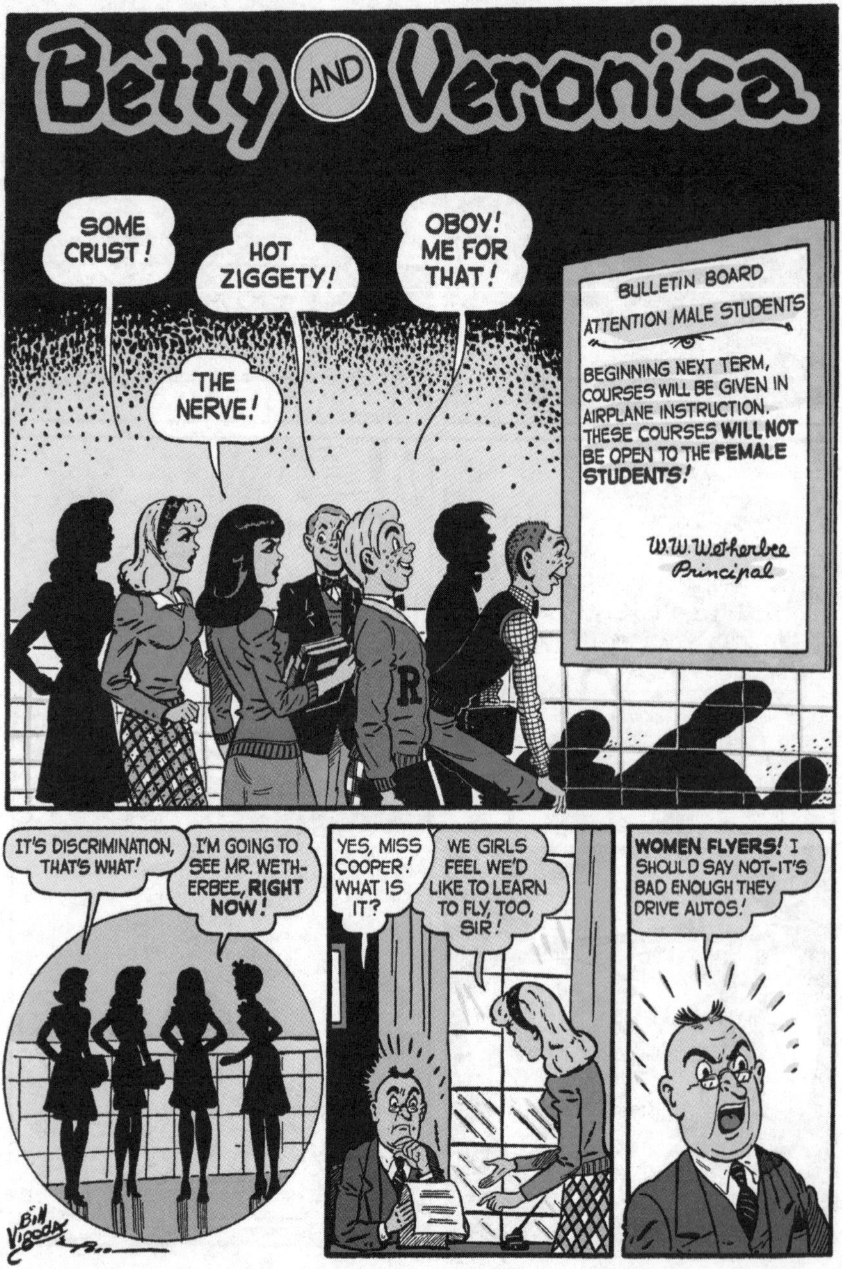
Betty AND Veronica
SOME CRUST!
HOT ZIGGETY!
OBOY! ME FOR THAT!
THE NERVE!
BULLETIN BOARD
ATTENTION MALE STUDENTS
BEGINNING NEXT TERM, COURSES WILL BE GIVEN IN AIRPLANE INSTRUCTION. THESE COURSES WILL NOT BE OPEN TO THE FEMALE STUDENTS!
W.W. Wetherbee Principal
R
IT'S DISCRIMINATION, THAT'S WHAT!
I'M GOING TO SEE MR. WETH-ERBEE, RIGHT NOW!
Bill Vigoda
YES, MISS COOPER! WHAT IS IT?
WE GIRLS FEEL WE'D LIKE TO LEARN TO FLY, TOO, SIR!
WOMEN FLYERS! I SHOULD SAY NOT-IT'S BAD ENOUGH THEY DRIVE AUTOS!

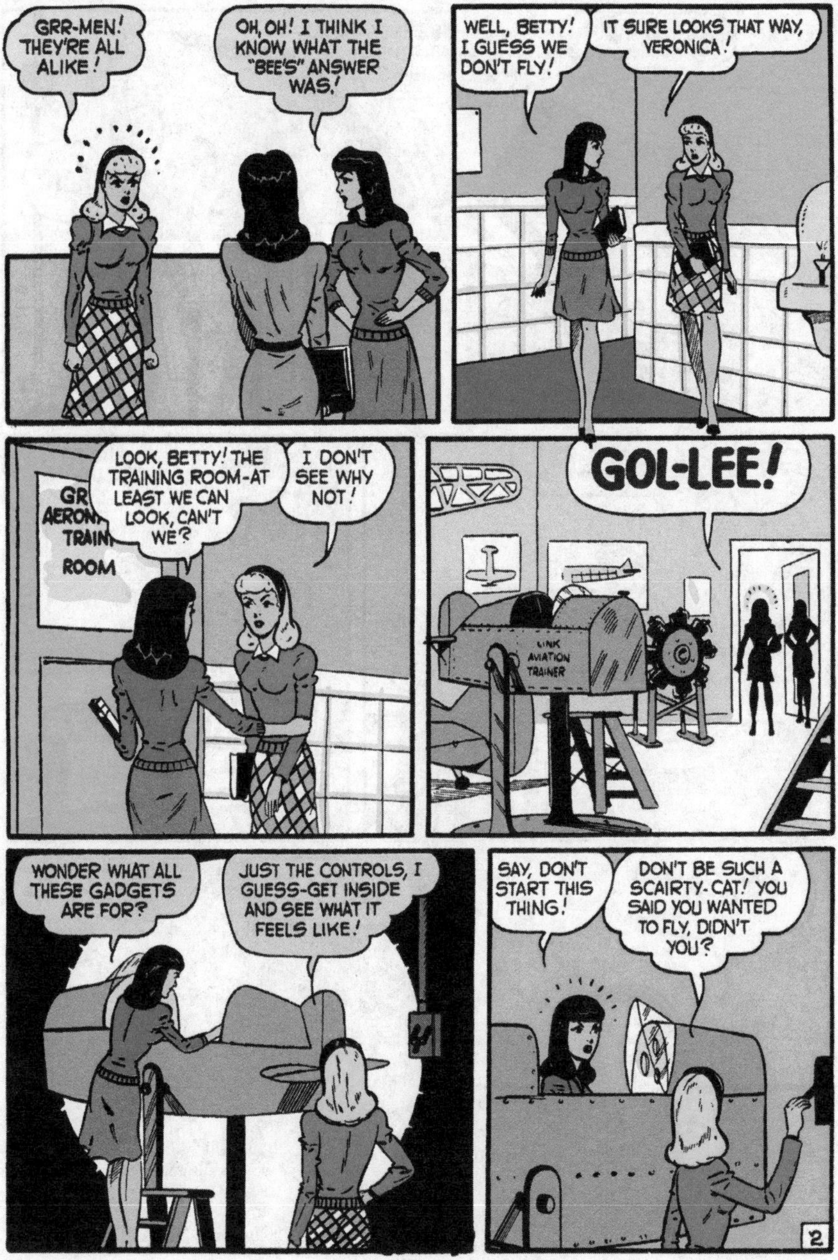
GRR-MEN! THEY'RE ALL ALIKE!
OH, OH! I THINK I KNOW WHAT THE "BEE'S" ANSWER WAS!
WELL, BETTY! I GUESS WE DON'T FLY!
IT SURE LOOKS THAT WAY, VERONICA!
LOOK, BETTY! THE TRAINING ROOM-AT LEAST WE CAN LOOK, CAN'T WE?
I DON'T SEE WHY NOT!
ROOM
GOL-LEE!
LINK AVIATION TRAINER
WONDER WHAT ALL THESE GADGETS ARE FOR?
JUST THE CONTROLS, I GUESS-GET INSIDE AND SEE WHAT IT FEELS LIKE!
SAY, DON'T START THIS THING!
DON'T BE SUCH A SCAIRTY-CAT! YOU SAID YOU WANTED TO FLY, DIDN'T YOU?
2

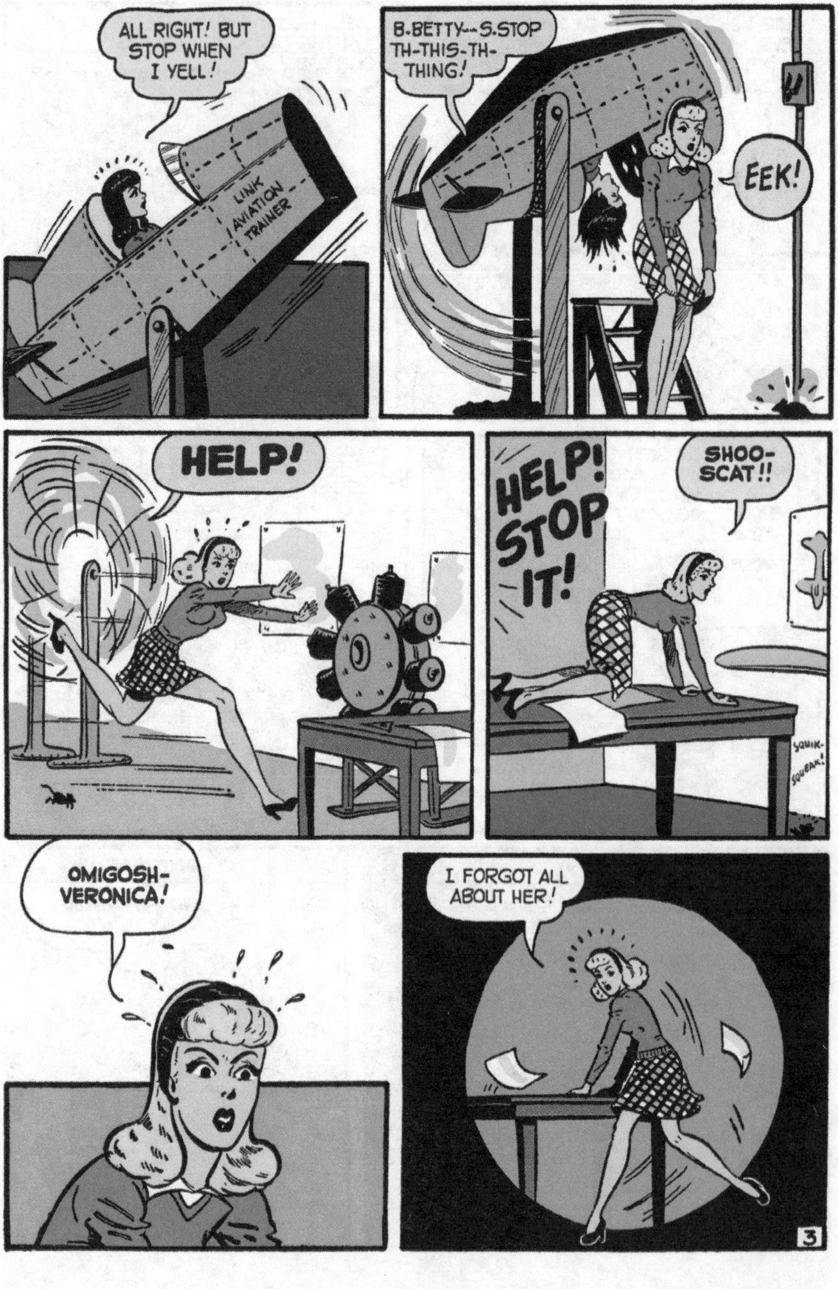
ALL RIGHT! BUT STOP WHEN I YELL!
LINK AVIATION TRAINER
B.BETTY--S.STOP TH-THIS-TH-THING!
EEK!
HELP!
HELP! STOP IT!
SHOO-SCAT!!
SQUIK-
SQUEAK!
OMIGOSH-VERONICA!
I FORGOT ALL ABOUT HER!
3

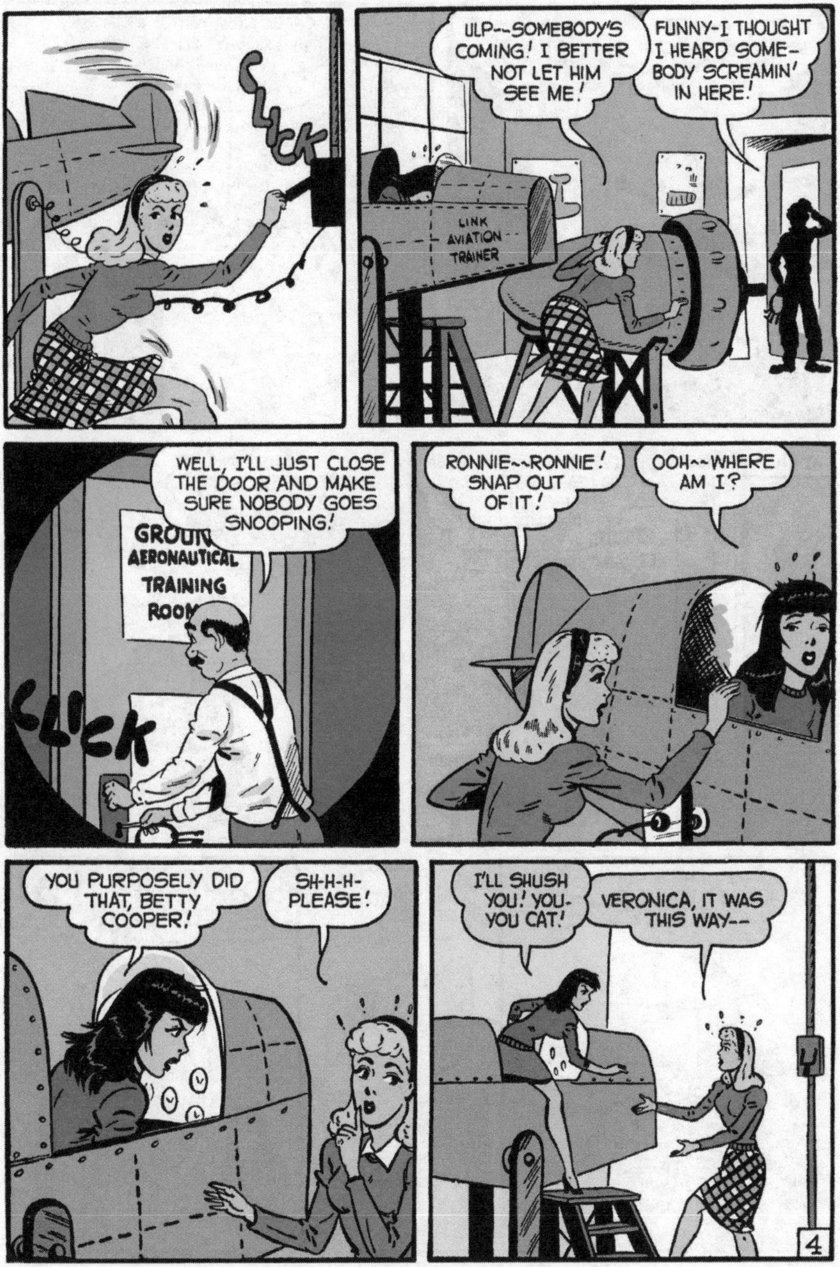
CLICK
ULP--SOMEBODY'S COMING! I BETTER NOT LET HIM SEE ME!
FUNNY-I THOUGHT I HEARD SOME-BODY SCREAMIN' IN HERE!
LINK AVIATION TRAINER
WELL, I'LL JUST CLOSE THE DOOR AND MAKE SURE NOBODY GOES SNOOPING!
GROUN AERONAUTICAL TRAINING ROOM
CLICK
RONNIE--RONNIE! SNAP OUT OF IT!
OOH--WHERE AM I?
YOU PURPOSELY DID THAT, BETTY COOPER!
SH-H-H- PLEASE!
I'LL SHUSH YOU! YOU- YOU CAT!
VERONICA, IT WAS THIS WAY--
4

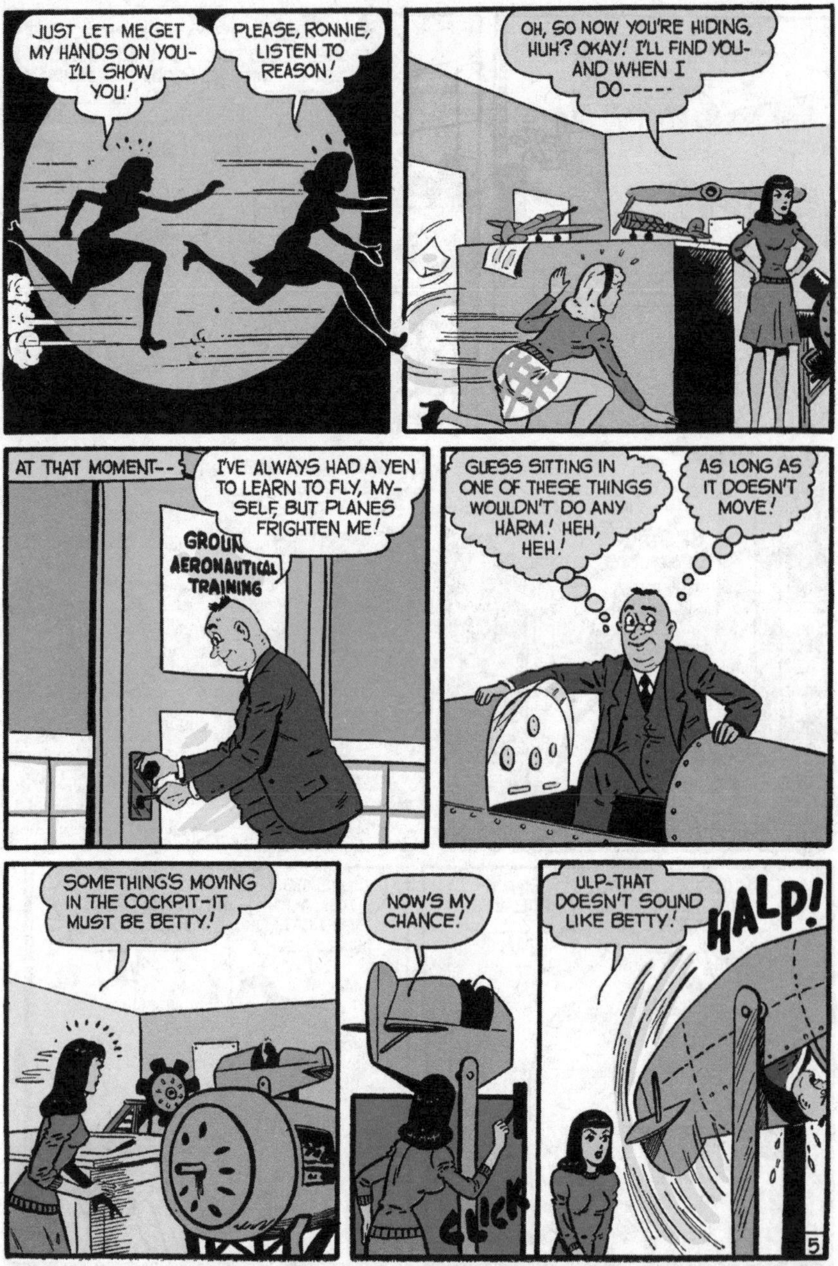

JUST LET ME GET MY HANDS ON YOU- I'LL SHOW YOU!
PLEASE, RONNIE, LISTEN TO REASON!
OH, SO NOW YOU'RE HIDING, HUH? OKAY! I'LL FIND YOU- AND WHEN I DO-----
AT THAT MOMENT--
I'VE ALWAYS HAD A YEN TO LEARN TO FLY, MY-SELF, BUT PLANES FRIGHTEN ME!
GROUN
AERONAUTICAL TRAINING
GUESS SITTING IN ONE OF THESE THINGS WOULDN'T DO ANY HARM! HEH, HEH!
AS LONG AS IT DOESN'T MOVE!
SOMETHING'S MOVING IN THE COCKPIT-IT MUST BE BETTY!
NOW'S MY CHANCE!
CLICK
ULP-THAT DOESN'T SOUND LIKE BETTY!
HALP!
5

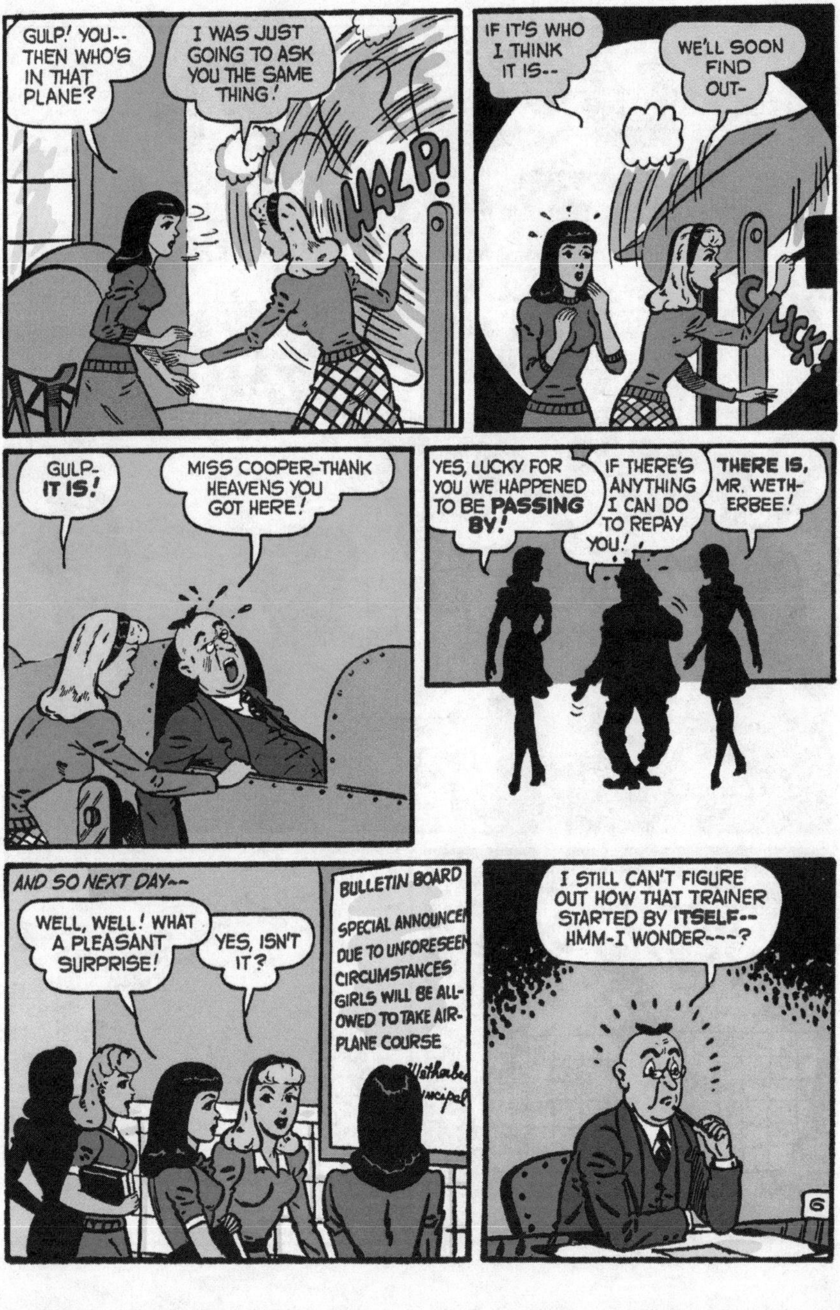

GULP! YOU-- THEN WHO'S IN THAT PLANE?
I WAS JUST GOING TO ASK YOU THE SAME THING!
HALP!
IF IT'S WHO I THINK IT IS--
WE'LL SOON FIND OUT-
CLICK!
GULP- IT IS!
MISS COOPER-THANK HEAVENS YOU GOT HERE!
YES, LUCKY FOR YOU WE HAPPENED TO BE PASSING BY!
IF THERE'S ANYTHING I CAN DO TO REPAY YOU!
THERE IS, MR. WETH-ERBEE!
AND SO NEXT DAY--
WELL, WELL! WHAT A PLEASANT SURPRISE!
YES, ISN'T IT?
BULLETIN BOARD
SPECIAL ANNOUNCE
DUE TO UNFORESEEN
CIRCUMSTANCES
GIRLS WILL BE ALL-
OWED TO TAKE AIR-
PLANE COURSE
I STILL CAN'T FIGURE OUT HOW THAT TRAINER STARTED BY ITSELF-- HMM-I WONDER---?
6

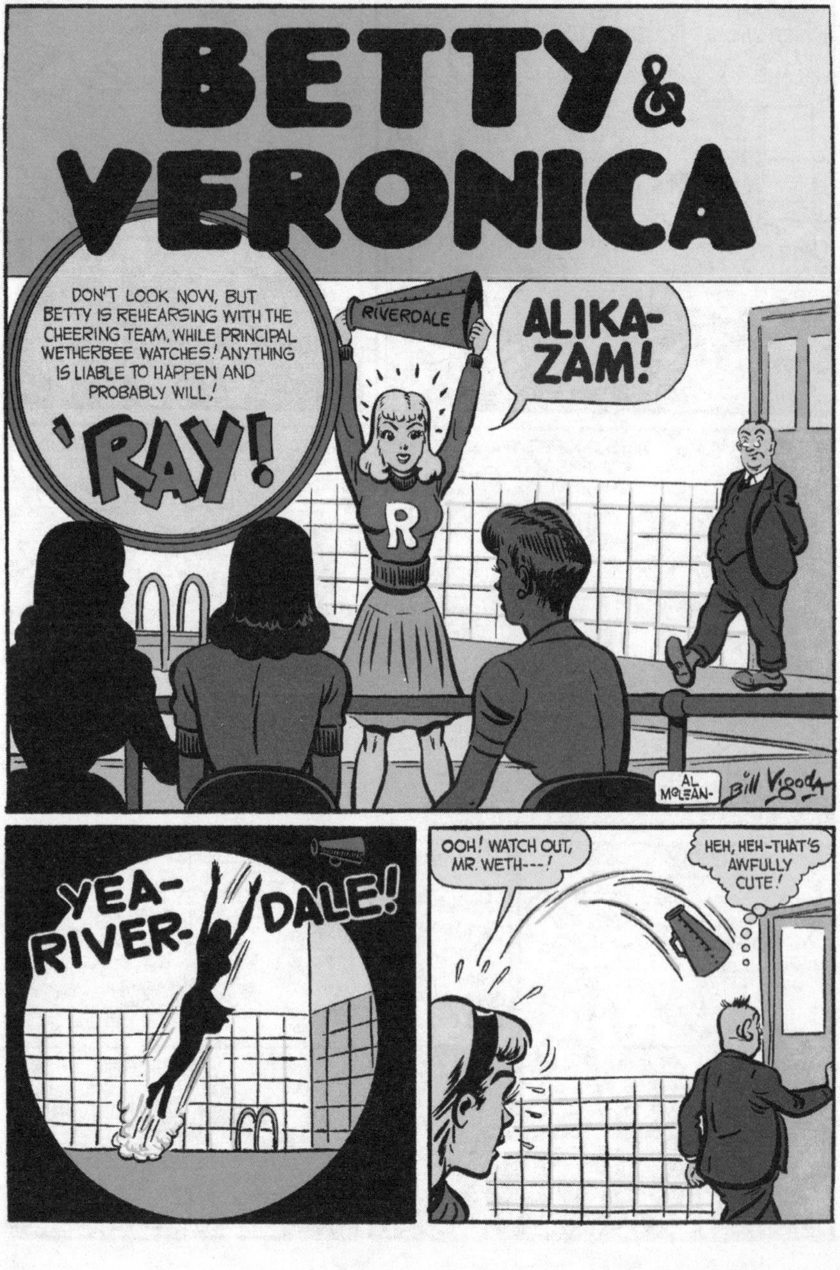
BETTY & VERONICA
DON'T LOOK NOW, BUT BETTY IS REHEARSING WITH THE CHEERING TEAM, WHILE PRINCIPAL WETHERBEE WATCHES! ANYTHING IS LIABLE TO HAPPEN AND PROBABLY WILL!
'RAY!
RIVERDALE
ALIKA-ZAM!
R
AL McLEAN-
Bill Vigoda
YEA-RIVER-DALE!
OOH! WATCH OUT, MR. WETH---!
HEH, HEH-THAT'S AWFULLY CUTE!

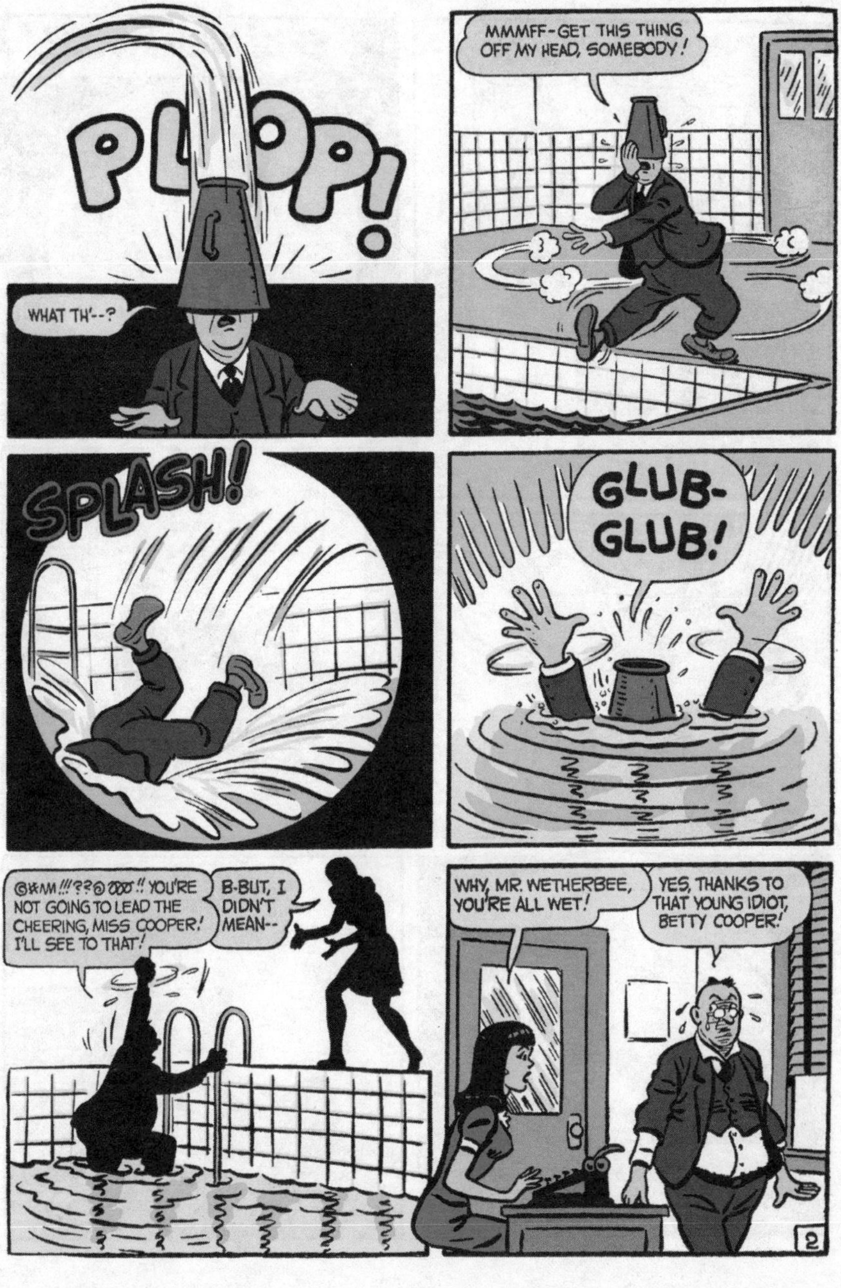
PLOOP!
WHAT TH'--?
MMMFF-GET THIS THING OFF MY HEAD, SOMEBODY!
SPLASH!
GLUB-GLUB!
@#*!!!??@ ✪✪!! YOU'RE NOT GOING TO LEAD THE CHEERING, MISS COOPER! I'LL SEE TO THAT!
B-BUT, I DIDN'T MEAN--
WHY, MR. WETHERBEE, YOU'RE ALL WET!
YES, THANKS TO THAT YOUNG IDIOT, BETTY COOPER!
2

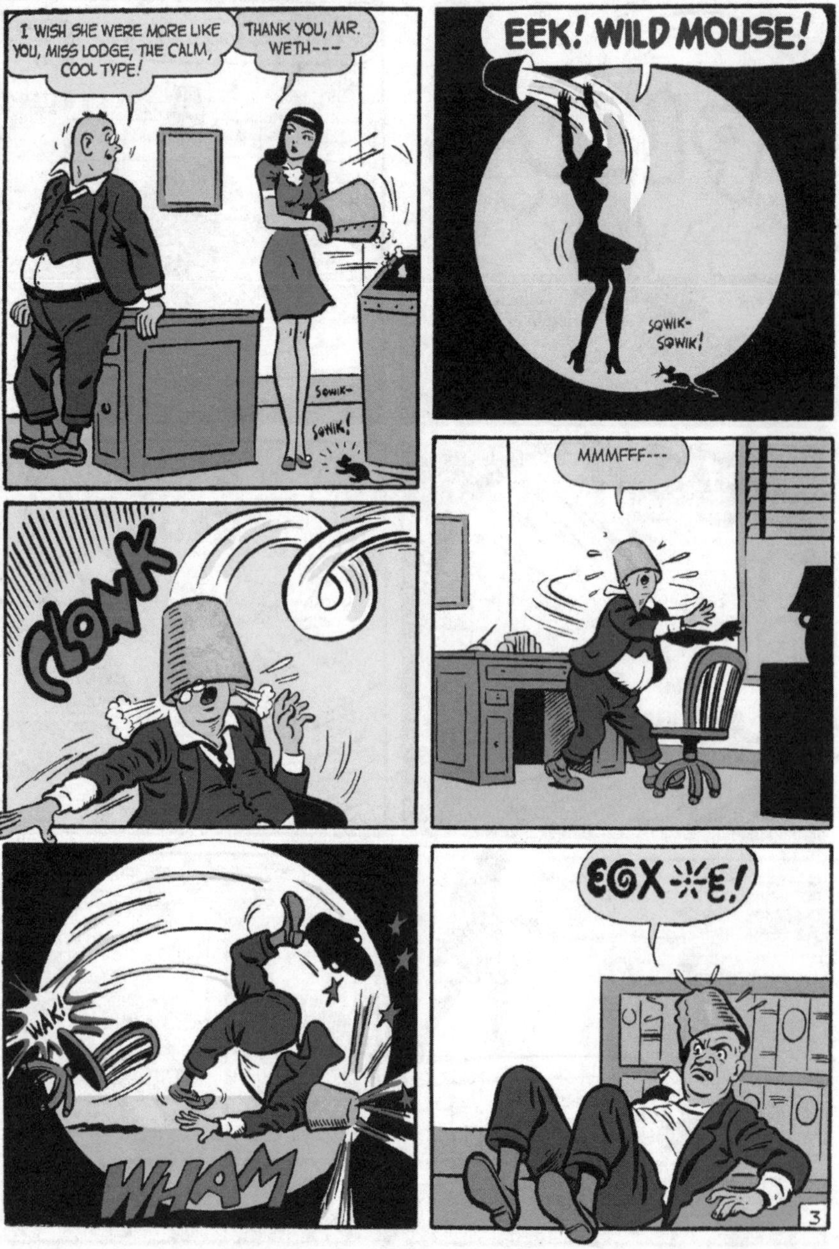

I WISH SHE WERE MORE LIKE YOU, MISS LODGE, THE CALM, COOL TYPE!
THANK YOU, MR. WETH---
SQWIK-
SQWIK!
EEK! WILD MOUSE!
SQWIK-
SQWIK!
CLONK
MMMFFF---
WAK!
WHAM

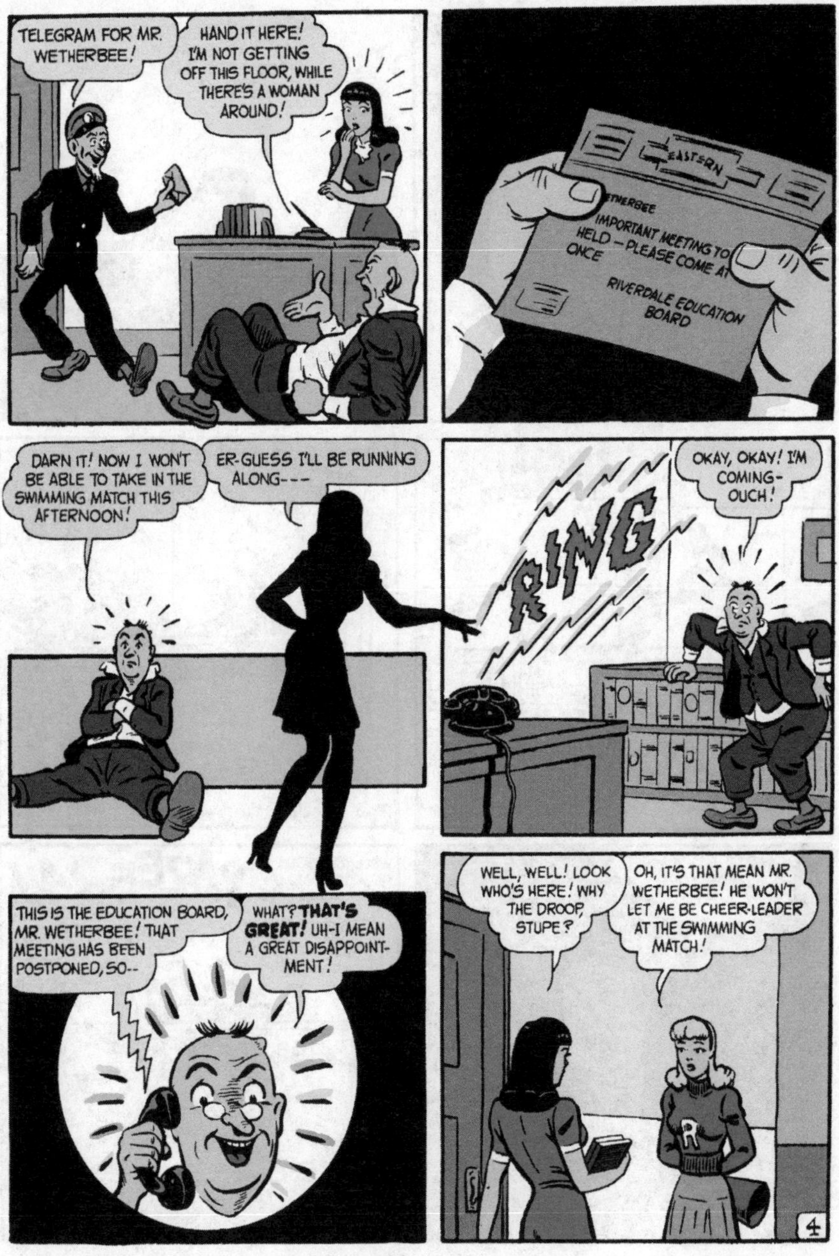
TELEGRAM FOR MR. WETHERBEE!
HAND IT HERE! I'M NOT GETTING OFF THIS FLOOR, WHILE THERE'S A WOMAN AROUND!
EASTERN
WETHERBEE
IMPORTANT MEETING TO BE HELD — PLEASE COME AT ONCE
RIVERDALE EDUCATION BOARD
DARN IT! NOW I WON'T BE ABLE TO TAKE IN THE SWIMMING MATCH THIS AFTERNOON!
ER-GUESS I'LL BE RUNNING ALONG---
RING
OKAY, OKAY! I'M COMING-OUCH!
THIS IS THE EDUCATION BOARD, MR. WETHERBEE! THAT MEETING HAS BEEN POSTPONED, SO--
WHAT? THAT'S GREAT! UH-I MEAN A GREAT DISAPPOINT-MENT!
WELL, WELL! LOOK WHO'S HERE! WHY THE DROOP, STUPE?
OH, IT'S THAT MEAN MR. WETHERBEE! HE WON'T LET ME BE CHEER-LEADER AT THE SWIMMING MATCH!
4

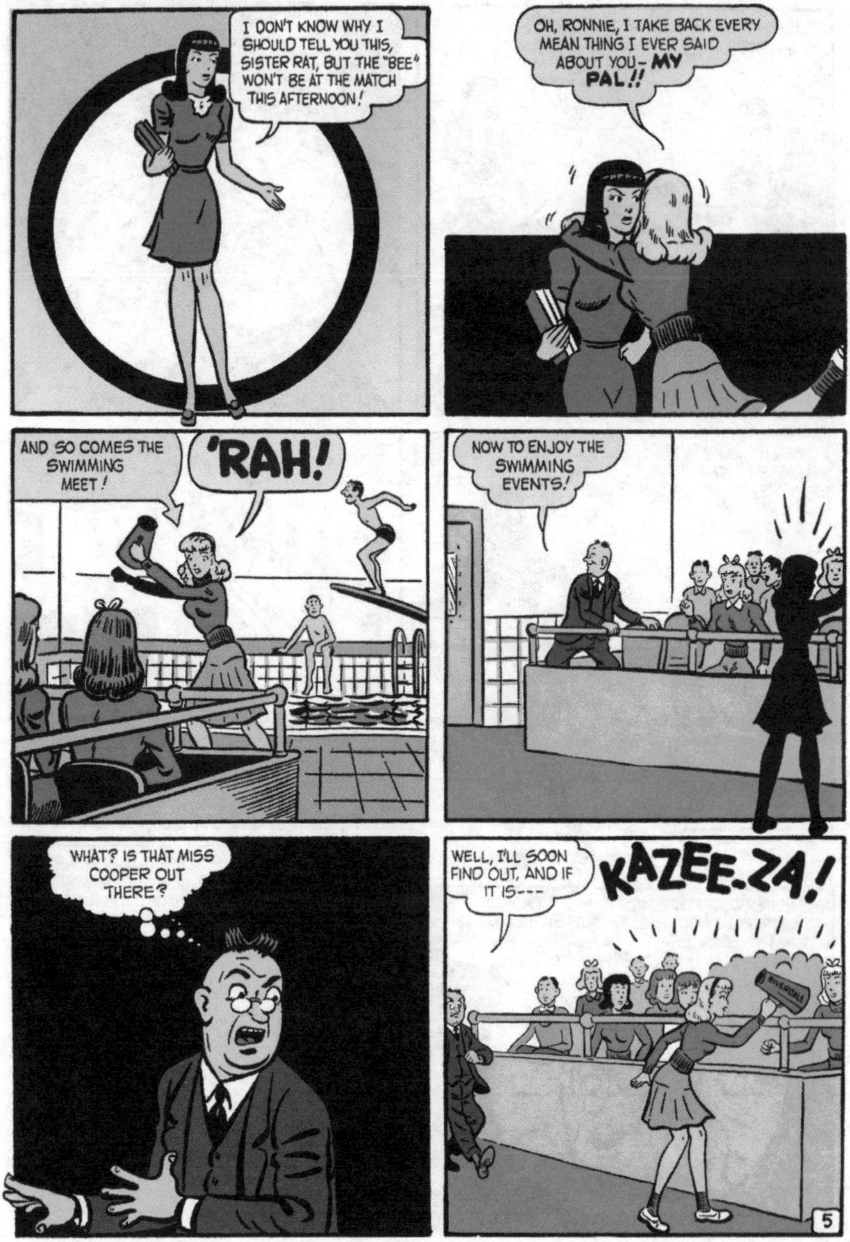
I DON'T KNOW WHY I SHOULD TELL YOU THIS, SISTER RAT, BUT THE "BEE" WON'T BE AT THE MATCH THIS AFTERNOON!
OH, RONNIE, I TAKE BACK EVERY MEAN THING I EVER SAID ABOUT YOU- MY PAL!!
AND SO COMES THE SWIMMING MEET!
'RAH!
NOW TO ENJOY THE SWIMMING EVENTS!
WHAT? IS THAT MISS COOPER OUT THERE?
WELL, I'LL SOON FIND OUT, AND IF IT IS---
KAZEE-ZA!
RIVERDALE
5

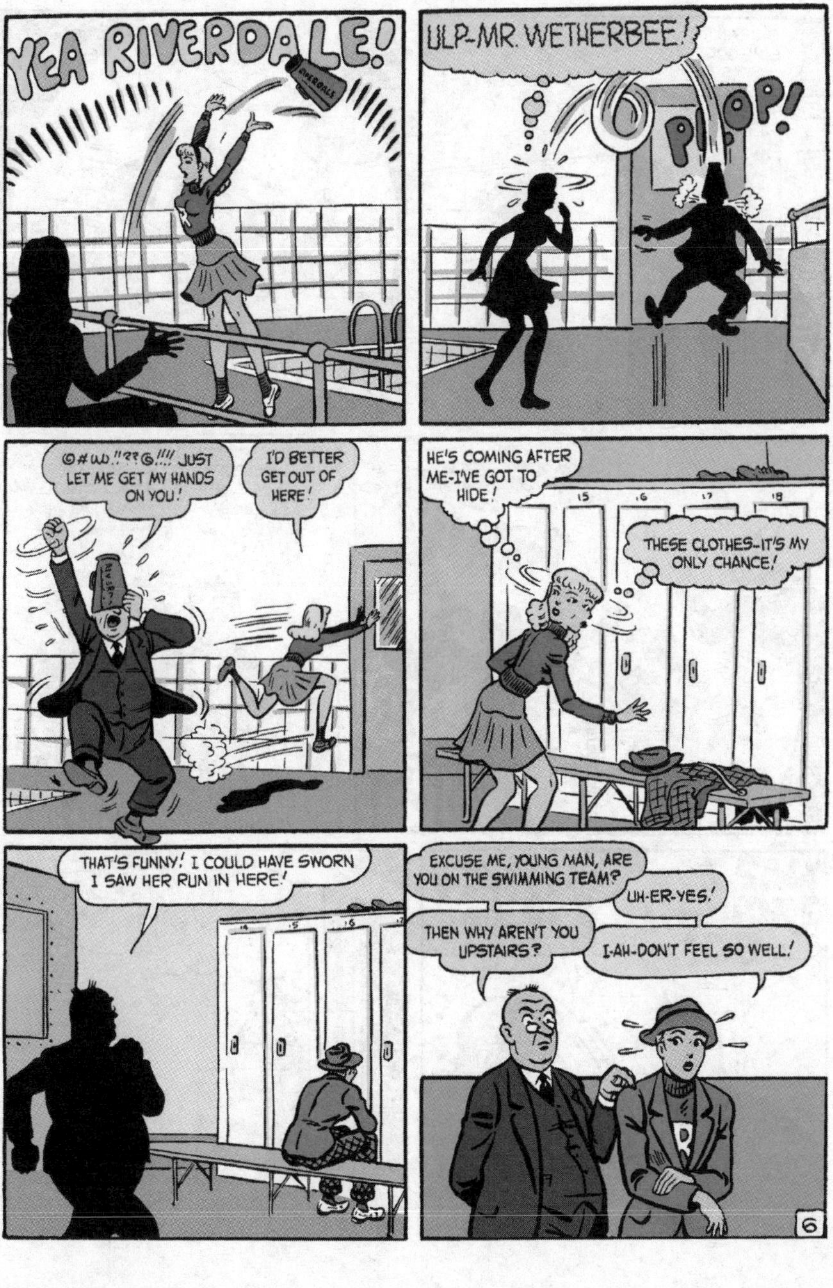
YEA RIVERDALE!
RIVERDALE
ULP-MR. WETHERBEE!
PLOP!
@#!!??@!!!! JUST LET ME GET MY HANDS ON YOU!
I'D BETTER GET OUT OF HERE!
HE'S COMING AFTER ME-I'VE GOT TO HIDE!
THESE CLOTHES-IT'S MY ONLY CHANCE!
THAT'S FUNNY! I COULD HAVE SWORN I SAW HER RUN IN HERE!
EXCUSE ME, YOUNG MAN, ARE YOU ON THE SWIMMING TEAM?
UH-ER-YES!
THEN WHY AREN'T YOU UPSTAIRS?
I-AH-DON'T FEEL SO WELL!
6

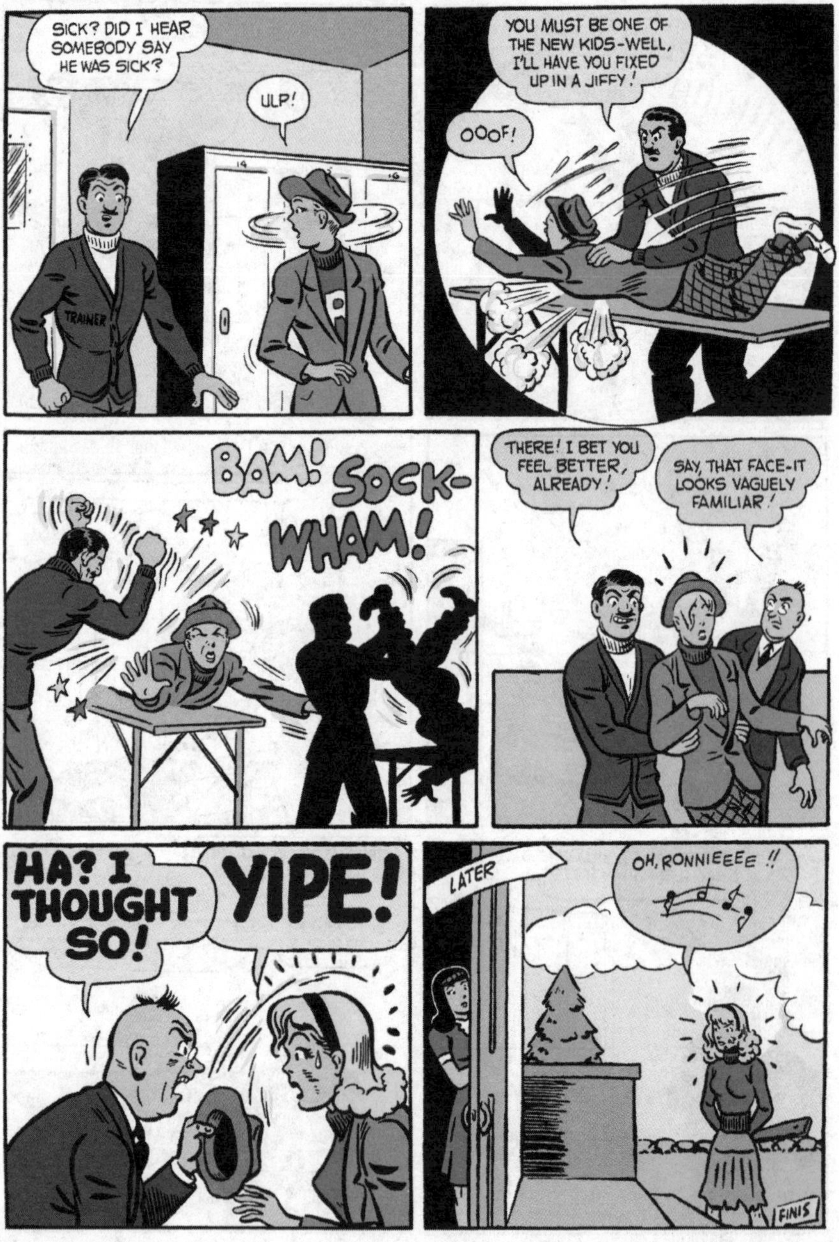
SICK? DID I HEAR SOMEBODY SAY HE WAS SICK?
ULP!
TRAINER
YOU MUST BE ONE OF THE NEW KIDS-WELL, I'LL HAVE YOU FIXED UP IN A JIFFY!
OOOF!
BAM! SOCK-WHAM!
THERE! I BET YOU FEEL BETTER, ALREADY!
SAY, THAT FACE-IT LOOKS VAGUELY FAMILIAR!
HA? I THOUGHT SO!
YIPE!
LATER
OH, RONNIEEEE !!
FINIS

THE BEST OF ARCHIE COMICS STARRING

BETTY & VERONICA

1950s

UN SEEKS TY
SHO CO)) ((RO
O RII)) RR

RIVERDALE GLOBE

GLOBE TO LAUNCH
"BLIND DATE" CONTEST
TOMORROW

Search On For
Most Popular
High School
Boy and Girl

WHAT'S COOKIN'?
BETTY & VERONICA #1, 1950
George Frese

FISH FOR DINNER
BETTY & VERONICA #4, 1951
Dan DeCarlo

SKI SICK
BETTY & VERONICA #12, 1954
Frank Doyle, Harry Lucey, Terry Szenics

LATE DATE
BETTY & VERONICA #20, 1955
Dan DeCarlo, Rudy Lapick

As a kid, every year I would count down the days to my favorite event—summer camp. At camp, I got to spend every day having fun with other girls my age, forming some of the most lasting friendships of my life. Little did I know at the time, but one of the longest-lasting of those was with the two girls in the title of this book, Betty and Veronica. I was known to always have a stash of Archie comics at my bunk, and my friends and I read them voraciously. I never expected that, years later, I'd be helping to make those same comics!

- KARI MCLACHLAN *Lead Designer, Archie Comics*

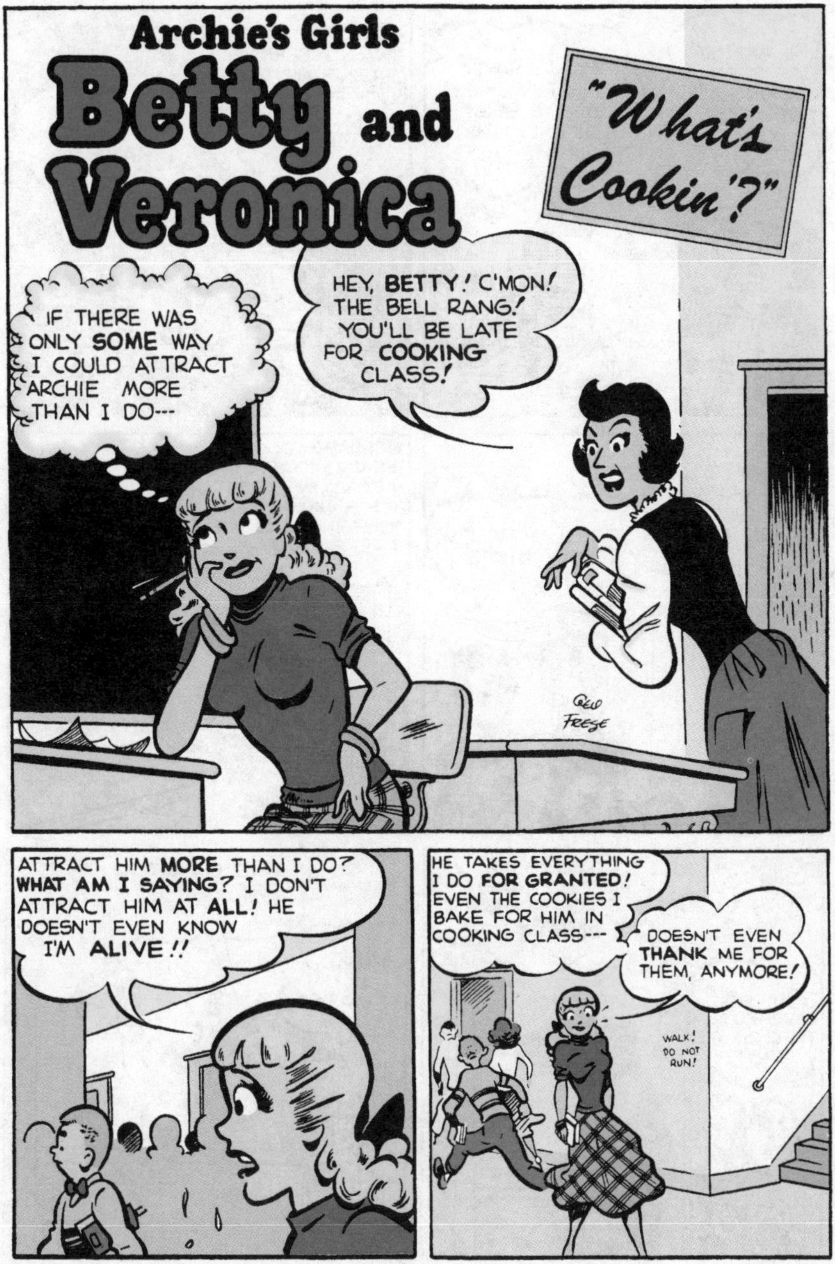
Archie's Girls
Betty and Veronica
"What's Cookin'?"
IF THERE WAS ONLY SOME WAY I COULD ATTRACT ARCHIE MORE THAN I DO---
HEY, BETTY! C'MON! THE BELL RANG! YOU'LL BE LATE FOR COOKING CLASS!
DeCARLO
FRESE
ATTRACT HIM MORE THAN I DO? WHAT AM I SAYING? I DON'T ATTRACT HIM AT ALL! HE DOESN'T EVEN KNOW I'M ALIVE!!
HE TAKES EVERYTHING I DO FOR GRANTED! EVEN THE COOKIES I BAKE FOR HIM IN COOKING CLASS---
DOESN'T EVEN THANK ME FOR THEM, ANYMORE!
WALK! DO NOT RUN!

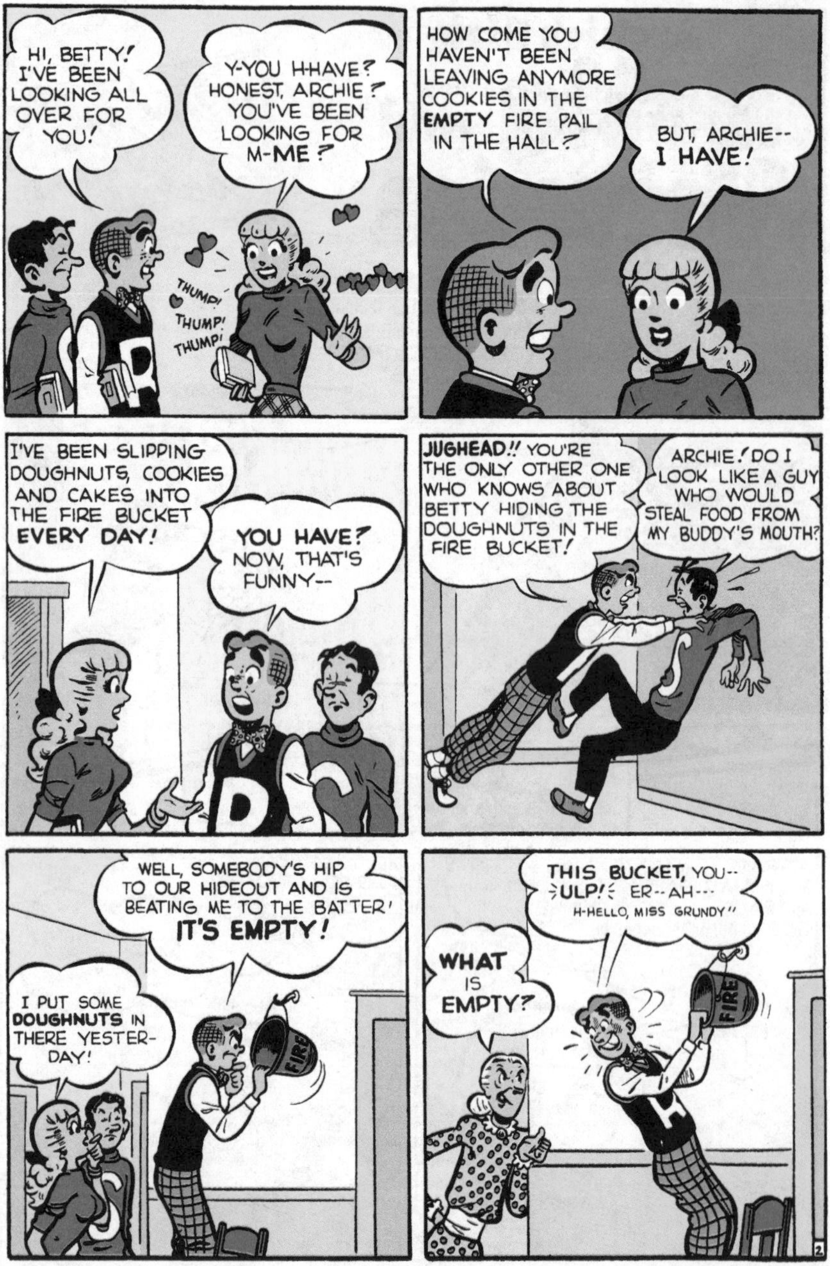
HI, BETTY! I'VE BEEN LOOKING ALL OVER FOR YOU!
Y-YOU H-HAVE? HONEST, ARCHIE? YOU'VE BEEN LOOKING FOR M-ME?
THUMP! THUMP! THUMP!
HOW COME YOU HAVEN'T BEEN LEAVING ANYMORE COOKIES IN THE EMPTY FIRE PAIL IN THE HALL?
BUT, ARCHIE-- I HAVE!
I'VE BEEN SLIPPING DOUGHNUTS, COOKIES AND CAKES INTO THE FIRE BUCKET EVERY DAY!
YOU HAVE? NOW, THAT'S FUNNY--
JUGHEAD!! YOU'RE THE ONLY OTHER ONE WHO KNOWS ABOUT BETTY HIDING THE DOUGHNUTS IN THE FIRE BUCKET!
ARCHIE! DO I LOOK LIKE A GUY WHO WOULD STEAL FOOD FROM MY BUDDY'S MOUTH?
WELL, SOMEBODY'S HIP TO OUR HIDEOUT AND IS BEATING ME TO THE BATTER! IT'S EMPTY!
I PUT SOME DOUGHNUTS IN THERE YESTER-DAY!
FIRE
WHAT IS EMPTY?
THIS BUCKET, YOU-- ULP! ER--AH--- H-HELLO, MISS GRUNDY"
FIRE
2

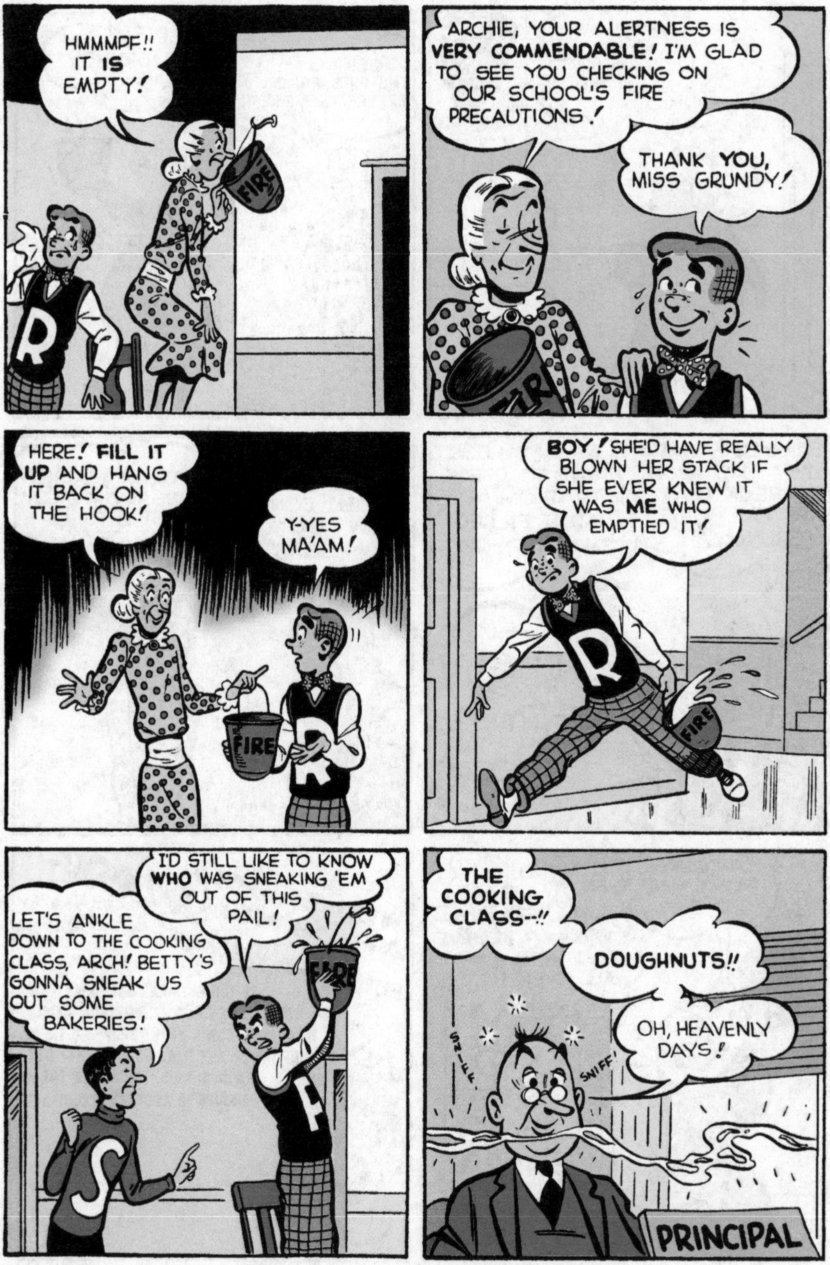
HMMMPF!! IT IS EMPTY!
ARCHIE, YOUR ALERTNESS IS VERY COMMENDABLE! I'M GLAD TO SEE YOU CHECKING ON OUR SCHOOL'S FIRE PRECAUTIONS!
THANK YOU, MISS GRUNDY!
HERE! FILL IT UP AND HANG IT BACK ON THE HOOK!
Y-YES MA'AM!
BOY! SHE'D HAVE REALLY BLOWN HER STACK IF SHE EVER KNEW IT WAS ME WHO EMPTIED IT!
LET'S ANKLE DOWN TO THE COOKING CLASS, ARCH! BETTY'S GONNA SNEAK US OUT SOME BAKERIES!
I'D STILL LIKE TO KNOW WHO WAS SNEAKING 'EM OUT OF THIS PAIL!
THE COOKING CLASS--!!
DOUGHNUTS!!
OH, HEAVENLY DAYS!
SNIFF
SNIFF!
PRINCIPAL

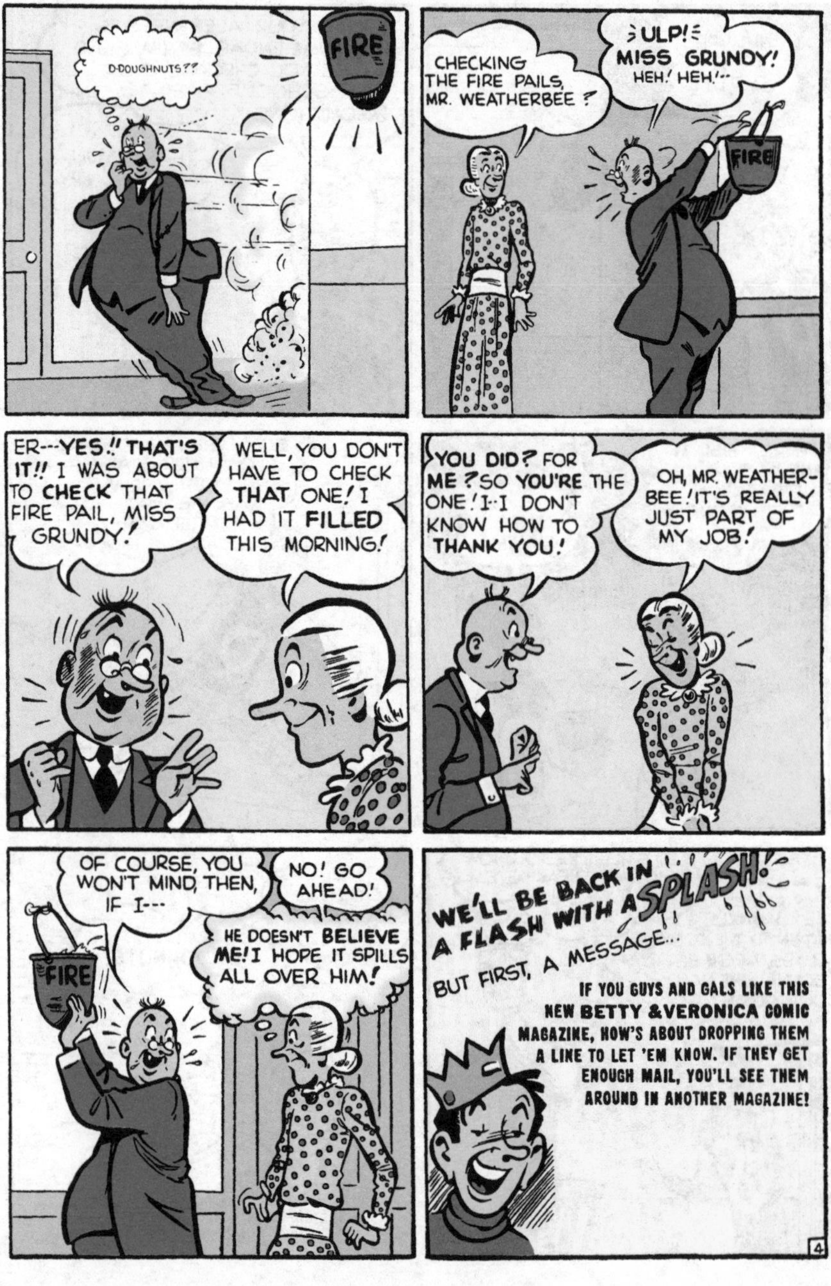
D-DOUGHNUTS??
FIRE
CHECKING THE FIRE PAILS, MR. WEATHERBEE ?
ULP! MISS GRUNDY! HEH! HEH!--
FIRE
ER---YES!! THAT'S IT!! I WAS ABOUT TO CHECK THAT FIRE PAIL, MISS GRUNDY!
WELL, YOU DON'T HAVE TO CHECK THAT ONE! I HAD IT FILLED THIS MORNING!
YOU DID? FOR ME? SO YOU'RE THE ONE! I-I DON'T KNOW HOW TO THANK YOU!
OH, MR. WEATHER-BEE! IT'S REALLY JUST PART OF MY JOB!
OF COURSE, YOU WON'T MIND, THEN, IF I---
NO! GO AHEAD!
HE DOESN'T BELIEVE ME! I HOPE IT SPILLS ALL OVER HIM!
FIRE
WE'LL BE BACK IN A FLASH WITH A SPLASH!
BUT FIRST, A MESSAGE...
IF YOU GUYS AND GALS LIKE THIS NEW BETTY & VERONICA COMIC MAGAZINE, HOW'S ABOUT DROPPING THEM A LINE TO LET 'EM KNOW. IF THEY GET ENOUGH MAIL, YOU'LL SEE THEM AROUND IN ANOTHER MAGAZINE!
4

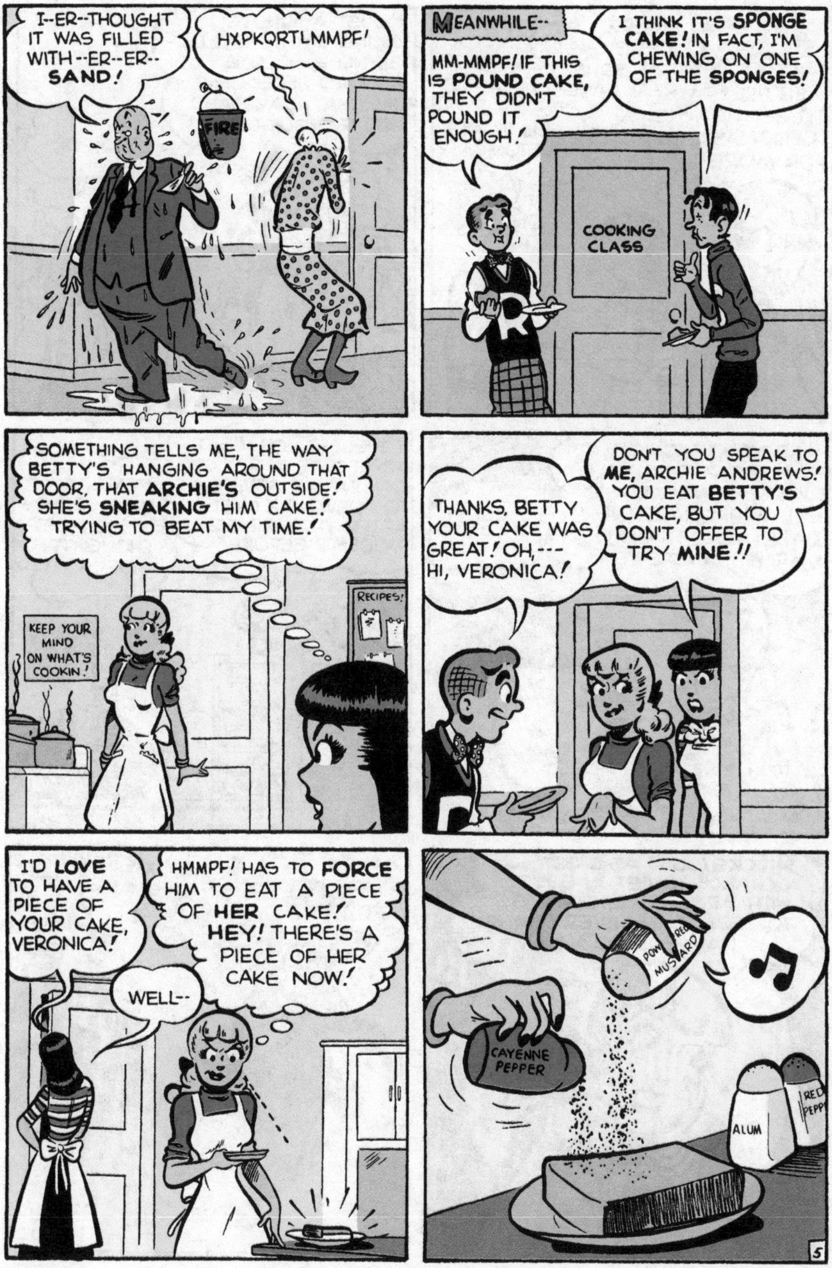

I--ER--THOUGHT IT WAS FILLED WITH--ER--ER-- SAND!
HXPKQRTLMMPF!
FIRE
MEANWHILE--
MM-MMPF! IF THIS IS POUND CAKE, THEY DIDN'T POUND IT ENOUGH!
I THINK IT'S SPONGE CAKE! IN FACT, I'M CHEWING ON ONE OF THE SPONGES!
COOKING CLASS
SOMETHING TELLS ME, THE WAY BETTY'S HANGING AROUND THAT DOOR, THAT ARCHIE'S OUTSIDE! SHE'S SNEAKING HIM CAKE! TRYING TO BEAT MY TIME!
RECIPES!
KEEP YOUR MIND ON WHAT'S COOKIN!
THANKS, BETTY YOUR CAKE WAS GREAT! OH,--- HI, VERONICA!
DON'T YOU SPEAK TO ME, ARCHIE ANDREWS! YOU EAT BETTY'S CAKE, BUT YOU DON'T OFFER TO TRY MINE!!
I'D LOVE TO HAVE A PIECE OF YOUR CAKE, VERONICA!
HMMPF! HAS TO FORCE HIM TO EAT A PIECE OF HER CAKE! HEY! THERE'S A PIECE OF HER CAKE NOW!
WELL--
MUSTARD
CAYENNE PEPPER
ALUM
RED
5

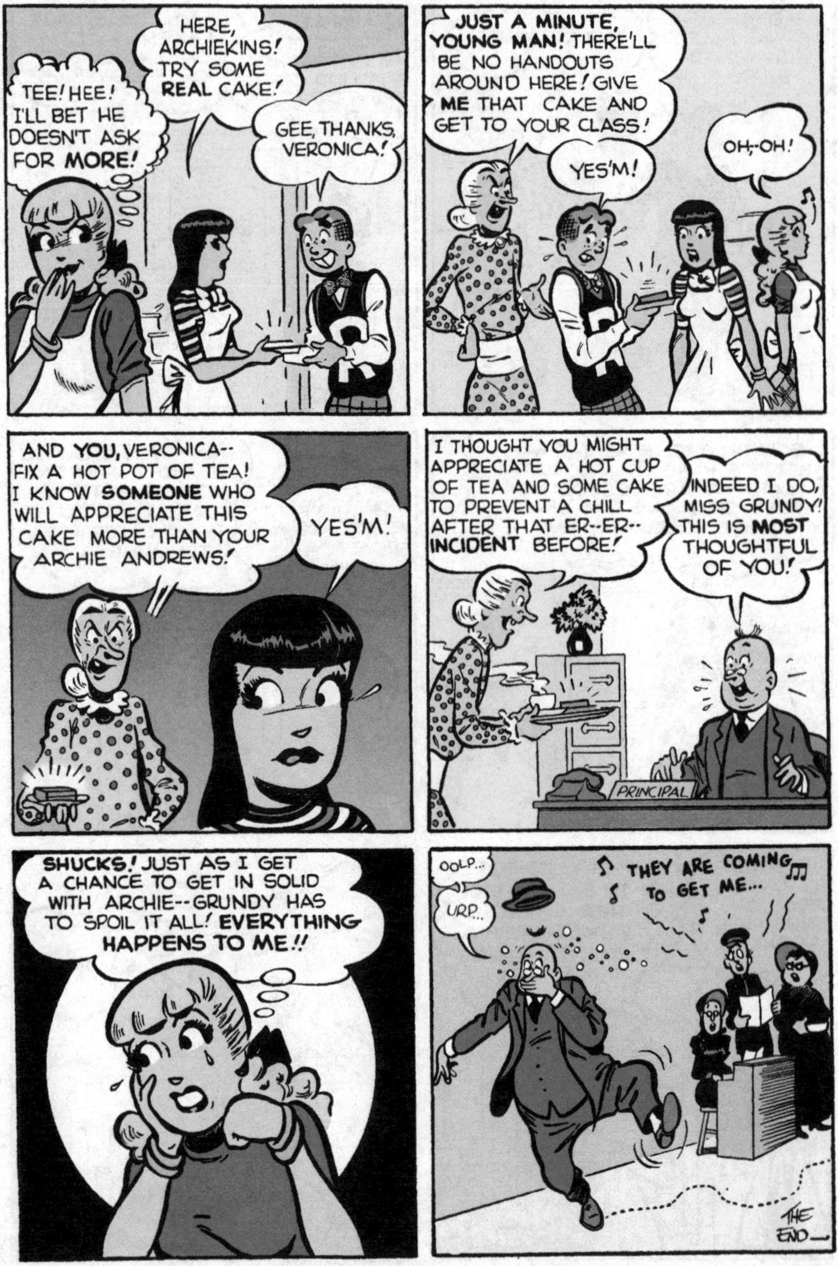
TEE! HEE! I'LL BET HE DOESN'T ASK FOR MORE!
HERE, ARCHIEKINS! TRY SOME REAL CAKE!
GEE, THANKS, VERONICA!
JUST A MINUTE, YOUNG MAN! THERE'LL BE NO HANDOUTS AROUND HERE! GIVE ME THAT CAKE AND GET TO YOUR CLASS!
YES'M!
OH,-OH!
AND YOU, VERONICA-- FIX A HOT POT OF TEA! I KNOW SOMEONE WHO WILL APPRECIATE THIS CAKE MORE THAN YOUR ARCHIE ANDREWS!
YES'M!
I THOUGHT YOU MIGHT APPRECIATE A HOT CUP OF TEA AND SOME CAKE TO PREVENT A CHILL AFTER THAT ER--ER-- INCIDENT BEFORE!
INDEED I DO, MISS GRUNDY! THIS IS MOST THOUGHTFUL OF YOU!
PRINCIPAL
SHUCKS! JUST AS I GET A CHANCE TO GET IN SOLID WITH ARCHIE--GRUNDY HAS TO SPOIL IT ALL! EVERYTHING HAPPENS TO ME!!
OOLP...
URP...
THEY ARE COMING TO GET ME...
THE END

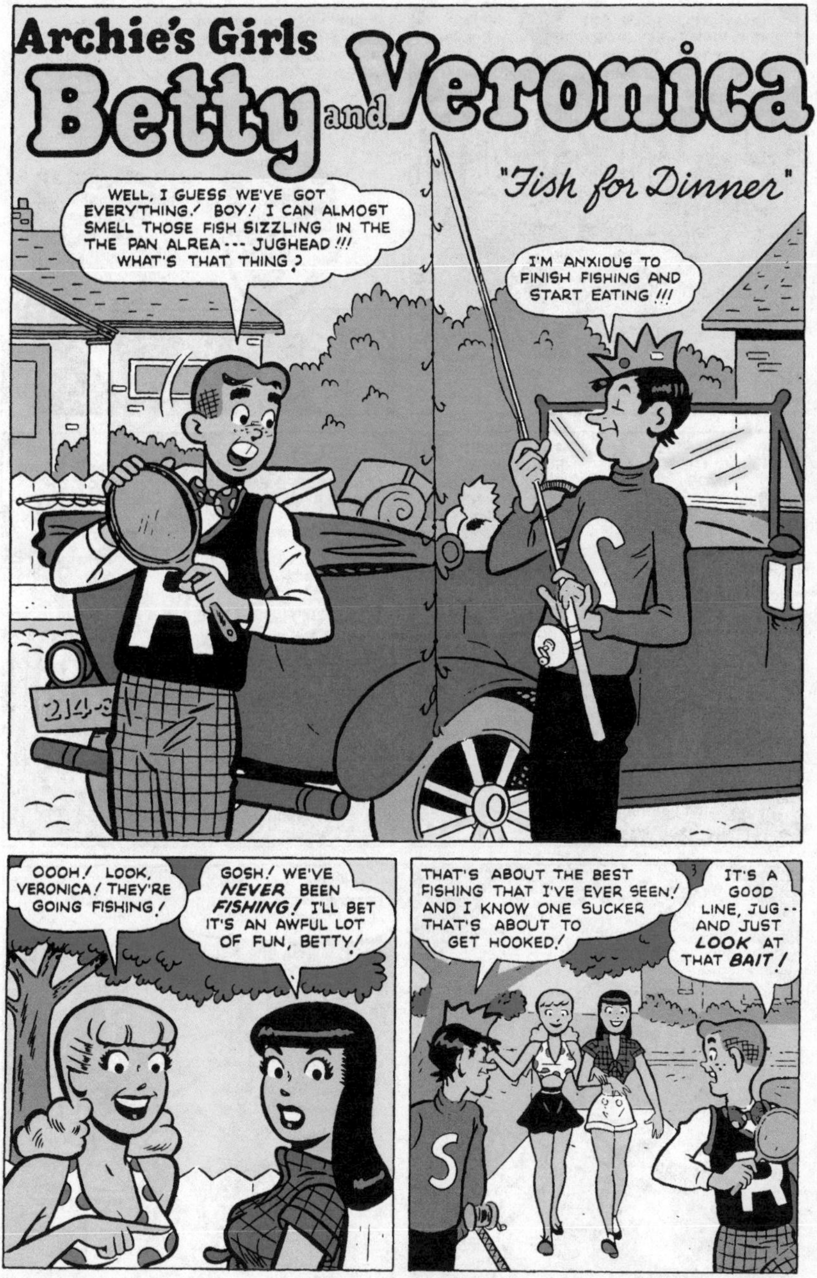
Archie's Girls
Betty and Veronica
"Fish for Dinner"
WELL, I GUESS WE'VE GOT EVERYTHING! BOY! I CAN ALMOST SMELL THOSE FISH SIZZLING IN THE THE PAN ALREA--- JUGHEAD!!! WHAT'S THAT THING?
I'M ANXIOUS TO FINISH FISHING AND START EATING!!!
214-3
OOOH! LOOK, VERONICA! THEY'RE GOING FISHING!
GOSH! WE'VE NEVER BEEN FISHING! I'LL BET IT'S AN AWFUL LOT OF FUN, BETTY!
THAT'S ABOUT THE BEST FISHING THAT I'VE EVER SEEN! AND I KNOW ONE SUCKER THAT'S ABOUT TO GET HOOKED!
IT'S A GOOD LINE, JUG-- AND JUST LOOK AT THAT BAIT!

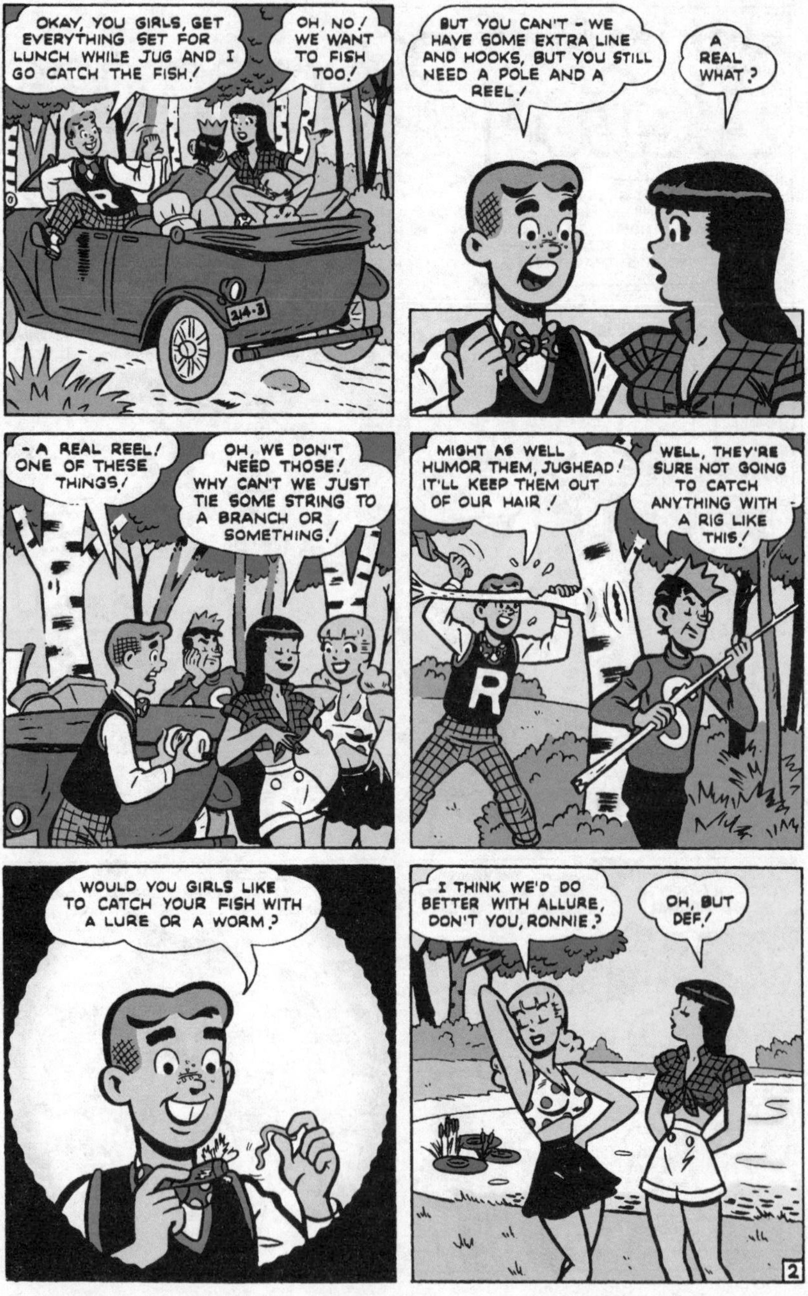
OKAY, YOU GIRLS, GET EVERYTHING SET FOR LUNCH WHILE JUG AND I GO CATCH THE FISH!
OH, NO! WE WANT TO FISH TOO!
2I4-3
BUT YOU CAN'T - WE HAVE SOME EXTRA LINE AND HOOKS, BUT YOU STILL NEED A POLE AND A REEL!
A REAL WHAT?
- A REAL REEL! ONE OF THESE THINGS!
OH, WE DON'T NEED THOSE! WHY CAN'T WE JUST TIE SOME STRING TO A BRANCH OR SOMETHING!
MIGHT AS WELL HUMOR THEM, JUGHEAD! IT'LL KEEP THEM OUT OF OUR HAIR!
WELL, THEY'RE SURE NOT GOING TO CATCH ANYTHING WITH A RIG LIKE THIS!
WOULD YOU GIRLS LIKE TO CATCH YOUR FISH WITH A LURE OR A WORM?
I THINK WE'D DO BETTER WITH ALLURE, DON'T YOU, RONNIE?
OH, BUT DEF!
2

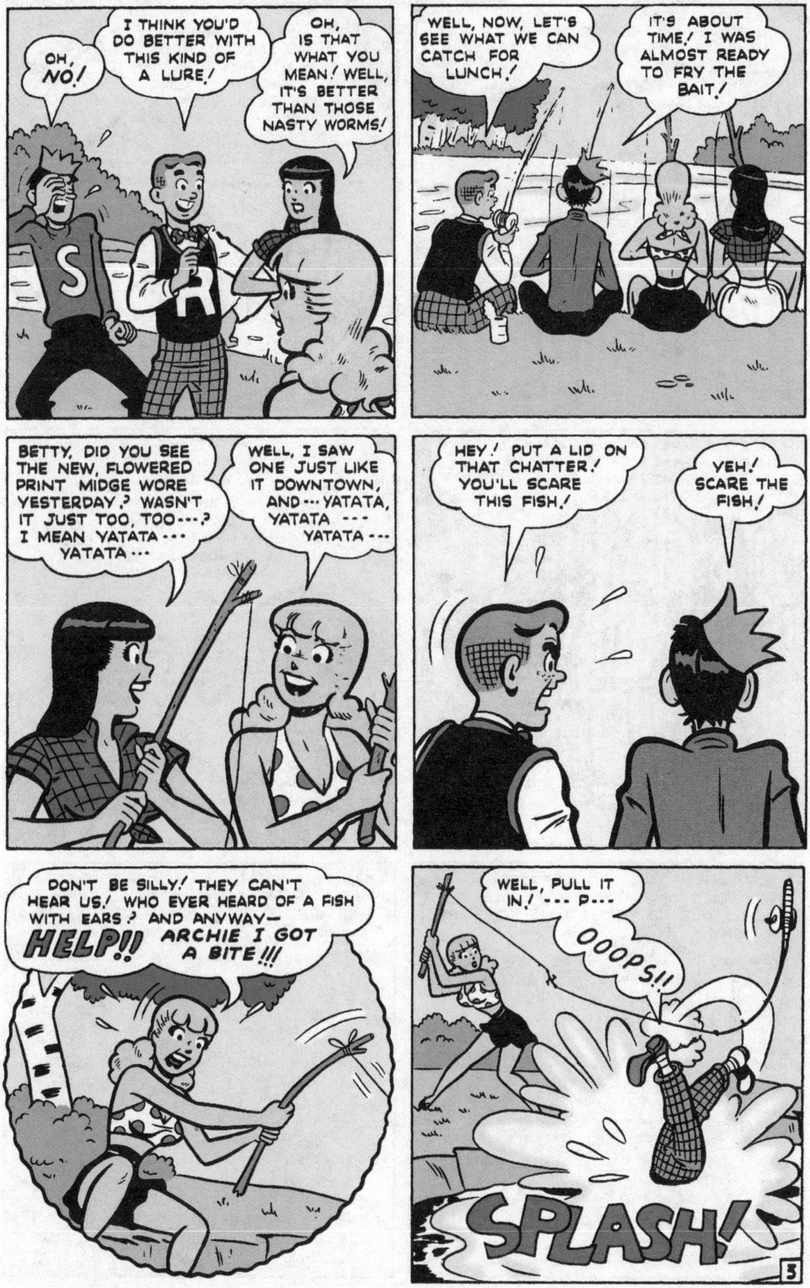
OH, NO!
I THINK YOU'D DO BETTER WITH THIS KIND OF A LURE!
OH, IS THAT WHAT YOU MEAN! WELL, IT'S BETTER THAN THOSE NASTY WORMS!
WELL, NOW, LET'S SEE WHAT WE CAN CATCH FOR LUNCH!
IT'S ABOUT TIME! I WAS ALMOST READY TO FRY THE BAIT!
BETTY, DID YOU SEE THE NEW, FLOWERED PRINT MIDGE WORE YESTERDAY? WASN'T IT JUST TOO, TOO---? I MEAN YATATA--- YATATA---
WELL, I SAW ONE JUST LIKE IT DOWNTOWN, AND---YATATA, YATATA --- YATATA ---
HEY! PUT A LID ON THAT CHATTER! YOU'LL SCARE THIS FISH!
YEH! SCARE THE FISH!
DON'T BE SILLY! THEY CAN'T HEAR US! WHO EVER HEARD OF A FISH WITH EARS? AND ANYWAY—
HELP!! ARCHIE I GOT A BITE!!!
WELL, PULL IT IN! --- P---
OOOPS!!
SPLASH!

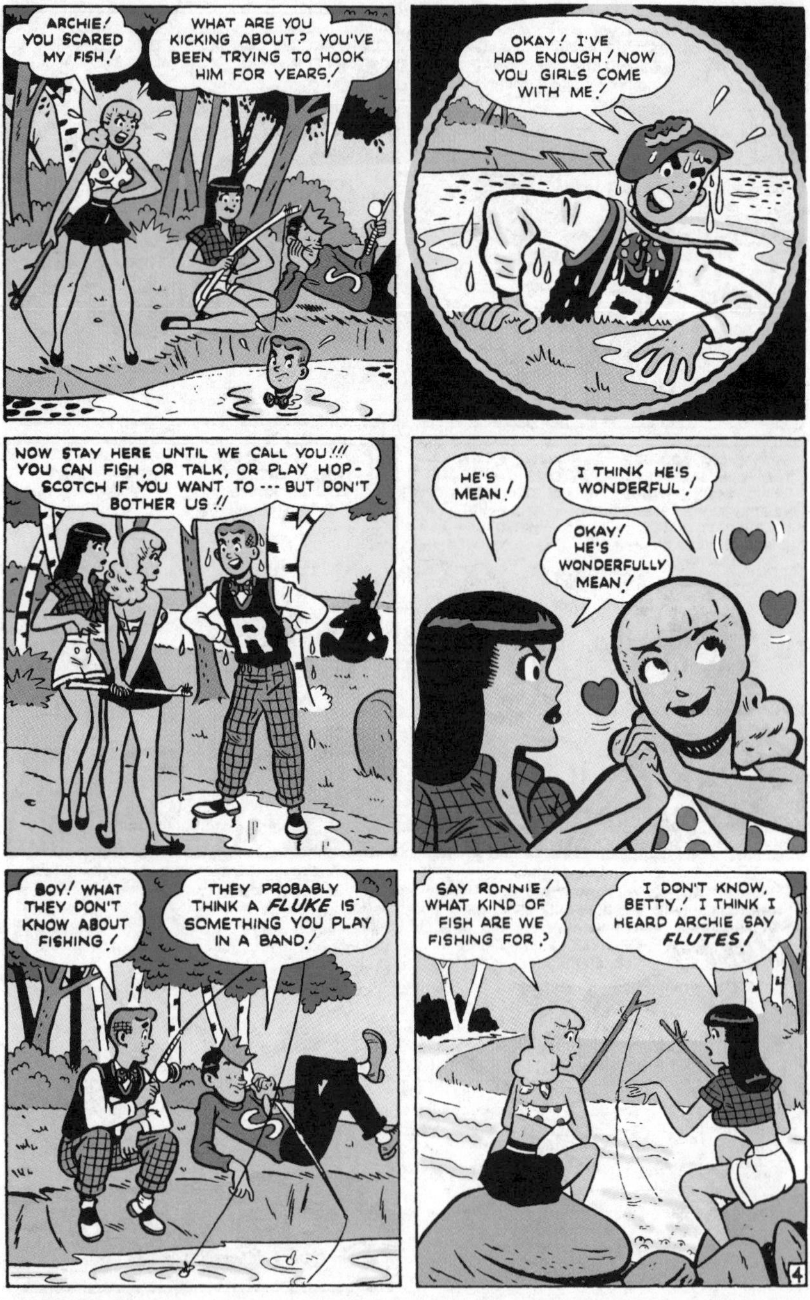
ARCHIE! YOU SCARED MY FISH!
WHAT ARE YOU KICKING ABOUT? YOU'VE BEEN TRYING TO HOOK HIM FOR YEARS!
OKAY! I'VE HAD ENOUGH! NOW YOU GIRLS COME WITH ME!
NOW STAY HERE UNTIL WE CALL YOU!!! YOU CAN FISH, OR TALK, OR PLAY HOP-SCOTCH IF YOU WANT TO --- BUT DON'T BOTHER US!!
HE'S MEAN!
I THINK HE'S WONDERFUL!
OKAY! HE'S WONDERFULLY MEAN!
BOY! WHAT THEY DON'T KNOW ABOUT FISHING!
THEY PROBABLY THINK A FLUKE IS SOMETHING YOU PLAY IN A BAND!
SAY RONNIE! WHAT KIND OF FISH ARE WE FISHING FOR?
I DON'T KNOW, BETTY! I THINK I HEARD ARCHIE SAY FLUTES!
4

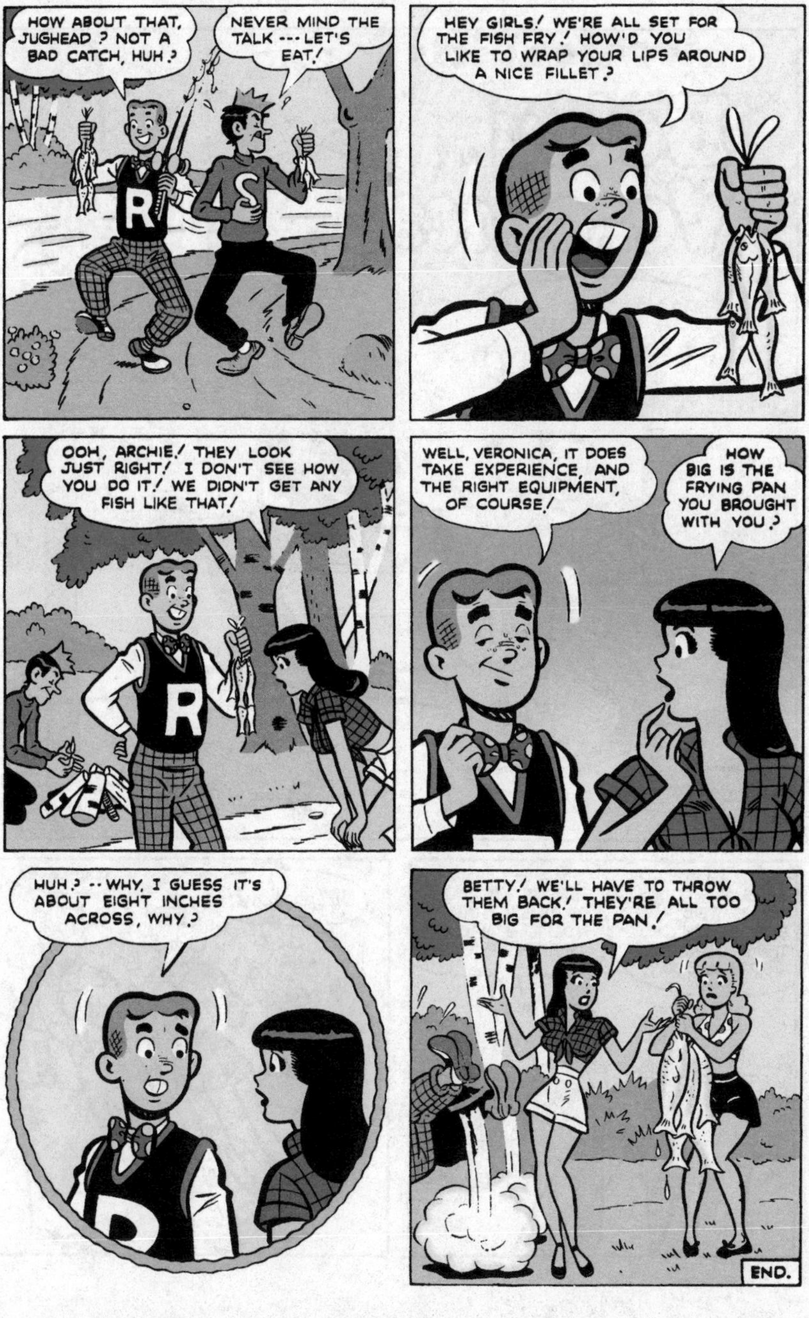

HOW ABOUT THAT, JUGHEAD ? NOT A BAD CATCH, HUH ?
NEVER MIND THE TALK --- LET'S EAT!
HEY GIRLS! WE'RE ALL SET FOR THE FISH FRY! HOW'D YOU LIKE TO WRAP YOUR LIPS AROUND A NICE FILLET ?
OOH, ARCHIE! THEY LOOK JUST RIGHT! I DON'T SEE HOW YOU DO IT! WE DIDN'T GET ANY FISH LIKE THAT!
WELL, VERONICA, IT DOES TAKE EXPERIENCE, AND THE RIGHT EQUIPMENT, OF COURSE!
HOW BIG IS THE FRYING PAN YOU BROUGHT WITH YOU ?
HUH ? -- WHY, I GUESS IT'S ABOUT EIGHT INCHES ACROSS, WHY ?
BETTY! WE'LL HAVE TO THROW THEM BACK! THEY'RE ALL TOO BIG FOR THE PAN!
END.

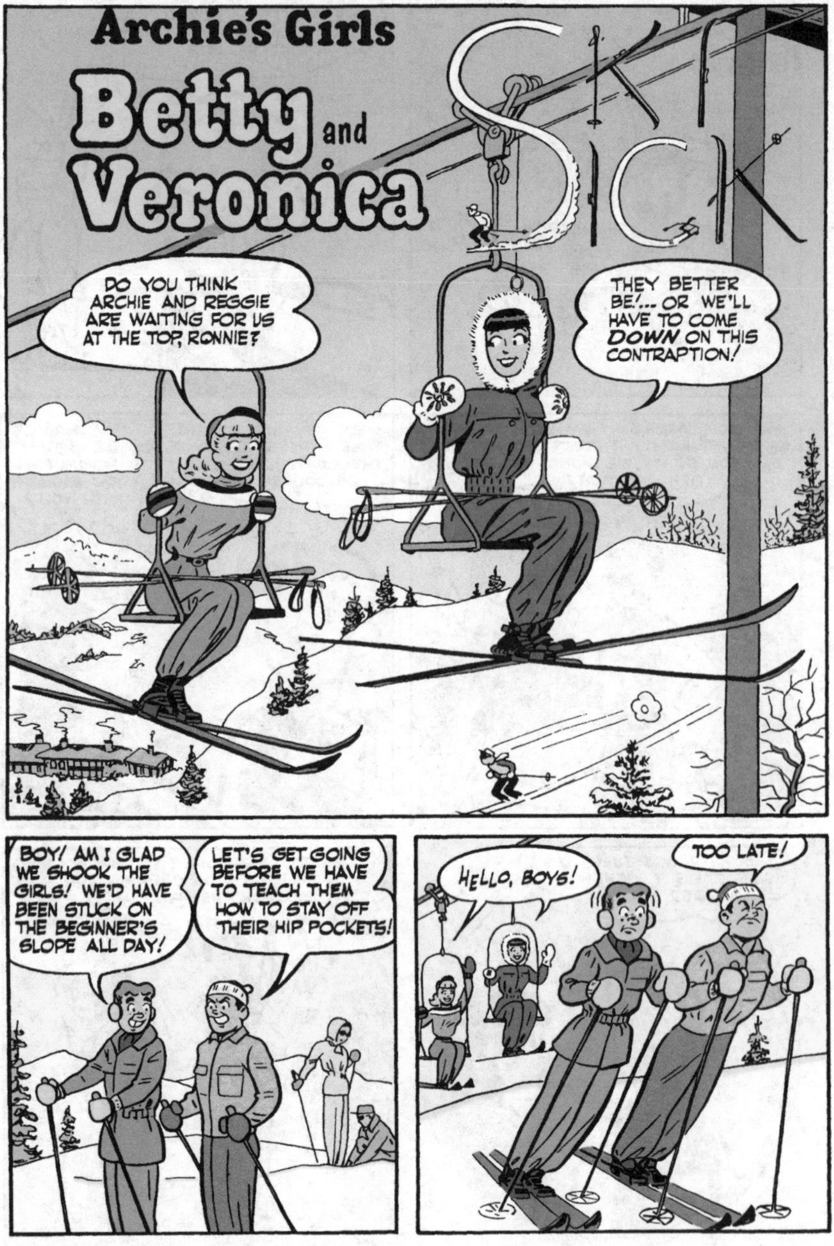
Archie's Girls
Betty and Veronica
SKI SICK
DO YOU THINK ARCHIE AND REGGIE ARE WAITING FOR US AT THE TOP, RONNIE?
THEY BETTER BE!... OR WE'LL HAVE TO COME DOWN ON THIS CONTRAPTION!
BOY! AM I GLAD WE SHOOK THE GIRLS! WE'D HAVE BEEN STUCK ON THE BEGINNER'S SLOPE ALL DAY!
LET'S GET GOING BEFORE WE HAVE TO TEACH THEM HOW TO STAY OFF THEIR HIP POCKETS!
HELLO, BOYS!
TOO LATE!

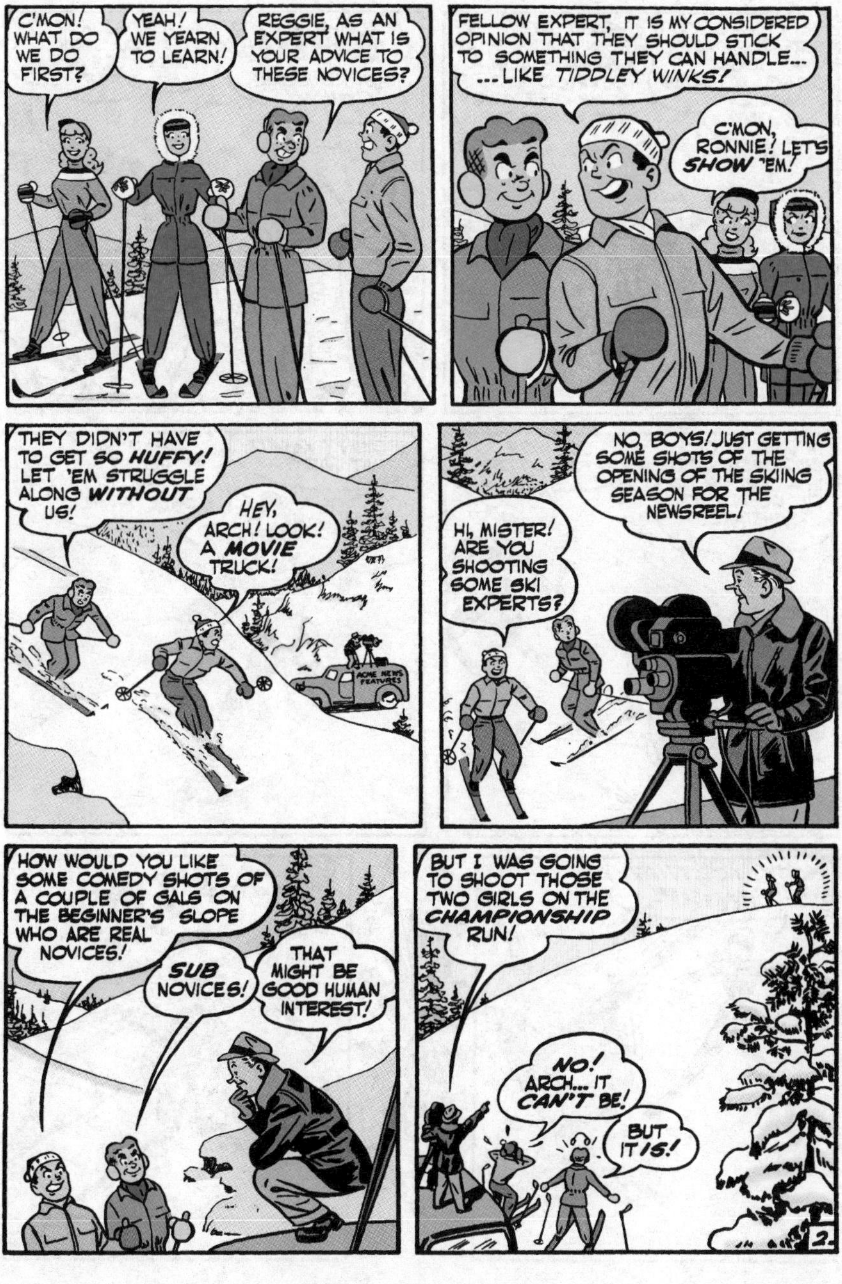

C'MON! WHAT DO WE DO FIRST?
YEAH! WE YEARN TO LEARN!
REGGIE, AS AN EXPERT WHAT IS YOUR ADVICE TO THESE NOVICES?
FELLOW EXPERT, IT IS MY CONSIDERED OPINION THAT THEY SHOULD STICK TO SOMETHING THEY CAN HANDLE... ...LIKE TIDDLEY WINKS!
C'MON, RONNIE! LET'S SHOW 'EM!
THEY DIDN'T HAVE TO GET SO HUFFY! LET 'EM STRUGGLE ALONG WITHOUT US!
HEY, ARCH! LOOK! A MOVIE TRUCK!
ACME NEWS FEATURES
HI, MISTER! ARE YOU SHOOTING SOME SKI EXPERTS?
NO, BOYS! JUST GETTING SOME SHOTS OF THE OPENING OF THE SKIING SEASON FOR THE NEWSREEL!
HOW WOULD YOU LIKE SOME COMEDY SHOTS OF A COUPLE OF GALS ON THE BEGINNER'S SLOPE WHO ARE REAL NOVICES!
SUB NOVICES!
THAT MIGHT BE GOOD HUMAN INTEREST!
BUT I WAS GOING TO SHOOT THOSE TWO GIRLS ON THE CHAMPIONSHIP RUN!
NO! ARCH... IT CAN'T BE!
BUT IT IS!
2

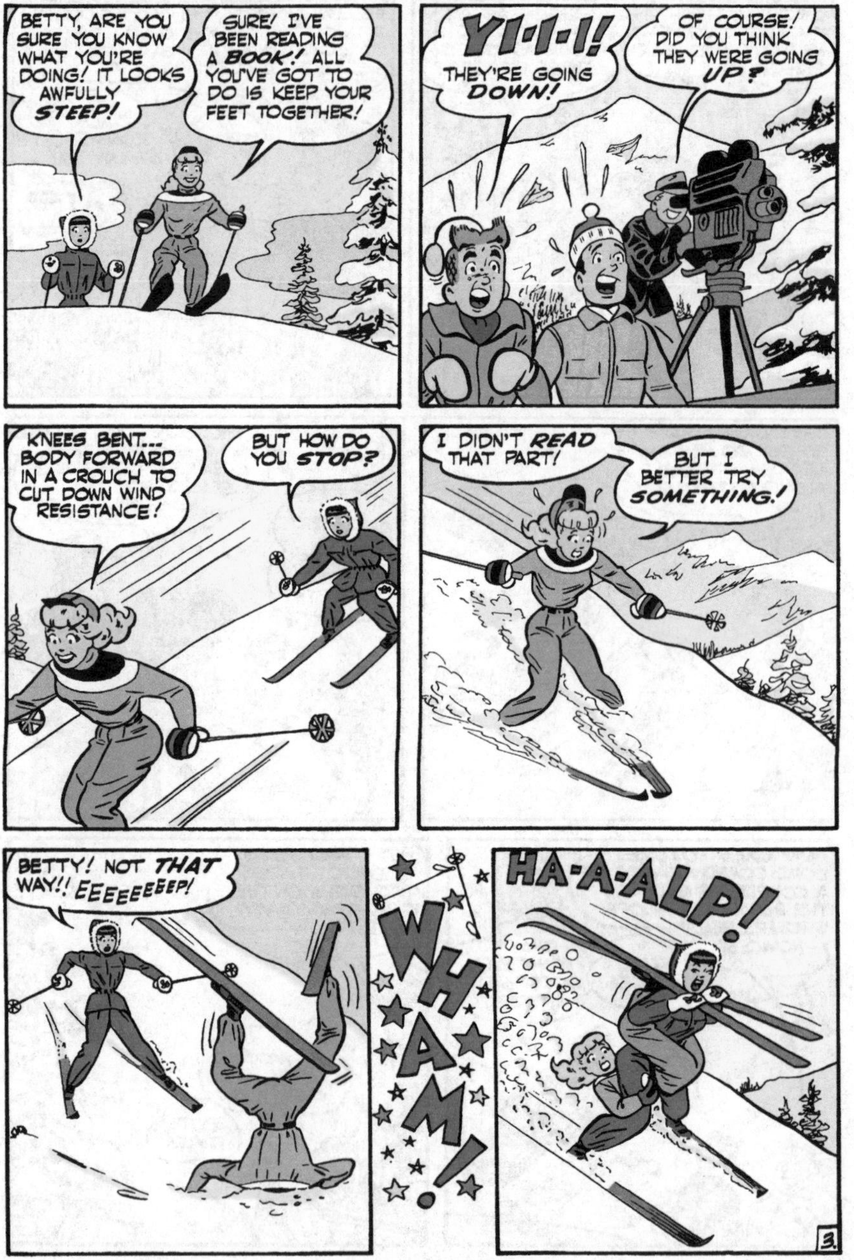

BETTY, ARE YOU SURE YOU KNOW WHAT YOU'RE DOING! IT LOOKS AWFULLY STEEP!
SURE! I'VE BEEN READING A BOOK! ALL YOU'VE GOT TO DO IS KEEP YOUR FEET TOGETHER!
YI-I-I! THEY'RE GOING DOWN!
OF COURSE! DID YOU THINK THEY WERE GOING UP?
KNEES BENT... BODY FORWARD IN A CROUCH TO CUT DOWN WIND RESISTANCE!
BUT HOW DO YOU STOP?
I DIDN'T READ THAT PART!
BUT I BETTER TRY SOMETHING!
BETTY! NOT THAT WAY!! EEEEEEEEEP!
WHAM!
HA-A-ALP!
3.

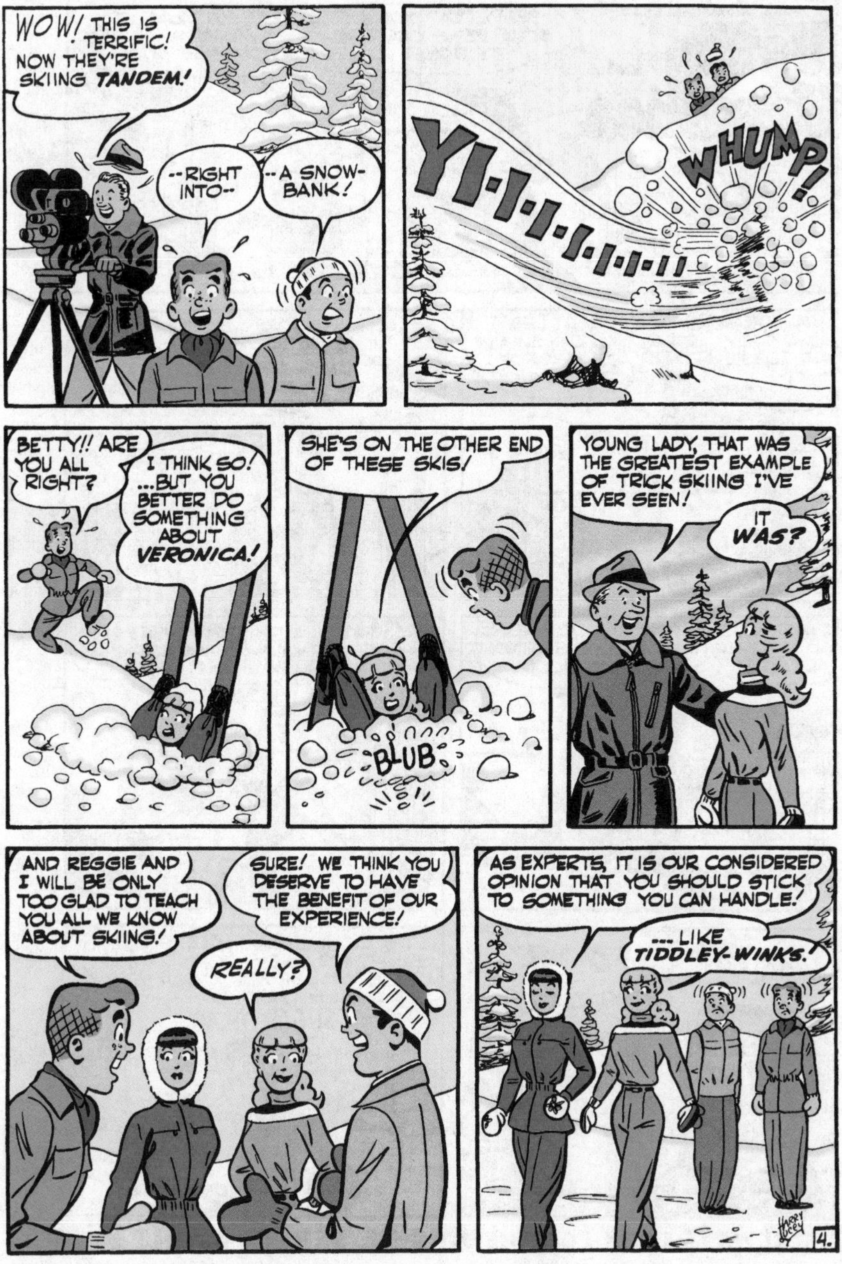
WOW! THIS IS TERRIFIC! NOW THEY'RE SKIING TANDEM!
--RIGHT INTO--
--A SNOW-BANK!
YI-I-I-I-I-I-I-II
WHUMP!
BETTY!! ARE YOU ALL RIGHT?
I THINK SO! ...BUT YOU BETTER DO SOMETHING ABOUT VERONICA!
SHE'S ON THE OTHER END OF THESE SKIS!
BLUB
YOUNG LADY, THAT WAS THE GREATEST EXAMPLE OF TRICK SKIING I'VE EVER SEEN!
IT WAS?
AND REGGIE AND I WILL BE ONLY TOO GLAD TO TEACH YOU ALL WE KNOW ABOUT SKIING!
SURE! WE THINK YOU DESERVE TO HAVE THE BENEFIT OF OUR EXPERIENCE!
REALLY?
AS EXPERTS, IT IS OUR CONSIDERED OPINION THAT YOU SHOULD STICK TO SOMETHING YOU CAN HANDLE!
... LIKE TIDDLEY-WINKS!
HARRY LUCEY
4.

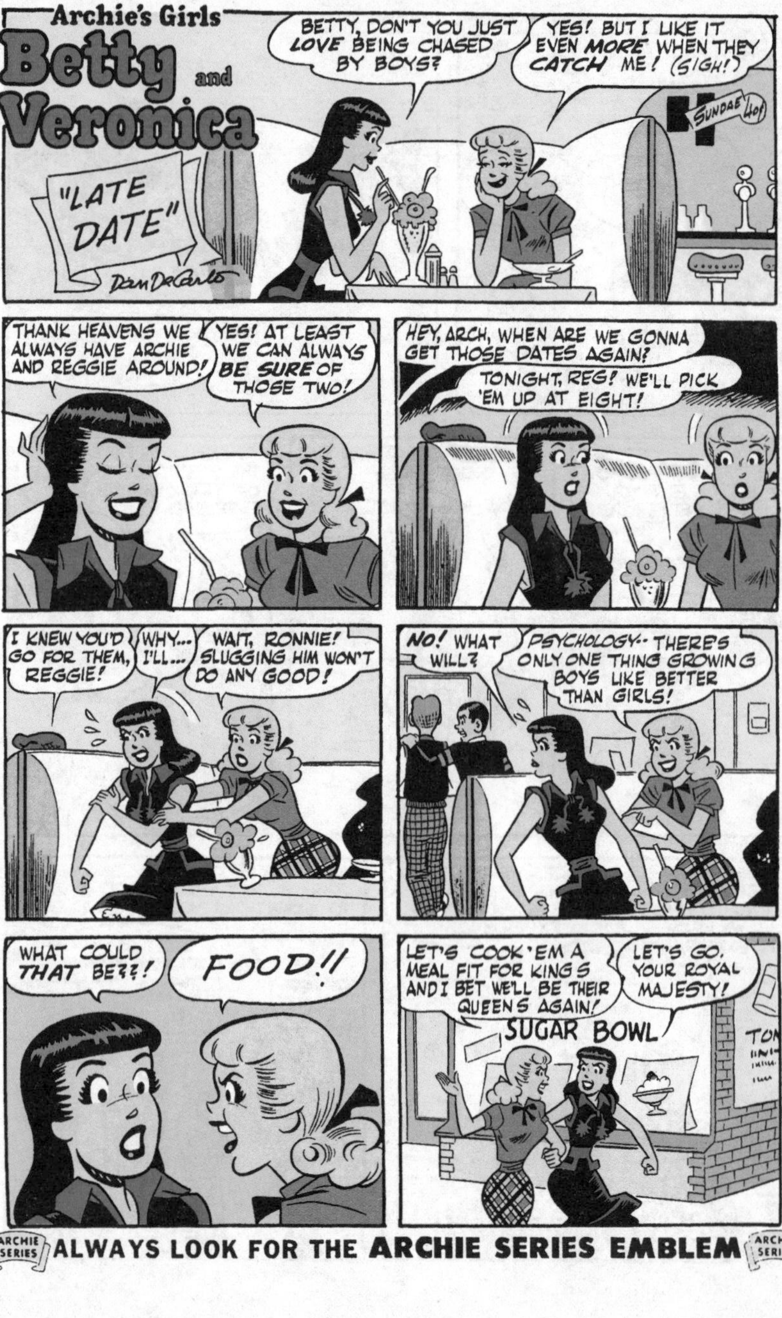
Archie's Girls
Betty and Veronica
"LATE DATE"
Dan DeCarlo
BETTY, DON'T YOU JUST LOVE BEING CHASED BY BOYS?
YES! BUT I LIKE IT EVEN MORE WHEN THEY CATCH ME! (SIGH!)
SUNDAE 40¢
THANK HEAVENS WE ALWAYS HAVE ARCHIE AND REGGIE AROUND!
YES! AT LEAST WE CAN ALWAYS BE SURE OF THOSE TWO!
HEY, ARCH, WHEN ARE WE GONNA GET THOSE DATES AGAIN?
TONIGHT, REG! WE'LL PICK 'EM UP AT EIGHT!
I KNEW YOU'D GO FOR THEM, REGGIE!
WHY... I'LL...
WAIT, RONNIE! SLUGGING HIM WON'T DO ANY GOOD!
NO! WHAT WILL?
PSYCHOLOGY-- THERE'S ONLY ONE THING GROWING BOYS LIKE BETTER THAN GIRLS!
WHAT COULD THAT BE???!
FOOD!!
LET'S COOK 'EM A MEAL FIT FOR KINGS AND I BET WE'LL BE THEIR QUEENS AGAIN!
LET'S GO, YOUR ROYAL MAJESTY!
SUGAR BOWL

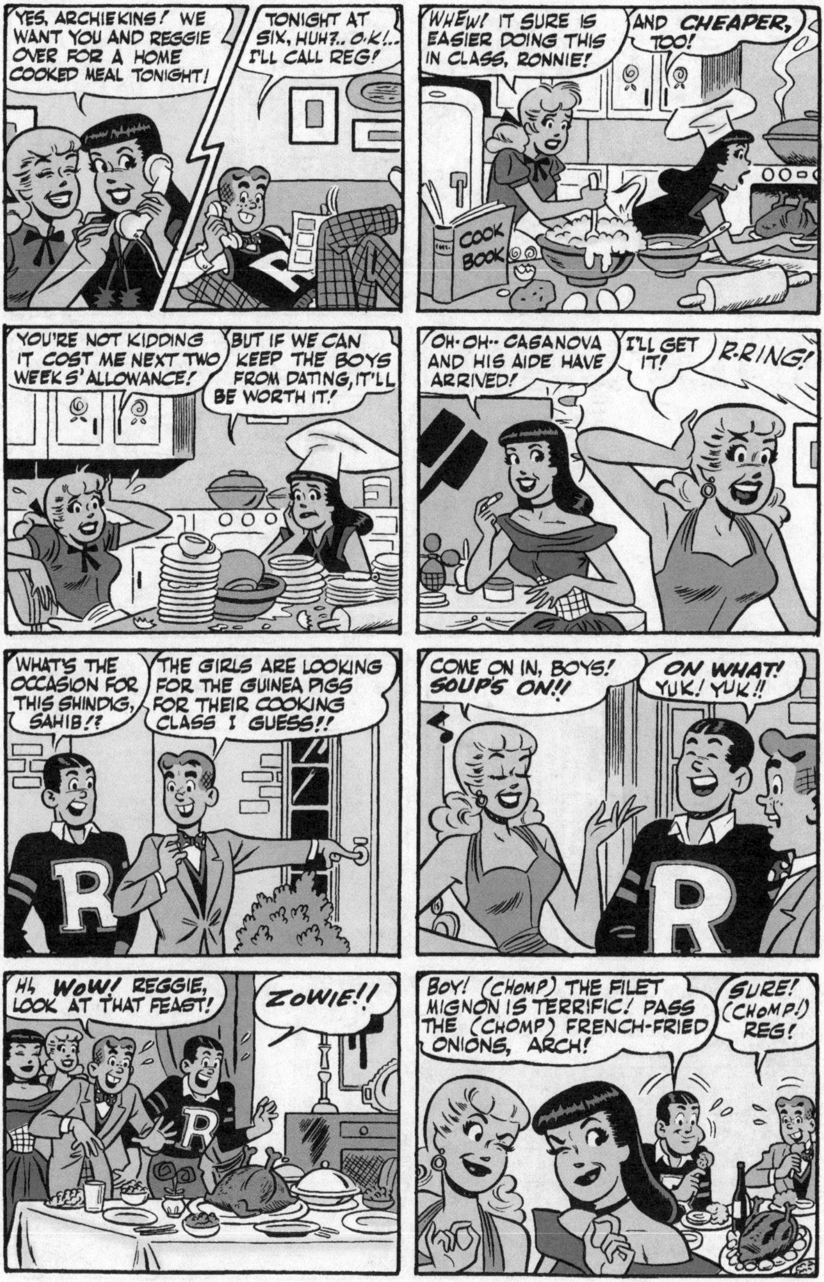
YES, ARCHIEKINS! WE WANT YOU AND REGGIE OVER FOR A HOME COOKED MEAL TONIGHT!
TONIGHT AT SIX, HUH?.. O.K!.. I'LL CALL REG!
WHEW! IT SURE IS EASIER DOING THIS IN CLASS, RONNIE!
AND CHEAPER, TOO!
COOK BOOK
YOU'RE NOT KIDDING IT COST ME NEXT TWO WEEK S' ALLOWANCE!
BUT IF WE CAN KEEP THE BOYS FROM DATING, IT'LL BE WORTH IT!
OH-OH-- CASANOVA AND HIS AIDE HAVE ARRIVED!
I'LL GET IT!
R-RING!
WHAT'S THE OCCASION FOR THIS SHINDIG, SAHIB!?
THE GIRLS ARE LOOKING FOR THE GUINEA PIGS FOR THEIR COOKING CLASS I GUESS!!
COME ON IN, BOYS! SOUP'S ON!!
ON WHAT! YUK! YUK!!
HI, WOW! REGGIE, LOOK AT THAT FEAST!
ZOWIE!!
BOY! (CHOMP) THE FILET MIGNON IS TERRIFIC! PASS THE (CHOMP) FRENCH-FRIED ONIONS, ARCH!
SURE! (CHOMP!) REG!

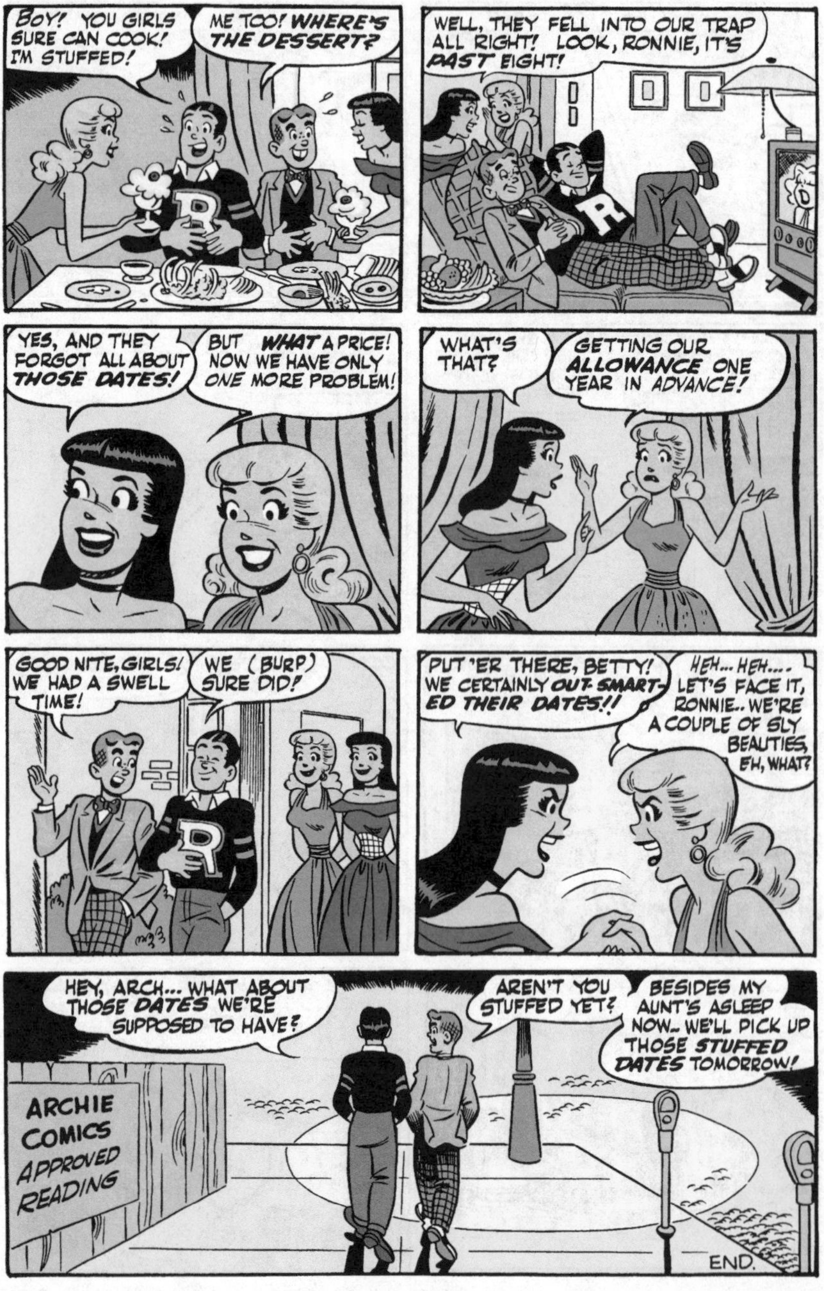
BOY! YOU GIRLS SURE CAN COOK! I'M STUFFED!
ME TOO! WHERE'S THE DESSERT?
WELL, THEY FELL INTO OUR TRAP ALL RIGHT! LOOK, RONNIE, IT'S PAST EIGHT!
YES, AND THEY FORGOT ALL ABOUT THOSE DATES!
BUT WHAT A PRICE! NOW WE HAVE ONLY ONE MORE PROBLEM!
WHAT'S THAT?
GETTING OUR ALLOWANCE ONE YEAR IN ADVANCE!
GOOD NITE, GIRLS! WE HAD A SWELL TIME!
WE (BURP) SURE DID!
PUT 'ER THERE, BETTY! WE CERTAINLY OUT-SMARTED THEIR DATES!!
HEH... HEH.... LET'S FACE IT, RONNIE.. WE'RE A COUPLE OF SLY BEAUTIES, EH, WHAT?
HEY, ARCH... WHAT ABOUT THOSE DATES WE'RE SUPPOSED TO HAVE?
AREN'T YOU STUFFED YET?
BESIDES MY AUNT'S ASLEEP NOW.. WE'LL PICK UP THOSE STUFFED DATES TOMORROW!
ARCHIE COMICS APPROVED READING
END.

CLICK CHICK
BETTY & VERONICA #26, 1956
Samm Schwartz, Barry Grossman

SOCK 'N ROLL
BETTY & VERONICA #26, 1956
Bob Bolling, Barry Grossman, Terry Szenics

POPULAR MECHANICS
BETTY & VERONICA #29, 1957
Frank Doyle, Harry Lucey

SHEEP SKINNED
BETTY & VERONICA #44, 1959
Frank Doyle, Dan DeCarlo, Rudy Lapick, Vincent DeCarlo

When I stopped to think about it, this one's a lay-up: "Popular Mechanics."
As much as I love Betty, it's fun to see one of those rare stories where she's
the schemer who gets karmaed in the end, not Ronnie. More importantly,
it's one of the very few B&V stories drawn by the incomparable Harry
Lucey, still my vote for favorite classic Archie artist of all time. His work is
so energetic, so expressive—and no one ever drew exasperation quite like
Lucey did.

- MARK WAID *Writer, Archie Comics*

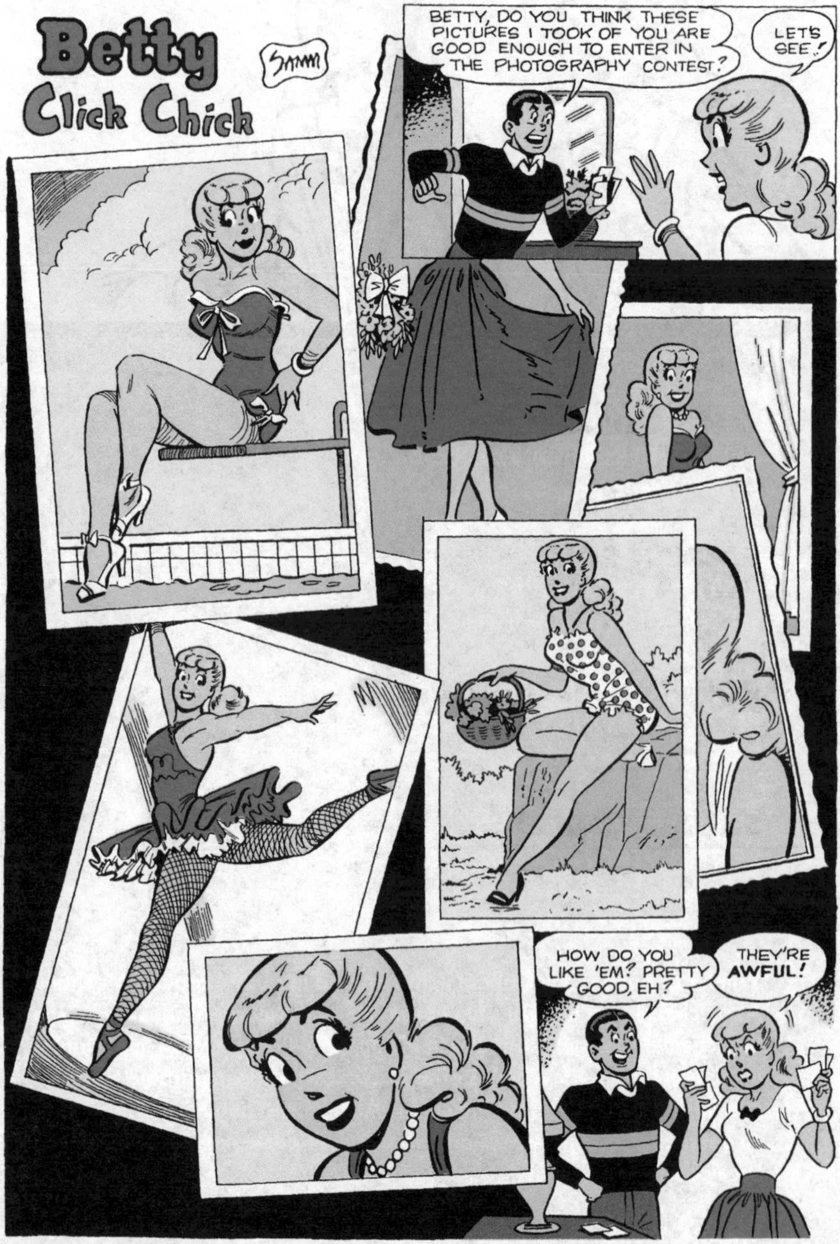

Betty
Click Chick
BETTY, DO YOU THINK THESE PICTURES I TOOK OF YOU ARE GOOD ENOUGH TO ENTER IN THE PHOTOGRAPHY CONTEST?
LET'S SEE!
HOW DO YOU LIKE 'EM? PRETTY GOOD, EH?
THEY'RE **AWFUL!**

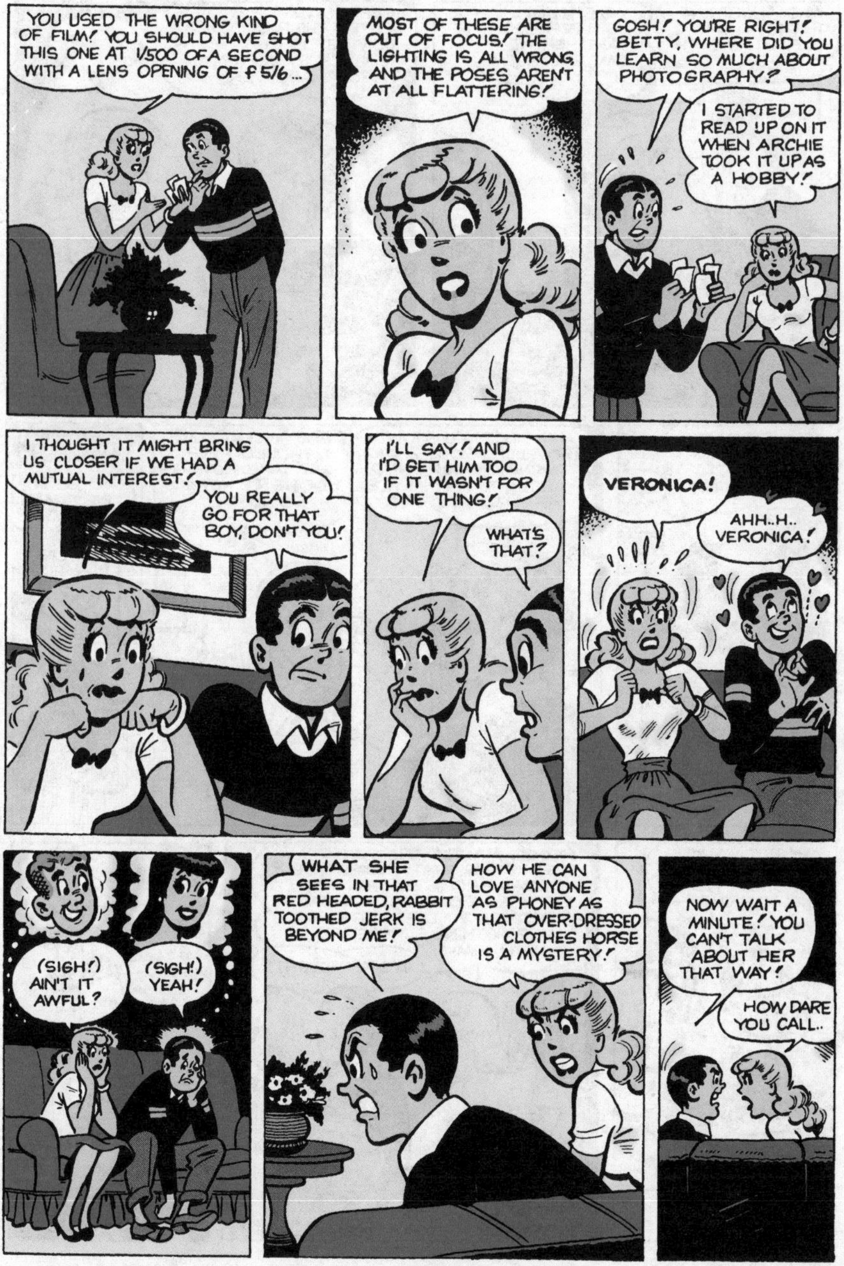
YOU USED THE WRONG KIND OF FILM! YOU SHOULD HAVE SHOT THIS ONE AT 1/500 OF A SECOND WITH A LENS OPENING OF f 5/6...
MOST OF THESE ARE OUT OF FOCUS! THE LIGHTING IS ALL WRONG, AND THE POSES AREN'T AT ALL FLATTERING!
GOSH! YOU'RE RIGHT! BETTY, WHERE DID YOU LEARN SO MUCH ABOUT PHOTOGRAPHY?
I STARTED TO READ UP ON IT WHEN ARCHIE TOOK IT UP AS A HOBBY!
I THOUGHT IT MIGHT BRING US CLOSER IF WE HAD A MUTUAL INTEREST!
YOU REALLY GO FOR THAT BOY, DON'T YOU!
I'LL SAY! AND I'D GET HIM TOO IF IT WASN'T FOR ONE THING!
WHAT'S THAT?
VERONICA!
AHH..H.. VERONICA!
(SIGH!) AIN'T IT AWFUL?
(SIGH!) YEAH!
WHAT SHE SEES IN THAT RED HEADED, RABBIT TOOTHED JERK IS BEYOND ME!
HOW HE CAN LOVE ANYONE AS PHONEY AS THAT OVER-DRESSED CLOTHES HORSE IS A MYSTERY!
NOW WAIT A MINUTE! YOU CAN'T TALK ABOUT HER THAT WAY!
HOW DARE YOU CALL..

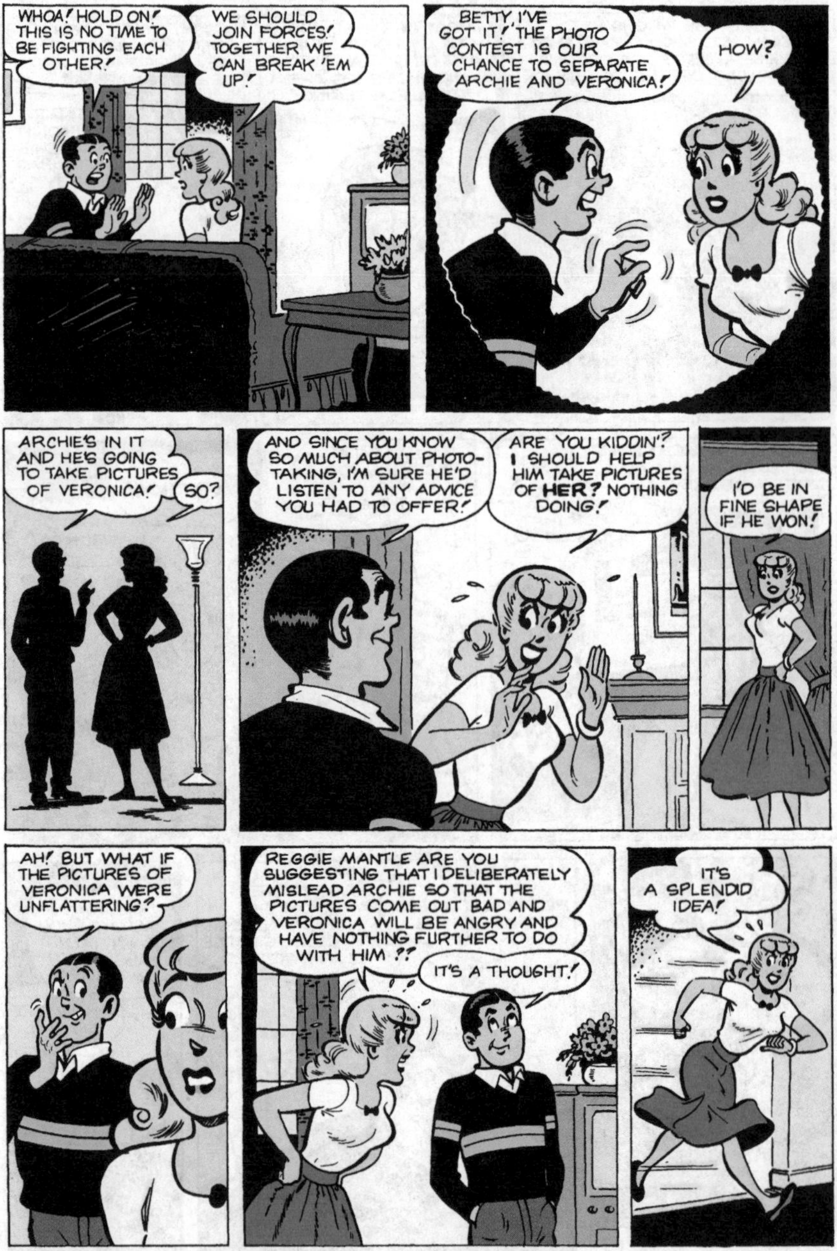
WHOA! HOLD ON! THIS IS NO TIME TO BE FIGHTING EACH OTHER!
WE SHOULD JOIN FORCES! TOGETHER WE CAN BREAK 'EM UP!
BETTY, I'VE GOT IT! THE PHOTO CONTEST IS OUR CHANCE TO SEPARATE ARCHIE AND VERONICA!
HOW?
ARCHIE'S IN IT AND HE'S GOING TO TAKE PICTURES OF VERONICA!
SO?
AND SINCE YOU KNOW SO MUCH ABOUT PHOTO-TAKING, I'M SURE HE'D LISTEN TO ANY ADVICE YOU HAD TO OFFER!
ARE YOU KIDDIN'? I SHOULD HELP HIM TAKE PICTURES OF HER? NOTHING DOING!
I'D BE IN FINE SHAPE IF HE WON!
AH! BUT WHAT IF THE PICTURES OF VERONICA WERE UNFLATTERING?
REGGIE MANTLE ARE YOU SUGGESTING THAT I DELIBERATELY MISLEAD ARCHIE SO THAT THE PICTURES COME OUT BAD AND VERONICA WILL BE ANGRY AND HAVE NOTHING FURTHER TO DO WITH HIM ??
IT'S A THOUGHT!
IT'S A SPLENDID IDEA!

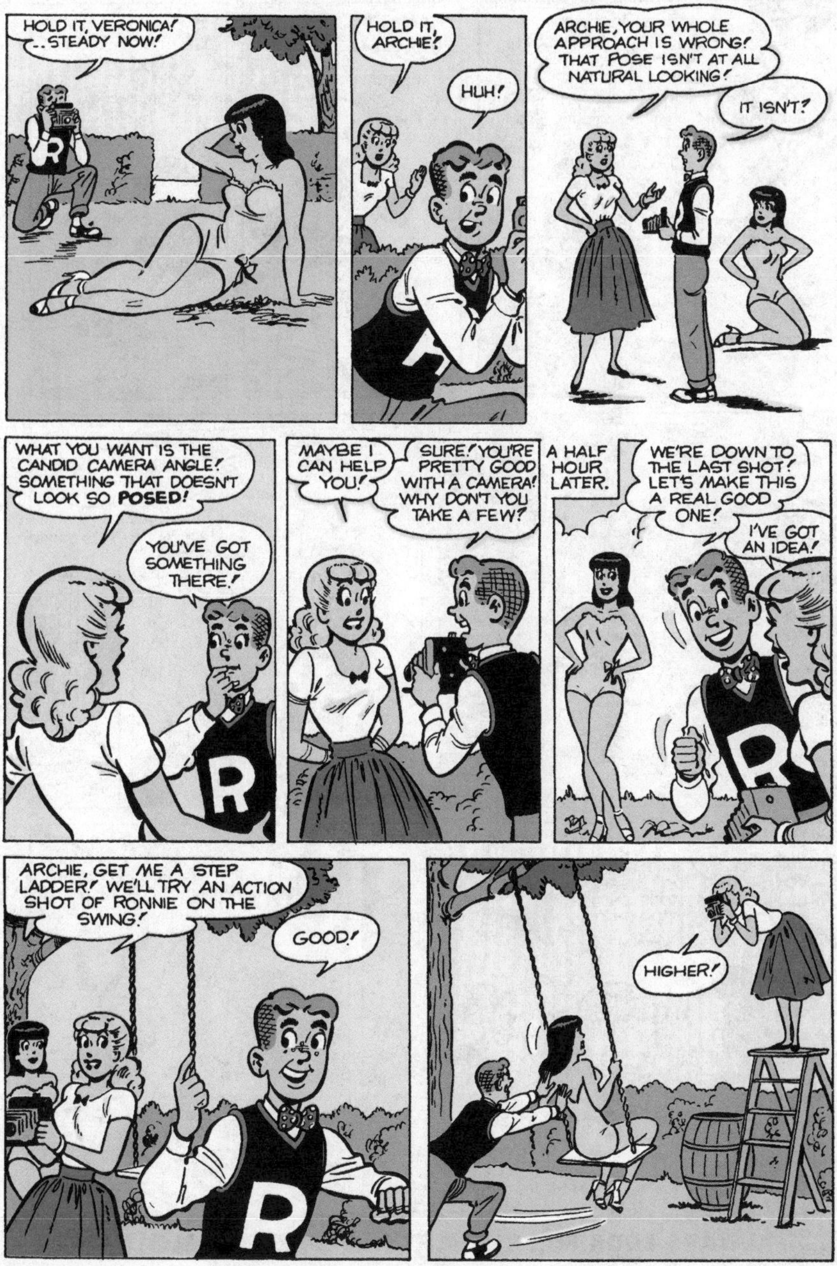
HOLD IT, VERONICA! ..STEADY NOW!
HOLD IT, ARCHIE!
HUH!
ARCHIE, YOUR WHOLE APPROACH IS WRONG! THAT POSE ISN'T AT ALL NATURAL LOOKING!
IT ISN'T?
WHAT YOU WANT IS THE CANDID CAMERA ANGLE! SOMETHING THAT DOESN'T LOOK SO **POSED**!
YOU'VE GOT SOMETHING THERE!
MAYBE I CAN HELP YOU!
SURE! YOU'RE PRETTY GOOD WITH A CAMERA! WHY DON'T YOU TAKE A FEW?
A HALF HOUR LATER.
WE'RE DOWN TO THE LAST SHOT! LET'S MAKE THIS A REAL GOOD ONE!
I'VE GOT AN IDEA!
ARCHIE, GET ME A STEP LADDER! WE'LL TRY AN ACTION SHOT OF RONNIE ON THE SWING!
GOOD!
HIGHER!

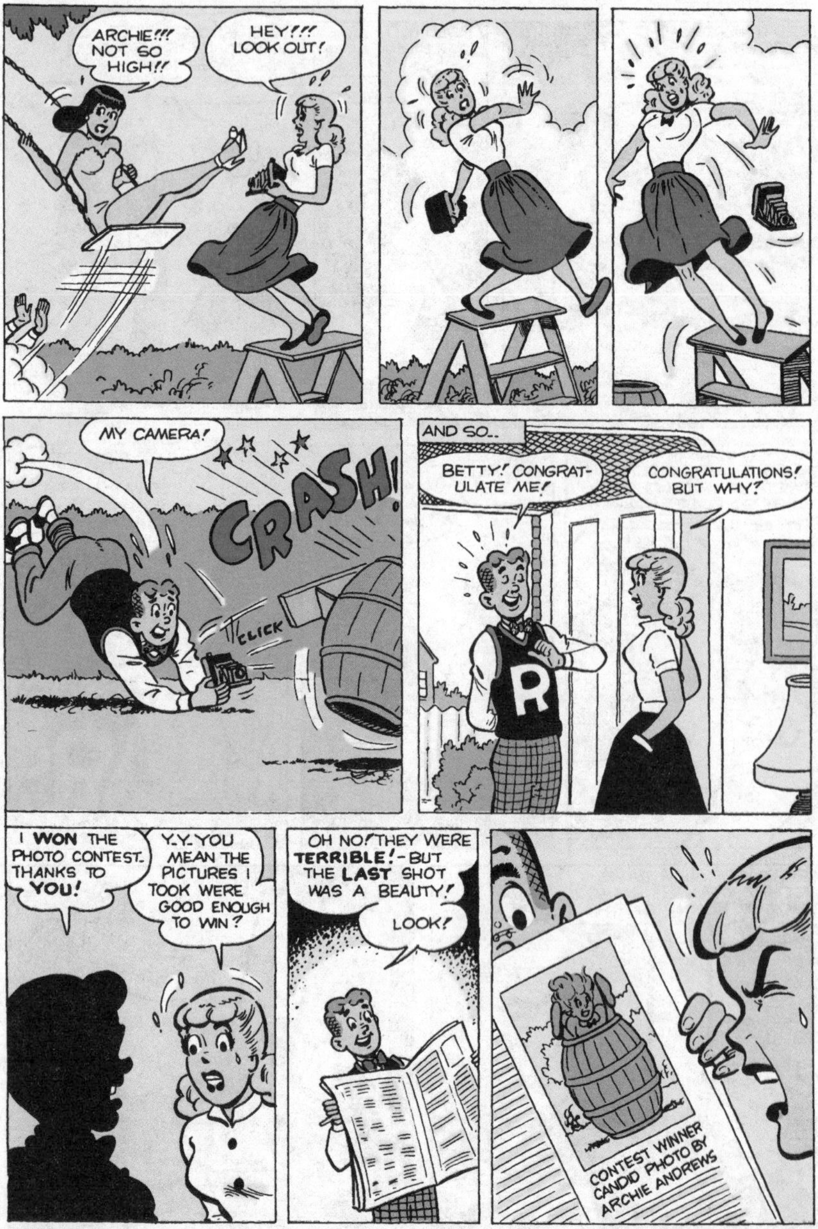
ARCHIE!!! NOT SO HIGH!!
HEY!!! LOOK OUT!
MY CAMERA!
CRASH!
CLICK
AND SO..
BETTY! CONGRAT-ULATE ME!
CONGRATULATIONS! BUT WHY?
I WON THE PHOTO CONTEST THANKS TO YOU!
Y-Y-YOU MEAN THE PICTURES I TOOK WERE GOOD ENOUGH TO WIN?
OH NO! THEY WERE TERRIBLE! - BUT THE LAST SHOT WAS A BEAUTY!
LOOK!
CONTEST WINNER CANDID PHOTO BY ARCHIE ANDREWS

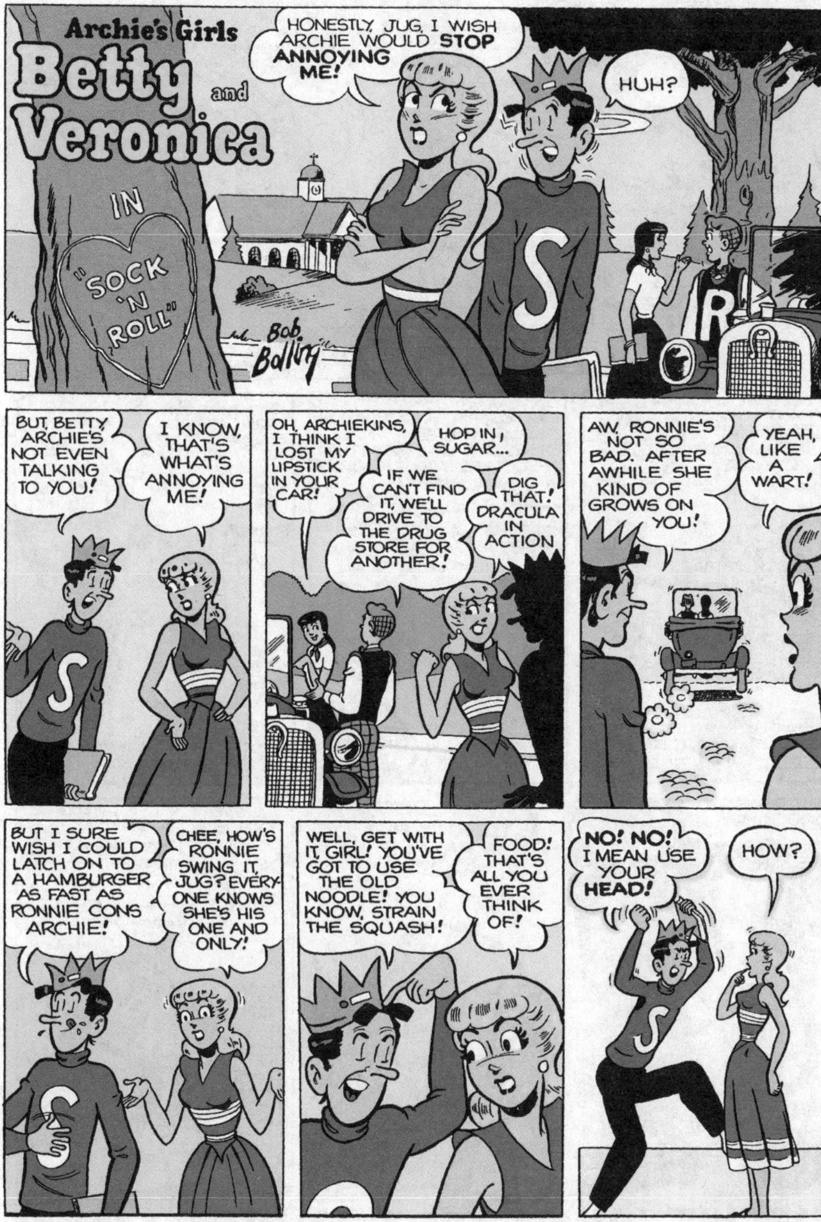
Archie's Girls
Betty and Veronica
IN
"SOCK 'N ROLL"
Bob Bolling
HONESTLY, JUG, I WISH ARCHIE WOULD STOP ANNOYING ME!
HUH?
BUT, BETTY, ARCHIE'S NOT EVEN TALKING TO YOU!
I KNOW, THAT'S WHAT'S ANNOYING ME!
OH, ARCHIEKINS, I THINK I LOST MY LIPSTICK IN YOUR CAR!
HOP IN, SUGAR...
IF WE CAN'T FIND IT, WE'LL DRIVE TO THE DRUG STORE FOR ANOTHER!
DIG THAT! DRACULA IN ACTION
AW, RONNIE'S NOT SO BAD. AFTER AWHILE SHE KIND OF GROWS ON YOU!
YEAH, LIKE A WART!
BUT I SURE WISH I COULD LATCH ON TO A HAMBURGER AS FAST AS RONNIE CONS ARCHIE!
CHEE, HOW'S RONNIE SWING IT, JUG? EVERY-ONE KNOWS SHE'S HIS ONE AND ONLY!
WELL, GET WITH IT, GIRL! YOU'VE GOT TO USE THE OLD NOODLE! YOU KNOW, STRAIN THE SQUASH!
FOOD! THAT'S ALL YOU EVER THINK OF!
NO! NO! I MEAN USE YOUR HEAD!
HOW?

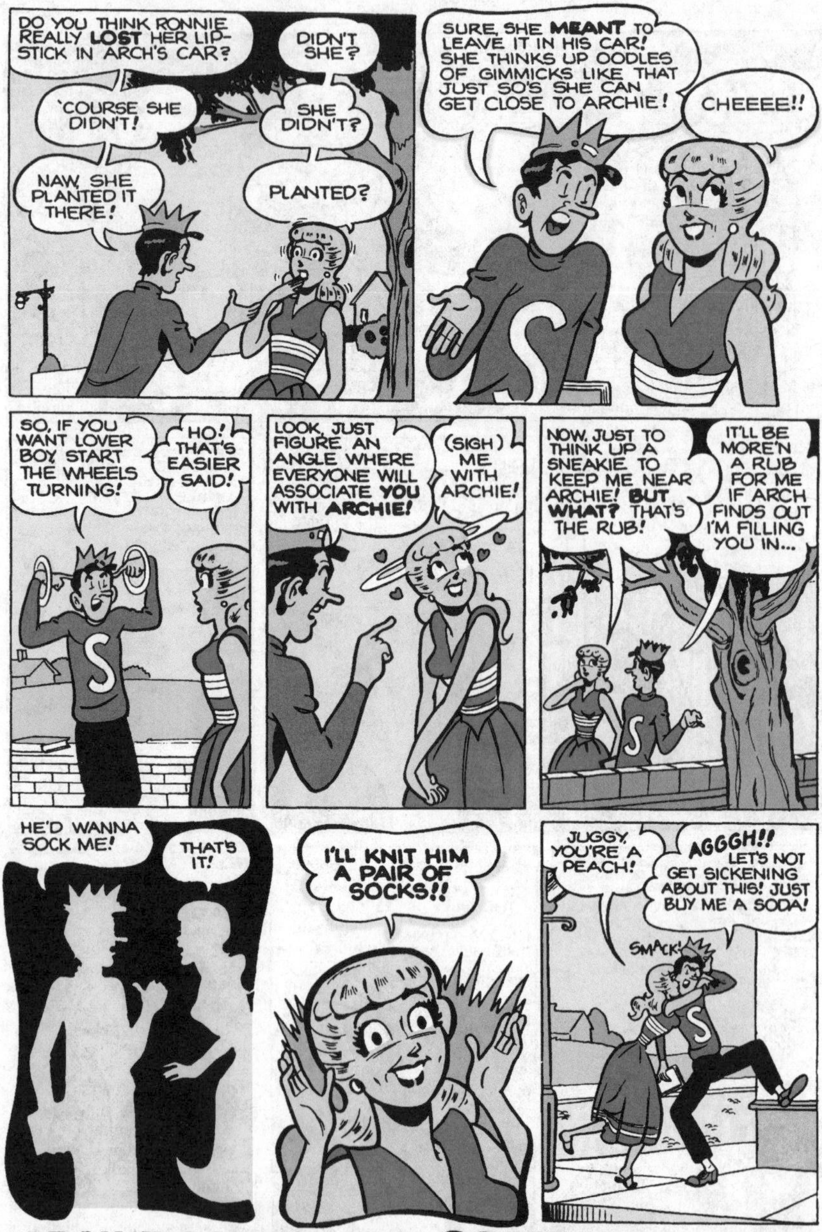
DO YOU THINK RONNIE REALLY LOST HER LIP-STICK IN ARCH'S CAR?
DIDN'T SHE?
`COURSE SHE DIDN'T!
SHE DIDN'T?
NAW, SHE PLANTED IT THERE!
PLANTED?
SURE, SHE MEANT TO LEAVE IT IN HIS CAR! SHE THINKS UP OODLES OF GIMMICKS LIKE THAT JUST SO'S SHE CAN GET CLOSE TO ARCHIE!
CHEEEE!!
SO, IF YOU WANT LOVER BOY, START THE WHEELS TURNING!
HO! THAT'S EASIER SAID!
LOOK, JUST FIGURE AN ANGLE WHERE EVERYONE WILL ASSOCIATE YOU WITH ARCHIE!
(SIGH) ME WITH ARCHIE!
NOW, JUST TO THINK UP A SNEAKIE TO KEEP ME NEAR ARCHIE! BUT WHAT? THAT'S THE RUB!
IT'LL BE MORE'N A RUB FOR ME IF ARCH FINDS OUT I'M FILLING YOU IN...
HE'D WANNA SOCK ME!
THAT'S IT!
I'LL KNIT HIM A PAIR OF SOCKS!!
JUGGY, YOU'RE A PEACH!
AGGGH!! LET'S NOT GET SICKENING ABOUT THIS! JUST BUY ME A SODA!
SMACK!

ARCHIE COMICS ARE **COMICAL** COMICS

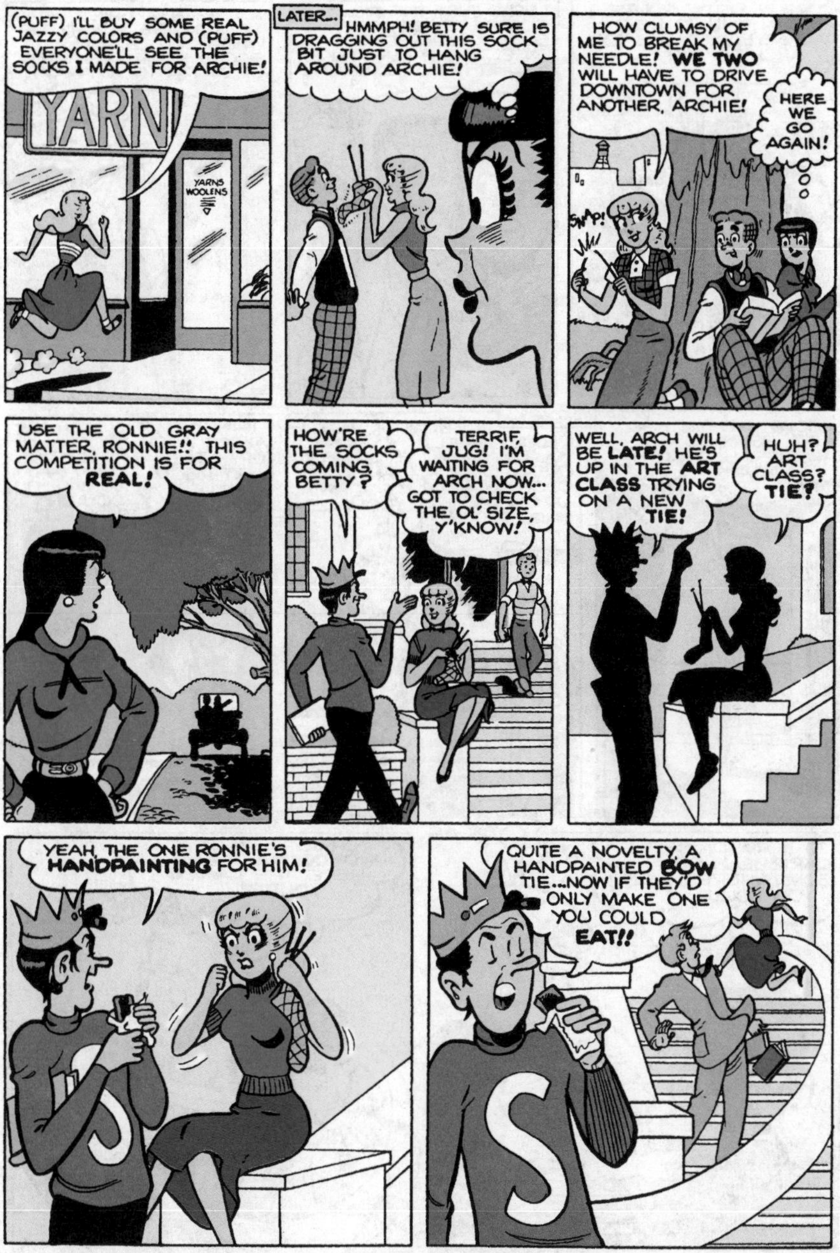

(PUFF) I'LL BUY SOME REAL JAZZY COLORS AND (PUFF) EVERYONE'LL SEE THE SOCKS I MADE FOR ARCHIE!
YARN
YARNS WOOLENS
LATER...
HMMPH! BETTY SURE IS DRAGGING OUT THIS SOCK BIT JUST TO HANG AROUND ARCHIE!
HOW CLUMSY OF ME TO BREAK MY NEEDLE! WE TWO WILL HAVE TO DRIVE DOWNTOWN FOR ANOTHER, ARCHIE!
HERE WE GO AGAIN!
SNAP!
USE THE OLD GRAY MATTER, RONNIE!! THIS COMPETITION IS FOR REAL!
HOW'RE THE SOCKS COMING, BETTY?
TERRIF, JUG! I'M WAITING FOR ARCH NOW... GOT TO CHECK THE OL' SIZE, Y'KNOW!
WELL, ARCH WILL BE LATE! HE'S UP IN THE ART CLASS TRYING ON A NEW TIE!
HUH? ART CLASS? TIE?
YEAH, THE ONE RONNIE'S HANDPAINTING FOR HIM!
QUITE A NOVELTY, A HANDPAINTED BOW TIE...NOW IF THEY'D ONLY MAKE ONE YOU COULD EAT!!

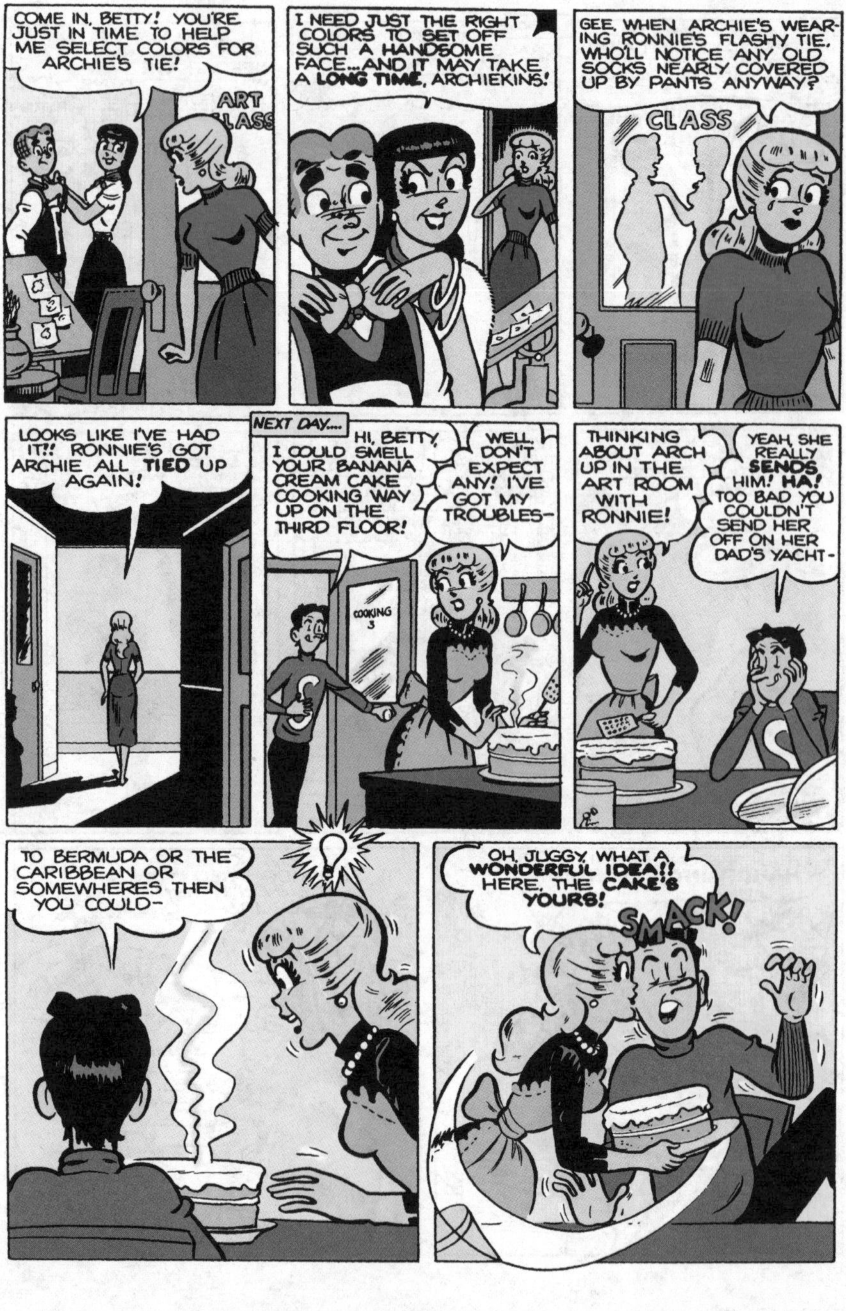

COME IN, BETTY! YOU'RE JUST IN TIME TO HELP ME SELECT COLORS FOR ARCHIE'S TIE!
ART CLASS
I NEED JUST THE RIGHT COLORS TO SET OFF SUCH A HANDSOME FACE...AND IT MAY TAKE A LONG TIME, ARCHIEKINS!
GEE, WHEN ARCHIE'S WEARING RONNIE'S FLASHY TIE, WHO'LL NOTICE ANY OLD SOCKS NEARLY COVERED UP BY PANTS ANYWAY?
CLASS
LOOKS LIKE I'VE HAD IT!! RONNIE'S GOT ARCHIE ALL TIED UP AGAIN!
NEXT DAY....
HI, BETTY, I COULD SMELL YOUR BANANA CREAM CAKE COOKING WAY UP ON THE THIRD FLOOR!
WELL, DON'T EXPECT ANY! I'VE GOT MY TROUBLES-
COOKING 3
THINKING ABOUT ARCH UP IN THE ART ROOM WITH RONNIE!
YEAH, SHE REALLY SENDS HIM! HA! TOO BAD YOU COULDN'T SEND HER OFF ON HER DAD'S YACHT-
TO BERMUDA OR THE CARIBBEAN OR SOMEWHERES THEN YOU COULD-
OH, JUGGY, WHAT A WONDERFUL IDEA!! HERE, THE CAKE'S YOURS!
SMACK!

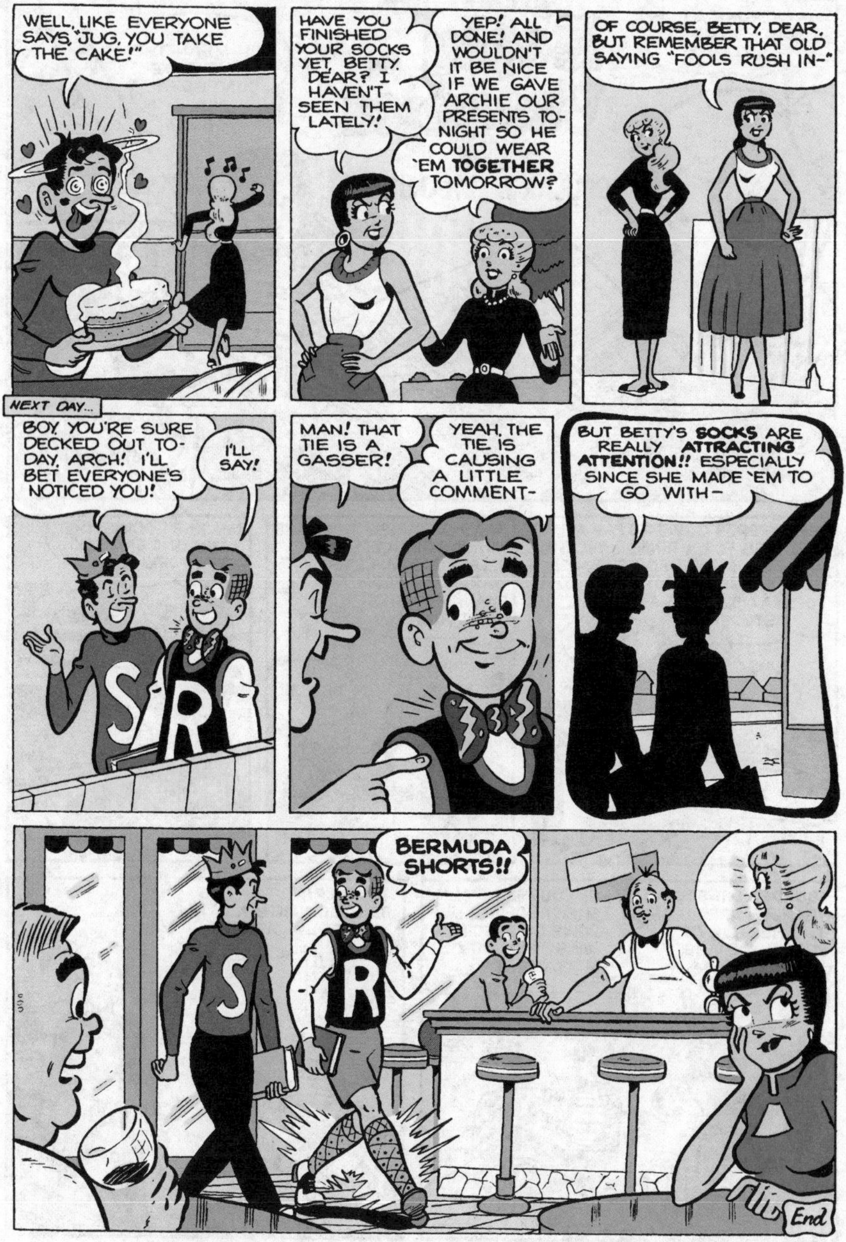
WELL, LIKE EVERYONE SAYS, "JUG, YOU TAKE THE CAKE!"
HAVE YOU FINISHED YOUR SOCKS YET, BETTY, DEAR? I HAVEN'T SEEN THEM LATELY!
YEP! ALL DONE! AND WOULDN'T IT BE NICE IF WE GAVE ARCHIE OUR PRESENTS TO-NIGHT SO HE COULD WEAR 'EM TOGETHER TOMORROW?
OF COURSE, BETTY, DEAR, BUT REMEMBER THAT OLD SAYING "FOOLS RUSH IN-"
NEXT DAY...
BOY, YOU'RE SURE DECKED OUT TO-DAY, ARCH! I'LL BET EVERYONE'S NOTICED YOU!
I'LL SAY!
MAN! THAT TIE IS A GASSER!
YEAH, THE TIE IS CAUSING A LITTLE COMMENT-
BUT BETTY'S SOCKS ARE REALLY ATTRACTING ATTENTION!! ESPECIALLY SINCE SHE MADE 'EM TO GO WITH-
BERMUDA SHORTS!!
End

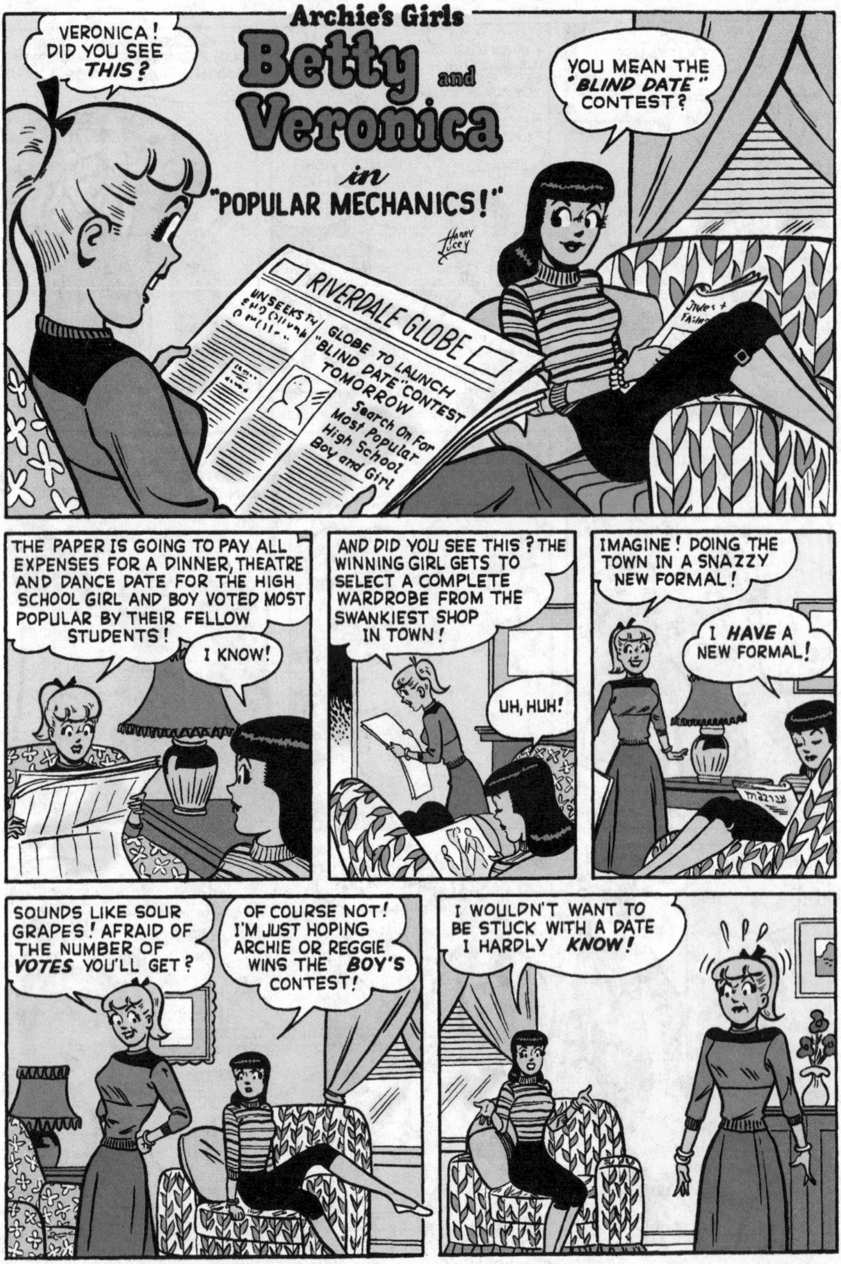

Archie's Girls
Betty and Veronica
in "POPULAR MECHANICS!"
HARRY LUCEY
VERONICA! DID YOU SEE THIS?
YOU MEAN THE "BLIND DATE" CONTEST?
RIVERDALE GLOBE
GLOBE TO LAUNCH "BLIND DATE" CONTEST TOMORROW
Search On For Most Popular High School Boy and Girl
THE PAPER IS GOING TO PAY ALL EXPENSES FOR A DINNER, THEATRE AND DANCE DATE FOR THE HIGH SCHOOL GIRL AND BOY VOTED MOST POPULAR BY THEIR FELLOW STUDENTS!
I KNOW!
AND DID YOU SEE THIS? THE WINNING GIRL GETS TO SELECT A COMPLETE WARDROBE FROM THE SWANKIEST SHOP IN TOWN!
UH, HUH!
IMAGINE! DOING THE TOWN IN A SNAZZY NEW FORMAL!
I HAVE A NEW FORMAL!
SOUNDS LIKE SOUR GRAPES! AFRAID OF THE NUMBER OF VOTES YOU'LL GET?
OF COURSE NOT! I'M JUST HOPING ARCHIE OR REGGIE WINS THE BOY'S CONTEST!
I WOULDN'T WANT TO BE STUCK WITH A DATE I HARDLY KNOW!

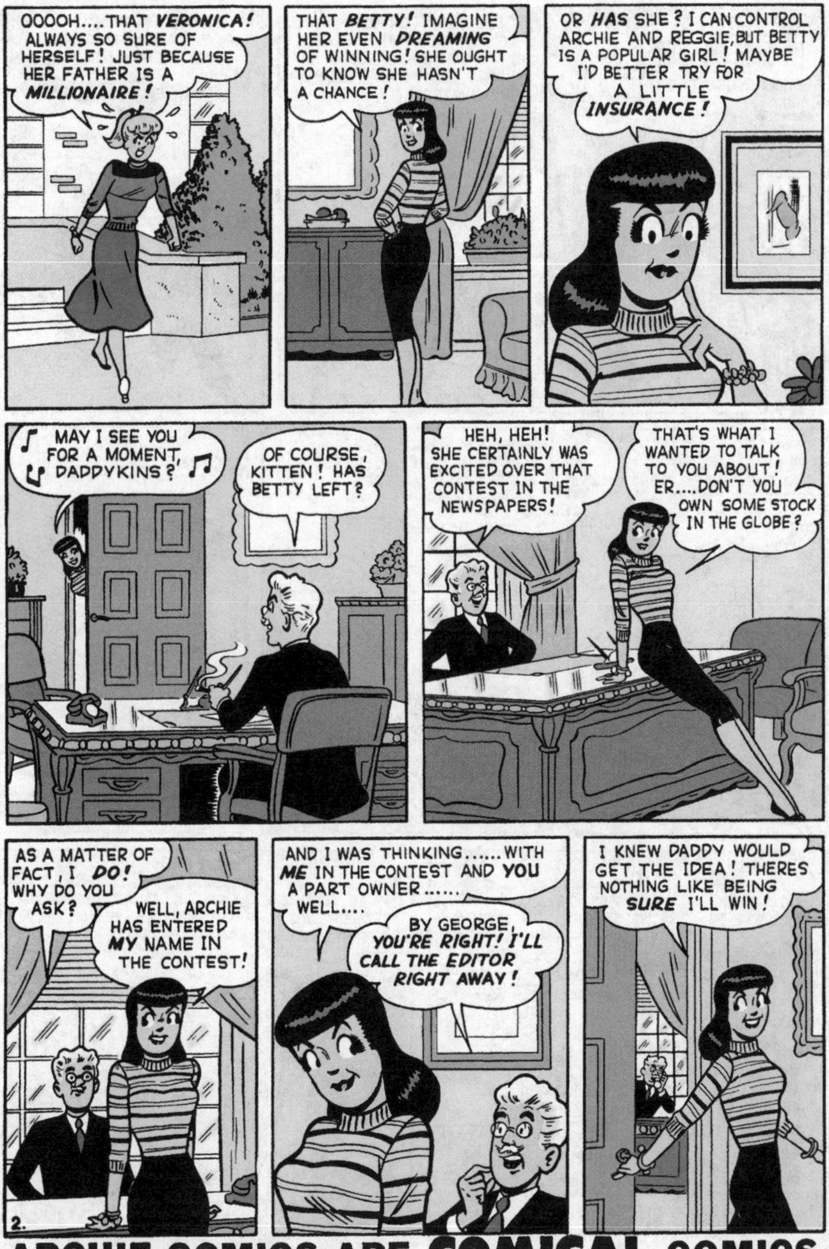

OOOOH....THAT *VERONICA!* ALWAYS SO SURE OF HERSELF! JUST BECAUSE HER FATHER IS A *MILLIONAIRE!*
THAT *BETTY!* IMAGINE HER EVEN *DREAMING* OF WINNING! SHE OUGHT TO KNOW SHE HASN'T A CHANCE!
OR *HAS* SHE? I CAN CONTROL ARCHIE AND REGGIE, BUT BETTY IS A POPULAR GIRL! MAYBE I'D BETTER TRY FOR A LITTLE *INSURANCE!*
MAY I SEE YOU FOR A MOMENT, DADDYKINS?
OF COURSE, KITTEN! HAS BETTY LEFT?
HEH, HEH! SHE CERTAINLY WAS EXCITED OVER THAT CONTEST IN THE NEWSPAPERS!
THAT'S WHAT I WANTED TO TALK TO YOU ABOUT! ER....DON'T YOU OWN SOME STOCK IN THE GLOBE?
AS A MATTER OF FACT, I *DO!* WHY DO YOU ASK?
WELL, ARCHIE HAS ENTERED *MY* NAME IN THE CONTEST!
AND I WAS THINKING......WITH *ME* IN THE CONTEST AND *YOU* A PART OWNER...... WELL....
BY GEORGE, *YOU'RE RIGHT! I'LL CALL THE EDITOR RIGHT AWAY!*
I KNEW DADDY WOULD GET THE IDEA! THERES NOTHING LIKE BEING *SURE* I'LL WIN!
2.

ARCHIE COMICS ARE COMICAL COMICS

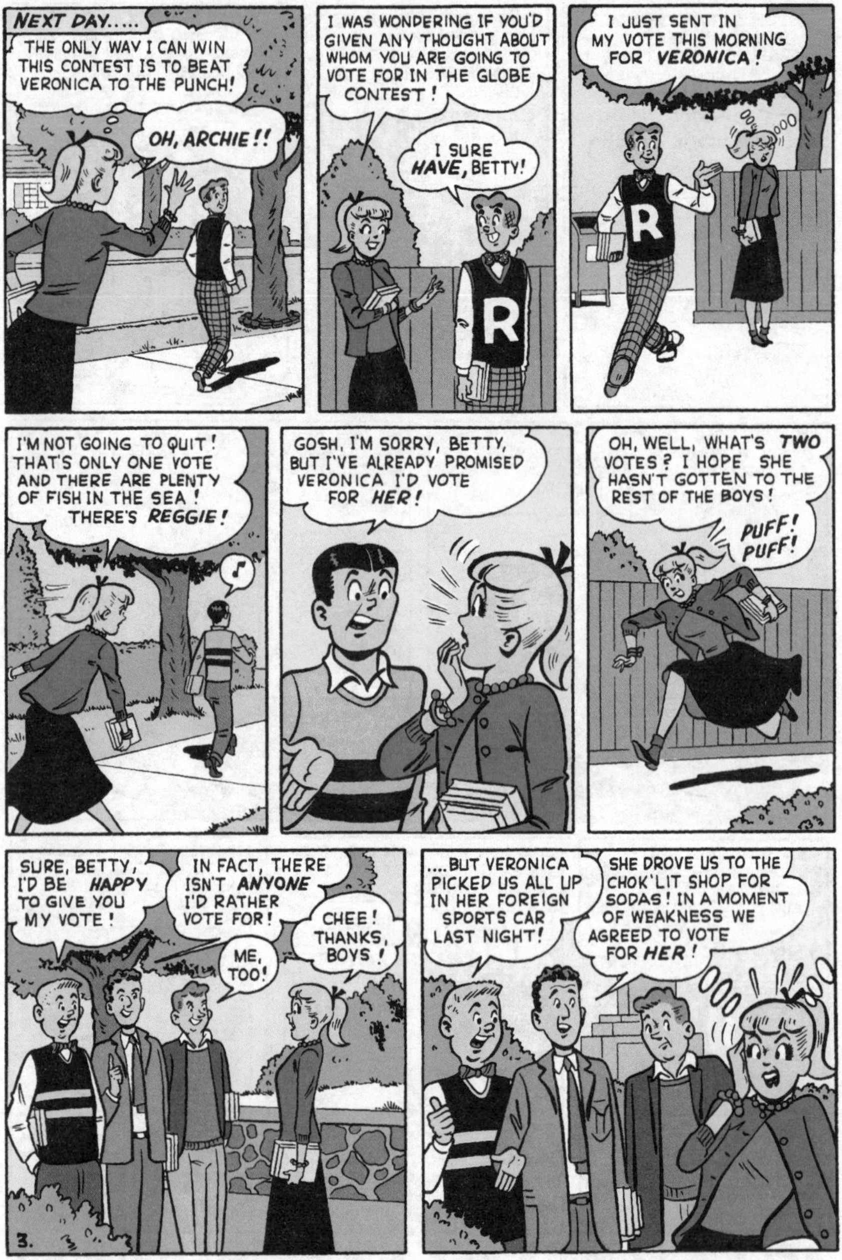
NEXT DAY.....
THE ONLY WAY I CAN WIN THIS CONTEST IS TO BEAT VERONICA TO THE PUNCH!
OH, ARCHIE!!
I WAS WONDERING IF YOU'D GIVEN ANY THOUGHT ABOUT WHOM YOU ARE GOING TO VOTE FOR IN THE GLOBE CONTEST!
I SURE HAVE, BETTY!
I JUST SENT IN MY VOTE THIS MORNING FOR VERONICA!
OOO OOO
I'M NOT GOING TO QUIT! THAT'S ONLY ONE VOTE AND THERE ARE PLENTY OF FISH IN THE SEA! THERE'S REGGIE!
GOSH, I'M SORRY, BETTY, BUT I'VE ALREADY PROMISED VERONICA I'D VOTE FOR HER!
OH, WELL, WHAT'S TWO VOTES? I HOPE SHE HASN'T GOTTEN TO THE REST OF THE BOYS!
PUFF! PUFF!
SURE, BETTY, I'D BE HAPPY TO GIVE YOU MY VOTE!
IN FACT, THERE ISN'T ANYONE I'D RATHER VOTE FOR!
ME, TOO!
CHEE! THANKS, BOYS!
3.
....BUT VERONICA PICKED US ALL UP IN HER FOREIGN SPORTS CAR LAST NIGHT!
SHE DROVE US TO THE CHOK'LIT SHOP FOR SODAS! IN A MOMENT OF WEAKNESS WE AGREED TO VOTE FOR HER!
OOO !!

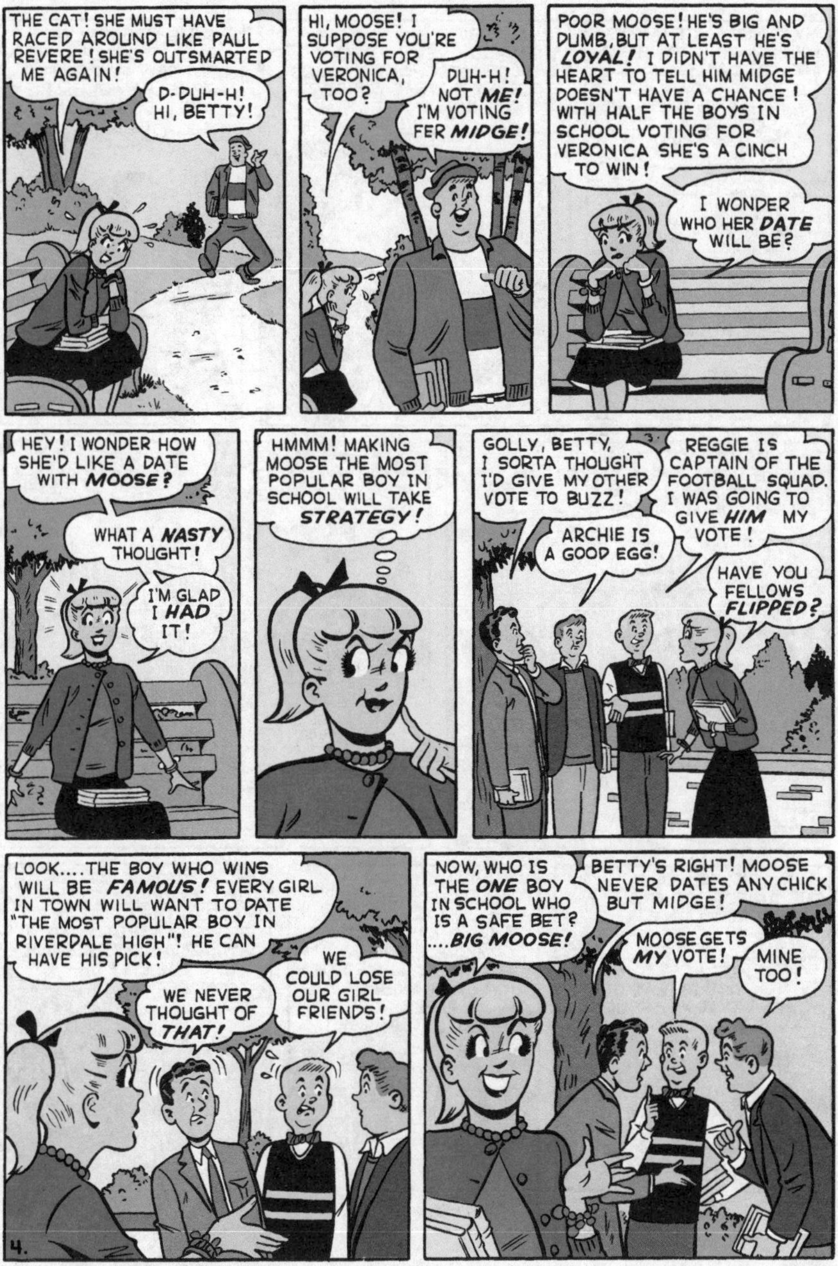
THE CAT! SHE MUST HAVE RACED AROUND LIKE PAUL REVERE! SHE'S OUTSMARTED ME AGAIN!
D-DUH-H! HI, BETTY!
HI, MOOSE! I SUPPOSE YOU'RE VOTING FOR VERONICA, TOO?
DUH-H! NOT ME! I'M VOTING FER MIDGE!
POOR MOOSE! HE'S BIG AND DUMB, BUT AT LEAST HE'S LOYAL! I DIDN'T HAVE THE HEART TO TELL HIM MIDGE DOESN'T HAVE A CHANCE! WITH HALF THE BOYS IN SCHOOL VOTING FOR VERONICA SHE'S A CINCH TO WIN!
I WONDER WHO HER DATE WILL BE?
HEY! I WONDER HOW SHE'D LIKE A DATE WITH MOOSE?
WHAT A NASTY THOUGHT!
I'M GLAD I HAD IT!
HMMM! MAKING MOOSE THE MOST POPULAR BOY IN SCHOOL WILL TAKE STRATEGY!
GOLLY, BETTY, I SORTA THOUGHT I'D GIVE MY OTHER VOTE TO BUZZ!
ARCHIE IS A GOOD EGG!
REGGIE IS CAPTAIN OF THE FOOTBALL SQUAD. I WAS GOING TO GIVE HIM MY VOTE!
HAVE YOU FELLOWS FLIPPED?
LOOK.... THE BOY WHO WINS WILL BE FAMOUS! EVERY GIRL IN TOWN WILL WANT TO DATE "THE MOST POPULAR BOY IN RIVERDALE HIGH"! HE CAN HAVE HIS PICK!
WE NEVER THOUGHT OF THAT!
WE COULD LOSE OUR GIRL FRIENDS!
4.
NOW, WHO IS THE ONE BOY IN SCHOOL WHO IS A SAFE BET? ....BIG MOOSE!
BETTY'S RIGHT! MOOSE NEVER DATES ANY CHICK BUT MIDGE!
MOOSE GETS MY VOTE!
MINE TOO!

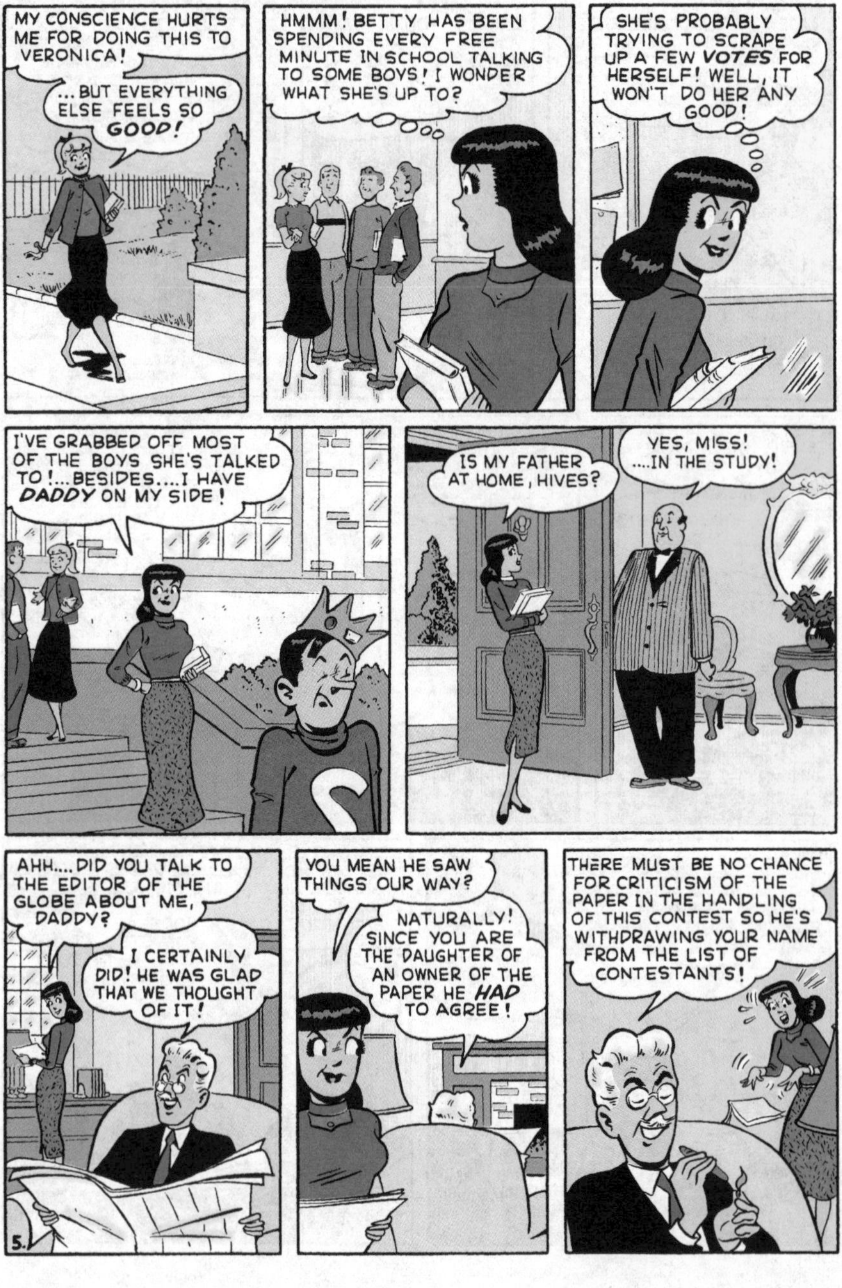
MY CONSCIENCE HURTS ME FOR DOING THIS TO VERONICA!
...BUT EVERYTHING ELSE FEELS SO GOOD!
HMMM! BETTY HAS BEEN SPENDING EVERY FREE MINUTE IN SCHOOL TALKING TO SOME BOYS! I WONDER WHAT SHE'S UP TO?
SHE'S PROBABLY TRYING TO SCRAPE UP A FEW VOTES FOR HERSELF! WELL, IT WON'T DO HER ANY GOOD!
I'VE GRABBED OFF MOST OF THE BOYS SHE'S TALKED TO!...BESIDES....I HAVE DADDY ON MY SIDE!
IS MY FATHER AT HOME, HIVES?
YES, MISS! ....IN THE STUDY!
AHH....DID YOU TALK TO THE EDITOR OF THE GLOBE ABOUT ME, DADDY?
I CERTAINLY DID! HE WAS GLAD THAT WE THOUGHT OF IT!
YOU MEAN HE SAW THINGS OUR WAY?
NATURALLY! SINCE YOU ARE THE DAUGHTER OF AN OWNER OF THE PAPER HE HAD TO AGREE!
THERE MUST BE NO CHANCE FOR CRITICISM OF THE PAPER IN THE HANDLING OF THIS CONTEST SO HE'S WITHDRAWING YOUR NAME FROM THE LIST OF CONTESTANTS!
5.

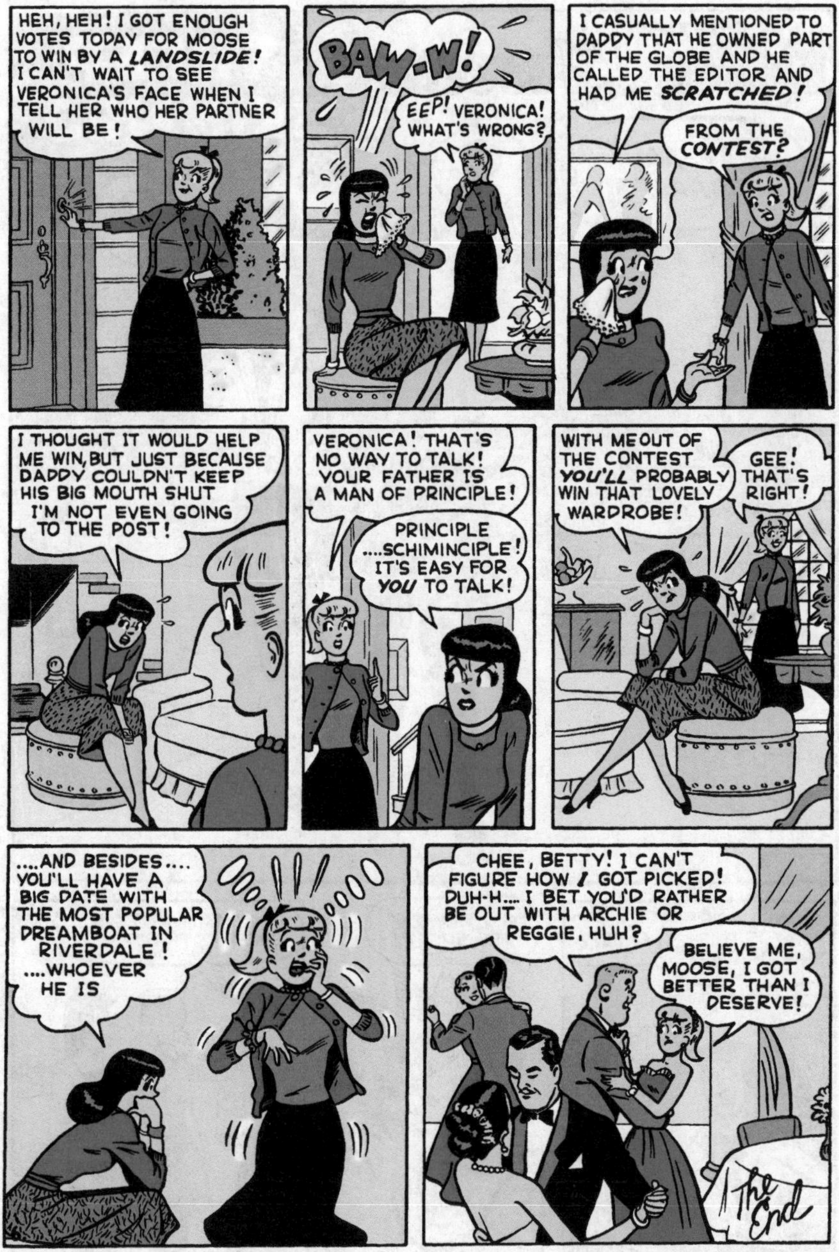
HEH, HEH! I GOT ENOUGH VOTES TODAY FOR MOOSE TO WIN BY A LANDSLIDE! I CAN'T WAIT TO SEE VERONICA'S FACE WHEN I TELL HER WHO HER PARTNER WILL BE!
BAW-W!
EEP! VERONICA! WHAT'S WRONG?
I CASUALLY MENTIONED TO DADDY THAT HE OWNED PART OF THE GLOBE AND HE CALLED THE EDITOR AND HAD ME SCRATCHED!
FROM THE CONTEST?
I THOUGHT IT WOULD HELP ME WIN, BUT JUST BECAUSE DADDY COULDN'T KEEP HIS BIG MOUTH SHUT I'M NOT EVEN GOING TO THE POST!
VERONICA! THAT'S NO WAY TO TALK! YOUR FATHER IS A MAN OF PRINCIPLE!
PRINCIPLE ....SCHIMINCIPLE! IT'S EASY FOR YOU TO TALK!
WITH ME OUT OF THE CONTEST YOU'LL PROBABLY WIN THAT LOVELY WARDROBE!
GEE! THAT'S RIGHT!
....AND BESIDES.... YOU'LL HAVE A BIG DATE WITH THE MOST POPULAR DREAMBOAT IN RIVERDALE! ....WHOEVER HE IS
CHEE, BETTY! I CAN'T FIGURE HOW I GOT PICKED! DUH-H.... I BET YOU'D RATHER BE OUT WITH ARCHIE OR REGGIE, HUH?
BELIEVE ME, MOOSE, I GOT BETTER THAN I DESERVE!
The End

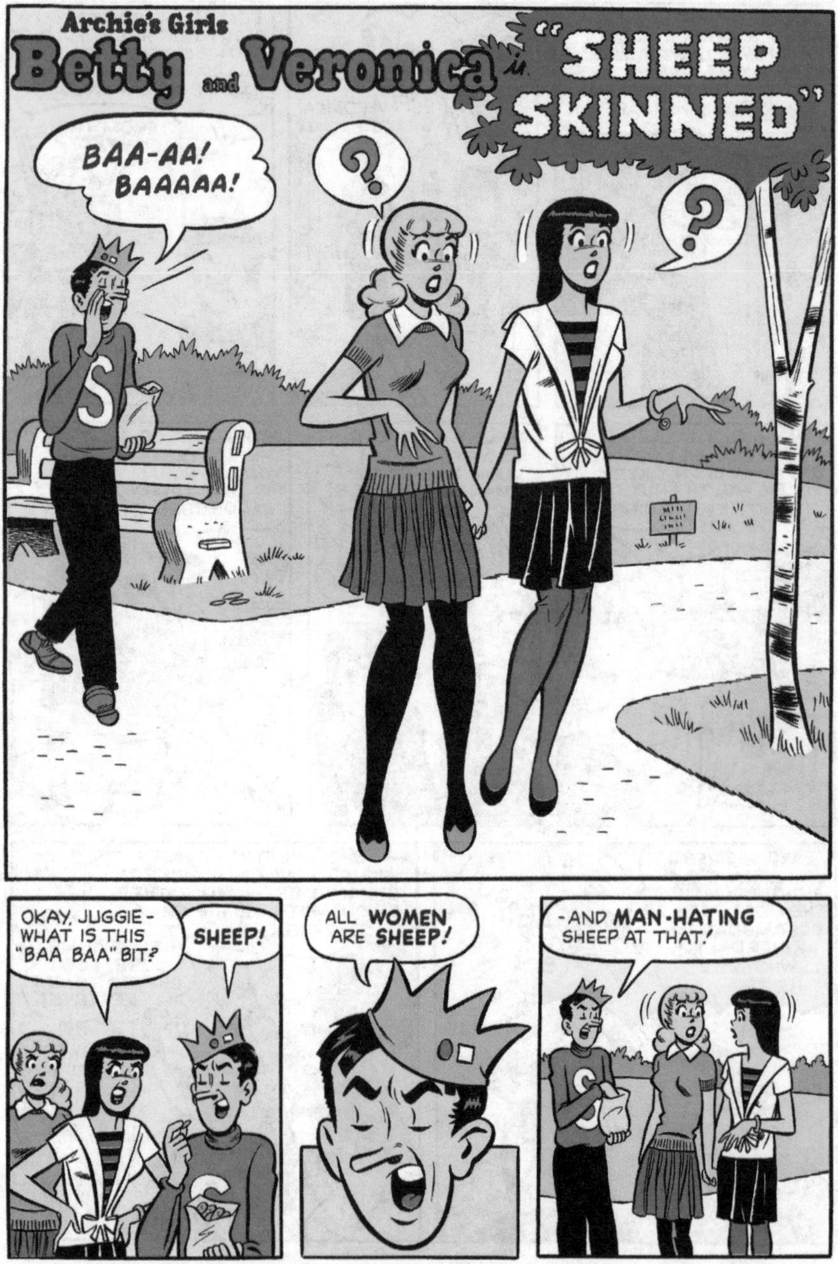
Archie's Girls
Betty and Veronica in
"SHEEP SKINNED"
BAA-AA! BAAAAA!
?
?
OKAY, JUGGIE - WHAT IS THIS "BAA BAA" BIT?
SHEEP!
ALL WOMEN ARE SHEEP!
-AND MAN-HATING SHEEP AT THAT!

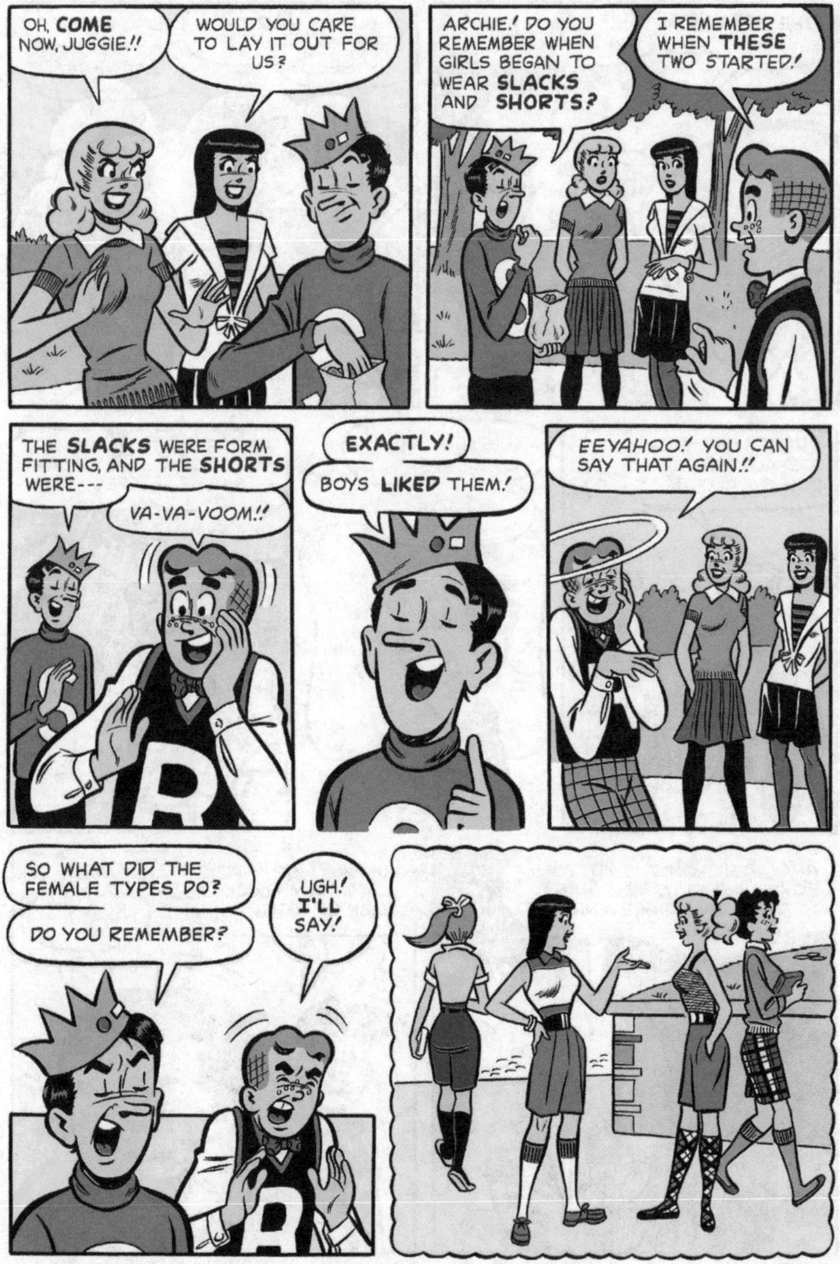
OH, COME NOW, JUGGIE.!!
WOULD YOU CARE TO LAY IT OUT FOR US?
ARCHIE.! DO YOU REMEMBER WHEN GIRLS BEGAN TO WEAR SLACKS AND SHORTS?
I REMEMBER WHEN THESE TWO STARTED.!
THE SLACKS WERE FORM FITTING, AND THE SHORTS WERE---
VA-VA-VOOM.!!
EXACTLY!
BOYS LIKED THEM.!
EEYAHOO.! YOU CAN SAY THAT AGAIN.!!
SO WHAT DID THE FEMALE TYPES DO?
DO YOU REMEMBER?
UGH! I'LL SAY!

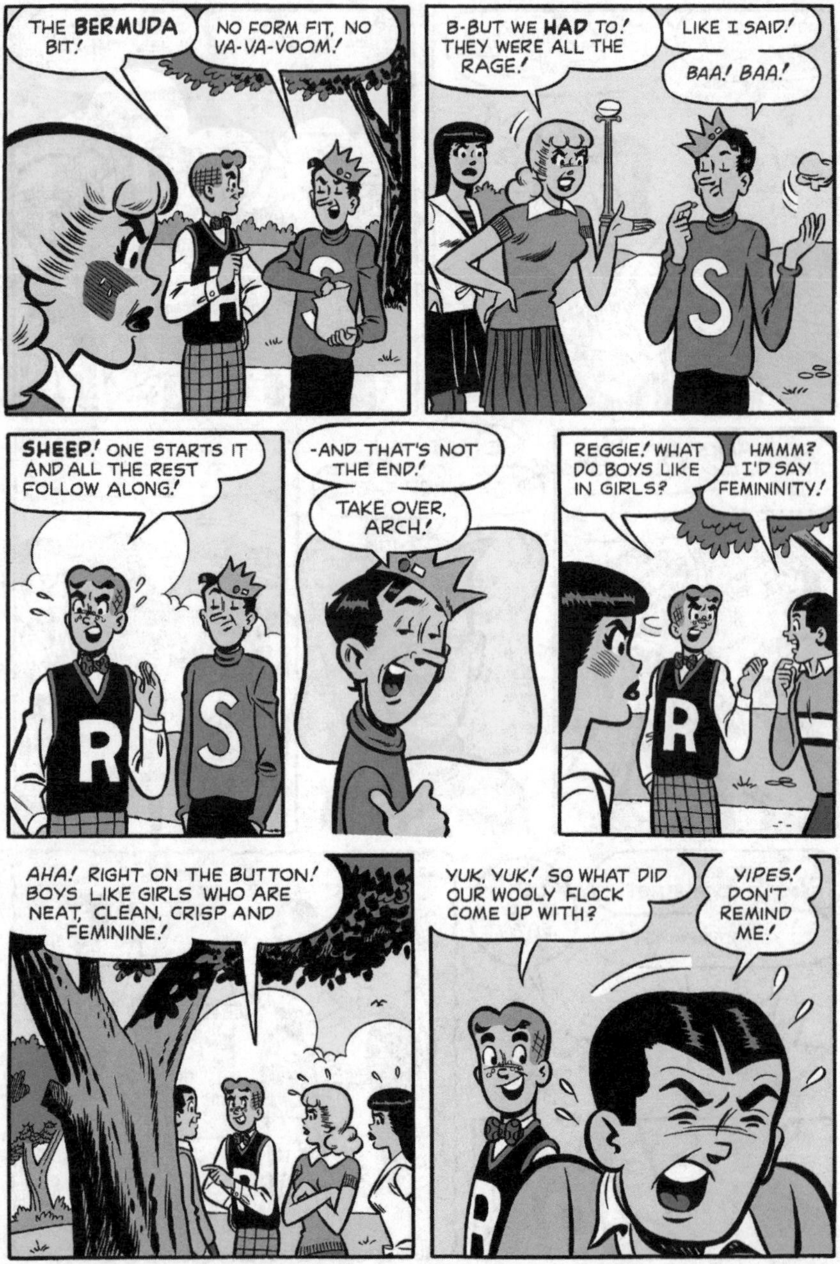
THE BERMUDA BIT!
NO FORM FIT, NO VA-VA-VOOM!
B-BUT WE HAD TO! THEY WERE ALL THE RAGE!
LIKE I SAID!
BAA! BAA!
SHEEP! ONE STARTS IT AND ALL THE REST FOLLOW ALONG!
-AND THAT'S NOT THE END!
TAKE OVER, ARCH!
REGGIE! WHAT DO BOYS LIKE IN GIRLS?
HMMM? I'D SAY FEMININITY!
AHA! RIGHT ON THE BUTTON! BOYS LIKE GIRLS WHO ARE NEAT, CLEAN, CRISP AND FEMININE!
YUK, YUK! SO WHAT DID OUR WOOLY FLOCK COME UP WITH?
YIPES! DON'T REMIND ME!

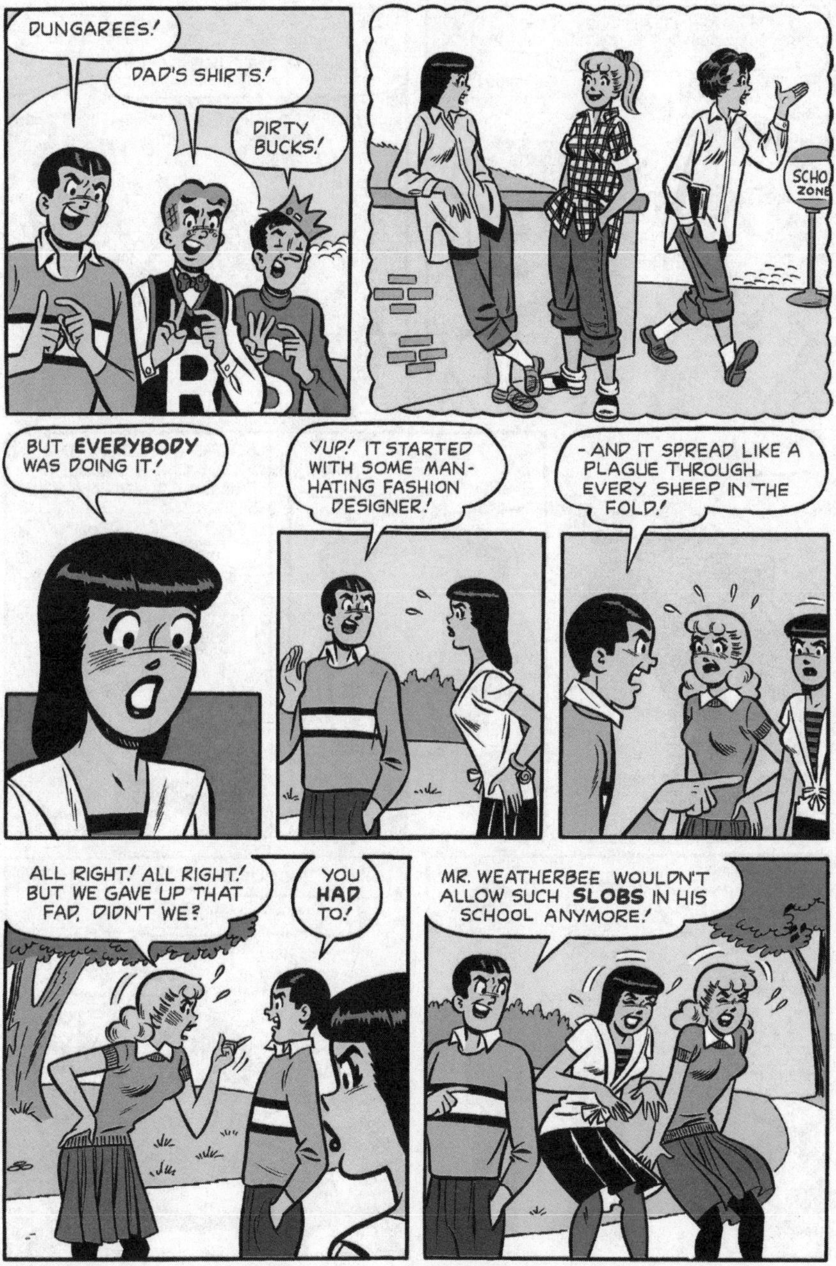
DUNGAREES!
DAD'S SHIRTS!
DIRTY BUCKS!
SCHO ZONE
BUT **EVERYBODY** WAS DOING IT!
YUP! IT STARTED WITH SOME MAN-HATING FASHION DESIGNER!
- AND IT SPREAD LIKE A PLAGUE THROUGH EVERY SHEEP IN THE FOLD!
ALL RIGHT! ALL RIGHT! BUT WE GAVE UP THAT FAD, DIDN'T WE?
YOU **HAD** TO!
MR. WEATHERBEE WOULDN'T ALLOW SUCH **SLOBS** IN HIS SCHOOL ANYMORE!

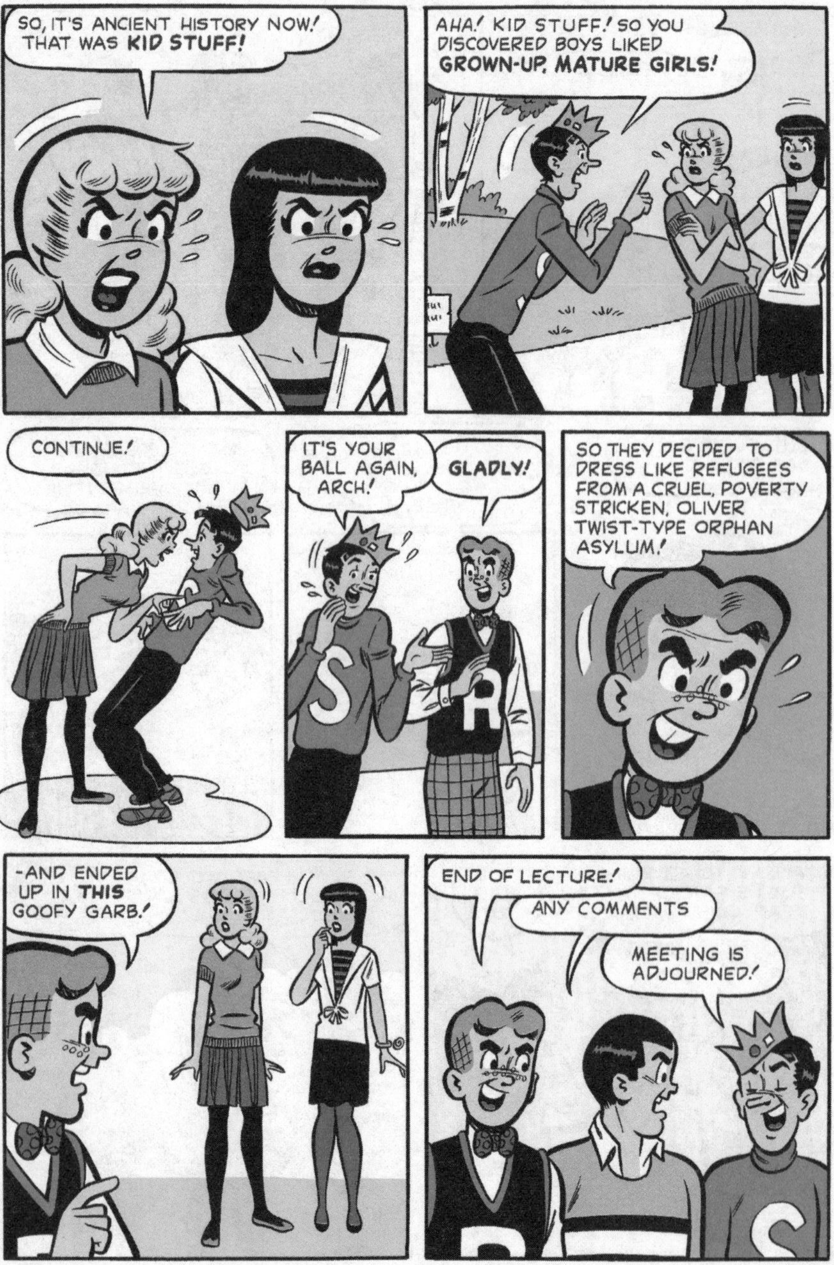

SO, IT'S ANCIENT HISTORY NOW! THAT WAS KID STUFF!
AHA! KID STUFF! SO YOU DISCOVERED BOYS LIKED GROWN-UP, MATURE GIRLS!
CONTINUE!
IT'S YOUR BALL AGAIN, ARCH!
GLADLY!
SO THEY DECIDED TO DRESS LIKE REFUGEES FROM A CRUEL, POVERTY STRICKEN, OLIVER TWIST-TYPE ORPHAN ASYLUM!
-AND ENDED UP IN THIS GOOFY GARB!
END OF LECTURE!
ANY COMMENTS
MEETING IS ADJOURNED!

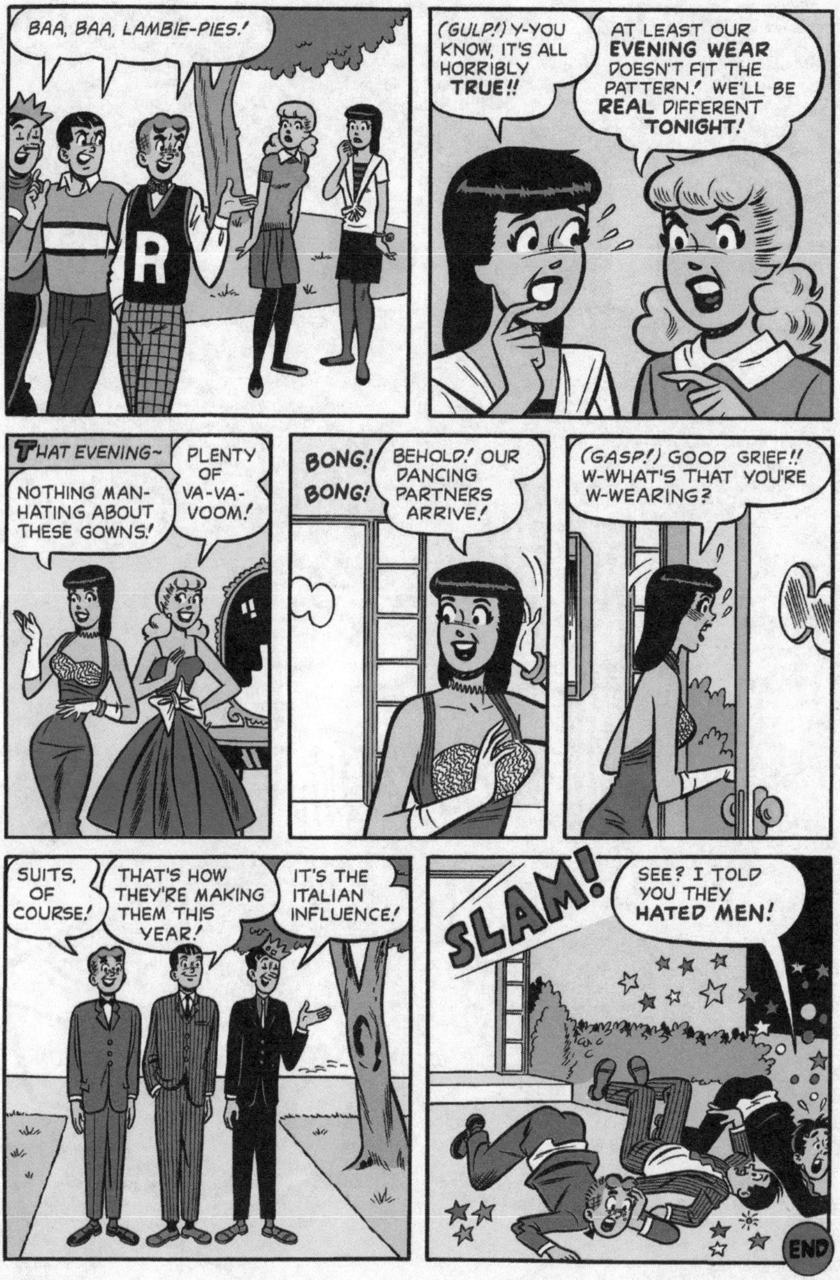
BAA, BAA, LAMBIE-PIES!
(GULP!) Y-YOU KNOW, IT'S ALL HORRIBLY TRUE!!
AT LEAST OUR EVENING WEAR DOESN'T FIT THE PATTERN! WE'LL BE REAL DIFFERENT TONIGHT!
THAT EVENING~
NOTHING MAN-HATING ABOUT THESE GOWNS!
PLENTY OF VA-VA-VOOM!
BONG! BONG!
BEHOLD! OUR DANCING PARTNERS ARRIVE!
(GASP!) GOOD GRIEF!! W-WHAT'S THAT YOU'RE W-WEARING?
SUITS, OF COURSE!
THAT'S HOW THEY'RE MAKING THEM THIS YEAR!
IT'S THE ITALIAN INFLUENCE!
SLAM!
SEE? I TOLD YOU THEY HATED MEN!
END

THE BEST OF ARCHIE COMICS STARRING

BETTY & VERONICA

1960s

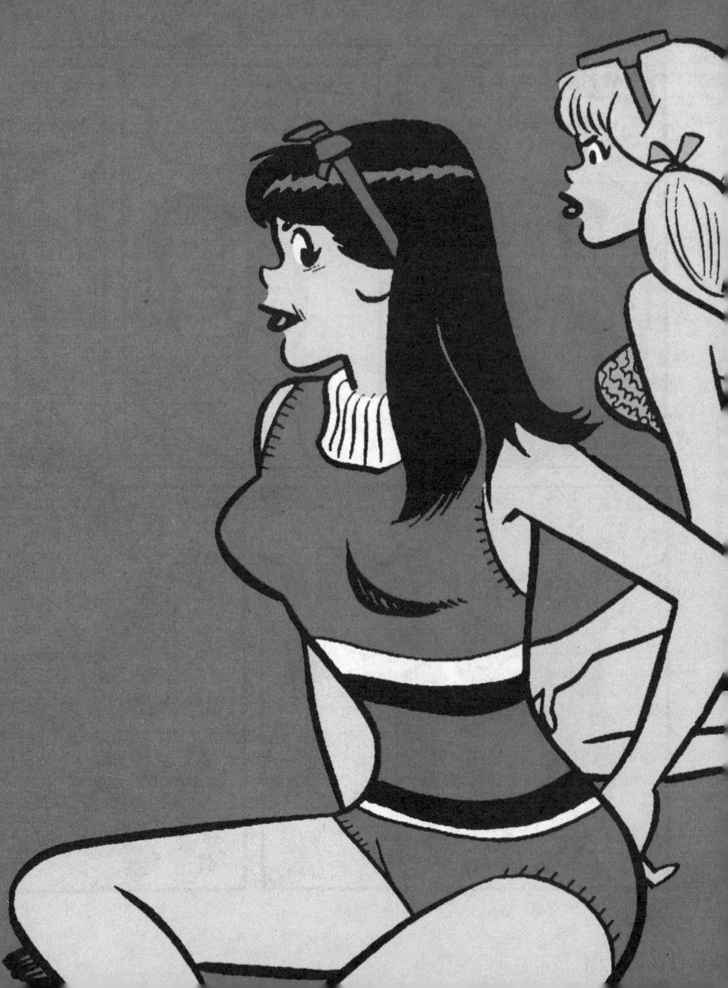

DRESS DILEMMA
BETTY & VERONICA #111, 1965
Frank Doyle, Dan DeCarlo, Rudy Lapick, Vincent DeCarlo, Barry Grossman

MIDAS MESS
BETTY & VERONICA #112, 1965
Frank Doyle, Dan DeCarlo, Rudy Lapick, Vincent DeCarlo, Barry Grossman

PRIZE PACKAGE
BETTY & VERONICA #112, 1965
Frank Doyle, Dan DeCarlo, Rudy Lapick, Vincent DeCarlo, Barry Grossman

Ever since I was a little kid, I've read Archie and his adventures. Betty and Veronica's friendship was something I always admired especially. Even though they were complete opposites they would support each other.

- EVA CABRERA *Artist, Archie Comics*

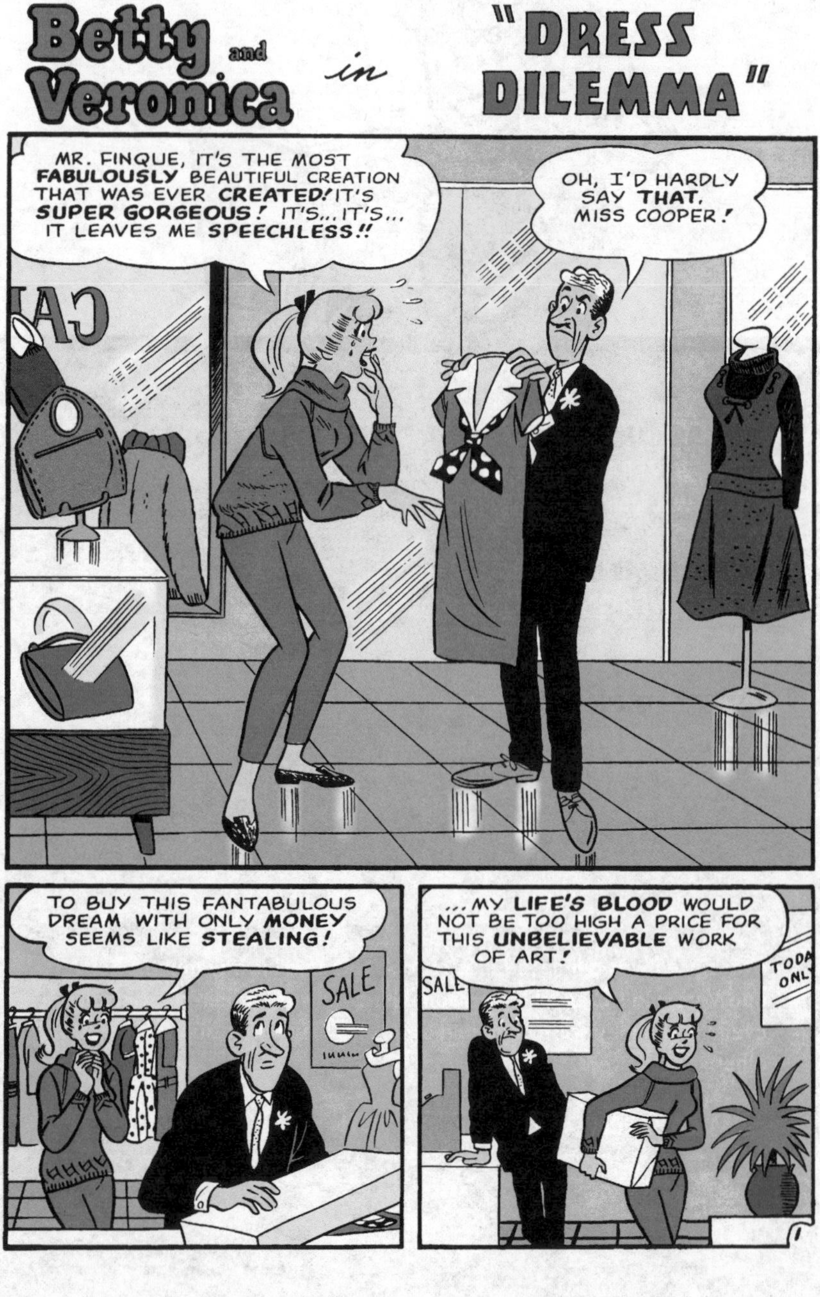
Betty and Veronica in "DRESS DILEMMA"
MR. FINQUE, IT'S THE MOST FABULOUSLY BEAUTIFUL CREATION THAT WAS EVER CREATED! IT'S SUPER GORGEOUS! IT'S... IT'S... IT LEAVES ME SPEECHLESS!!
OH, I'D HARDLY SAY THAT, MISS COOPER!
TO BUY THIS FANTABULOUS DREAM WITH ONLY MONEY SEEMS LIKE STEALING!
SALE
...MY LIFE'S BLOOD WOULD NOT BE TOO HIGH A PRICE FOR THIS UNBELIEVABLE WORK OF ART!
SALE
1

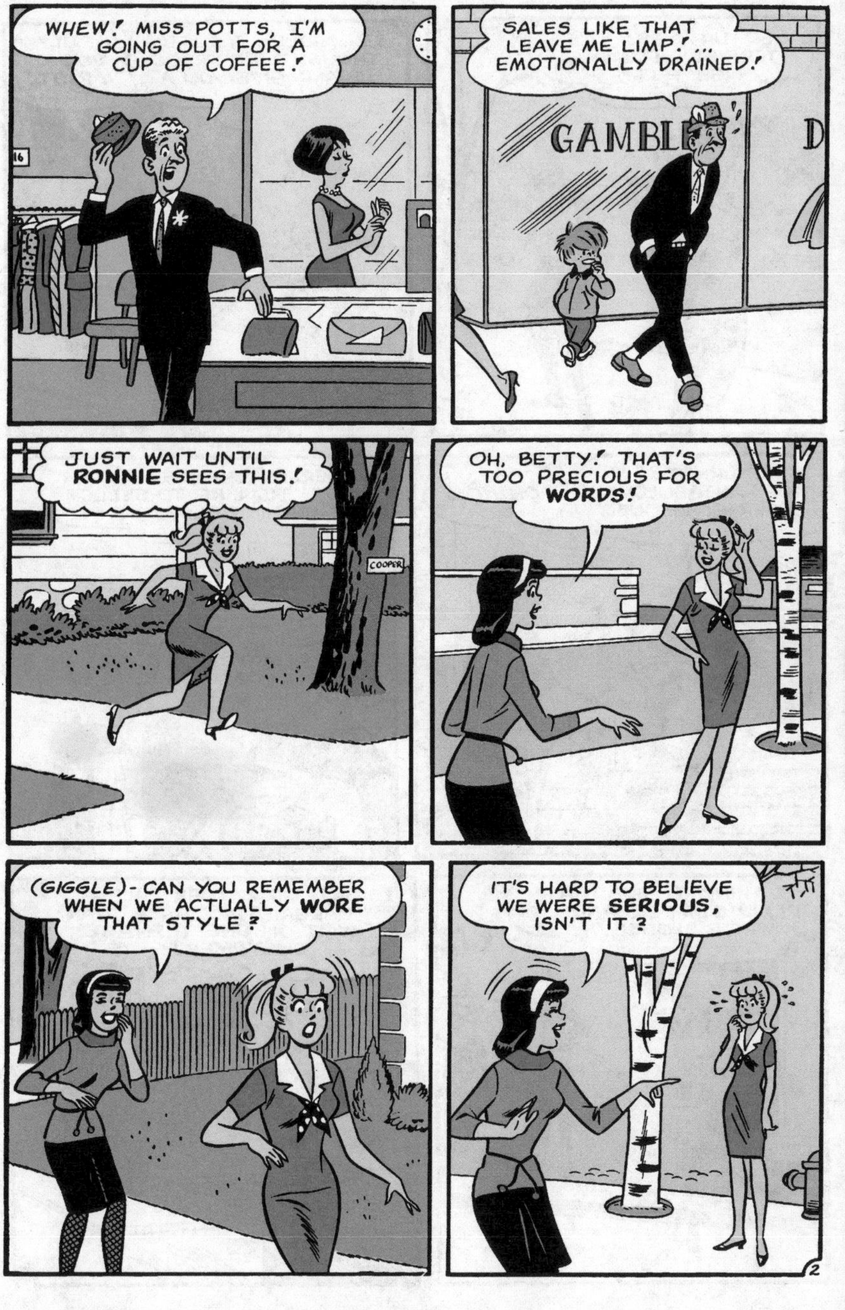
WHEW! MISS POTTS, I'M GOING OUT FOR A CUP OF COFFEE!
16
SALES LIKE THAT LEAVE ME LIMP! ... EMOTIONALLY DRAINED!
GAMBLE
D
JUST WAIT UNTIL **RONNIE** SEES THIS!
COOPER
OH, BETTY! THAT'S TOO PRECIOUS FOR **WORDS!**
(GIGGLE)- CAN YOU REMEMBER WHEN WE ACTUALLY **WORE** THAT STYLE?
IT'S HARD TO BELIEVE WE WERE **SERIOUS,** ISN'T IT?
2

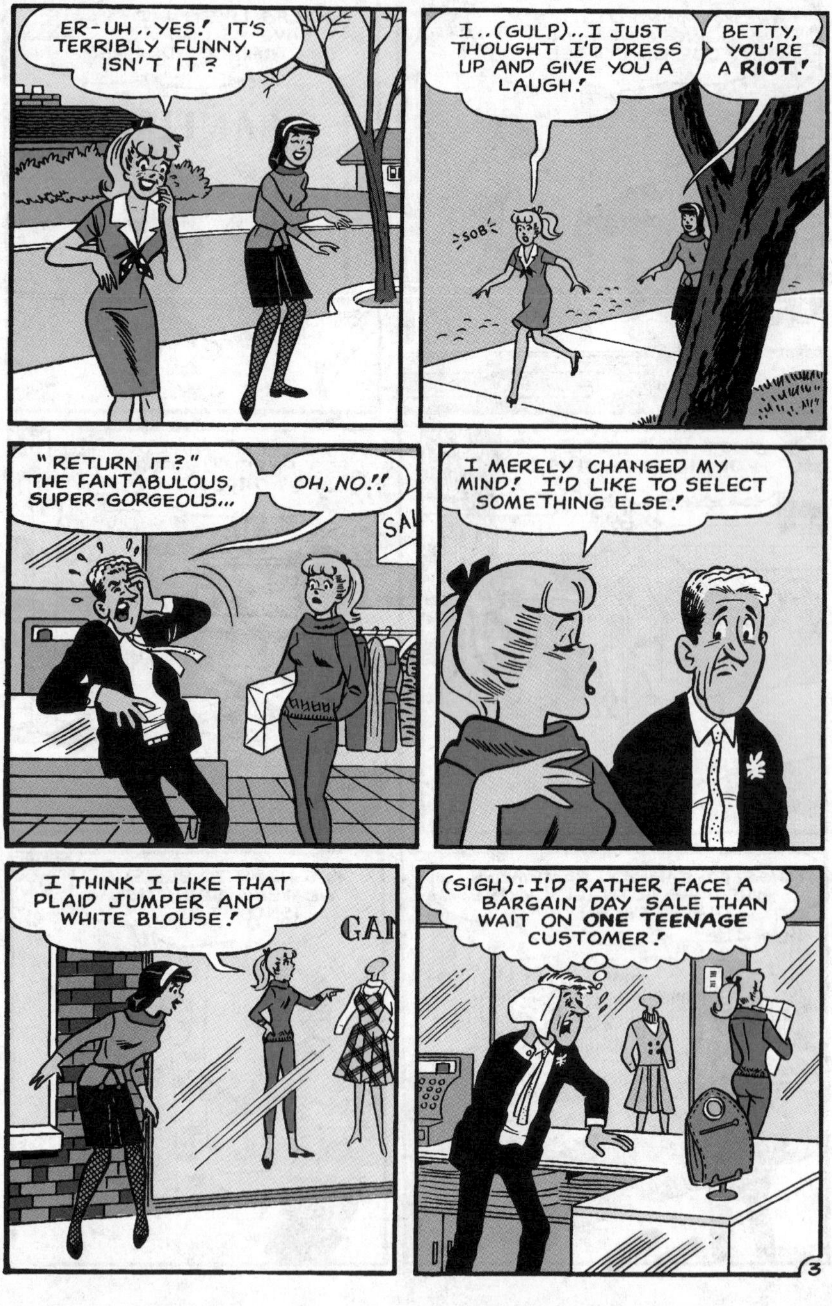
ER-UH..YES! IT'S TERRIBLY FUNNY, ISN'T IT?
I..(GULP)..I JUST THOUGHT I'D DRESS UP AND GIVE YOU A LAUGH!
SOB
BETTY, YOU'RE A **RIOT**!
"RETURN IT?" THE FANTABULOUS, SUPER-GORGEOUS...
OH, NO!!
I MERELY CHANGED MY MIND! I'D LIKE TO SELECT SOMETHING ELSE!
I THINK I LIKE THAT PLAID JUMPER AND WHITE BLOUSE!
(SIGH)- I'D RATHER FACE A BARGAIN DAY SALE THAN WAIT ON **ONE TEENAGE** CUSTOMER!

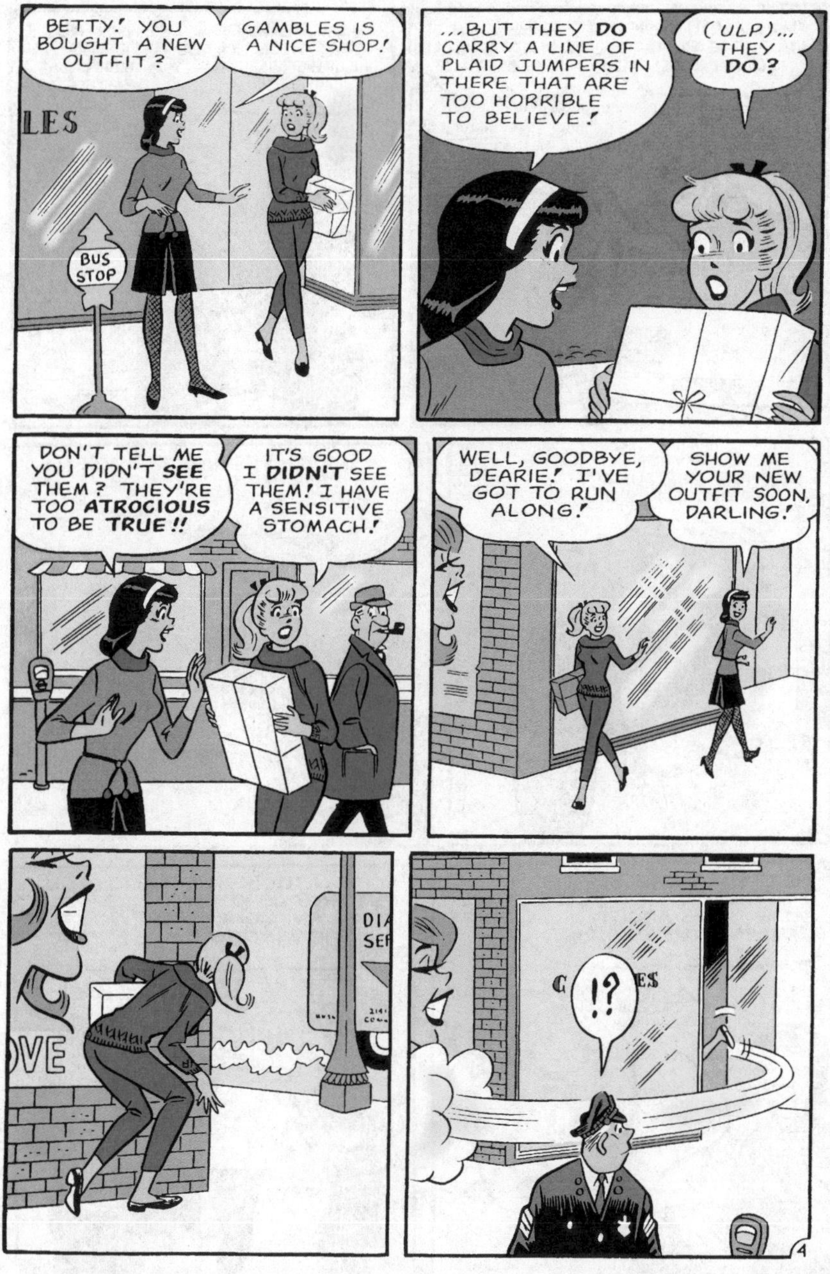
BETTY! YOU BOUGHT A NEW OUTFIT?
GAMBLES IS A NICE SHOP!
LES
BUS STOP
...BUT THEY DO CARRY A LINE OF PLAID JUMPERS IN THERE THAT ARE TOO HORRIBLE TO BELIEVE!
(ULP)... THEY DO?
DON'T TELL ME YOU DIDN'T SEE THEM? THEY'RE TOO ATROCIOUS TO BE TRUE!!
IT'S GOOD I DIDN'T SEE THEM! I HAVE A SENSITIVE STOMACH!
WELL, GOODBYE, DEARIE! I'VE GOT TO RUN ALONG!
SHOW ME YOUR NEW OUTFIT SOON, DARLING!
OVE
!?
4

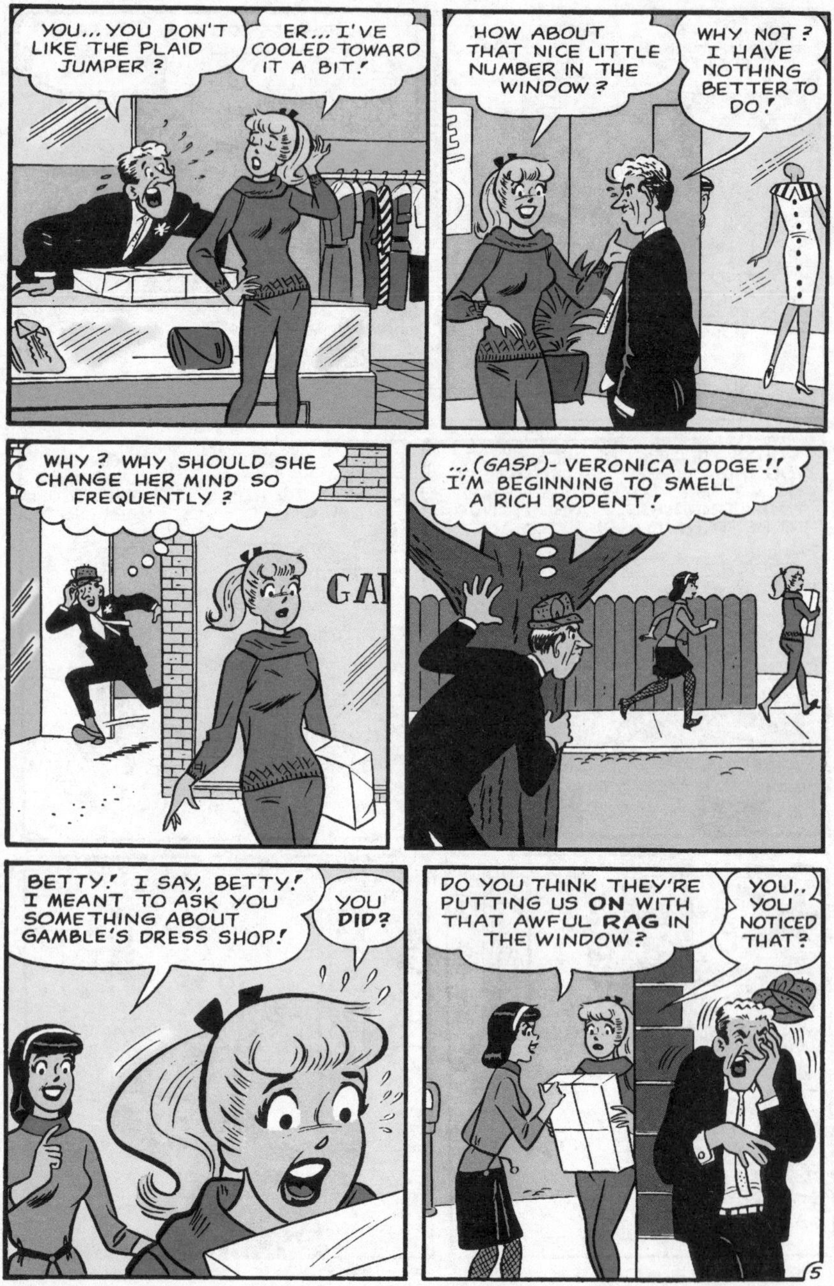
YOU... YOU DON'T LIKE THE PLAID JUMPER?
ER... I'VE COOLED TOWARD IT A BIT!
HOW ABOUT THAT NICE LITTLE NUMBER IN THE WINDOW?
WHY NOT? I HAVE NOTHING BETTER TO DO!
WHY? WHY SHOULD SHE CHANGE HER MIND SO FREQUENTLY?
GA
...(GASP)- VERONICA LODGE!! I'M BEGINNING TO SMELL A RICH RODENT!
BETTY! I SAY, BETTY! I MEANT TO ASK YOU SOMETHING ABOUT GAMBLE'S DRESS SHOP!
YOU DID?
DO YOU THINK THEY'RE PUTTING US ON WITH THAT AWFUL RAG IN THE WINDOW?
YOU.. YOU NOTICED THAT?
5

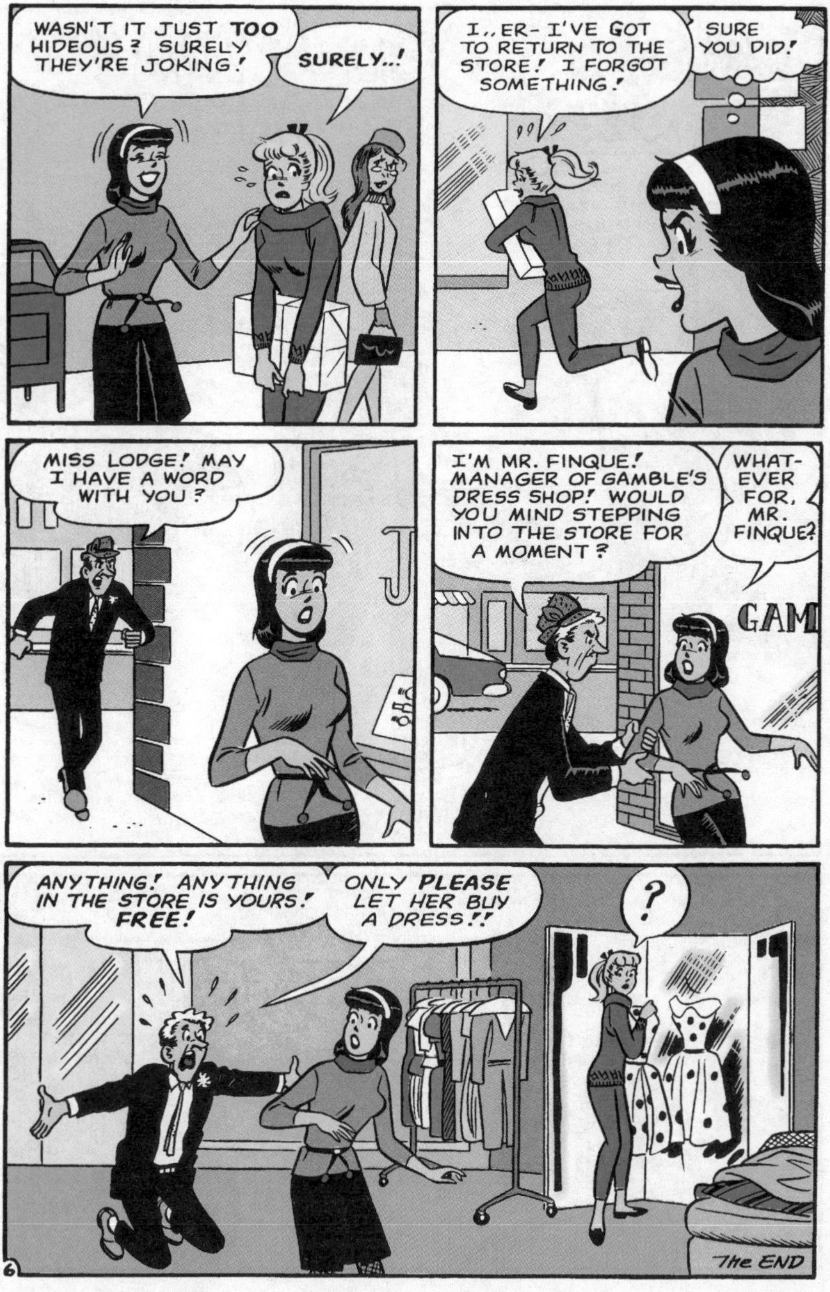
WASN'T IT JUST TOO HIDEOUS? SURELY THEY'RE JOKING!
SURELY..!
I.,ER- I'VE GOT TO RETURN TO THE STORE! I FORGOT SOMETHING!
SURE YOU DID!
MISS LODGE! MAY I HAVE A WORD WITH YOU?
I'M MR. FINQUE! MANAGER OF GAMBLE'S DRESS SHOP! WOULD YOU MIND STEPPING INTO THE STORE FOR A MOMENT?
WHAT-EVER FOR, MR. FINQUE?
GAM
ANYTHING! ANYTHING IN THE STORE IS YOURS! FREE!
ONLY PLEASE LET HER BUY A DRESS!!
?
The END

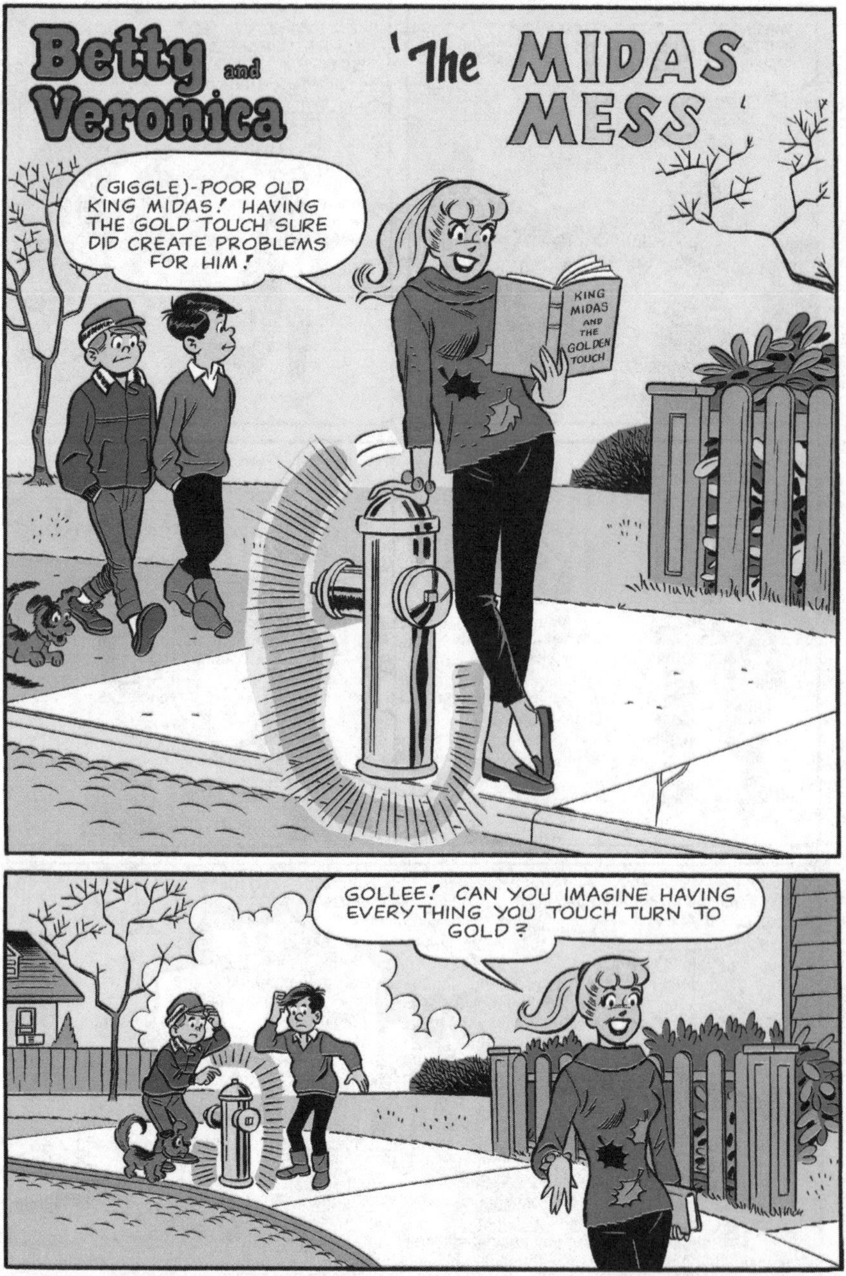
Betty and Veronica
'The MIDAS MESS'
(GIGGLE)-POOR OLD KING MIDAS! HAVING THE GOLD TOUCH SURE DID CREATE PROBLEMS FOR HIM!
KING MIDAS AND THE GOLDEN TOUCH
GOLLEE! CAN YOU IMAGINE HAVING EVERYTHING YOU TOUCH TURN TO GOLD?

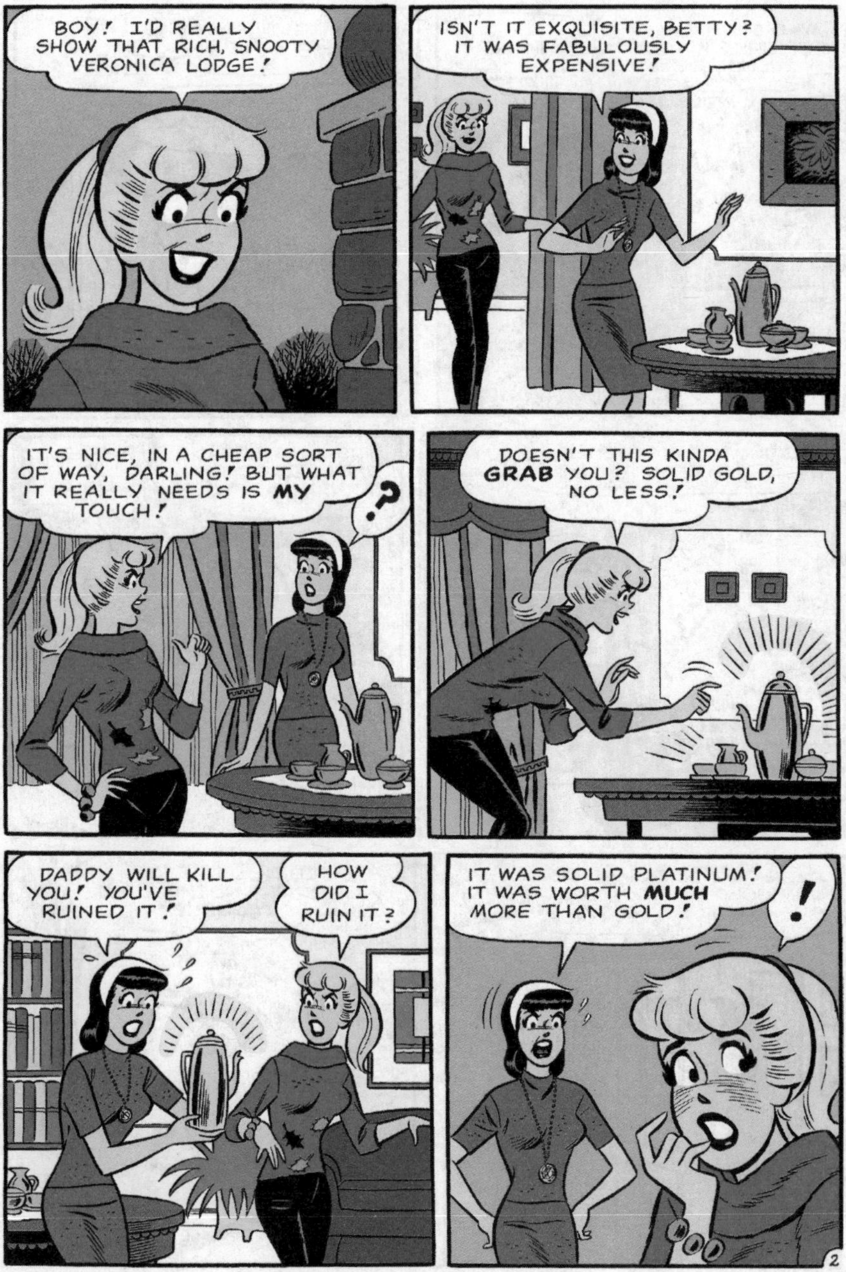
BOY! I'D REALLY SHOW THAT RICH, SNOOTY VERONICA LODGE!
ISN'T IT EXQUISITE, BETTY? IT WAS FABULOUSLY EXPENSIVE!
IT'S NICE, IN A CHEAP SORT OF WAY, DARLING! BUT WHAT IT REALLY NEEDS IS **MY** TOUCH!
?
DOESN'T THIS KINDA **GRAB** YOU? SOLID GOLD, NO LESS!
DADDY WILL KILL YOU! YOU'VE RUINED IT!
HOW DID I RUIN IT?
IT WAS SOLID PLATINUM! IT WAS WORTH **MUCH** MORE THAN GOLD!
!

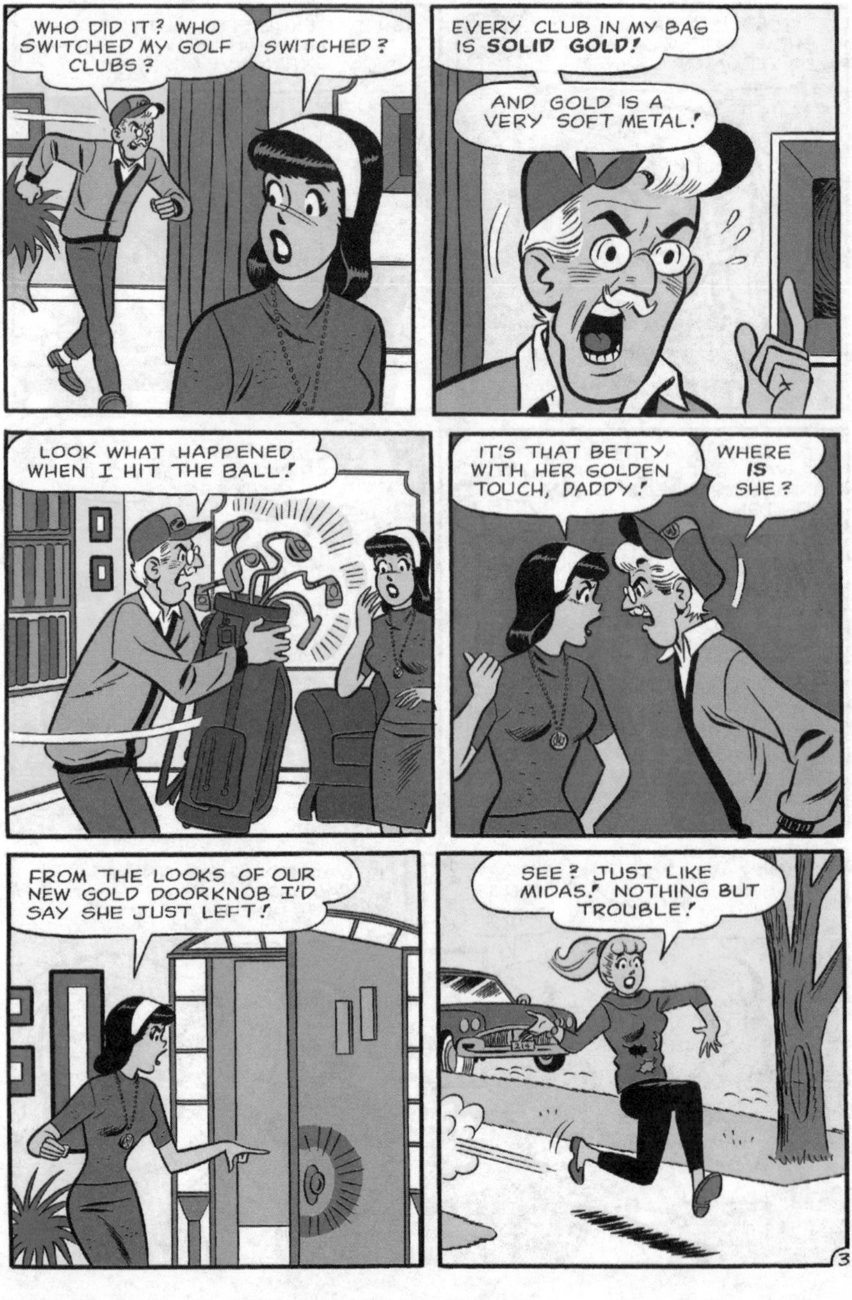
WHO DID IT? WHO SWITCHED MY GOLF CLUBS?
SWITCHED?
EVERY CLUB IN MY BAG IS **SOLID GOLD!**
AND GOLD IS A VERY SOFT METAL!
LOOK WHAT HAPPENED WHEN I HIT THE BALL!
IT'S THAT BETTY WITH HER GOLDEN TOUCH, DADDY!
WHERE **IS** SHE?
FROM THE LOOKS OF OUR NEW GOLD DOORKNOB I'D SAY SHE JUST LEFT!
SEE? JUST LIKE MIDAS! NOTHING BUT TROUBLE!
214

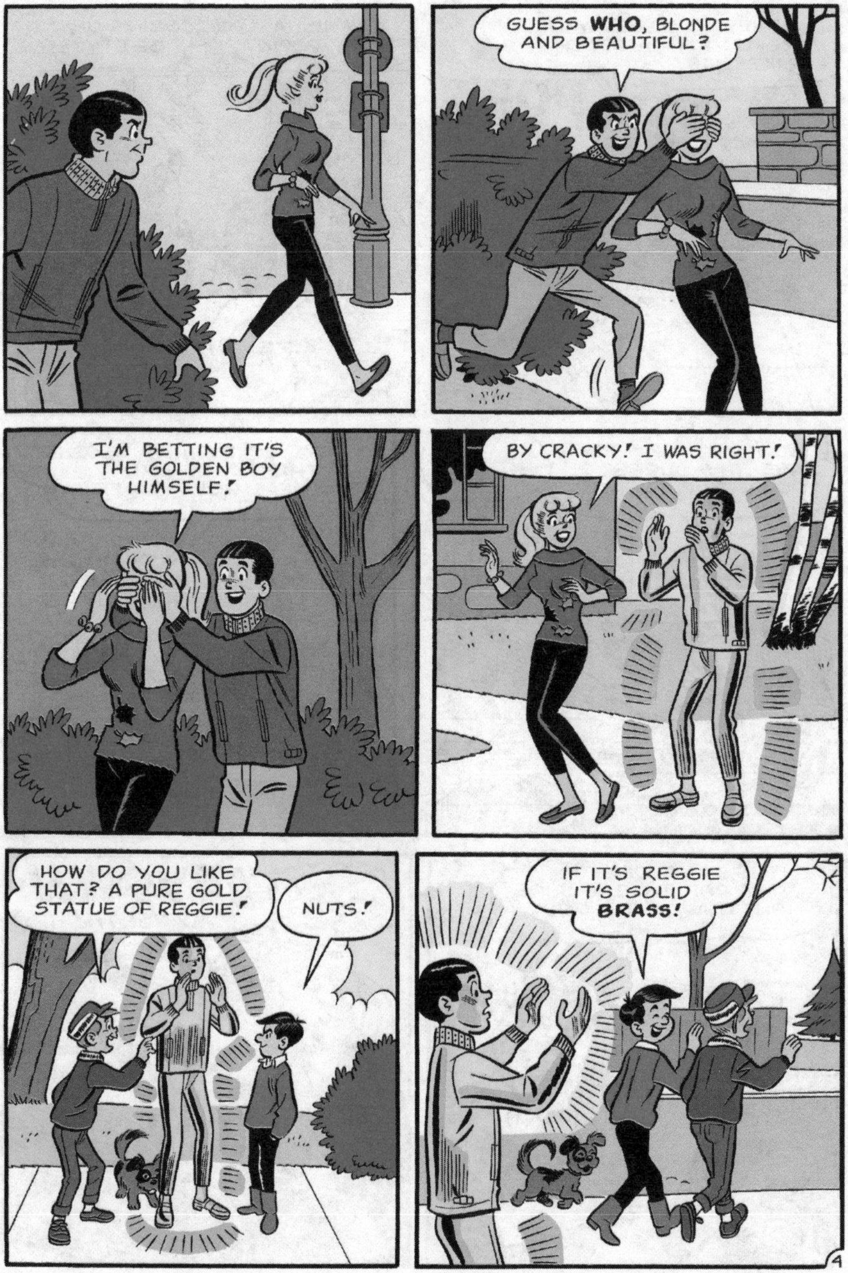
GUESS **WHO**, BLONDE AND BEAUTIFUL?
I'M BETTING IT'S THE GOLDEN BOY HIMSELF!
BY CRACKY! I WAS RIGHT!
HOW DO YOU LIKE THAT? A PURE GOLD STATUE OF REGGIE!
NUTS!
IF IT'S REGGIE IT'S SOLID **BRASS!**
4

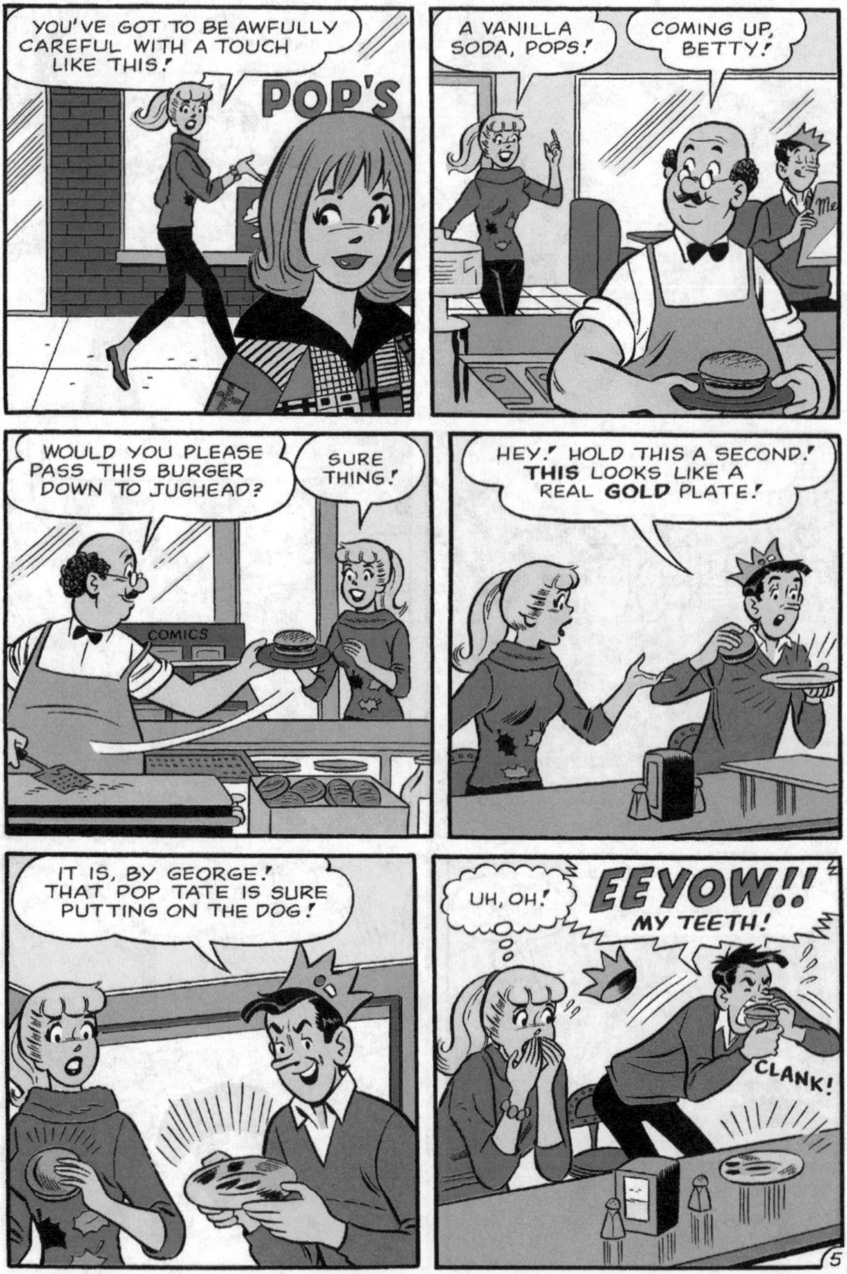
YOU'VE GOT TO BE AWFULLY CAREFUL WITH A TOUCH LIKE THIS!
POP'S
A VANILLA SODA, POPS!
COMING UP, BETTY!
WOULD YOU PLEASE PASS THIS BURGER DOWN TO JUGHEAD?
SURE THING!
COMICS
HEY! HOLD THIS A SECOND! **THIS** LOOKS LIKE A REAL **GOLD** PLATE!
IT IS, BY GEORGE! THAT POP TATE IS SURE PUTTING ON THE DOG!
UH, OH!
EEYOW!! MY TEETH!
CLANK!

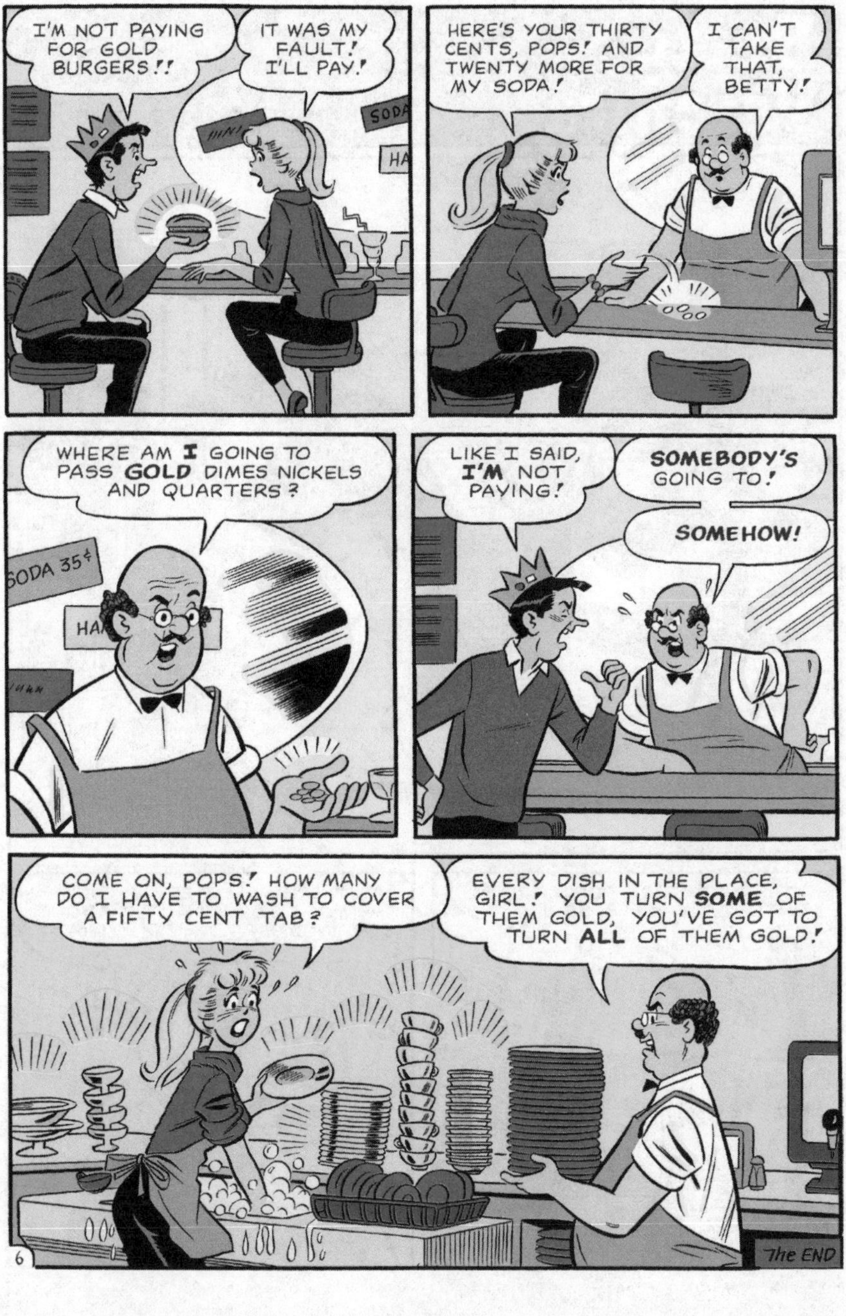
I'M NOT PAYING FOR GOLD BURGERS!!
IT WAS MY FAULT! I'LL PAY!
SODA
HERE'S YOUR THIRTY CENTS, POPS! AND TWENTY MORE FOR MY SODA!
I CAN'T TAKE THAT, BETTY!
WHERE AM I GOING TO PASS GOLD DIMES NICKELS AND QUARTERS?
SODA 35¢
LIKE I SAID, I'M NOT PAYING!
SOMEBODY'S GOING TO!
SOMEHOW!
COME ON, POPS! HOW MANY DO I HAVE TO WASH TO COVER A FIFTY CENT TAB?
EVERY DISH IN THE PLACE, GIRL! YOU TURN SOME OF THEM GOLD, YOU'VE GOT TO TURN ALL OF THEM GOLD!
The END

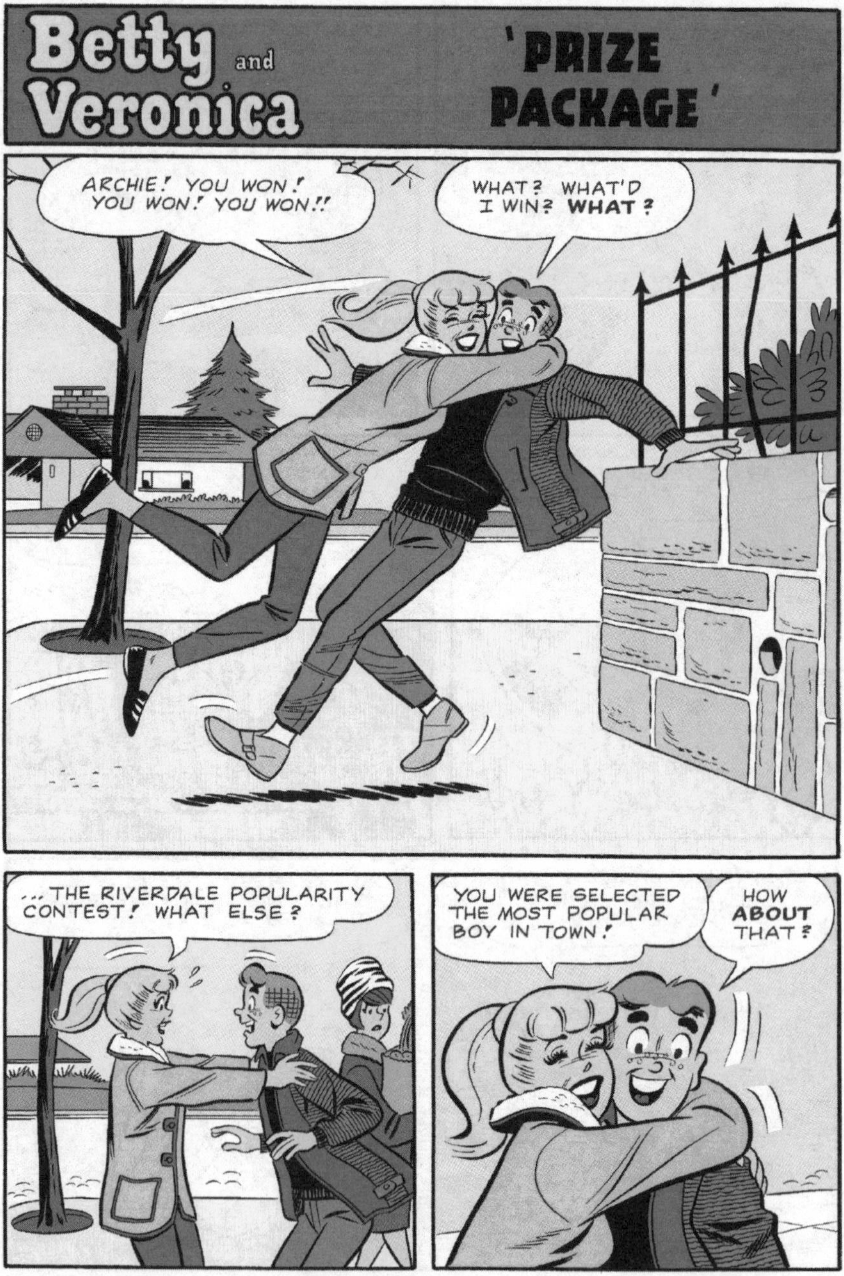

Betty and Veronica
'PRIZE PACKAGE'
ARCHIE! YOU WON! YOU WON! YOU WON!!
WHAT? WHAT'D I WIN? WHAT?
... THE RIVERDALE POPULARITY CONTEST! WHAT ELSE?
YOU WERE SELECTED THE MOST POPULAR BOY IN TOWN!
HOW ABOUT THAT?

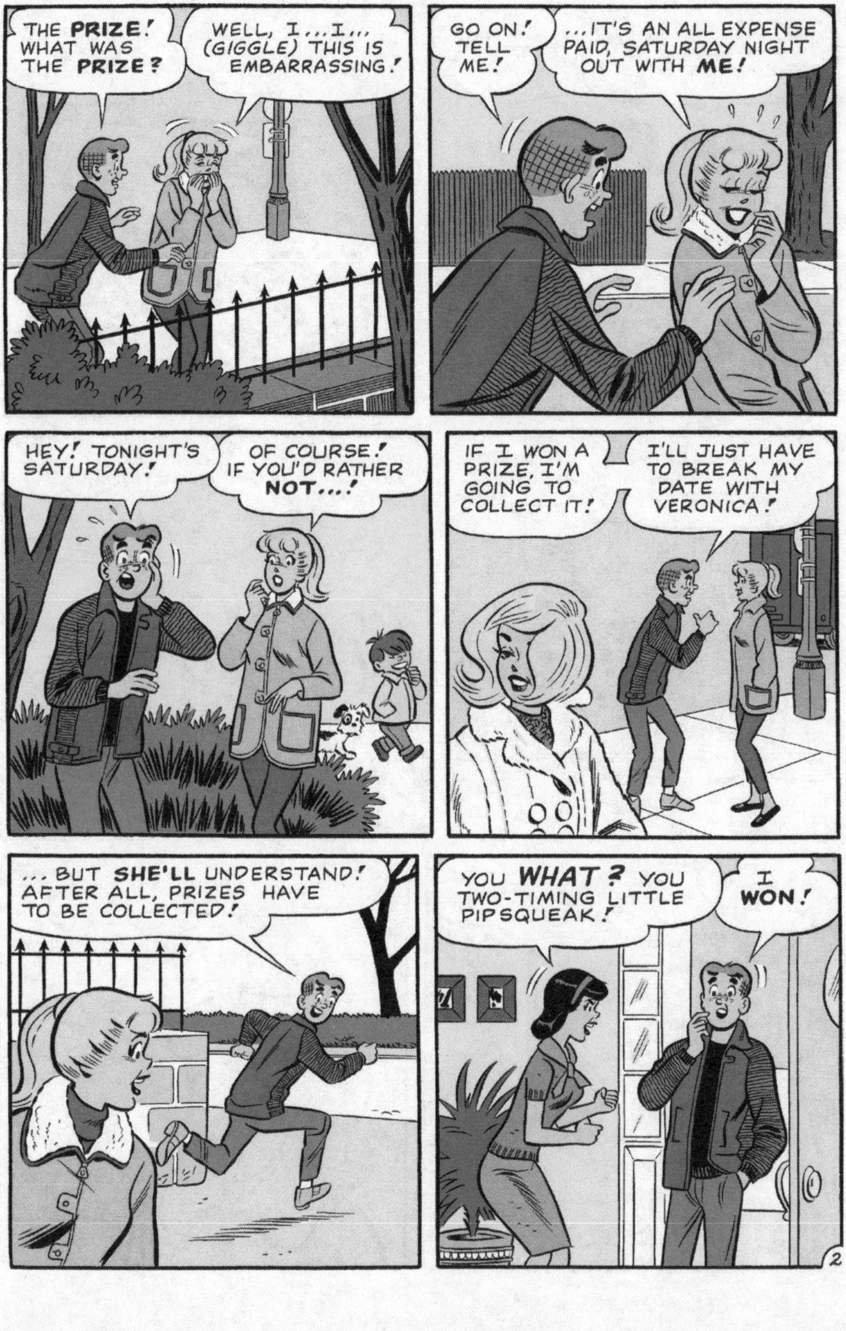
THE PRIZE! WHAT WAS THE PRIZE?
WELL, I...I... (GIGGLE) THIS IS EMBARRASSING!
GO ON! TELL ME!
...IT'S AN ALL EXPENSE PAID, SATURDAY NIGHT OUT WITH ME!
HEY! TONIGHT'S SATURDAY!
OF COURSE! IF YOU'D RATHER NOT...!
IF I WON A PRIZE, I'M GOING TO COLLECT IT!
I'LL JUST HAVE TO BREAK MY DATE WITH VERONICA!
... BUT SHE'LL UNDERSTAND! AFTER ALL, PRIZES HAVE TO BE COLLECTED!
I WON!
YOU WHAT? YOU TWO-TIMING LITTLE PIPSQUEAK!
2

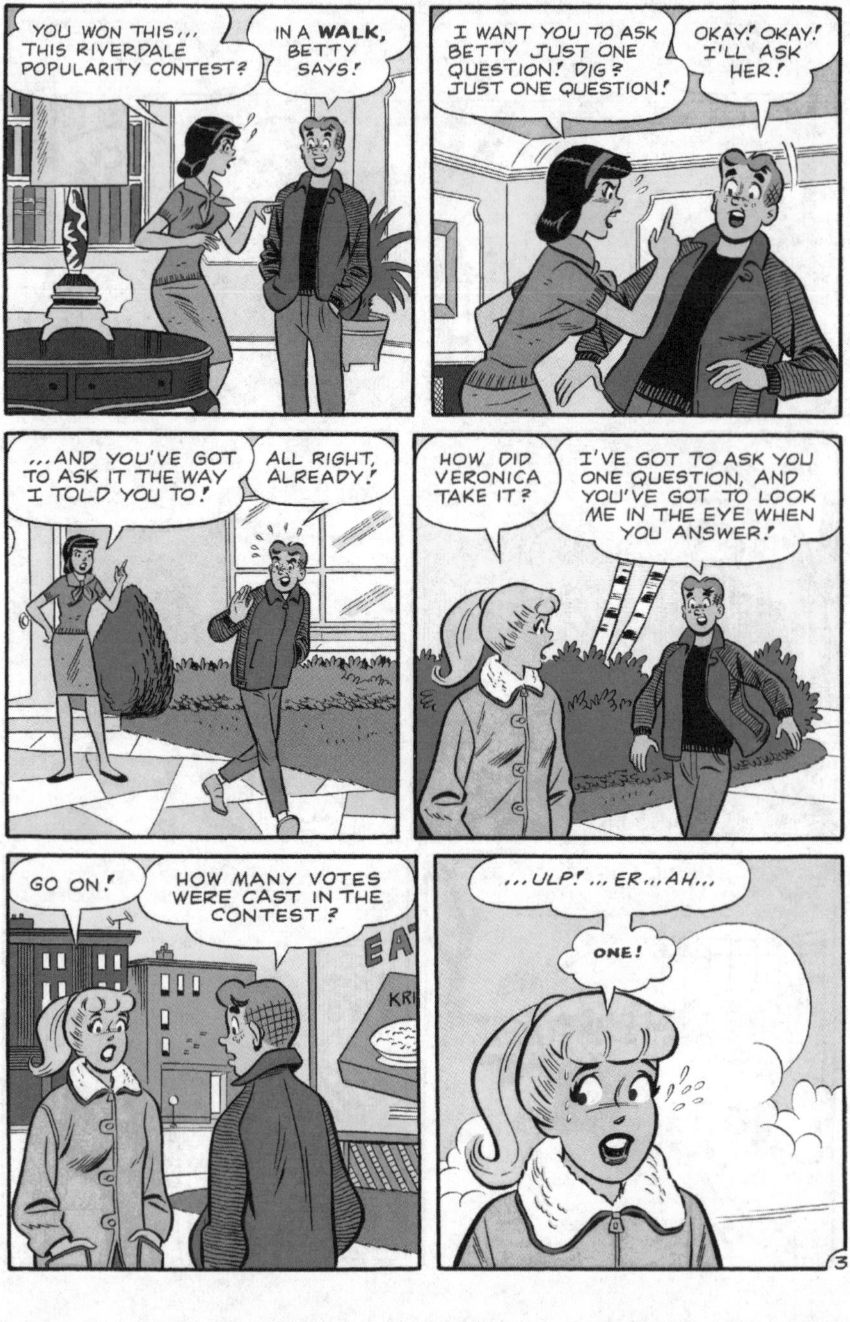
YOU WON THIS... THIS RIVERDALE POPULARITY CONTEST?
IN A **WALK,** BETTY SAYS!
I WANT YOU TO ASK BETTY JUST ONE QUESTION! DIG? JUST ONE QUESTION!
OKAY! OKAY! I'LL ASK HER!
...AND YOU'VE GOT TO ASK IT THE WAY I TOLD YOU TO!
ALL RIGHT, ALREADY!
HOW DID VERONICA TAKE IT?
I'VE GOT TO ASK YOU ONE QUESTION, AND YOU'VE GOT TO LOOK ME IN THE EYE WHEN YOU ANSWER!
GO ON!
HOW MANY VOTES WERE CAST IN THE CONTEST?
...ULP! ...ER...AH...
ONE!

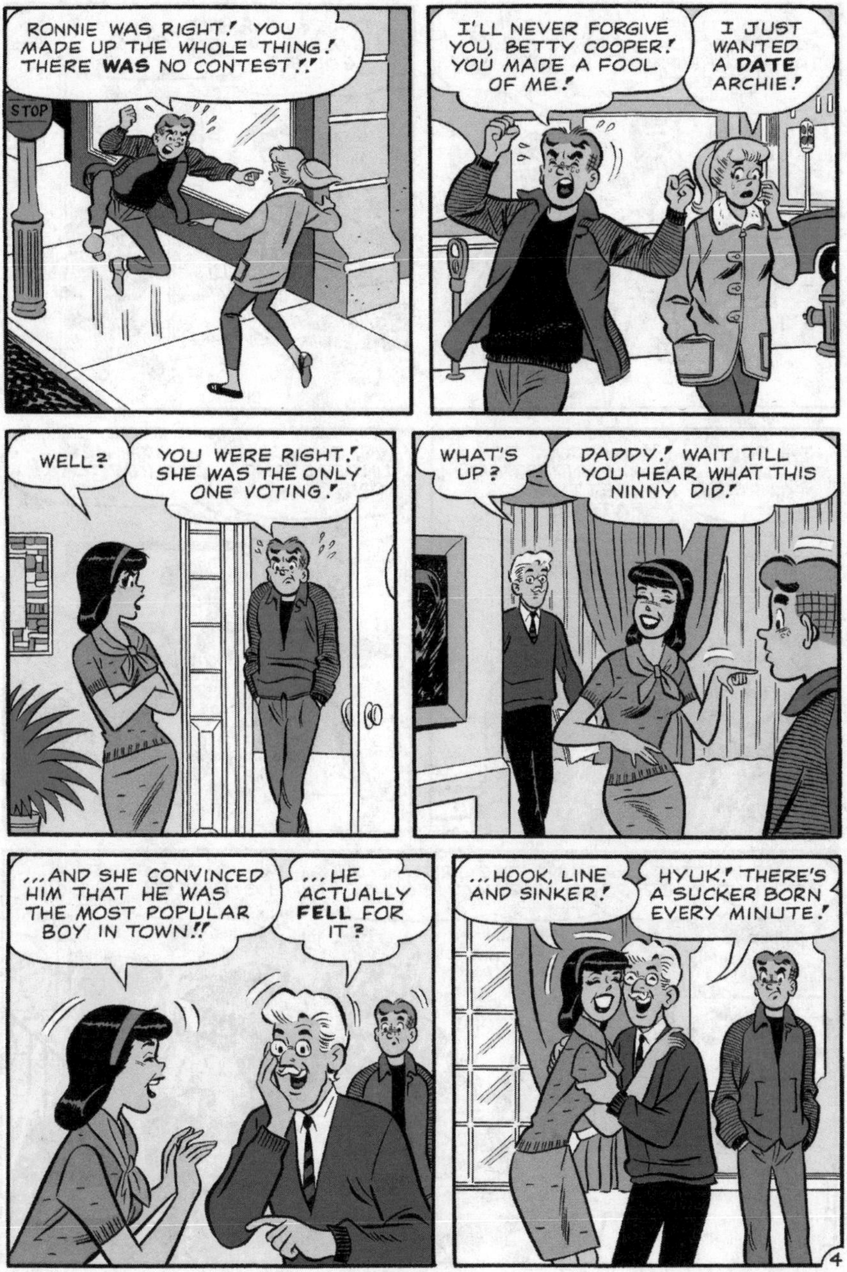
RONNIE WAS RIGHT! YOU MADE UP THE WHOLE THING! THERE WAS NO CONTEST!!
STOP
I'LL NEVER FORGIVE YOU, BETTY COOPER! YOU MADE A FOOL OF ME!
I JUST WANTED A DATE ARCHIE!
WELL?
YOU WERE RIGHT! SHE WAS THE ONLY ONE VOTING!
WHAT'S UP?
DADDY! WAIT TILL YOU HEAR WHAT THIS NINNY DID!
...AND SHE CONVINCED HIM THAT HE WAS THE MOST POPULAR BOY IN TOWN!!
...HE ACTUALLY FELL FOR IT?
...HOOK, LINE AND SINKER!
HYUK! THERE'S A SUCKER BORN EVERY MINUTE!

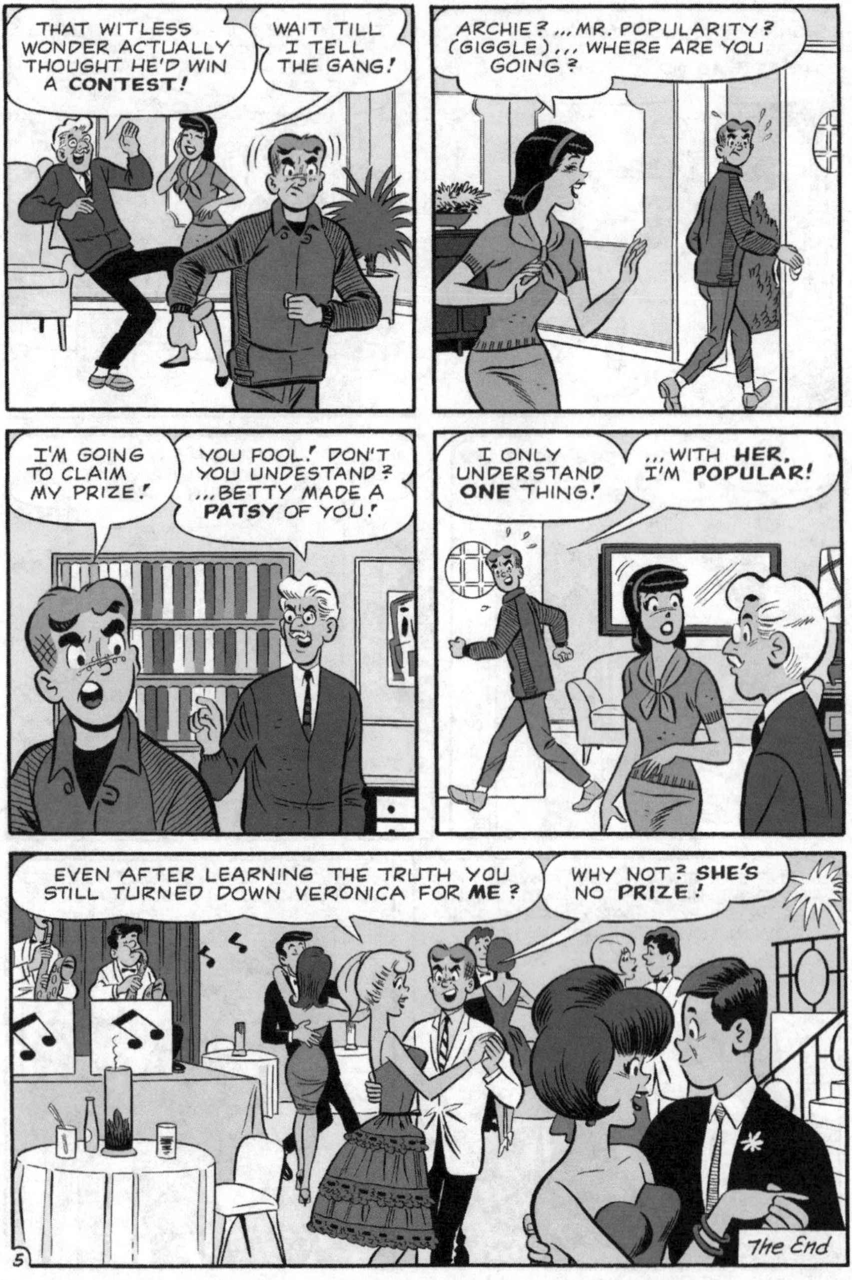
THAT WITLESS WONDER ACTUALLY THOUGHT HE'D WIN A **CONTEST!**
WAIT TILL I TELL THE GANG!
ARCHIE? ... MR. POPULARITY? (GIGGLE)... WHERE ARE YOU GOING?
I'M GOING TO CLAIM MY PRIZE!
YOU FOOL! DON'T YOU UNDESTAND? ...BETTY MADE A **PATSY** OF YOU!
I ONLY UNDERSTAND **ONE** THING!
...WITH **HER**, I'M **POPULAR!**
EVEN AFTER LEARNING THE TRUTH YOU STILL TURNED DOWN VERONICA FOR **ME**?
WHY NOT? **SHE'S** NO **PRIZE!**
The End
5

THE ESCORT
BETTY & VERONICA #113, 1965
Frank Doyle, Dan DeCarlo, Rudy Lapick, Victor Gorelick

TILT
BETTY & VERONICA #122, 1965
Frank Doyle, Dan DeCarlo, Rudy Lapick, Vincent DeCarlo, Barry Grossman

NEW GIRL IN TOWN
BETTY & VERONICA #142, 1967
George Gladir, Dan DeCarlo, Rudy Lapick, Bill Yoshida, Barry Grossman

Betty and Veronica gave me a window into a world unlike my own. I grew up in the city in a home where English was a language we learned after my oldest sister Fay began kindergarten. I learned about suburban life through the adventures of Archie and his friends. In the classic storylines, Betty and Veronica were playing tug of war for Archie's attention. Veronica had unpleasant characteristics which very similar to the "mean girls' at school. Yes, I identified with Betty who had a more compassionate nature.

- JANICE CHIANG *Letterer, Archie Comics*

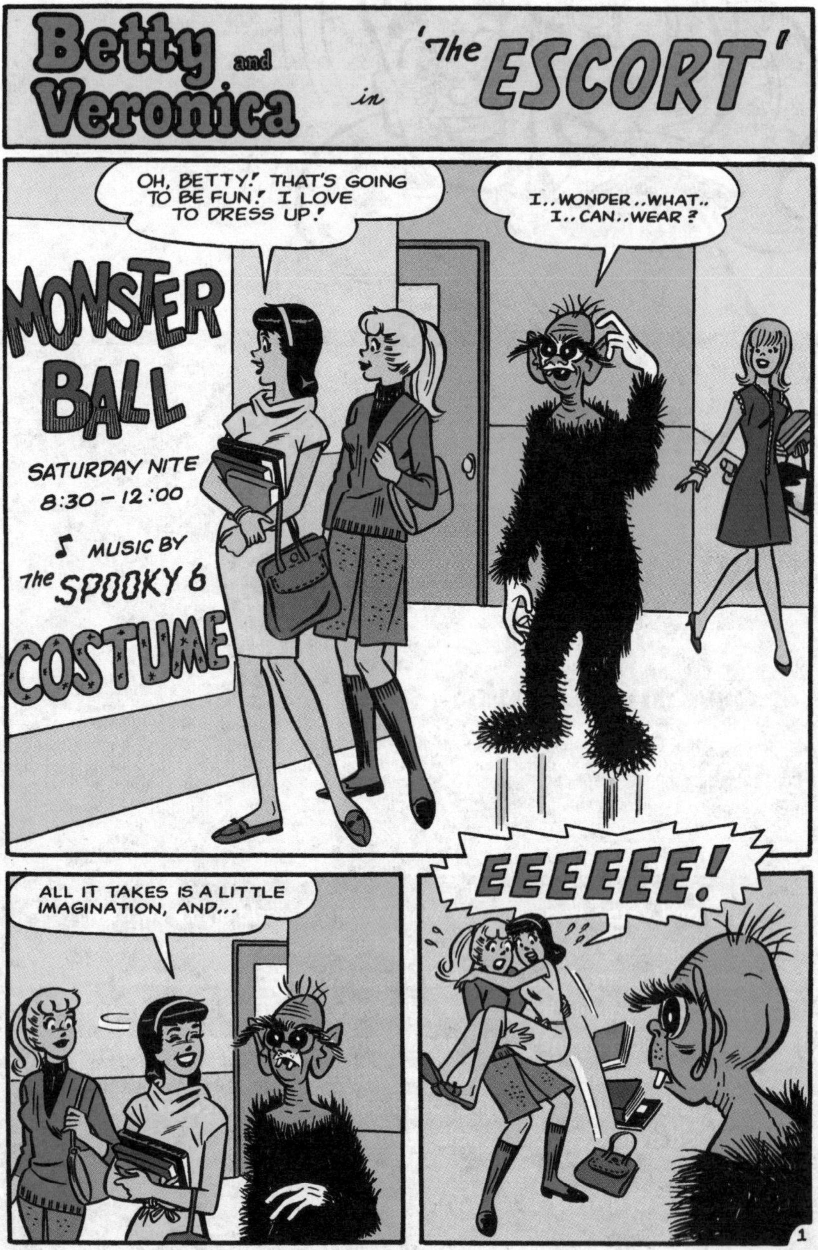
Betty and Veronica in 'The ESCORT'
OH, BETTY! THAT'S GOING TO BE FUN! I LOVE TO DRESS UP!
MONSTER BALL
SATURDAY NITE
8:30 - 12:00
MUSIC BY
The SPOOKY 6
COSTUME
I.. WONDER.. WHAT.. I.. CAN.. WEAR?
ALL IT TAKES IS A LITTLE IMAGINATION, AND...
EEEEEE!

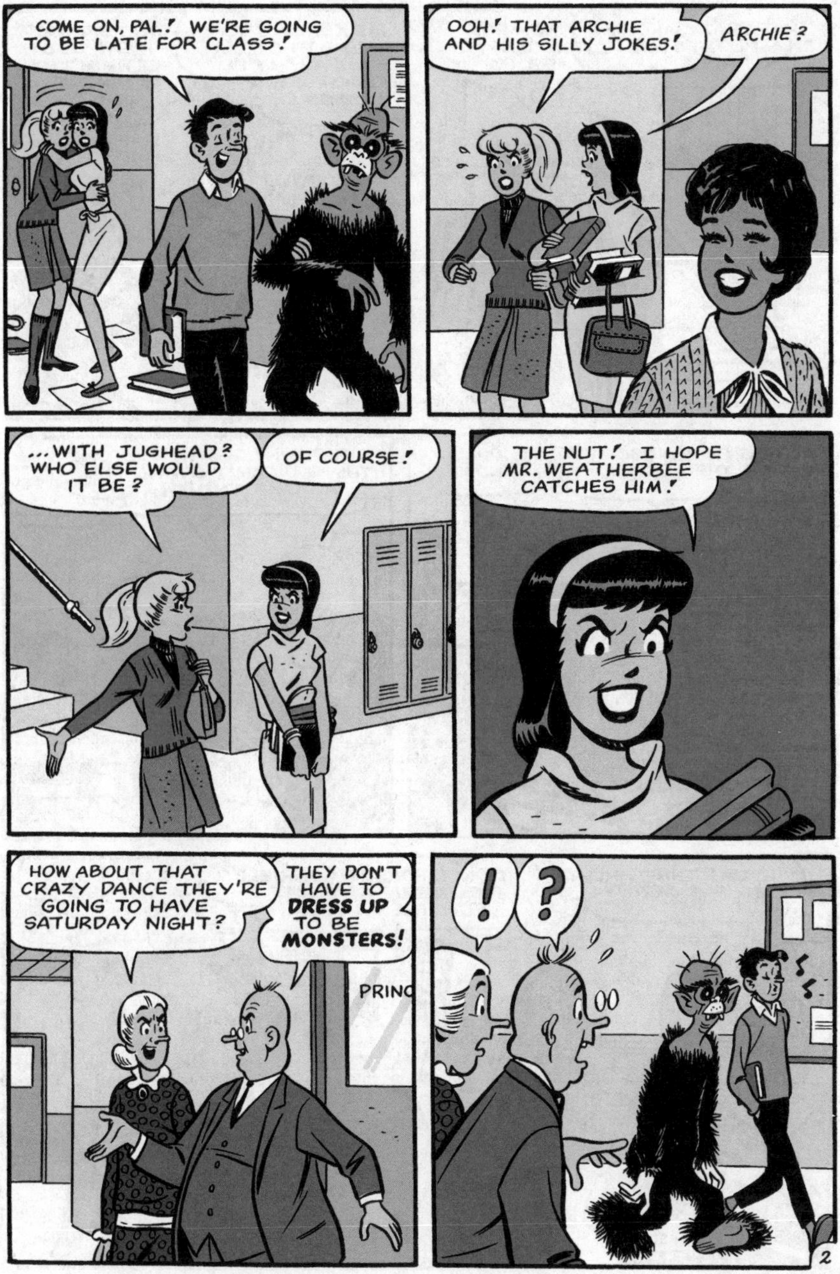
COME ON, PAL! WE'RE GOING TO BE LATE FOR CLASS!
OOH! THAT ARCHIE AND HIS SILLY JOKES!
ARCHIE?
...WITH JUGHEAD? WHO ELSE WOULD IT BE?
OF COURSE!
THE NUT! I HOPE MR. WEATHERBEE CATCHES HIM!
HOW ABOUT THAT CRAZY DANCE THEY'RE GOING TO HAVE SATURDAY NIGHT?
THEY DON'T HAVE TO **DRESS UP** TO BE **MONSTERS!**
PRINC
!
?
2

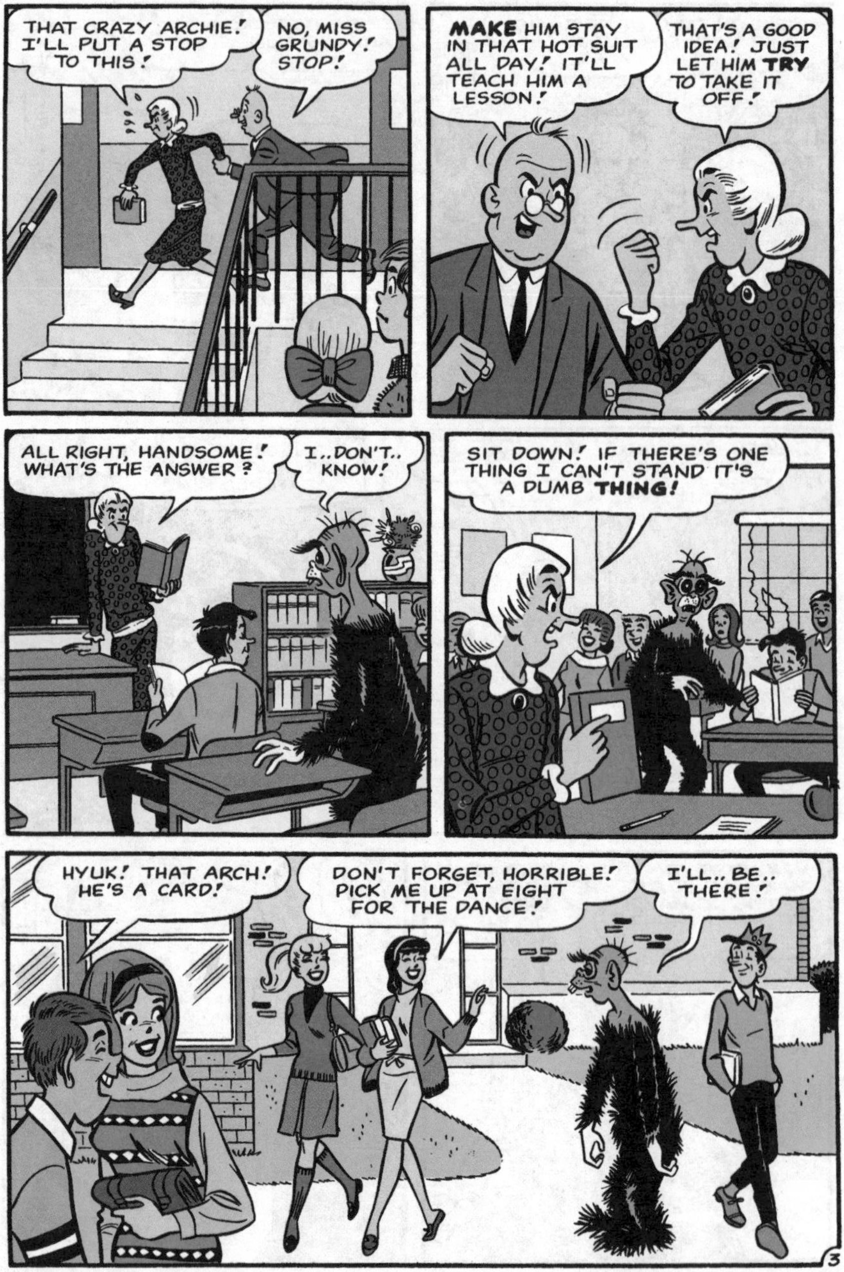
THAT CRAZY ARCHIE! I'LL PUT A STOP TO THIS!
NO, MISS GRUNDY! STOP!
MAKE HIM STAY IN THAT HOT SUIT ALL DAY! IT'LL TEACH HIM A LESSON!
THAT'S A GOOD IDEA! JUST LET HIM TRY TO TAKE IT OFF!
ALL RIGHT, HANDSOME! WHAT'S THE ANSWER?
I..DON'T.. KNOW!
SIT DOWN! IF THERE'S ONE THING I CAN'T STAND IT'S A DUMB THING!
HYUK! THAT ARCH! HE'S A CARD!
DON'T FORGET, HORRIBLE! PICK ME UP AT EIGHT FOR THE DANCE!
I'LL.. BE.. THERE!
3

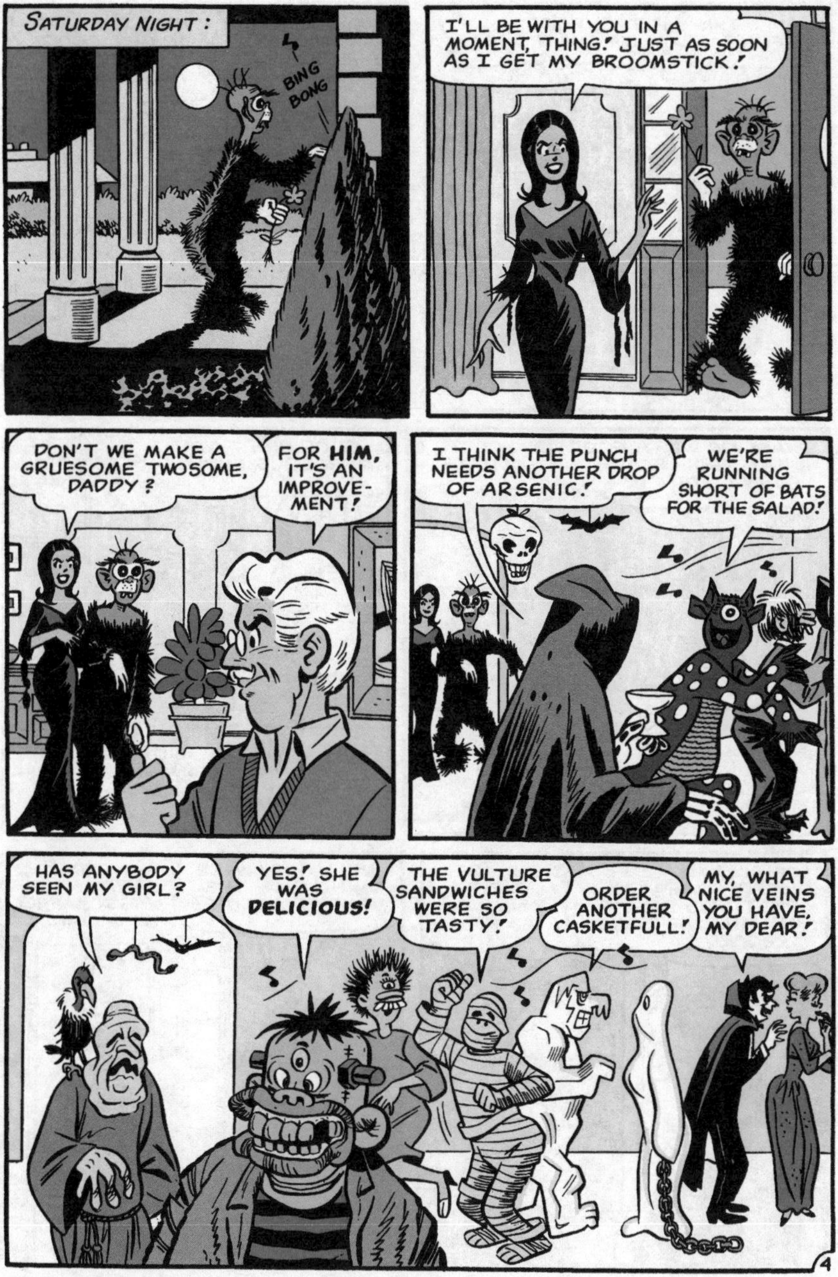
SATURDAY NIGHT:
BING BONG
I'LL BE WITH YOU IN A MOMENT, THING! JUST AS SOON AS I GET MY BROOMSTICK!
DON'T WE MAKE A GRUESOME TWOSOME, DADDY?
FOR HIM, IT'S AN IMPROVE-MENT!
I THINK THE PUNCH NEEDS ANOTHER DROP OF ARSENIC!
WE'RE RUNNING SHORT OF BATS FOR THE SALAD!
HAS ANYBODY SEEN MY GIRL?
YES! SHE WAS DELICIOUS!
THE VULTURE SANDWICHES WERE SO TASTY!
ORDER ANOTHER CASKETFULL!
MY, WHAT NICE VEINS YOU HAVE, MY DEAR!

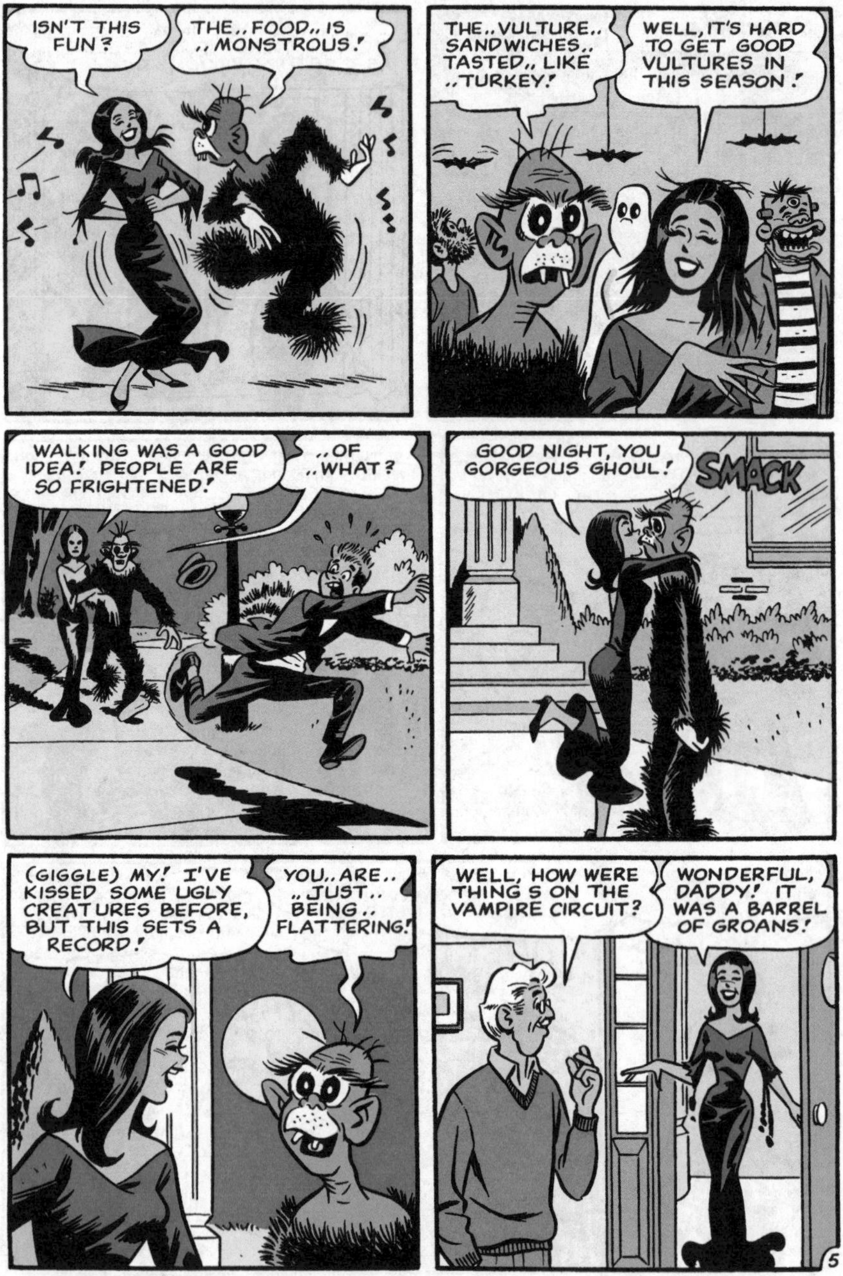
ISN'T THIS FUN?
THE.. FOOD.. IS .. MONSTROUS!
THE.. VULTURE.. SANDWICHES.. TASTED.. LIKE ..TURKEY!
WELL, IT'S HARD TO GET GOOD VULTURES IN THIS SEASON!
WALKING WAS A GOOD IDEA! PEOPLE ARE SO FRIGHTENED!
..OF ..WHAT?
GOOD NIGHT, YOU GORGEOUS GHOUL!
SMACK
(GIGGLE) MY! I'VE KISSED SOME UGLY CREATURES BEFORE, BUT THIS SETS A RECORD!
YOU.. ARE.. ..JUST.. BEING.. FLATTERING!
WELL, HOW WERE THING S ON THE VAMPIRE CIRCUIT?
WONDERFUL, DADDY! IT WAS A BARREL OF GROANS!
5

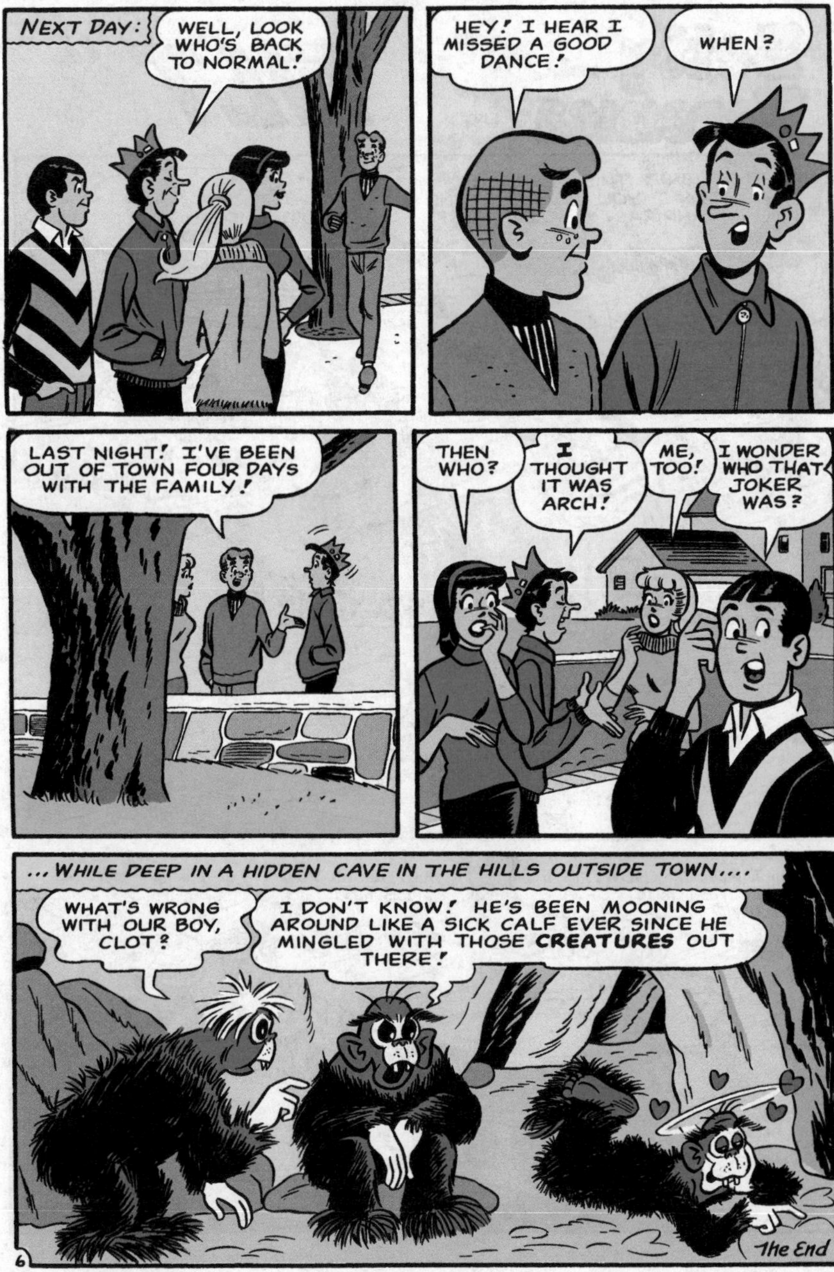
NEXT DAY:
WELL, LOOK WHO'S BACK TO NORMAL!
HEY! I HEAR I MISSED A GOOD DANCE!
WHEN?
LAST NIGHT! I'VE BEEN OUT OF TOWN FOUR DAYS WITH THE FAMILY!
THEN WHO?
I THOUGHT IT WAS ARCH!
ME, TOO!
I WONDER WHO THAT JOKER WAS?
...WHILE DEEP IN A HIDDEN CAVE IN THE HILLS OUTSIDE TOWN....
WHAT'S WRONG WITH OUR BOY, CLOT?
I DON'T KNOW! HE'S BEEN MOONING AROUND LIKE A SICK CALF EVER SINCE HE MINGLED WITH THOSE **CREATURES** OUT THERE!
The End
6

Betty and Veronica in "TILT"

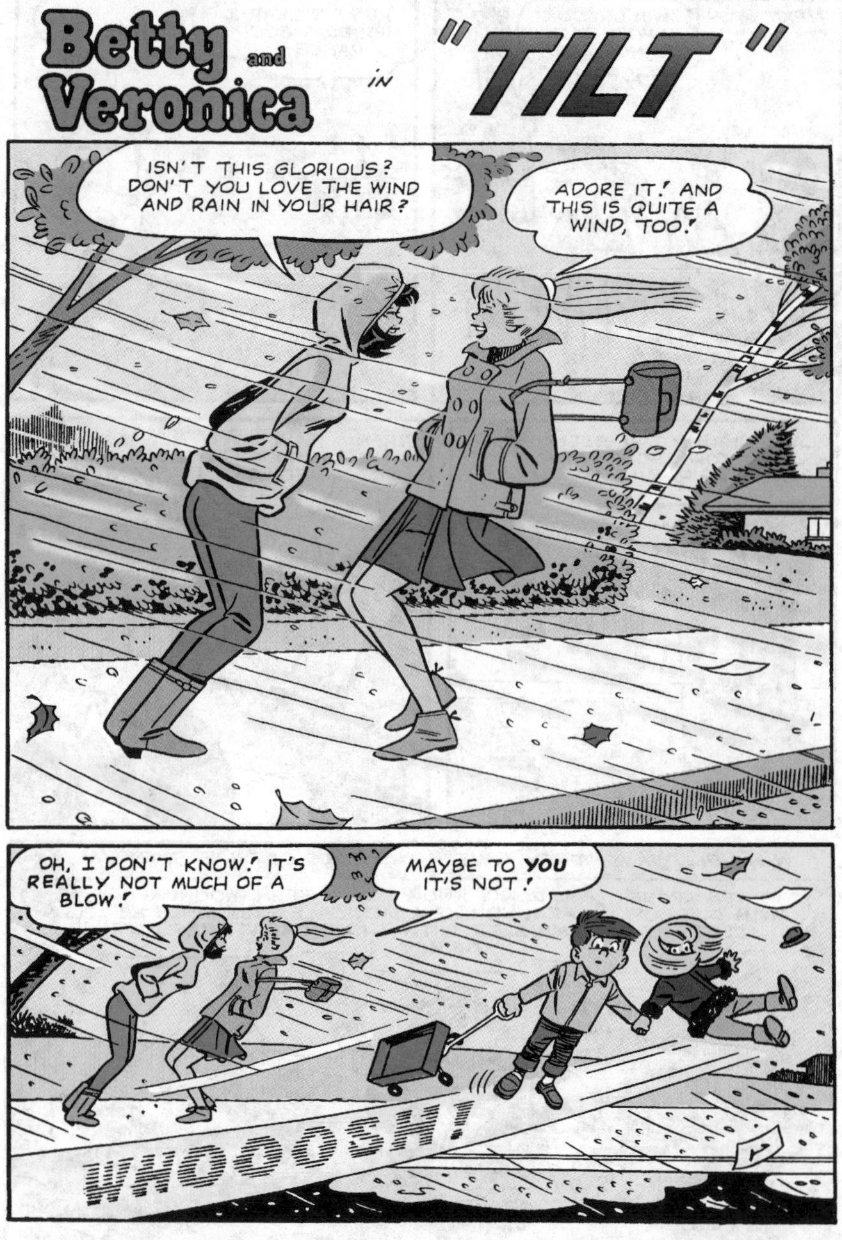
ISN'T THIS GLORIOUS? DON'T YOU LOVE THE WIND AND RAIN IN YOUR HAIR?
ADORE IT! AND THIS IS QUITE A WIND, TOO!
OH, I DON'T KNOW! IT'S REALLY NOT MUCH OF A BLOW!
MAYBE TO **YOU** IT'S NOT!
WHOOOOSH!

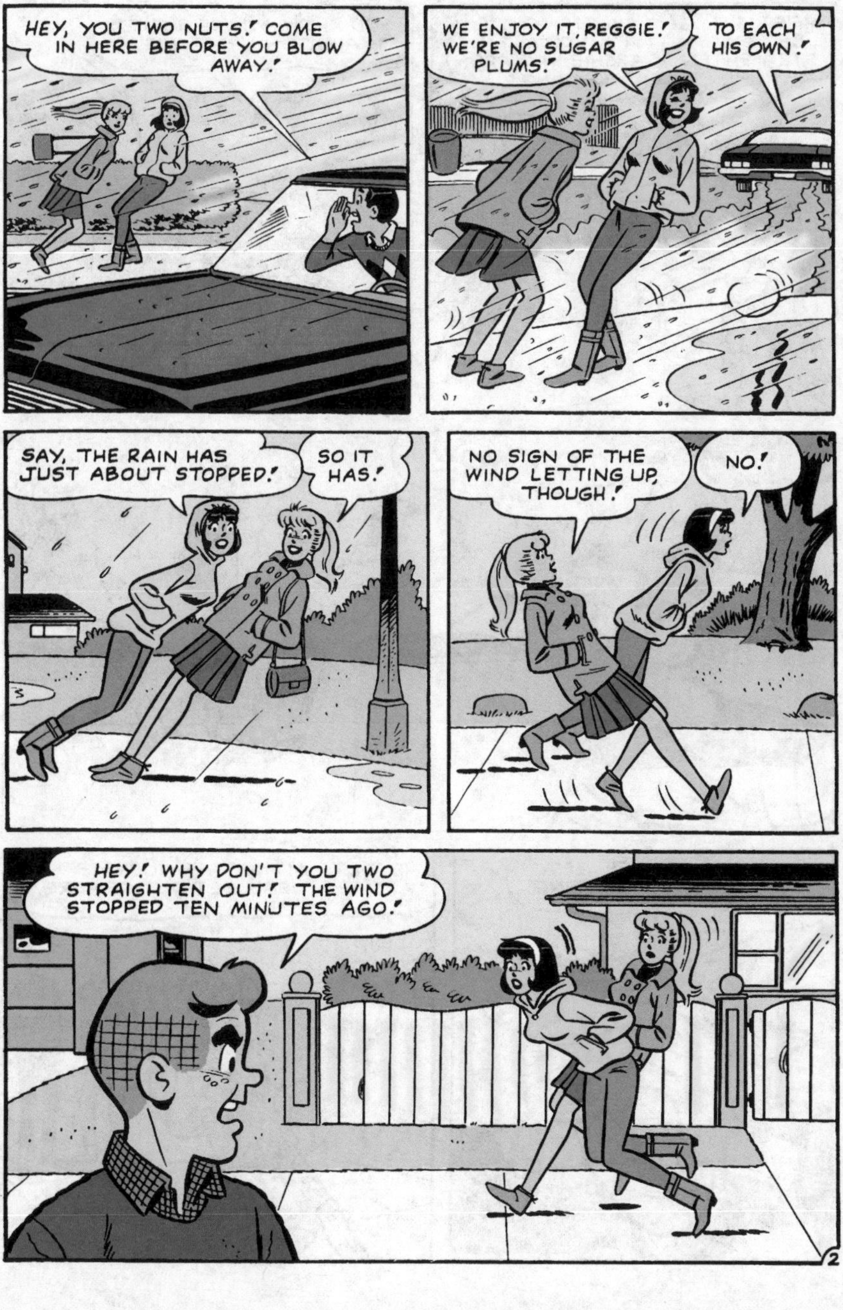
HEY, YOU TWO NUTS! COME IN HERE BEFORE YOU BLOW AWAY!
WE ENJOY IT, REGGIE! WE'RE NO SUGAR PLUMS!
TO EACH HIS OWN!
SAY, THE RAIN HAS JUST ABOUT STOPPED!
SO IT HAS!
NO SIGN OF THE WIND LETTING UP, THOUGH!
NO!
HEY! WHY DON'T YOU TWO STRAIGHTEN OUT! THE WIND STOPPED TEN MINUTES AGO!

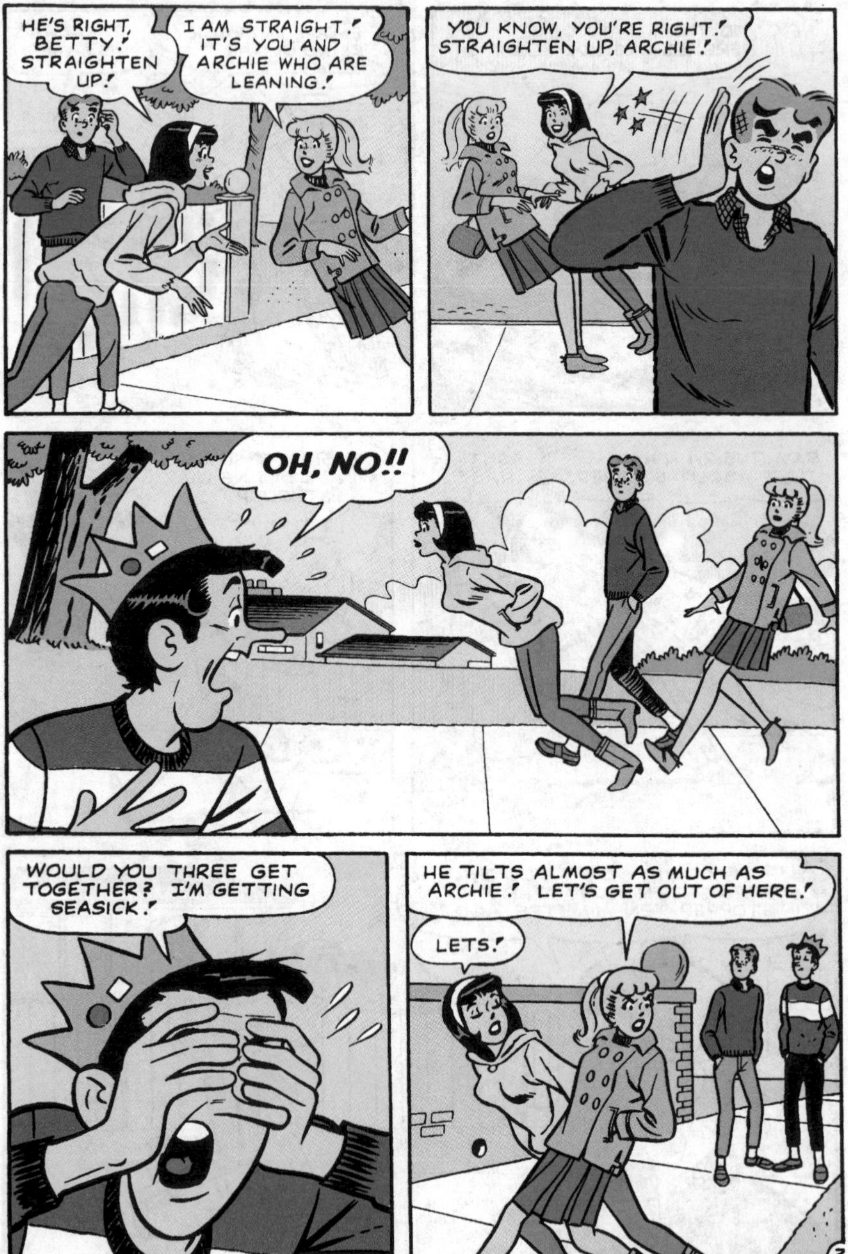
HE'S RIGHT, BETTY! STRAIGHTEN UP!
I AM STRAIGHT! IT'S YOU AND ARCHIE WHO ARE LEANING!
YOU KNOW, YOU'RE RIGHT! STRAIGHTEN UP, ARCHIE!
OH, NO!!
WOULD YOU THREE GET TOGETHER? I'M GETTING SEASICK!
HE TILTS ALMOST AS MUCH AS ARCHIE! LET'S GET OUT OF HERE!
LETS!
3

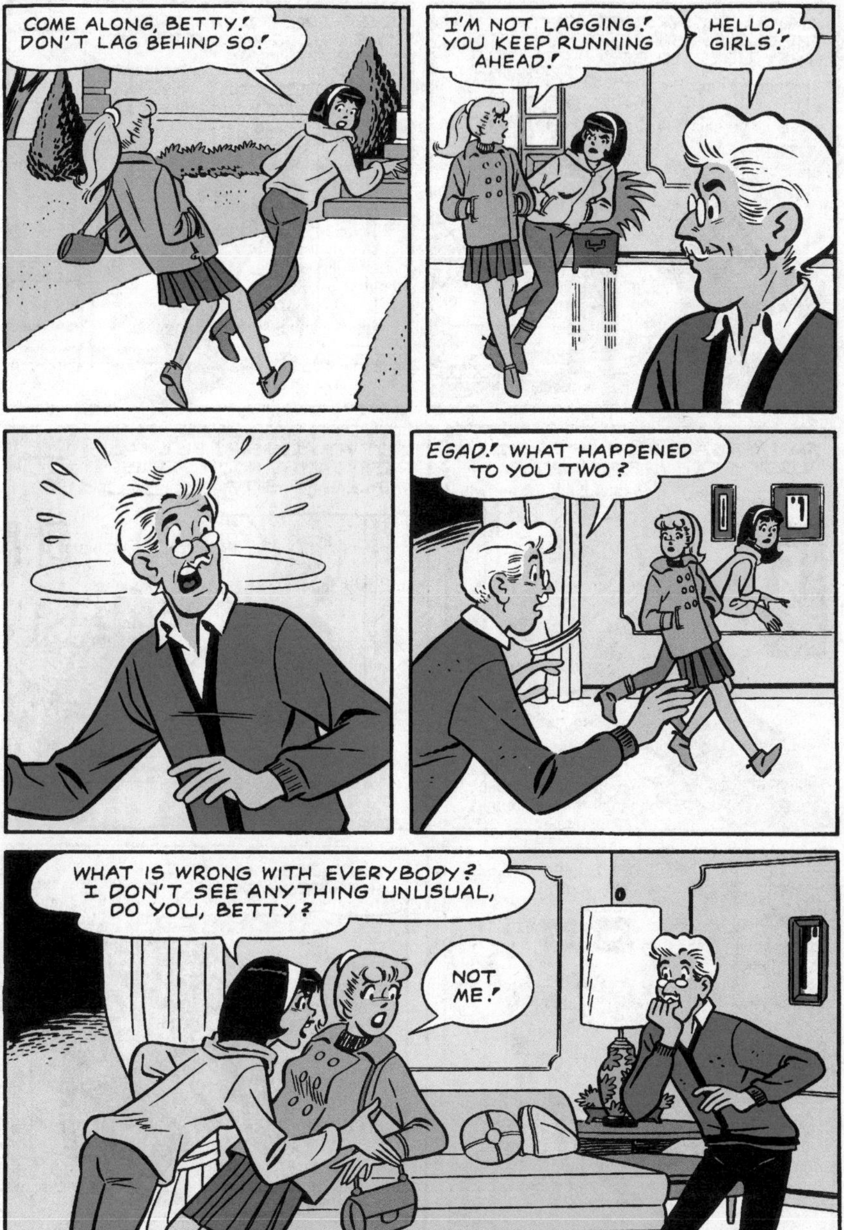
COME ALONG, BETTY! DON'T LAG BEHIND SO!
I'M NOT LAGGING! YOU KEEP RUNNING AHEAD!
HELLO, GIRLS!
EGAD! WHAT HAPPENED TO YOU TWO?
WHAT IS WRONG WITH EVERYBODY? I DON'T SEE ANYTHING UNUSUAL, DO YOU, BETTY?
NOT ME!
4

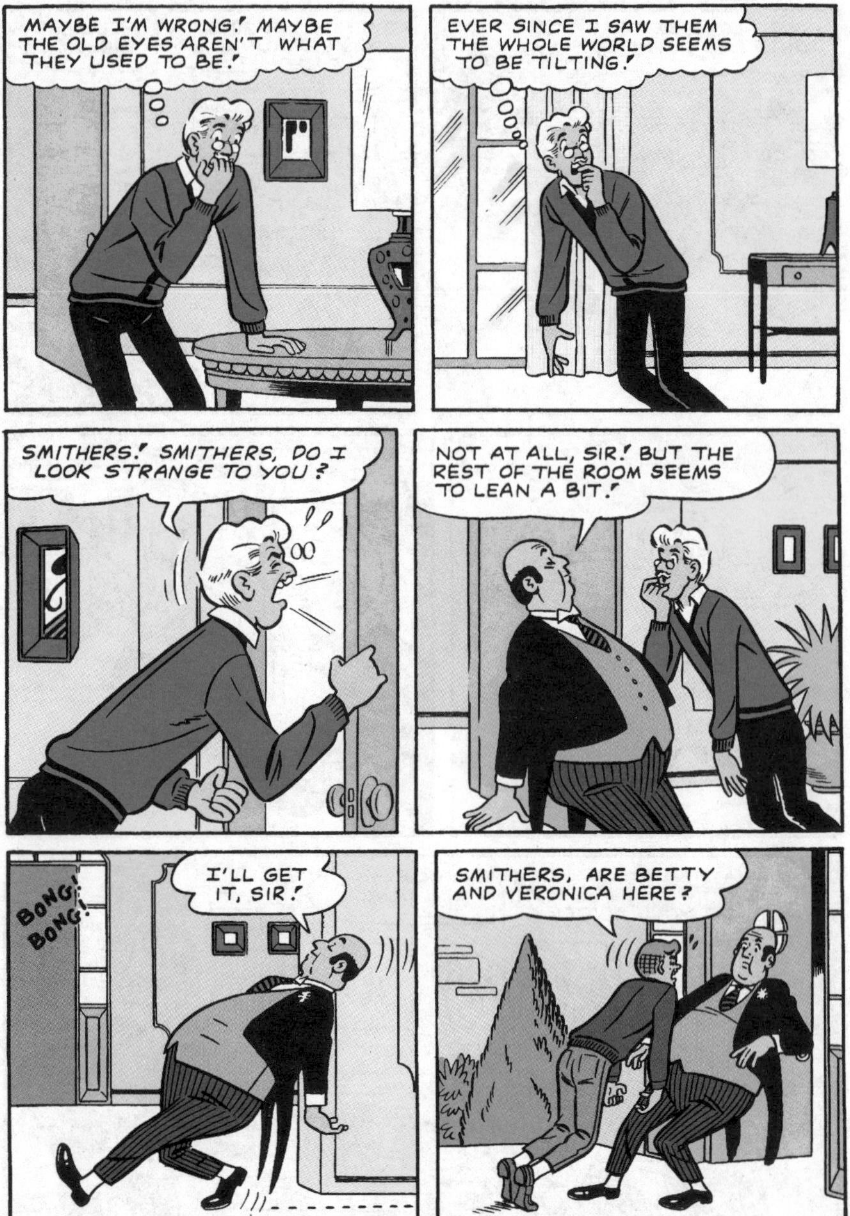
MAYBE I'M WRONG! MAYBE THE OLD EYES AREN'T WHAT THEY USED TO BE!
EVER SINCE I SAW THEM THE WHOLE WORLD SEEMS TO BE TILTING!
SMITHERS! SMITHERS, DO I LOOK STRANGE TO YOU?
NOT AT ALL, SIR! BUT THE REST OF THE ROOM SEEMS TO LEAN A BIT!
BONG! BONG!
I'LL GET IT, SIR!
SMITHERS, ARE BETTY AND VERONICA HERE?
5

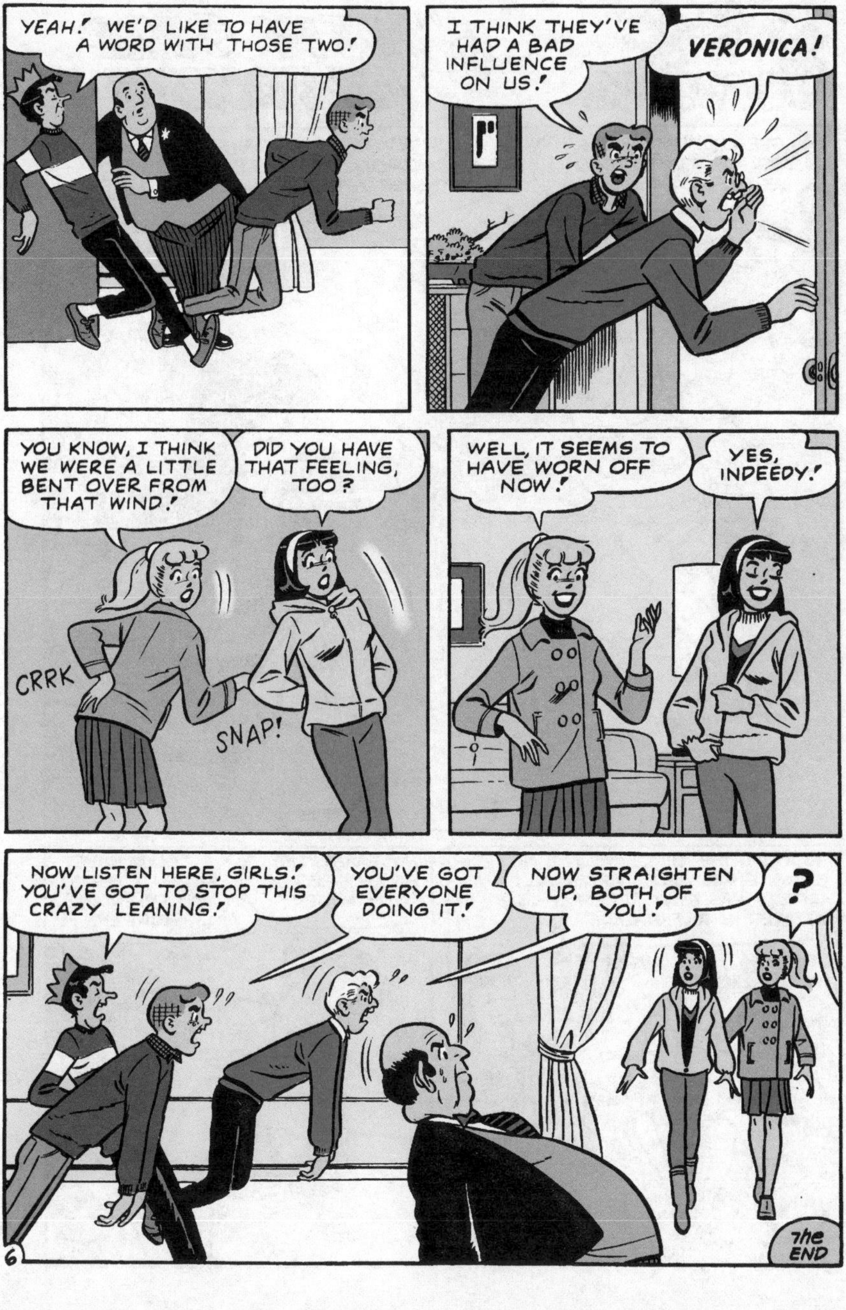
YEAH! WE'D LIKE TO HAVE A WORD WITH THOSE TWO!
I THINK THEY'VE HAD A BAD INFLUENCE ON US!
VERONICA!
YOU KNOW, I THINK WE WERE A LITTLE BENT OVER FROM THAT WIND!
DID YOU HAVE THAT FEELING, TOO?
CRRK
SNAP!
WELL, IT SEEMS TO HAVE WORN OFF NOW!
YES, INDEEDY!
NOW LISTEN HERE, GIRLS! YOU'VE GOT TO STOP THIS CRAZY LEANING!
YOU'VE GOT EVERYONE DOING IT!
NOW STRAIGHTEN UP, BOTH OF YOU!
?
THE END

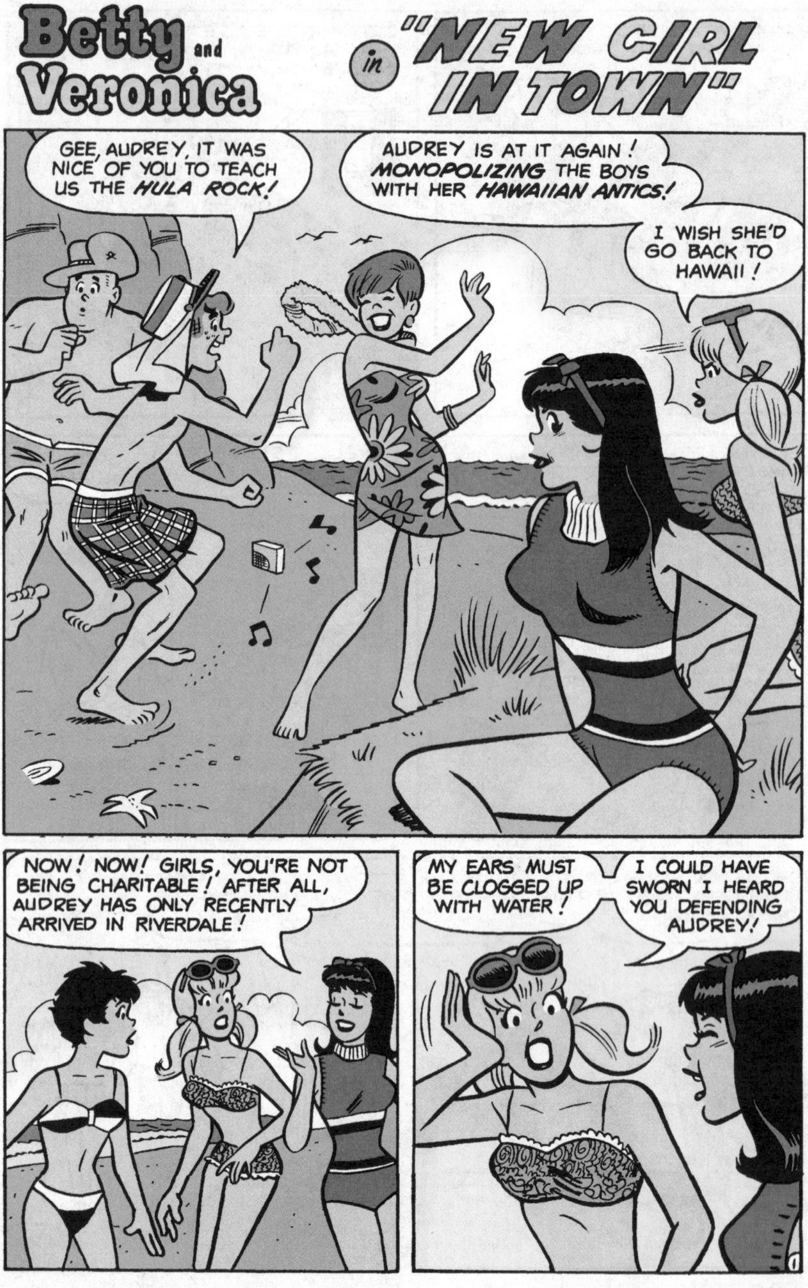
Betty and Veronica
in "NEW GIRL IN TOWN"
GEE, AUDREY, IT WAS NICE OF YOU TO TEACH US THE HULA ROCK!
AUDREY IS AT IT AGAIN! MONOPOLIZING THE BOYS WITH HER HAWAIIAN ANTICS!
I WISH SHE'D GO BACK TO HAWAII!
NOW! NOW! GIRLS, YOU'RE NOT BEING CHARITABLE! AFTER ALL, AUDREY HAS ONLY RECENTLY ARRIVED IN RIVERDALE!
MY EARS MUST BE CLOGGED UP WITH WATER!
I COULD HAVE SWORN I HEARD YOU DEFENDING AUDREY!

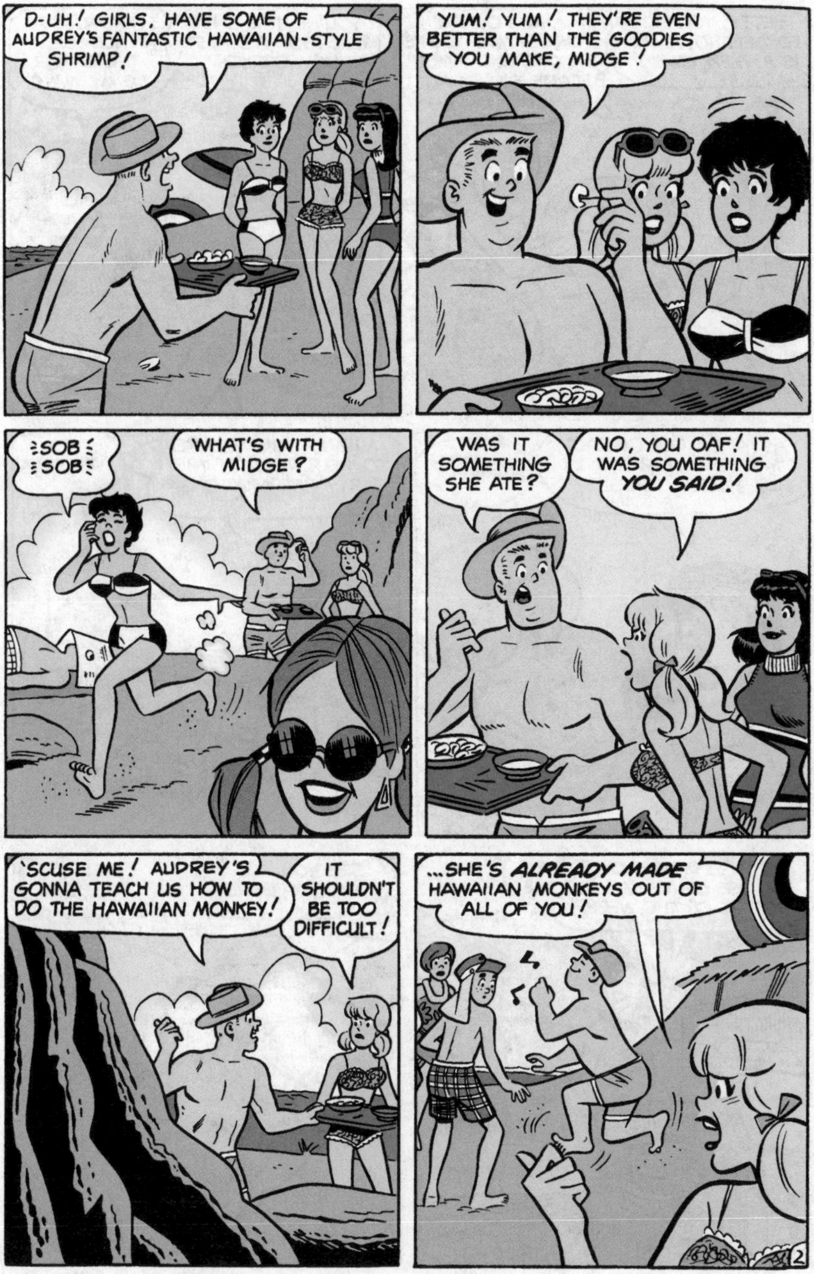
D-UH! GIRLS, HAVE SOME OF AUDREY'S FANTASTIC HAWAIIAN-STYLE SHRIMP!
YUM! YUM! THEY'RE EVEN BETTER THAN THE GOODIES YOU MAKE, MIDGE!
SOB SOB
WHAT'S WITH MIDGE?
WAS IT SOMETHING SHE ATE?
NO, YOU OAF! IT WAS SOMETHING YOU SAID!
'SCUSE ME! AUDREY'S GONNA TEACH US HOW TO DO THE HAWAIIAN MONKEY!
IT SHOULDN'T BE TOO DIFFICULT!
...SHE'S ALREADY MADE HAWAIIAN MONKEYS OUT OF ALL OF YOU!

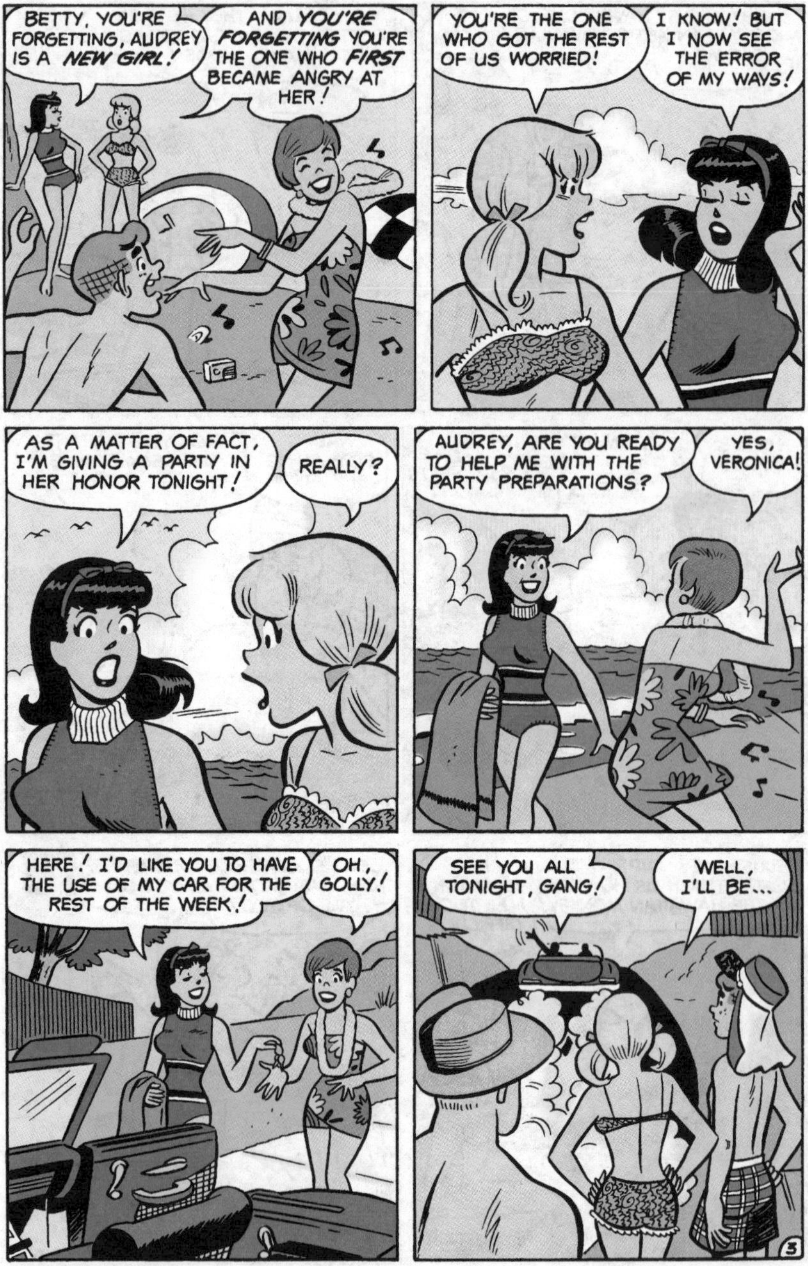
BETTY, YOU'RE FORGETTING, AUDREY IS A NEW GIRL!
AND YOU'RE FORGETTING YOU'RE THE ONE WHO FIRST BECAME ANGRY AT HER!
YOU'RE THE ONE WHO GOT THE REST OF US WORRIED!
I KNOW! BUT I NOW SEE THE ERROR OF MY WAYS!
AS A MATTER OF FACT, I'M GIVING A PARTY IN HER HONOR TONIGHT!
REALLY?
AUDREY, ARE YOU READY TO HELP ME WITH THE PARTY PREPARATIONS?
YES, VERONICA!
HERE! I'D LIKE YOU TO HAVE THE USE OF MY CAR FOR THE REST OF THE WEEK!
OH, GOLLY!
SEE YOU ALL TONIGHT, GANG!
WELL, I'LL BE...
3

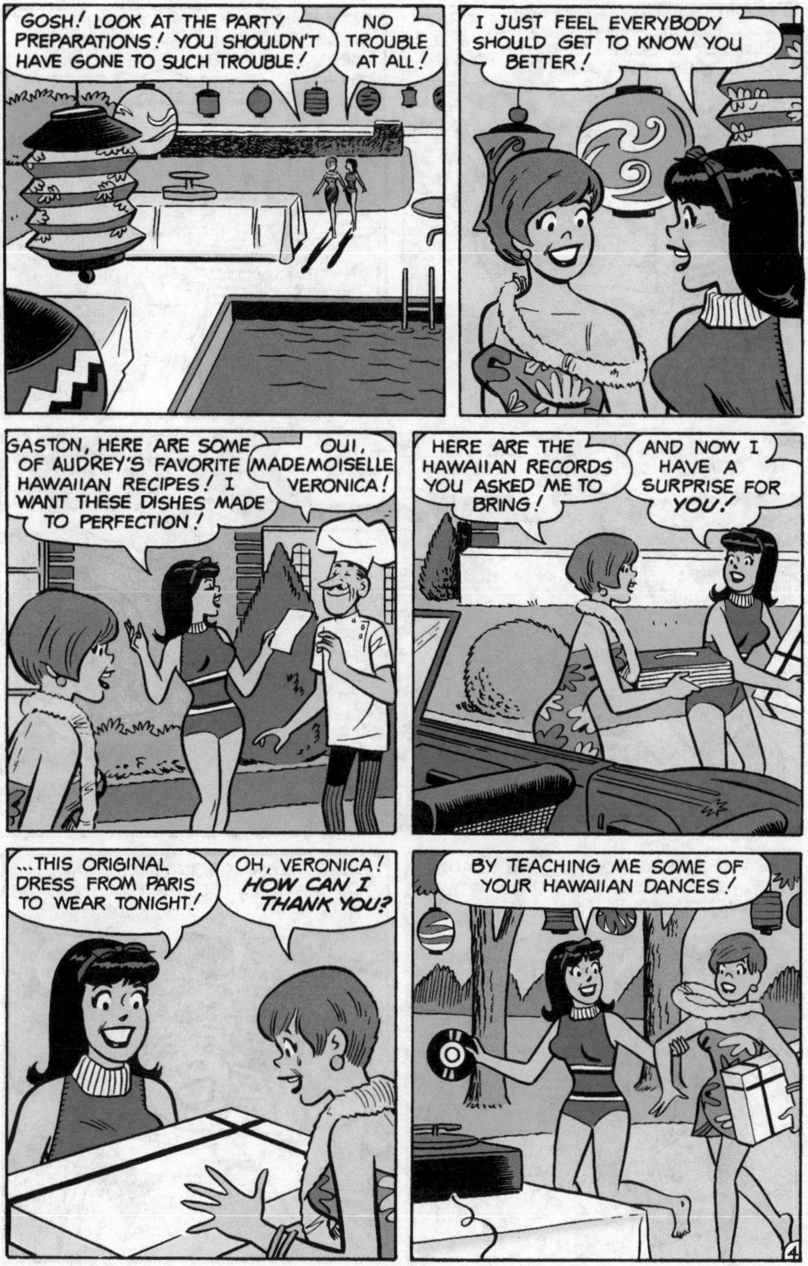
GOSH! LOOK AT THE PARTY PREPARATIONS! YOU SHOULDN'T HAVE GONE TO SUCH TROUBLE!
NO TROUBLE AT ALL!
I JUST FEEL EVERYBODY SHOULD GET TO KNOW YOU BETTER!
GASTON, HERE ARE SOME OF AUDREY'S FAVORITE HAWAIIAN RECIPES! I WANT THESE DISHES MADE TO PERFECTION!
OUI, MADEMOISELLE VERONICA!
HERE ARE THE HAWAIIAN RECORDS YOU ASKED ME TO BRING!
AND NOW I HAVE A SURPRISE FOR *YOU!*
...THIS ORIGINAL DRESS FROM PARIS TO WEAR TONIGHT!
OH, VERONICA! *HOW CAN I THANK YOU?*
BY TEACHING ME SOME OF YOUR HAWAIIAN DANCES!
4

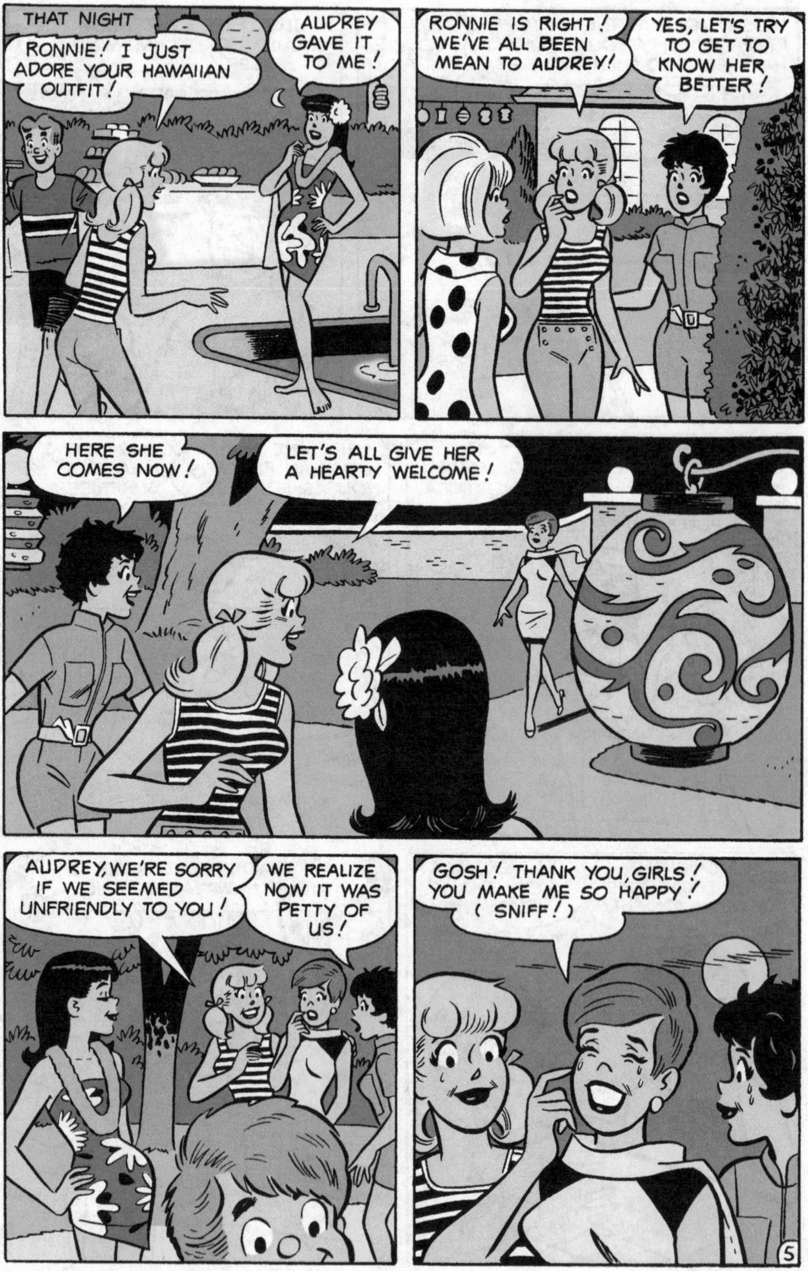
THAT NIGHT
RONNIE! I JUST ADORE YOUR HAWAIIAN OUTFIT!
AUDREY GAVE IT TO ME!
RONNIE IS RIGHT! WE'VE ALL BEEN MEAN TO AUDREY!
YES, LET'S TRY TO GET TO KNOW HER BETTER!
HERE SHE COMES NOW!
LET'S ALL GIVE HER A HEARTY WELCOME!
AUDREY, WE'RE SORRY IF WE SEEMED UNFRIENDLY TO YOU!
WE REALIZE NOW IT WAS PETTY OF US!
GOSH! THANK YOU, GIRLS! YOU MAKE ME SO HAPPY! (SNIFF!)
5

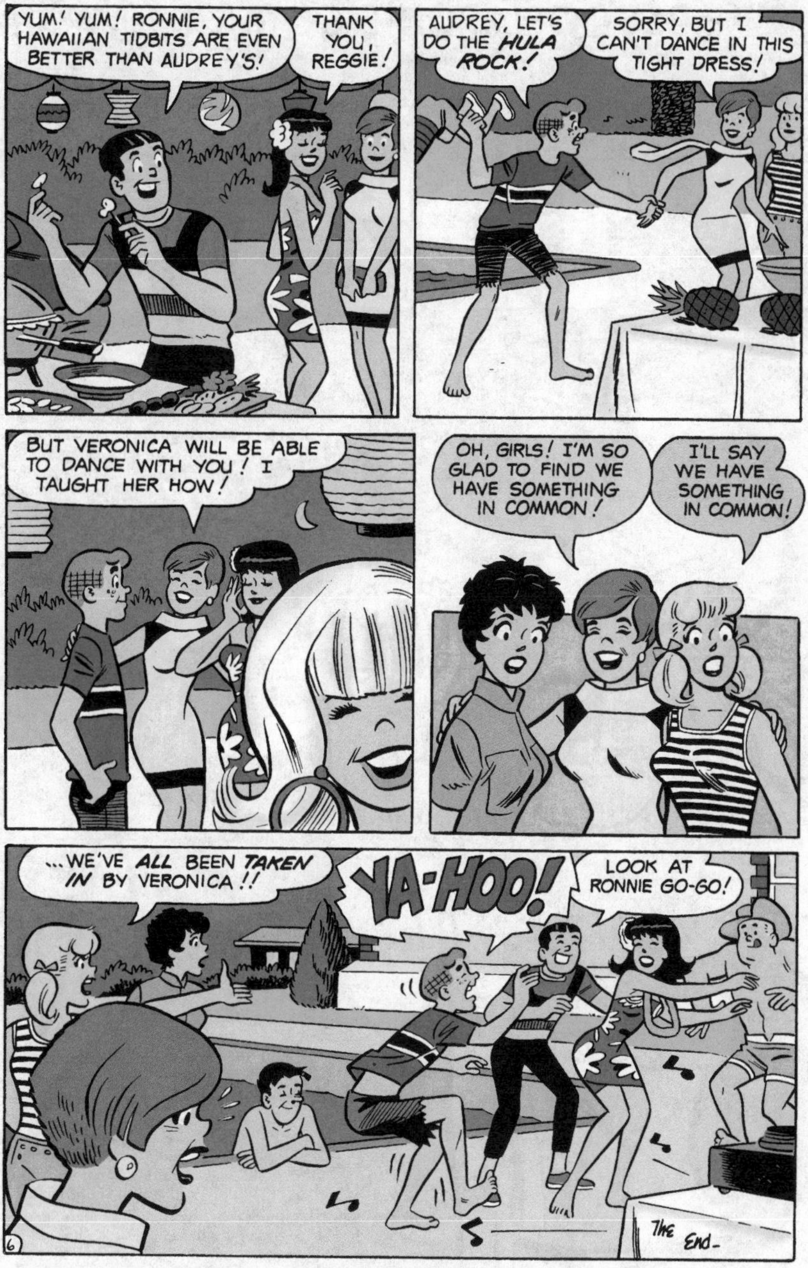
YUM! YUM! RONNIE, YOUR HAWAIIAN TIDBITS ARE EVEN BETTER THAN AUDREY'S!
THANK YOU, REGGIE!
AUDREY, LET'S DO THE HULA ROCK!
SORRY, BUT I CAN'T DANCE IN THIS TIGHT DRESS!
BUT VERONICA WILL BE ABLE TO DANCE WITH YOU! I TAUGHT HER HOW!
OH, GIRLS! I'M SO GLAD TO FIND WE HAVE SOMETHING IN COMMON!
I'LL SAY WE HAVE SOMETHING IN COMMON!
...WE'VE ALL BEEN TAKEN IN BY VERONICA!!
YA-HOO!
LOOK AT RONNIE GO-GO!
The End-
6

THE BEST OF ARCHIE COMICS STARRING

BETTY & VERONICA

1970s

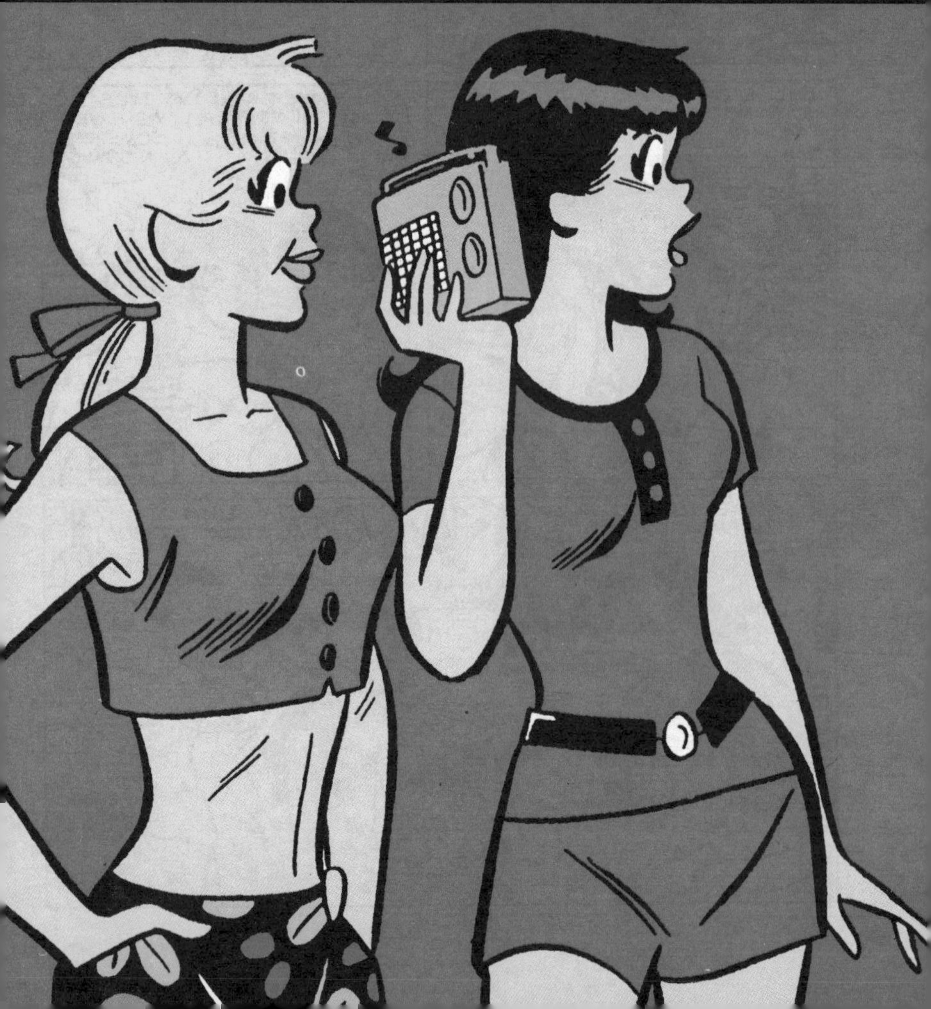

CRABBY COUPLE
BETTY & VERONICA #177, 1970
Dick Malmgren, Dan DeCarlo, Rudy Lapick, Bill Yoshida

FROM STEM TO STERN
BETTY & VERONICA #193, 1972
Frank Doyle, Dan DeCarlo, Rudy Lapick, Bill Yoshida, Barry Grossman

SUCCESS STORY
BETTY & VERONICA #206, 1973
Frank Doyle, Dan DeCarlo, Jim DeCarlo, Barry Grossman

TEMPTATION
BETTY & VERONICA #220, 1974
Frank Doyle, Dan DeCarlo, Rudy Lapick, Bill Yoshida, Barry Grossman

Like a lot of comic readers, I've grown up with Betty and Veronica. For better or worse, boxed into a hair color or personality type, they remain a common part of the vocabulary of life. Those 'send in outfits' columns left me breathless: I could draw their clothes or adventuring packs?! Having drawn as soon as I could grasp a crayon, this was a revelation. Cutting out and playing with paper dolls never interested me but designing them? Woof!

- JEN VAUGHN *Artist, Archie Comics*

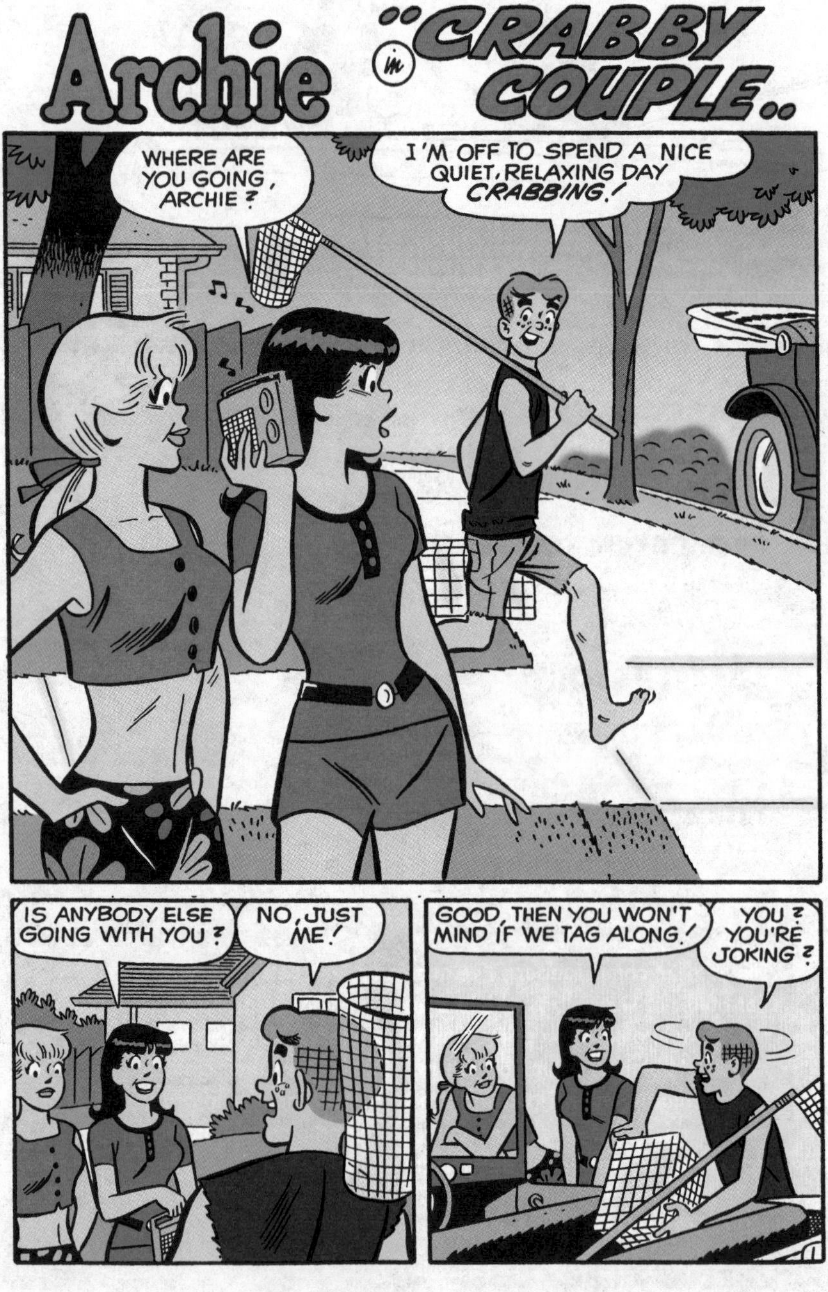
Archie in "CRABBY COUPLE"
WHERE ARE YOU GOING, ARCHIE?
I'M OFF TO SPEND A NICE QUIET, RELAXING DAY CRABBING!
IS ANYBODY ELSE GOING WITH YOU?
NO, JUST ME!
GOOD, THEN YOU WON'T MIND IF WE TAG ALONG!
YOU? YOU'RE JOKING?

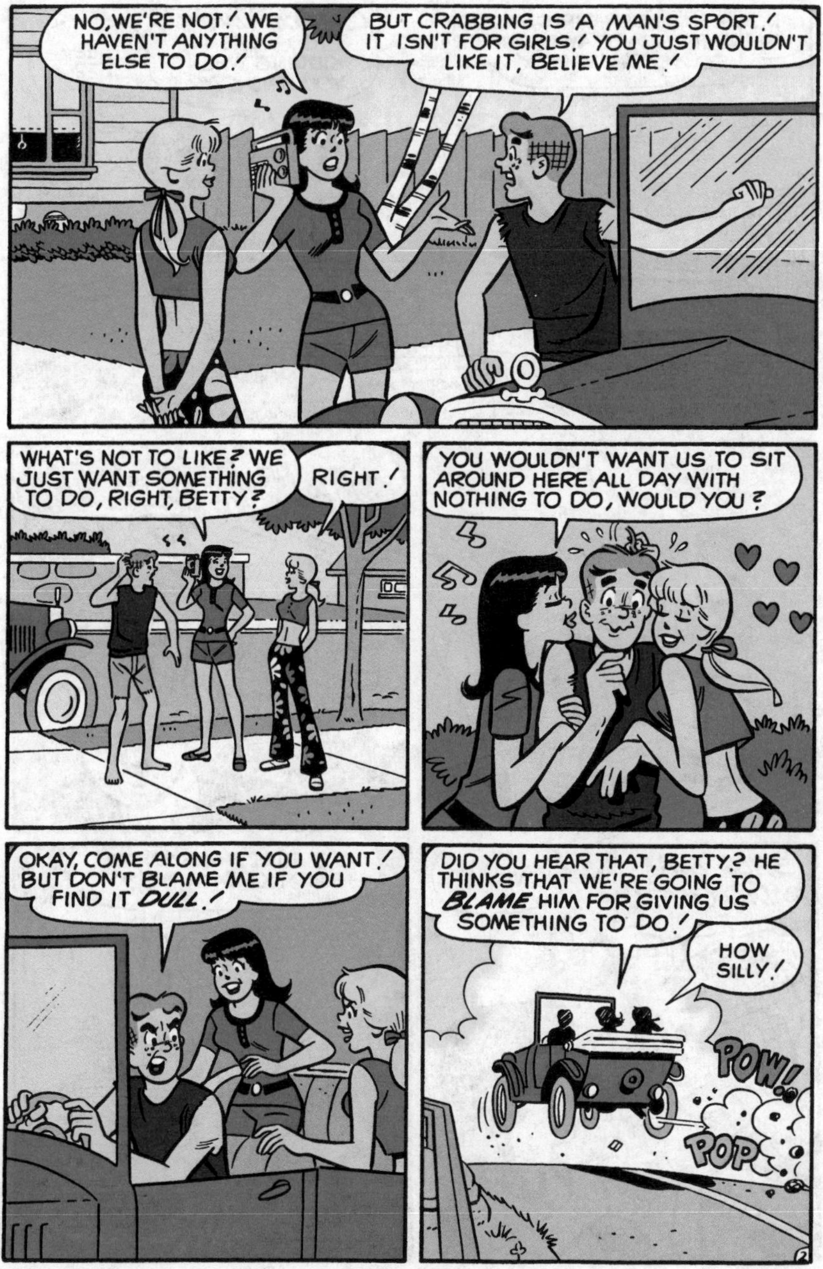
NO, WE'RE NOT! WE HAVEN'T ANYTHING ELSE TO DO!
BUT CRABBING IS A MAN'S SPORT! IT ISN'T FOR GIRLS! YOU JUST WOULDN'T LIKE IT, BELIEVE ME!
WHAT'S NOT TO LIKE? WE JUST WANT SOMETHING TO DO, RIGHT, BETTY?
RIGHT!
YOU WOULDN'T WANT US TO SIT AROUND HERE ALL DAY WITH NOTHING TO DO, WOULD YOU?
OKAY, COME ALONG IF YOU WANT! BUT DON'T BLAME ME IF YOU FIND IT *DULL*!
DID YOU HEAR THAT, BETTY? HE THINKS THAT WE'RE GOING TO *BLAME* HIM FOR GIVING US SOMETHING TO DO!
HOW SILLY!
POW!
POP
2

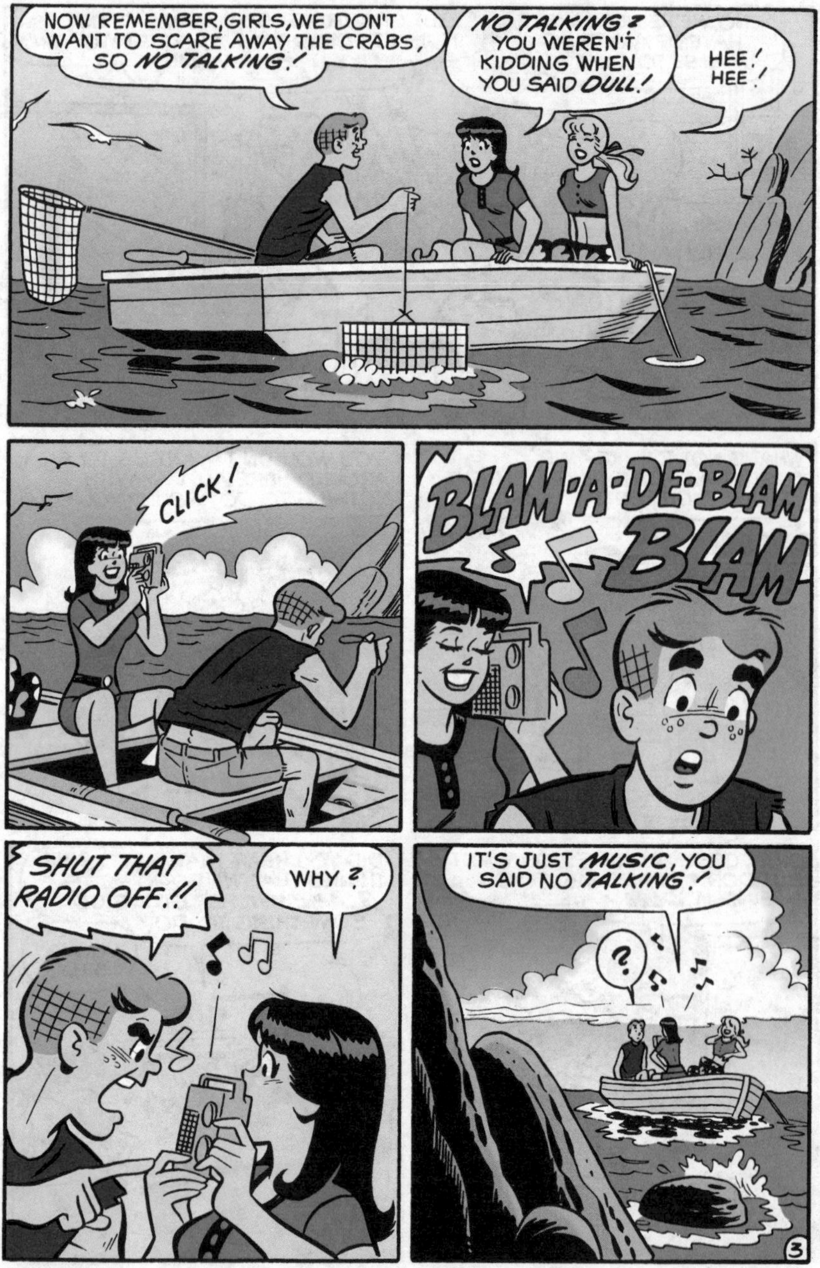
NOW REMEMBER, GIRLS, WE DON'T WANT TO SCARE AWAY THE CRABS, SO *NO TALKING*!
NO TALKING? YOU WEREN'T KIDDING WHEN YOU SAID *DULL*!
HEE! HEE!
CLICK!
BLAM-A-DE-BLAM
BLAM
SHUT THAT RADIO OFF!!
WHY?
IT'S JUST *MUSIC*, YOU SAID NO *TALKING*!
?
3

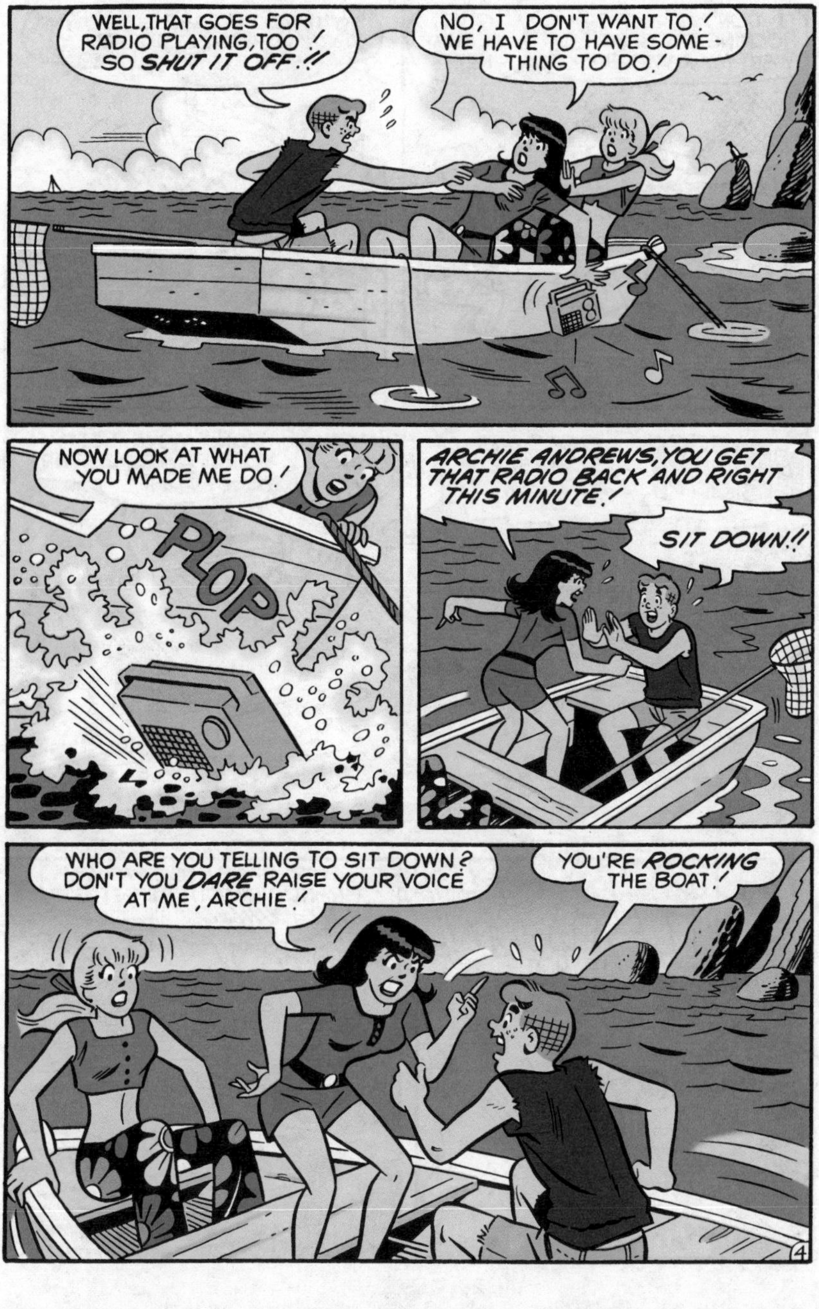
WELL, THAT GOES FOR RADIO PLAYING, TOO! SO SHUT IT OFF!!
NO, I DON'T WANT TO! WE HAVE TO HAVE SOME-THING TO DO!
NOW LOOK AT WHAT YOU MADE ME DO!
PLOP
ARCHIE ANDREWS, YOU GET THAT RADIO BACK AND RIGHT THIS MINUTE!
SIT DOWN!!
WHO ARE YOU TELLING TO SIT DOWN? DON'T YOU DARE RAISE YOUR VOICE AT ME, ARCHIE!
YOU'RE ROCKING THE BOAT!
4

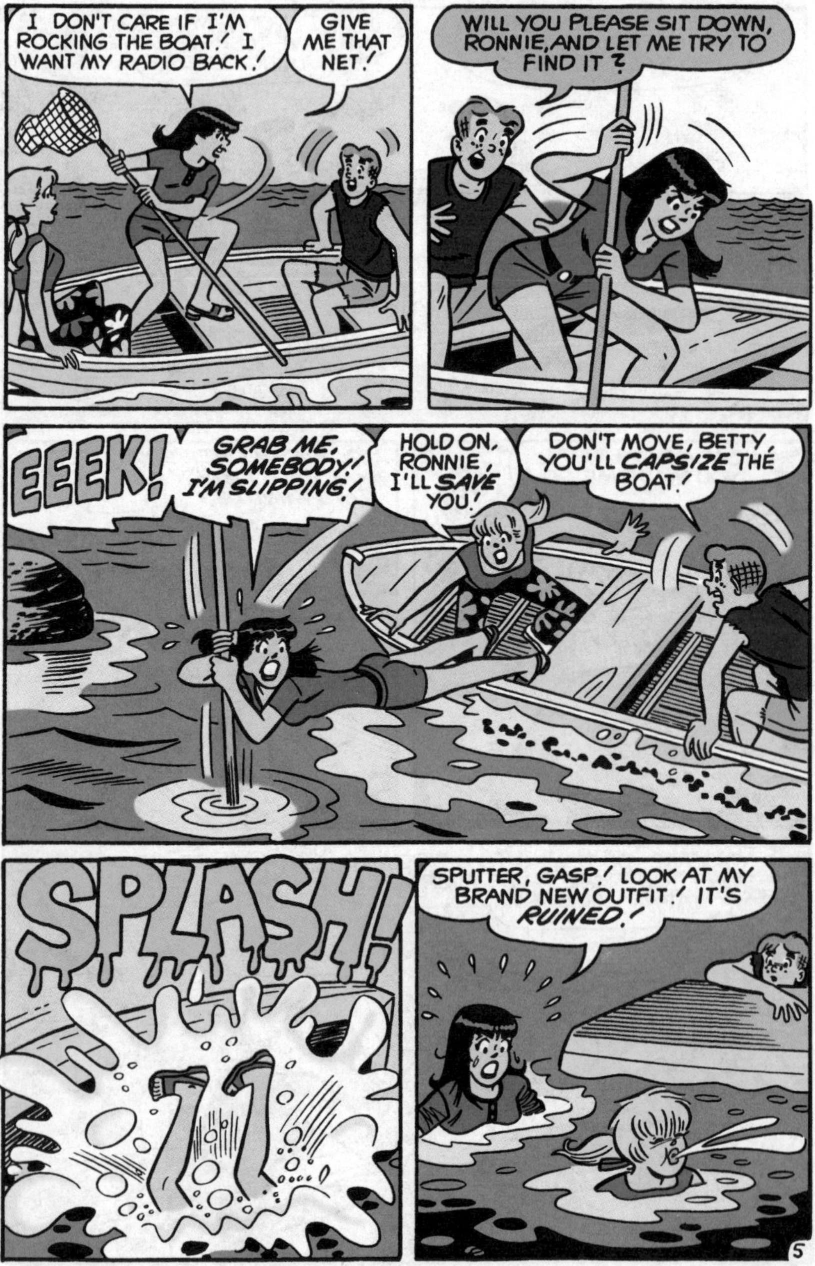
I DON'T CARE IF I'M ROCKING THE BOAT! I WANT MY RADIO BACK!
GIVE ME THAT NET!
WILL YOU PLEASE SIT DOWN, RONNIE, AND LET ME TRY TO FIND IT?
EEEK!
GRAB ME, SOMEBODY! I'M SLIPPING!
HOLD ON, RONNIE, I'LL SAVE YOU!
DON'T MOVE, BETTY, YOU'LL CAPSIZE THE BOAT!
SPLASH!
SPUTTER, GASP! LOOK AT MY BRAND NEW OUTFIT! IT'S RUINED!

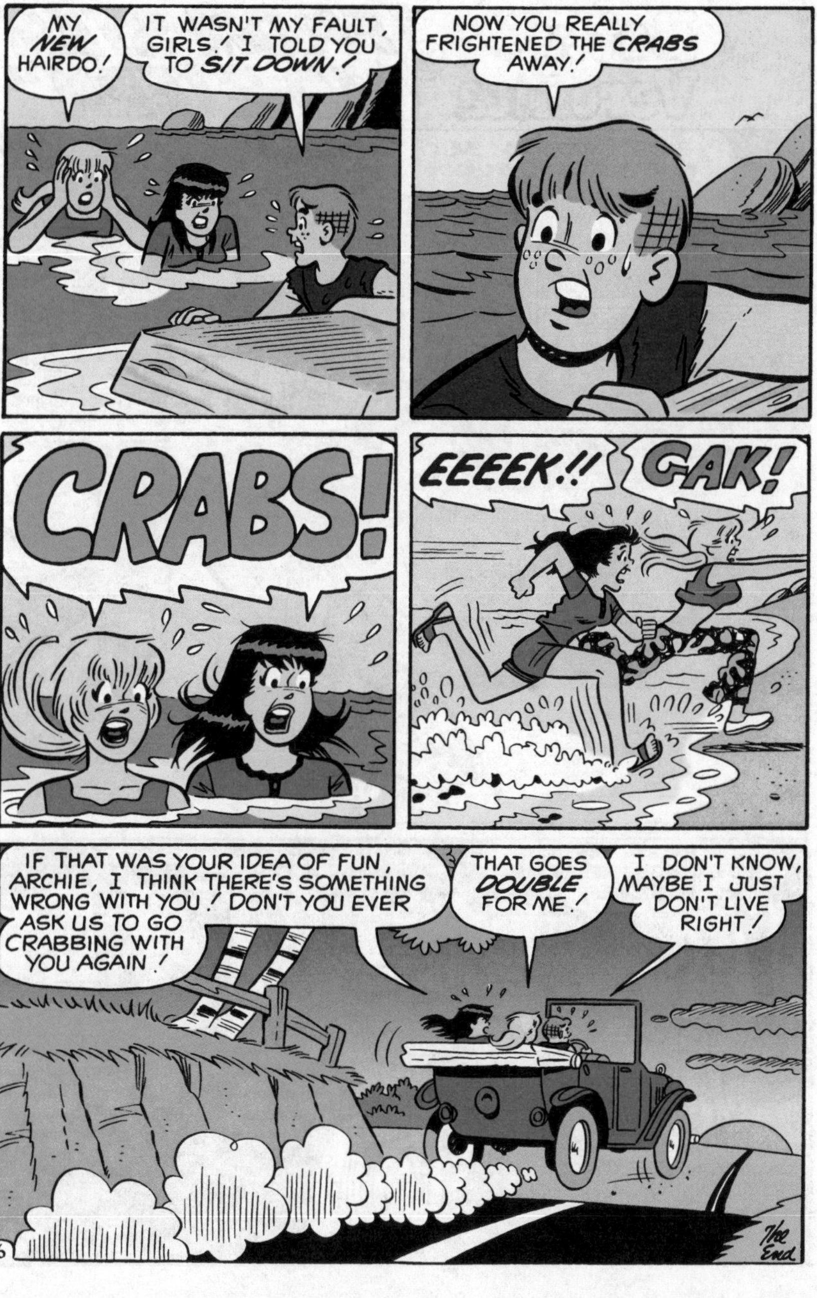

MY NEW HAIRDO!
IT WASN'T MY FAULT, GIRLS! I TOLD YOU TO SIT DOWN!
NOW YOU REALLY FRIGHTENED THE CRABS AWAY!
CRABS!
EEEEK!!
GAK!
IF THAT WAS YOUR IDEA OF FUN, ARCHIE, I THINK THERE'S SOMETHING WRONG WITH YOU! DON'T YOU EVER ASK US TO GO CRABBING WITH YOU AGAIN!
THAT GOES DOUBLE FOR ME!
I DON'T KNOW, MAYBE I JUST DON'T LIVE RIGHT!
End

Betty and Veronica in "FROM STEM TO STERN"

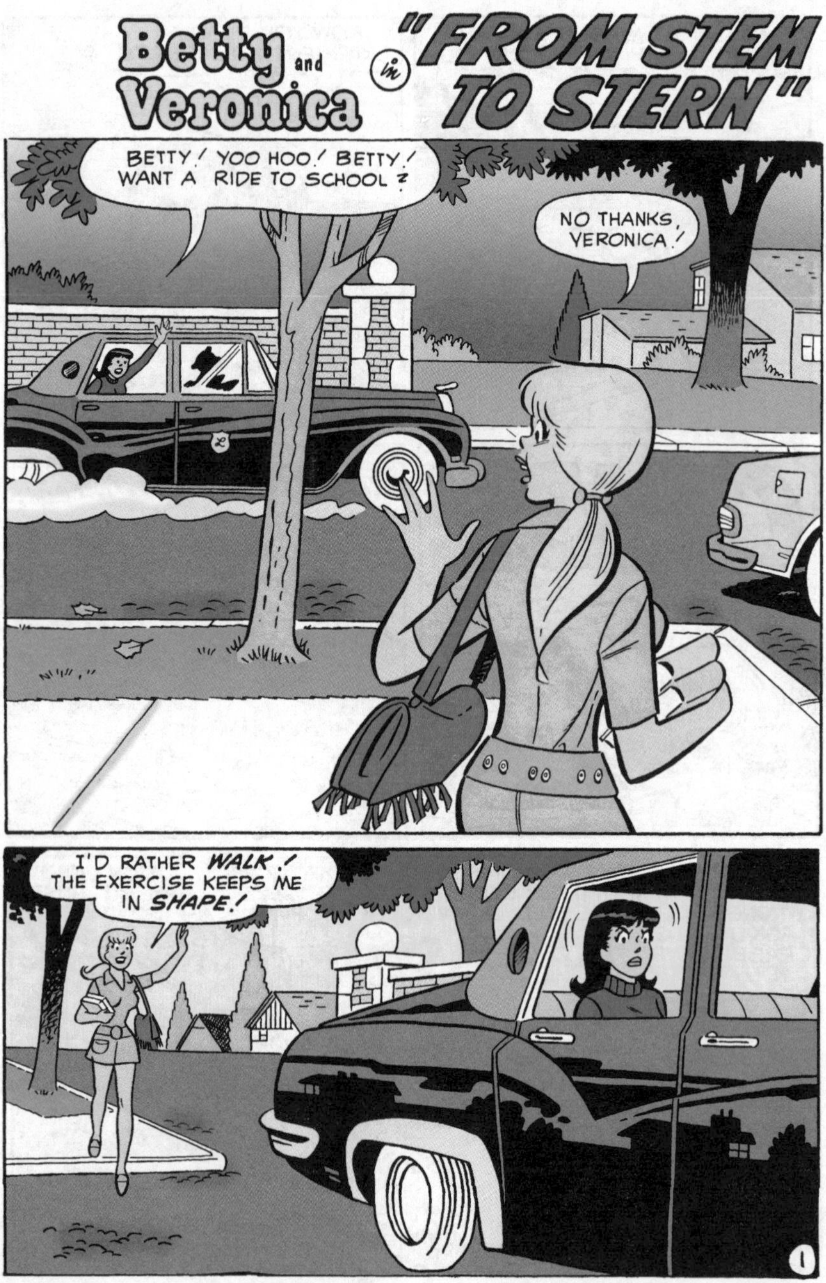
BETTY! YOO HOO! BETTY! WANT A RIDE TO SCHOOL?
NO THANKS, VERONICA!
I'D RATHER WALK! THE EXERCISE KEEPS ME IN SHAPE!
1

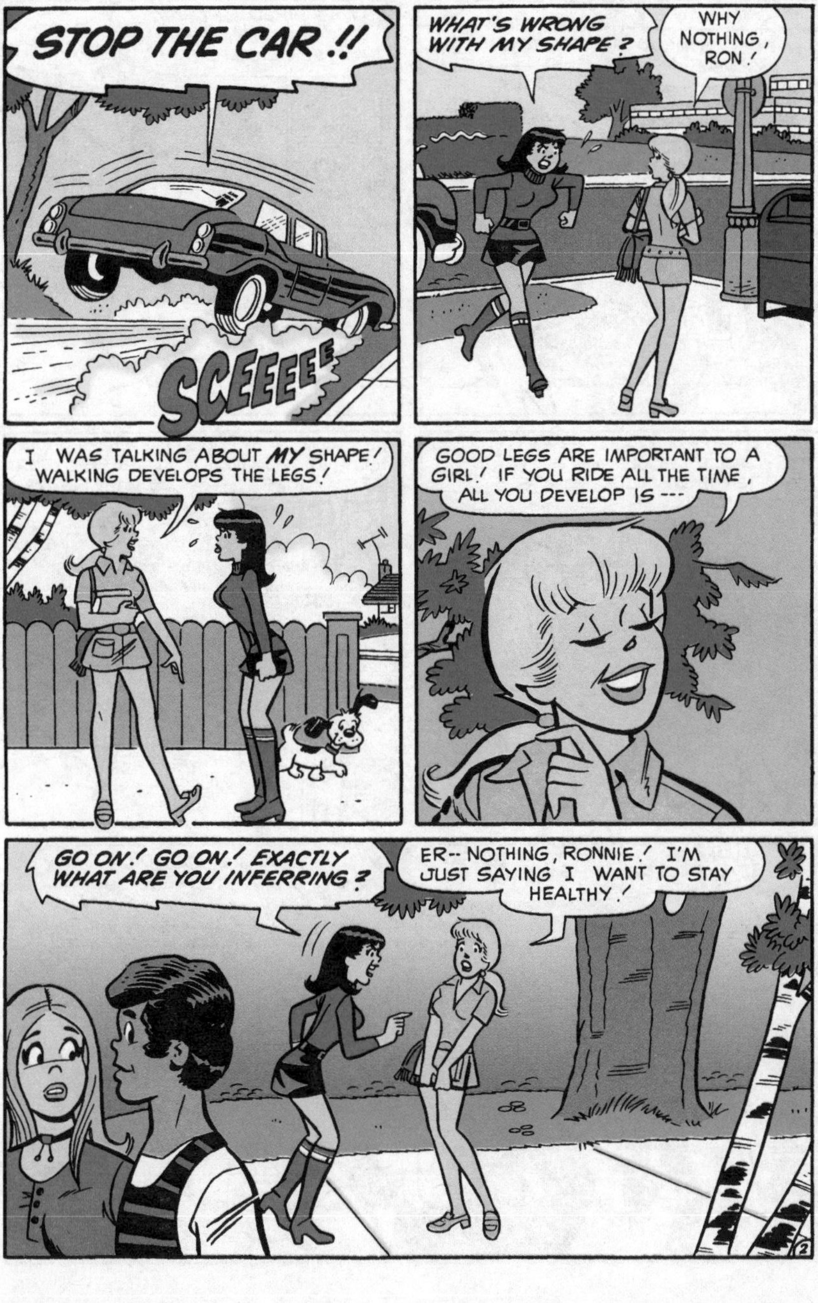
STOP THE CAR !!
SCEEEEE
WHAT'S WRONG WITH MY SHAPE ?
WHY NOTHING, RON !
I WAS TALKING ABOUT MY SHAPE ! WALKING DEVELOPS THE LEGS !
GOOD LEGS ARE IMPORTANT TO A GIRL ! IF YOU RIDE ALL THE TIME, ALL YOU DEVELOP IS ---
GO ON ! GO ON ! EXACTLY WHAT ARE YOU INFERRING ?
ER-- NOTHING, RONNIE ! I'M JUST SAYING I WANT TO STAY HEALTHY !
2

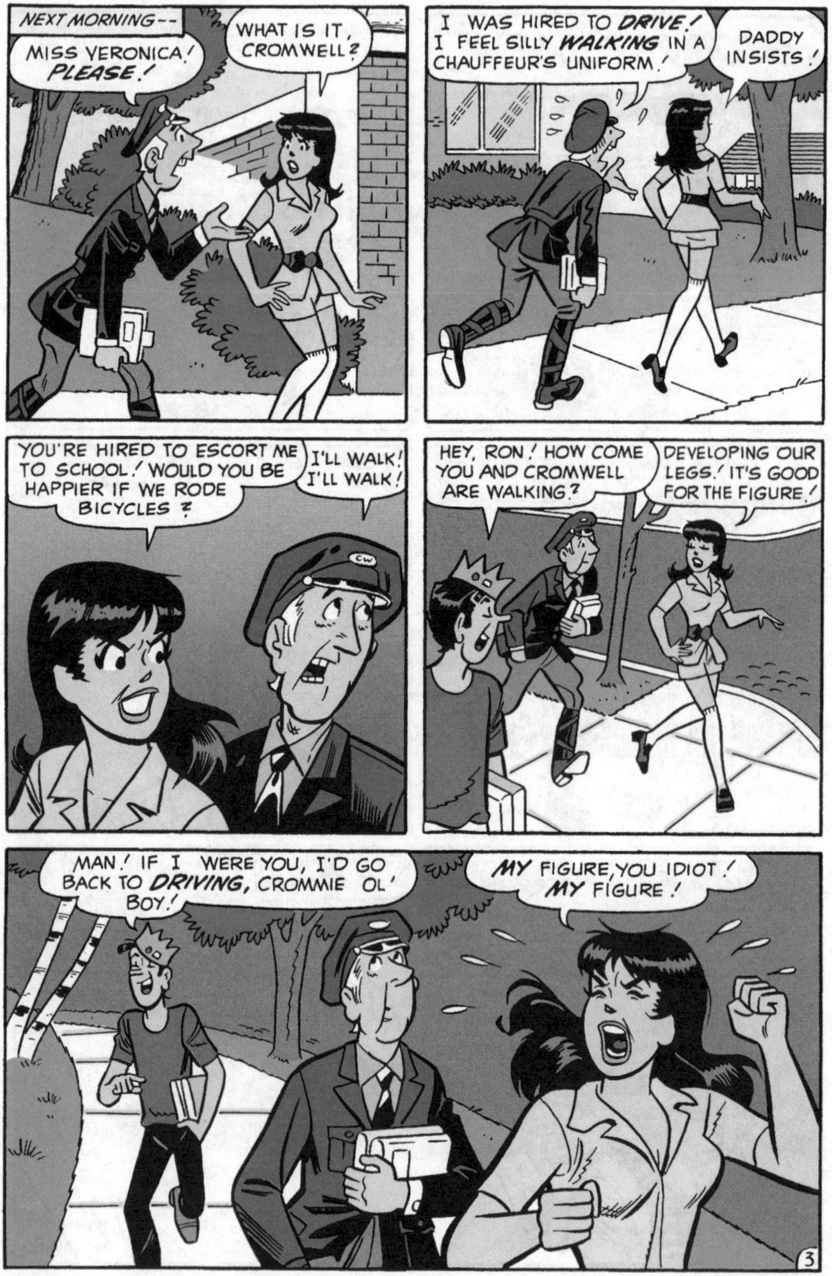
NEXT MORNING--
MISS VERONICA! PLEASE!
WHAT IS IT, CROMWELL?
I WAS HIRED TO DRIVE! I FEEL SILLY WALKING IN A CHAUFFEUR'S UNIFORM!
DADDY INSISTS!
YOU'RE HIRED TO ESCORT ME TO SCHOOL! WOULD YOU BE HAPPIER IF WE RODE BICYCLES?
I'LL WALK! I'LL WALK!
HEY, RON! HOW COME YOU AND CROMWELL ARE WALKING?
DEVELOPING OUR LEGS! IT'S GOOD FOR THE FIGURE!
MAN! IF I WERE YOU, I'D GO BACK TO DRIVING, CROMMIE OL' BOY!
MY FIGURE, YOU IDIOT! MY FIGURE!
3

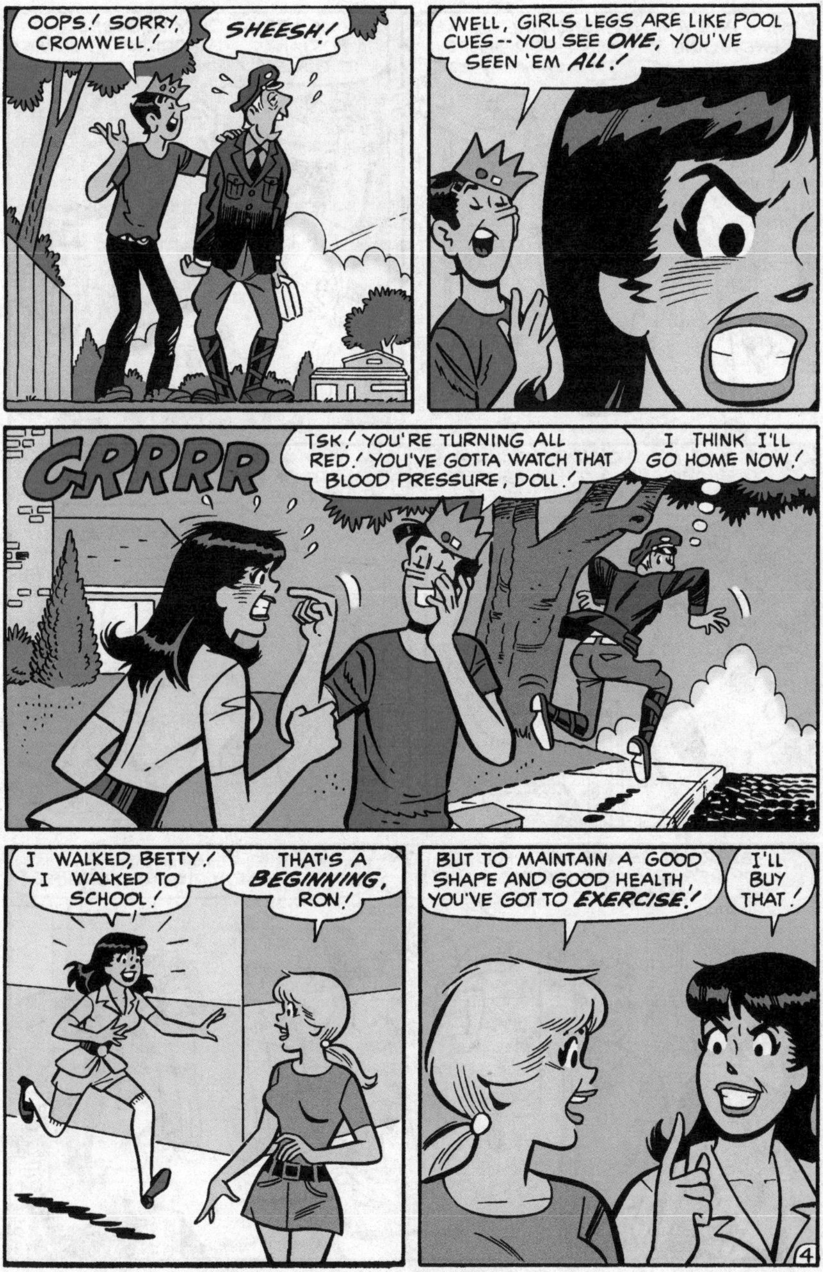
OOPS! SORRY, CROMWELL!
SHEESH!
WELL, GIRLS LEGS ARE LIKE POOL CUES -- YOU SEE ONE, YOU'VE SEEN 'EM ALL!
GRRRR
TSK! YOU'RE TURNING ALL RED! YOU'VE GOTTA WATCH THAT BLOOD PRESSURE, DOLL!
I THINK I'LL GO HOME NOW!
I WALKED, BETTY! I WALKED TO SCHOOL!
THAT'S A BEGINNING, RON!
BUT TO MAINTAIN A GOOD SHAPE AND GOOD HEALTH, YOU'VE GOT TO EXERCISE!
I'LL BUY THAT!
4

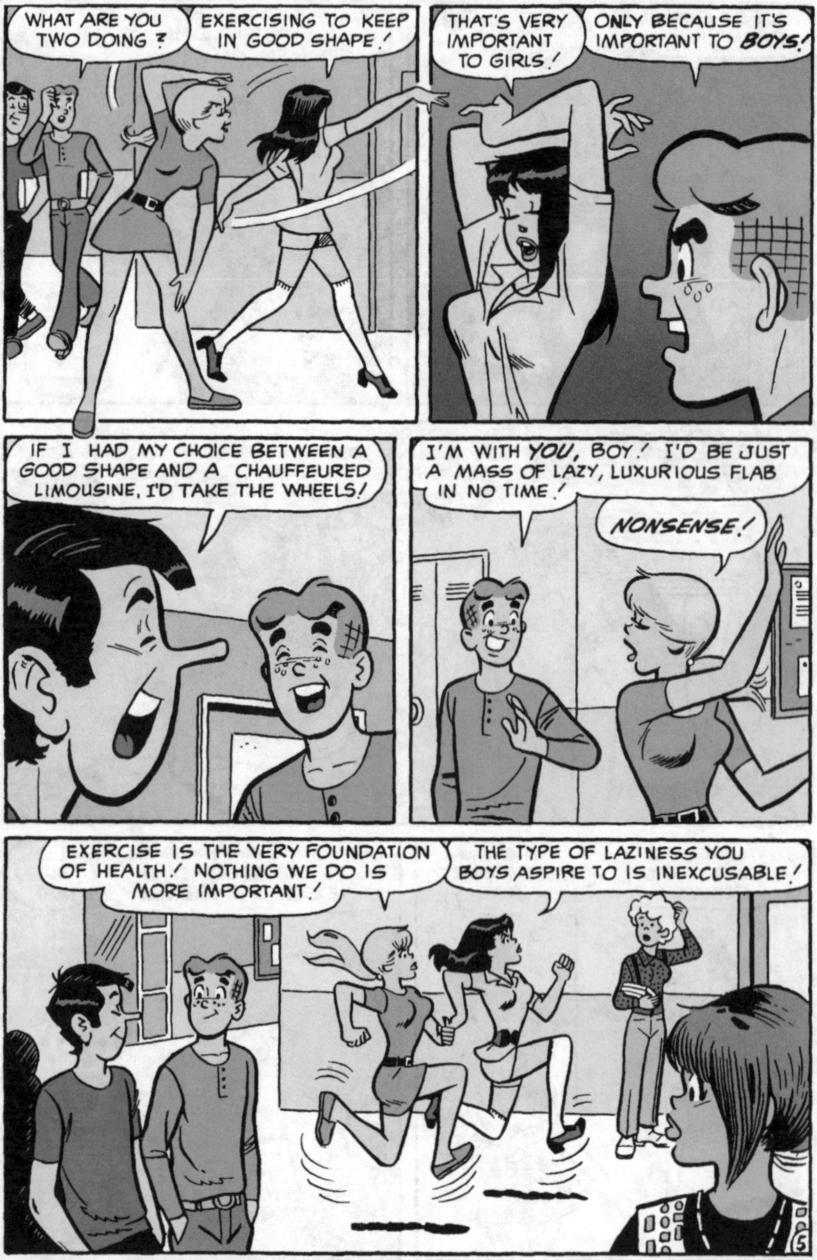
WHAT ARE YOU TWO DOING ?
EXERCISING TO KEEP IN GOOD SHAPE!
THAT'S VERY IMPORTANT TO GIRLS!
ONLY BECAUSE IT'S IMPORTANT TO BOYS!
IF I HAD MY CHOICE BETWEEN A GOOD SHAPE AND A CHAUFFEURED LIMOUSINE, I'D TAKE THE WHEELS!
I'M WITH YOU, BOY! I'D BE JUST A MASS OF LAZY, LUXURIOUS FLAB IN NO TIME!
NONSENSE!
EXERCISE IS THE VERY FOUNDATION OF HEALTH! NOTHING WE DO IS MORE IMPORTANT!
THE TYPE OF LAZINESS YOU BOYS ASPIRE TO IS INEXCUSABLE!
5

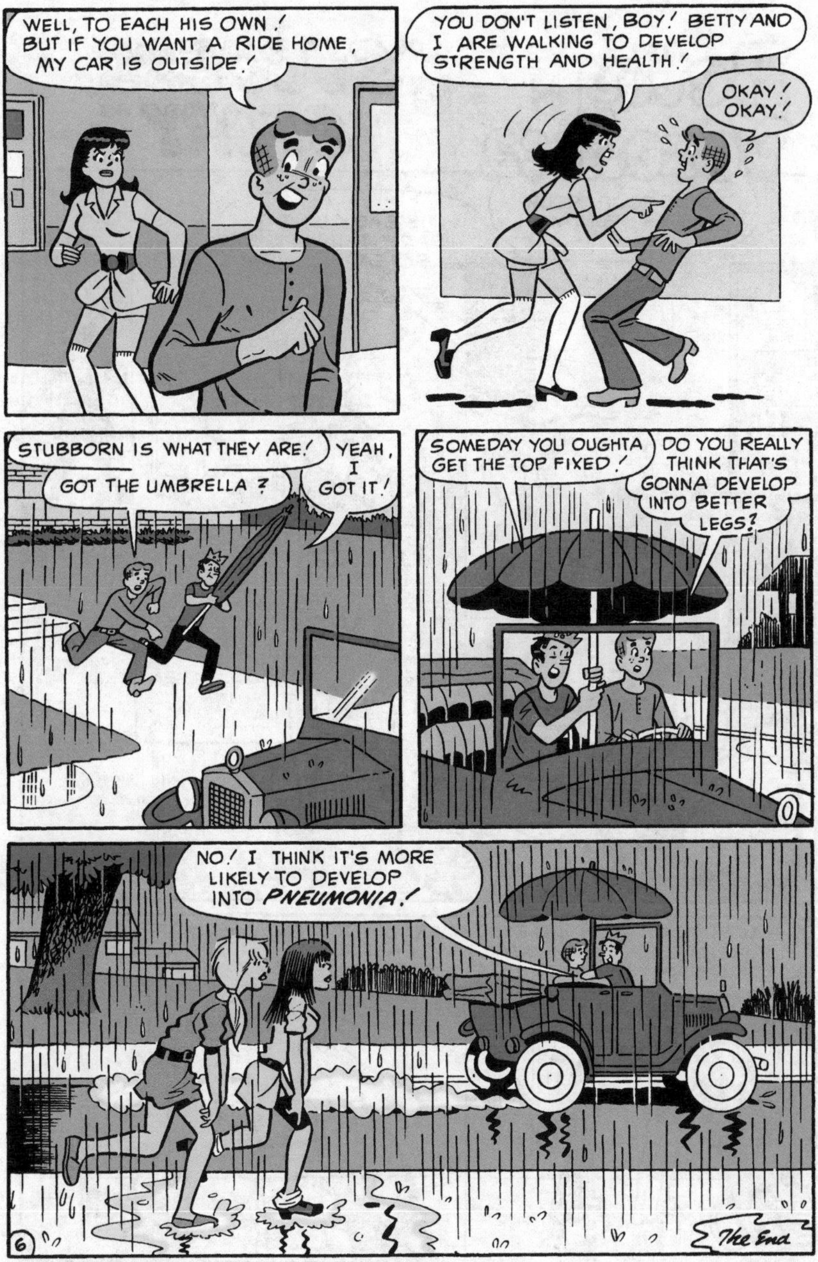
WELL, TO EACH HIS OWN! BUT IF YOU WANT A RIDE HOME, MY CAR IS OUTSIDE!
YOU DON'T LISTEN, BOY! BETTY AND I ARE WALKING TO DEVELOP STRENGTH AND HEALTH!
OKAY! OKAY!
STUBBORN IS WHAT THEY ARE!
GOT THE UMBRELLA ?
YEAH, I GOT IT!
SOMEDAY YOU OUGHTA GET THE TOP FIXED!
DO YOU REALLY THINK THAT'S GONNA DEVELOP INTO BETTER LEGS?
NO! I THINK IT'S MORE LIKELY TO DEVELOP INTO *PNEUMONIA*!
6
The End

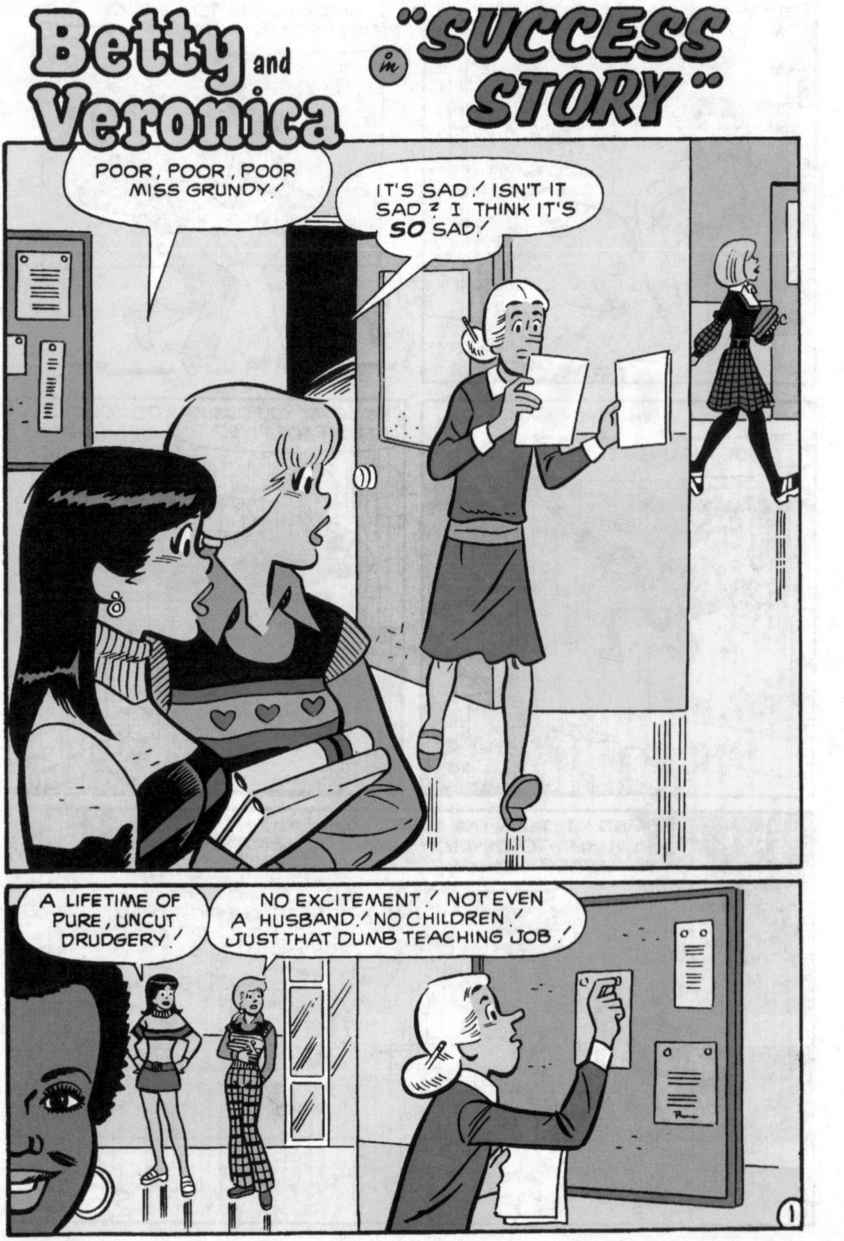
Betty and Veronica
in
"SUCCESS STORY"
POOR, POOR, POOR MISS GRUNDY!
IT'S SAD! ISN'T IT SAD? I THINK IT'S SO SAD!
A LIFETIME OF PURE, UNCUT DRUDGERY!
NO EXCITEMENT! NOT EVEN A HUSBAND! NO CHILDREN! JUST THAT DUMB TEACHING JOB!
1

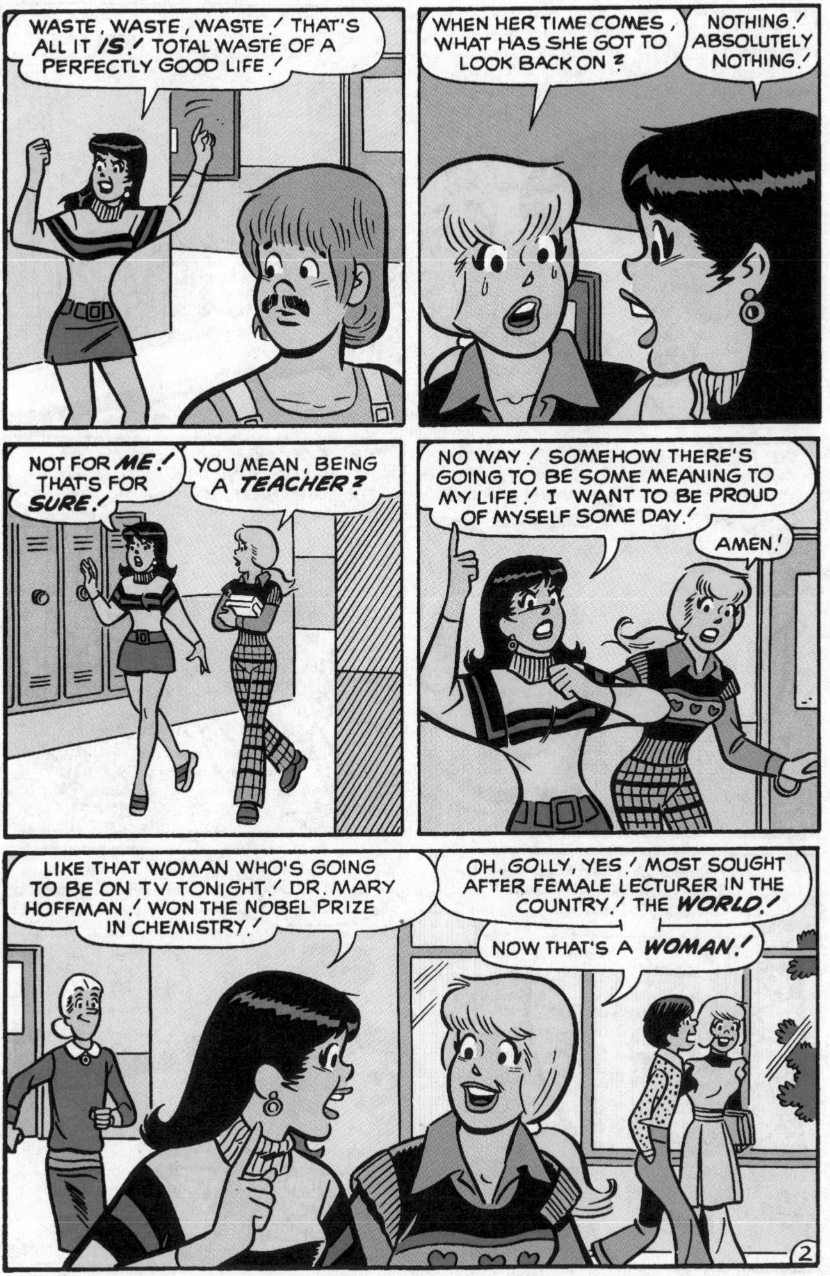
WASTE, WASTE, WASTE! THAT'S ALL IT IS! TOTAL WASTE OF A PERFECTLY GOOD LIFE!
WHEN HER TIME COMES, WHAT HAS SHE GOT TO LOOK BACK ON?
NOTHING! ABSOLUTELY NOTHING!
NOT FOR ME! THAT'S FOR SURE!
YOU MEAN, BEING A TEACHER?
NO WAY! SOMEHOW THERE'S GOING TO BE SOME MEANING TO MY LIFE! I WANT TO BE PROUD OF MYSELF SOME DAY!
AMEN!
LIKE THAT WOMAN WHO'S GOING TO BE ON TV TONIGHT! DR. MARY HOFFMAN! WON THE NOBEL PRIZE IN CHEMISTRY!
OH, GOLLY, YES! MOST SOUGHT AFTER FEMALE LECTURER IN THE COUNTRY! THE WORLD!
NOW THAT'S A WOMAN!
2

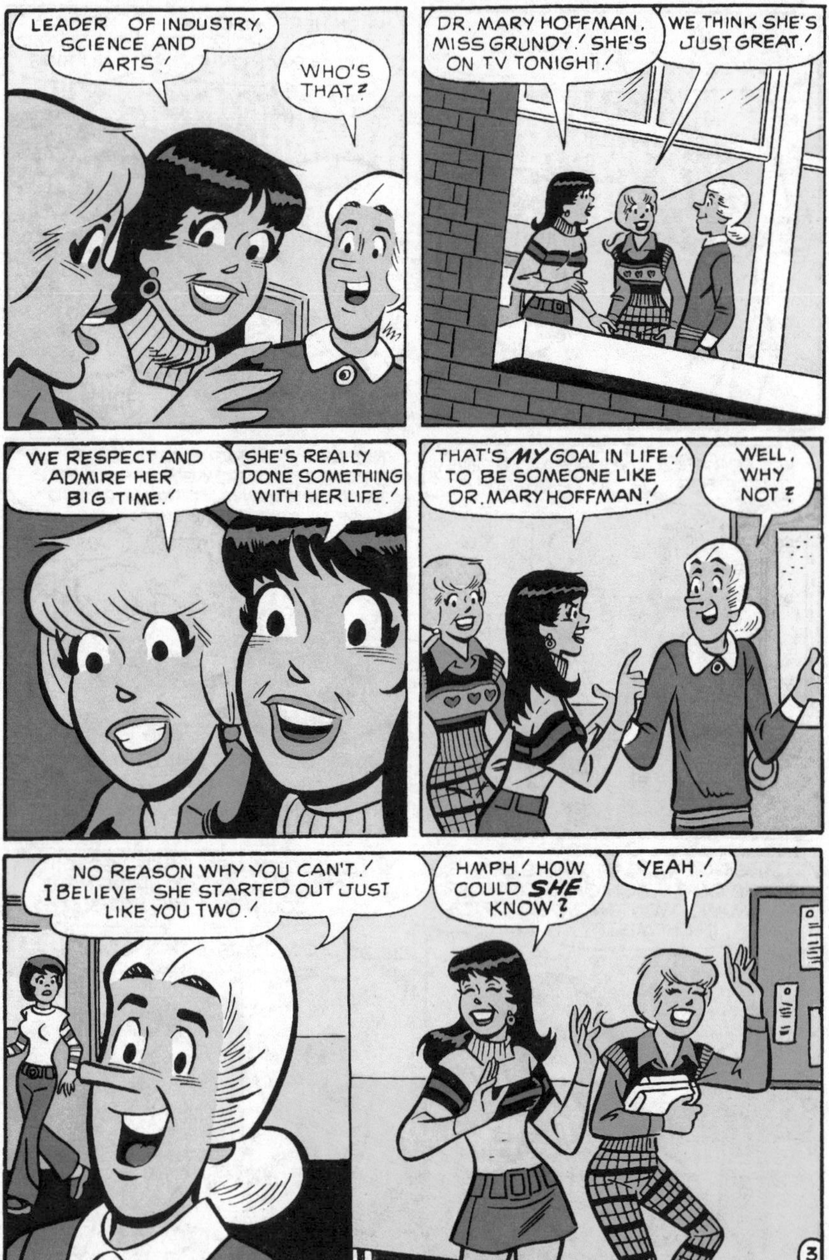
LEADER OF INDUSTRY, SCIENCE AND ARTS!
WHO'S THAT?
DR. MARY HOFFMAN, MISS GRUNDY! SHE'S ON TV TONIGHT!
WE THINK SHE'S JUST GREAT!
WE RESPECT AND ADMIRE HER BIG TIME!
SHE'S REALLY DONE SOMETHING WITH HER LIFE!
THAT'S MY GOAL IN LIFE! TO BE SOMEONE LIKE DR. MARY HOFFMAN!
WELL, WHY NOT?
NO REASON WHY YOU CAN'T! I BELIEVE SHE STARTED OUT JUST LIKE YOU TWO!
HMPH! HOW COULD SHE KNOW?
YEAH!
3

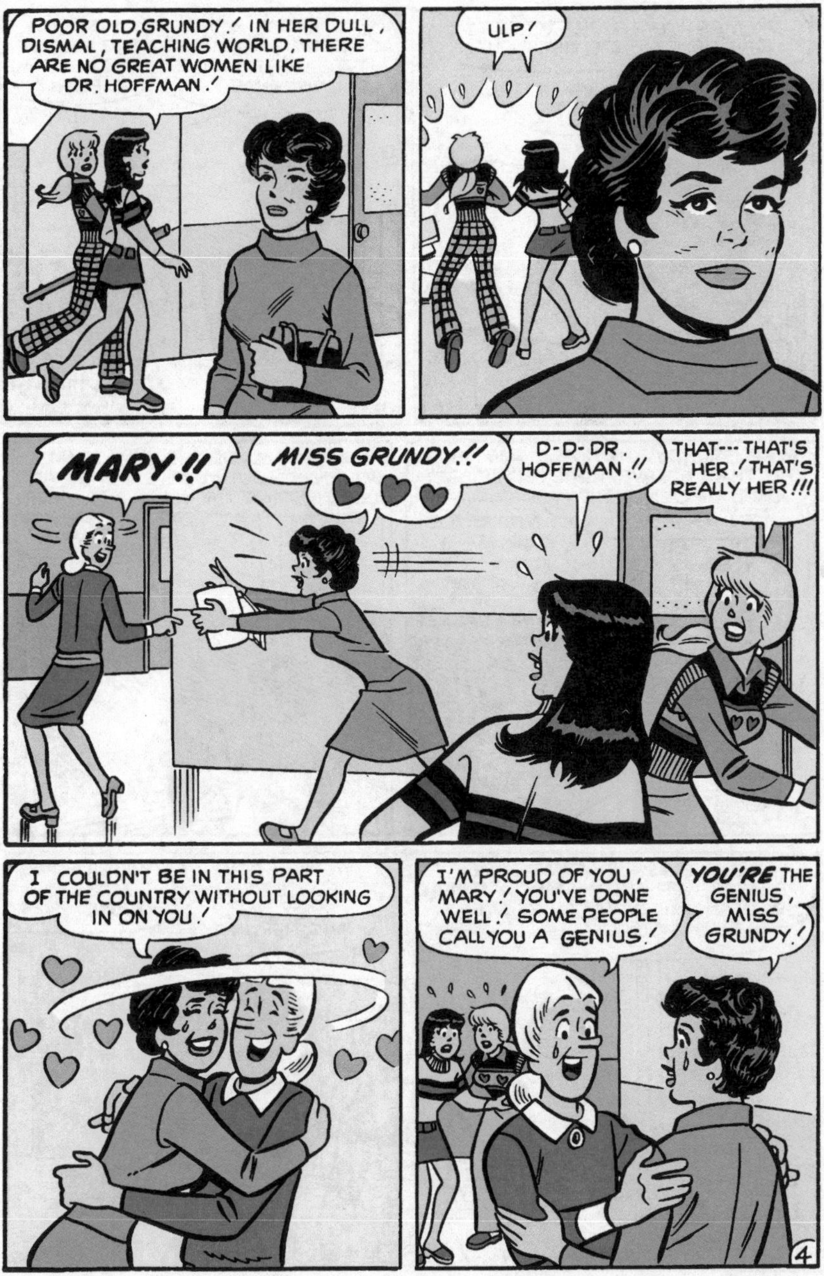
POOR OLD, GRUNDY! IN HER DULL, DISMAL, TEACHING WORLD, THERE ARE NO GREAT WOMEN LIKE DR. HOFFMAN!
ULP!
MARY!!
MISS GRUNDY!!
D-D-DR. HOFFMAN!!
THAT--- THAT'S HER! THAT'S REALLY HER!!!
I COULDN'T BE IN THIS PART OF THE COUNTRY WITHOUT LOOKING IN ON YOU!
I'M PROUD OF YOU, MARY! YOU'VE DONE WELL! SOME PEOPLE CALL YOU A GENIUS!
YOU'RE THE GENIUS, MISS GRUNDY!
4

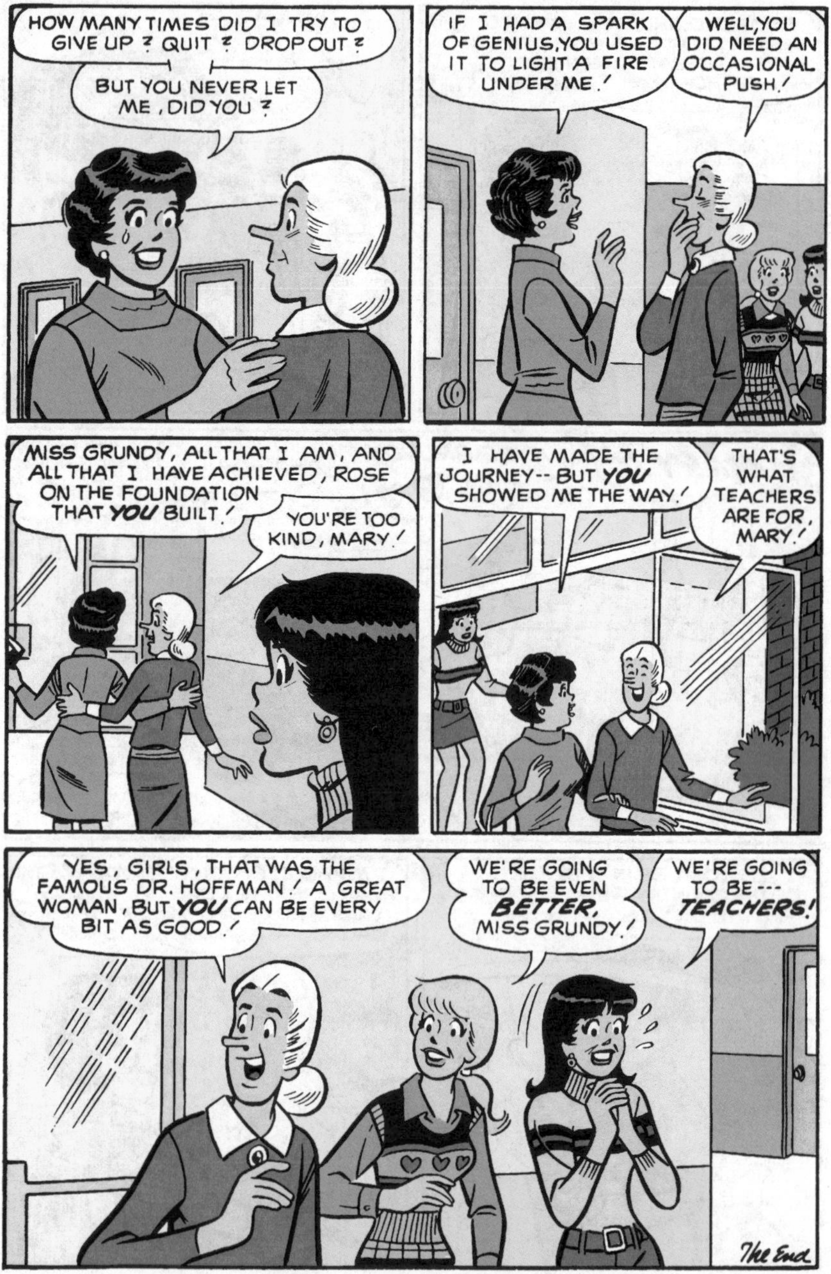
HOW MANY TIMES DID I TRY TO GIVE UP? QUIT? DROP OUT?
BUT YOU NEVER LET ME, DID YOU?
IF I HAD A SPARK OF GENIUS, YOU USED IT TO LIGHT A FIRE UNDER ME!
WELL, YOU DID NEED AN OCCASIONAL PUSH!
MISS GRUNDY, ALL THAT I AM, AND ALL THAT I HAVE ACHIEVED, ROSE ON THE FOUNDATION THAT YOU BUILT!
YOU'RE TOO KIND, MARY!
I HAVE MADE THE JOURNEY-- BUT YOU SHOWED ME THE WAY!
THAT'S WHAT TEACHERS ARE FOR, MARY!
YES, GIRLS, THAT WAS THE FAMOUS DR. HOFFMAN! A GREAT WOMAN, BUT YOU CAN BE EVERY BIT AS GOOD!
WE'RE GOING TO BE EVEN BETTER, MISS GRUNDY!
WE'RE GOING TO BE --- TEACHERS!
The End

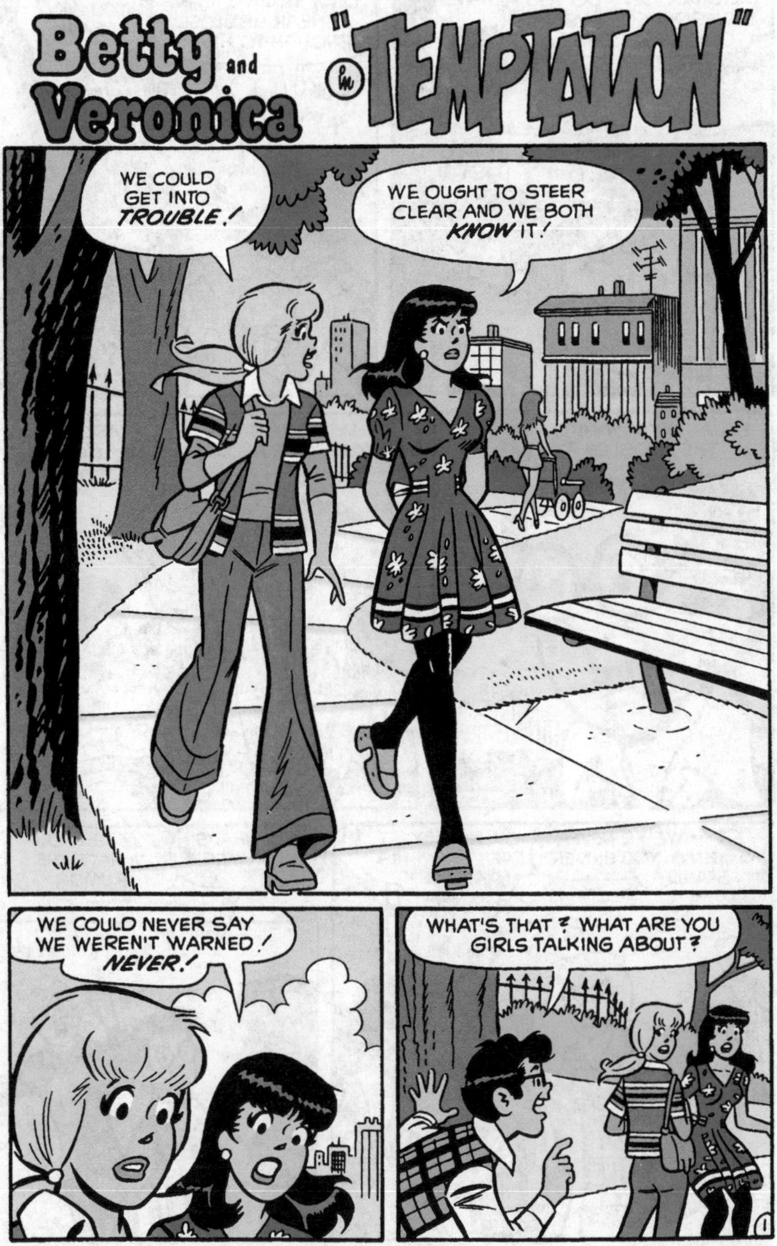
Betty and Veronica
in "TEMPTATION"
WE COULD GET INTO TROUBLE!
WE OUGHT TO STEER CLEAR AND WE BOTH KNOW IT!
WE COULD NEVER SAY WE WEREN'T WARNED! NEVER!
WHAT'S THAT? WHAT ARE YOU GIRLS TALKING ABOUT?
1

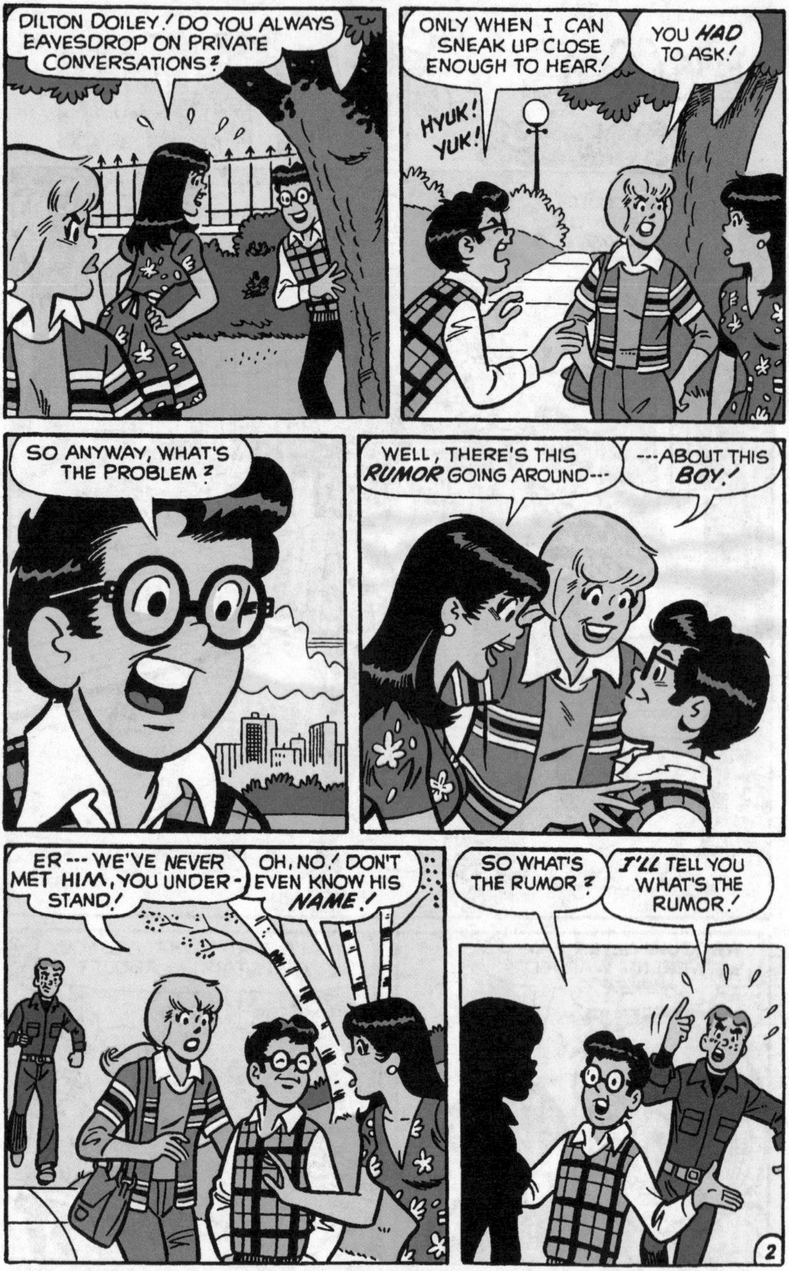
DILTON DOILEY! DO YOU ALWAYS EAVESDROP ON PRIVATE CONVERSATIONS?
ONLY WHEN I CAN SNEAK UP CLOSE ENOUGH TO HEAR!
HYUK! YUK!
YOU HAD TO ASK!
SO ANYWAY, WHAT'S THE PROBLEM?
WELL, THERE'S THIS RUMOR GOING AROUND---
---ABOUT THIS BOY!
ER--- WE'VE NEVER MET HIM, YOU UNDER-STAND!
OH, NO! DON'T EVEN KNOW HIS NAME!
SO WHAT'S THE RUMOR?
I'LL TELL YOU WHAT'S THE RUMOR!
2

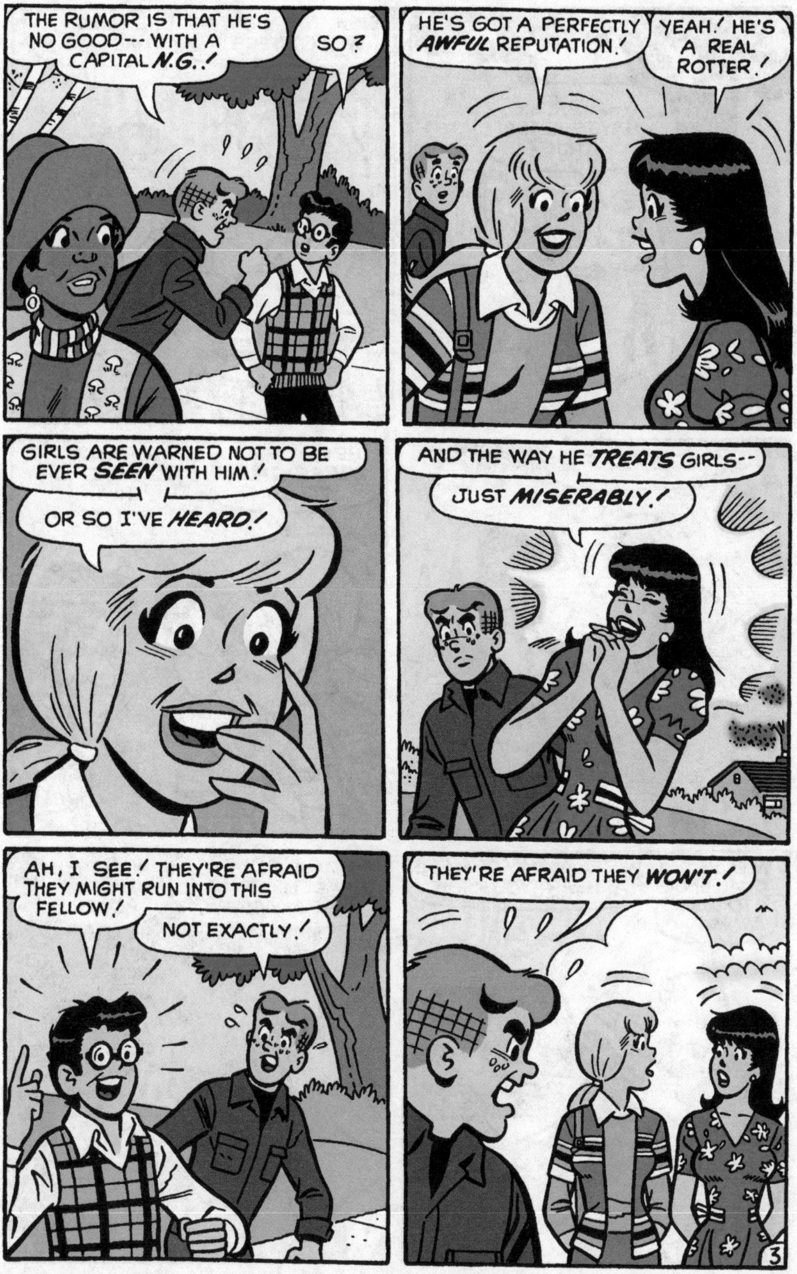
THE RUMOR IS THAT HE'S NO GOOD--- WITH A CAPITAL N.G.!
SO?
HE'S GOT A PERFECTLY AWFUL REPUTATION!
YEAH! HE'S A REAL ROTTER!
GIRLS ARE WARNED NOT TO BE EVER SEEN WITH HIM!
OR SO I'VE HEARD!
AND THE WAY HE TREATS GIRLS--
JUST MISERABLY!
AH, I SEE! THEY'RE AFRAID THEY MIGHT RUN INTO THIS FELLOW!
NOT EXACTLY!
THEY'RE AFRAID THEY WON'T!
3

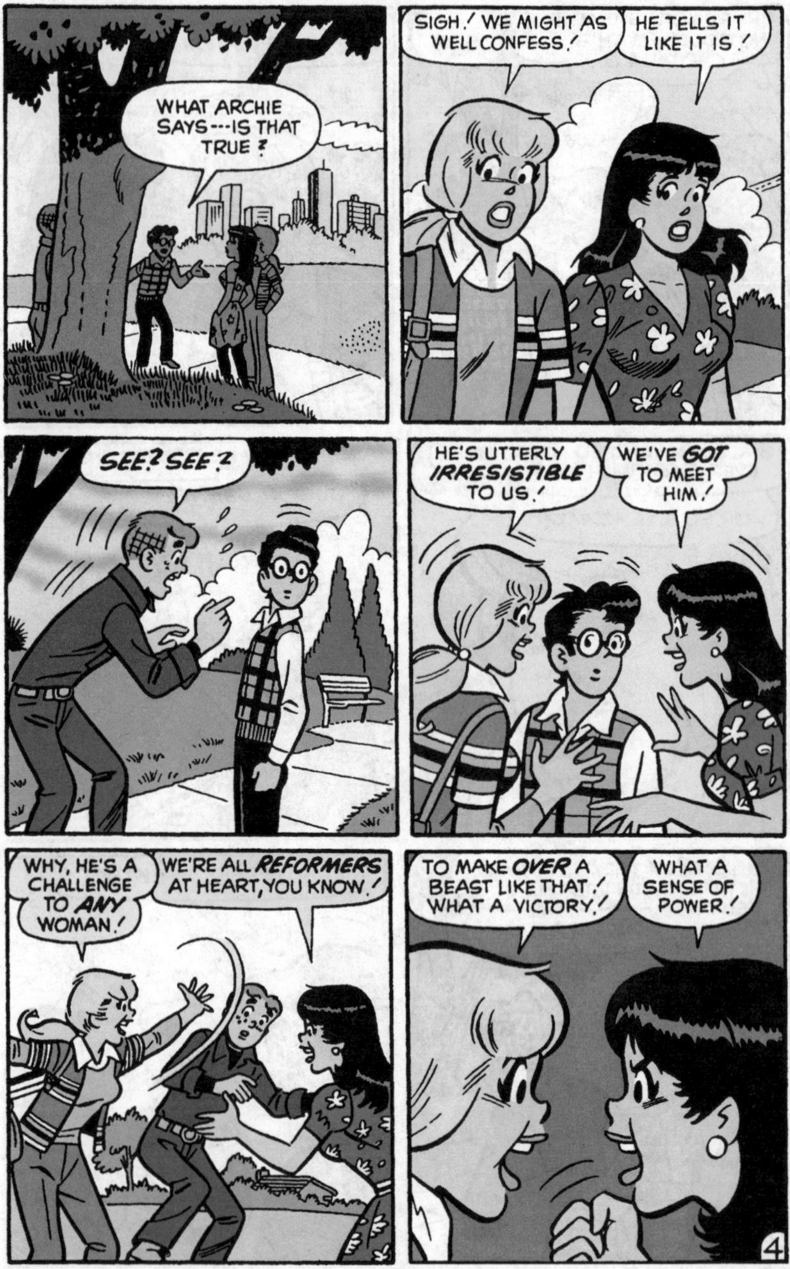
WHAT ARCHIE SAYS---IS THAT TRUE?
SIGH! WE MIGHT AS WELL CONFESS!
HE TELLS IT LIKE IT IS!
SEE? SEE?
HE'S UTTERLY IRRESISTIBLE TO US!
WE'VE GOT TO MEET HIM!
WHY, HE'S A CHALLENGE TO ANY WOMAN!
WE'RE ALL REFORMERS AT HEART, YOU KNOW!
TO MAKE OVER A BEAST LIKE THAT! WHAT A VICTORY!
WHAT A SENSE OF POWER!
4

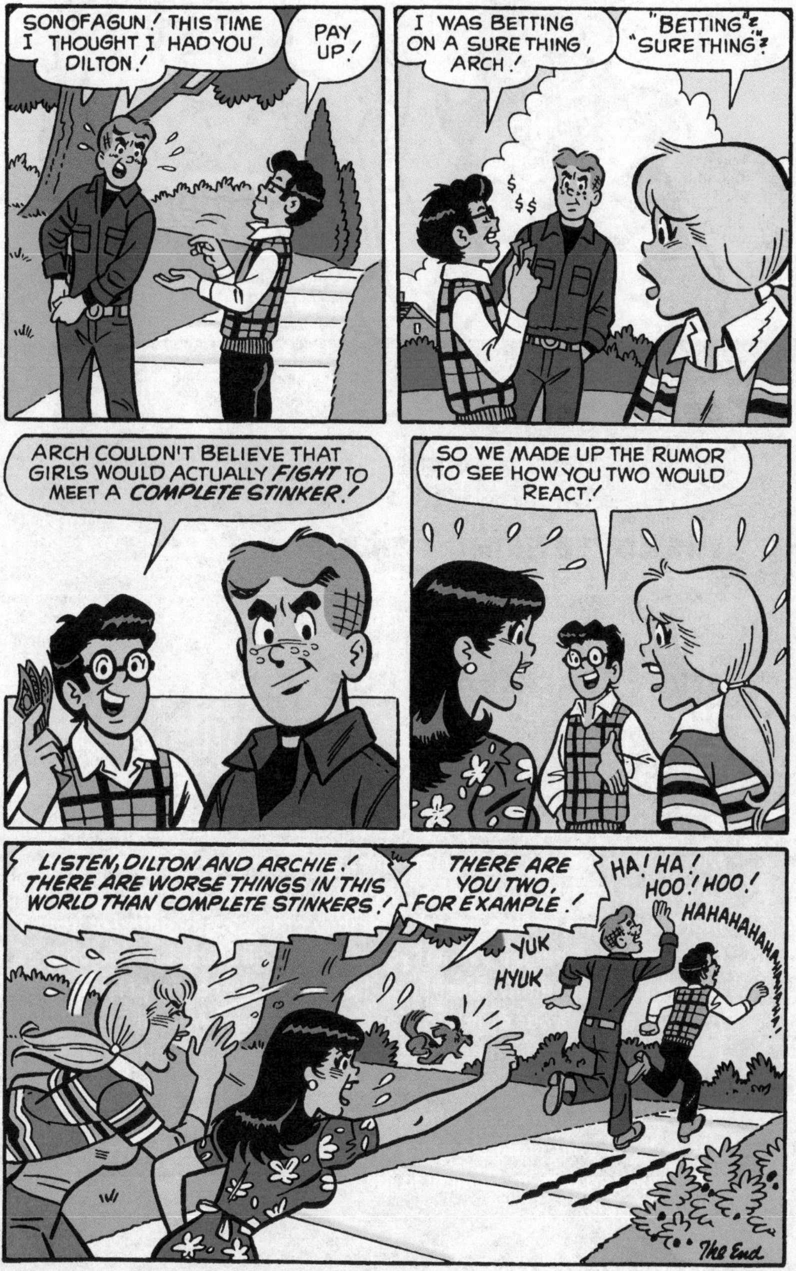
SONOFAGUN! THIS TIME I THOUGHT I HAD YOU, DILTON!
PAY UP!
I WAS BETTING ON A SURE THING, ARCH!
"BETTING"? "SURE THING"?
ARCH COULDN'T BELIEVE THAT GIRLS WOULD ACTUALLY FIGHT TO MEET A COMPLETE STINKER!
SO WE MADE UP THE RUMOR TO SEE HOW YOU TWO WOULD REACT!
LISTEN, DILTON AND ARCHIE! THERE ARE WORSE THINGS IN THIS WORLD THAN COMPLETE STINKERS!
THERE ARE YOU TWO, FOR EXAMPLE!
HA! HA! HOO! HOO!
HAHAHAHAHA
YUK
HYUK
The End

BREATH TAKING
BETTY & VERONICA #222, 1974
Frank Doyle, Dan DeCarlo, Rudy Lapick, Bill Yoshida, Barry Grossman

THE ADVERTISING GAME
BETTY & VERONICA #243, 1976
Frank Doyle, Dan DeCarlo, Rudy Lapick, Bill Yoshida

SNAP, CRACKLE AND POP
BETTY & VERONICA #287, 1979
Frank Doyle, Dan DeCarlo, Rudy Lapick, Bill Yoshida, Barry Grossman

Part of the appeal of Betty and Veronica isn't just that they're two best friends who have strong personalities and manage to uphold a long-standing friendship despite both being in love with the same boy, but that the two are friends even though they are so vastly different from one another. A human yin and yang, the two girls embody radically different ends of many spectrums—be it socio-economic, personality types and even your standard high school cliques. While the two are able to overcome these differences, it's always interesting to see stories where their dissimilarities are brought to the forefront. Seeing them acknowledge these variances, go toe-to-toe about them and end with a better understanding of each other (at least most of the time!), adds a human element to their stories that speaks to people of all walks of life.

- JAMIE LEE ROTANTE *Writer/Editor, Archie Comics*

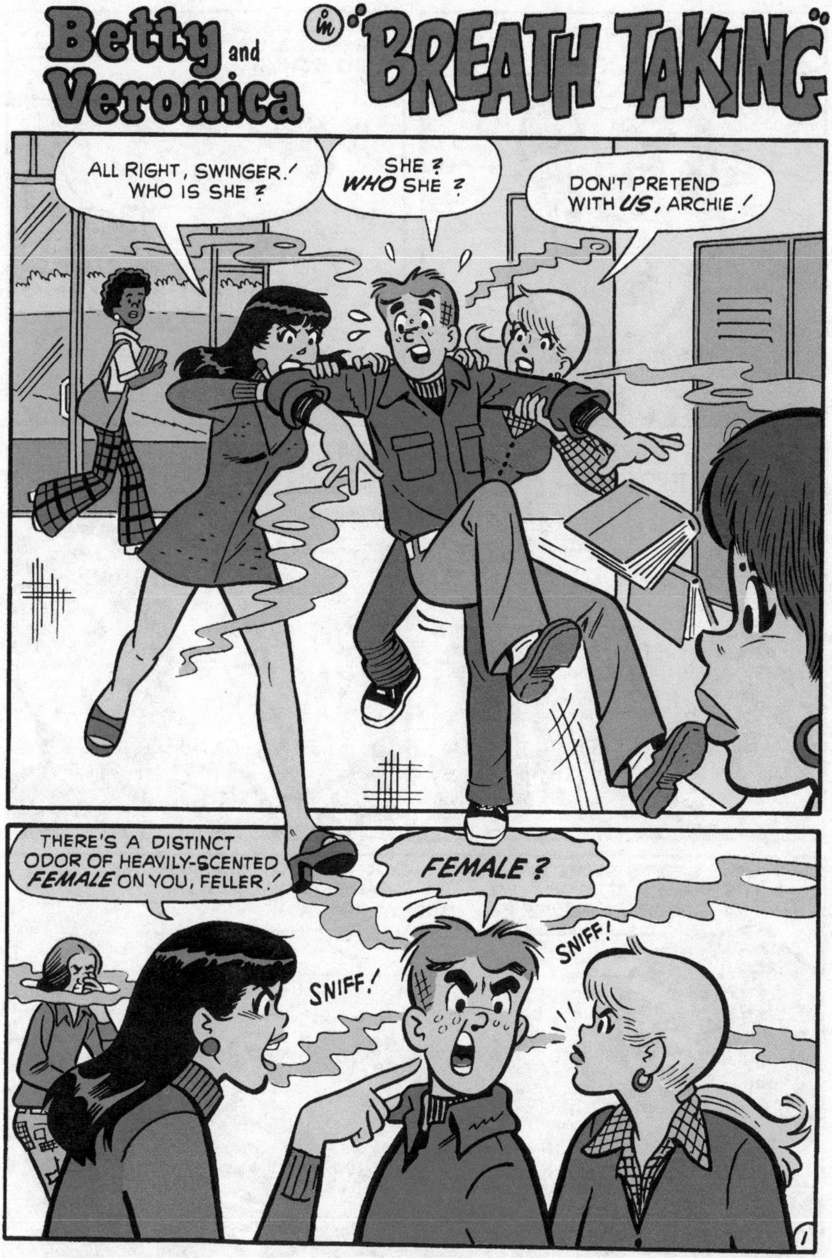
Betty and Veronica in "BREATH TAKING"
ALL RIGHT, SWINGER! WHO IS SHE?
SHE? WHO SHE?
DON'T PRETEND WITH US, ARCHIE!
THERE'S A DISTINCT ODOR OF HEAVILY-SCENTED FEMALE ON YOU, FELLER!
FEMALE?
SNIFF!
SNIFF!
1

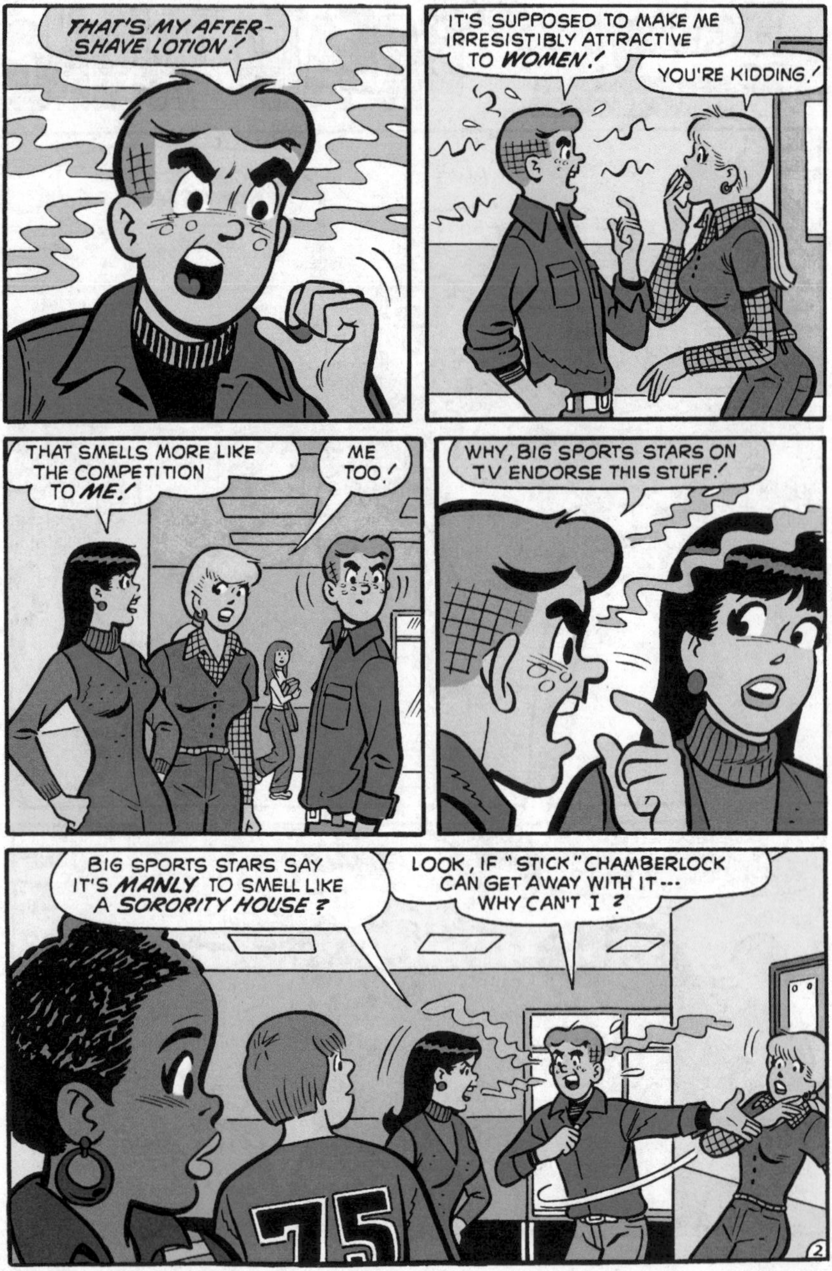
THAT'S MY AFTER-SHAVE LOTION!
IT'S SUPPOSED TO MAKE ME IRRESISTIBLY ATTRACTIVE TO WOMEN!
YOU'RE KIDDING!
THAT SMELLS MORE LIKE THE COMPETITION TO ME!
ME TOO!
WHY, BIG SPORTS STARS ON TV ENDORSE THIS STUFF!
BIG SPORTS STARS SAY IT'S MANLY TO SMELL LIKE A SORORITY HOUSE?
LOOK, IF "STICK" CHAMBERLOCK CAN GET AWAY WITH IT --- WHY CAN'T I?
75
2

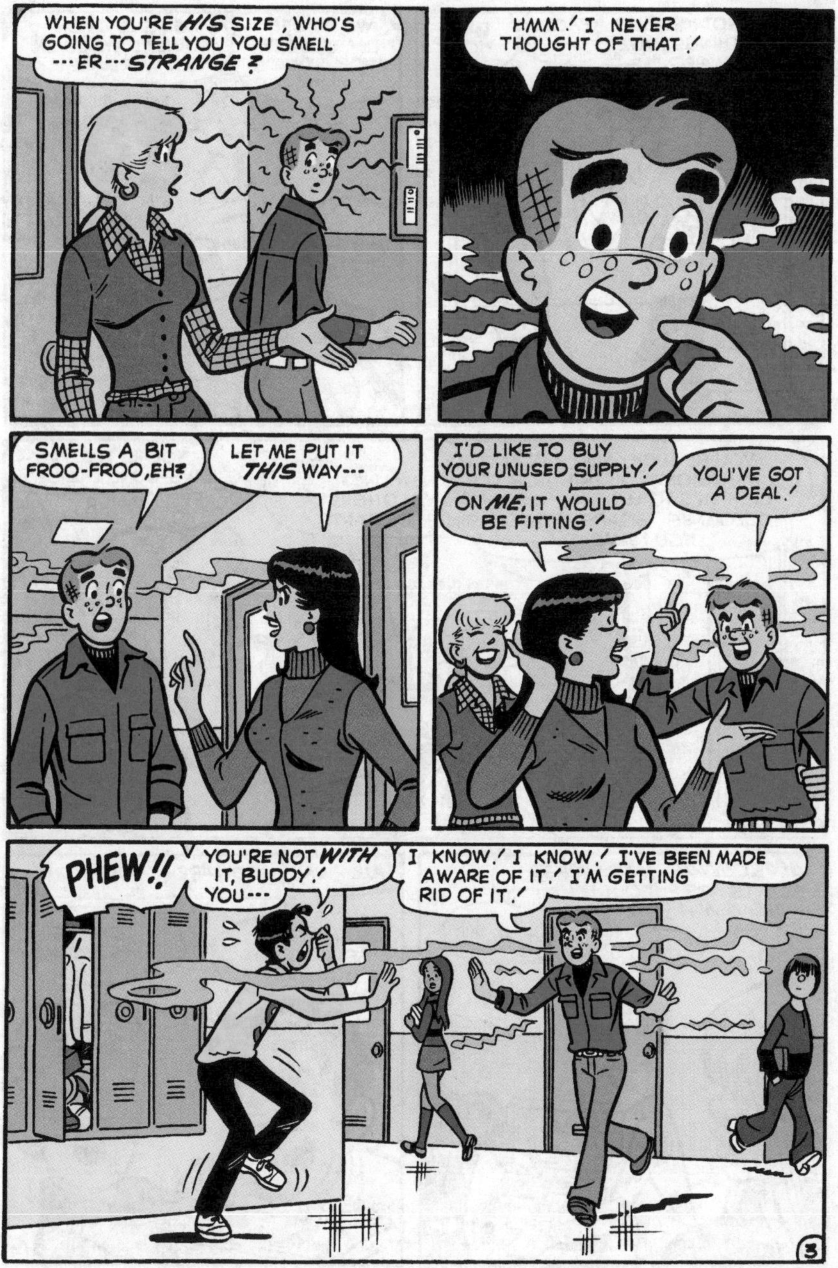
WHEN YOU'RE HIS SIZE, WHO'S GOING TO TELL YOU YOU SMELL ---ER---STRANGE?
HMM! I NEVER THOUGHT OF THAT!
SMELLS A BIT FROO-FROO, EH?
LET ME PUT IT THIS WAY---
I'D LIKE TO BUY YOUR UNUSED SUPPLY!
ON ME, IT WOULD BE FITTING!
YOU'VE GOT A DEAL!
PHEW!!
YOU'RE NOT WITH IT, BUDDY! YOU---
I KNOW! I KNOW! I'VE BEEN MADE AWARE OF IT! I'M GETTING RID OF IT!
3

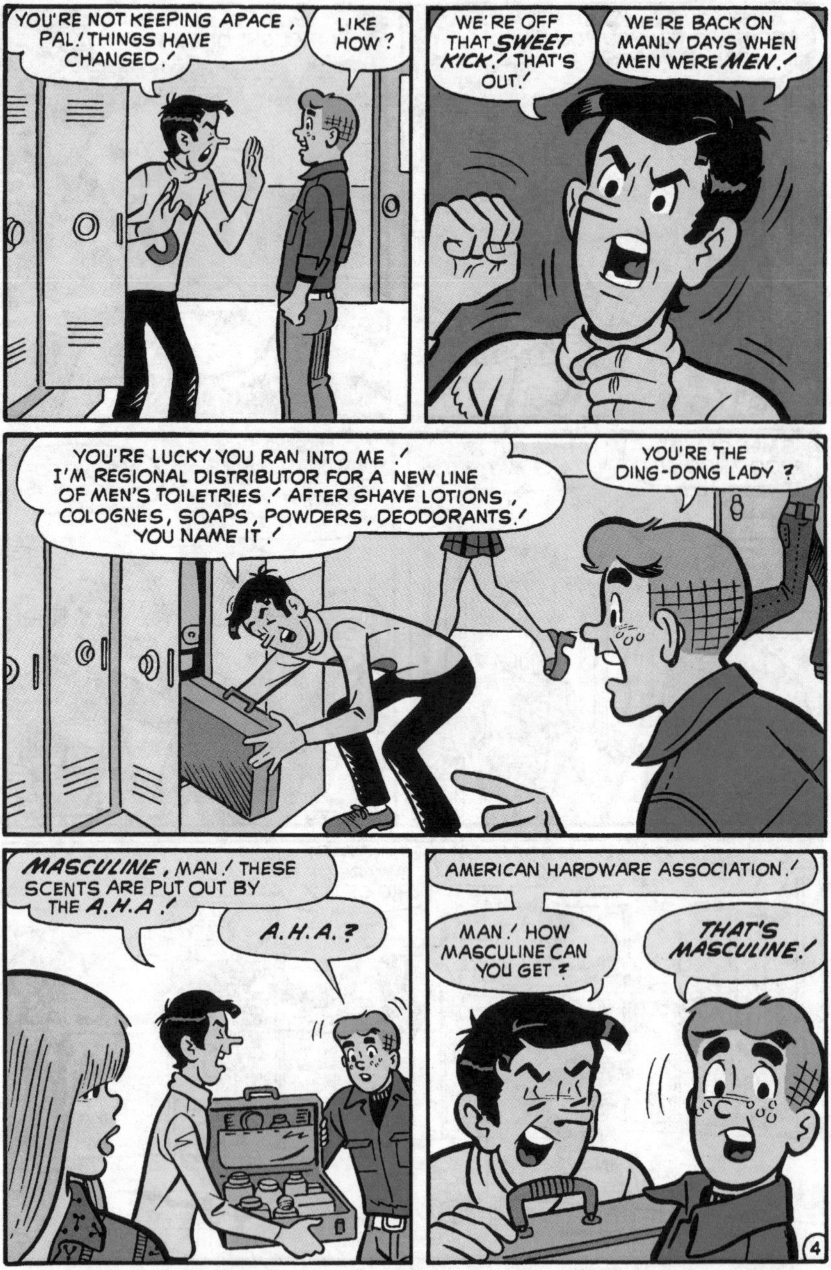
YOU'RE NOT KEEPING APACE, PAL! THINGS HAVE CHANGED!
LIKE HOW?
WE'RE OFF THAT SWEET KICK! THAT'S OUT!
WE'RE BACK ON MANLY DAYS WHEN MEN WERE MEN!
YOU'RE LUCKY YOU RAN INTO ME! I'M REGIONAL DISTRIBUTOR FOR A NEW LINE OF MEN'S TOILETRIES! AFTER SHAVE LOTIONS, COLOGNES, SOAPS, POWDERS, DEODORANTS! YOU NAME IT!
YOU'RE THE DING-DONG LADY?
MASCULINE, MAN! THESE SCENTS ARE PUT OUT BY THE A.H.A!
A.H.A.?
AMERICAN HARDWARE ASSOCIATION!
MAN! HOW MASCULINE CAN YOU GET?
THAT'S MASCULINE!
4

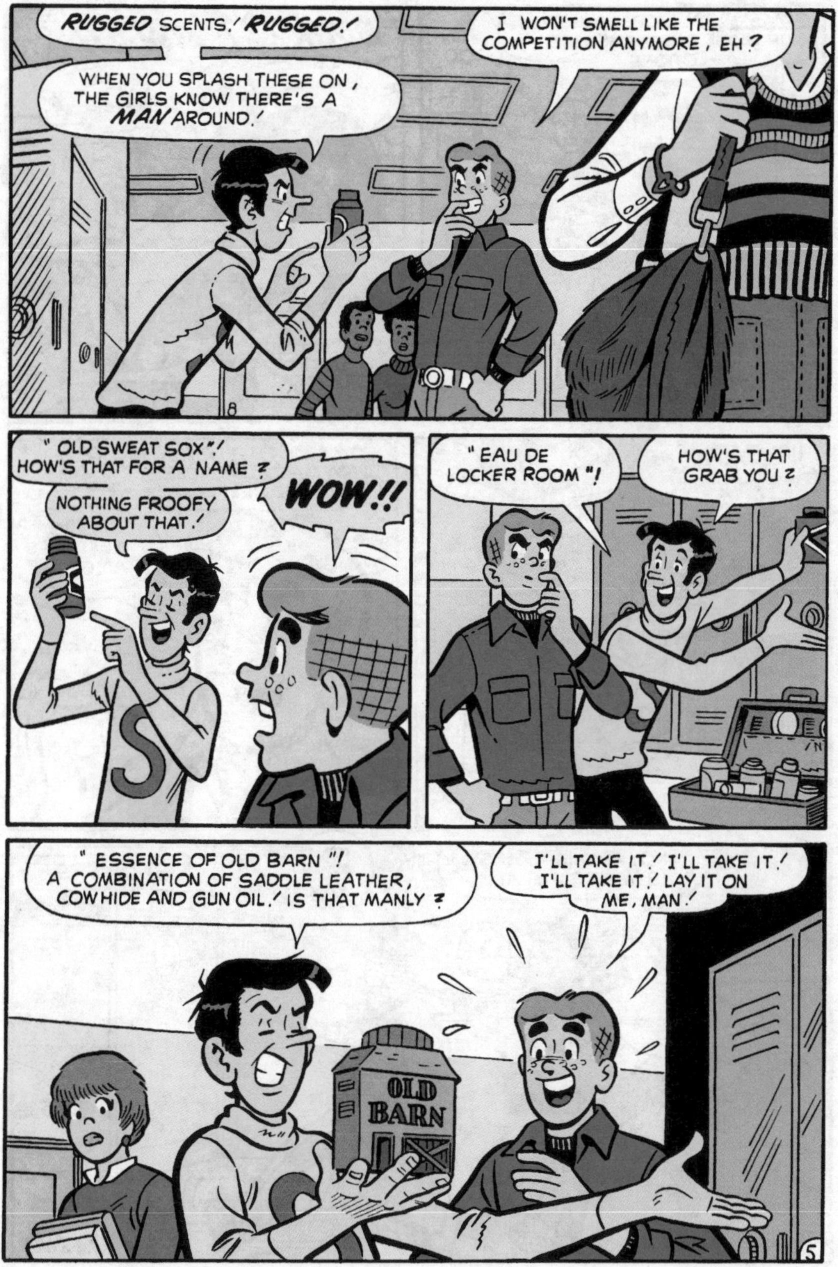
RUGGED SCENTS! RUGGED!
WHEN YOU SPLASH THESE ON, THE GIRLS KNOW THERE'S A MAN AROUND!
I WON'T SMELL LIKE THE COMPETITION ANYMORE, EH?
"OLD SWEAT SOX"! HOW'S THAT FOR A NAME?
NOTHING FROOFY ABOUT THAT!
WOW!!
"EAU DE LOCKER ROOM"!
HOW'S THAT GRAB YOU?
"ESSENCE OF OLD BARN"! A COMBINATION OF SADDLE LEATHER, COWHIDE AND GUN OIL! IS THAT MANLY?
I'LL TAKE IT! I'LL TAKE IT! I'LL TAKE IT! LAY IT ON ME, MAN!
OLD BARN
5

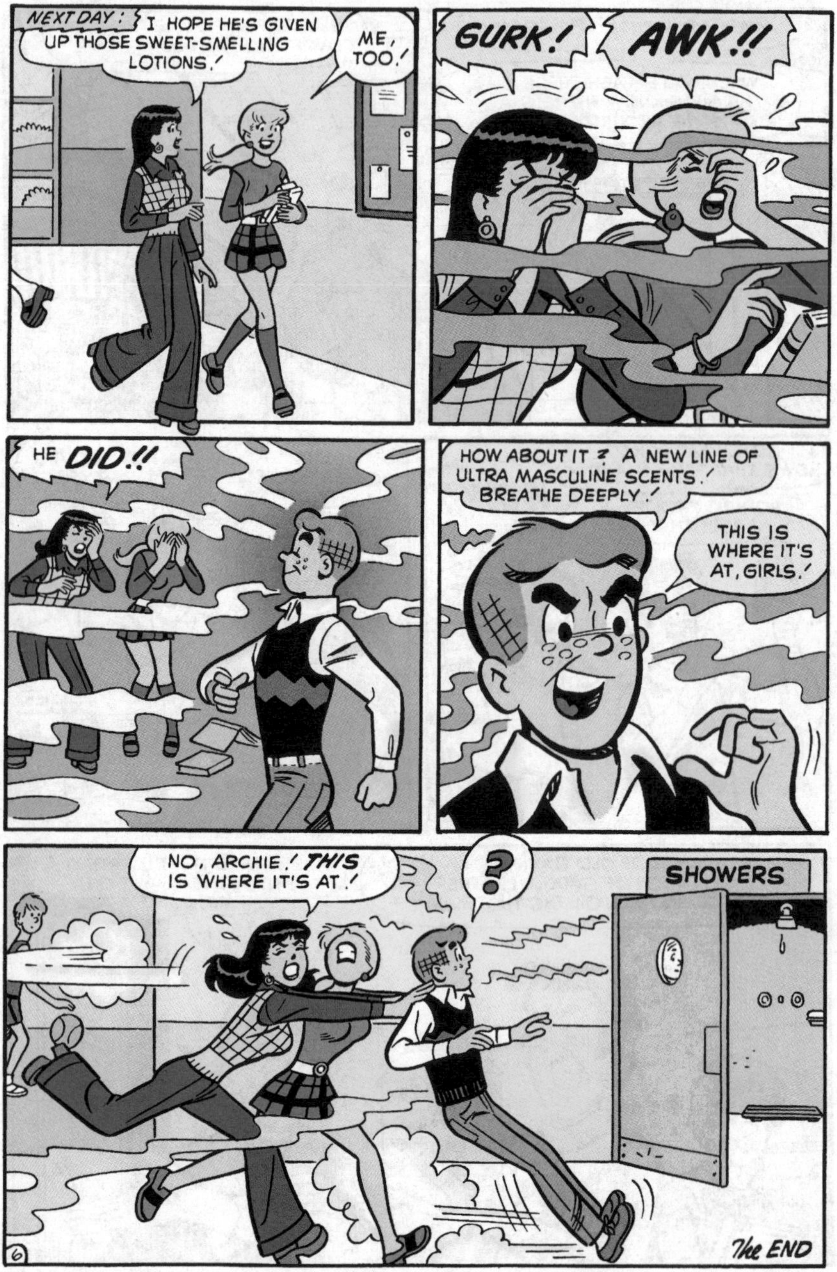
NEXT DAY:
I HOPE HE'S GIVEN UP THOSE SWEET-SMELLING LOTIONS!
ME, TOO!
GURK!
AWK!!
HE DID!!
HOW ABOUT IT? A NEW LINE OF ULTRA MASCULINE SCENTS! BREATHE DEEPLY!
THIS IS WHERE IT'S AT, GIRLS!
NO, ARCHIE! THIS IS WHERE IT'S AT!
?
SHOWERS
6
The END

Betty and Veronica in "The Advertising Game"

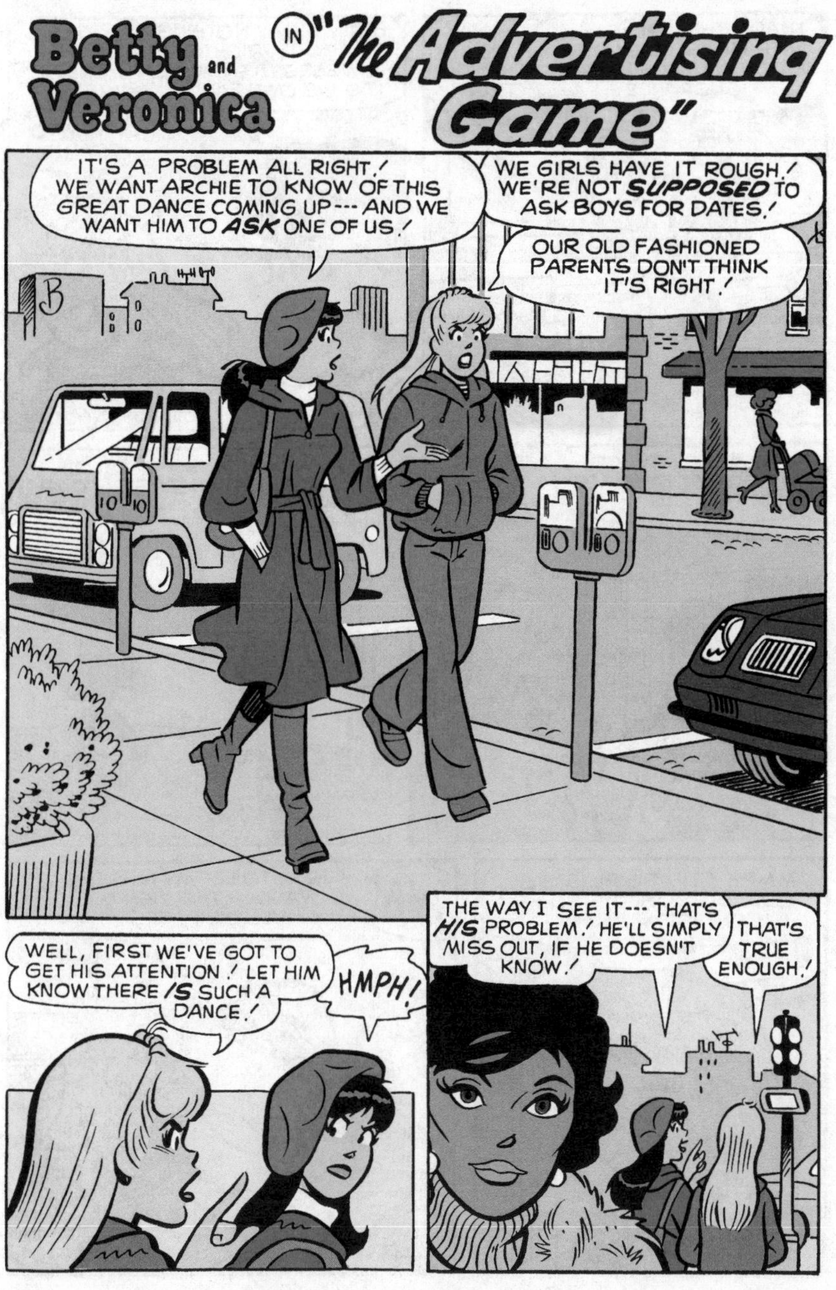

IT'S A PROBLEM ALL RIGHT! WE WANT ARCHIE TO KNOW OF THIS GREAT DANCE COMING UP --- AND WE WANT HIM TO ASK ONE OF US!
WE GIRLS HAVE IT ROUGH! WE'RE NOT SUPPOSED TO ASK BOYS FOR DATES!
OUR OLD FASHIONED PARENTS DON'T THINK IT'S RIGHT!
WELL, FIRST WE'VE GOT TO GET HIS ATTENTION! LET HIM KNOW THERE IS SUCH A DANCE!
HMPH!
THE WAY I SEE IT --- THAT'S HIS PROBLEM! HE'LL SIMPLY MISS OUT, IF HE DOESN'T KNOW!
THAT'S TRUE ENOUGH!

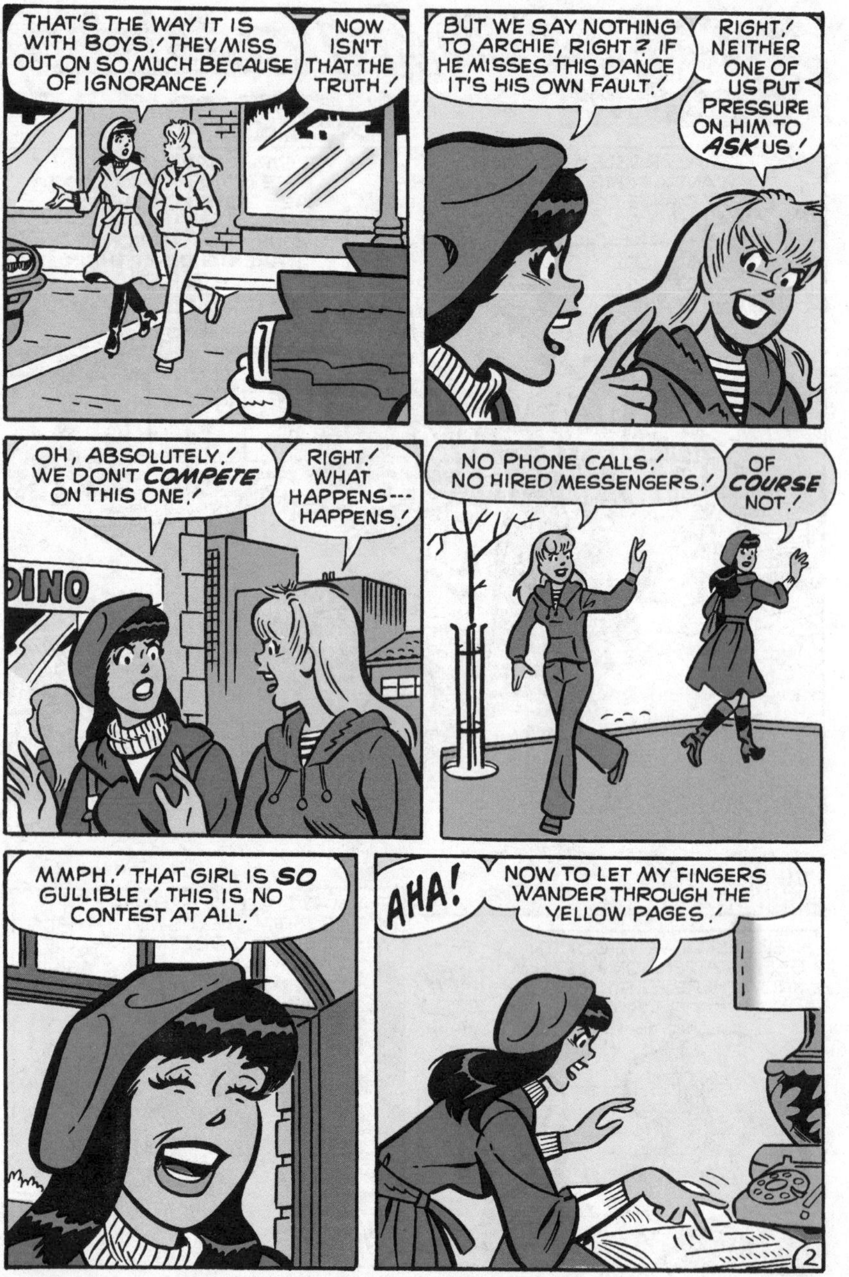
THAT'S THE WAY IT IS WITH BOYS! THEY MISS OUT ON SO MUCH BECAUSE OF IGNORANCE!
NOW ISN'T THAT THE TRUTH!
BUT WE SAY NOTHING TO ARCHIE, RIGHT? IF HE MISSES THIS DANCE IT'S HIS OWN FAULT!
RIGHT! NEITHER ONE OF US PUT PRESSURE ON HIM TO ASK US!
OH, ABSOLUTELY! WE DON'T COMPETE ON THIS ONE!
RIGHT! WHAT HAPPENS--- HAPPENS!
DINO
NO PHONE CALLS! NO HIRED MESSENGERS!
OF COURSE NOT!
MMPH! THAT GIRL IS SO GULLIBLE! THIS IS NO CONTEST AT ALL!
AHA!
NOW TO LET MY FINGERS WANDER THROUGH THE YELLOW PAGES!
2

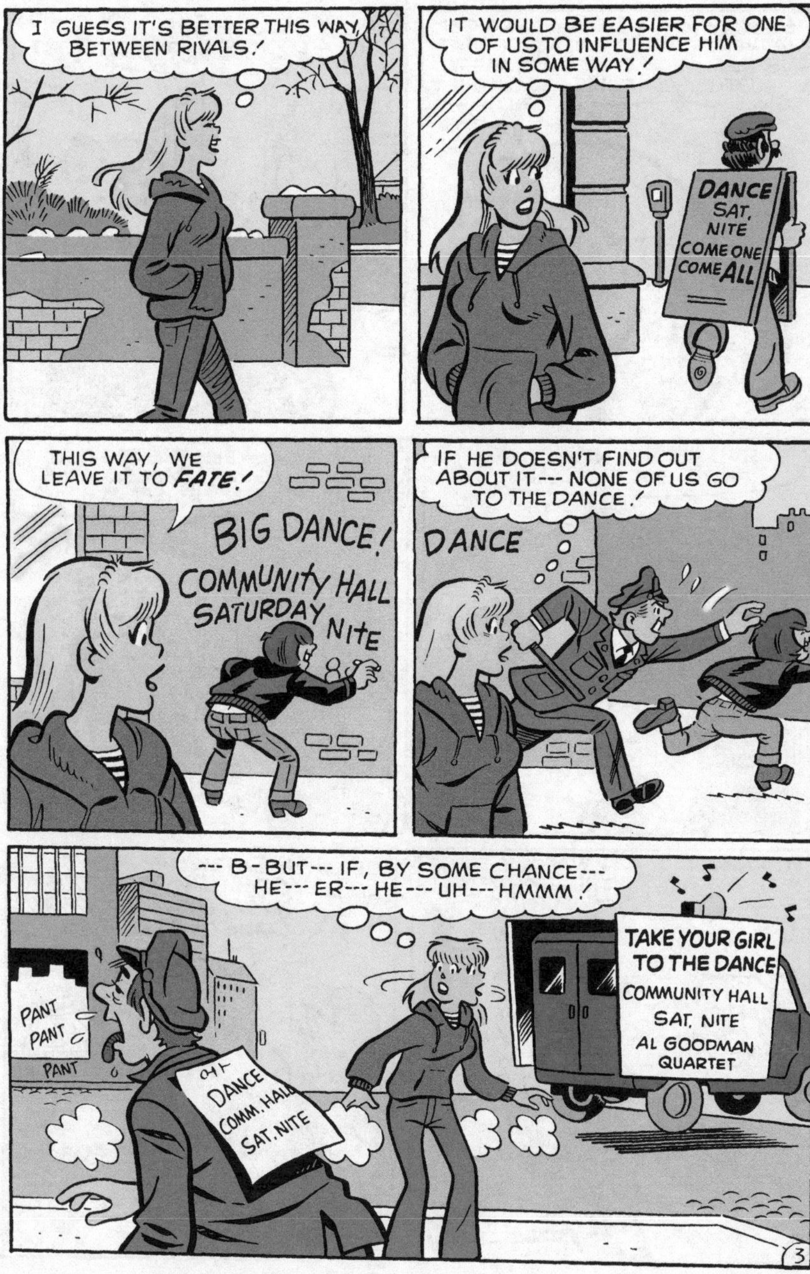

I GUESS IT'S BETTER THIS WAY, BETWEEN RIVALS.!
IT WOULD BE EASIER FOR ONE OF US TO INFLUENCE HIM IN SOME WAY.!
DANCE SAT. NITE COME ONE COME ALL
THIS WAY, WE LEAVE IT TO FATE.!
BIG DANCE! COMMUNITY HALL SATURDAY NITE
IF HE DOESN'T FIND OUT ABOUT IT --- NONE OF US GO TO THE DANCE.!
DANCE
--- B-BUT--- IF, BY SOME CHANCE--- HE--- ER--- HE--- UH--- HMMM.!
TAKE YOUR GIRL TO THE DANCE
COMMUNITY HALL
SAT. NITE
AL GOODMAN QUARTET
PANT PANT PANT
DANCE COMM. HALL SAT. NITE

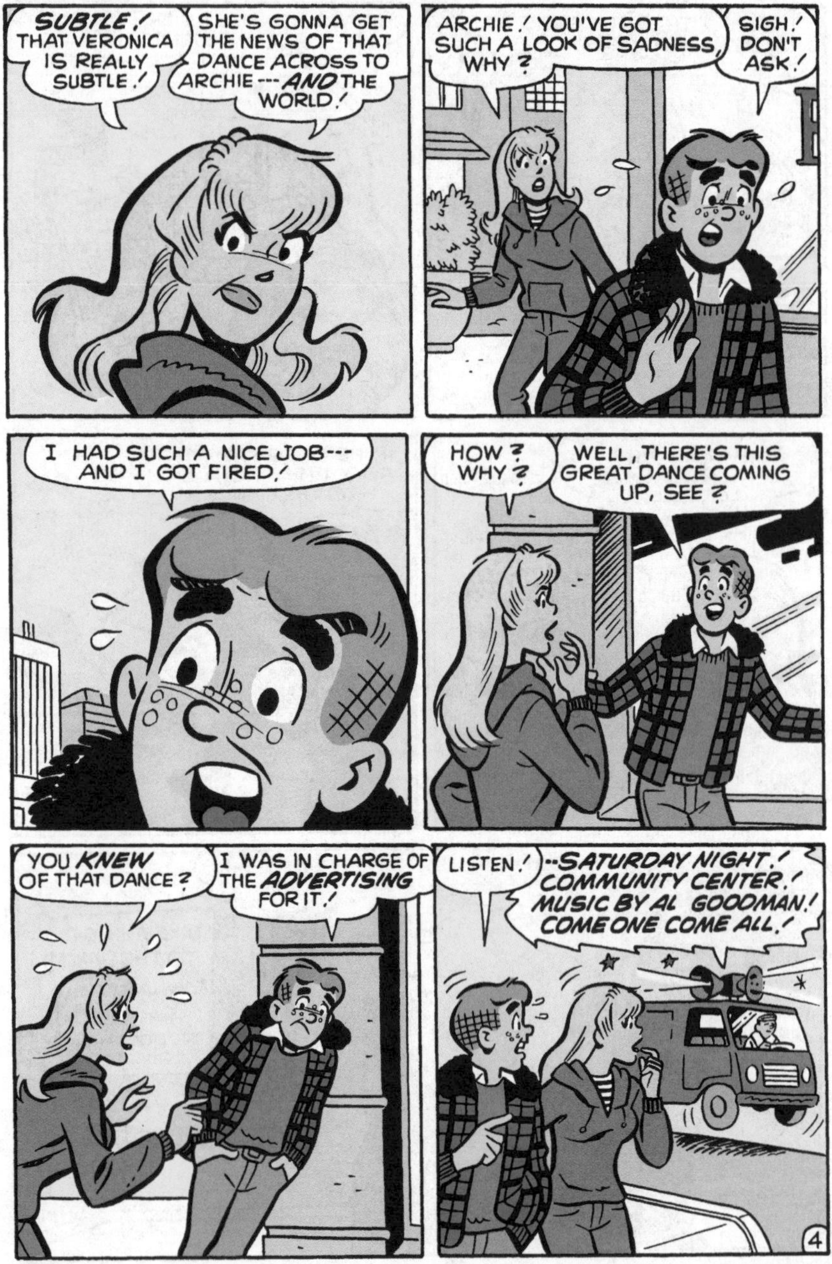
SUBTLE! THAT VERONICA IS REALLY SUBTLE!
SHE'S GONNA GET THE NEWS OF THAT DANCE ACROSS TO ARCHIE --- AND THE WORLD!
ARCHIE! YOU'VE GOT SUCH A LOOK OF SADNESS, WHY?
SIGH! DON'T ASK!
I HAD SUCH A NICE JOB--- AND I GOT FIRED!
HOW? WHY?
WELL, THERE'S THIS GREAT DANCE COMING UP, SEE?
YOU KNEW OF THAT DANCE?
I WAS IN CHARGE OF THE ADVERTISING FOR IT!
LISTEN!
--SATURDAY NIGHT! COMMUNITY CENTER! MUSIC BY AL GOODMAN! COME ONE COME ALL!
4

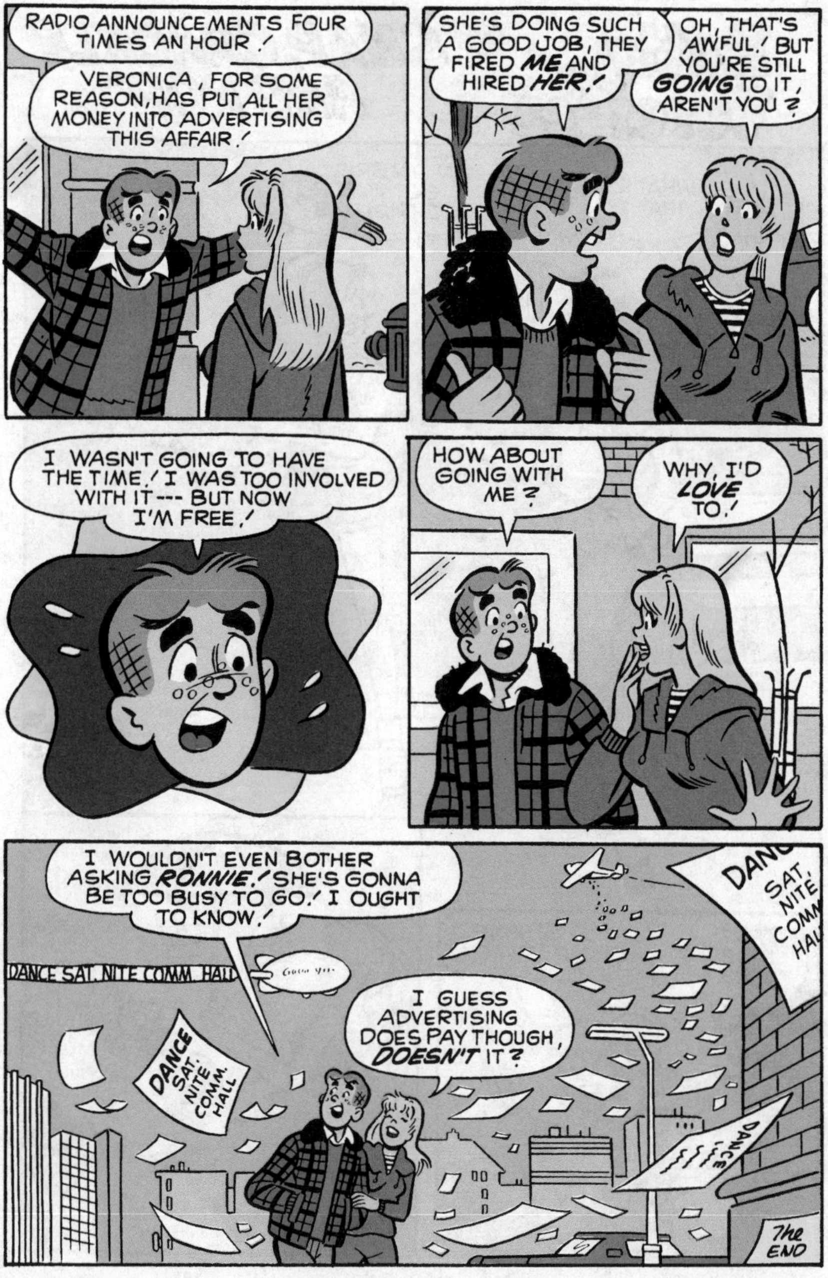

RADIO ANNOUNCEMENTS FOUR TIMES AN HOUR!
VERONICA, FOR SOME REASON, HAS PUT ALL HER MONEY INTO ADVERTISING THIS AFFAIR!
SHE'S DOING SUCH A GOOD JOB, THEY FIRED *ME* AND HIRED *HER*!
OH, THAT'S AWFUL! BUT YOU'RE STILL *GOING* TO IT, AREN'T YOU?
I WASN'T GOING TO HAVE THE TIME! I WAS TOO INVOLVED WITH IT --- BUT NOW I'M FREE!
HOW ABOUT GOING WITH ME?
WHY, I'D *LOVE* TO!
I WOULDN'T EVEN BOTHER ASKING *RONNIE*! SHE'S GONNA BE TOO BUSY TO GO! I OUGHT TO KNOW!
DANCE SAT. NITE COMM. HALL
DANCE SAT. NITE COMM. HALL
I GUESS ADVERTISING DOES PAY THOUGH, *DOESN'T* IT?
The END

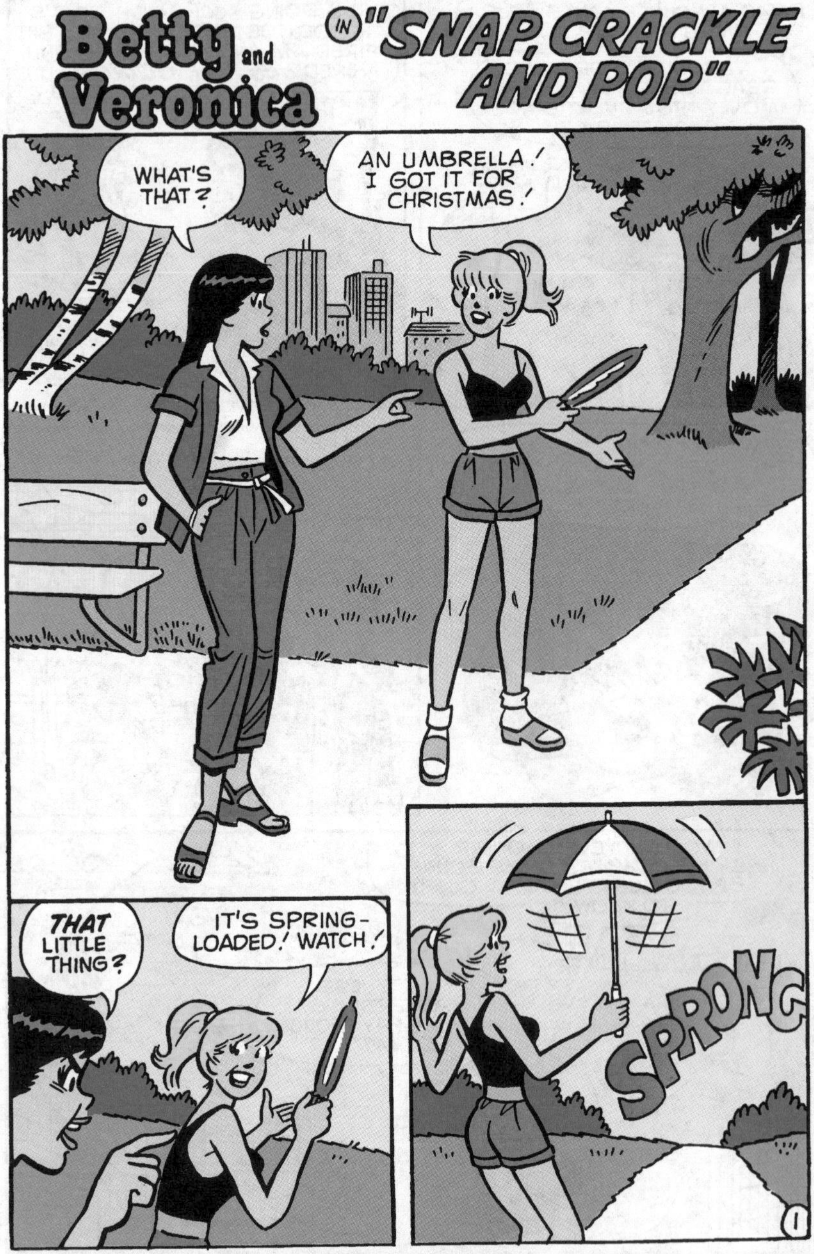
Betty and Veronica
IN "SNAP, CRACKLE AND POP"
WHAT'S THAT?
AN UMBRELLA! I GOT IT FOR CHRISTMAS!
THAT LITTLE THING?
IT'S SPRING-LOADED! WATCH!
SPRONG
1

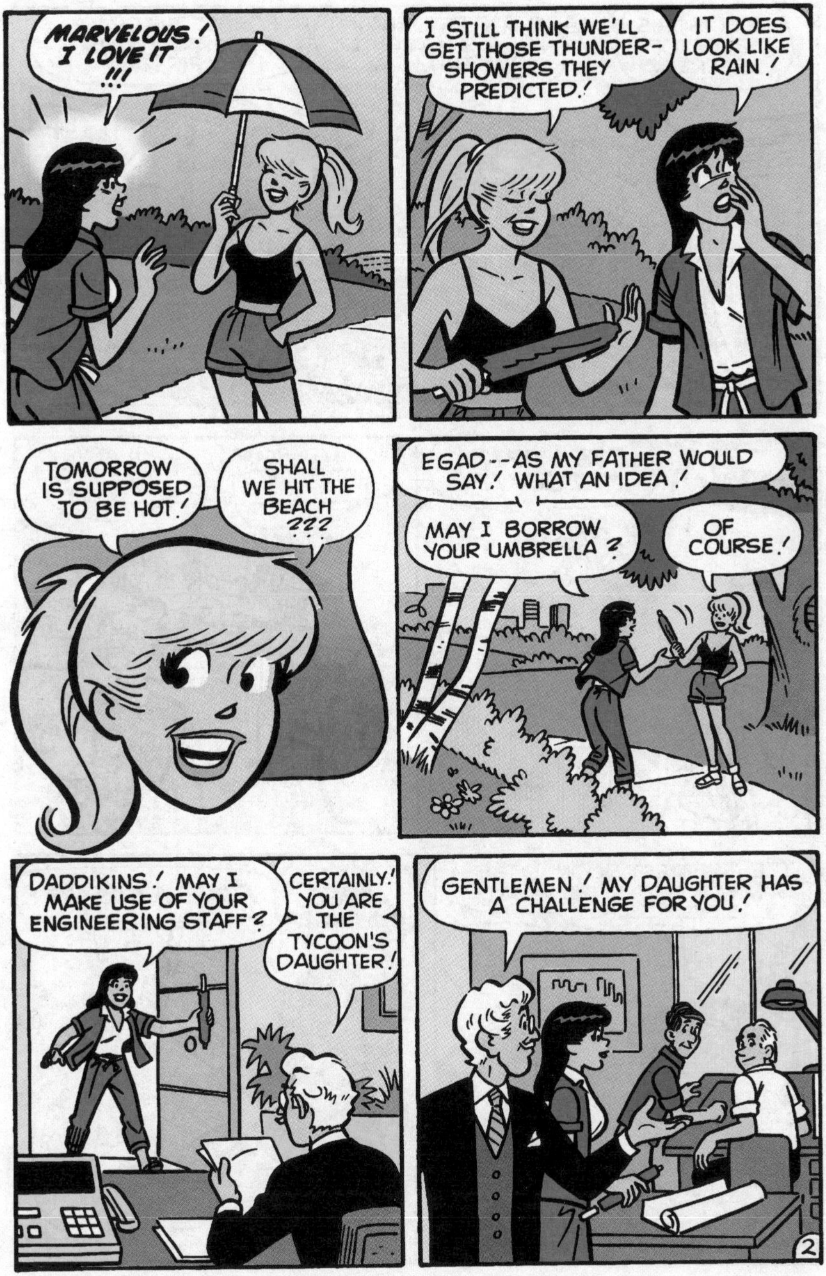
MARVELOUS! I LOVE IT !!!
I STILL THINK WE'LL GET THOSE THUNDER-SHOWERS THEY PREDICTED!
IT DOES LOOK LIKE RAIN!
TOMORROW IS SUPPOSED TO BE HOT!
SHALL WE HIT THE BEACH ???
EGAD--AS MY FATHER WOULD SAY! WHAT AN IDEA!
MAY I BORROW YOUR UMBRELLA?
OF COURSE!
DADDIKINS! MAY I MAKE USE OF YOUR ENGINEERING STAFF?
CERTAINLY! YOU ARE THE TYCOON'S DAUGHTER!
GENTLEMEN! MY DAUGHTER HAS A CHALLENGE FOR YOU!
2

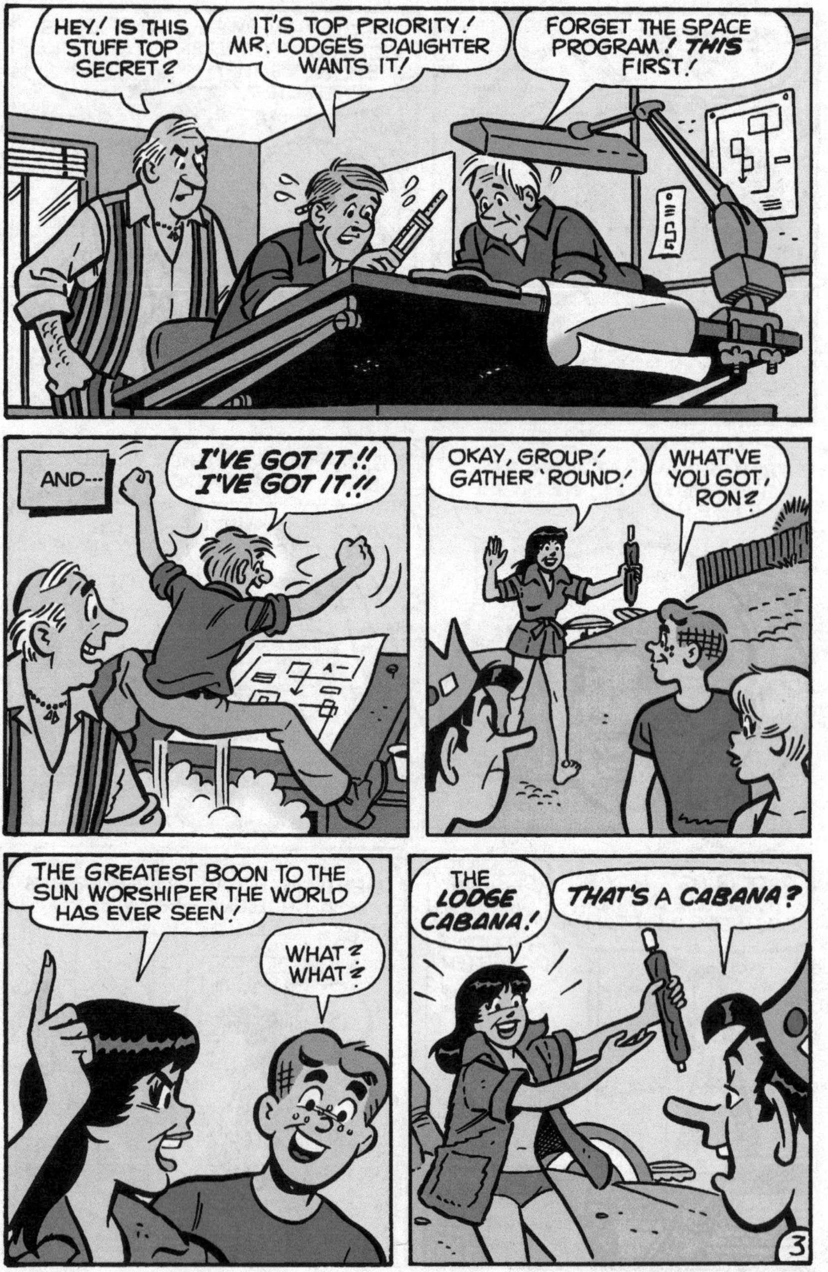
HEY! IS THIS STUFF TOP SECRET?
IT'S TOP PRIORITY! MR. LODGE'S DAUGHTER WANTS IT!
FORGET THE SPACE PROGRAM! THIS FIRST!
AND---
I'VE GOT IT!! I'VE GOT IT!!
OKAY, GROUP! GATHER 'ROUND!
WHAT'VE YOU GOT, RON?
THE GREATEST BOON TO THE SUN WORSHIPER THE WORLD HAS EVER SEEN!
WHAT? WHAT?
THE LODGE CABANA!
THAT'S A CABANA?
3

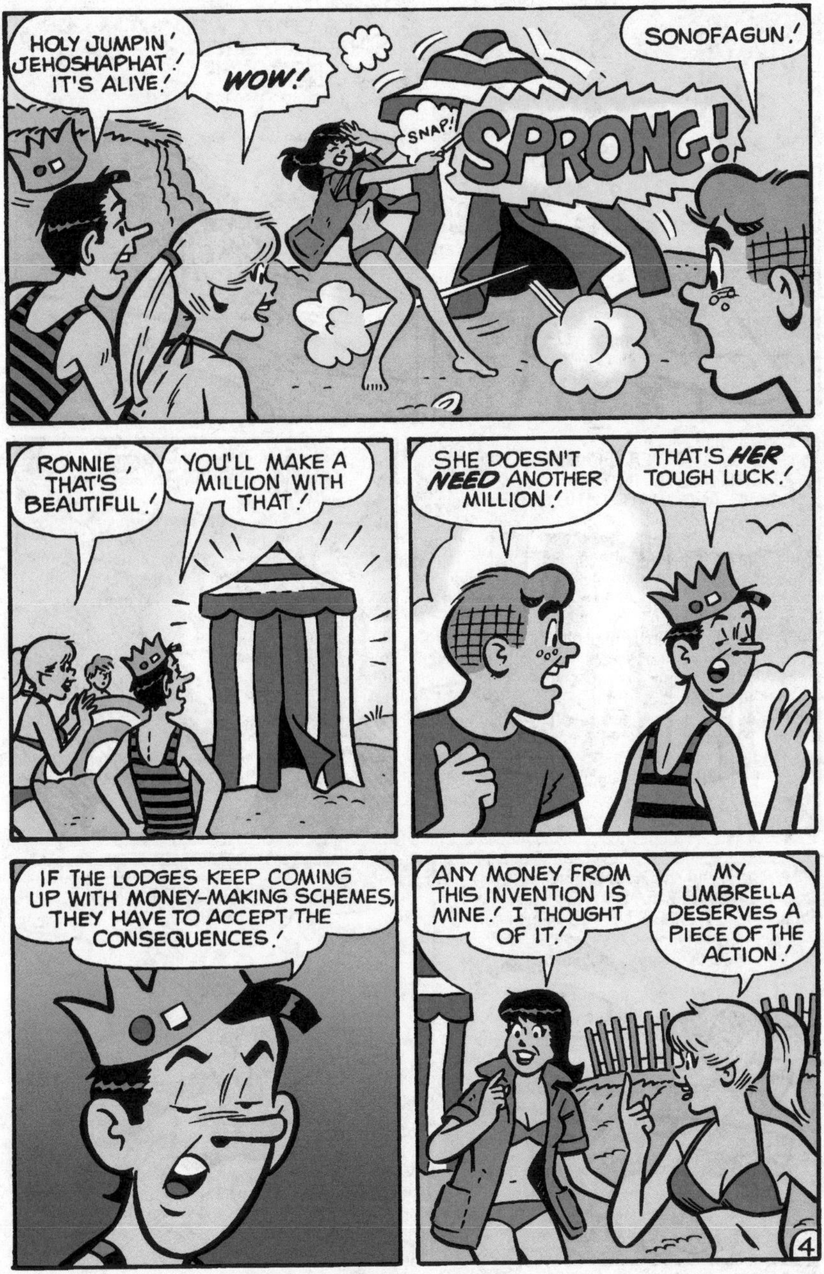
HOLY JUMPIN' JEHOSHAPHAT! IT'S ALIVE!
WOW!
SNAP!
SPRONG!
SONOFAGUN!
RONNIE, THAT'S BEAUTIFUL!
YOU'LL MAKE A MILLION WITH THAT!
SHE DOESN'T NEED ANOTHER MILLION!
THAT'S HER TOUGH LUCK!
IF THE LODGES KEEP COMING UP WITH MONEY-MAKING SCHEMES, THEY HAVE TO ACCEPT THE CONSEQUENCES!
ANY MONEY FROM THIS INVENTION IS MINE! I THOUGHT OF IT!
MY UMBRELLA DESERVES A PIECE OF THE ACTION!
4

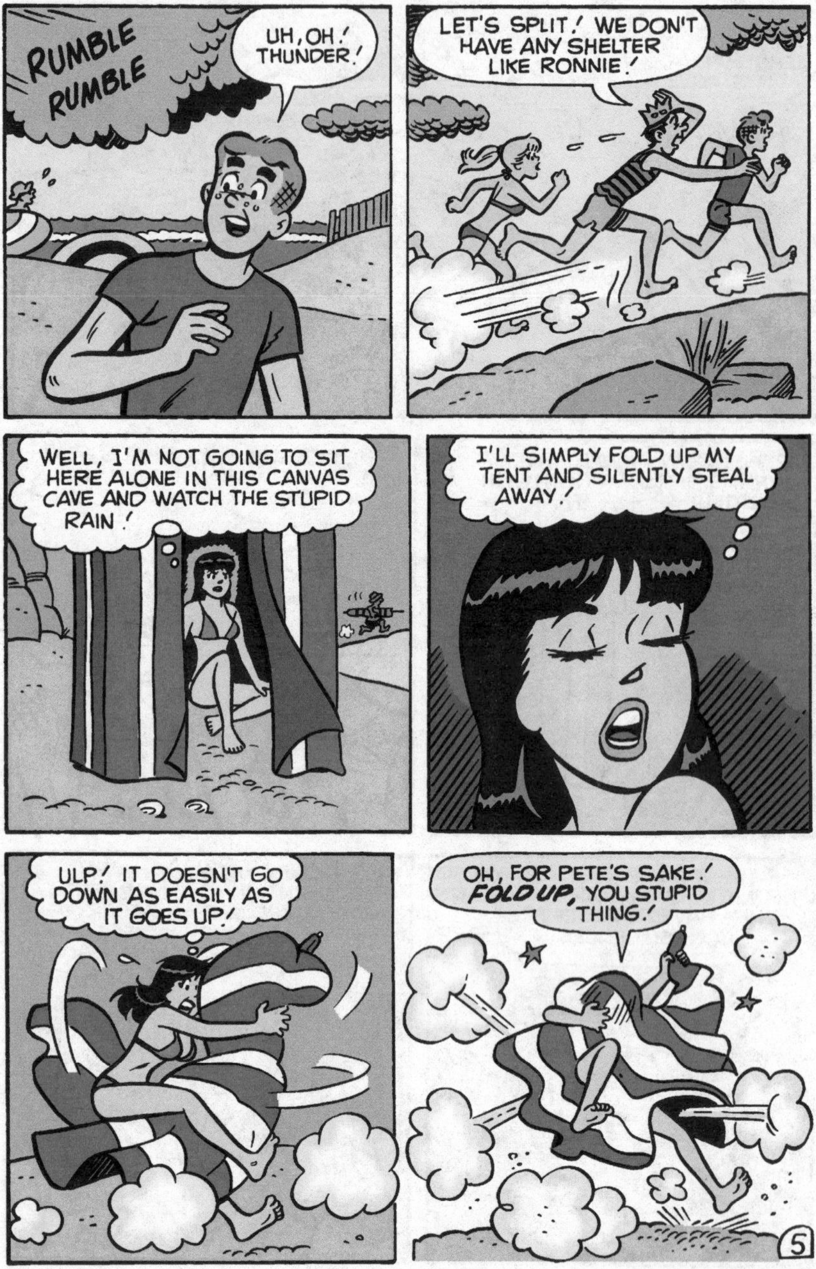
RUMBLE RUMBLE
UH, OH! THUNDER!
LET'S SPLIT! WE DON'T HAVE ANY SHELTER LIKE RONNIE!
WELL, I'M NOT GOING TO SIT HERE ALONE IN THIS CANVAS CAVE AND WATCH THE STUPID RAIN!
I'LL SIMPLY FOLD UP MY TENT AND SILENTLY STEAL AWAY!
ULP! IT DOESN'T GO DOWN AS EASILY AS IT GOES UP!
OH, FOR PETE'S SAKE! FOLD UP, YOU STUPID THING!
5

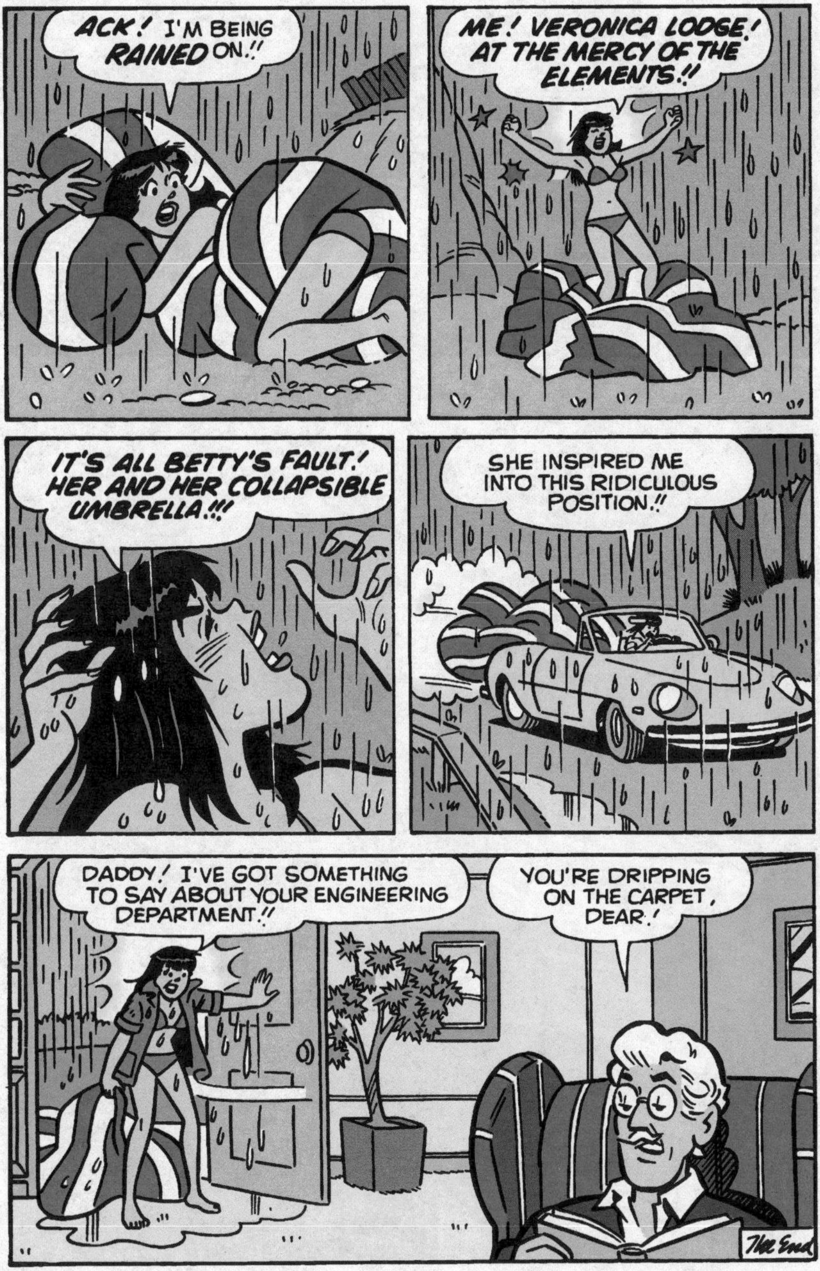
ACK! I'M BEING RAINED ON!!
ME! VERONICA LODGE! AT THE MERCY OF THE ELEMENTS!!
IT'S ALL BETTY'S FAULT! HER AND HER COLLAPSIBLE UMBRELLA!!!
SHE INSPIRED ME INTO THIS RIDICULOUS POSITION!!
DADDY! I'VE GOT SOMETHING TO SAY ABOUT YOUR ENGINEERING DEPARTMENT!!
YOU'RE DRIPPING ON THE CARPET, DEAR!
The End

THE BEST OF ARCHIE COMICS STARRING

BETTY & VERONICA

1980s

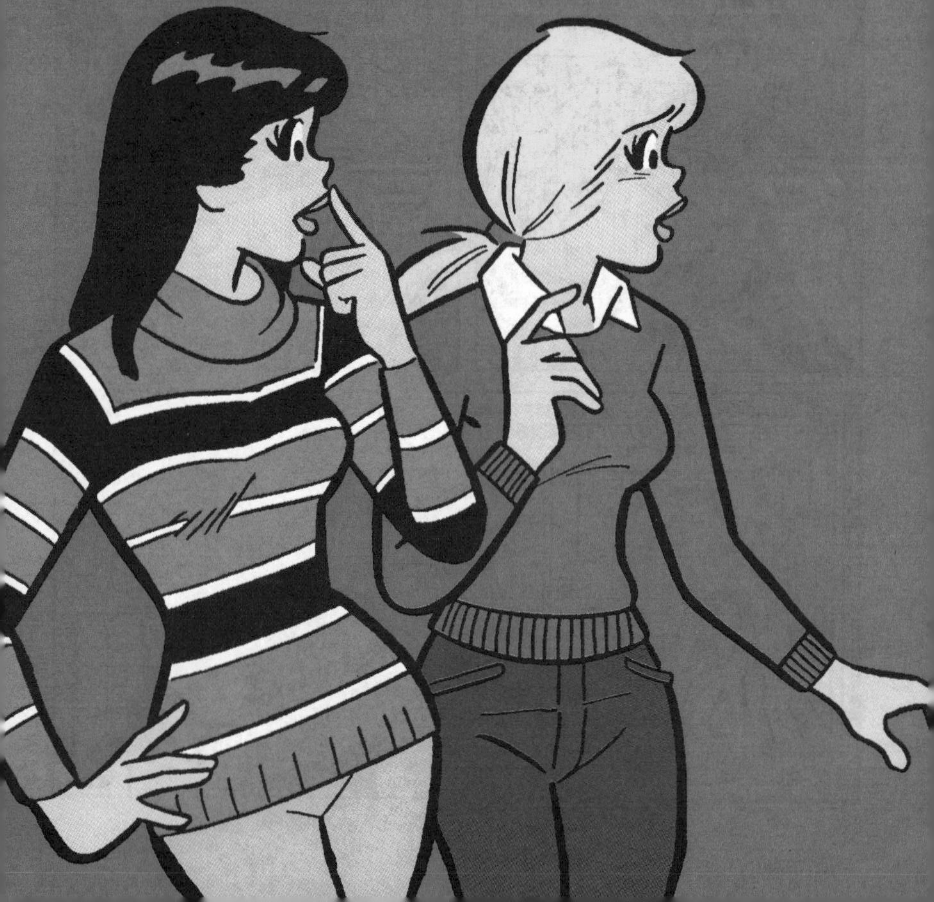

VOICES OF CHANGE
BETTY & VERONICA #289, 1980
Frank Doyle, Dan DeCarlo, Jim DeCarlo, Bill Yoshida, Barry Grossman

SCULPTURE SCHEMER
BETTY & VERONICA #303, 1981
George Gladir, Dan DeCarlo, Jim DeCarlo, Bill Yoshida, Barry Grossman

CHILLER
BETTY & VERONICA #333, 1984
George Gladir, Dan DeCarlo, Rudy Lapick, Bill Yoshida, Barry Grossman

IS THERE AN ARCHIE IN THE HOUSE?
BETTY & VERONICA #333, 1984
Adam Phillips, Dan DeCarlo, Jim DeCarlo, Bill Yoshida, Barry Grossman

My very first comic books were Archie Comics, and while I always enjoyed guys' adventures, Betty and Veronica's relationship was the center of it all for me. They were never the perfect pair: they were "frenemies" as often as they were friends, but still always seemed to have each other's backs. Like a begrudging respect for one another. I think that combination of sweet, spice and salt somehow made them more real. As a kid, I ate it up, and as an adult, I'm lucky enough to help bring them to life myself.

- SANYA ANWAR *Artist, Archie Comics*

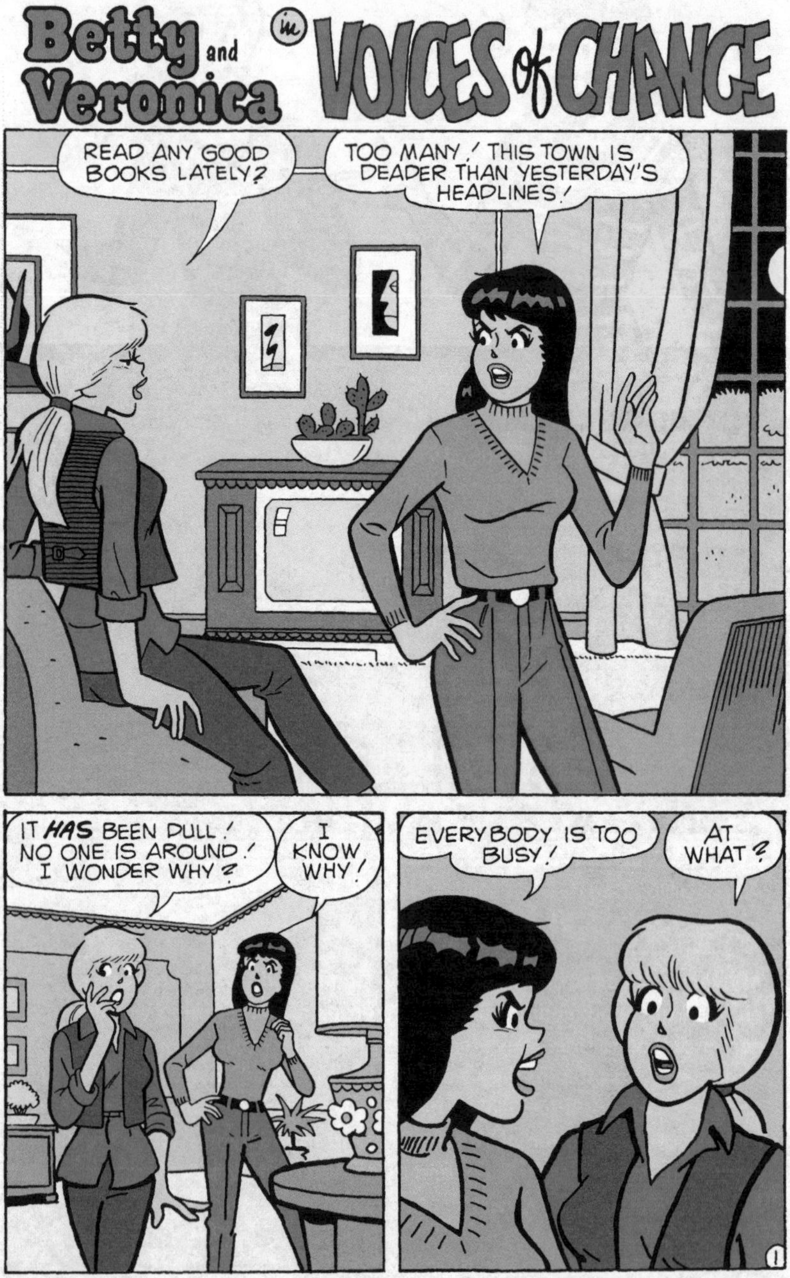
Betty and Veronica in VOICES of CHANGE
READ ANY GOOD BOOKS LATELY?
TOO MANY! THIS TOWN IS DEADER THAN YESTERDAY'S HEADLINES!
IT HAS BEEN DULL! NO ONE IS AROUND! I WONDER WHY?
I KNOW WHY!
EVERYBODY IS TOO BUSY!
AT WHAT?
1

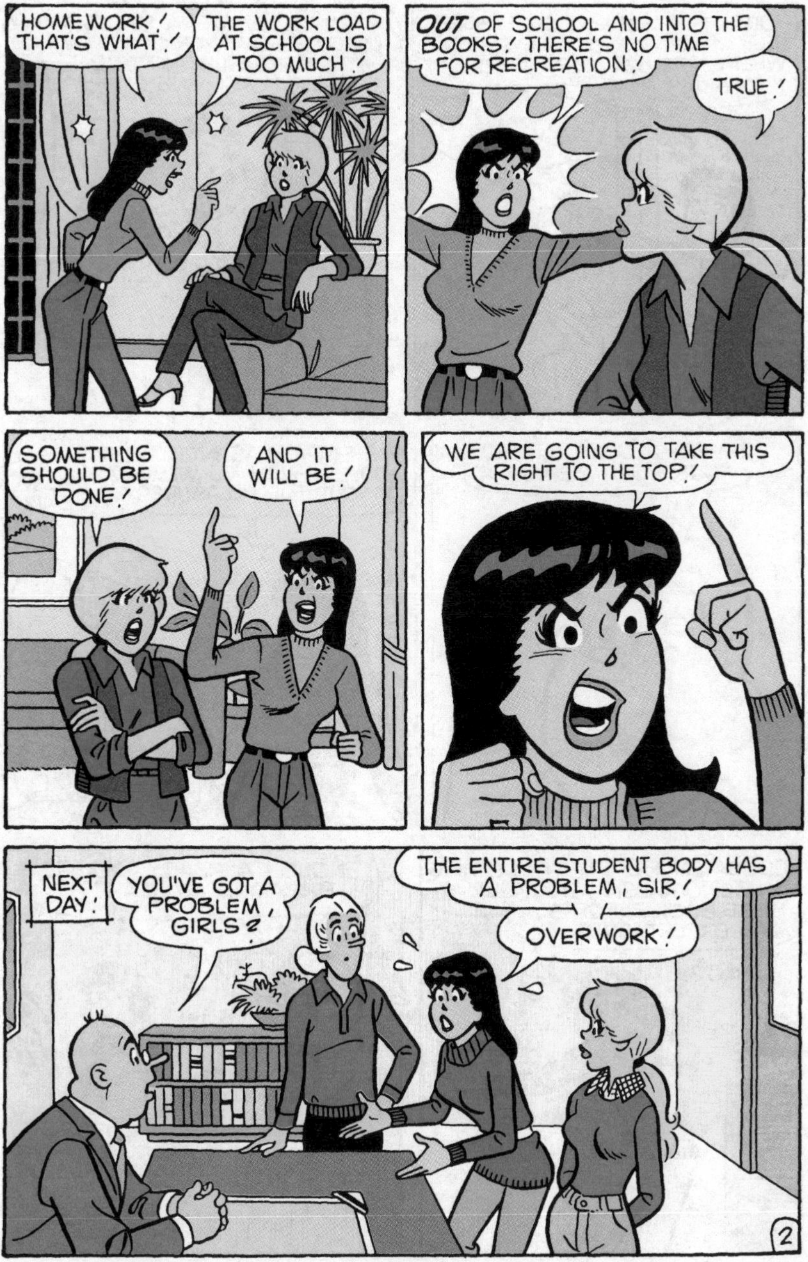
HOMEWORK! THAT'S WHAT!
THE WORK LOAD AT SCHOOL IS TOO MUCH!
OUT OF SCHOOL AND INTO THE BOOKS! THERE'S NO TIME FOR RECREATION!
TRUE!
SOMETHING SHOULD BE DONE!
AND IT WILL BE!
WE ARE GOING TO TAKE THIS RIGHT TO THE TOP!
NEXT DAY!
YOU'VE GOT A PROBLEM, GIRLS?
THE ENTIRE STUDENT BODY HAS A PROBLEM, SIR!
OVERWORK!
2

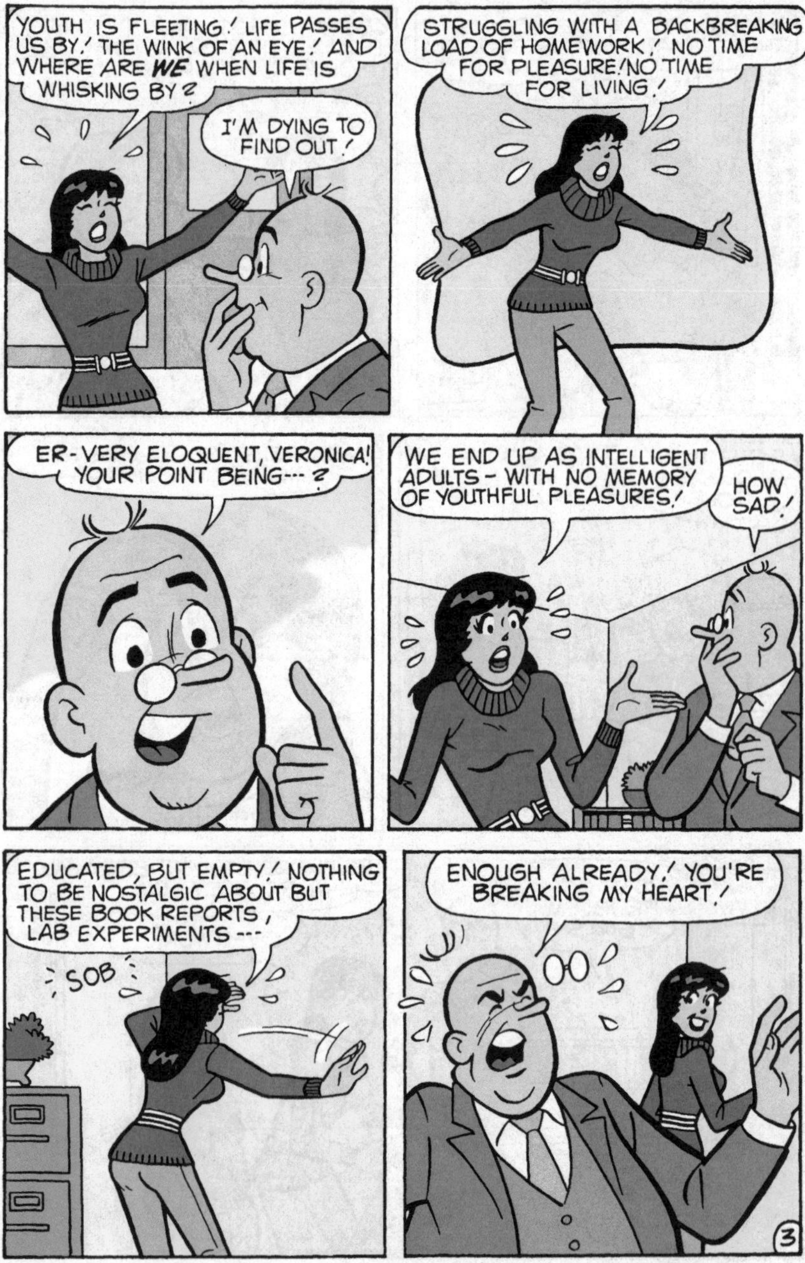
YOUTH IS FLEETING! LIFE PASSES US BY! THE WINK OF AN EYE! AND WHERE ARE WE WHEN LIFE IS WHISKING BY?
I'M DYING TO FIND OUT!
STRUGGLING WITH A BACKBREAKING LOAD OF HOMEWORK! NO TIME FOR PLEASURE! NO TIME FOR LIVING!
ER-VERY ELOQUENT, VERONICA! YOUR POINT BEING---?
WE END UP AS INTELLIGENT ADULTS - WITH NO MEMORY OF YOUTHFUL PLEASURES!
HOW SAD!
EDUCATED, BUT EMPTY! NOTHING TO BE NOSTALGIC ABOUT BUT THESE BOOK REPORTS, LAB EXPERIMENTS---
SOB
ENOUGH ALREADY! YOU'RE BREAKING MY HEART!
3

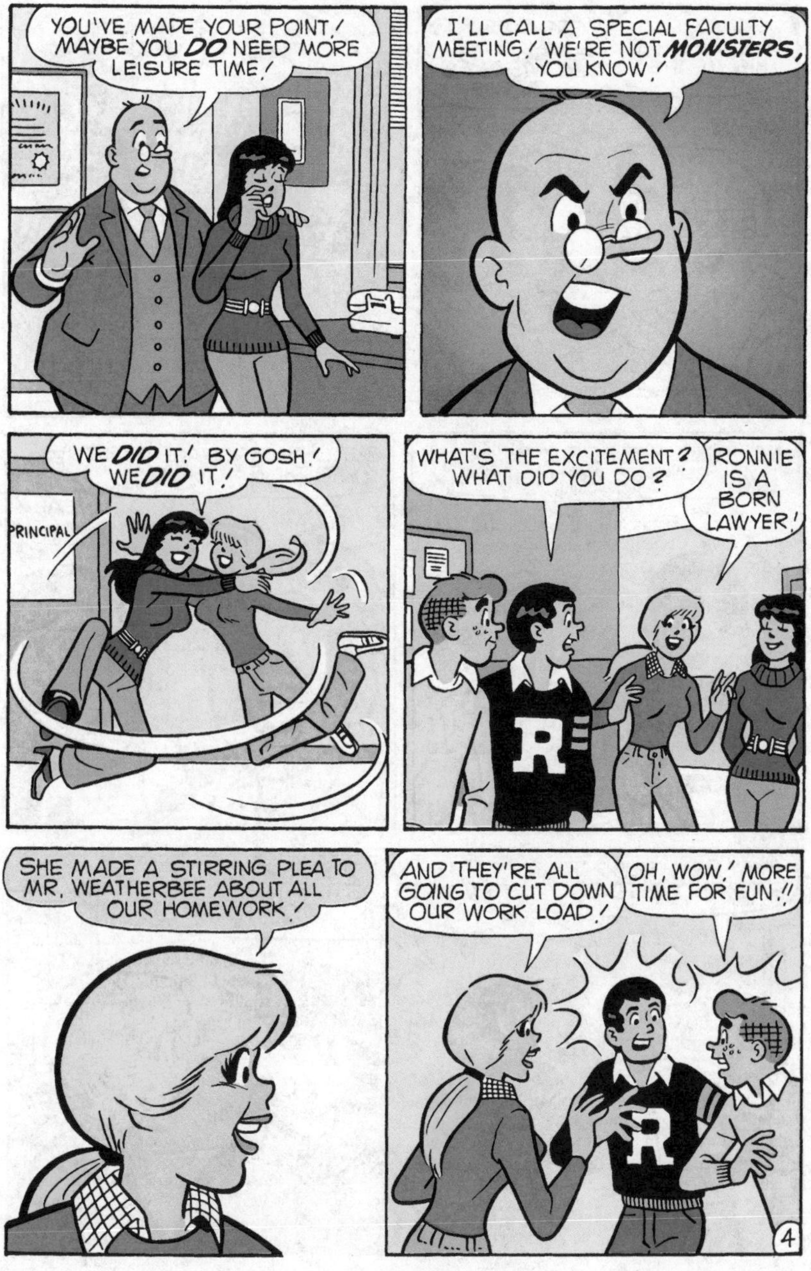
YOU'VE MADE YOUR POINT! MAYBE YOU DO NEED MORE LEISURE TIME!
I'LL CALL A SPECIAL FACULTY MEETING! WE'RE NOT MONSTERS, YOU KNOW!
WE DID IT! BY GOSH! WE DID IT!
PRINCIPAL
WHAT'S THE EXCITEMENT? WHAT DID YOU DO?
RONNIE IS A BORN LAWYER!
SHE MADE A STIRRING PLEA TO MR. WEATHERBEE ABOUT ALL OUR HOMEWORK!
AND THEY'RE ALL GOING TO CUT DOWN OUR WORK LOAD!
OH, WOW! MORE TIME FOR FUN!!
4

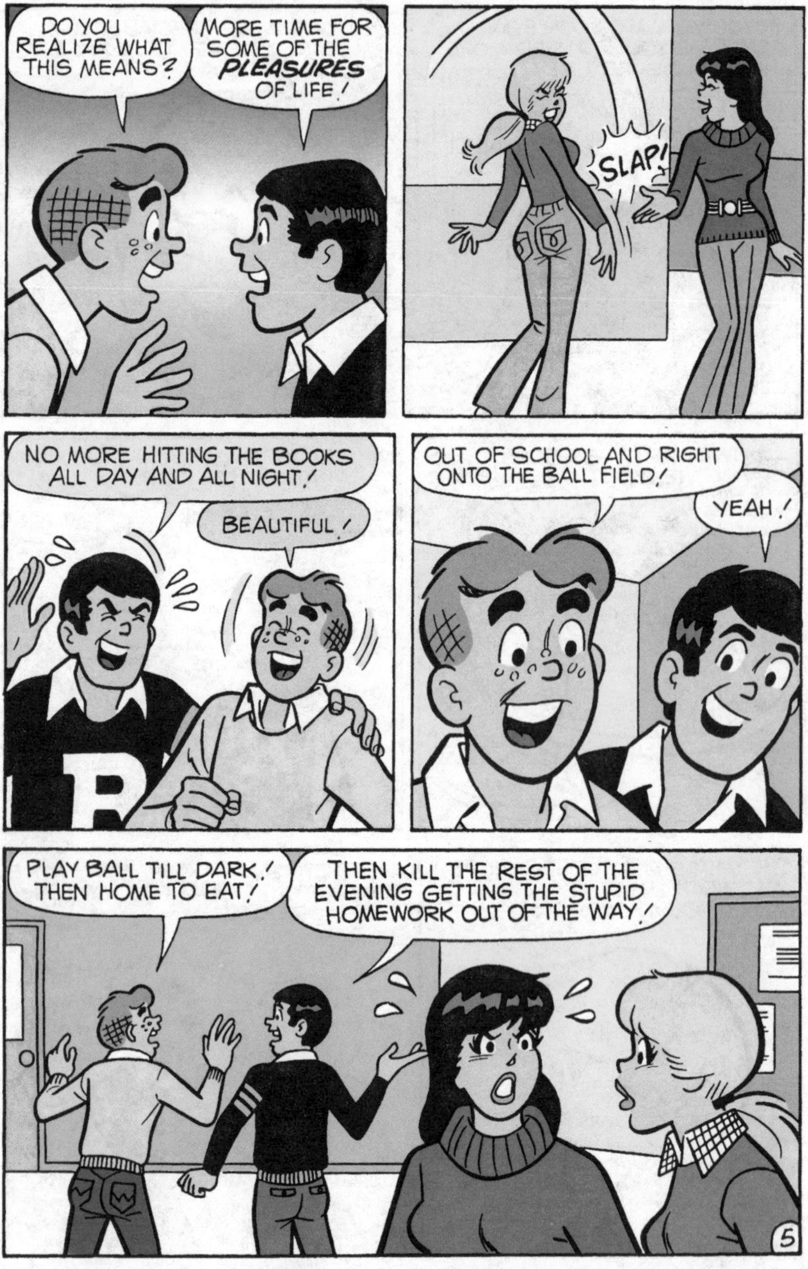
DO YOU REALIZE WHAT THIS MEANS?
MORE TIME FOR SOME OF THE PLEASURES OF LIFE!
SLAP!
NO MORE HITTING THE BOOKS ALL DAY AND ALL NIGHT!
BEAUTIFUL!
OUT OF SCHOOL AND RIGHT ONTO THE BALL FIELD!
YEAH!
PLAY BALL TILL DARK! THEN HOME TO EAT!
THEN KILL THE REST OF THE EVENING GETTING THE STUPID HOMEWORK OUT OF THE WAY!
5

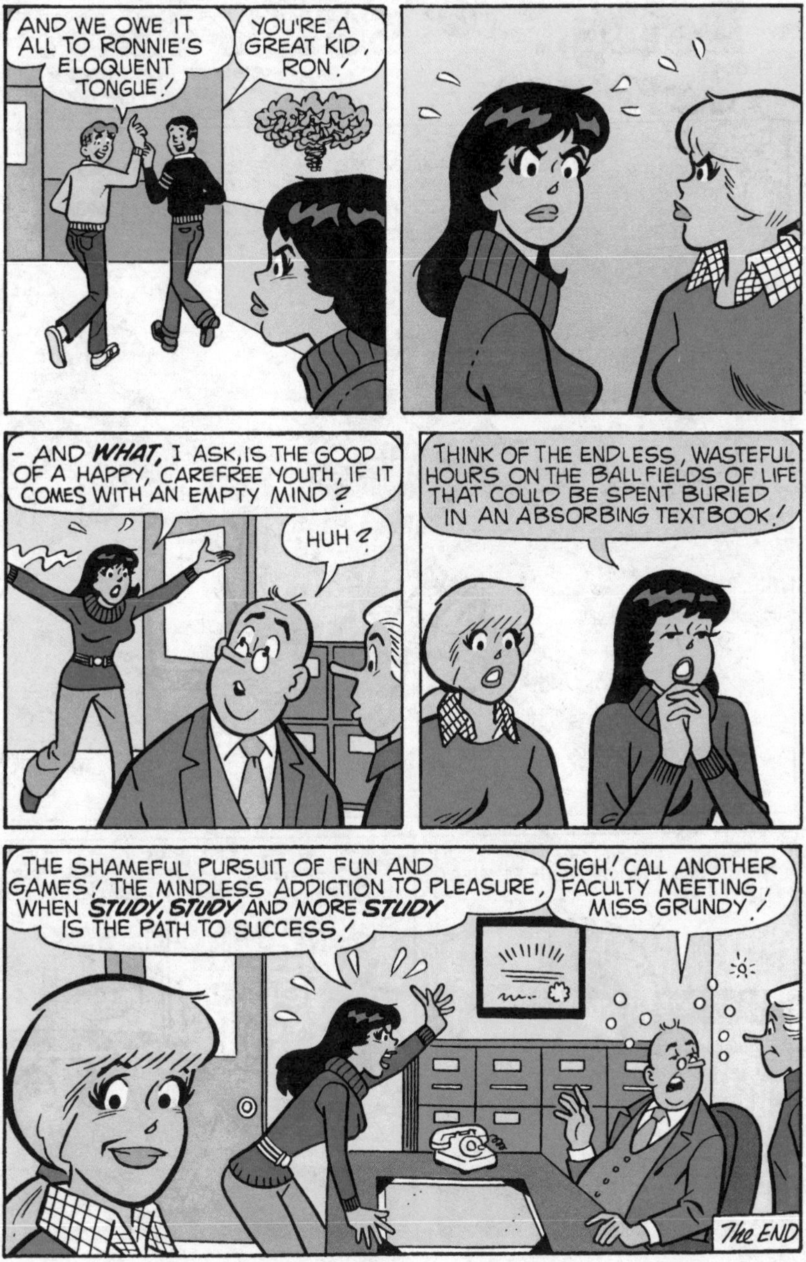
AND WE OWE IT ALL TO RONNIE'S ELOQUENT TONGUE!
YOU'RE A GREAT KID, RON!
- AND WHAT, I ASK, IS THE GOOD OF A HAPPY, CAREFREE YOUTH, IF IT COMES WITH AN EMPTY MIND?
HUH?
THINK OF THE ENDLESS, WASTEFUL HOURS ON THE BALLFIELDS OF LIFE THAT COULD BE SPENT BURIED IN AN ABSORBING TEXTBOOK!
THE SHAMEFUL PURSUIT OF FUN AND GAMES! THE MINDLESS ADDICTION TO PLEASURE, WHEN STUDY, STUDY AND MORE STUDY IS THE PATH TO SUCCESS!
SIGH! CALL ANOTHER FACULTY MEETING, MISS GRUNDY!
The END

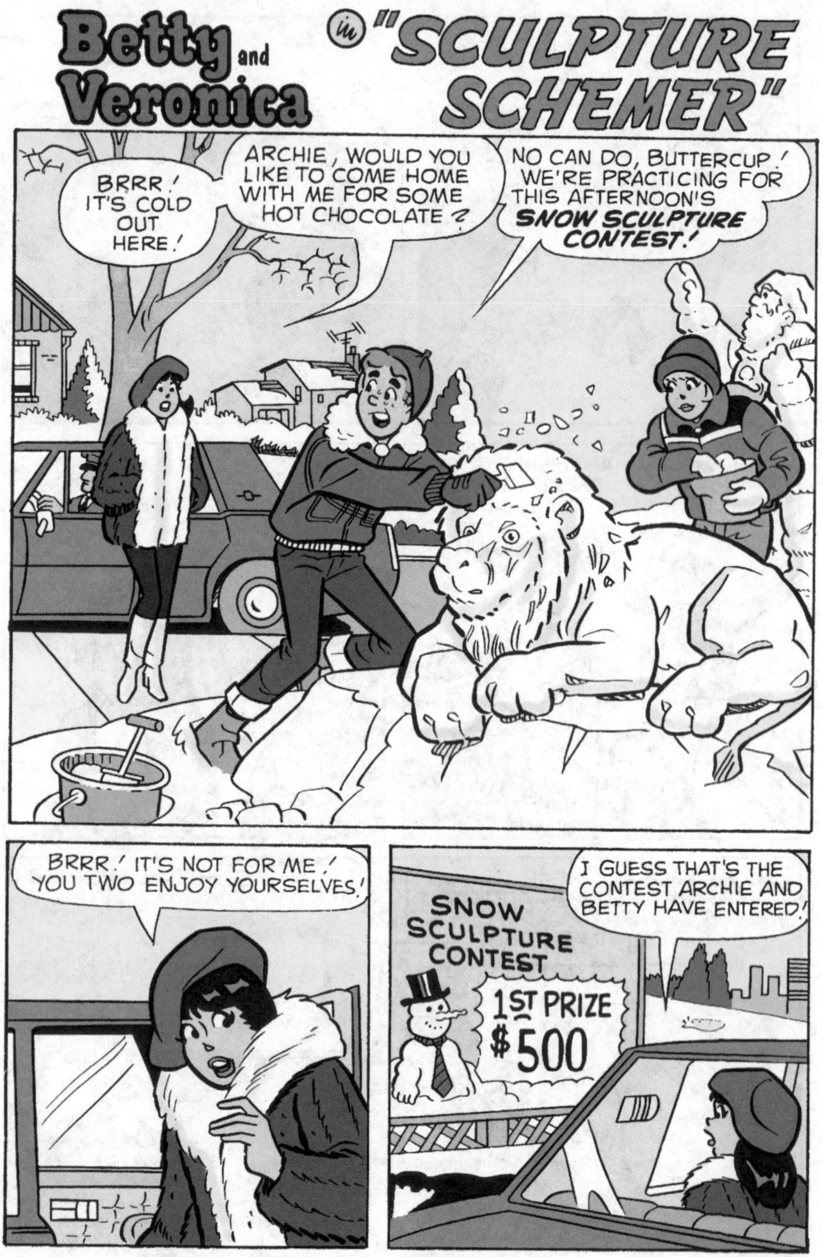
Betty and Veronica
in "SCULPTURE SCHEMER"
BRRR! IT'S COLD OUT HERE!
ARCHIE, WOULD YOU LIKE TO COME HOME WITH ME FOR SOME HOT CHOCOLATE?
NO CAN DO, BUTTERCUP! WE'RE PRACTICING FOR THIS AFTERNOON'S SNOW SCULPTURE CONTEST!
BRRR! IT'S NOT FOR ME! YOU TWO ENJOY YOURSELVES!
SNOW SCULPTURE CONTEST
1ST PRIZE $500
I GUESS THAT'S THE CONTEST ARCHIE AND BETTY HAVE ENTERED!

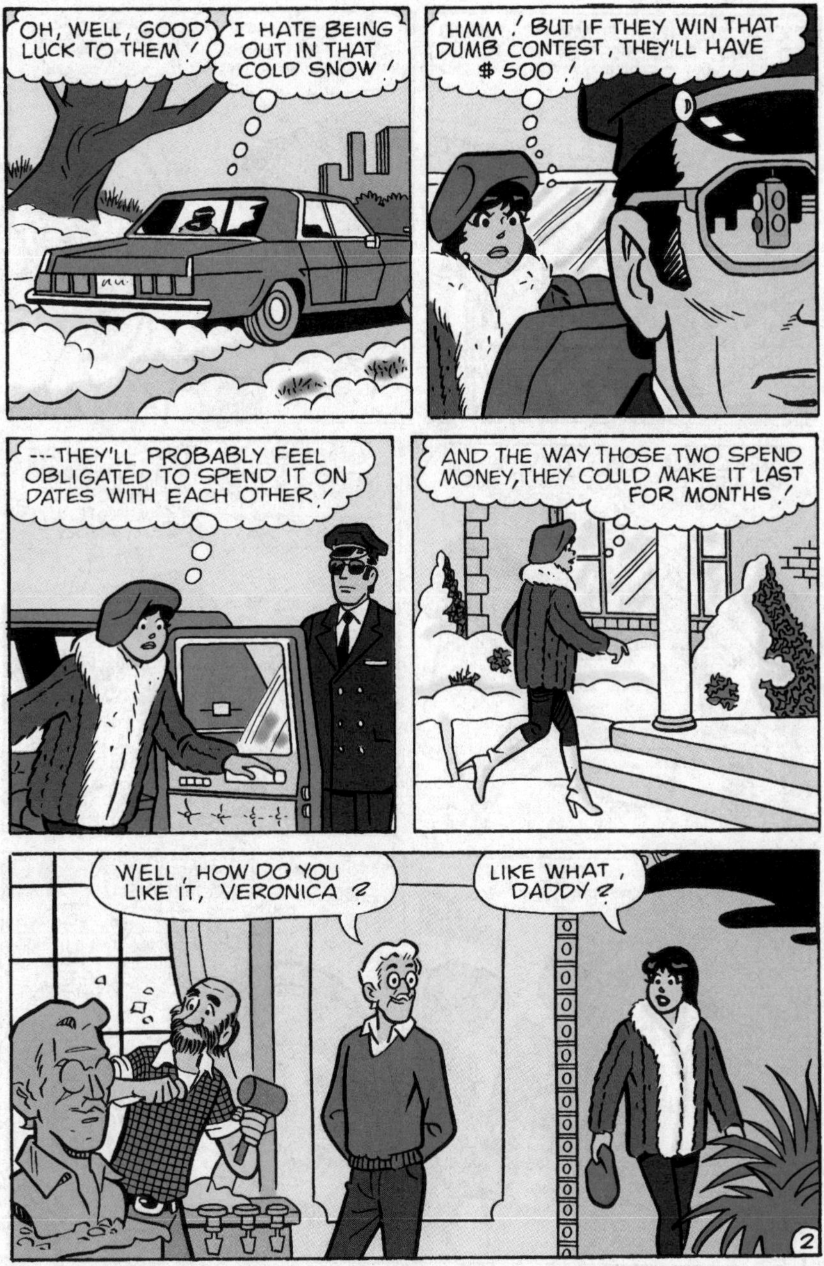
OH, WELL, GOOD LUCK TO THEM!
I HATE BEING OUT IN THAT COLD SNOW!
HMM! BUT IF THEY WIN THAT DUMB CONTEST, THEY'LL HAVE $500!
---THEY'LL PROBABLY FEEL OBLIGATED TO SPEND IT ON DATES WITH EACH OTHER!
AND THE WAY THOSE TWO SPEND MONEY, THEY COULD MAKE IT LAST FOR MONTHS!
WELL, HOW DO YOU LIKE IT, VERONICA?
LIKE WHAT, DADDY?
2

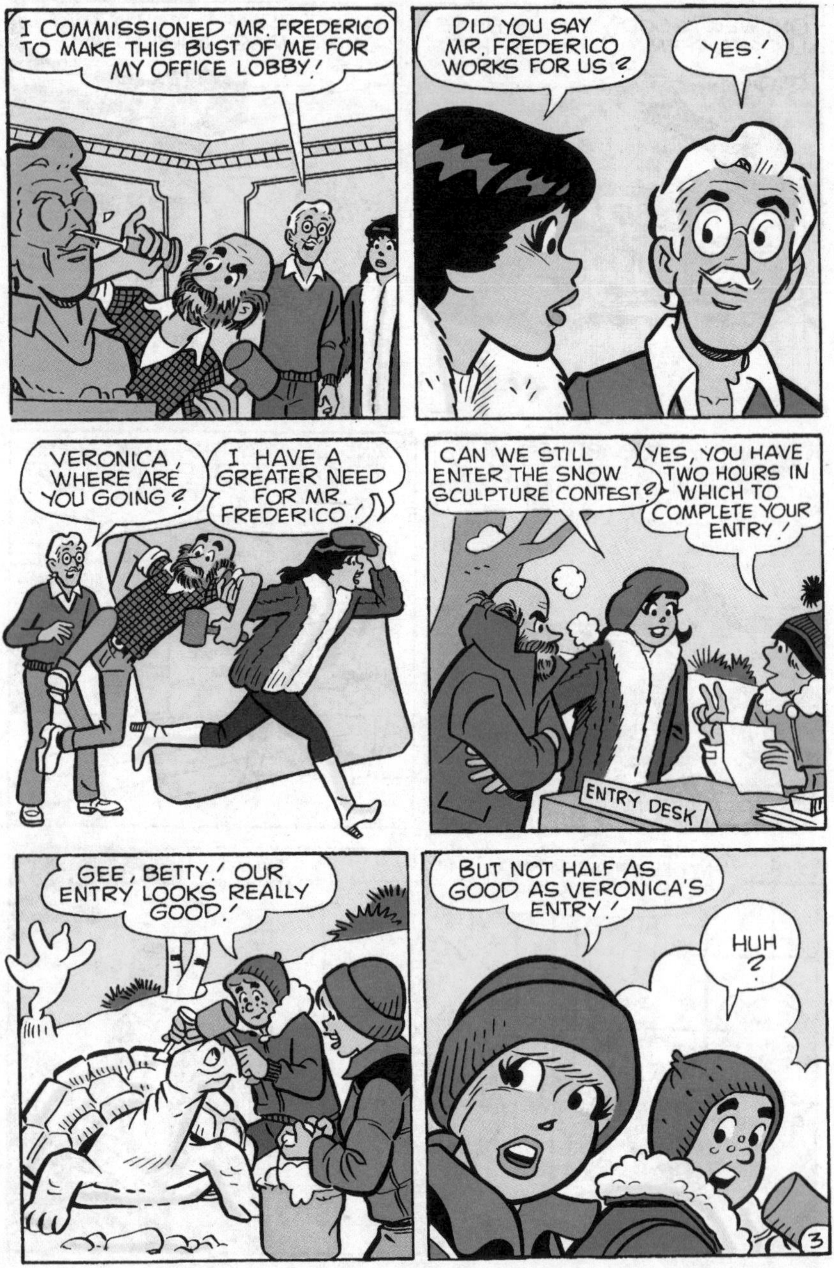
I COMMISSIONED MR. FREDERICO TO MAKE THIS BUST OF ME FOR MY OFFICE LOBBY!
DID YOU SAY MR. FREDERICO WORKS FOR US?
YES!
VERONICA, WHERE ARE YOU GOING?
I HAVE A GREATER NEED FOR MR. FREDERICO!
CAN WE STILL ENTER THE SNOW SCULPTURE CONTEST?
YES, YOU HAVE TWO HOURS IN WHICH TO COMPLETE YOUR ENTRY!
ENTRY DESK
GEE, BETTY! OUR ENTRY LOOKS REALLY GOOD!
BUT NOT HALF AS GOOD AS VERONICA'S ENTRY!
HUH?
3

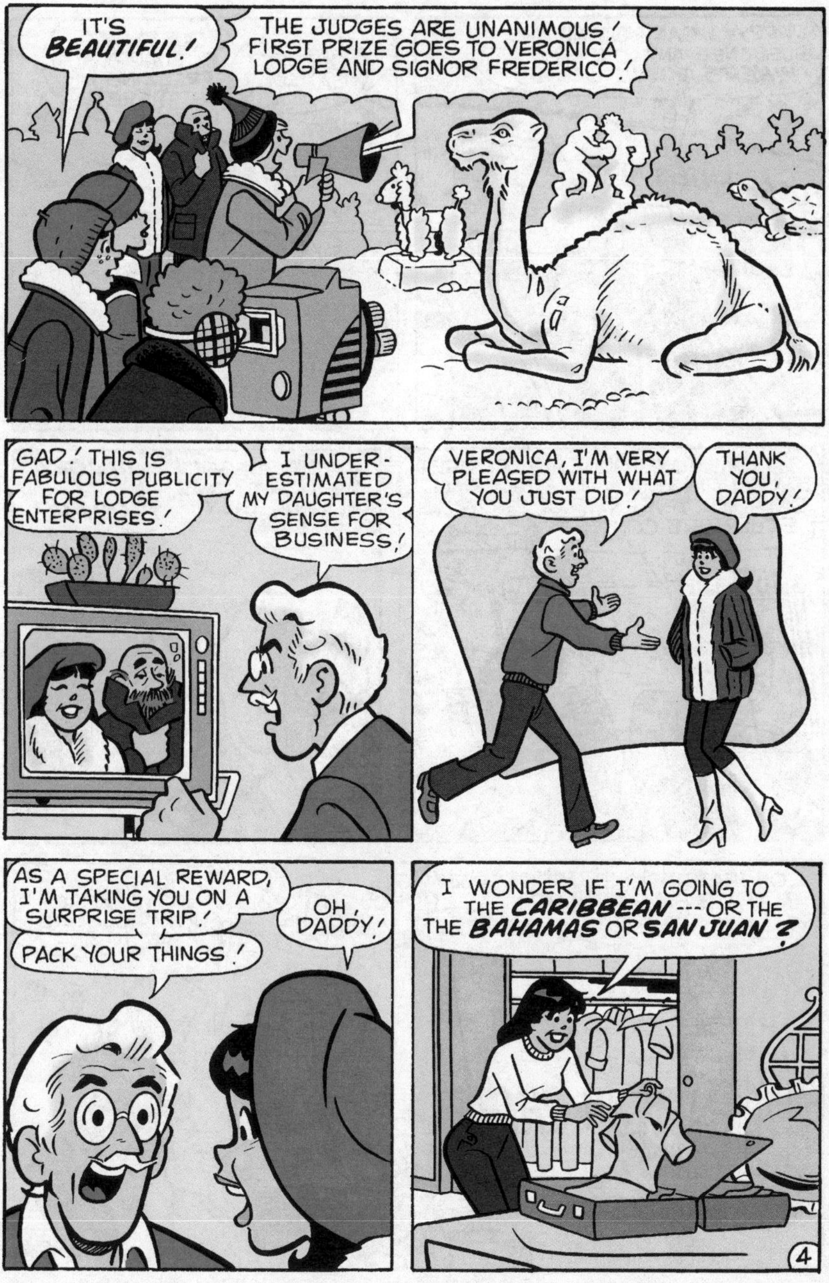
IT'S BEAUTIFUL!
THE JUDGES ARE UNANIMOUS! FIRST PRIZE GOES TO VERONICA LODGE AND SIGNOR FREDERICO!
GAD! THIS IS FABULOUS PUBLICITY FOR LODGE ENTERPRISES!
I UNDER-ESTIMATED MY DAUGHTER'S SENSE FOR BUSINESS!
VERONICA, I'M VERY PLEASED WITH WHAT YOU JUST DID!
THANK YOU, DADDY!
AS A SPECIAL REWARD, I'M TAKING YOU ON A SURPRISE TRIP!
PACK YOUR THINGS!
OH, DADDY!
I WONDER IF I'M GOING TO THE CARIBBEAN --- OR THE THE BAHAMAS OR SAN JUAN?
4

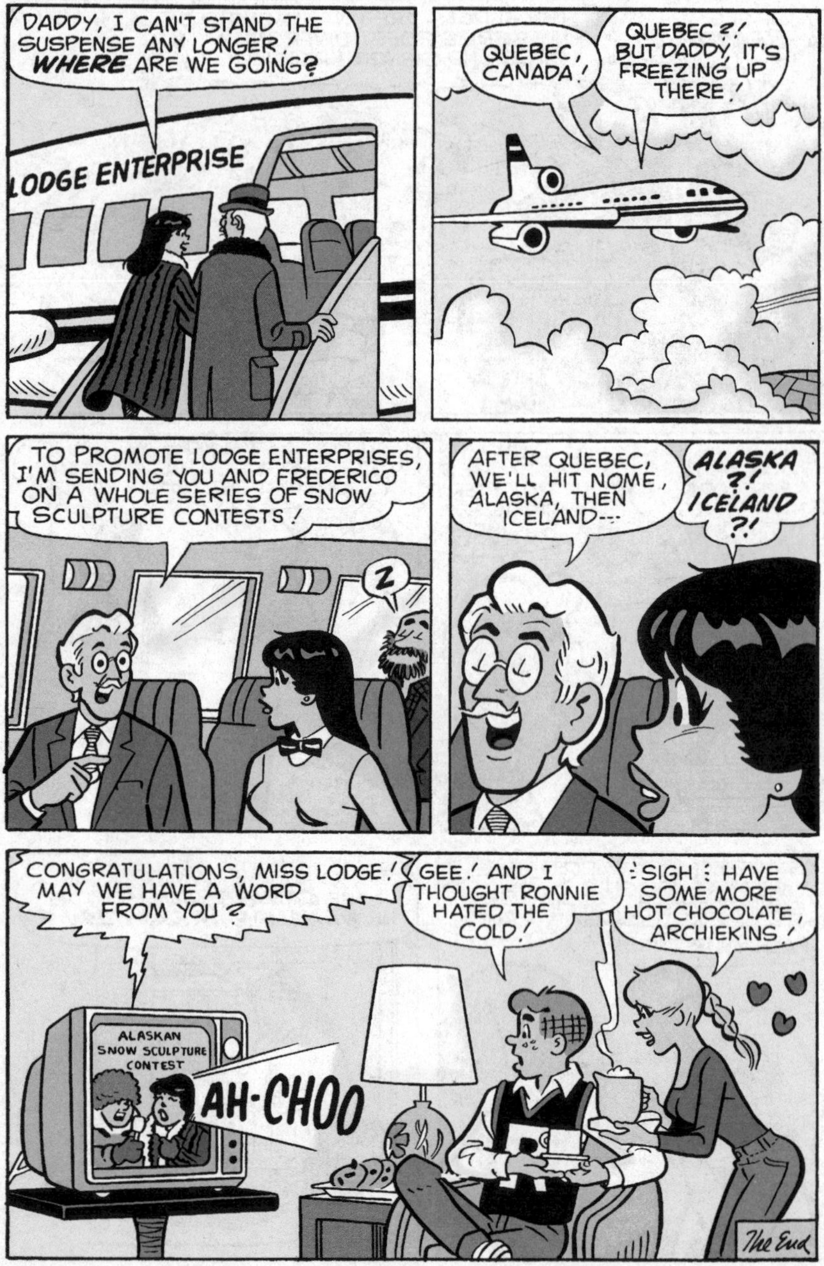
DADDY, I CAN'T STAND THE SUSPENSE ANY LONGER! WHERE ARE WE GOING?
LODGE ENTERPRISE
QUEBEC, CANADA!
QUEBEC?! BUT DADDY, IT'S FREEZING UP THERE!
TO PROMOTE LODGE ENTERPRISES, I'M SENDING YOU AND FREDERICO ON A WHOLE SERIES OF SNOW SCULPTURE CONTESTS!
Z
AFTER QUEBEC, WE'LL HIT NOME, ALASKA, THEN ICELAND---
ALASKA?! ICELAND?!
CONGRATULATIONS, MISS LODGE! MAY WE HAVE A WORD FROM YOU?
ALASKAN SNOW SCULPTURE CONTEST
AH-CHOO
GEE! AND I THOUGHT RONNIE HATED THE COLD!
SIGH HAVE SOME MORE HOT CHOCOLATE, ARCHIEKINS!
The End

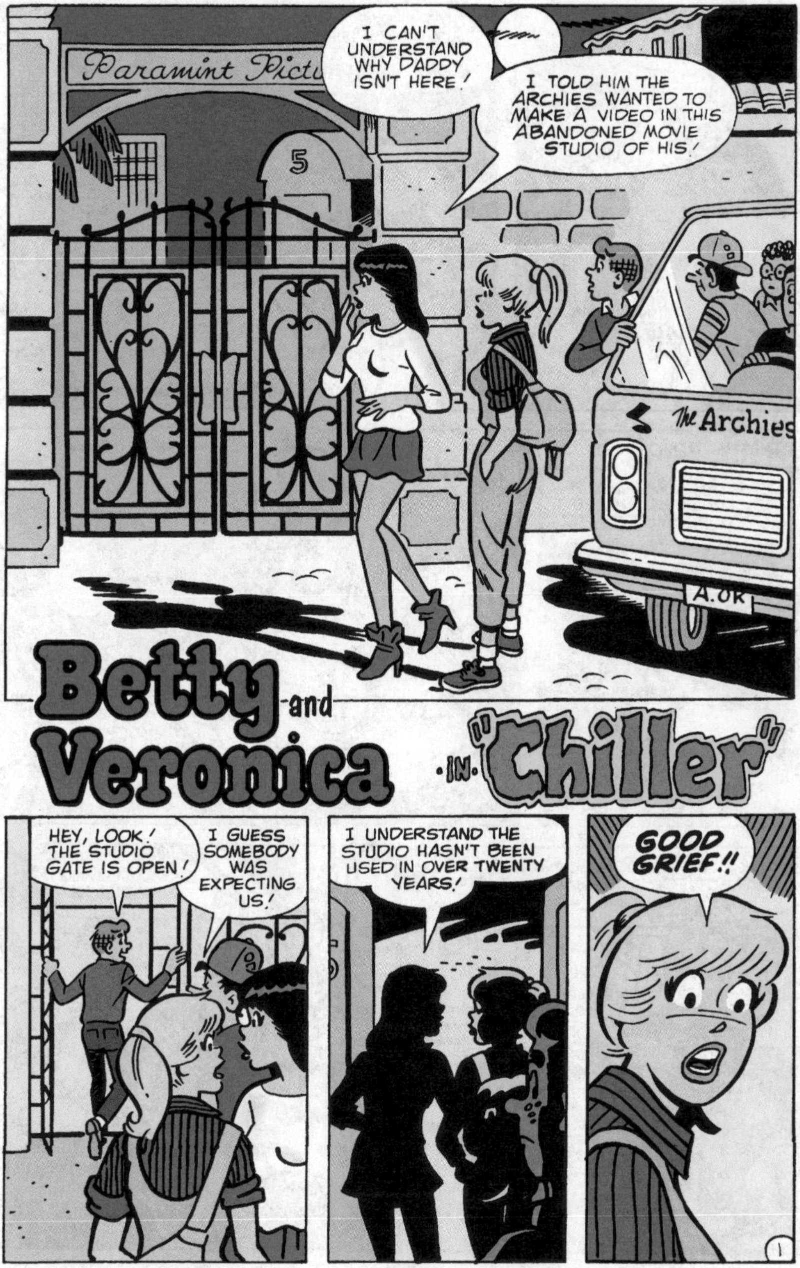

Paramint Pictu
5
I CAN'T UNDERSTAND WHY DADDY ISN'T HERE!
I TOLD HIM THE ARCHIES WANTED TO MAKE A VIDEO IN THIS ABANDONED MOVIE STUDIO OF HIS!
The Archies
A.OK
Betty and Veronica in "Chiller"
HEY, LOOK! THE STUDIO GATE IS OPEN!
I GUESS SOMEBODY WAS EXPECTING US!
I UNDERSTAND THE STUDIO HASN'T BEEN USED IN OVER TWENTY YEARS!
GOOD GRIEF!!
1

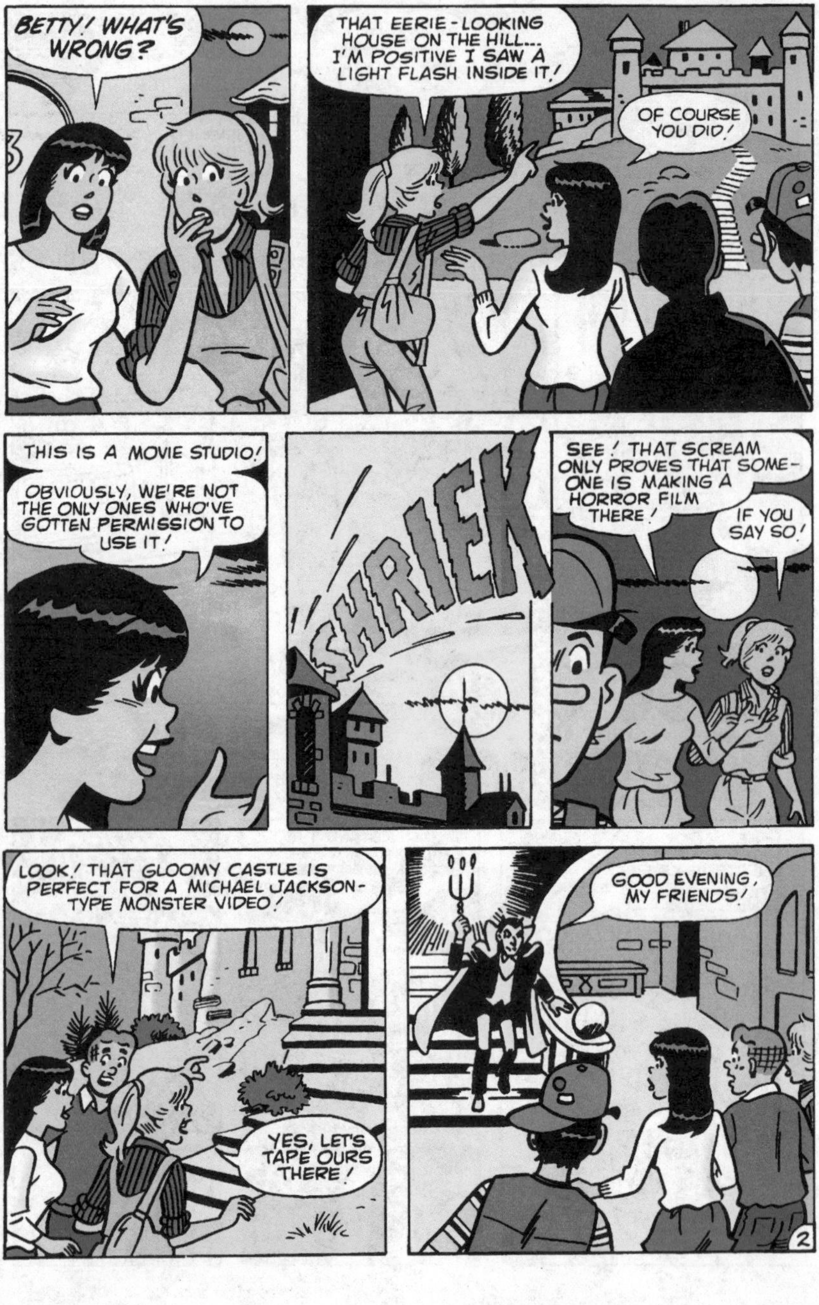

BETTY! WHAT'S WRONG?
THAT EERIE-LOOKING HOUSE ON THE HILL... I'M POSITIVE I SAW A LIGHT FLASH INSIDE IT!
OF COURSE YOU DID!
THIS IS A MOVIE STUDIO!
OBVIOUSLY, WE'RE NOT THE ONLY ONES WHO'VE GOTTEN PERMISSION TO USE IT!
SHRIEK
SEE! THAT SCREAM ONLY PROVES THAT SOME-ONE IS MAKING A HORROR FILM THERE!
IF YOU SAY SO!
LOOK! THAT GLOOMY CASTLE IS PERFECT FOR A MICHAEL JACKSON-TYPE MONSTER VIDEO!
YES, LET'S TAPE OURS THERE!
GOOD EVENING, MY FRIENDS!
2

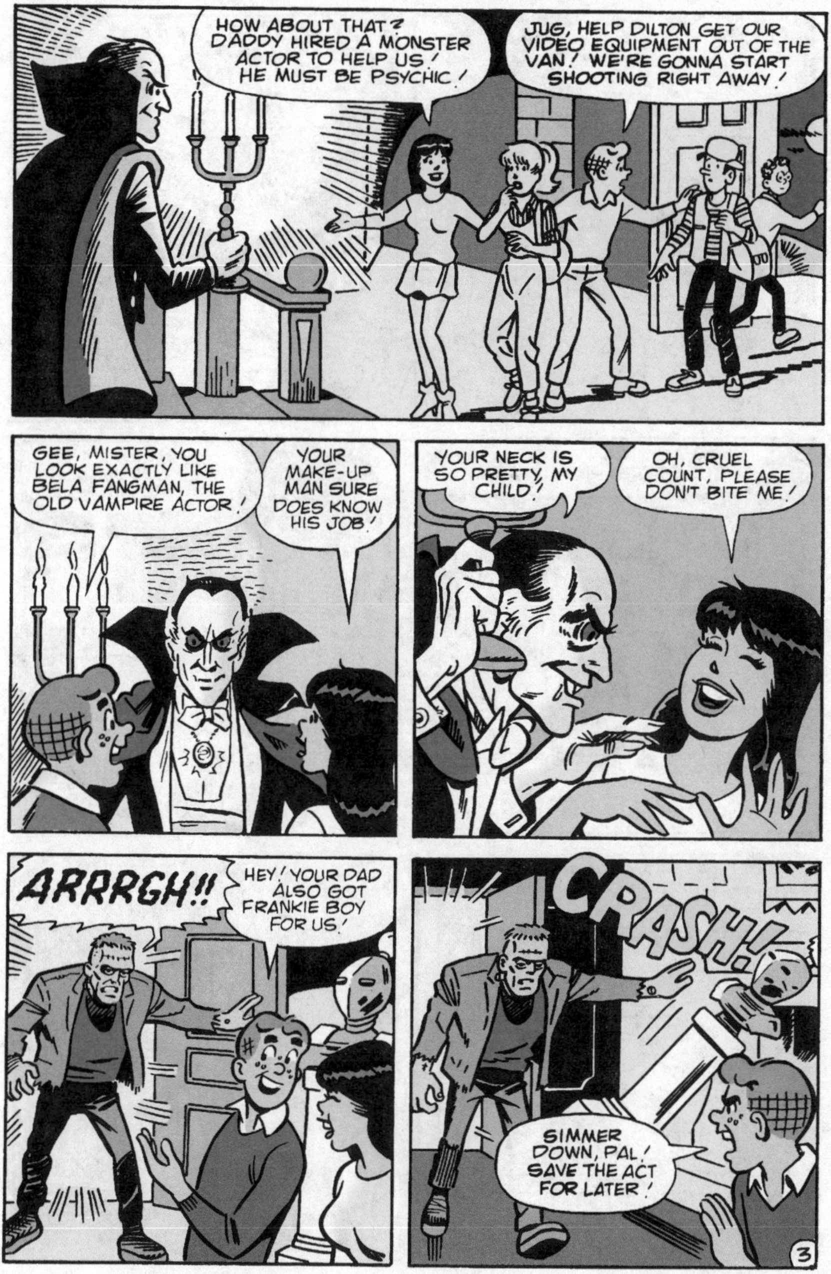
HOW ABOUT THAT? DADDY HIRED A MONSTER ACTOR TO HELP US! HE MUST BE PSYCHIC!
JUG, HELP DILTON GET OUR VIDEO EQUIPMENT OUT OF THE VAN! WE'RE GONNA START SHOOTING RIGHT AWAY!
GEE, MISTER, YOU LOOK EXACTLY LIKE BELA FANGMAN, THE OLD VAMPIRE ACTOR!
YOUR MAKE-UP MAN SURE DOES KNOW HIS JOB!
YOUR NECK IS SO PRETTY, MY CHILD!
OH, CRUEL COUNT, PLEASE DON'T BITE ME!
ARRRGH!!
HEY! YOUR DAD ALSO GOT FRANKIE BOY FOR US!
CRASH!
SIMMER DOWN, PAL! SAVE THE ACT FOR LATER!
3

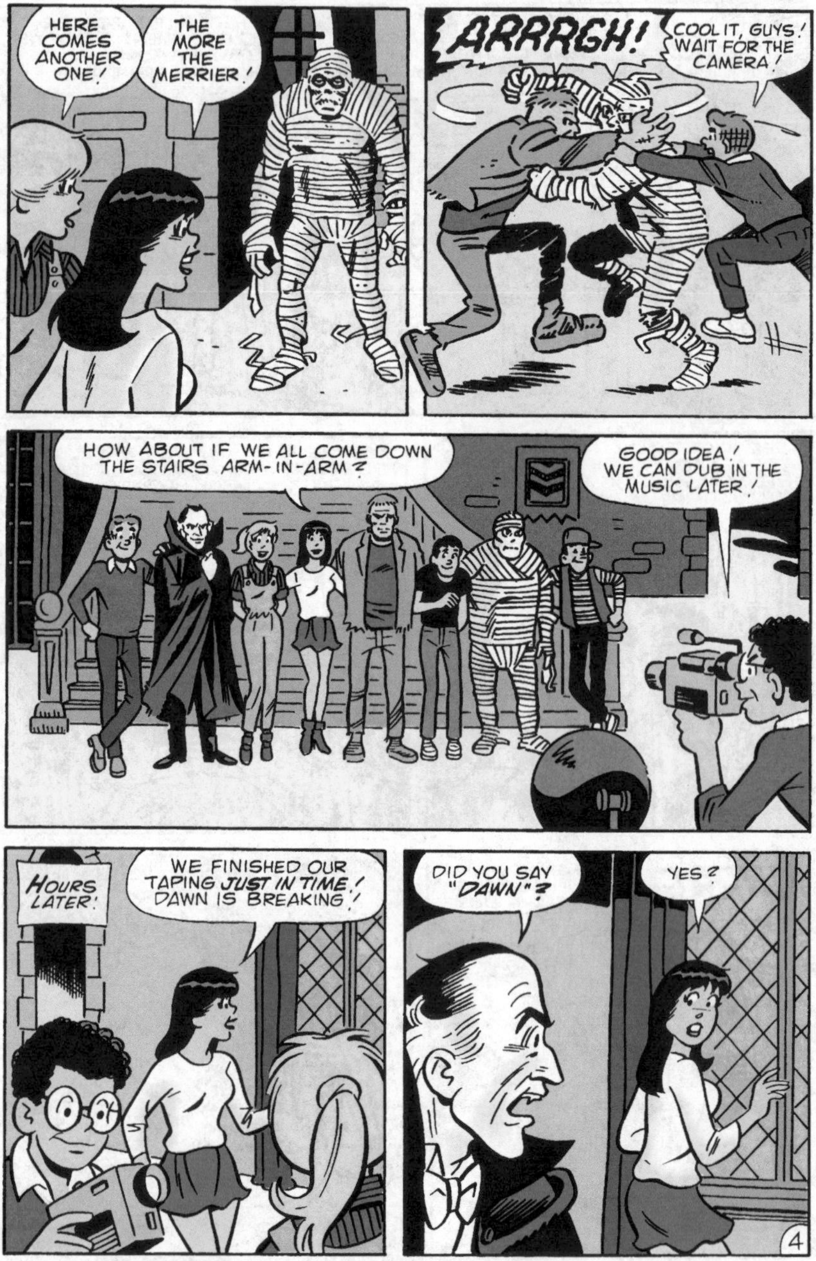
HERE COMES ANOTHER ONE!
THE MORE THE MERRIER!
ARRRGH!
COOL IT, GUYS! WAIT FOR THE CAMERA!
HOW ABOUT IF WE ALL COME DOWN THE STAIRS ARM-IN-ARM?
GOOD IDEA! WE CAN DUB IN THE MUSIC LATER!
HOURS LATER.
WE FINISHED OUR TAPING JUST IN TIME! DAWN IS BREAKING!
DID YOU SAY "DAWN"?
YES?
4

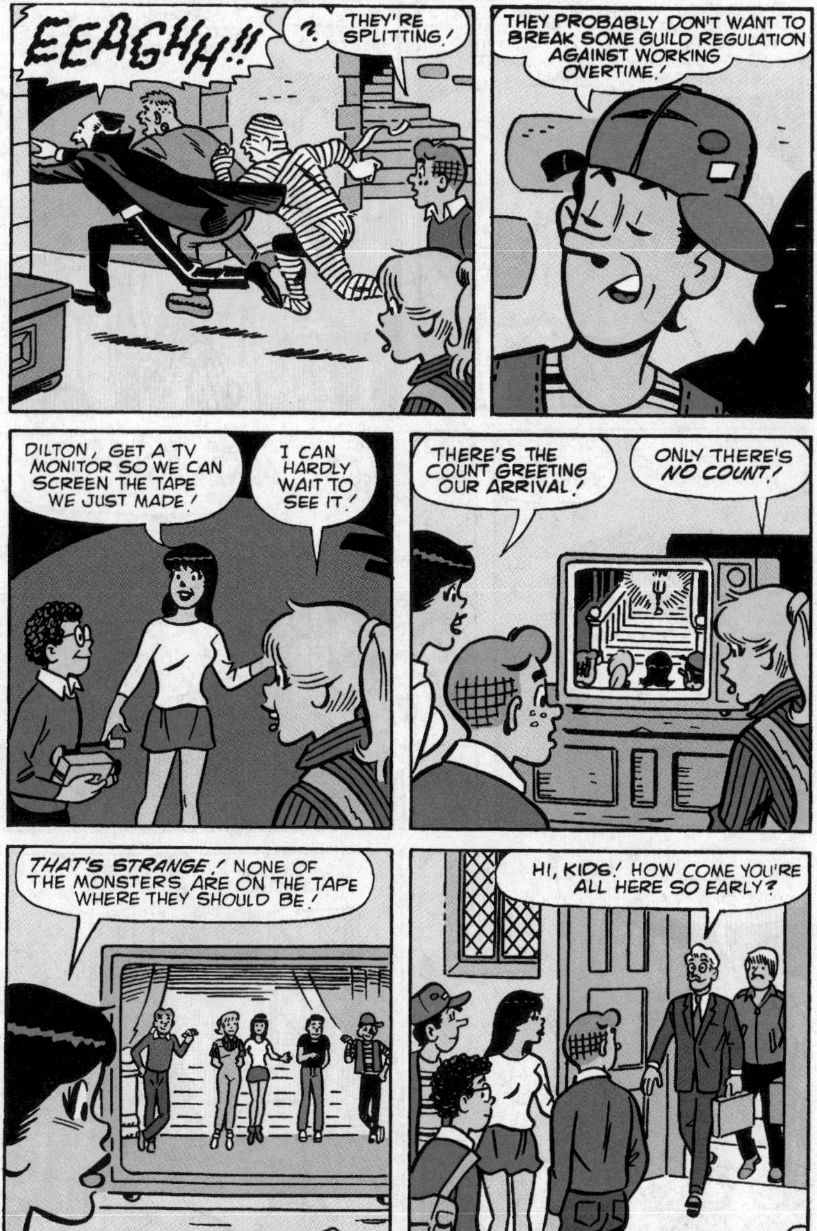
EEAGHH!!
? THEY'RE SPLITTING!
THEY PROBABLY DON'T WANT TO BREAK SOME GUILD REGULATION AGAINST WORKING OVERTIME!
DILTON, GET A TV MONITOR SO WE CAN SCREEN THE TAPE WE JUST MADE!
I CAN HARDLY WAIT TO SEE IT!
THERE'S THE COUNT GREETING OUR ARRIVAL!
ONLY THERE'S NO COUNT!
THAT'S STRANGE! NONE OF THE MONSTERS ARE ON THE TAPE WHERE THEY SHOULD BE!
HI, KIDS! HOW COME YOU'RE ALL HERE SO EARLY?
5

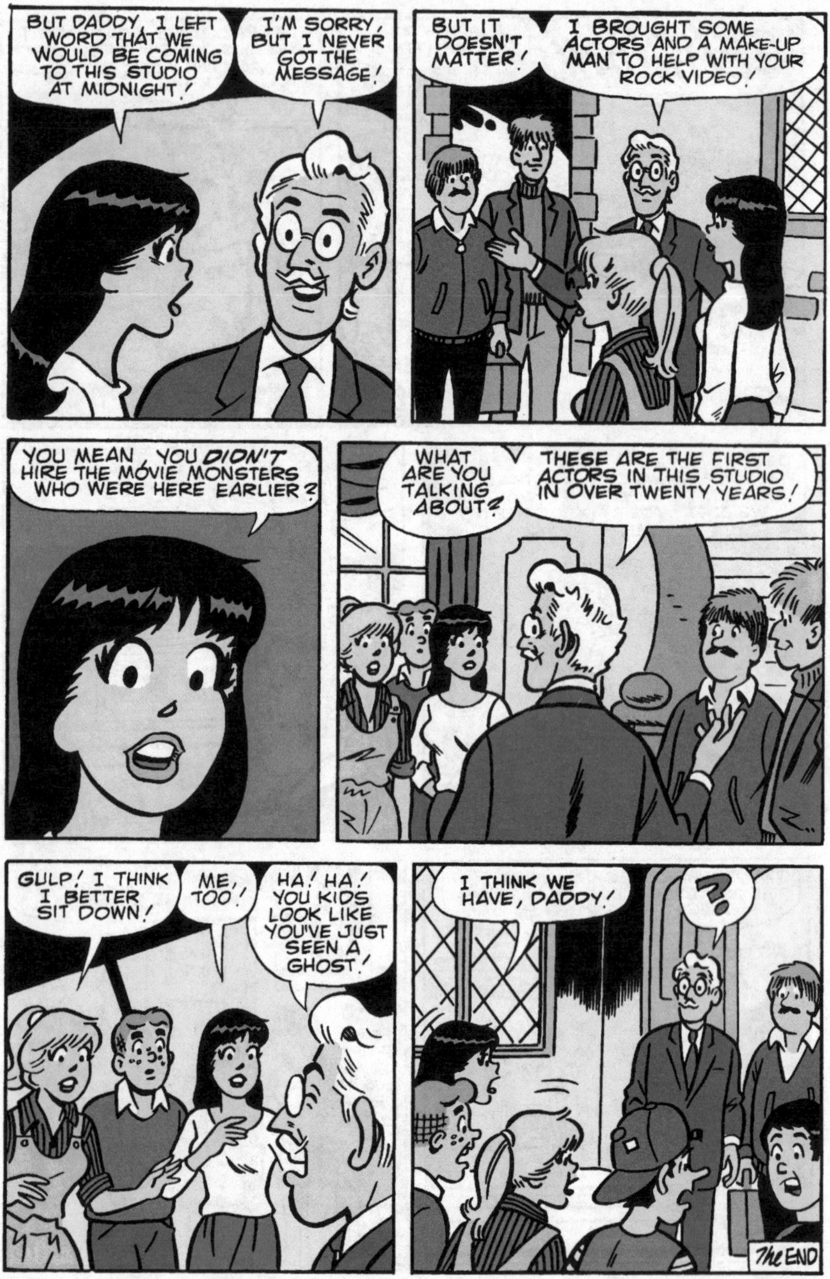
BUT DADDY, I LEFT WORD THAT WE WOULD BE COMING TO THIS STUDIO AT MIDNIGHT!
I'M SORRY, BUT I NEVER GOT THE MESSAGE!
BUT IT DOESN'T MATTER!
I BROUGHT SOME ACTORS AND A MAKE-UP MAN TO HELP WITH YOUR ROCK VIDEO!
YOU MEAN, YOU DIDN'T HIRE THE MOVIE MONSTERS WHO WERE HERE EARLIER?
WHAT ARE YOU TALKING ABOUT?
THESE ARE THE FIRST ACTORS IN THIS STUDIO IN OVER TWENTY YEARS!
GULP! I THINK I BETTER SIT DOWN!
ME, TOO!
HA! HA! YOU KIDS LOOK LIKE YOU'VE JUST SEEN A GHOST!
I THINK WE HAVE, DADDY!
?
The END

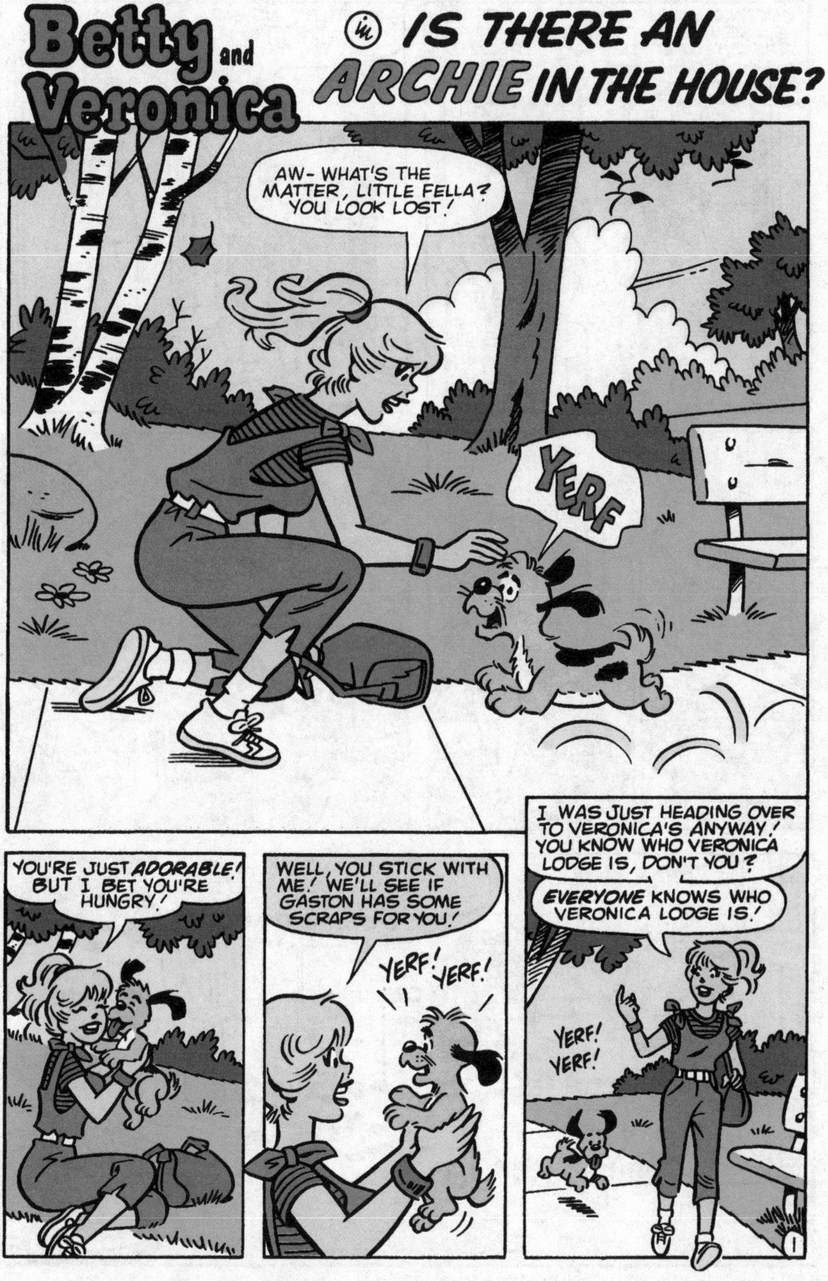
Betty and Veronica
IS THERE AN ARCHIE IN THE HOUSE?
AW- WHAT'S THE MATTER, LITTLE FELLA? YOU LOOK LOST!
YERF
YOU'RE JUST ADORABLE! BUT I BET YOU'RE HUNGRY!
WELL, YOU STICK WITH ME! WE'LL SEE IF GASTON HAS SOME SCRAPS FOR YOU!
YERF! YERF!
I WAS JUST HEADING OVER TO VERONICA'S ANYWAY! YOU KNOW WHO VERONICA LODGE IS, DON'T YOU?
EVERYONE KNOWS WHO VERONICA LODGE IS!
YERF! YERF!
1

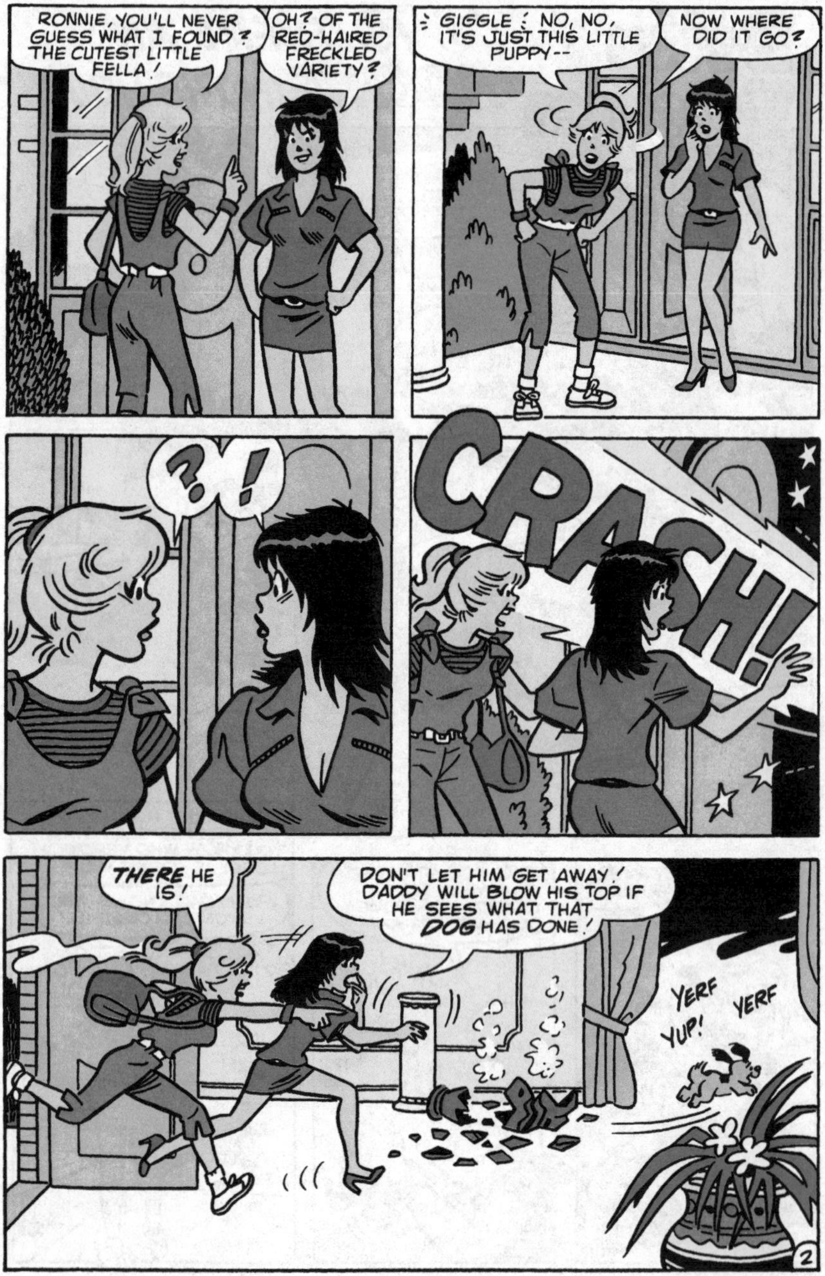
RONNIE, YOU'LL NEVER GUESS WHAT I FOUND ? THE CUTEST LITTLE FELLA !
OH? OF THE RED-HAIRED FRECKLED VARIETY ?
GIGGLE ! NO, NO, IT'S JUST THIS LITTLE PUPPY--
NOW WHERE DID IT GO ?
?
!
CRASH!
THERE HE IS !
DON'T LET HIM GET AWAY ! DADDY WILL BLOW HIS TOP IF HE SEES WHAT THAT DOG HAS DONE !
YERF
YUP!
YERF
2

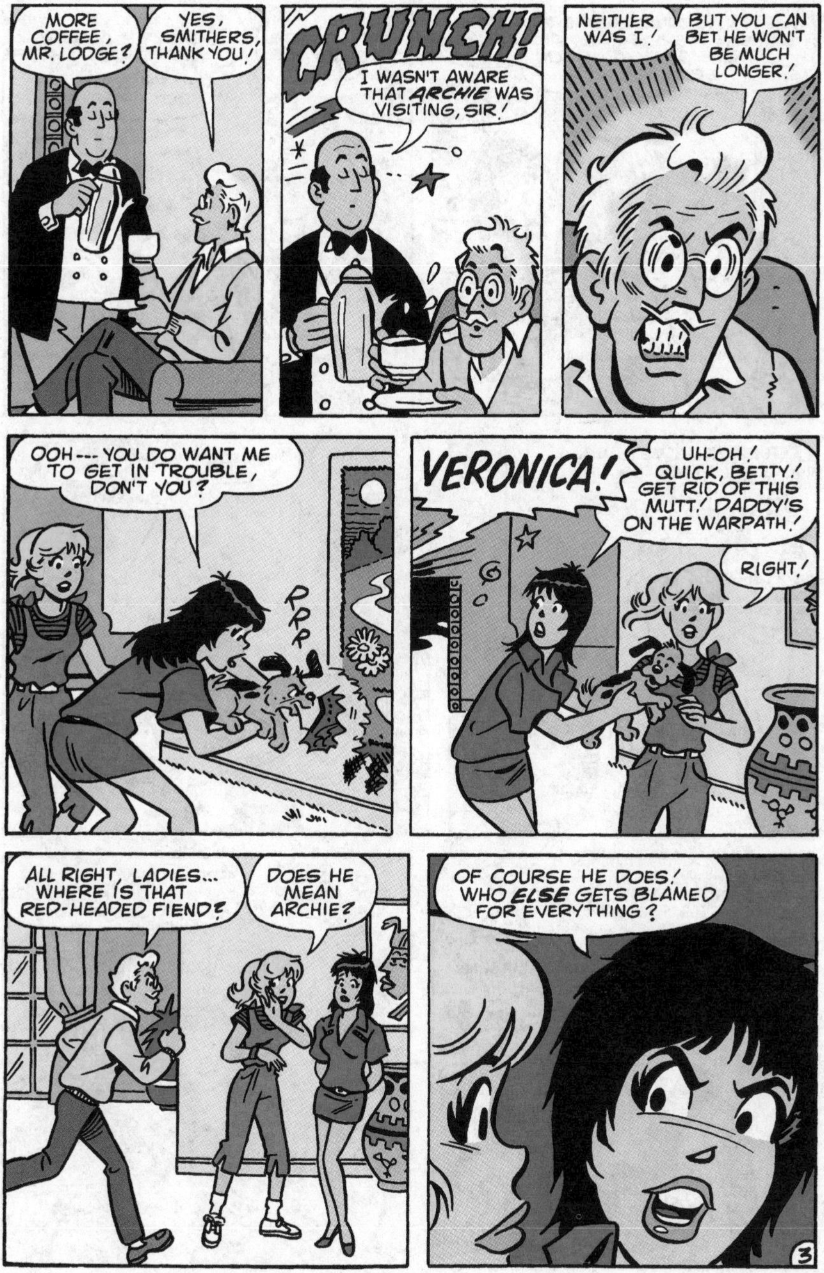
MORE COFFEE, MR. LODGE?
YES, SMITHERS, THANK YOU!
CRUNCH!
I WASN'T AWARE THAT ARCHIE WAS VISITING, SIR!
NEITHER WAS I!
BUT YOU CAN BET HE WON'T BE MUCH LONGER!
OOH--- YOU DO WANT ME TO GET IN TROUBLE, DON'T YOU?
RRR
VERONICA!
UH-OH! QUICK, BETTY! GET RID OF THIS MUTT! DADDY'S ON THE WARPATH!
RIGHT!
ALL RIGHT, LADIES... WHERE IS THAT RED-HEADED FIEND?
DOES HE MEAN ARCHIE?
OF COURSE HE DOES! WHO ELSE GETS BLAMED FOR EVERYTHING?
3

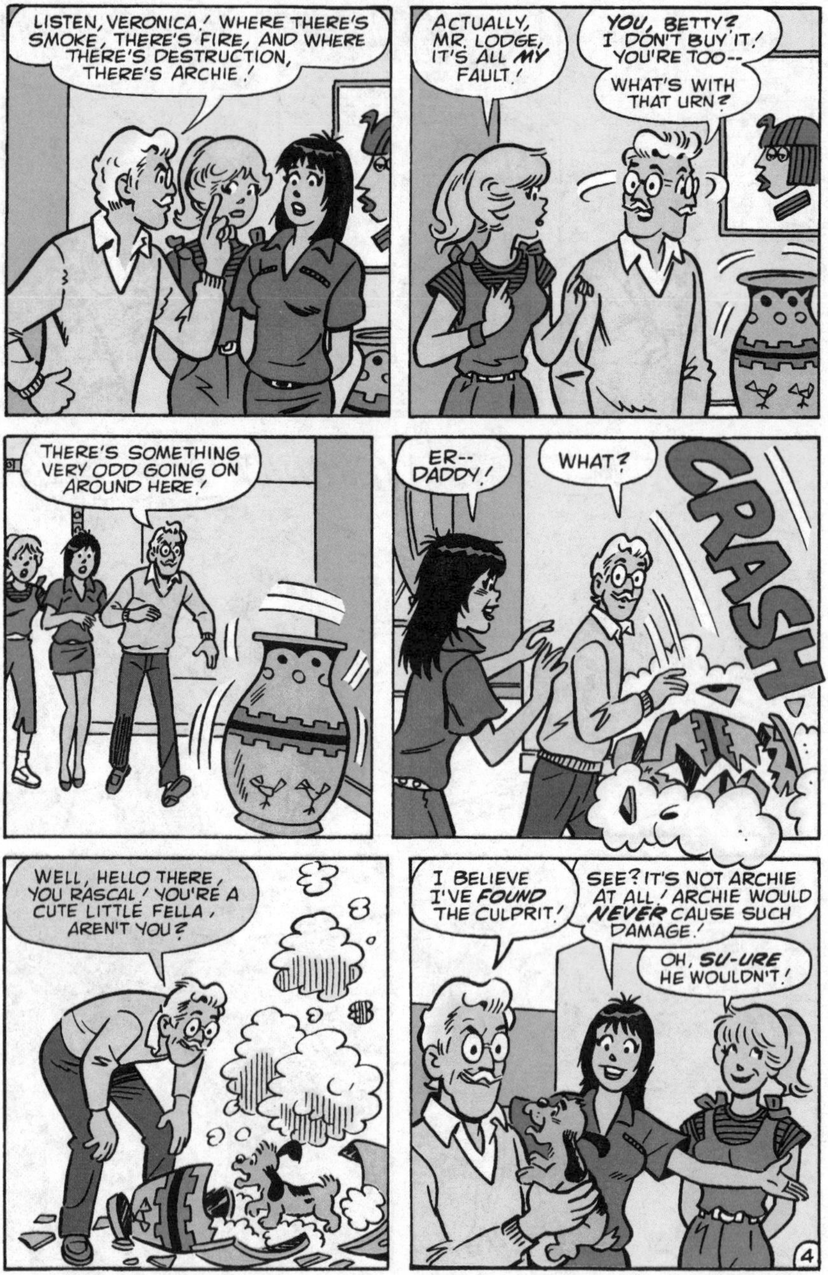
LISTEN, VERONICA! WHERE THERE'S SMOKE, THERE'S FIRE, AND WHERE THERE'S DESTRUCTION, THERE'S ARCHIE!
ACTUALLY, MR. LODGE, IT'S ALL MY FAULT!
YOU, BETTY? I DON'T BUY IT! YOU'RE TOO--
WHAT'S WITH THAT URN?
THERE'S SOMETHING VERY ODD GOING ON AROUND HERE!
ER-- DADDY!
WHAT?
CRASH
WELL, HELLO THERE, YOU RASCAL! YOU'RE A CUTE LITTLE FELLA, AREN'T YOU?
I BELIEVE I'VE FOUND THE CULPRIT!
SEE? IT'S NOT ARCHIE AT ALL! ARCHIE WOULD NEVER CAUSE SUCH DAMAGE!
OH, SU-URE HE WOULDN'T!
4

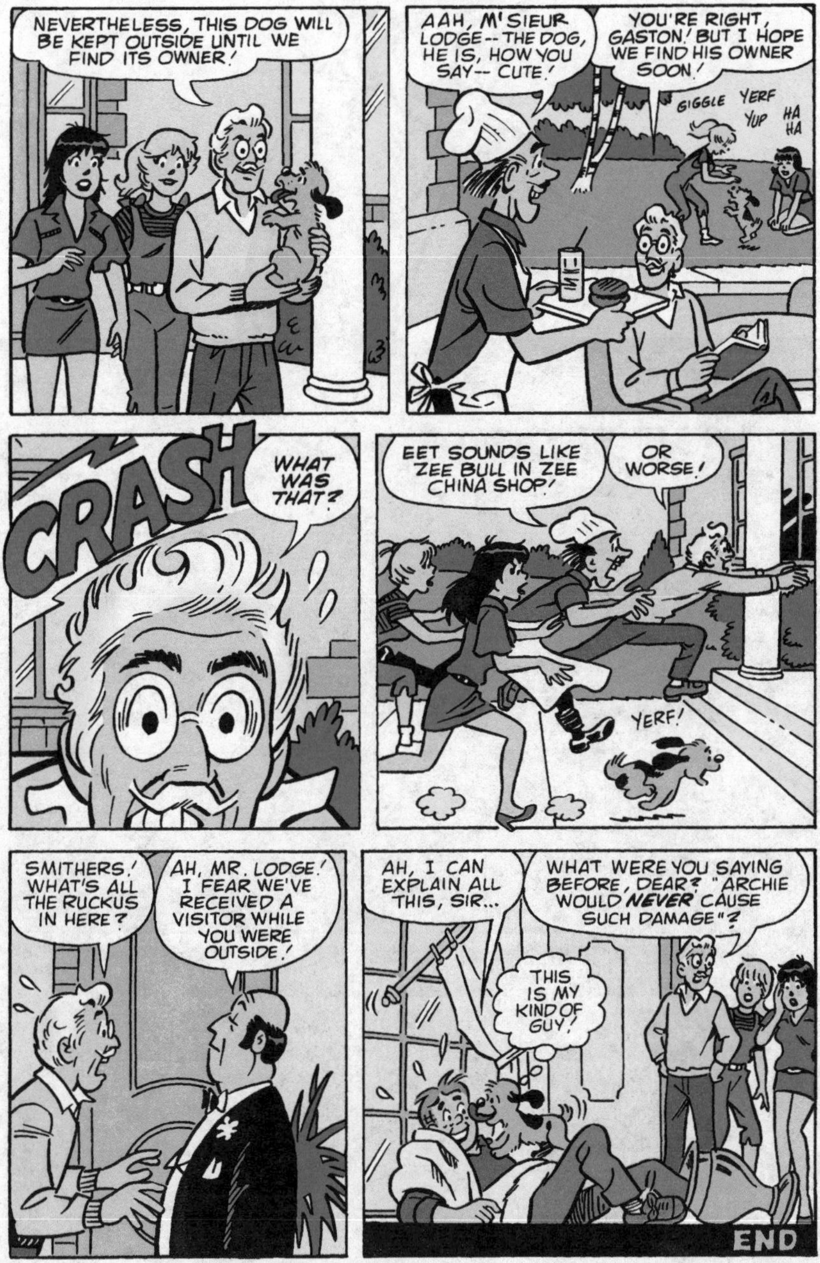
NEVERTHELESS, THIS DOG WILL BE KEPT OUTSIDE UNTIL WE FIND ITS OWNER!
AAH, M'SIEUR LODGE -- THE DOG, HE IS, HOW YOU SAY -- CUTE!
YOU'RE RIGHT, GASTON! BUT I HOPE WE FIND HIS OWNER SOON!
GIGGLE
YERF
YUP
HA HA
CRASH
WHAT WAS THAT?
EET SOUNDS LIKE ZEE BULL IN ZEE CHINA SHOP!
OR WORSE!
YERF!
SMITHERS! WHAT'S ALL THE RUCKUS IN HERE?
AH, MR. LODGE! I FEAR WE'VE RECEIVED A VISITOR WHILE YOU WERE OUTSIDE!
AH, I CAN EXPLAIN ALL THIS, SIR...
WHAT WERE YOU SAYING BEFORE, DEAR? "ARCHIE WOULD NEVER CAUSE SUCH DAMAGE"?
THIS IS MY KIND OF GUY!
END

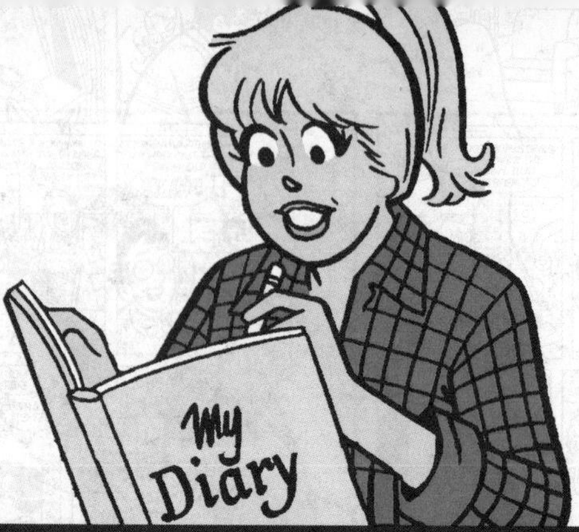
My
Diary

THE UNTOUCHABLE

BETTY & VERONICA #335, 1985

Frank Doyle, Dan DeCarlo, Jim DeCarlo, Bill Yoshida, Barry Grossman

THE ART LESSON

BETTY'S DIARY #1, 1986

Sam Kujava, Dan DeCarlo, Jim DeCarlo, Barry Grossman, Bill Yoshida

RIGHT FOR THE PART

BETTY & VERONICA VOL. 2 #1, 1987

Frank Doyle, Dan DeCarlo, Jim DeCarlo

The most interesting stories to me as a kid and now were not the heart-pounding will-Archie-or-won't-he but when B&V adventured out together or solo. They represent sisterly love across class and background. They can't be stopped! Watching B&V evolve is a joy, working on some of the Archie books as a colorist and cover artist, a pleasure. Here's to 80+ more years of their friendship!

- JEN VAUGHN *Artist, Archie Comics*

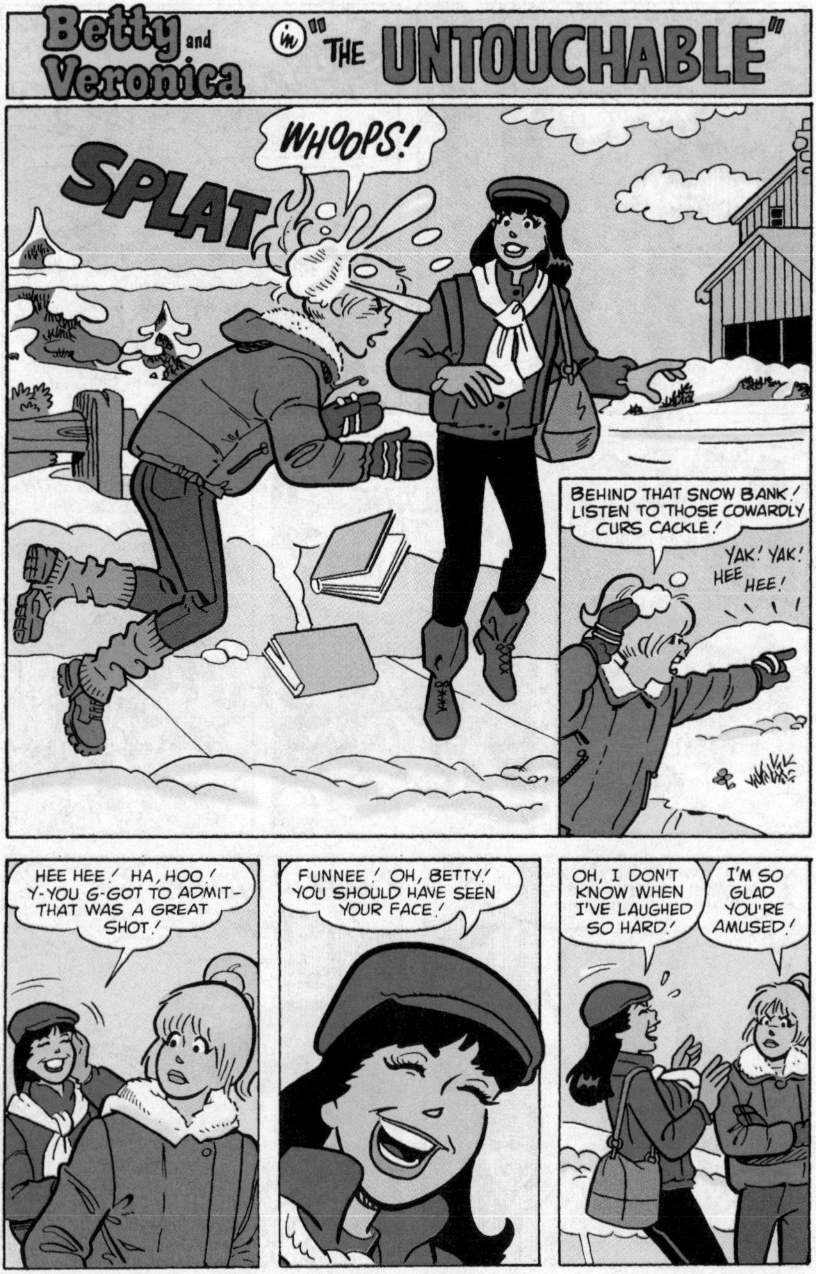

Betty and Veronica in "THE UNTOUCHABLE"
WHOOPS!
SPLAT
BEHIND THAT SNOW BANK! LISTEN TO THOSE COWARDLY CURS CACKLE!
YAK! YAK!
HEE HEE!
HEE HEE! HA, HOO! Y-YOU G-GOT TO ADMIT-THAT WAS A GREAT SHOT!
FUNNEE! OH, BETTY! YOU SHOULD HAVE SEEN YOUR FACE!
OH, I DON'T KNOW WHEN I'VE LAUGHED SO HARD!
I'M SO GLAD YOU'RE AMUSED!

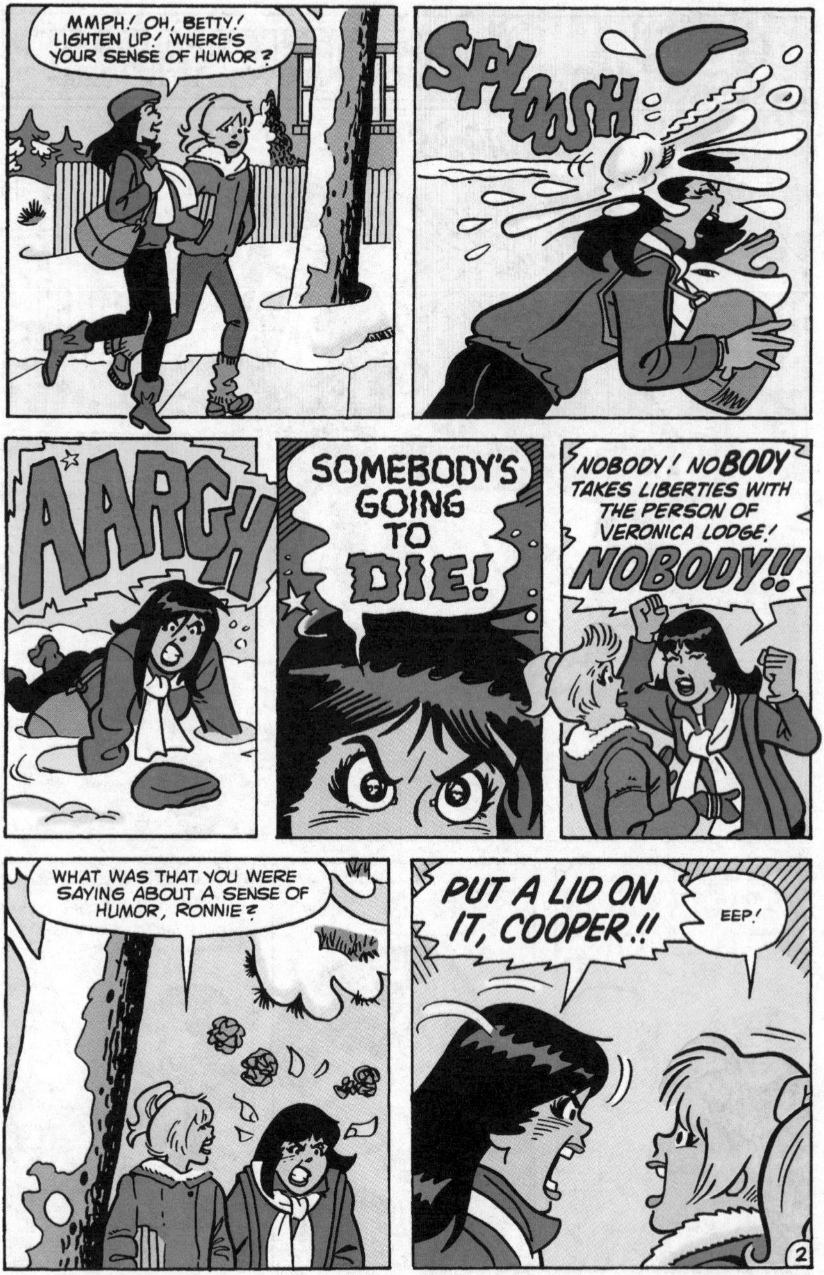
MMPH! OH, BETTY! LIGHTEN UP! WHERE'S YOUR SENSE OF HUMOR?
SPLOOSH
AARGH
SOMEBODY'S GOING TO DIE!
NOBODY! NOBODY TAKES LIBERTIES WITH THE PERSON OF VERONICA LODGE! NOBODY!!
WHAT WAS THAT YOU WERE SAYING ABOUT A SENSE OF HUMOR, RONNIE?
PUT A LID ON IT, COOPER!!
EEP!
2

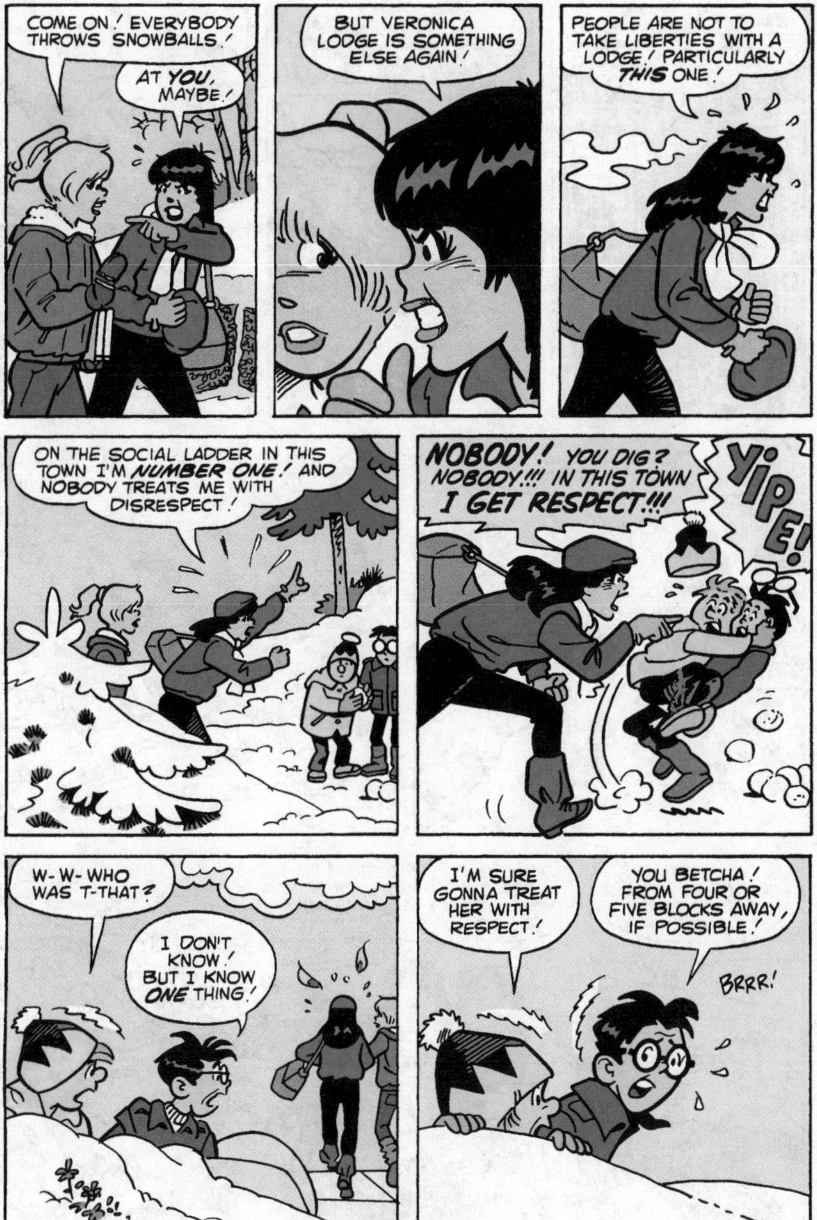
COME ON! EVERYBODY THROWS SNOWBALLS!
AT YOU, MAYBE!
BUT VERONICA LODGE IS SOMETHING ELSE AGAIN!
PEOPLE ARE NOT TO TAKE LIBERTIES WITH A LODGE! PARTICULARLY THIS ONE!
ON THE SOCIAL LADDER IN THIS TOWN I'M NUMBER ONE! AND NOBODY TREATS ME WITH DISRESPECT!
NOBODY! YOU DIG? NOBODY!!! IN THIS TOWN I GET RESPECT!!!
YIPE!
W-W-WHO WAS T-THAT?
I DON'T KNOW! BUT I KNOW ONE THING!
I'M SURE GONNA TREAT HER WITH RESPECT!
YOU BETCHA! FROM FOUR OR FIVE BLOCKS AWAY, IF POSSIBLE!
BRRR!
3

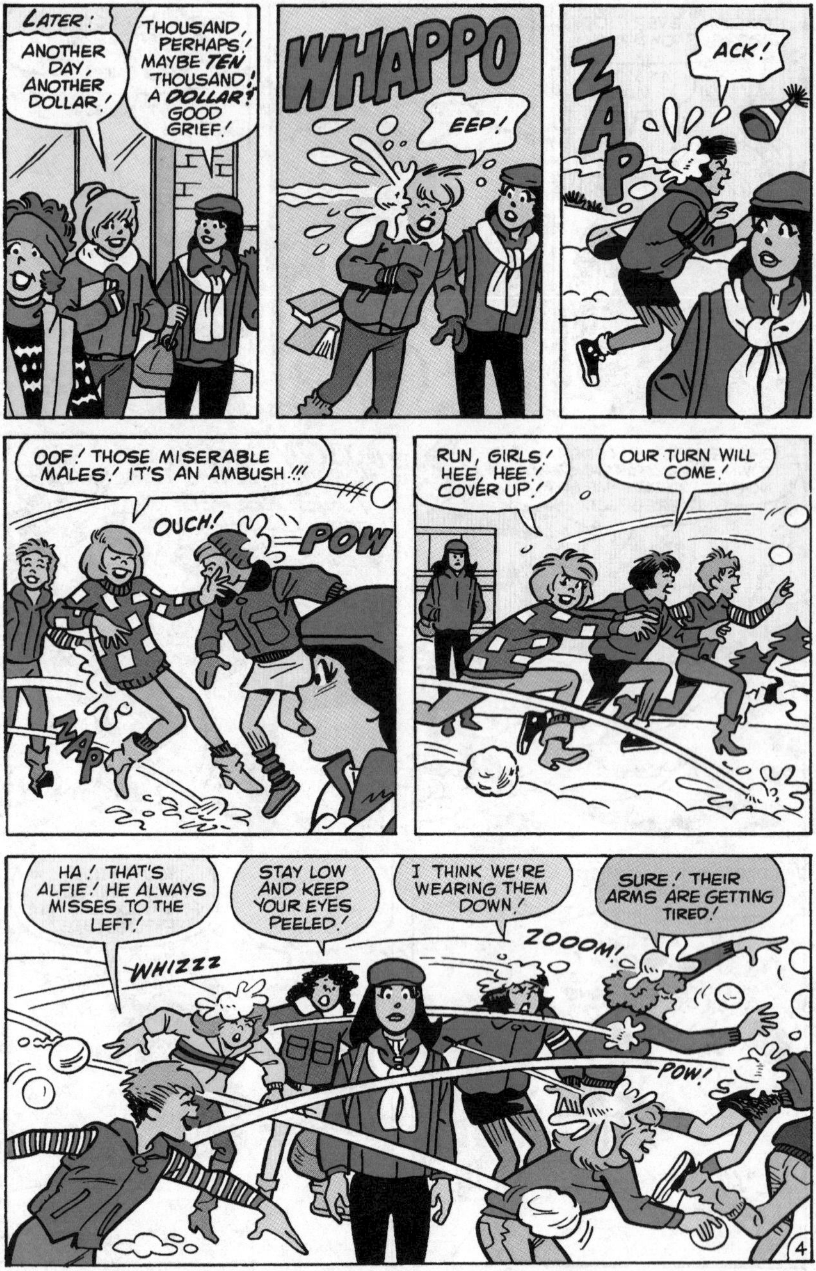
LATER:
ANOTHER DAY, ANOTHER DOLLAR!
THOUSAND, PERHAPS! MAYBE TEN THOUSAND! A DOLLAR? GOOD GRIEF!
WHAPPO
EEP!
ZAP
ACK!
OOF! THOSE MISERABLE MALES! IT'S AN AMBUSH!!!
OUCH!
POW
WAP
RUN, GIRLS! HEE, HEE! COVER UP!
OUR TURN WILL COME!
HA! THAT'S ALFIE! HE ALWAYS MISSES TO THE LEFT!
STAY LOW AND KEEP YOUR EYES PEELED!
I THINK WE'RE WEARING THEM DOWN!
SURE! THEIR ARMS ARE GETTING TIRED!
ZOOOM!
WHIZZZ
POW!
4

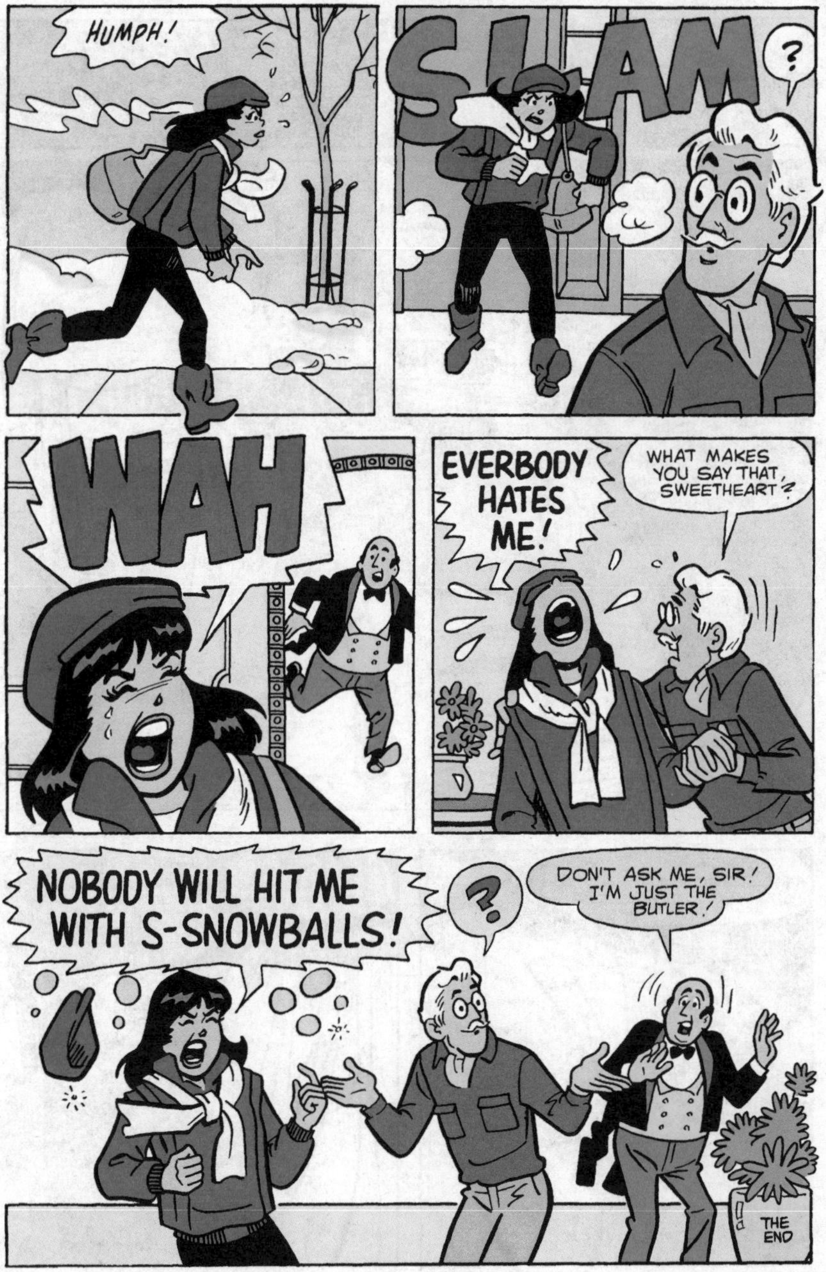
HUMPH!
SLAM
?
WAH
EVERBODY HATES ME!
WHAT MAKES YOU SAY THAT, SWEETHEART?
NOBODY WILL HIT ME WITH S-SNOWBALLS!
?
DON'T ASK ME, SIR! I'M JUST THE BUTLER!
THE END

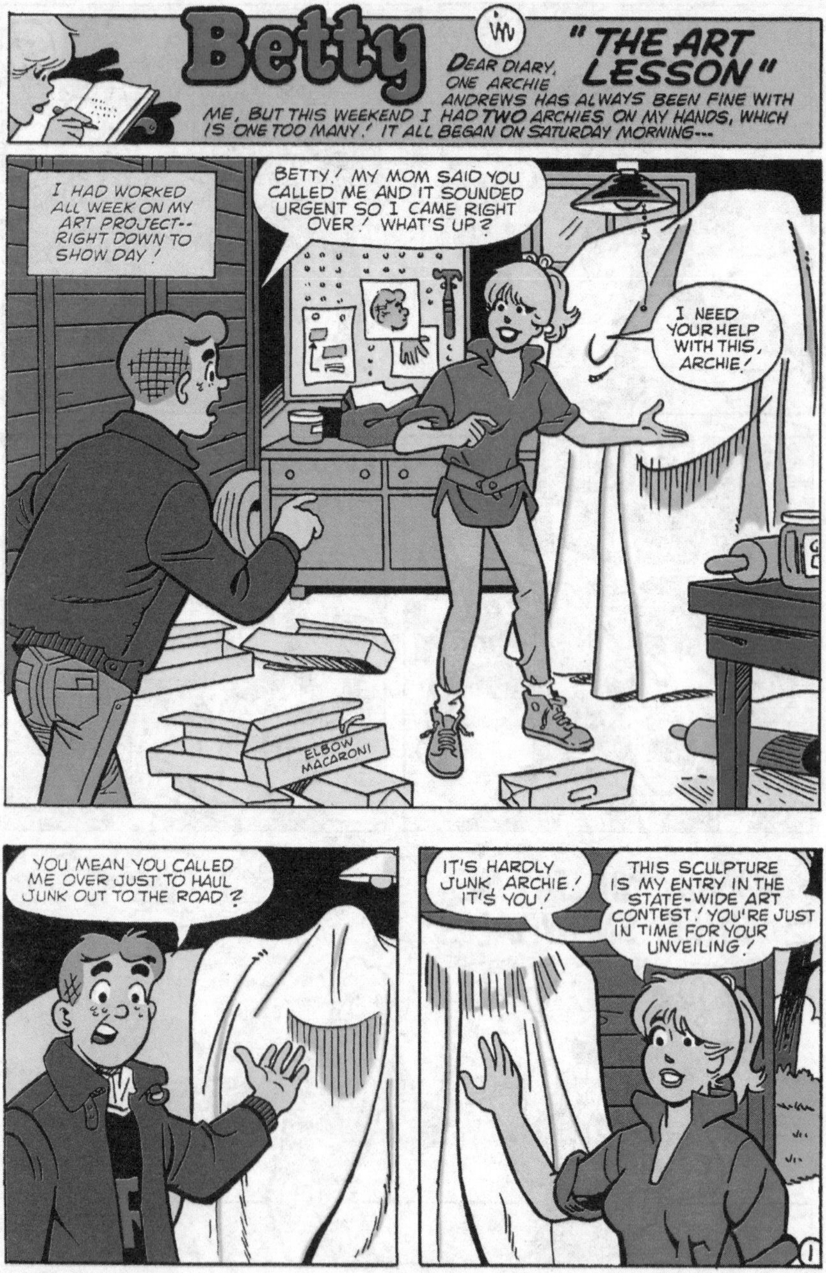
Betty
"THE ART LESSON"
DEAR DIARY, ONE ARCHIE ANDREWS HAS ALWAYS BEEN FINE WITH ME, BUT THIS WEEKEND I HAD TWO ARCHIES ON MY HANDS, WHICH IS ONE TOO MANY! IT ALL BEGAN ON SATURDAY MORNING---
I HAD WORKED ALL WEEK ON MY ART PROJECT-- RIGHT DOWN TO SHOW DAY!
BETTY! MY MOM SAID YOU CALLED ME AND IT SOUNDED URGENT SO I CAME RIGHT OVER! WHAT'S UP?
I NEED YOUR HELP WITH THIS, ARCHIE!
ELBOW MACARONI
YOU MEAN YOU CALLED ME OVER JUST TO HAUL JUNK OUT TO THE ROAD?
IT'S HARDLY JUNK, ARCHIE! IT'S YOU!
THIS SCULPTURE IS MY ENTRY IN THE STATE-WIDE ART CONTEST! YOU'RE JUST IN TIME FOR YOUR UNVEILING!
1

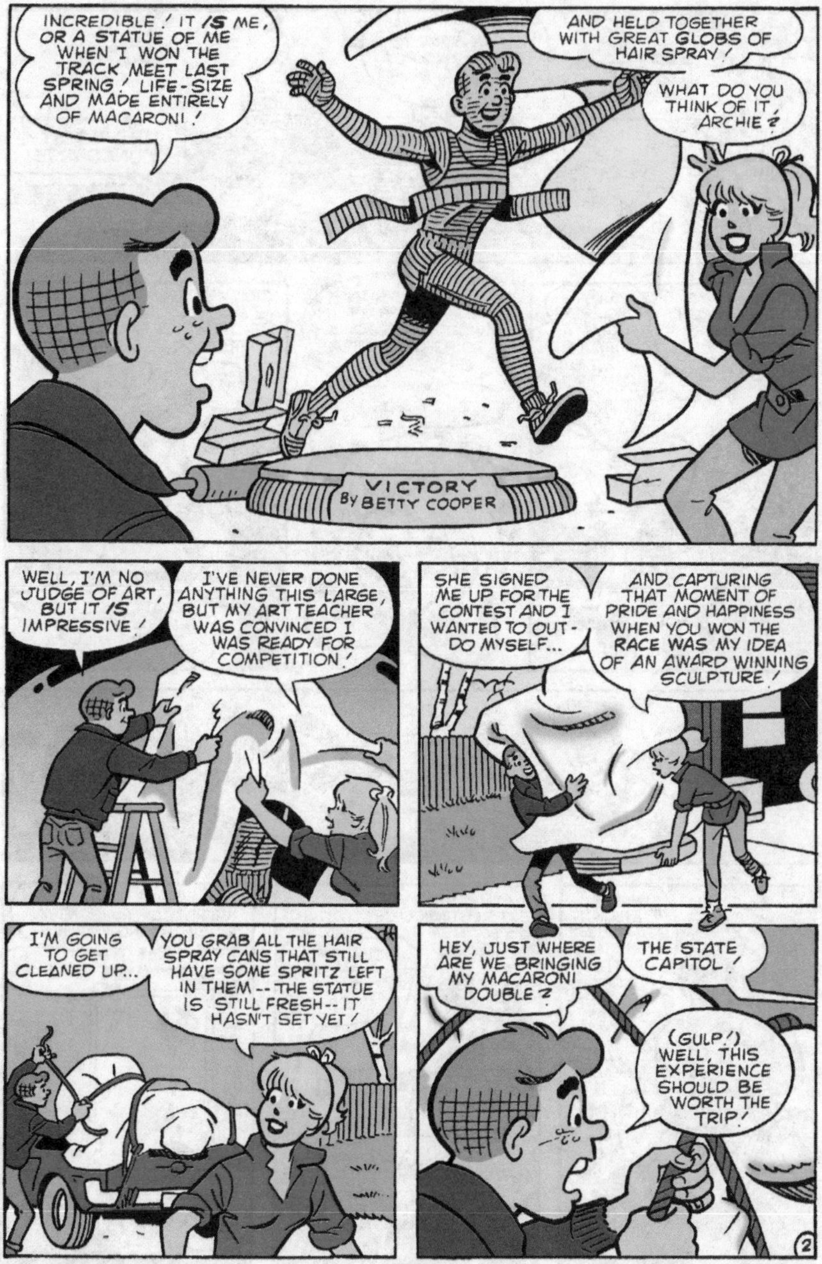
INCREDIBLE! IT IS ME, OR A STATUE OF ME WHEN I WON THE TRACK MEET LAST SPRING! LIFE-SIZE AND MADE ENTIRELY OF MACARONI!
AND HELD TOGETHER WITH GREAT GLOBS OF HAIR SPRAY!
WHAT DO YOU THINK OF IT, ARCHIE?
VICTORY
BY BETTY COOPER
WELL, I'M NO JUDGE OF ART, BUT IT IS IMPRESSIVE!
I'VE NEVER DONE ANYTHING THIS LARGE, BUT MY ART TEACHER WAS CONVINCED I WAS READY FOR COMPETITION!
SHE SIGNED ME UP FOR THE CONTEST AND I WANTED TO OUT-DO MYSELF...
AND CAPTURING THAT MOMENT OF PRIDE AND HAPPINESS WHEN YOU WON THE RACE WAS MY IDEA OF AN AWARD WINNING SCULPTURE!
I'M GOING TO GET CLEANED UP...
YOU GRAB ALL THE HAIR SPRAY CANS THAT STILL HAVE SOME SPRITZ LEFT IN THEM -- THE STATUE IS STILL FRESH-- IT HASN'T SET YET!
HEY, JUST WHERE ARE WE BRINGING MY MACARONI DOUBLE?
THE STATE CAPITOL!
(GULP!) WELL, THIS EXPERIENCE SHOULD BE WORTH THE TRIP!
2

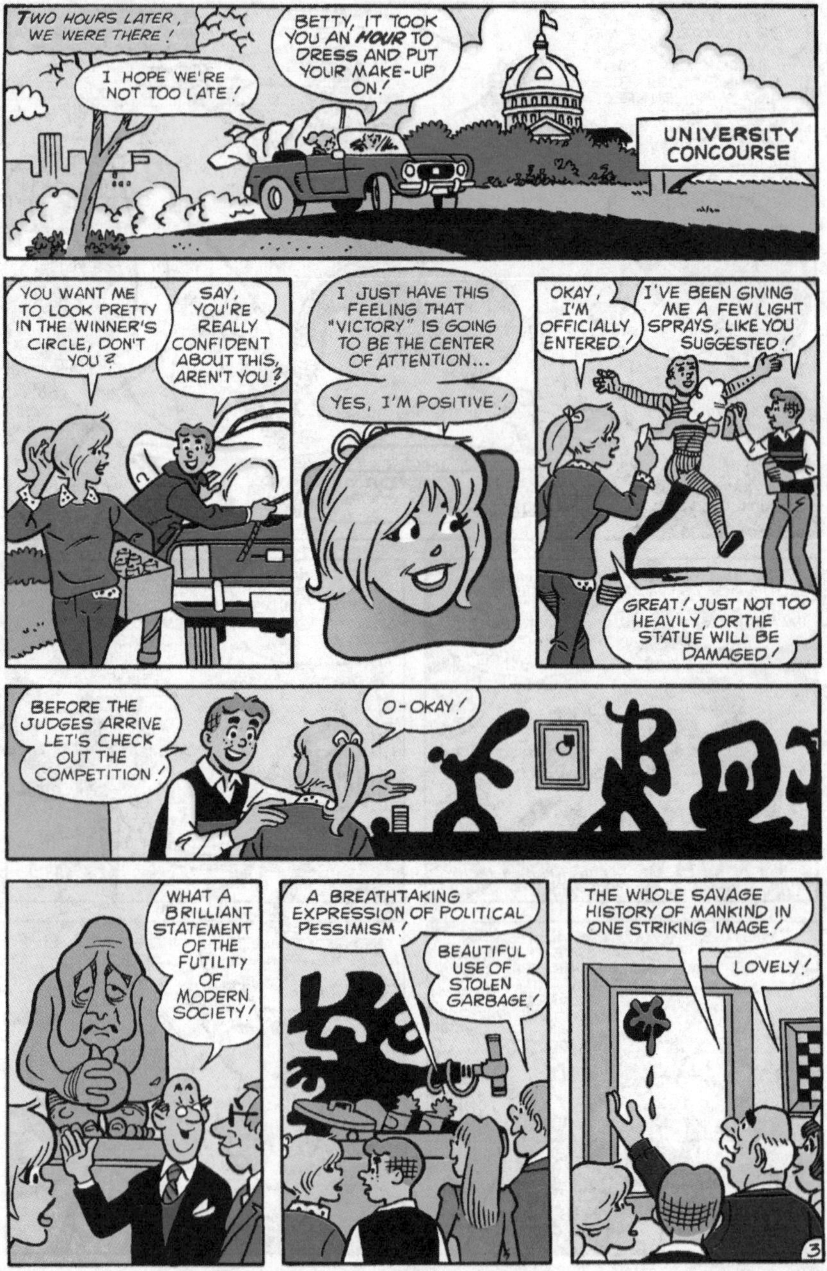
TWO HOURS LATER, WE WERE THERE!
I HOPE WE'RE NOT TOO LATE!
BETTY, IT TOOK YOU AN HOUR TO DRESS AND PUT YOUR MAKE-UP ON!
UNIVERSITY CONCOURSE
YOU WANT ME TO LOOK PRETTY IN THE WINNER'S CIRCLE, DON'T YOU?
SAY, YOU'RE REALLY CONFIDENT ABOUT THIS, AREN'T YOU?
I JUST HAVE THIS FEELING THAT "VICTORY" IS GOING TO BE THE CENTER OF ATTENTION...
YES, I'M POSITIVE!
OKAY, I'M OFFICIALLY ENTERED!
I'VE BEEN GIVING ME A FEW LIGHT SPRAYS, LIKE YOU SUGGESTED!
GREAT! JUST NOT TOO HEAVILY, OR THE STATUE WILL BE DAMAGED!
BEFORE THE JUDGES ARRIVE LET'S CHECK OUT THE COMPETITION!
O-OKAY!
WHAT A BRILLIANT STATEMENT OF THE FUTILITY OF MODERN SOCIETY!
A BREATHTAKING EXPRESSION OF POLITICAL PESSIMISM!
BEAUTIFUL USE OF STOLEN GARBAGE!
THE WHOLE SAVAGE HISTORY OF MANKIND IN ONE STRIKING IMAGE!
LOVELY!
3

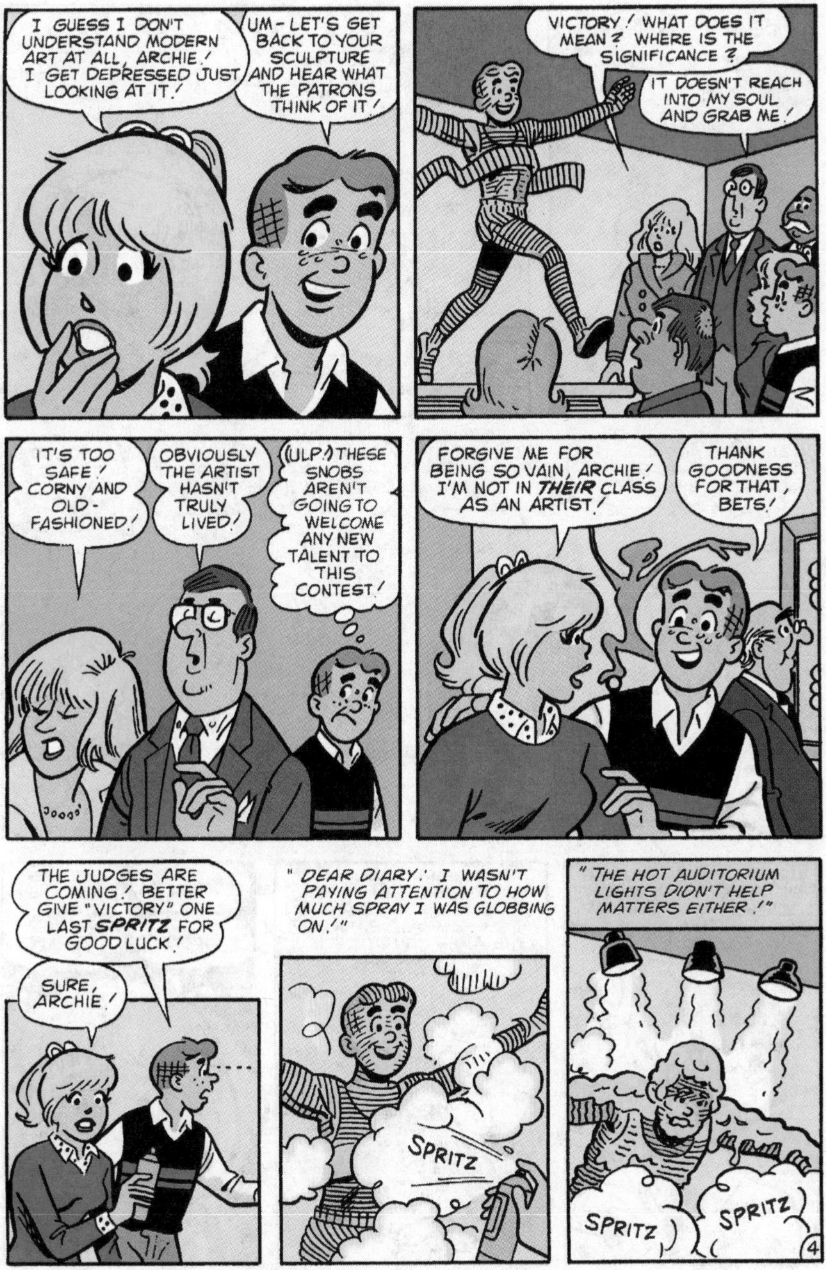
I GUESS I DON'T UNDERSTAND MODERN ART AT ALL, ARCHIE! I GET DEPRESSED JUST LOOKING AT IT!
UM - LET'S GET BACK TO YOUR SCULPTURE AND HEAR WHAT THE PATRONS THINK OF IT!
VICTORY! WHAT DOES IT MEAN? WHERE IS THE SIGNIFICANCE?
IT DOESN'T REACH INTO MY SOUL AND GRAB ME!
IT'S TOO SAFE! CORNY AND OLD-FASHIONED!
OBVIOUSLY THE ARTIST HASN'T TRULY LIVED!
(ULP!) THESE SNOBS AREN'T GOING TO WELCOME ANY NEW TALENT TO THIS CONTEST!
FORGIVE ME FOR BEING SO VAIN, ARCHIE! I'M NOT IN THEIR CLASS AS AN ARTIST!
THANK GOODNESS FOR THAT, BETS!
THE JUDGES ARE COMING! BETTER GIVE "VICTORY" ONE LAST SPRITZ FOR GOOD LUCK!
SURE, ARCHIE!
"DEAR DIARY: I WASN'T PAYING ATTENTION TO HOW MUCH SPRAY I WAS GLOBBING ON!"
SPRITZ
"THE HOT AUDITORIUM LIGHTS DIDN'T HELP MATTERS EITHER!"
SPRITZ
SPRITZ
4

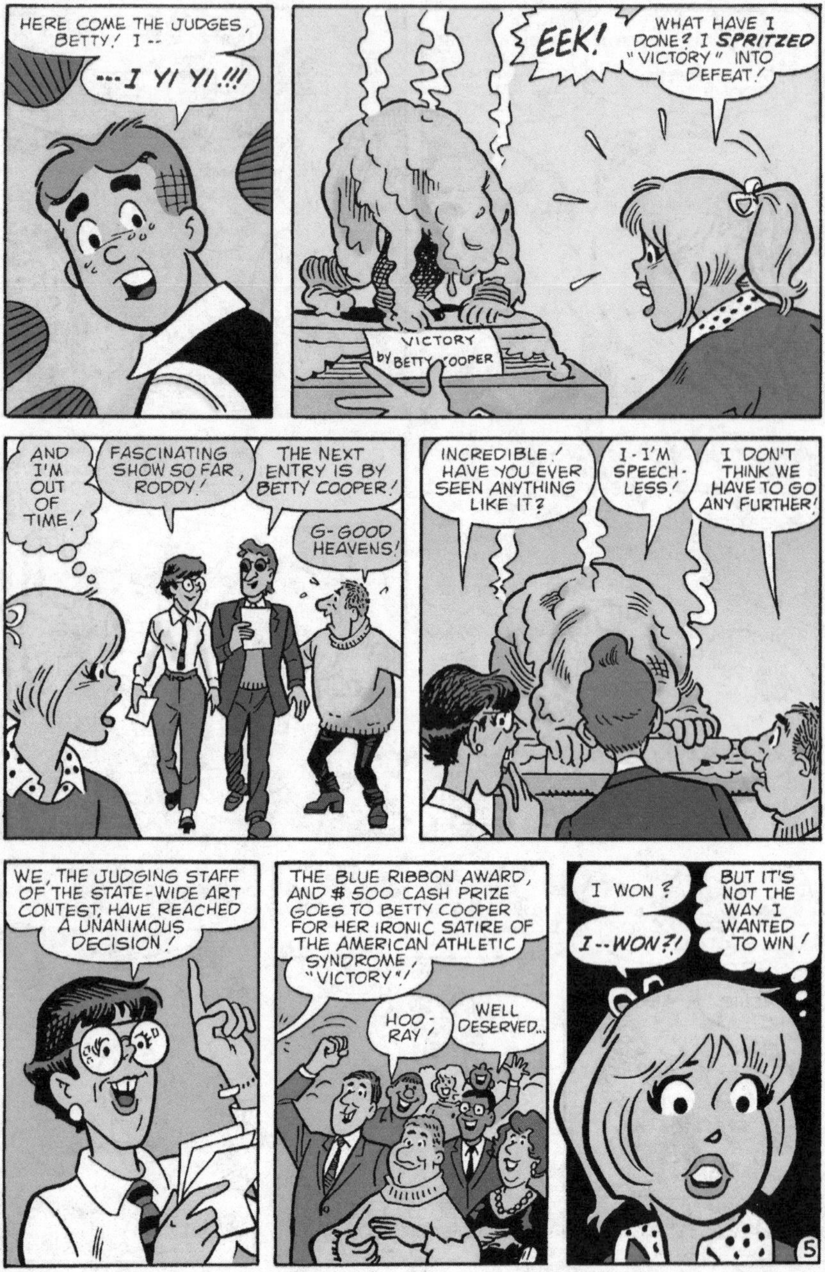
HERE COME THE JUDGES, BETTY! I --
---I YI YI!!!
EEK!
WHAT HAVE I DONE? I SPRITZED "VICTORY" INTO DEFEAT!
VICTORY by BETTY COOPER
AND I'M OUT OF TIME!
FASCINATING SHOW SO FAR, RODDY!
THE NEXT ENTRY IS BY BETTY COOPER!
G-GOOD HEAVENS!
INCREDIBLE! HAVE YOU EVER SEEN ANYTHING LIKE IT?
I-I'M SPEECH-LESS!
I DON'T THINK WE HAVE TO GO ANY FURTHER!
WE, THE JUDGING STAFF OF THE STATE-WIDE ART CONTEST, HAVE REACHED A UNANIMOUS DECISION!
THE BLUE RIBBON AWARD, AND $ 500 CASH PRIZE GOES TO BETTY COOPER FOR HER IRONIC SATIRE OF THE AMERICAN ATHLETIC SYNDROME, "VICTORY"!
HOO-RAY!
WELL DESERVED...
I WON?
I--WON?!
BUT IT'S NOT THE WAY I WANTED TO WIN!
5

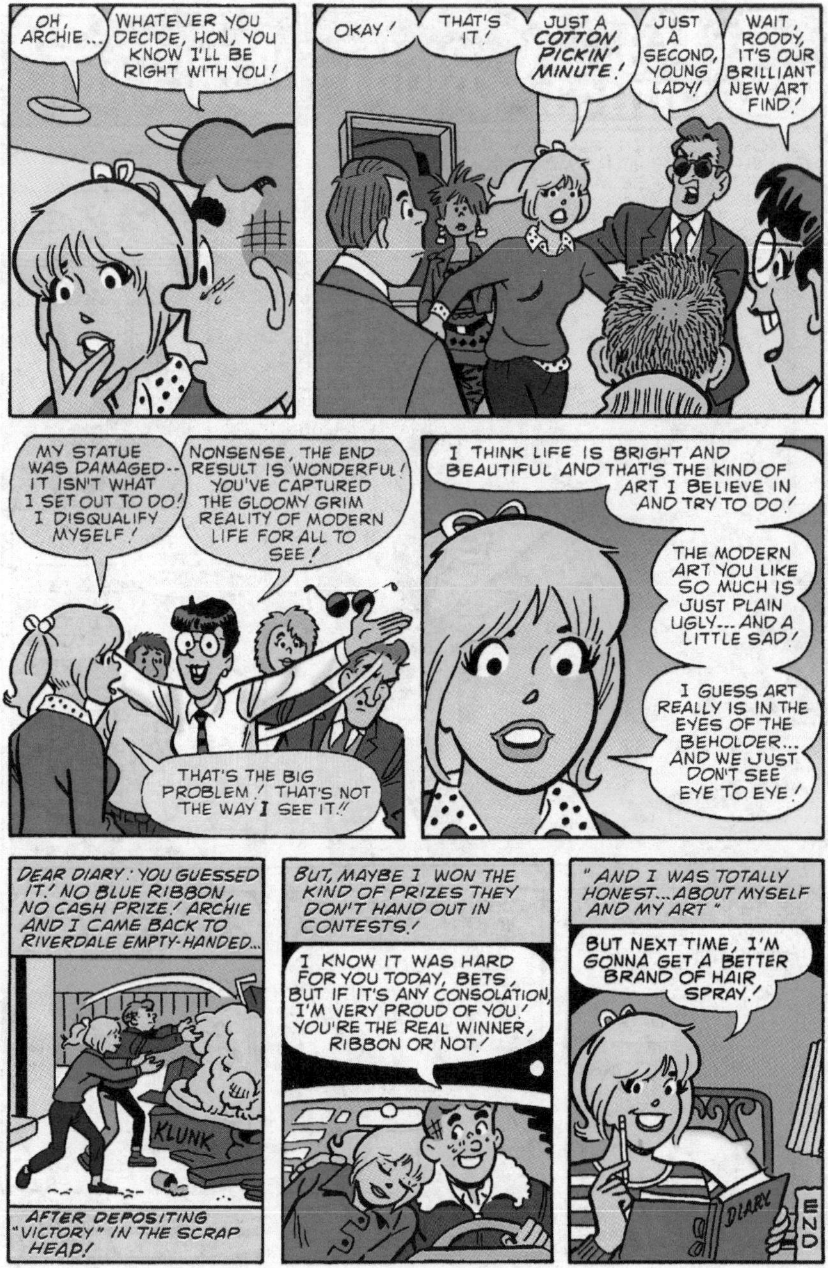
OH, ARCHIE...
WHATEVER YOU DECIDE, HON, YOU KNOW I'LL BE RIGHT WITH YOU!
OKAY!
THAT'S IT!
JUST A COTTON PICKIN' MINUTE!
JUST A SECOND, YOUNG LADY!
WAIT, RODDY, IT'S OUR BRILLIANT NEW ART FIND!
MY STATUE WAS DAMAGED-- IT ISN'T WHAT I SET OUT TO DO! I DISQUALIFY MYSELF!
NONSENSE, THE END RESULT IS WONDERFUL! YOU'VE CAPTURED THE GLOOMY GRIM REALITY OF MODERN LIFE FOR ALL TO SEE!
THAT'S THE BIG PROBLEM! THAT'S NOT THE WAY I SEE IT!!
I THINK LIFE IS BRIGHT AND BEAUTIFUL AND THAT'S THE KIND OF ART I BELIEVE IN AND TRY TO DO!
THE MODERN ART YOU LIKE SO MUCH IS JUST PLAIN UGLY... AND A LITTLE SAD!
I GUESS ART REALLY IS IN THE EYES OF THE BEHOLDER... AND WE JUST DON'T SEE EYE TO EYE!
DEAR DIARY: YOU GUESSED IT! NO BLUE RIBBON, NO CASH PRIZE! ARCHIE AND I CAME BACK TO RIVERDALE EMPTY-HANDED...
KLUNK
AFTER DEPOSITING "VICTORY" IN THE SCRAP HEAP!
BUT, MAYBE I WON THE KIND OF PRIZES THEY DON'T HAND OUT IN CONTESTS!
I KNOW IT WAS HARD FOR YOU TODAY, BETS, BUT IF IT'S ANY CONSOLATION, I'M VERY PROUD OF YOU! YOU'RE THE REAL WINNER, RIBBON OR NOT!
"AND I WAS TOTALLY HONEST... ABOUT MYSELF AND MY ART"
BUT NEXT TIME, I'M GONNA GET A BETTER BRAND OF HAIR SPRAY!
DIARY
END

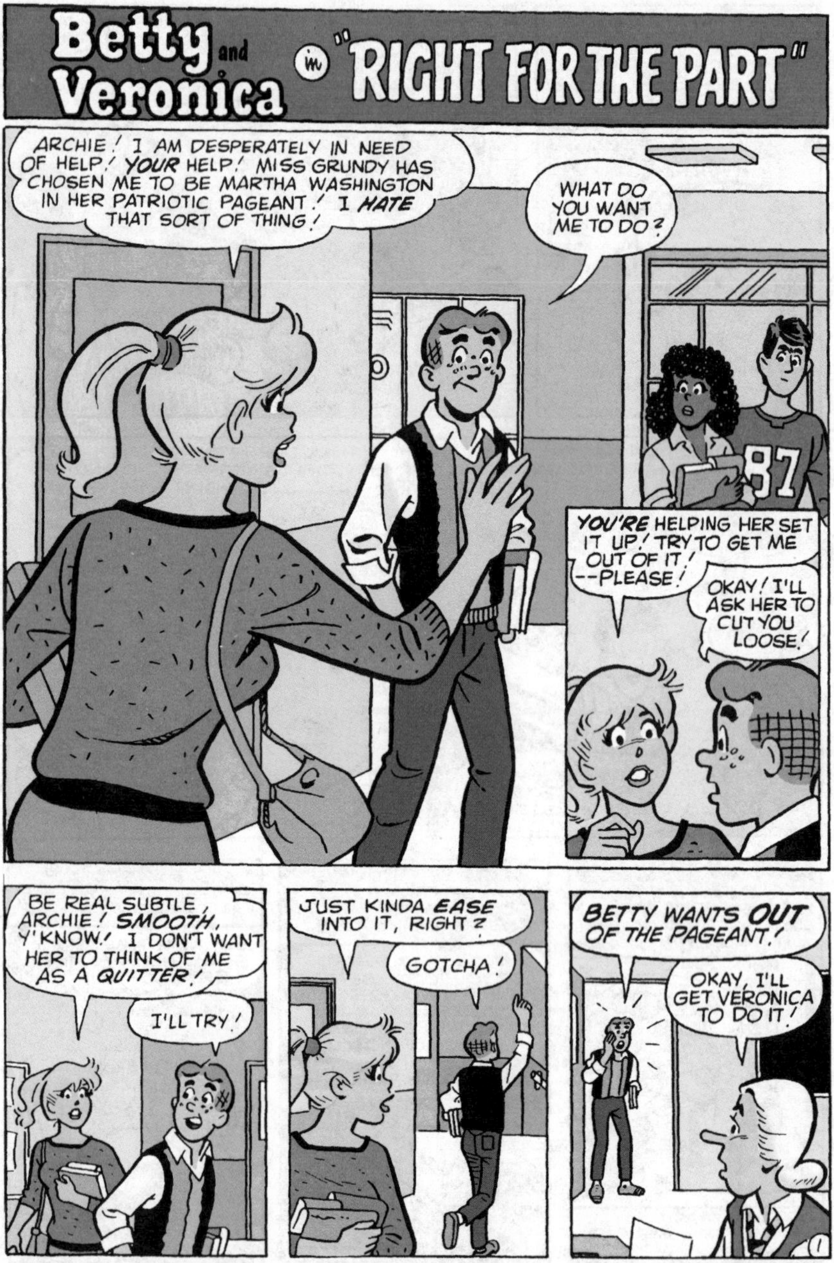
Betty and Veronica in "RIGHT FOR THE PART"
ARCHIE! I AM DESPERATELY IN NEED OF HELP! YOUR HELP! MISS GRUNDY HAS CHOSEN ME TO BE MARTHA WASHINGTON IN HER PATRIOTIC PAGEANT! I HATE THAT SORT OF THING!
WHAT DO YOU WANT ME TO DO?
87
YOU'RE HELPING HER SET IT UP! TRY TO GET ME OUT OF IT! --PLEASE!
OKAY! I'LL ASK HER TO CUT YOU LOOSE!
BE REAL SUBTLE, ARCHIE! SMOOTH, Y'KNOW! I DON'T WANT HER TO THINK OF ME AS A QUITTER!
I'LL TRY!
JUST KINDA EASE INTO IT, RIGHT?
GOTCHA!
BETTY WANTS OUT OF THE PAGEANT!
OKAY, I'LL GET VERONICA TO DO IT!
1

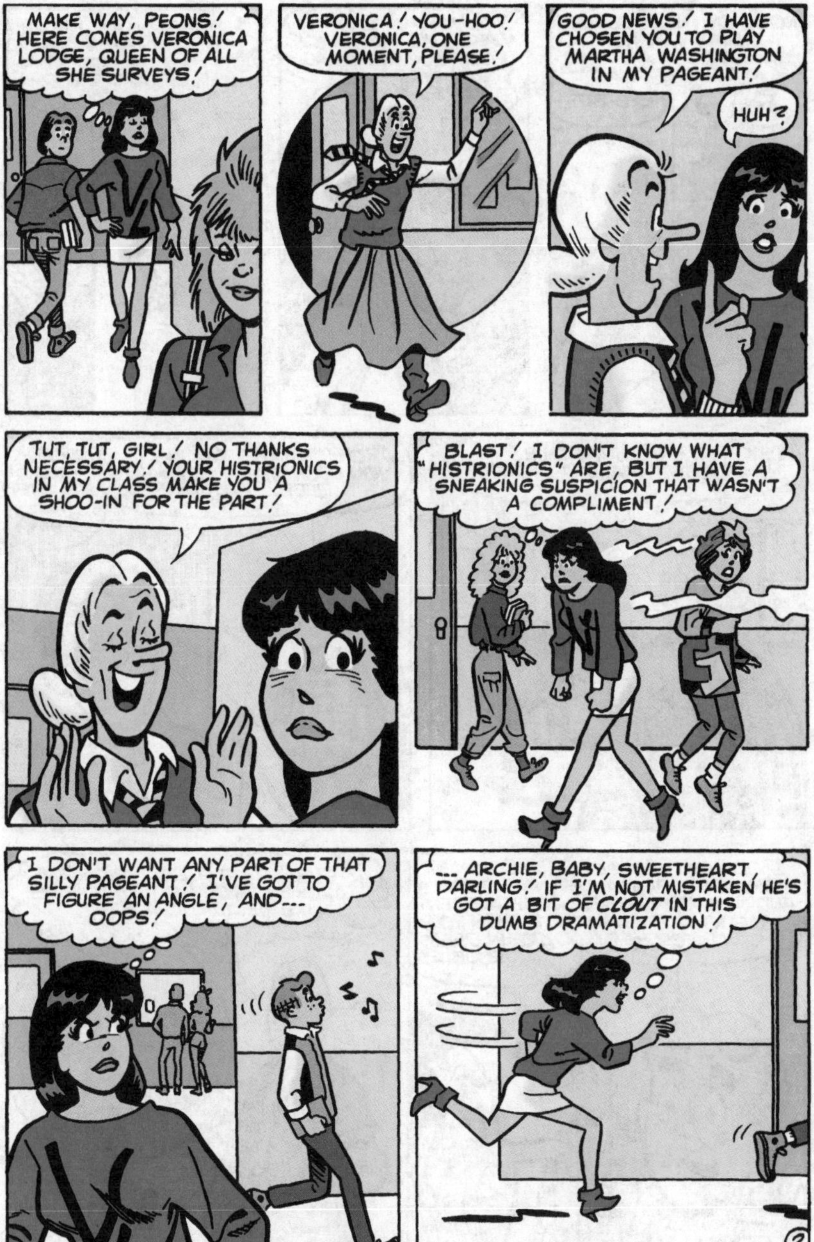
MAKE WAY, PEONS! HERE COMES VERONICA LODGE, QUEEN OF ALL SHE SURVEYS!
VERONICA! YOU-HOO! VERONICA, ONE MOMENT, PLEASE!
GOOD NEWS! I HAVE CHOSEN YOU TO PLAY MARTHA WASHINGTON IN MY PAGEANT!
HUH?
TUT, TUT, GIRL! NO THANKS NECESSARY! YOUR HISTRIONICS IN MY CLASS MAKE YOU A SHOO-IN FOR THE PART!
BLAST! I DON'T KNOW WHAT "HISTRIONICS" ARE, BUT I HAVE A SNEAKING SUSPICION THAT WASN'T A COMPLIMENT!
I DON'T WANT ANY PART OF THAT SILLY PAGEANT! I'VE GOT TO FIGURE AN ANGLE, AND--- OOPS!
--- ARCHIE, BABY, SWEETHEART, DARLING! IF I'M NOT MISTAKEN HE'S GOT A BIT OF CLOUT IN THIS DUMB DRAMATIZATION!
2

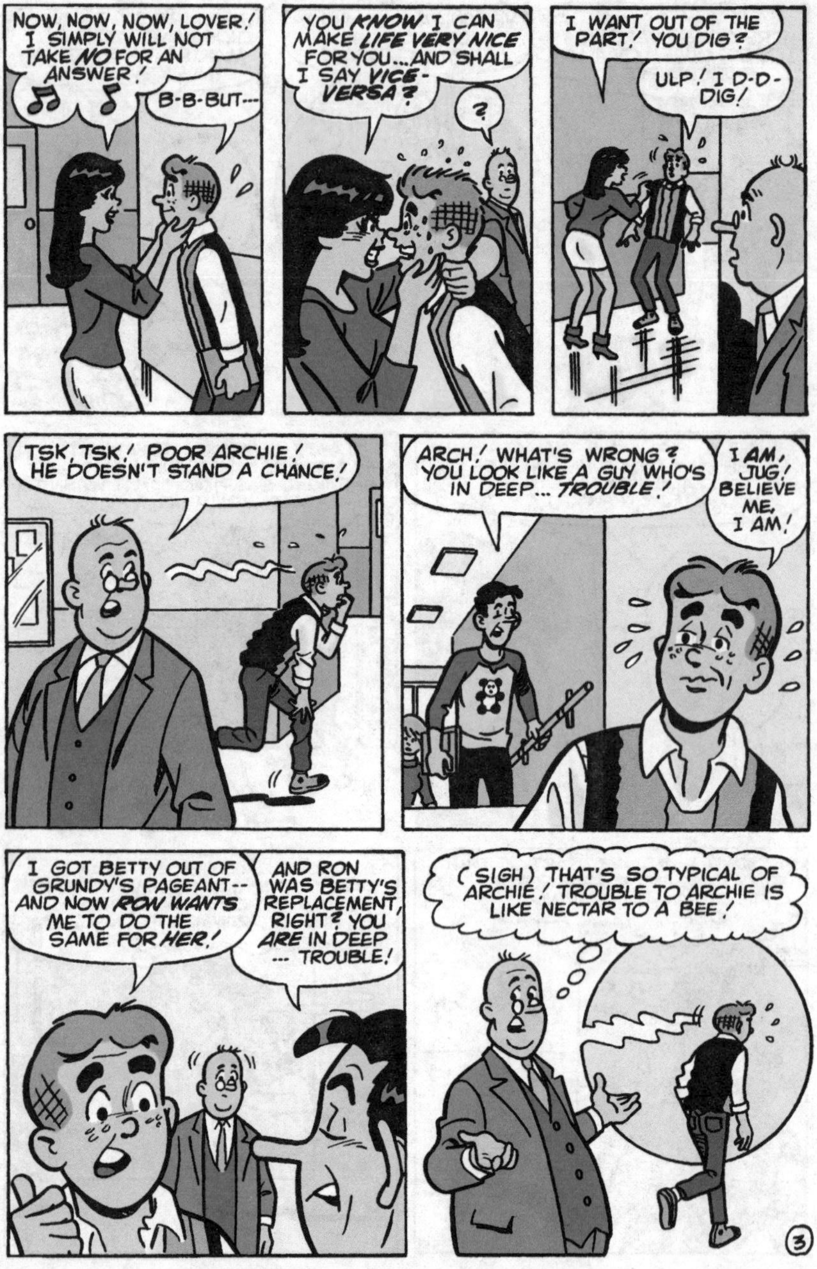

NOW, NOW, NOW, LOVER! I SIMPLY WILL NOT TAKE NO FOR AN ANSWER!
B-B-BUT---
YOU KNOW I CAN MAKE LIFE VERY NICE FOR YOU... AND SHALL I SAY VICE-VERSA?
?
I WANT OUT OF THE PART! YOU DIG?
ULP! I D-D-DIG!
TSK, TSK! POOR ARCHIE! HE DOESN'T STAND A CHANCE!
ARCH! WHAT'S WRONG? YOU LOOK LIKE A GUY WHO'S IN DEEP... TROUBLE!
I AM, JUG! BELIEVE ME, I AM!
I GOT BETTY OUT OF GRUNDY'S PAGEANT-- AND NOW RON WANTS ME TO DO THE SAME FOR HER!
AND RON WAS BETTY'S REPLACEMENT, RIGHT? YOU ARE IN DEEP --- TROUBLE!
(SIGH) THAT'S SO TYPICAL OF ARCHIE! TROUBLE TO ARCHIE IS LIKE NECTAR TO A BEE!
3

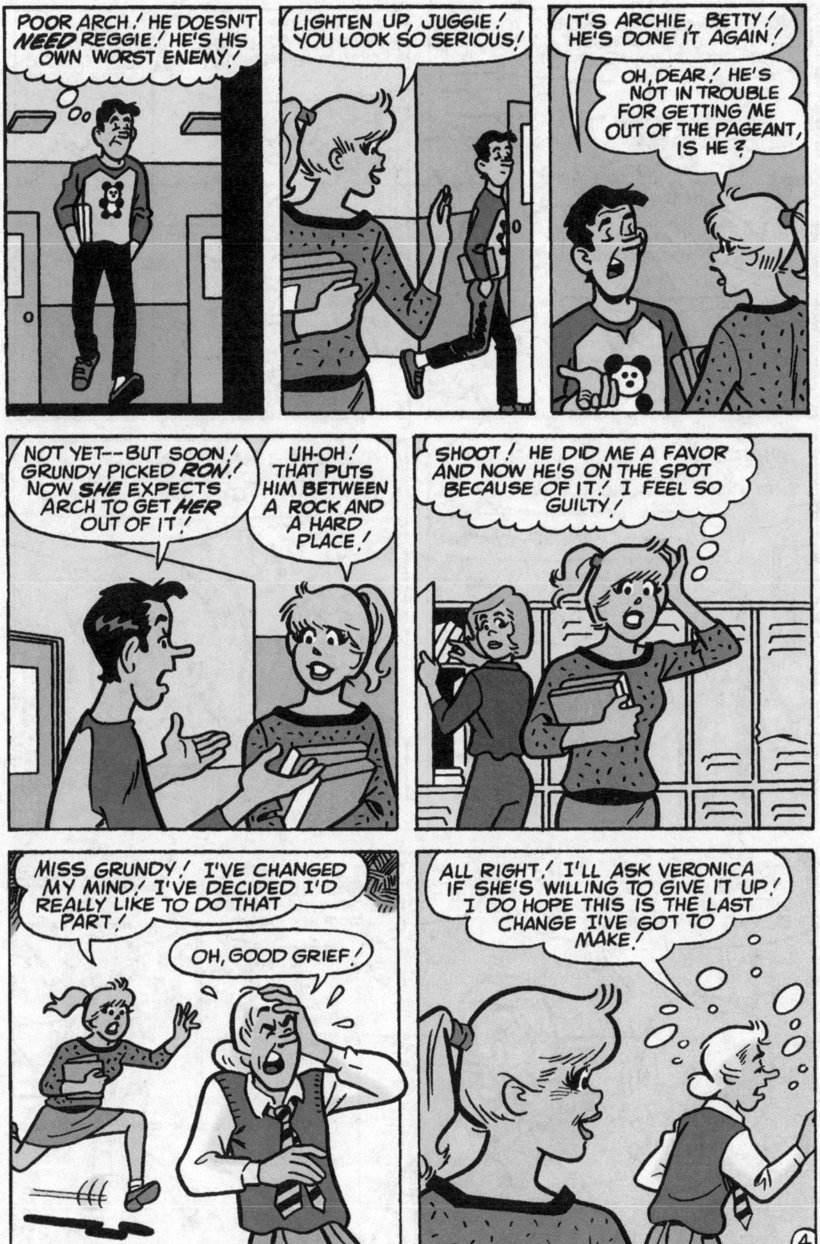
POOR ARCH! HE DOESN'T NEED REGGIE! HE'S HIS OWN WORST ENEMY!
LIGHTEN UP, JUGGIE! YOU LOOK SO SERIOUS!
IT'S ARCHIE, BETTY! HE'S DONE IT AGAIN!
OH, DEAR! HE'S NOT IN TROUBLE FOR GETTING ME OUT OF THE PAGEANT, IS HE?
NOT YET--BUT SOON! GRUNDY PICKED RON! NOW SHE EXPECTS ARCH TO GET HER OUT OF IT!
UH-OH! THAT PUTS HIM BETWEEN A ROCK AND A HARD PLACE!
SHOOT! HE DID ME A FAVOR AND NOW HE'S ON THE SPOT BECAUSE OF IT! I FEEL SO GUILTY!
MISS GRUNDY! I'VE CHANGED MY MIND! I'VE DECIDED I'D REALLY LIKE TO DO THAT PART!
OH, GOOD GRIEF!
ALL RIGHT! I'LL ASK VERONICA IF SHE'S WILLING TO GIVE IT UP! I DO HOPE THIS IS THE LAST CHANGE I'VE GOT TO MAKE!
4

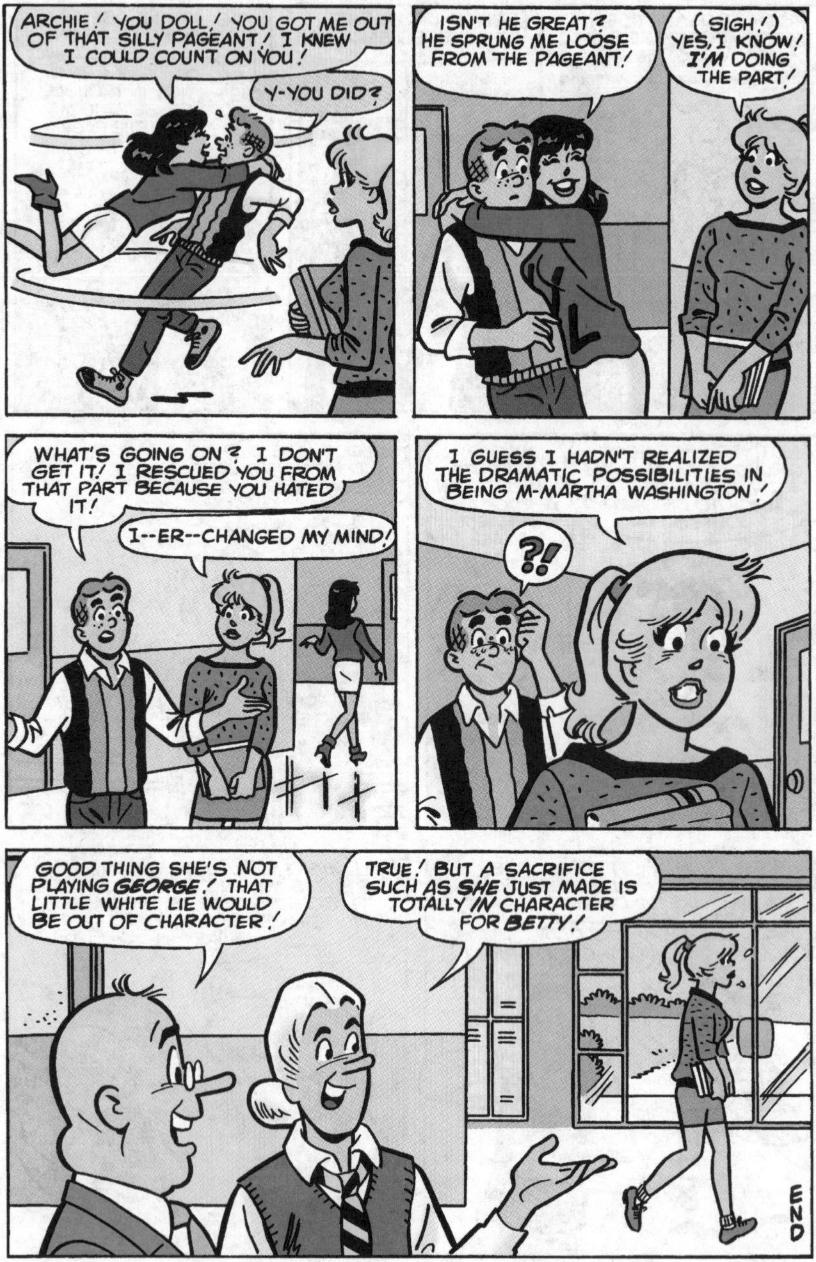
ARCHIE! YOU DOLL! YOU GOT ME OUT OF THAT SILLY PAGEANT! I KNEW I COULD COUNT ON YOU!
Y-YOU DID?
ISN'T HE GREAT? HE SPRUNG ME LOOSE FROM THE PAGEANT!
(SIGH!) YES, I KNOW! I'M DOING THE PART!
WHAT'S GOING ON? I DON'T GET IT! I RESCUED YOU FROM THAT PART BECAUSE YOU HATED IT!
I--ER--CHANGED MY MIND!
I GUESS I HADN'T REALIZED THE DRAMATIC POSSIBILITIES IN BEING M-MARTHA WASHINGTON!
?!
GOOD THING SHE'S NOT PLAYING GEORGE! THAT LITTLE WHITE LIE WOULD BE OUT OF CHARACTER!
TRUE! BUT A SACRIFICE SUCH AS SHE JUST MADE IS TOTALLY IN CHARACTER FOR BETTY!
END

THE BEST OF ARCHIE COMICS STARRING

BETTY & VERONICA

1990s

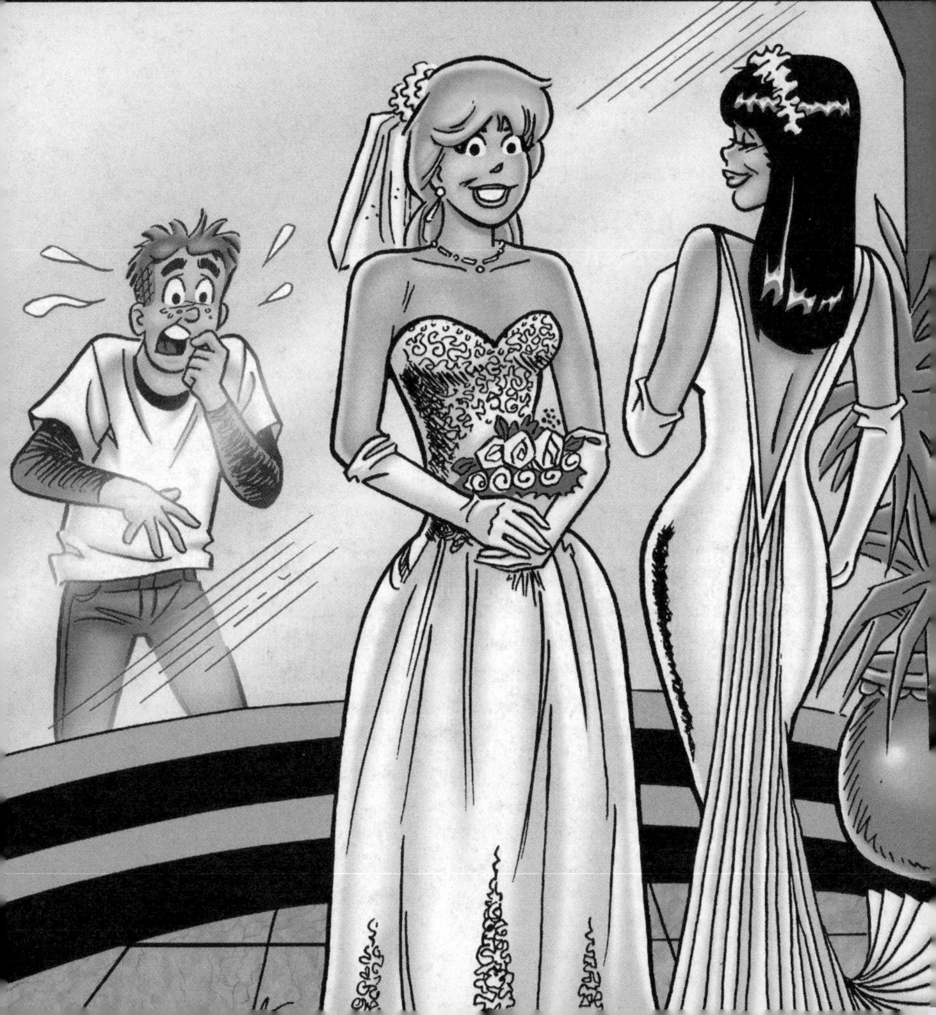

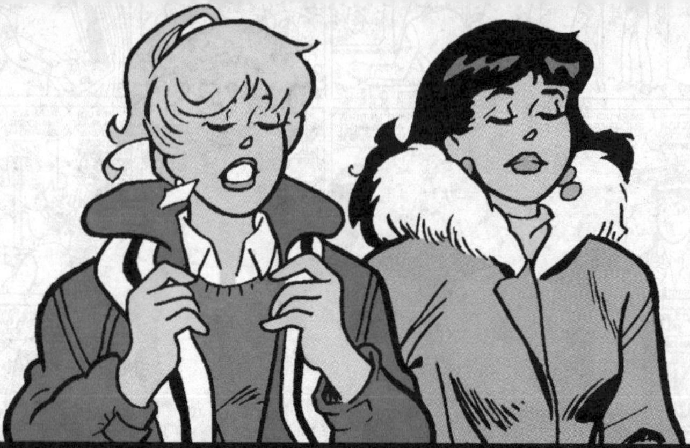

INNER VOICES
BETTY & VERONICA VOL. 2 #26, 1990
Frank Doyle, Dan DeCarlo, Jim DeCarlo, Bill Yoshida, Barry Grossman

AS EASY AS 12-26-83
BETTY & VERONICA VOL. 2 #39, 1991
Frank Doyle, Dan DeCarlo, Alison Flood, Bill Yoshida, Barry Grossman

PAINT THE MARSH MELLOW
BETTY & VERONICA VOL. 2 #67, 1993
Bob Bolling, Dan DeCarlo, Alison Flood, Bill Yoshida, Barry Grossman

As the iconic duo of Betty & Veronica entered their fifth decade together, the stories took a thoughtful and engaging twist—still dealing with the eternal love triangle, but also putting the focus squarely on the long-running and powerful friendship between the two girls. Whether competing for the red-headed Archie or dealing with school hijinks or other, myriad misadventures, one thing always held true in these stories: Betty and Veronica were best friends—forever.

- **ALEX SEGURA** *Co-President, Archie Comics*

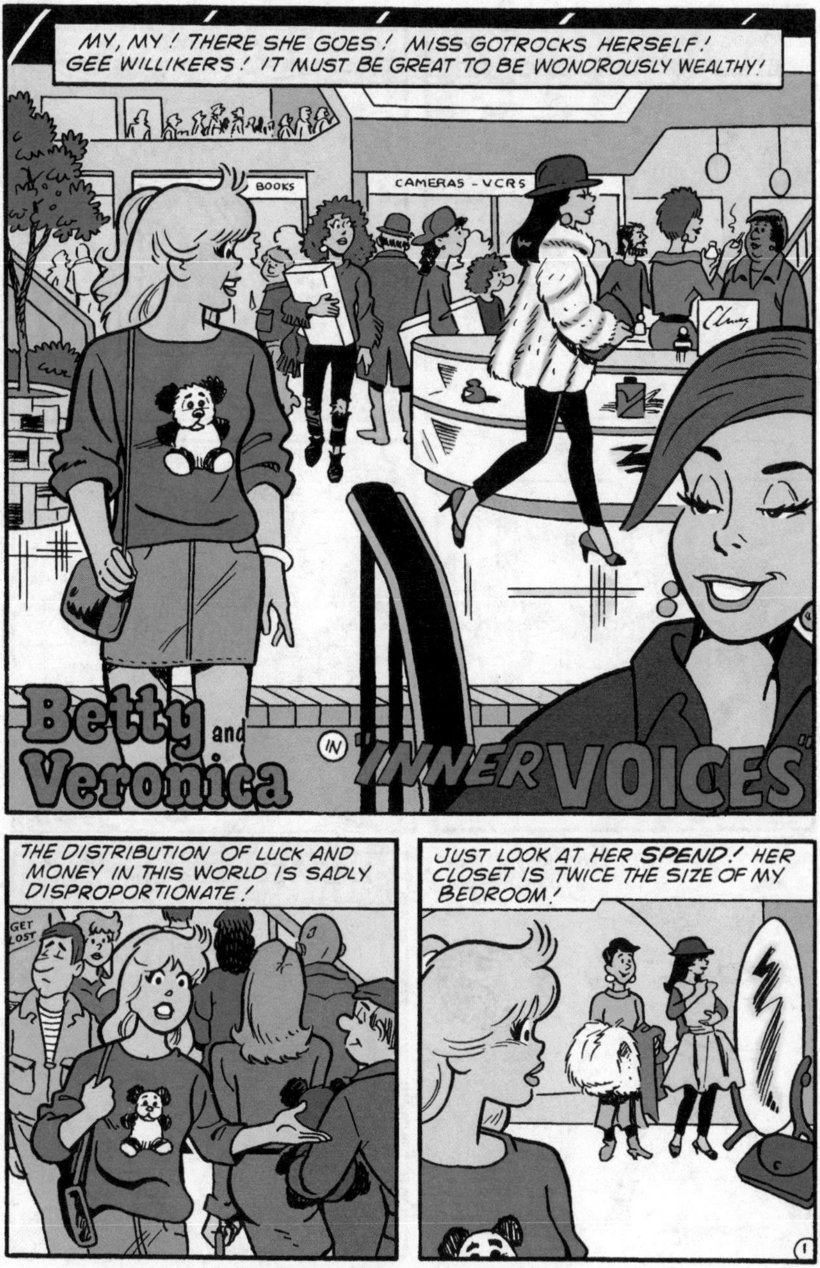
MY, MY! THERE SHE GOES! MISS GOTROCKS HERSELF! GEE WILLIKERS! IT MUST BE GREAT TO BE WONDROUSLY WEALTHY!
BOOKS
CAMERAS - VCRS
Betty and Veronica IN "INNER VOICES"
THE DISTRIBUTION OF LUCK AND MONEY IN THIS WORLD IS SADLY DISPROPORTIONATE!
GET LOST
JUST LOOK AT HER SPEND! HER CLOSET IS TWICE THE SIZE OF MY BEDROOM!
1

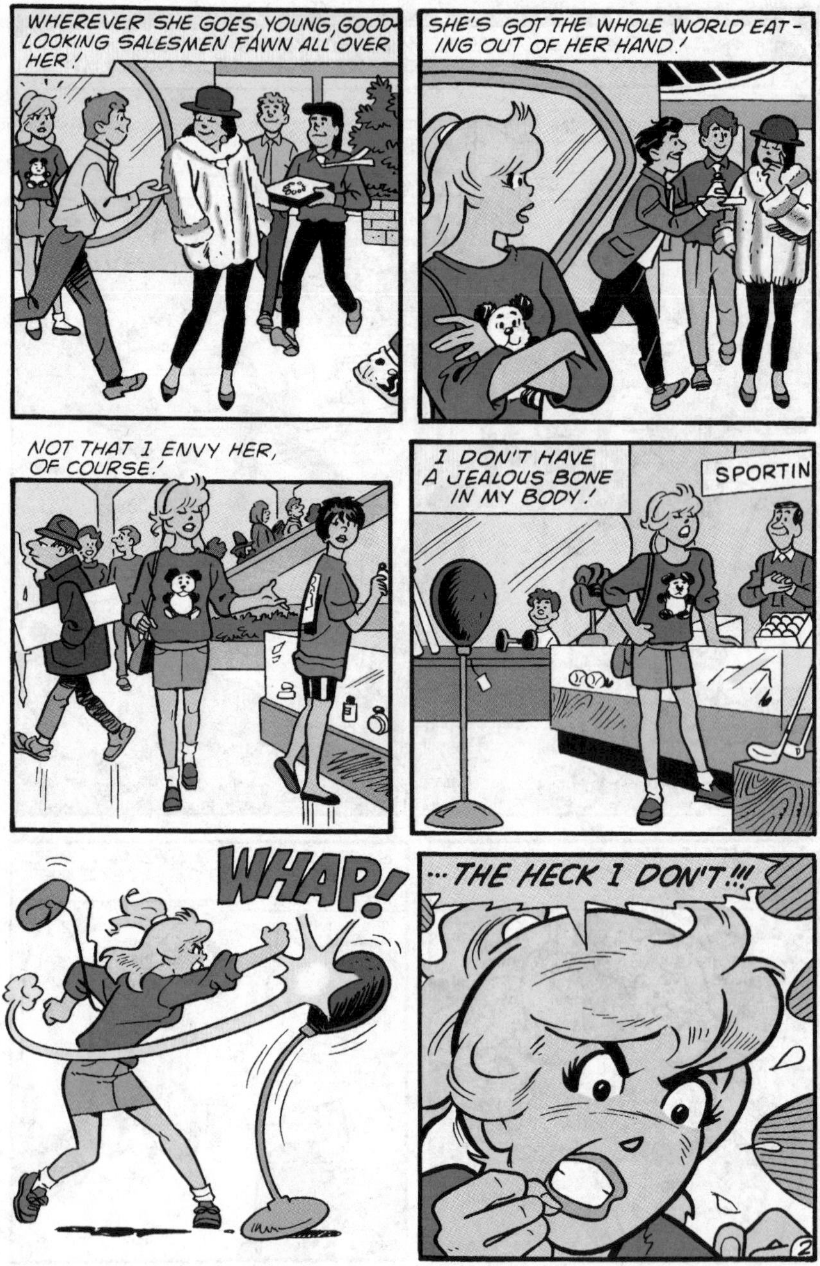
WHEREVER SHE GOES YOUNG, GOOD-LOOKING SALESMEN FAWN ALL OVER HER!
SHE'S GOT THE WHOLE WORLD EATING OUT OF HER HAND!
NOT THAT I ENVY HER, OF COURSE!
I DON'T HAVE A JEALOUS BONE IN MY BODY!
SPORTIN
WHAP!
...THE HECK I DON'T!!!

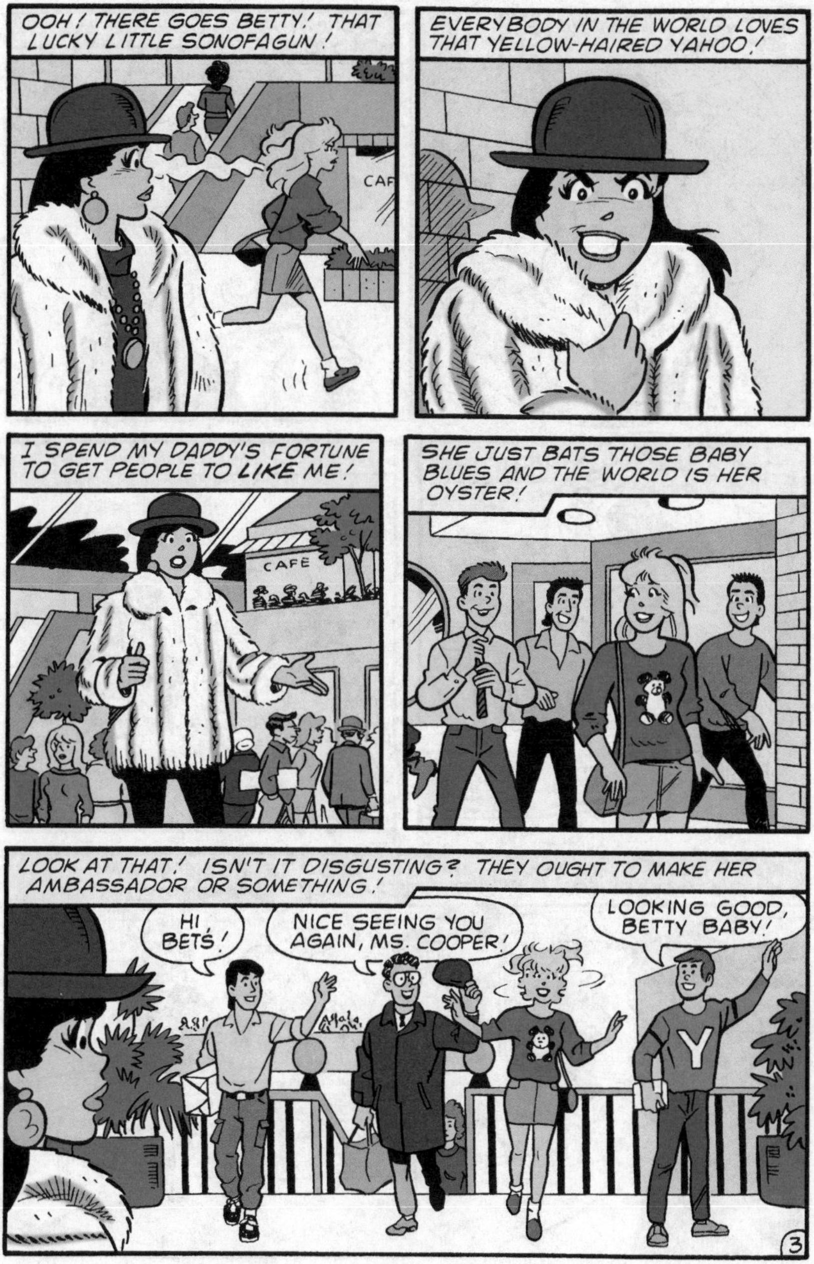
OOH! THERE GOES BETTY! THAT LUCKY LITTLE SONOFAGUN!
CAFÉ
EVERYBODY IN THE WORLD LOVES THAT YELLOW-HAIRED YAHOO!
I SPEND MY DADDY'S FORTUNE TO GET PEOPLE TO LIKE ME!
CAFÉ
SHE JUST BATS THOSE BABY BLUES AND THE WORLD IS HER OYSTER!
LOOK AT THAT! ISN'T IT DISGUSTING? THEY OUGHT TO MAKE HER AMBASSADOR OR SOMETHING!
HI, BETS!
NICE SEEING YOU AGAIN, MS. COOPER!
LOOKING GOOD, BETTY BABY!
Y
3

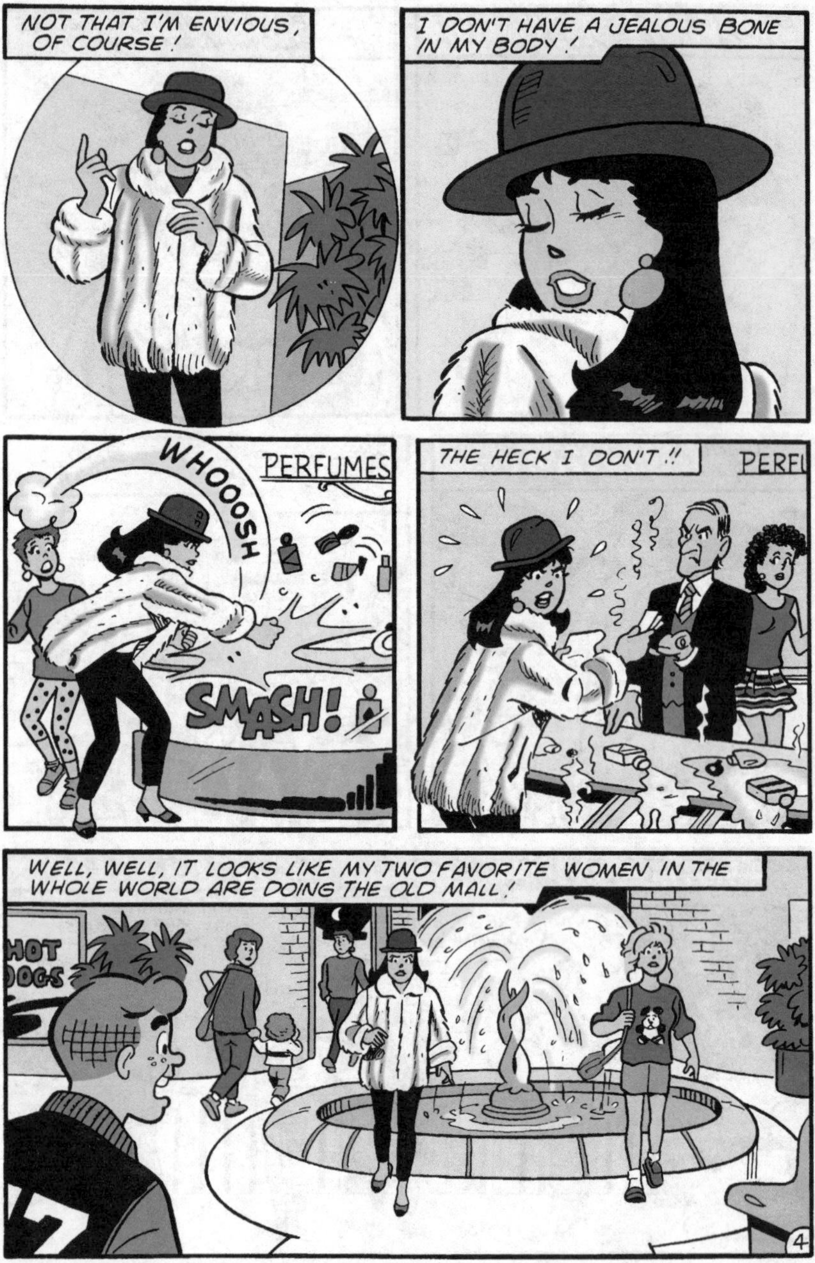
NOT THAT I'M ENVIOUS, OF COURSE!
I DON'T HAVE A JEALOUS BONE IN MY BODY!
PERFUMES
WHOOOSH
SMASH!
THE HECK I DON'T!!
PERFU
WELL, WELL, IT LOOKS LIKE MY TWO FAVORITE WOMEN IN THE WHOLE WORLD ARE DOING THE OLD MALL!
HOT DOGS
4

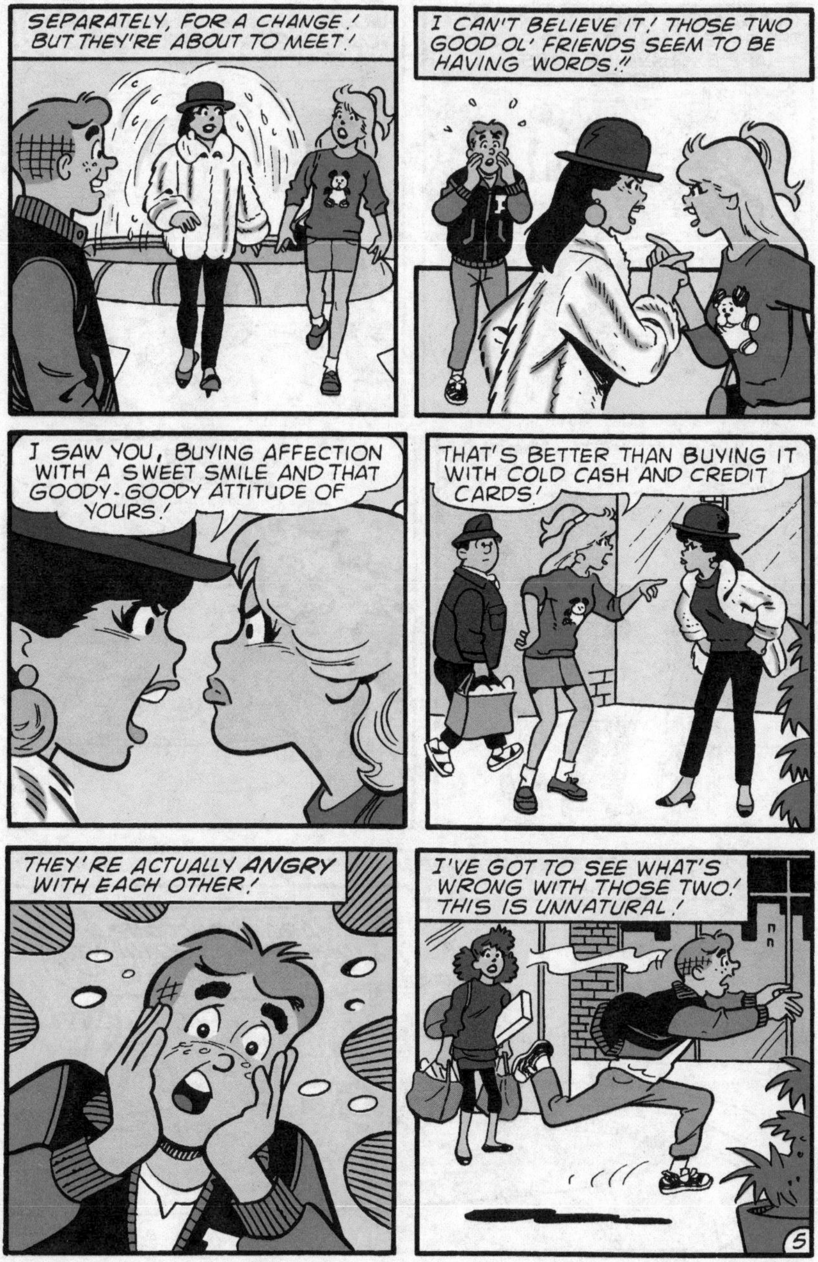
SEPARATELY, FOR A CHANGE! BUT THEY'RE ABOUT TO MEET!
I CAN'T BELIEVE IT! THOSE TWO GOOD OL' FRIENDS SEEM TO BE HAVING WORDS!!
I SAW YOU, BUYING AFFECTION WITH A SWEET SMILE AND THAT GOODY-GOODY ATTITUDE OF YOURS!
THAT'S BETTER THAN BUYING IT WITH COLD CASH AND CREDIT CARDS!
THEY'RE ACTUALLY ANGRY WITH EACH OTHER!
I'VE GOT TO SEE WHAT'S WRONG WITH THOSE TWO! THIS IS UNNATURAL!
5

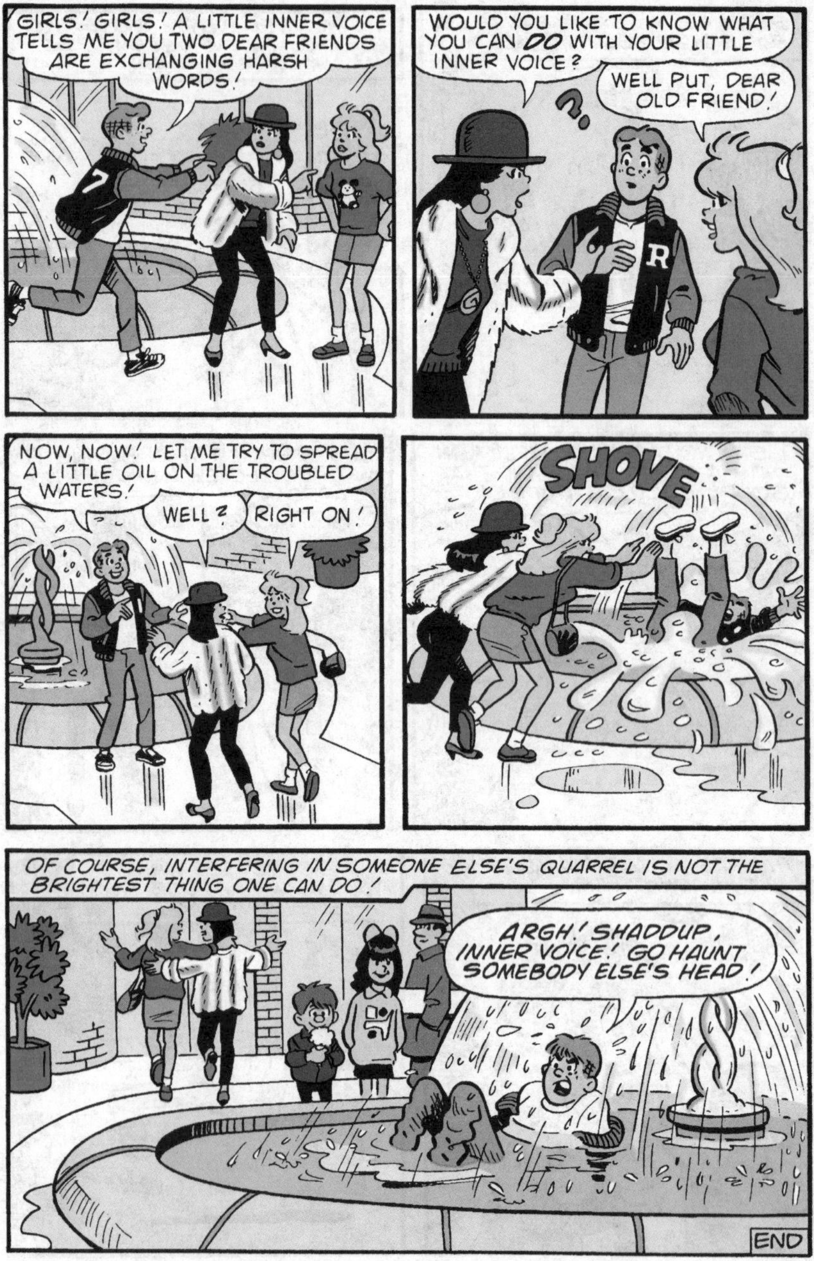
GIRLS! GIRLS! A LITTLE INNER VOICE TELLS ME YOU TWO DEAR FRIENDS ARE EXCHANGING HARSH WORDS!
WOULD YOU LIKE TO KNOW WHAT YOU CAN DO WITH YOUR LITTLE INNER VOICE?
?
WELL PUT, DEAR OLD FRIEND!
NOW, NOW! LET ME TRY TO SPREAD A LITTLE OIL ON THE TROUBLED WATERS!
WELL?
RIGHT ON!
SHOVE
OF COURSE, INTERFERING IN SOMEONE ELSE'S QUARREL IS NOT THE BRIGHTEST THING ONE CAN DO!
ARGH! SHADDUP, INNER VOICE! GO HAUNT SOMEBODY ELSE'S HEAD!
END

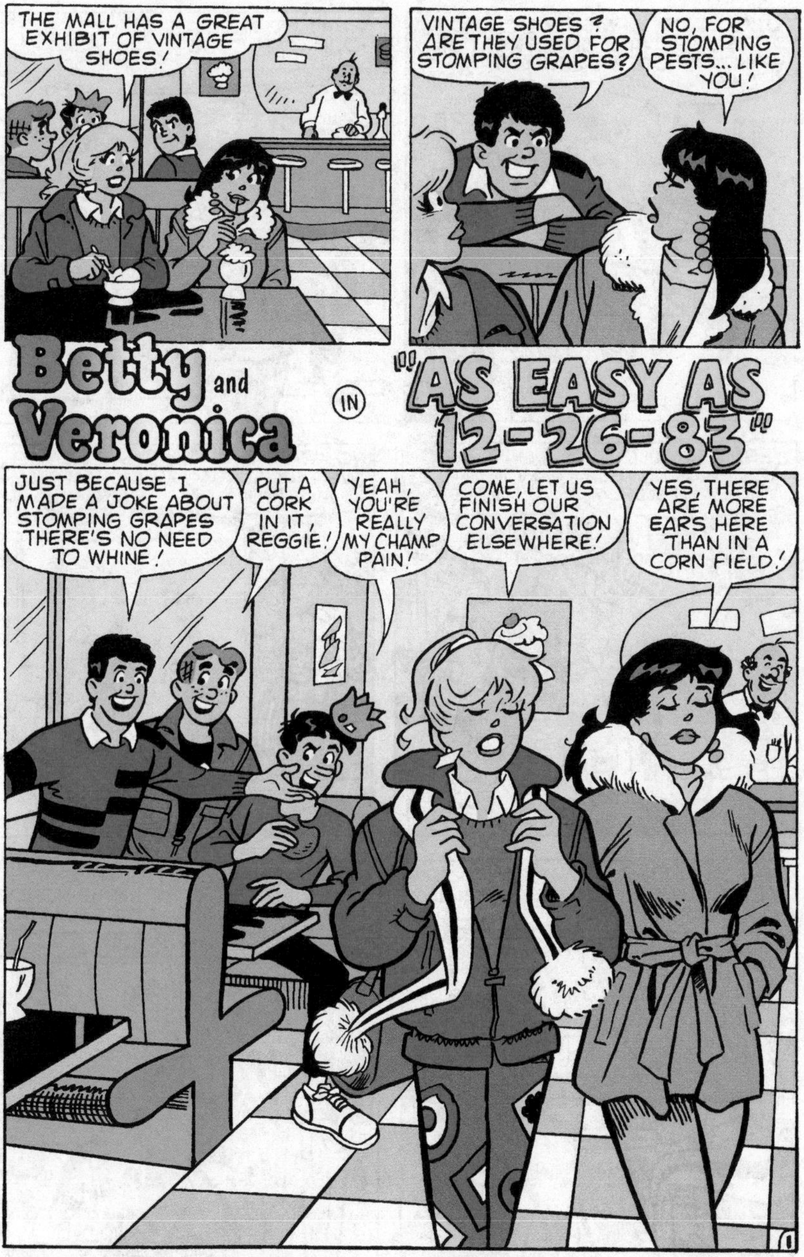
THE MALL HAS A GREAT EXHIBIT OF VINTAGE SHOES!
VINTAGE SHOES? ARE THEY USED FOR STOMPING GRAPES?
NO, FOR STOMPING PESTS... LIKE YOU!
Betty and Veronica
IN
"AS EASY AS 12-26-83"
JUST BECAUSE I MADE A JOKE ABOUT STOMPING GRAPES THERE'S NO NEED TO WHINE!
PUT A CORK IN IT, REGGIE!
YEAH, YOU'RE REALLY MY CHAMP PAIN!
COME, LET US FINISH OUR CONVERSATION ELSEWHERE!
YES, THERE ARE MORE EARS HERE THAN IN A CORN FIELD!
1

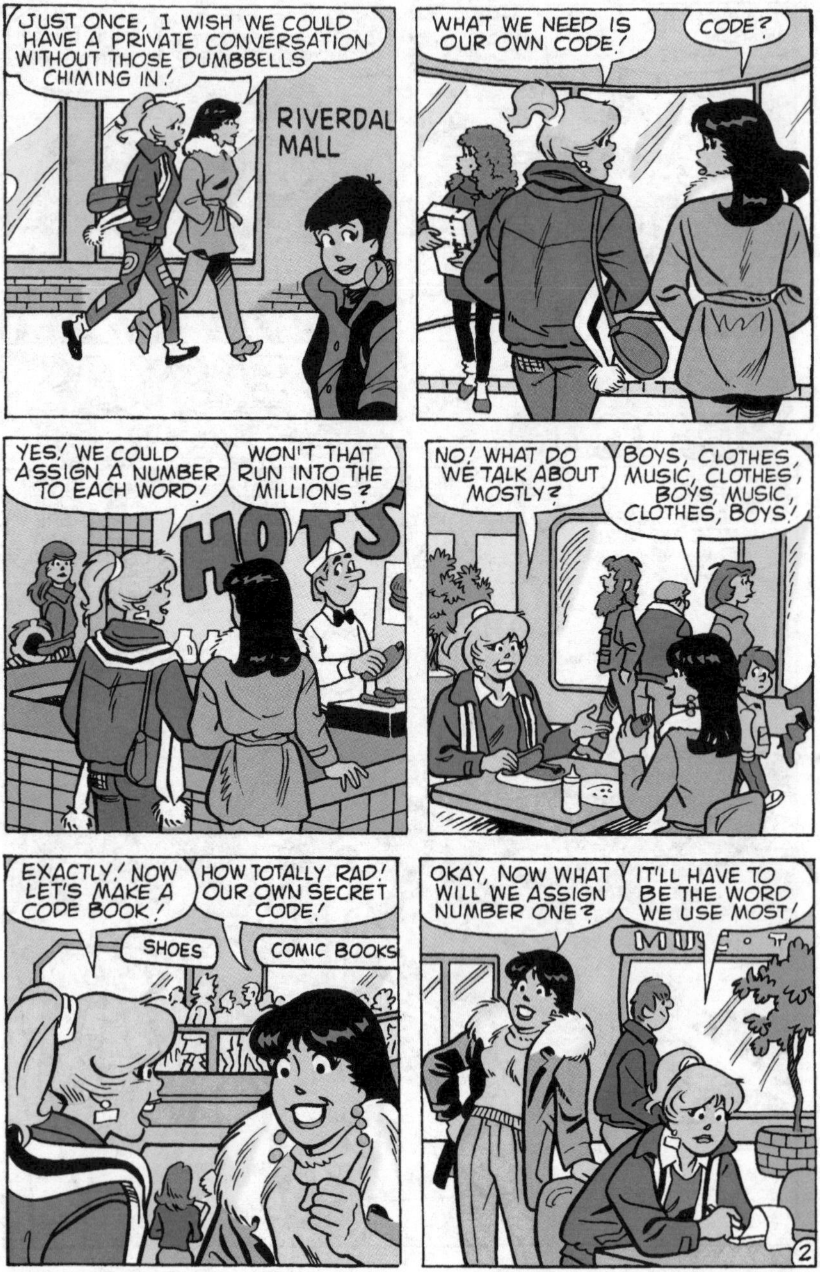
JUST ONCE, I WISH WE COULD HAVE A PRIVATE CONVERSATION WITHOUT THOSE DUMBBELLS CHIMING IN!
RIVERDAL MALL
WHAT WE NEED IS OUR OWN CODE!
CODE?
YES! WE COULD ASSIGN A NUMBER TO EACH WORD!
WON'T THAT RUN INTO THE MILLIONS?
HOTS
NO! WHAT DO WE TALK ABOUT MOSTLY?
BOYS, CLOTHES, MUSIC, CLOTHES, BOYS, MUSIC, CLOTHES, BOYS!
EXACTLY! NOW LET'S MAKE A CODE BOOK!
HOW TOTALLY RAD! OUR OWN SECRET CODE!
SHOES
COMIC BOOKS
OKAY, NOW WHAT WILL WE ASSIGN NUMBER ONE?
IT'LL HAVE TO BE THE WORD WE USE MOST!
2

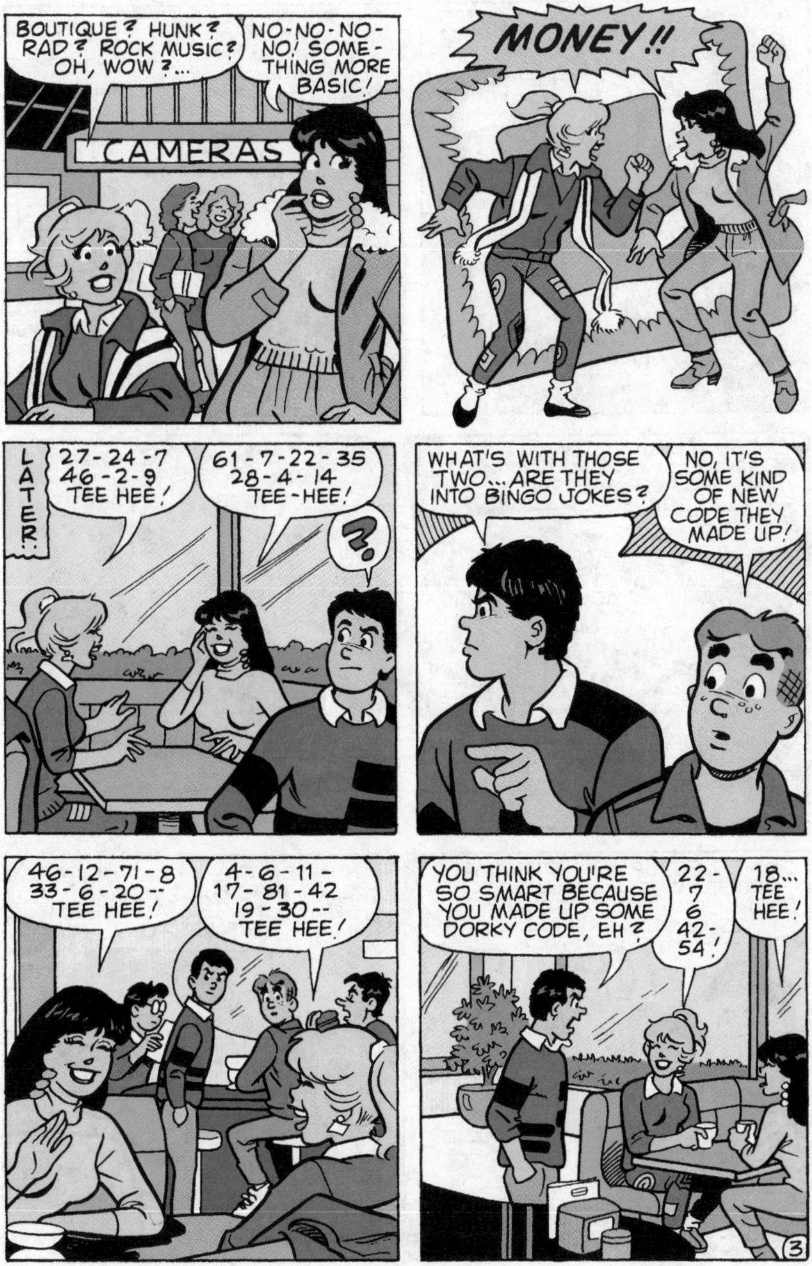
BOUTIQUE? HUNK? RAD? ROCK MUSIC? OH, WOW?...
NO-NO-NO-NO! SOMETHING MORE BASIC!
CAMERAS
MONEY!!
LATER:
27-24-7 46-2-9 TEE HEE!
61-7-22-35 28-4-14 TEE-HEE!
?
WHAT'S WITH THOSE TWO... ARE THEY INTO BINGO JOKES?
NO, IT'S SOME KIND OF NEW CODE THEY MADE UP!
46-12-71-8 33-6-20-- TEE HEE!
4-6-11-17-81-42 19-30-- TEE HEE!
YOU THINK YOU'RE SO SMART BECAUSE YOU MADE UP SOME DORKY CODE, EH?
22-7 6 42-54!
18... TEE HEE!
3

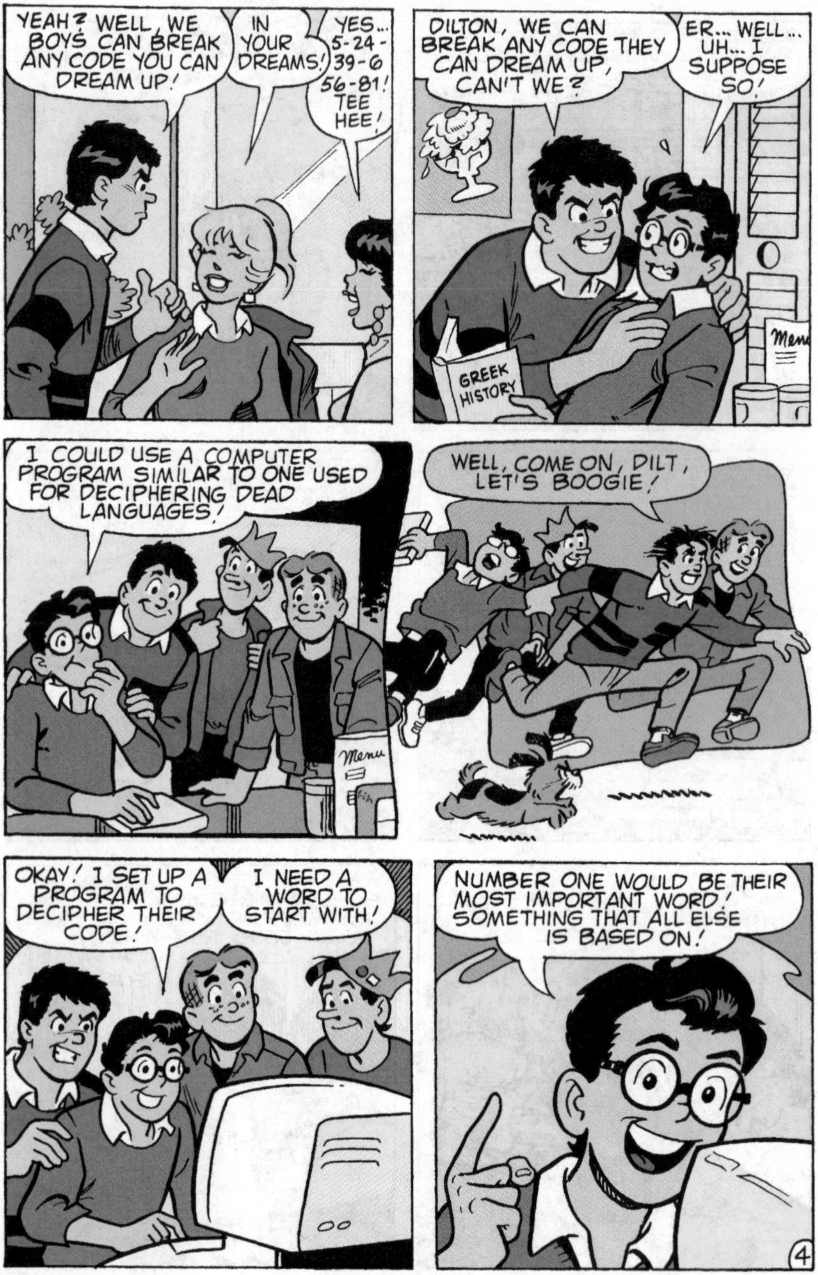
YEAH? WELL, WE BOYS CAN BREAK ANY CODE YOU CAN DREAM UP!
IN YOUR DREAMS!
YES... 5-24-39-6 56-81! TEE HEE!
DILTON, WE CAN BREAK ANY CODE THEY CAN DREAM UP, CAN'T WE?
ER... WELL... UH... I SUPPOSE SO!
GREEK HISTORY
Menu
I COULD USE A COMPUTER PROGRAM SIMILAR TO ONE USED FOR DECIPHERING DEAD LANGUAGES!
Menu
WELL, COME ON, DILT, LET'S BOOGIE!
OKAY! I SET UP A PROGRAM TO DECIPHER THEIR CODE!
I NEED A WORD TO START WITH!
NUMBER ONE WOULD BE THEIR MOST IMPORTANT WORD! SOMETHING THAT ALL ELSE IS BASED ON!
4

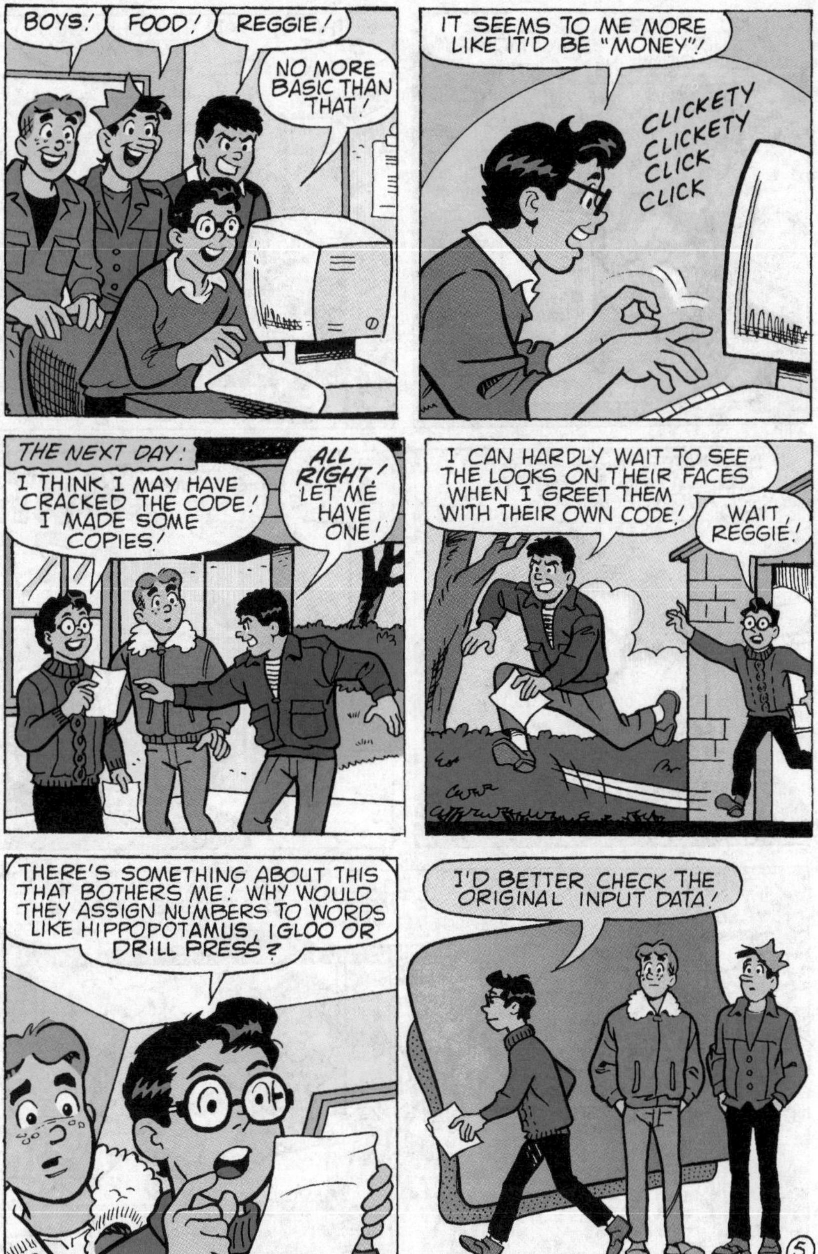

BOYS!
FOOD!
REGGIE!
NO MORE BASIC THAN THAT!
IT SEEMS TO ME MORE LIKE IT'D BE "MONEY"!
CLICKETY CLICKETY CLICK CLICK
THE NEXT DAY:
I THINK I MAY HAVE CRACKED THE CODE! I MADE SOME COPIES!
ALL RIGHT! LET ME HAVE ONE!
I CAN HARDLY WAIT TO SEE THE LOOKS ON THEIR FACES WHEN I GREET THEM WITH THEIR OWN CODE!
WAIT, REGGIE!
THERE'S SOMETHING ABOUT THIS THAT BOTHERS ME! WHY WOULD THEY ASSIGN NUMBERS TO WORDS LIKE HIPPOPOTAMUS, IGLOO OR DRILL PRESS?
I'D BETTER CHECK THE ORIGINAL INPUT DATA!
5

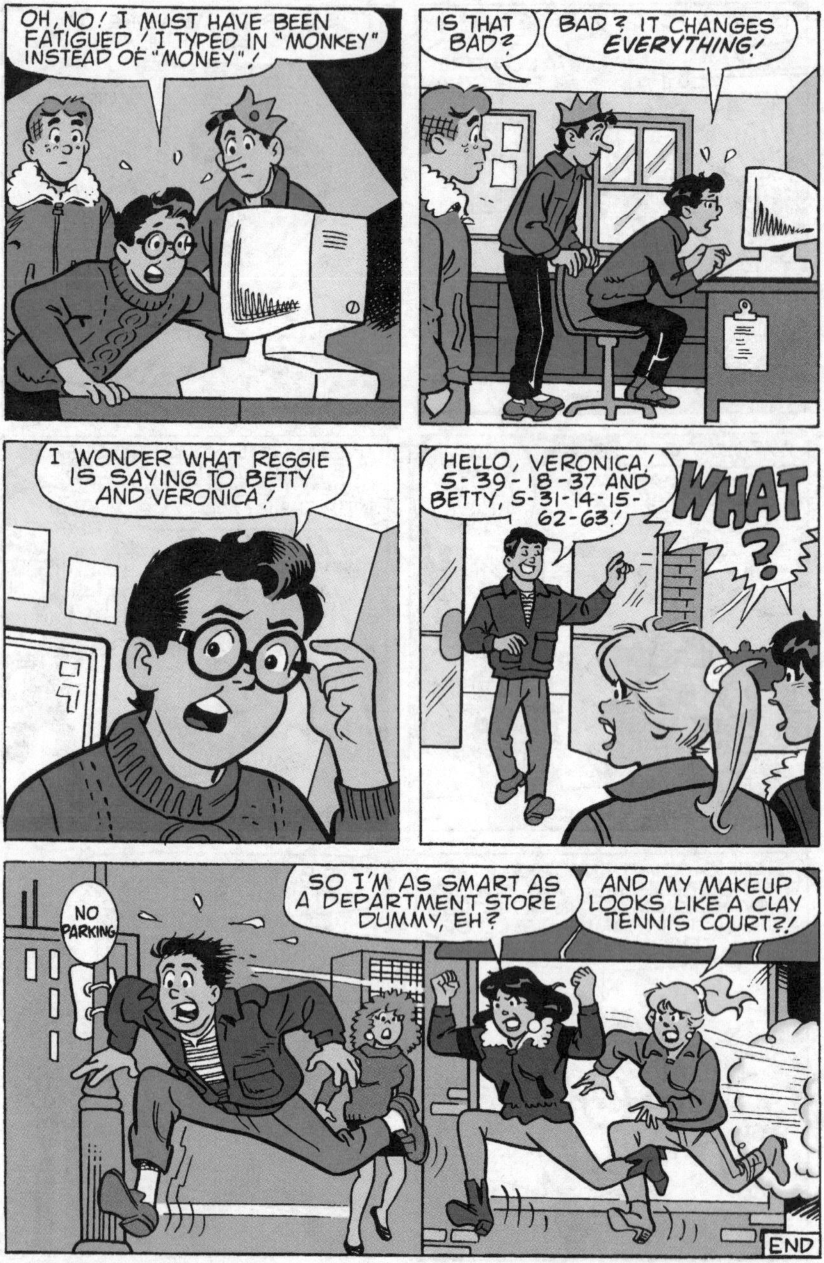
OH, NO! I MUST HAVE BEEN FATIGUED! I TYPED IN "MONKEY" INSTEAD OF "MONEY"!
IS THAT BAD?
BAD? IT CHANGES EVERYTHING!
I WONDER WHAT REGGIE IS SAYING TO BETTY AND VERONICA!
HELLO, VERONICA! 5-39-18-37 AND BETTY, 5-31-14-15-62-63!
WHAT?
NO PARKING
SO I'M AS SMART AS A DEPARTMENT STORE DUMMY, EH?
AND MY MAKEUP LOOKS LIKE A CLAY TENNIS COURT?!
END

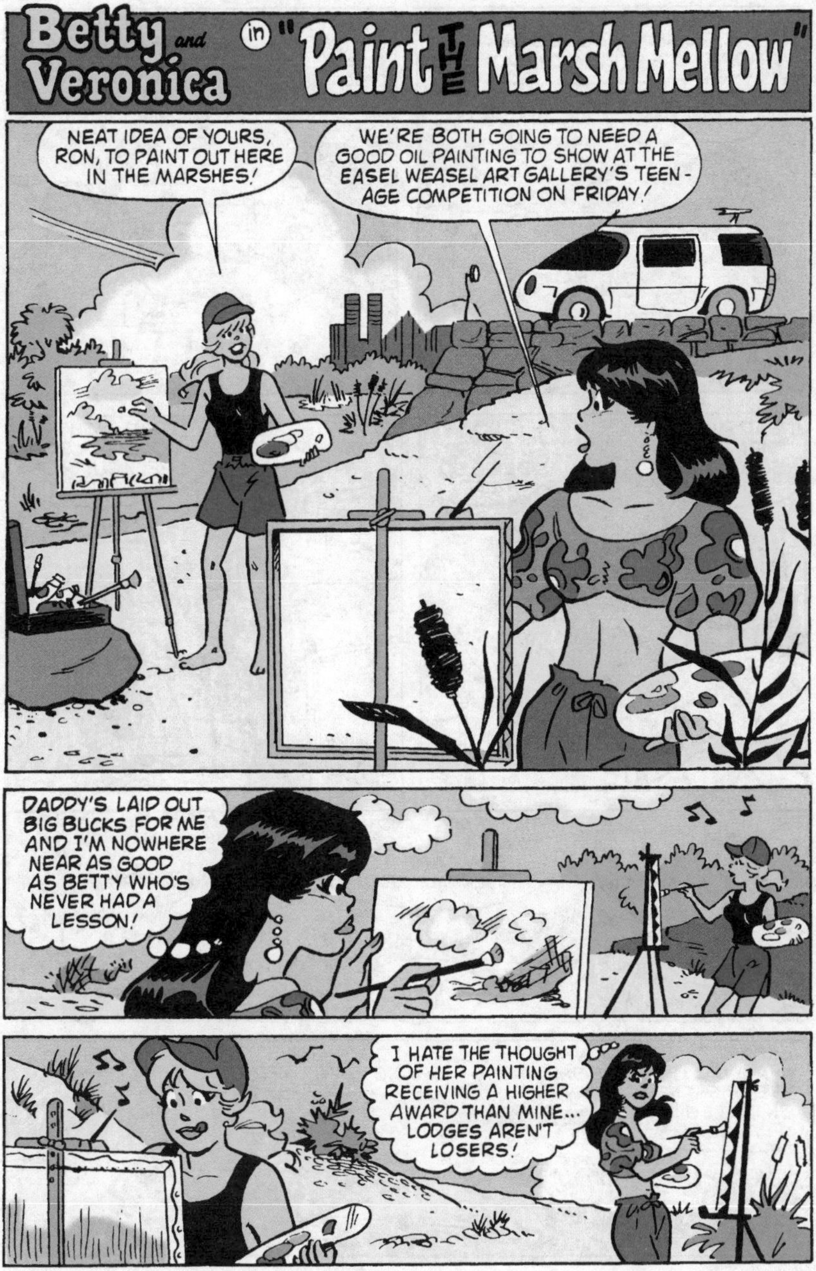
Betty and Veronica
in "Paint the Marsh Mellow"
NEAT IDEA OF YOURS, RON, TO PAINT OUT HERE IN THE MARSHES!
WE'RE BOTH GOING TO NEED A GOOD OIL PAINTING TO SHOW AT THE EASEL WEASEL ART GALLERY'S TEEN-AGE COMPETITION ON FRIDAY!
DADDY'S LAID OUT BIG BUCKS FOR ME AND I'M NOWHERE NEAR AS GOOD AS BETTY WHO'S NEVER HAD A LESSON!
I HATE THE THOUGHT OF HER PAINTING RECEIVING A HIGHER AWARD THAN MINE... LODGES AREN'T LOSERS!

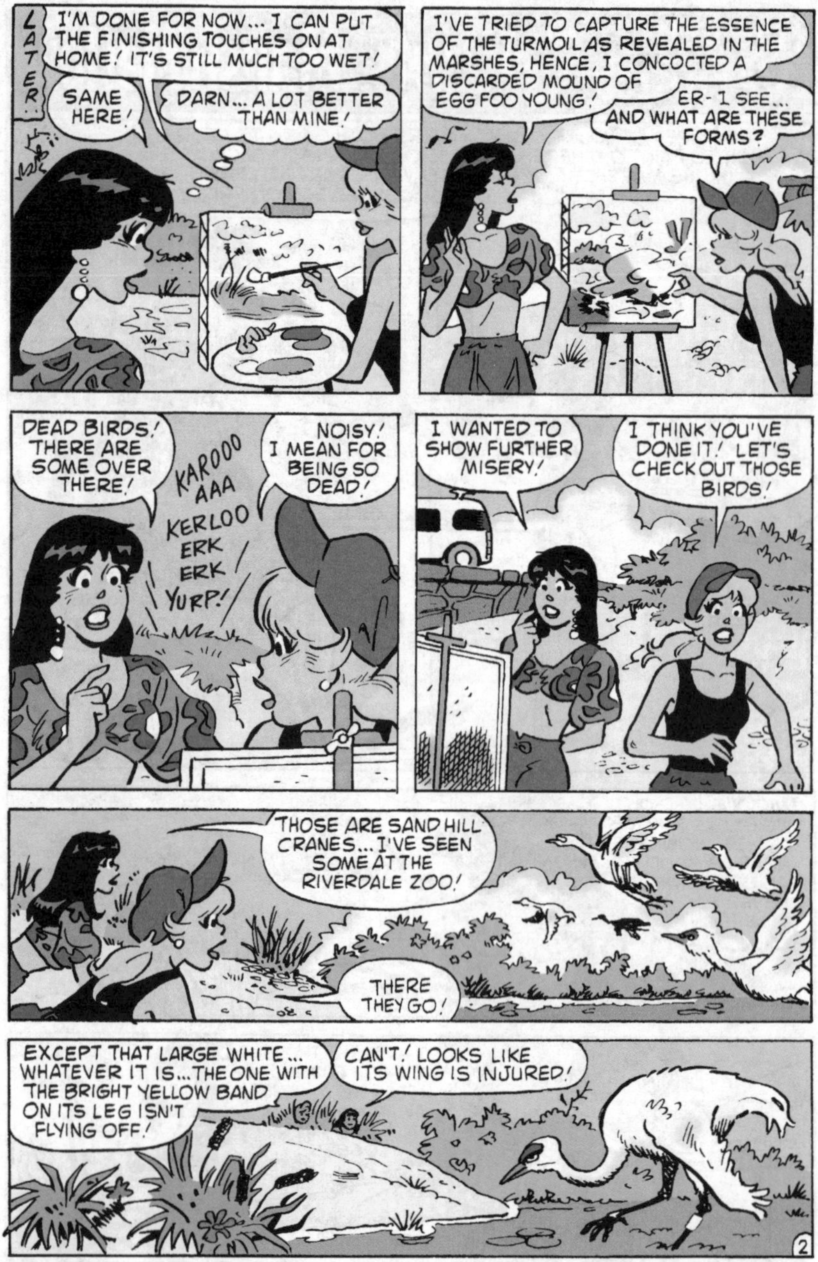
LATER...
I'M DONE FOR NOW... I CAN PUT THE FINISHING TOUCHES ON AT HOME! IT'S STILL MUCH TOO WET!
SAME HERE!
DARN... A LOT BETTER THAN MINE!
I'VE TRIED TO CAPTURE THE ESSENCE OF THE TURMOIL AS REVEALED IN THE MARSHES, HENCE, I CONCOCTED A DISCARDED MOUND OF EGG FOO YOUNG!
ER- I SEE... AND WHAT ARE THESE FORMS?
DEAD BIRDS! THERE ARE SOME OVER THERE!
KAROOO
AAA
KERLOO
ERK
ERK
YURP!
NOISY! I MEAN FOR BEING SO DEAD!
I WANTED TO SHOW FURTHER MISERY!
I THINK YOU'VE DONE IT! LET'S CHECK OUT THOSE BIRDS!
THOSE ARE SAND HILL CRANES... I'VE SEEN SOME AT THE RIVERDALE ZOO!
THERE THEY GO!
EXCEPT THAT LARGE WHITE... WHATEVER IT IS... THE ONE WITH THE BRIGHT YELLOW BAND ON ITS LEG ISN'T FLYING OFF!
CAN'T! LOOKS LIKE ITS WING IS INJURED!
2

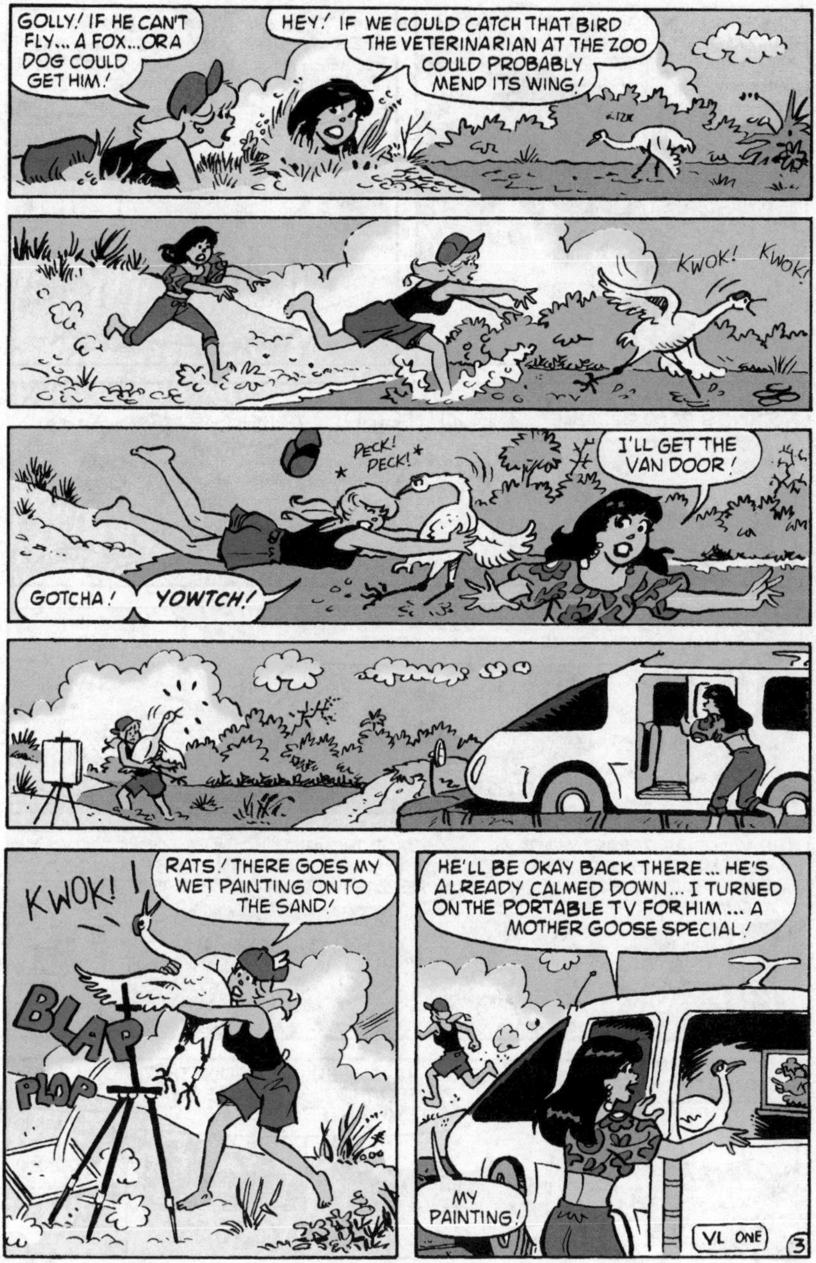
GOLLY! IF HE CAN'T FLY... A FOX...OR A DOG COULD GET HIM!
HEY! IF WE COULD CATCH THAT BIRD THE VETERINARIAN AT THE ZOO COULD PROBABLY MEND ITS WING!
KWOK! KWOK!
PECK! PECK!
I'LL GET THE VAN DOOR!
GOTCHA!
YOWTCH!
KWOK!
RATS! THERE GOES MY WET PAINTING ONTO THE SAND!
BLAP
PLOP
HE'LL BE OKAY BACK THERE... HE'S ALREADY CALMED DOWN... I TURNED ON THE PORTABLE TV FOR HIM... A MOTHER GOOSE SPECIAL!
MY PAINTING!
VL ONE
3

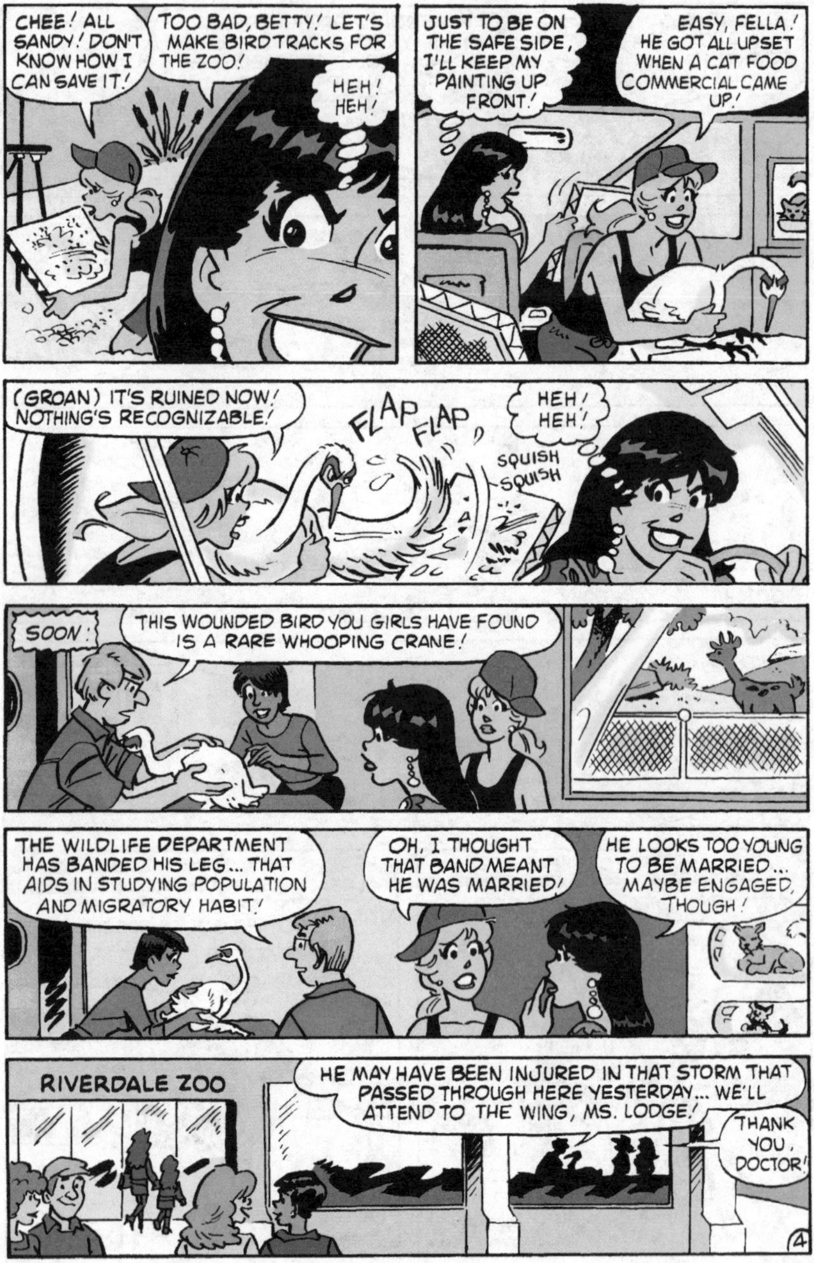
CHEE! ALL SANDY! DON'T KNOW HOW I CAN SAVE IT!
TOO BAD, BETTY! LET'S MAKE BIRD TRACKS FOR THE ZOO!
HEH! HEH!
JUST TO BE ON THE SAFE SIDE, I'LL KEEP MY PAINTING UP FRONT!
EASY, FELLA! HE GOT ALL UPSET WHEN A CAT FOOD COMMERCIAL CAME UP!
(GROAN) IT'S RUINED NOW! NOTHING'S RECOGNIZABLE!
FLAP FLAP
HEH! HEH!
SQUISH SQUISH
SOON:
THIS WOUNDED BIRD YOU GIRLS HAVE FOUND IS A RARE WHOOPING CRANE!
THE WILDLIFE DEPARTMENT HAS BANDED HIS LEG... THAT AIDS IN STUDYING POPULATION AND MIGRATORY HABIT!
OH, I THOUGHT THAT BAND MEANT HE WAS MARRIED!
HE LOOKS TOO YOUNG TO BE MARRIED... MAYBE ENGAGED, THOUGH!
RIVERDALE ZOO
HE MAY HAVE BEEN INJURED IN THAT STORM THAT PASSED THROUGH HERE YESTERDAY... WE'LL ATTEND TO THE WING, MS. LODGE!
THANK YOU, DOCTOR!
4

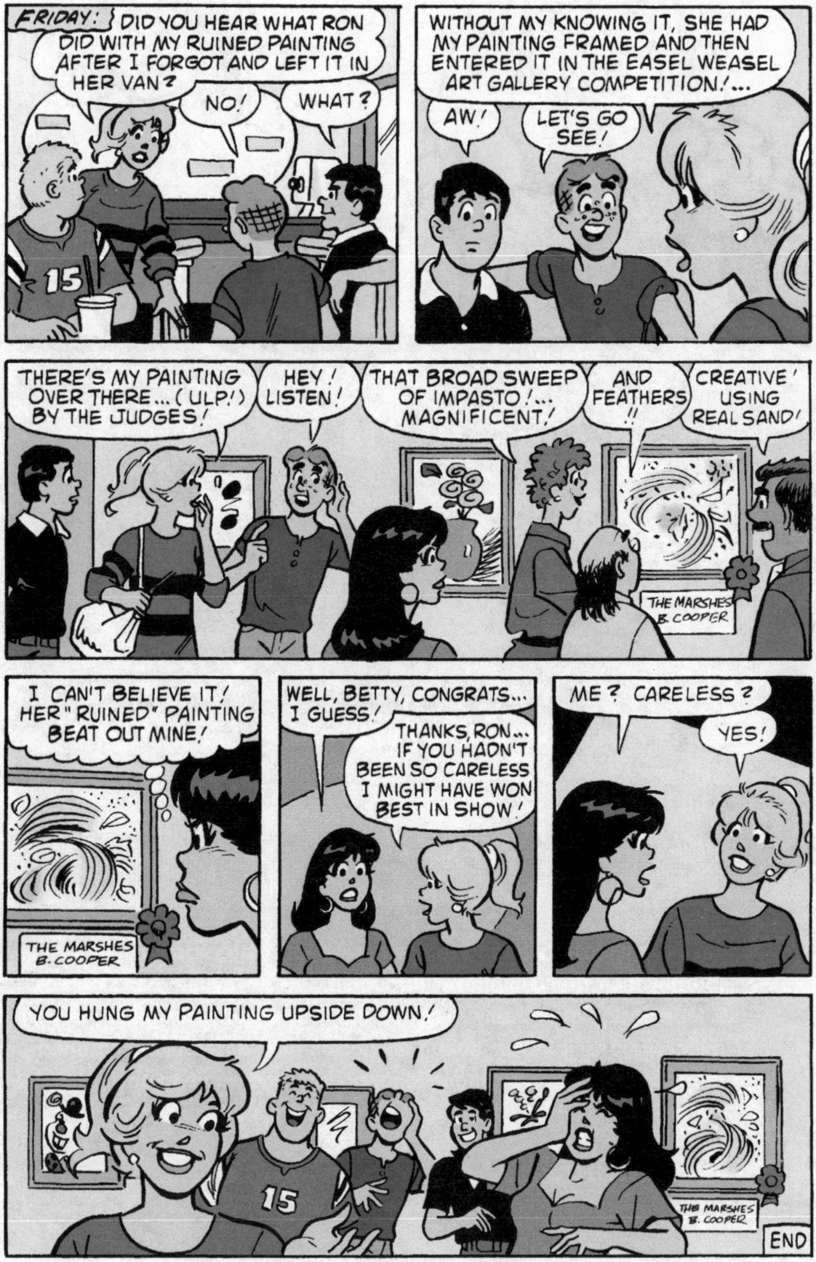
FRIDAY:
DID YOU HEAR WHAT RON DID WITH MY RUINED PAINTING AFTER I FORGOT AND LEFT IT IN HER VAN?
NO!
WHAT?
WITHOUT MY KNOWING IT, SHE HAD MY PAINTING FRAMED AND THEN ENTERED IT IN THE EASEL WEASEL ART GALLERY COMPETITION!...
AW!
LET'S GO SEE!
THERE'S MY PAINTING OVER THERE... (ULP!) BY THE JUDGES!
HEY! LISTEN!
THAT BROAD SWEEP OF IMPASTO!... MAGNIFICENT!
AND FEATHERS !!
CREATIVE USING REAL SAND!
THE MARSHES B. COOPER
I CAN'T BELIEVE IT! HER "RUINED" PAINTING BEAT OUT MINE!
THE MARSHES B. COOPER
WELL, BETTY, CONGRATS... I GUESS!
THANKS, RON... IF YOU HADN'T BEEN SO CARELESS I MIGHT HAVE WON BEST IN SHOW!
ME? CARELESS?
YES!
YOU HUNG MY PAINTING UPSIDE DOWN!
15
THE MARSHES B. COOPER
END

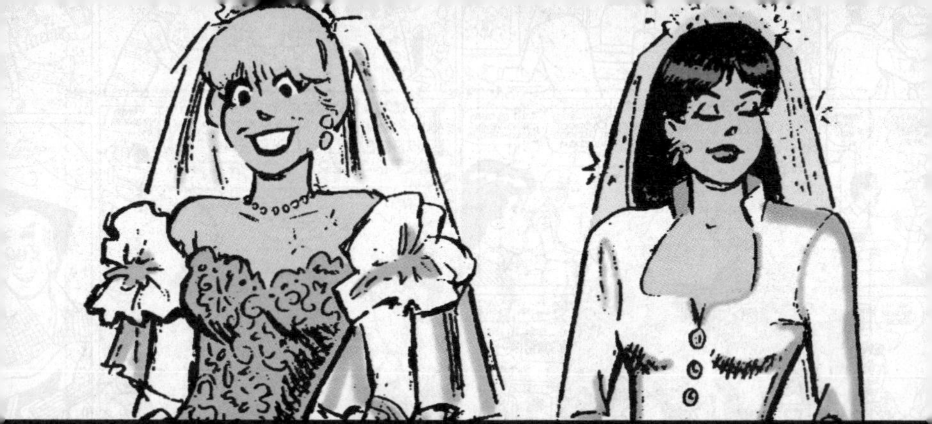

SUPER SLEUTHER

BETTY #15, 1994

Bob Bolling, Doug Crane, Rudy Lapick, Bill Yoshida, Barry Grossman

ARCHIE'S CHOICE

BETTY & VERONICA VOL. 2 #112, 1997

Barbara Slate, Dan DeCarlo, Bill Yoshida, Barry Grossman

BETTER FASHIONABLY LATE THAN NEVER

BETTY & VERONICA VOL. 2 #136, 1999

Kathleen Webb, Dan DeCarlo, Henry Scarpelli, Bill Yoshida, Barry Grossman

The charm of Betty and Veronica is not their rivalry for Archie, but the journey their friendship takes through it. This is why they still stand as a team today after many decades: they embolden each other through their relationship. Even though they come from different backgrounds, they choose to try and understand, accept, and relate to each other. At the end of the day, Betty and Veronica are sisters for life.

- ELAINA UNGER *Colorist, Archie Comics*

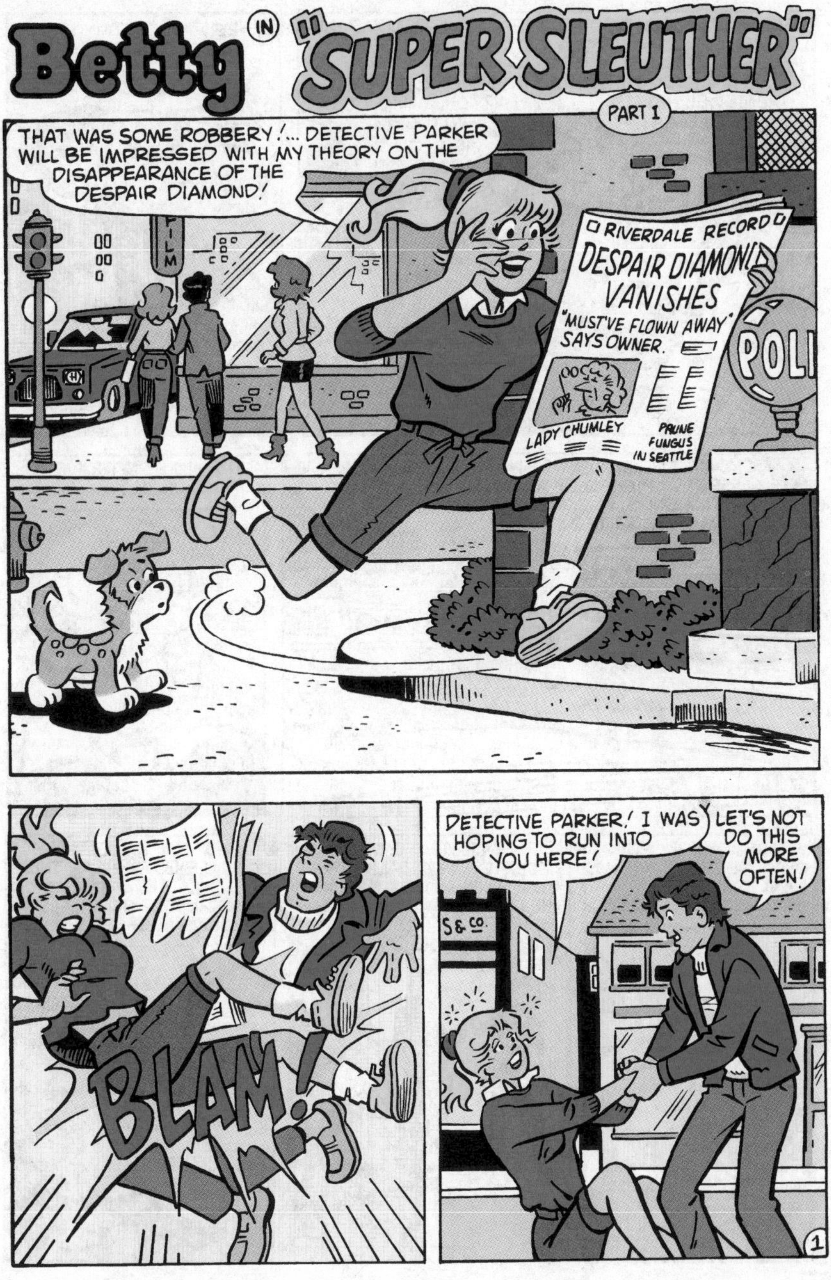
Betty IN "SUPER SLEUTHER"
PART 1
THAT WAS SOME ROBBERY!... DETECTIVE PARKER WILL BE IMPRESSED WITH MY THEORY ON THE DISAPPEARANCE OF THE DESPAIR DIAMOND!
FILM
RIVERDALE RECORD
DESPAIR DIAMOND VANISHES
"MUST'VE FLOWN AWAY" SAYS OWNER.
LADY CHUMLEY
PRUNE FUNGUS IN SEATTLE
POLI
BLAM!
DETECTIVE PARKER! I WAS HOPING TO RUN INTO YOU HERE!
LET'S NOT DO THIS MORE OFTEN!
S&CO.
1

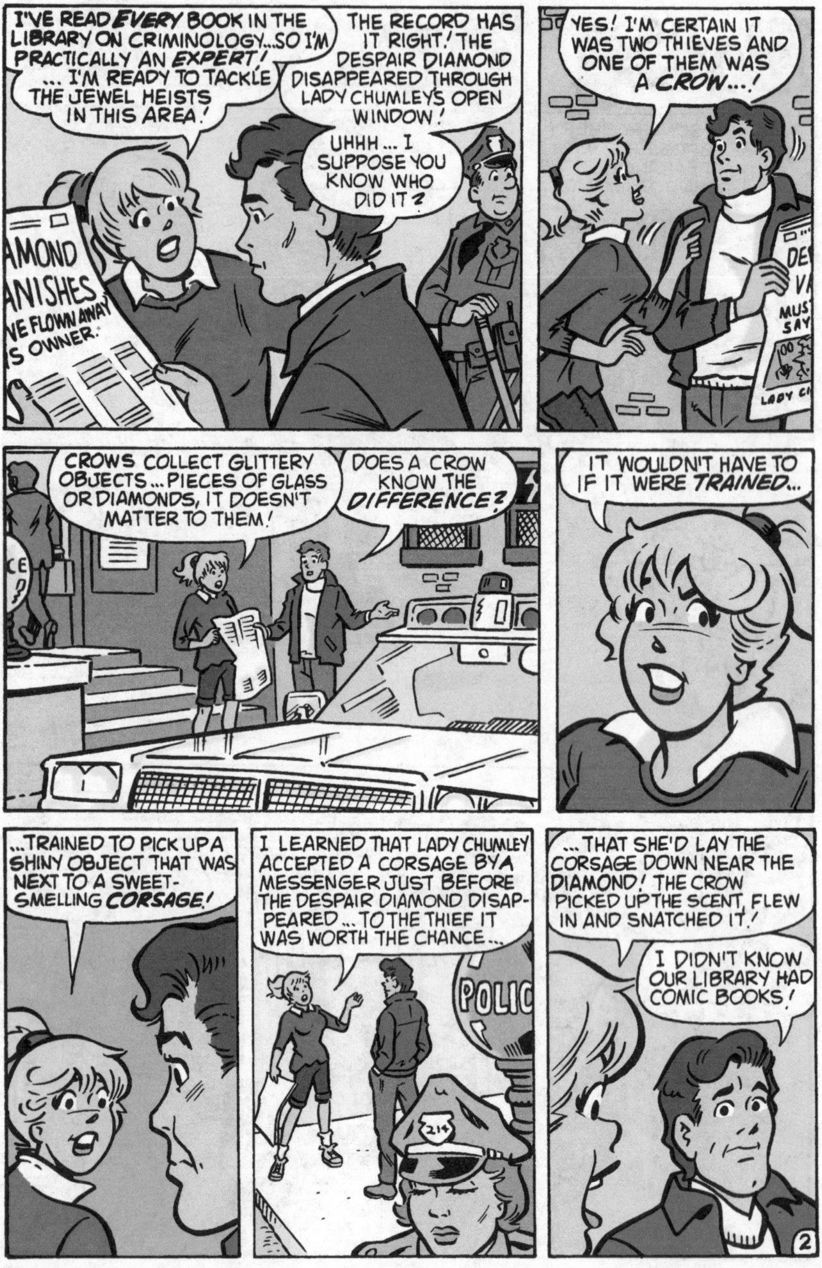
I'VE READ EVERY BOOK IN THE LIBRARY ON CRIMINOLOGY...SO I'M PRACTICALLY AN EXPERT! ... I'M READY TO TACKLE THE JEWEL HEISTS IN THIS AREA!
THE RECORD HAS IT RIGHT! THE DESPAIR DIAMOND DISAPPEARED THROUGH LADY CHUMLEY'S OPEN WINDOW!
UHHH ... I SUPPOSE YOU KNOW WHO DID IT?
AMOND
ANISHES
VE FLOWN AWAY
S OWNER.
YES! I'M CERTAIN IT WAS TWO THIEVES AND ONE OF THEM WAS A CROW...!
CROWS COLLECT GLITTERY OBJECTS ... PIECES OF GLASS OR DIAMONDS, IT DOESN'T MATTER TO THEM!
DOES A CROW KNOW THE DIFFERENCE?
IT WOULDN'T HAVE TO IF IT WERE TRAINED...
...TRAINED TO PICK UP A SHINY OBJECT THAT WAS NEXT TO A SWEET-SMELLING CORSAGE!
I LEARNED THAT LADY CHUMLEY ACCEPTED A CORSAGE BY A MESSENGER JUST BEFORE THE DESPAIR DIAMOND DISAPPEARED ... TO THE THIEF IT WAS WORTH THE CHANCE...
POLIC
... THAT SHE'D LAY THE CORSAGE DOWN NEAR THE DIAMOND! THE CROW PICKED UP THE SCENT, FLEW IN AND SNATCHED IT!
I DIDN'T KNOW OUR LIBRARY HAD COMIC BOOKS!
2

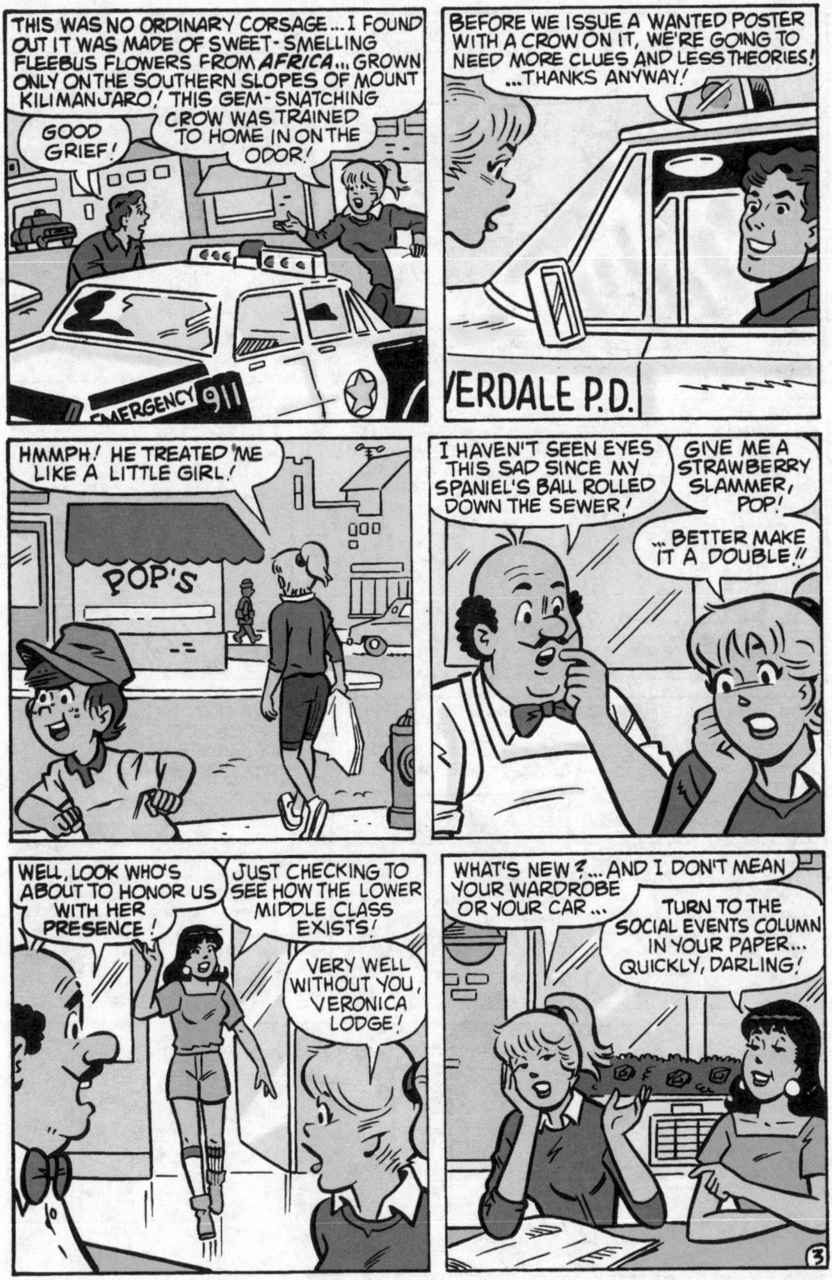
THIS WAS NO ORDINARY CORSAGE... I FOUND OUT IT WAS MADE OF SWEET-SMELLING FLEEBUS FLOWERS FROM AFRICA... GROWN ONLY ON THE SOUTHERN SLOPES OF MOUNT KILIMANJARO! THIS GEM-SNATCHING CROW WAS TRAINED TO HOME IN ON THE ODOR!
GOOD GRIEF!
EMERGENCY 911
BEFORE WE ISSUE A WANTED POSTER WITH A CROW ON IT, WE'RE GOING TO NEED MORE CLUES AND LESS THEORIES! ...THANKS ANYWAY!
VERDALE P.D.
HMMPH! HE TREATED ME LIKE A LITTLE GIRL!
POP'S
I HAVEN'T SEEN EYES THIS SAD SINCE MY SPANIEL'S BALL ROLLED DOWN THE SEWER!
GIVE ME A STRAWBERRY SLAMMER, POP!
... BETTER MAKE IT A DOUBLE!!
WELL, LOOK WHO'S ABOUT TO HONOR US WITH HER PRESENCE!
JUST CHECKING TO SEE HOW THE LOWER MIDDLE CLASS EXISTS!
VERY WELL WITHOUT YOU, VERONICA LODGE!
WHAT'S NEW?... AND I DON'T MEAN YOUR WARDROBE OR YOUR CAR...
TURN TO THE SOCIAL EVENTS COLUMN IN YOUR PAPER... QUICKLY, DARLING!
3

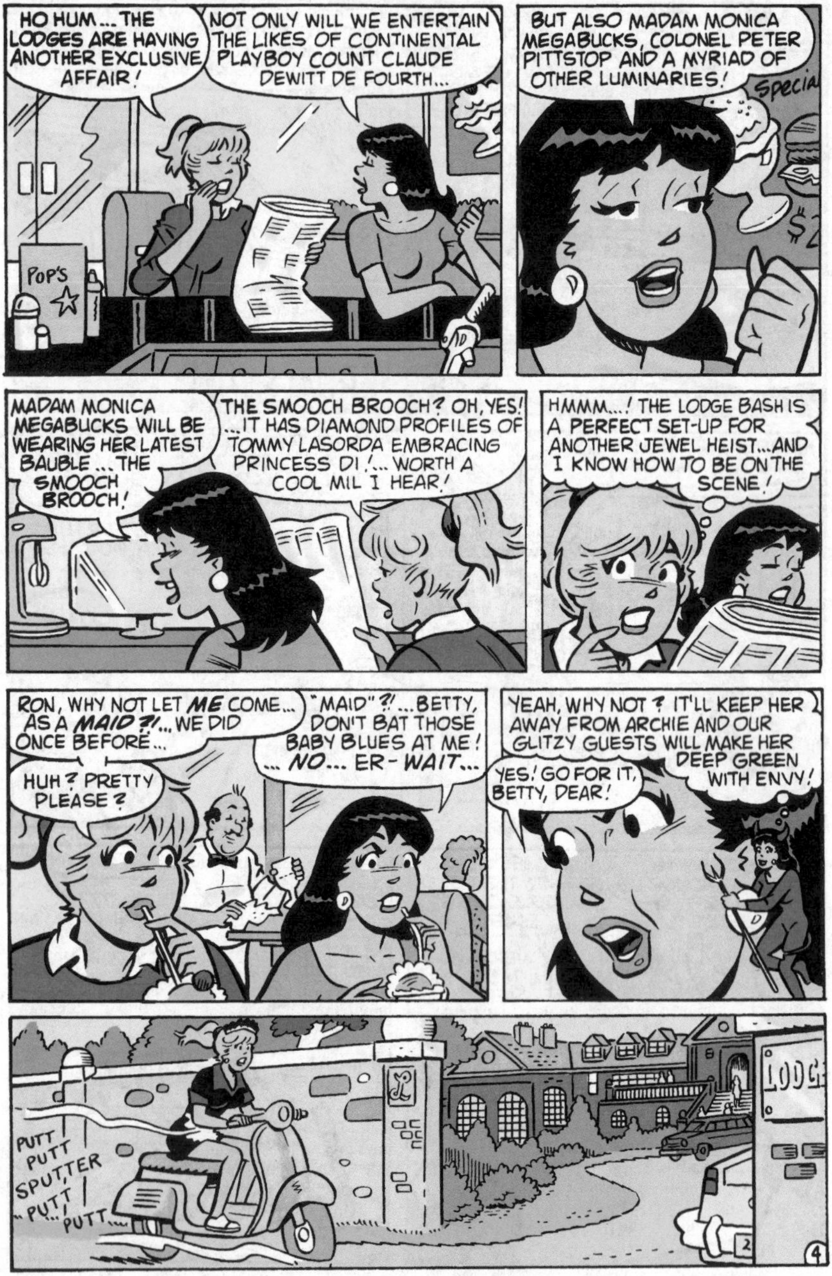
HO HUM... THE LODGES ARE HAVING ANOTHER EXCLUSIVE AFFAIR!
NOT ONLY WILL WE ENTERTAIN THE LIKES OF CONTINENTAL PLAYBOY COUNT CLAUDE DEWITT DE FOURTH...
POP'S
BUT ALSO MADAM MONICA MEGABUCKS, COLONEL PETER PITTSTOP AND A MYRIAD OF OTHER LUMINARIES!
MADAM MONICA MEGABUCKS WILL BE WEARING HER LATEST BAUBLE... THE SMOOCH BROOCH!
THE SMOOCH BROOCH? OH, YES! ...IT HAS DIAMOND PROFILES OF TOMMY LASORDA EMBRACING PRINCESS DI!... WORTH A COOL MIL I HEAR!
HMMM...! THE LODGE BASH IS A PERFECT SET-UP FOR ANOTHER JEWEL HEIST...AND I KNOW HOW TO BE ON THE SCENE!
RON, WHY NOT LET ME COME... AS A MAID?!... WE DID ONCE BEFORE...
"MAID"?! ...BETTY, DON'T BAT THOSE BABY BLUES AT ME! ...NO... ER-WAIT...
HUH? PRETTY PLEASE?
YEAH, WHY NOT? IT'LL KEEP HER AWAY FROM ARCHIE AND OUR GLITZY GUESTS WILL MAKE HER DEEP GREEN WITH ENVY!
YES! GO FOR IT, BETTY, DEAR!
PUTT PUTT SPUTTER PUTT! PUTT...
LODGE
4

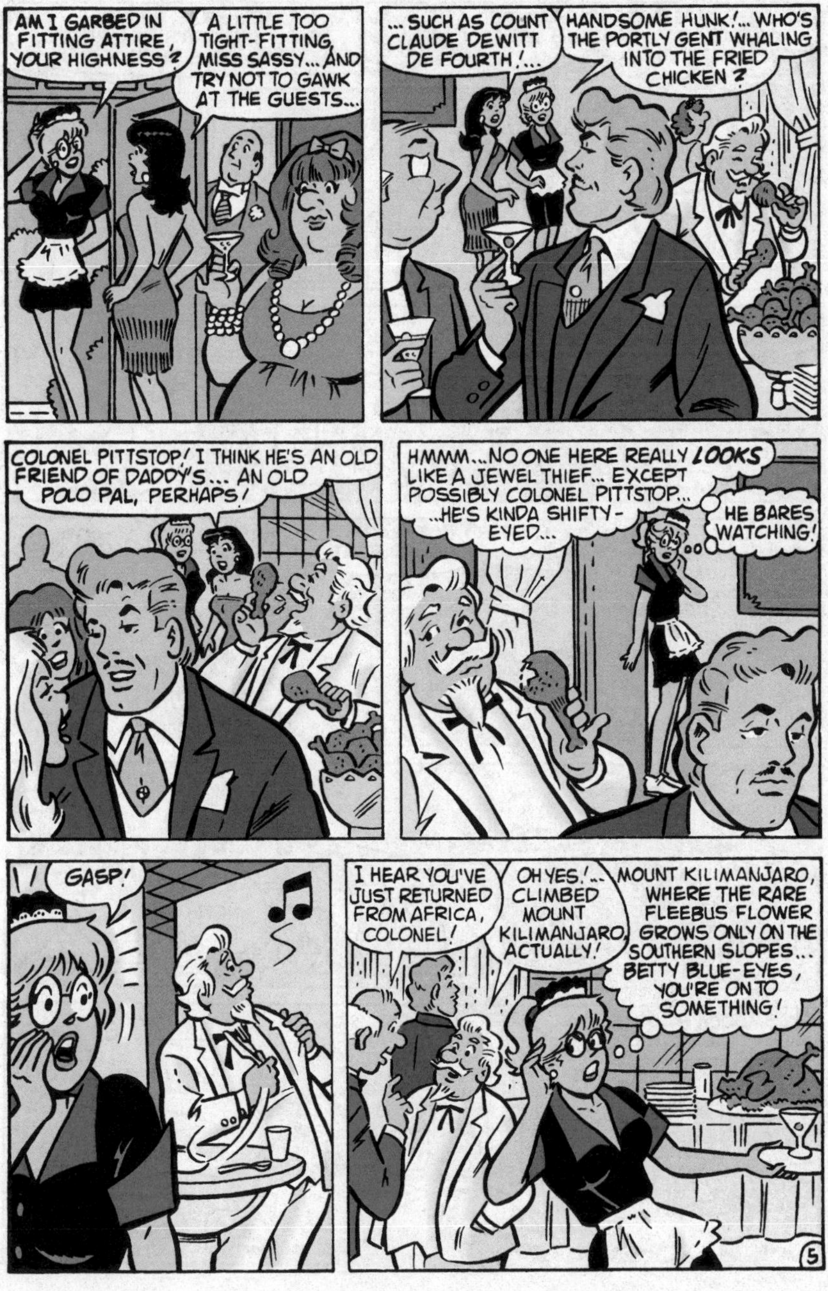
AM I GARBED IN FITTING ATTIRE, YOUR HIGHNESS?
A LITTLE TOO TIGHT-FITTING, MISS SASSY... AND TRY NOT TO GAWK AT THE GUESTS...
... SUCH AS COUNT CLAUDE DEWITT DE FOURTH!...
HANDSOME HUNK!... WHO'S THE PORTLY GENT WHALING INTO THE FRIED CHICKEN?
COLONEL PITTSTOP! I THINK HE'S AN OLD FRIEND OF DADDY'S... AN OLD POLO PAL, PERHAPS!
HMMM...NO ONE HERE REALLY LOOKS LIKE A JEWEL THIEF... EXCEPT POSSIBLY COLONEL PITTSTOP... ...HE'S KINDA SHIFTY-EYED...
HE BARES WATCHING!
GASP!
I HEAR YOU'VE JUST RETURNED FROM AFRICA, COLONEL!
OH YES!... CLIMBED MOUNT KILIMANJARO, ACTUALLY!
MOUNT KILIMANJARO, WHERE THE RARE FLEEBUS FLOWER GROWS ONLY ON THE SOUTHERN SLOPES... BETTY BLUE-EYES, YOU'RE ON TO SOMETHING!
5

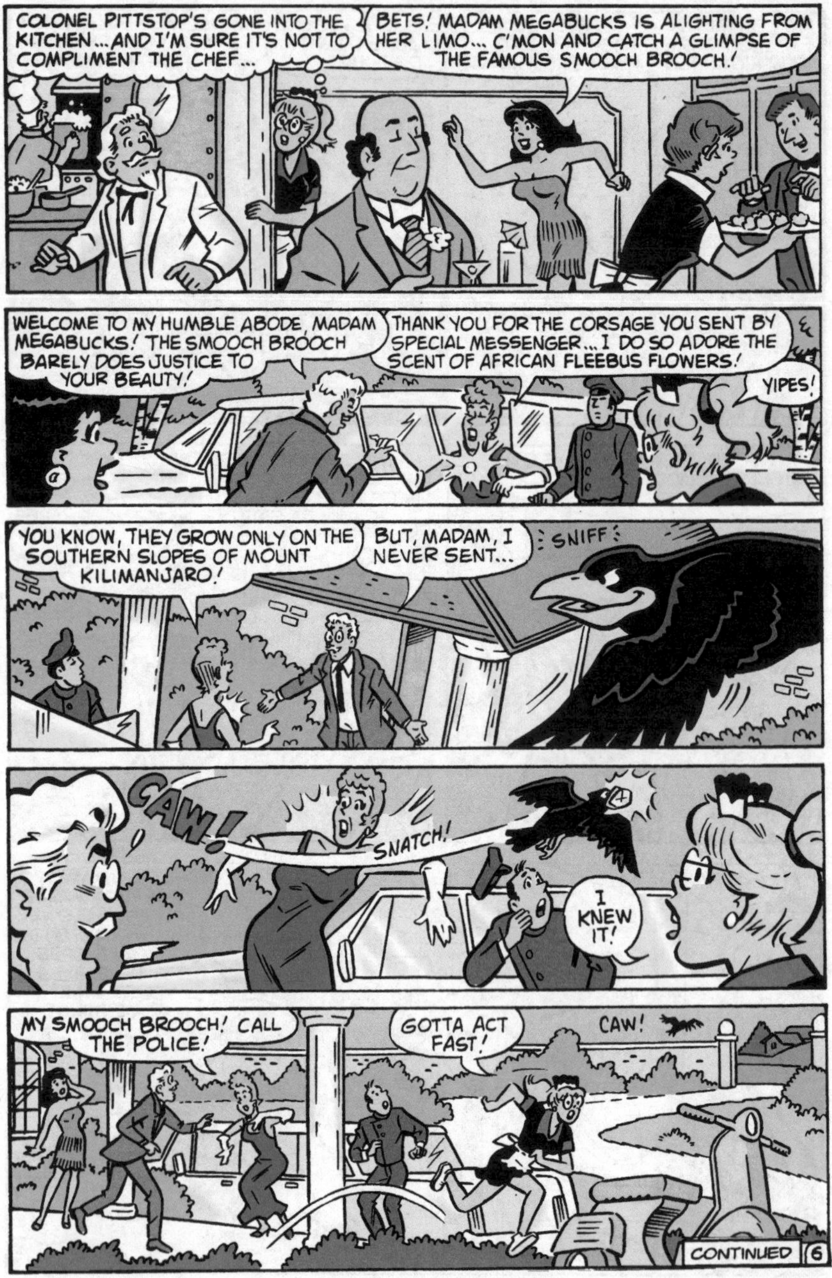
COLONEL PITTSTOP'S GONE INTO THE KITCHEN ... AND I'M SURE IT'S NOT TO COMPLIMENT THE CHEF...
BETS! MADAM MEGABUCKS IS ALIGHTING FROM HER LIMO... C'MON AND CATCH A GLIMPSE OF THE FAMOUS SMOOCH BROOCH!
WELCOME TO MY HUMBLE ABODE, MADAM MEGABUCKS! THE SMOOCH BROOCH BARELY DOES JUSTICE TO YOUR BEAUTY!
THANK YOU FOR THE CORSAGE YOU SENT BY SPECIAL MESSENGER... I DO SO ADORE THE SCENT OF AFRICAN FLEEBUS FLOWERS!
YIPES!
YOU KNOW, THEY GROW ONLY ON THE SOUTHERN SLOPES OF MOUNT KILIMANJARO!
BUT, MADAM, I NEVER SENT...
SNIFF
CAW!
SNATCH!
I KNEW IT!
MY SMOOCH BROOCH! CALL THE POLICE!
GOTTA ACT FAST!
CAW!
CONTINUED
6

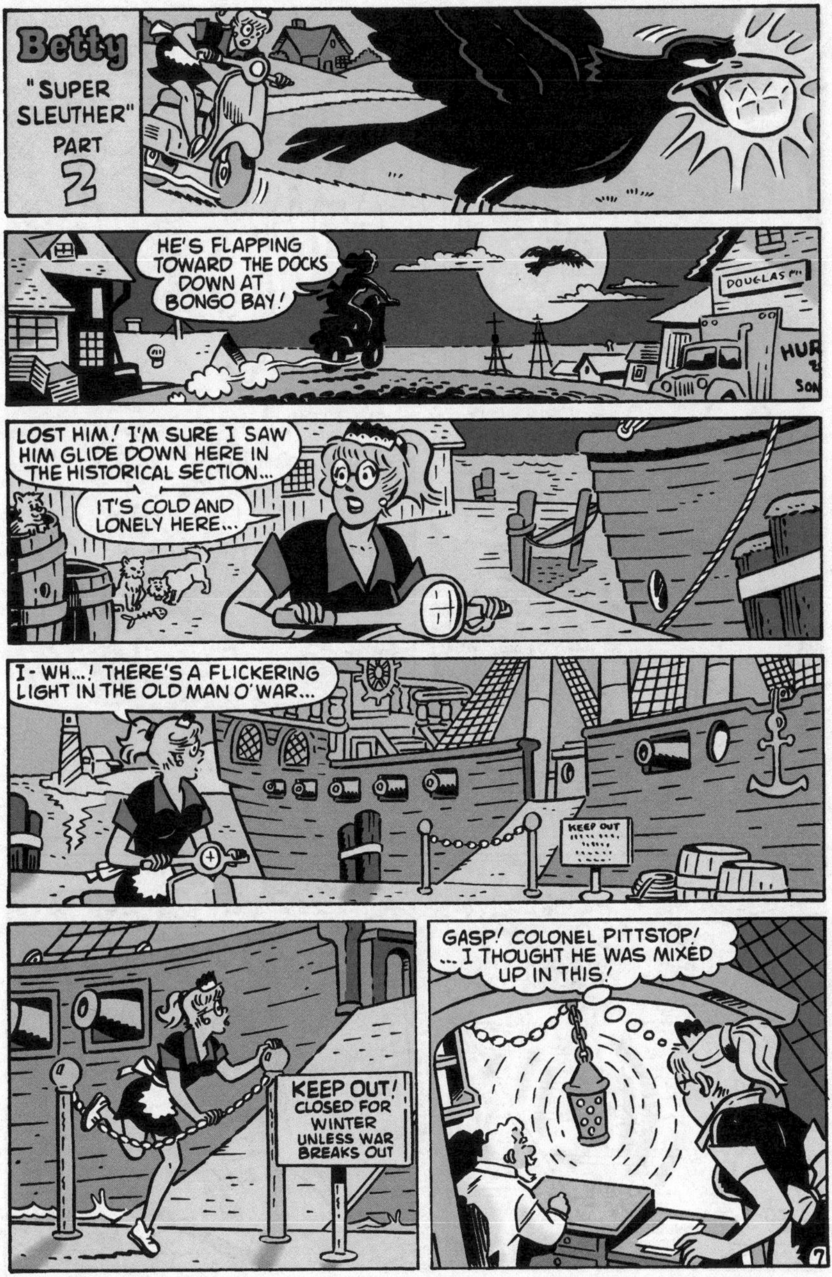
Betty
"SUPER SLEUTHER" PART 2
HE'S FLAPPING TOWARD THE DOCKS DOWN AT BONGO BAY!
DOUGLAS
LOST HIM! I'M SURE I SAW HIM GLIDE DOWN HERE IN THE HISTORICAL SECTION...
IT'S COLD AND LONELY HERE...
I-WH...! THERE'S A FLICKERING LIGHT IN THE OLD MAN O'WAR...
KEEP OUT
KEEP OUT! CLOSED FOR WINTER UNLESS WAR BREAKS OUT
GASP! COLONEL PITTSTOP! ...I THOUGHT HE WAS MIXED UP IN THIS!
7

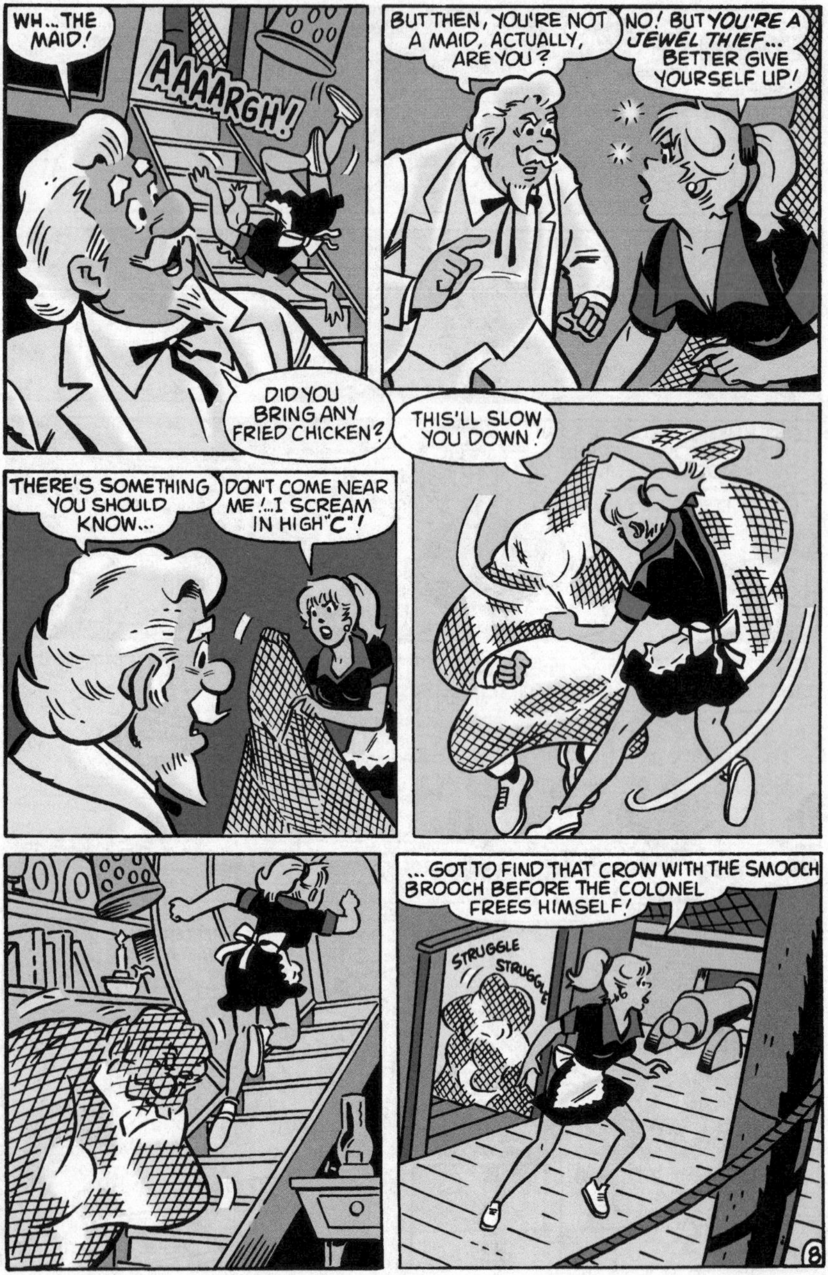
WH... THE MAID!
AAAARGH!
DID YOU BRING ANY FRIED CHICKEN?
BUT THEN, YOU'RE NOT A MAID, ACTUALLY, ARE YOU?
NO! BUT YOU'RE A JEWEL THIEF... BETTER GIVE YOURSELF UP!
THERE'S SOMETHING YOU SHOULD KNOW...
DON'T COME NEAR ME!...I SCREAM IN HIGH "C"!
THIS'LL SLOW YOU DOWN!
...GOT TO FIND THAT CROW WITH THE SMOOCH BROOCH BEFORE THE COLONEL FREES HIMSELF!
STRUGGLE
STRUGGLE
8

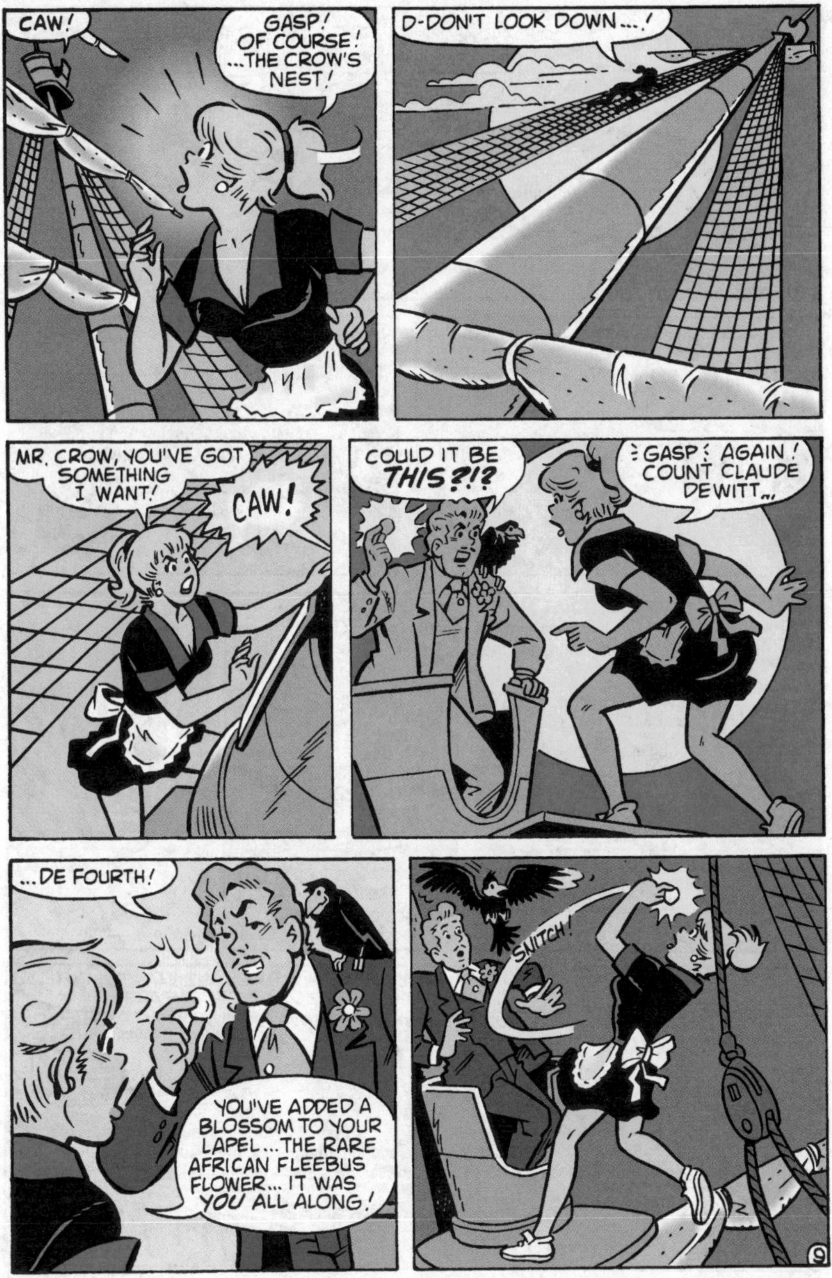
CAW!
GASP! OF COURSE! ...THE CROW'S NEST!
D-DON'T LOOK DOWN....!
MR. CROW, YOU'VE GOT SOMETHING I WANT!
CAW!
COULD IT BE THIS?!?
GASP! AGAIN! COUNT CLAUDE DEWITT...
...DE FOURTH!
YOU'VE ADDED A BLOSSOM TO YOUR LAPEL... THE RARE AFRICAN FLEEBUS FLOWER... IT WAS YOU ALL ALONG!
SNITCH!
9

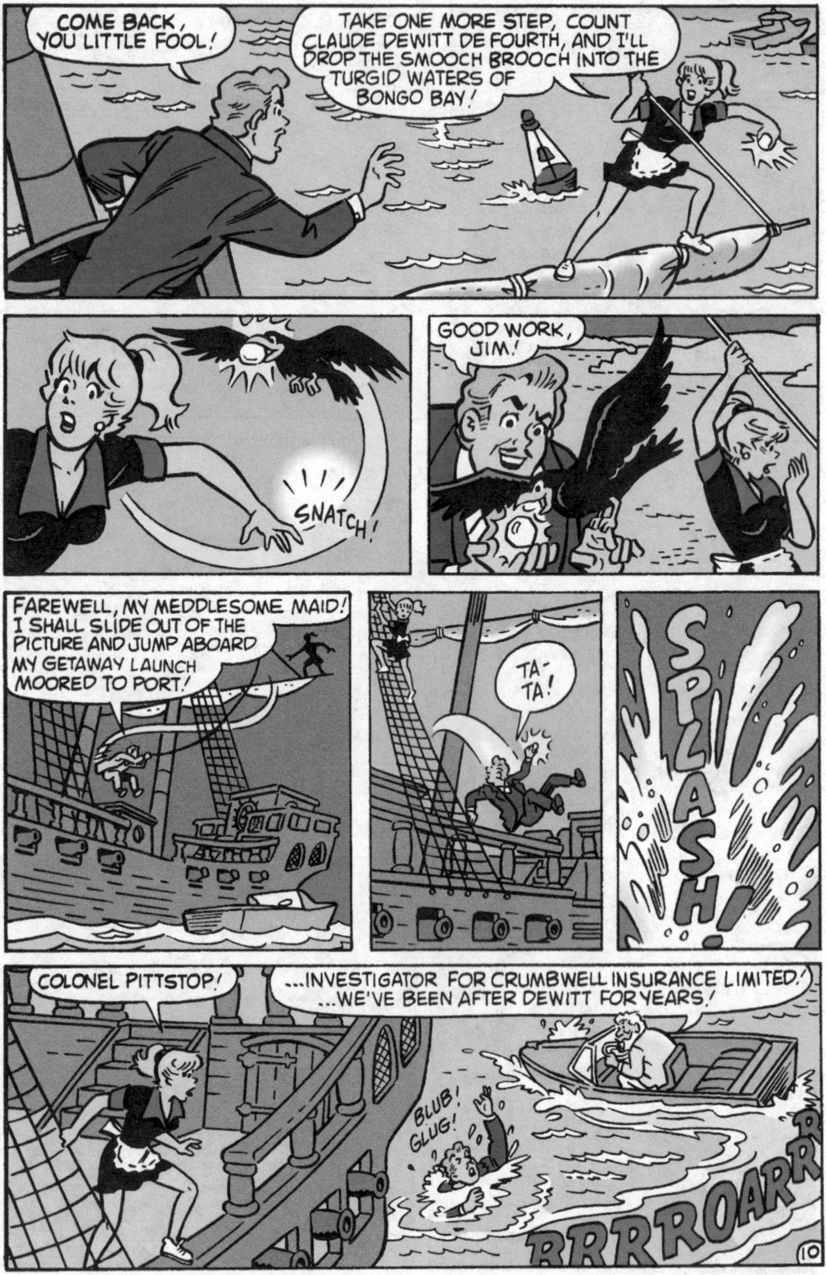

COME BACK, YOU LITTLE FOOL!
TAKE ONE MORE STEP, COUNT CLAUDE DEWITT DE FOURTH, AND I'LL DROP THE SMOOCH BROOCH INTO THE TURGID WATERS OF BONGO BAY!
SNATCH!
GOOD WORK, JIM!
FAREWELL, MY MEDDLESOME MAID! I SHALL SLIDE OUT OF THE PICTURE AND JUMP ABOARD MY GETAWAY LAUNCH MOORED TO PORT!
TA-TA!
SPLASH!
COLONEL PITTSTOP!
...INVESTIGATOR FOR CRUMBWELL INSURANCE LIMITED! ...WE'VE BEEN AFTER DEWITT FOR YEARS!
BLUB! GLUG!
RRRROARRR
10

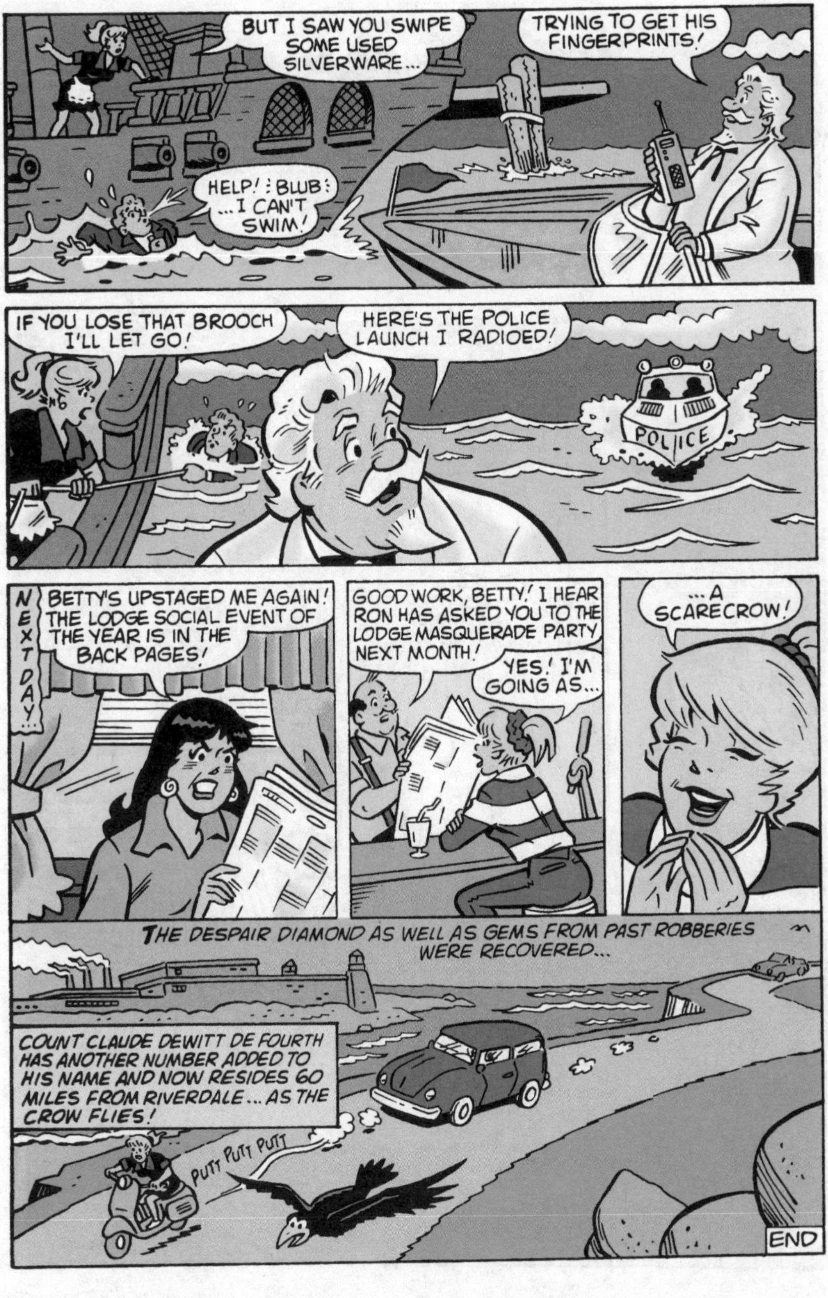
BUT I SAW YOU SWIPE SOME USED SILVERWARE...
TRYING TO GET HIS FINGERPRINTS!
HELP! :BLUB: ...I CAN'T SWIM!
IF YOU LOSE THAT BROOCH I'LL LET GO!
HERE'S THE POLICE LAUNCH I RADIOED!
POLICE
NEXT DAY...
BETTY'S UPSTAGED ME AGAIN! THE LODGE SOCIAL EVENT OF THE YEAR IS IN THE BACK PAGES!
GOOD WORK, BETTY! I HEAR RON HAS ASKED YOU TO THE LODGE MASQUERADE PARTY NEXT MONTH!
YES! I'M GOING AS...
...A SCARECROW!
THE DESPAIR DIAMOND AS WELL AS GEMS FROM PAST ROBBERIES WERE RECOVERED...
COUNT CLAUDE DEWITT DE FOURTH HAS ANOTHER NUMBER ADDED TO HIS NAME AND NOW RESIDES 60 MILES FROM RIVERDALE... AS THE CROW FLIES!
PUTT PUTT PUTT
END

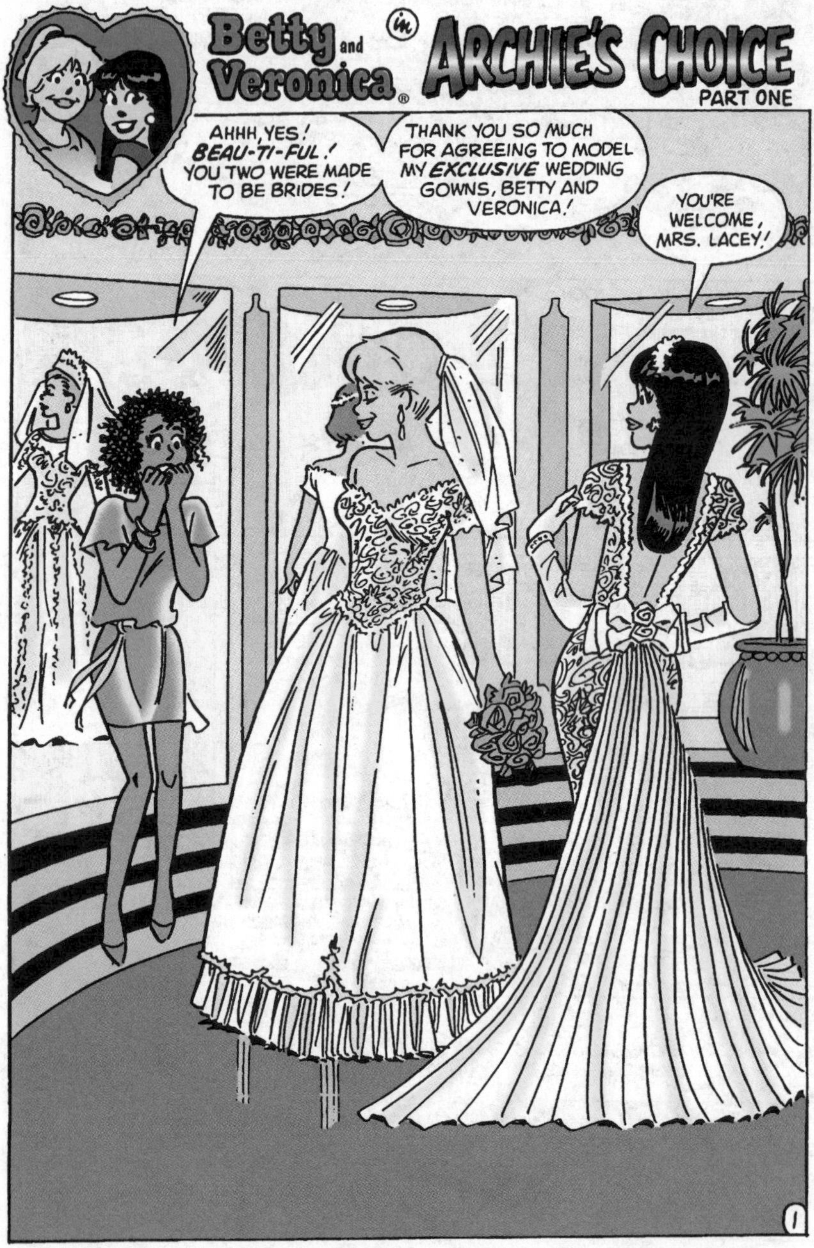
Betty and Veronica in
ARCHIE'S CHOICE
PART ONE
AHHH, YES! BEAU-TI-FUL! YOU TWO WERE MADE TO BE BRIDES!
THANK YOU SO MUCH FOR AGREEING TO MODEL MY EXCLUSIVE WEDDING GOWNS, BETTY AND VERONICA!
YOU'RE WELCOME, MRS. LACEY!
1

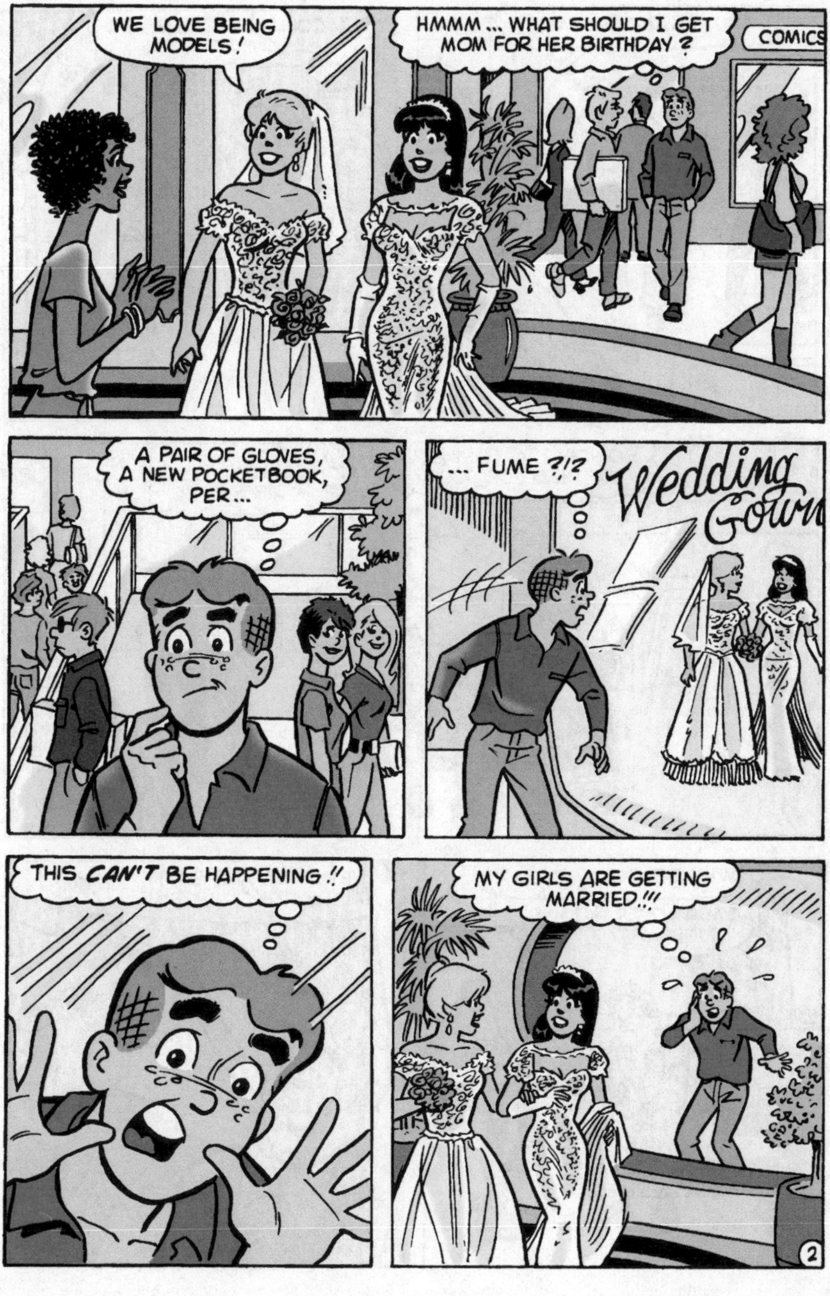
WE LOVE BEING MODELS!
HMMM... WHAT SHOULD I GET MOM FOR HER BIRTHDAY?
COMICS
A PAIR OF GLOVES, A NEW POCKETBOOK, PER...
... FUME ?!?
Wedding Gown
THIS CAN'T BE HAPPENING!!
MY GIRLS ARE GETTING MARRIED!!!
2

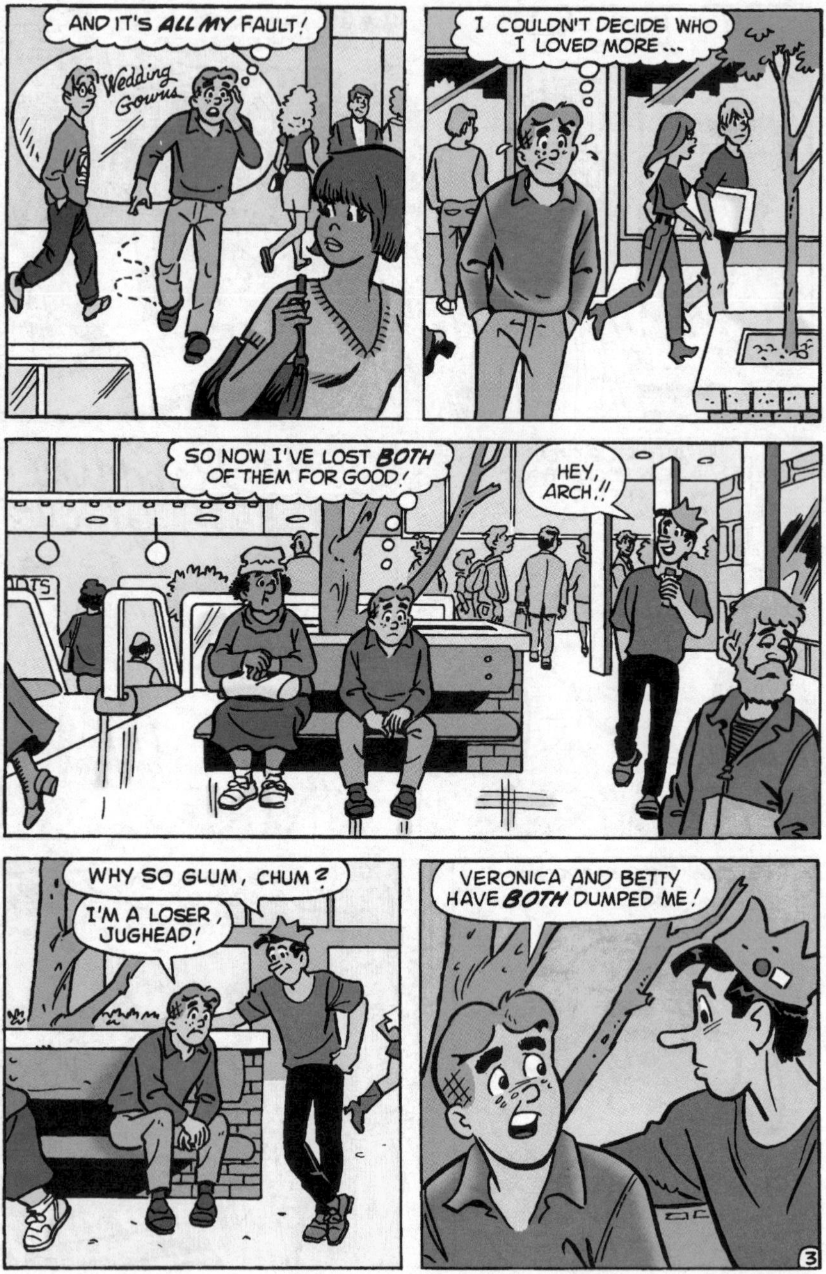
AND IT'S ALL MY FAULT!
Wedding Gowns
I COULDN'T DECIDE WHO I LOVED MORE...
SO NOW I'VE LOST BOTH OF THEM FOR GOOD!
HEY, ARCH!!
WHY SO GLUM, CHUM?
I'M A LOSER, JUGHEAD!
VERONICA AND BETTY HAVE BOTH DUMPED ME!

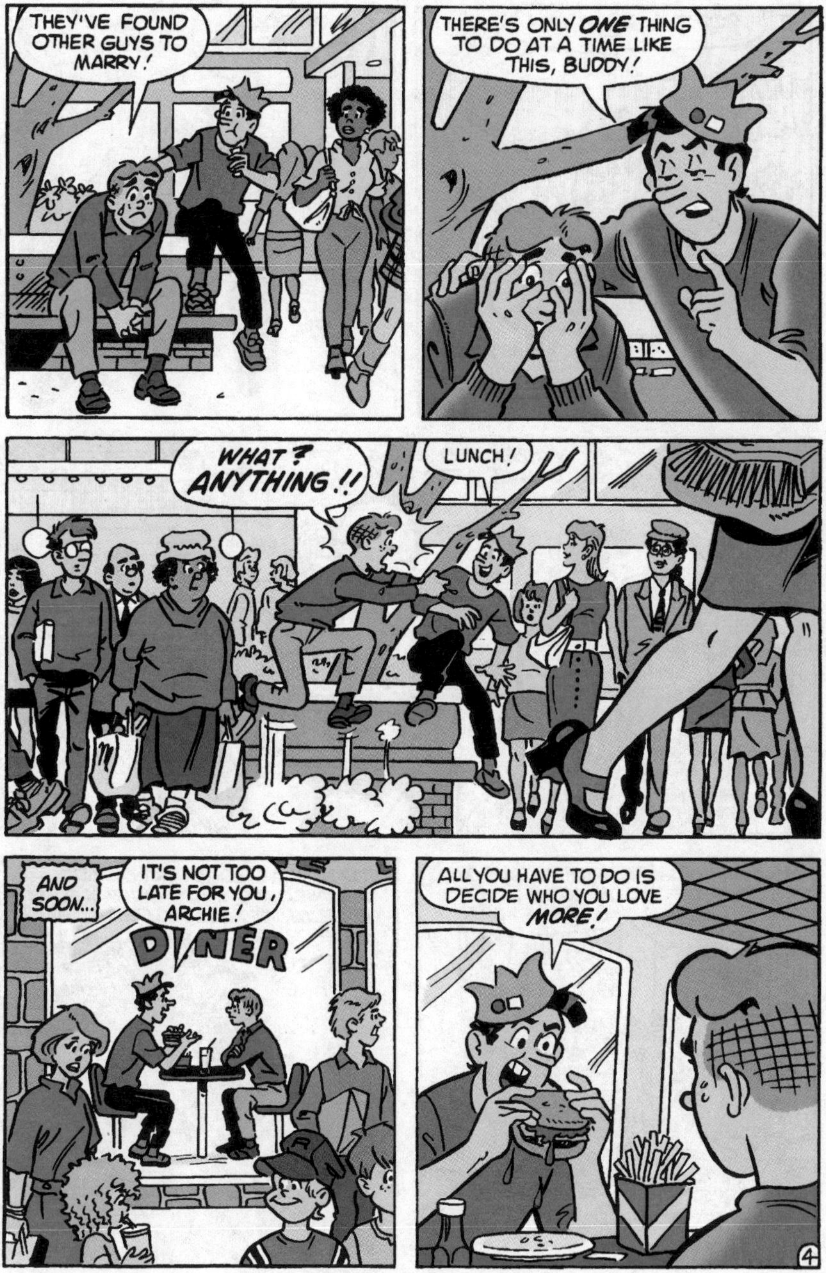
THEY'VE FOUND OTHER GUYS TO MARRY!
THERE'S ONLY ONE THING TO DO AT A TIME LIKE THIS, BUDDY!
WHAT? ANYTHING!!
LUNCH!
AND SOON...
IT'S NOT TOO LATE FOR YOU, ARCHIE!
DINER
ALL YOU HAVE TO DO IS DECIDE WHO YOU LOVE MORE!
4

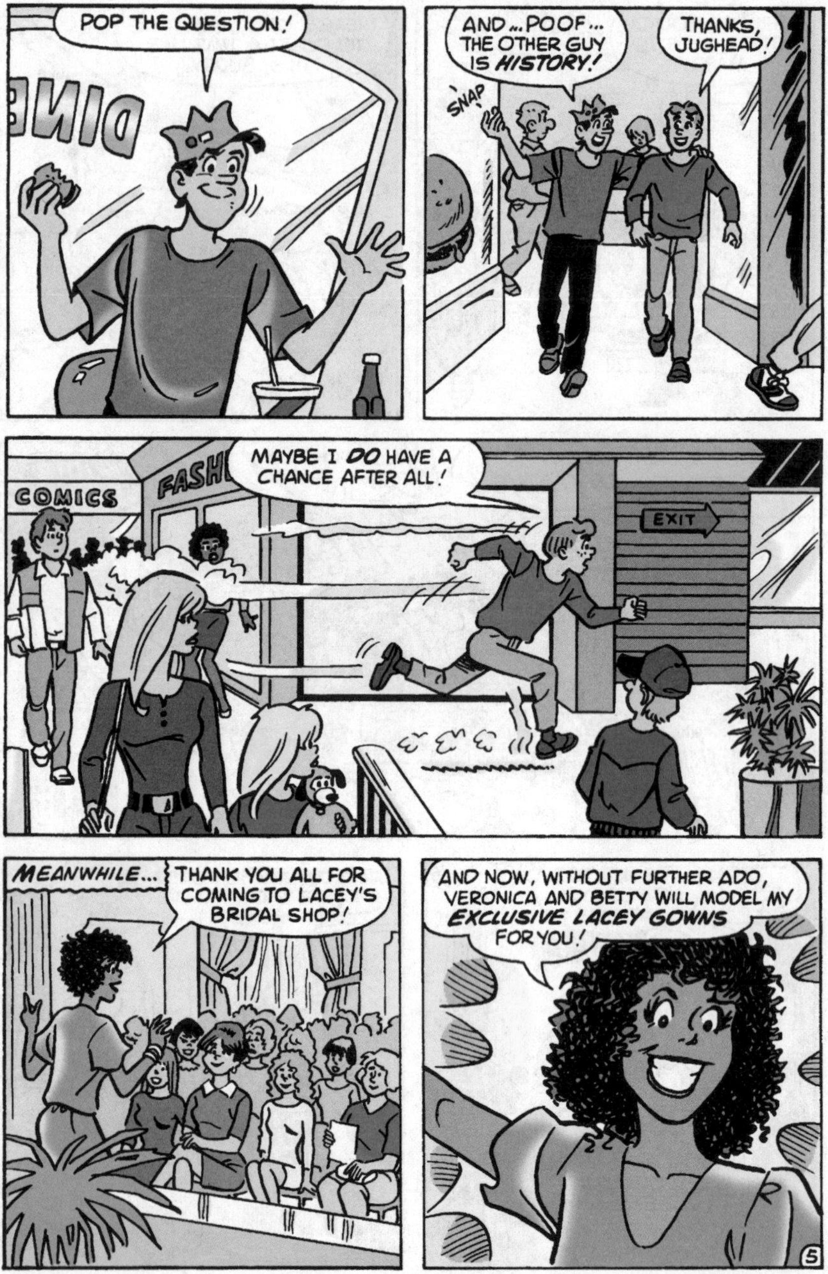
DINE
POP THE QUESTION!
AND ... POOF ... THE OTHER GUY IS HISTORY!
SNAP
THANKS, JUGHEAD!
COMICS
FASH
MAYBE I DO HAVE A CHANCE AFTER ALL!
EXIT
MEANWHILE...
THANK YOU ALL FOR COMING TO LACEY'S BRIDAL SHOP!
AND NOW, WITHOUT FURTHER ADO, VERONICA AND BETTY WILL MODEL MY EXCLUSIVE LACEY GOWNS FOR YOU!
5

Betty the MODEL BRIDE

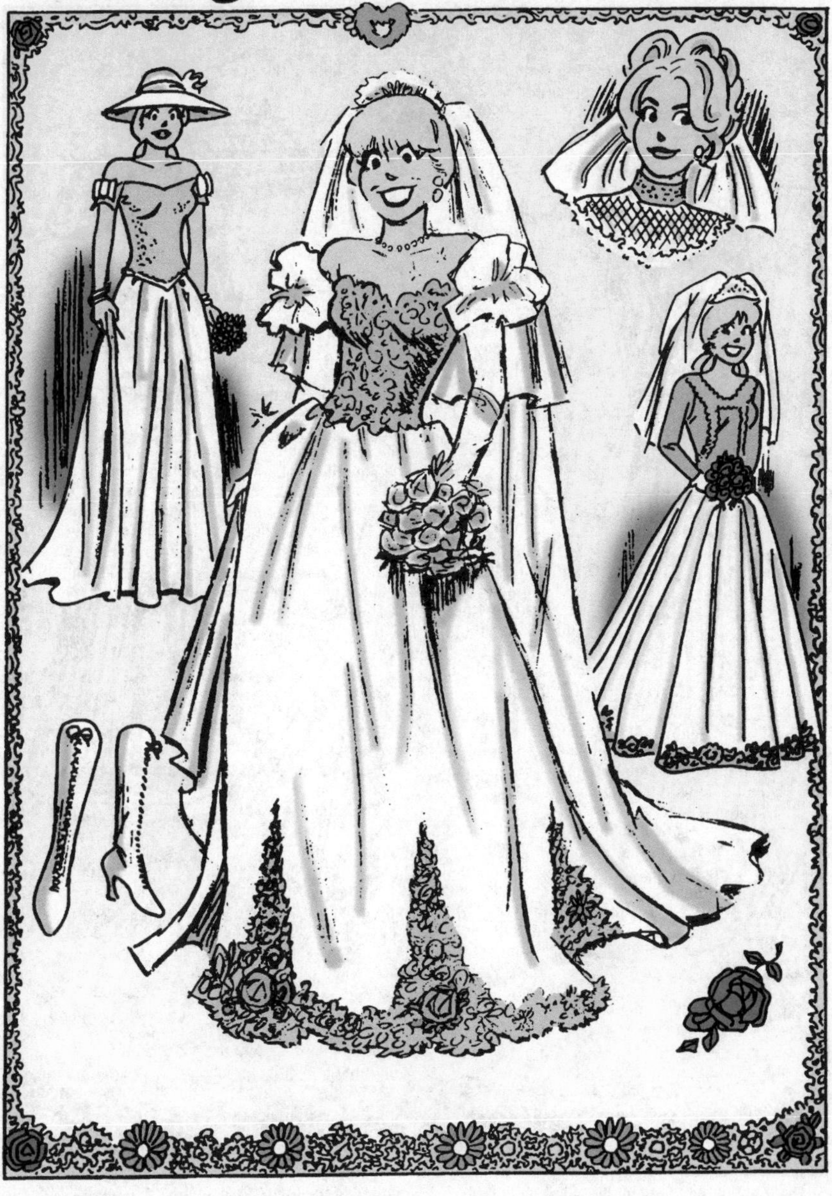

Veronica the MODEL BRIDE

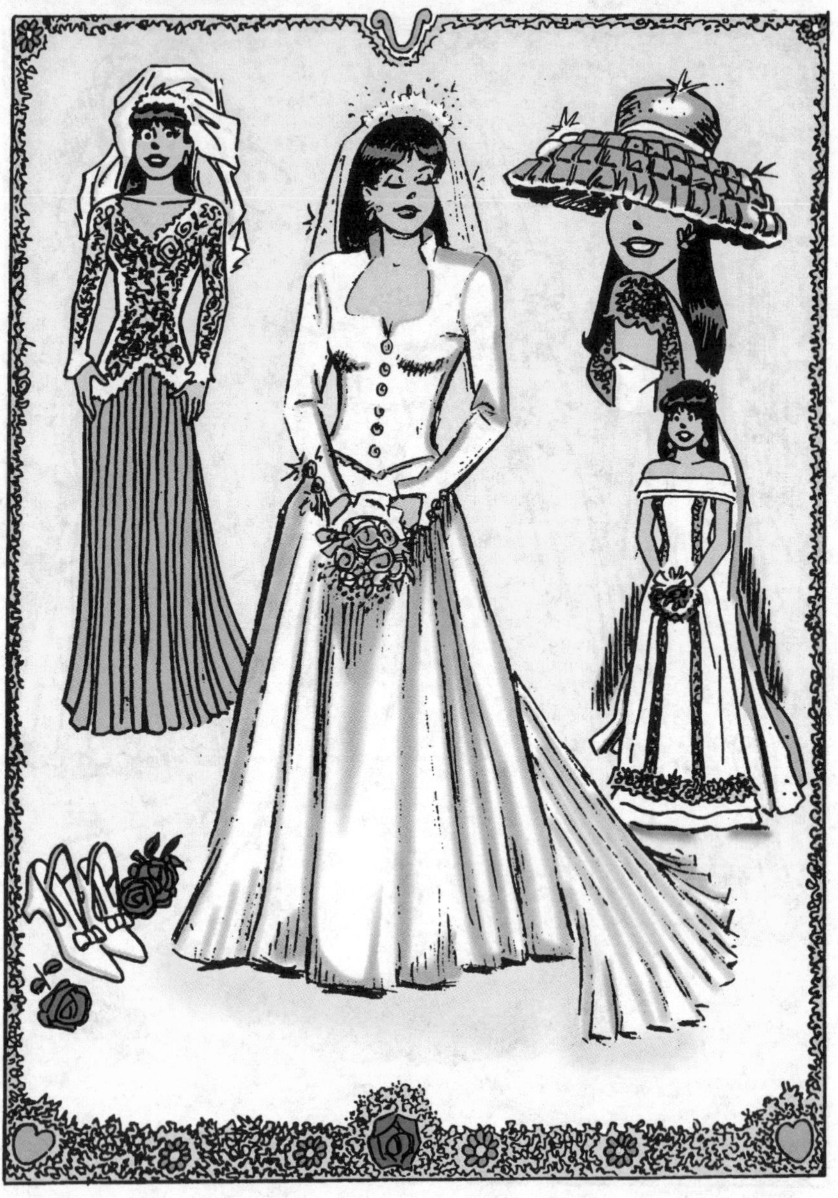

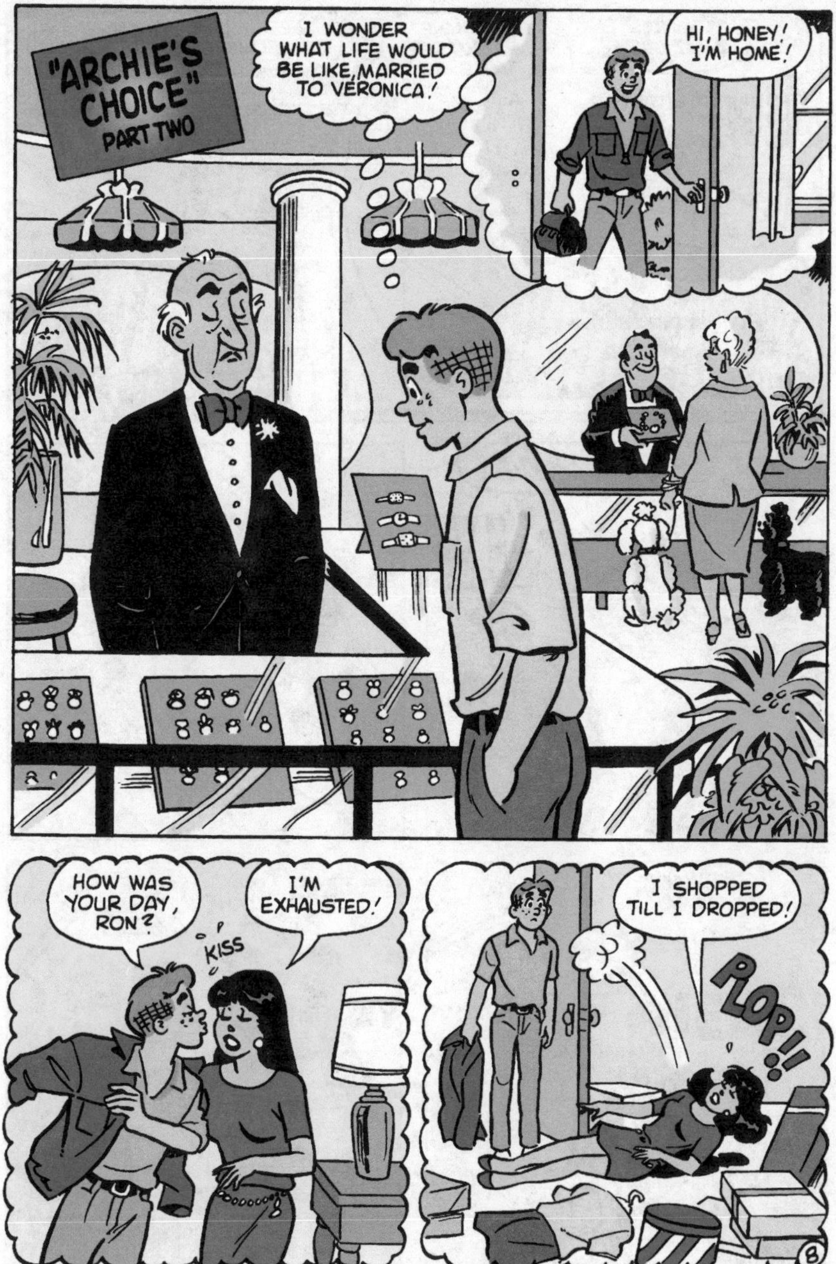
"ARCHIE'S CHOICE" PART TWO
I WONDER WHAT LIFE WOULD BE LIKE, MARRIED TO VERONICA!
HI, HONEY! I'M HOME!
HOW WAS YOUR DAY, RON?
KISS
I'M EXHAUSTED!
I SHOPPED TILL I DROPPED!
PLOP!!
8

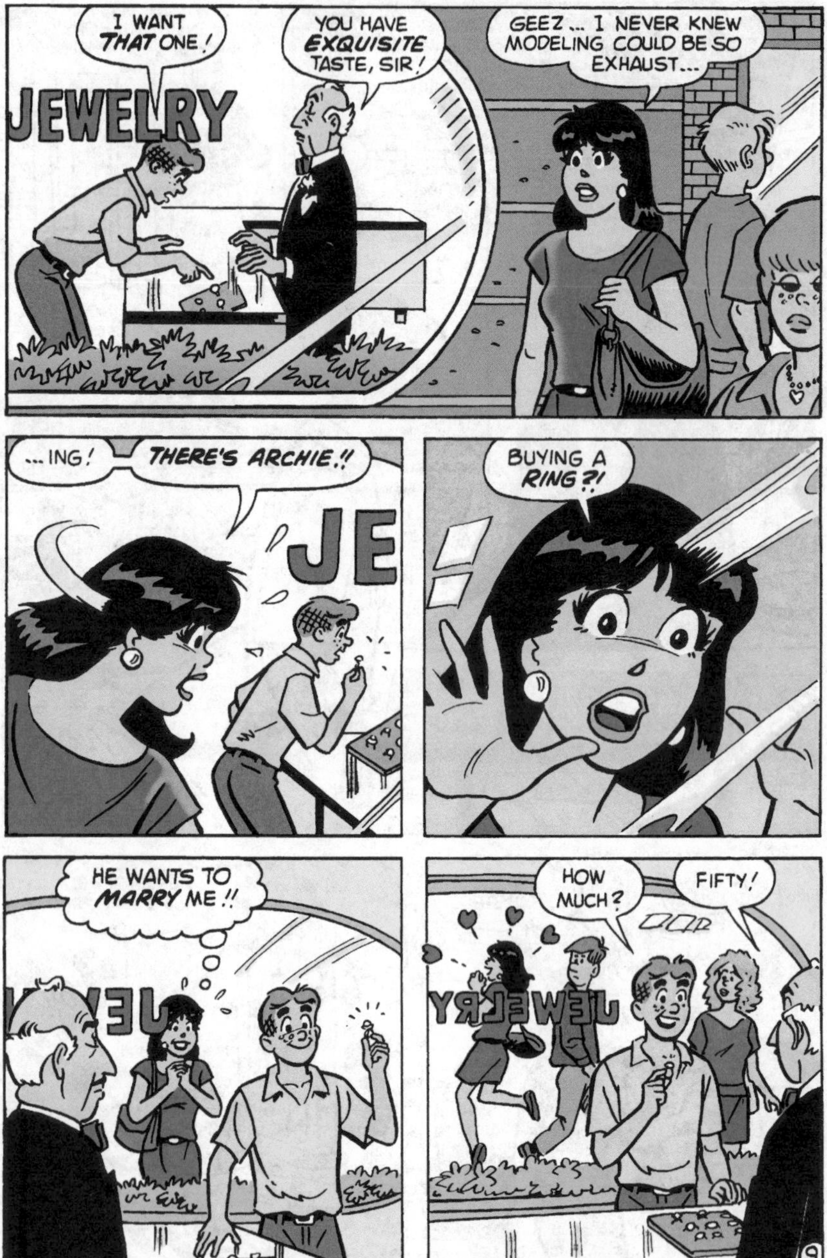
I WANT THAT ONE!
YOU HAVE EXQUISITE TASTE, SIR!
JEWELRY
GEEZ ... I NEVER KNEW MODELING COULD BE SO EXHAUST...
...ING! THERE'S ARCHIE.!!
JE
BUYING A RING?!
HE WANTS TO MARRY ME!!
HOW MUCH?
FIFTY!
9

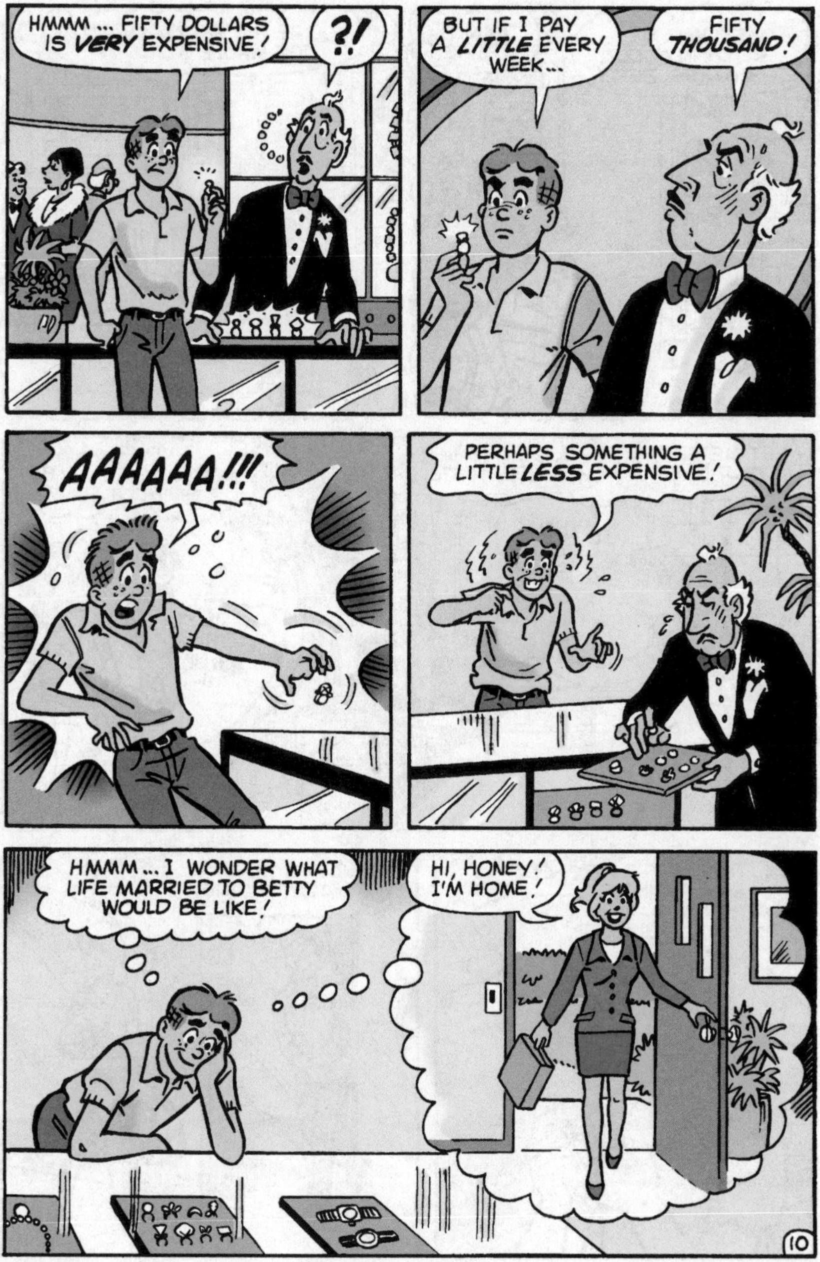
HMMM ... FIFTY DOLLARS IS VERY EXPENSIVE!
?!
BUT IF I PAY A LITTLE EVERY WEEK...
FIFTY THOUSAND!
AAAAAA!!!
PERHAPS SOMETHING A LITTLE LESS EXPENSIVE!
HMMM ... I WONDER WHAT LIFE MARRIED TO BETTY WOULD BE LIKE!
HI, HONEY! I'M HOME!
10

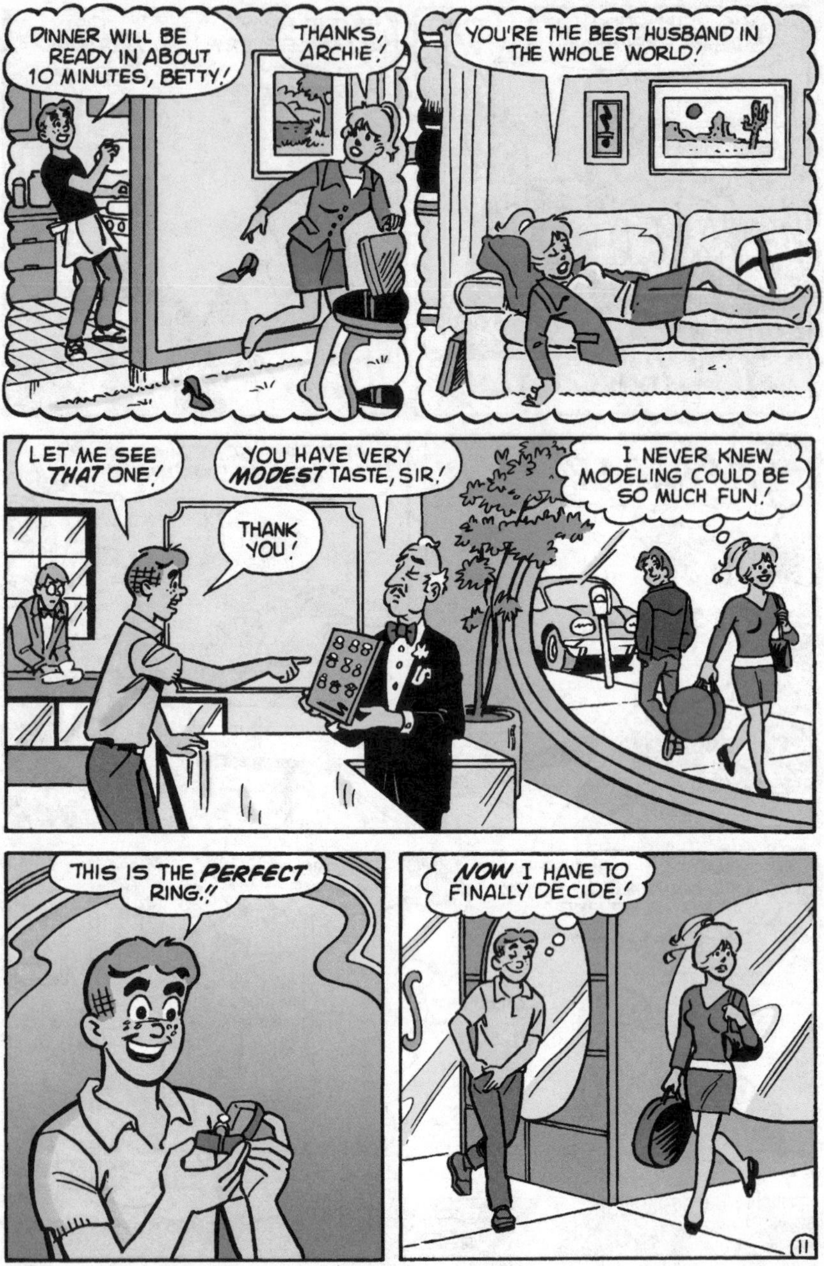
DINNER WILL BE READY IN ABOUT 10 MINUTES, BETTY!
THANKS, ARCHIE!
YOU'RE THE BEST HUSBAND IN THE WHOLE WORLD!
LET ME SEE THAT ONE!
YOU HAVE VERY MODEST TASTE, SIR!
THANK YOU!
I NEVER KNEW MODELING COULD BE SO MUCH FUN!
THIS IS THE PERFECT RING!!
NOW I HAVE TO FINALLY DECIDE!
11

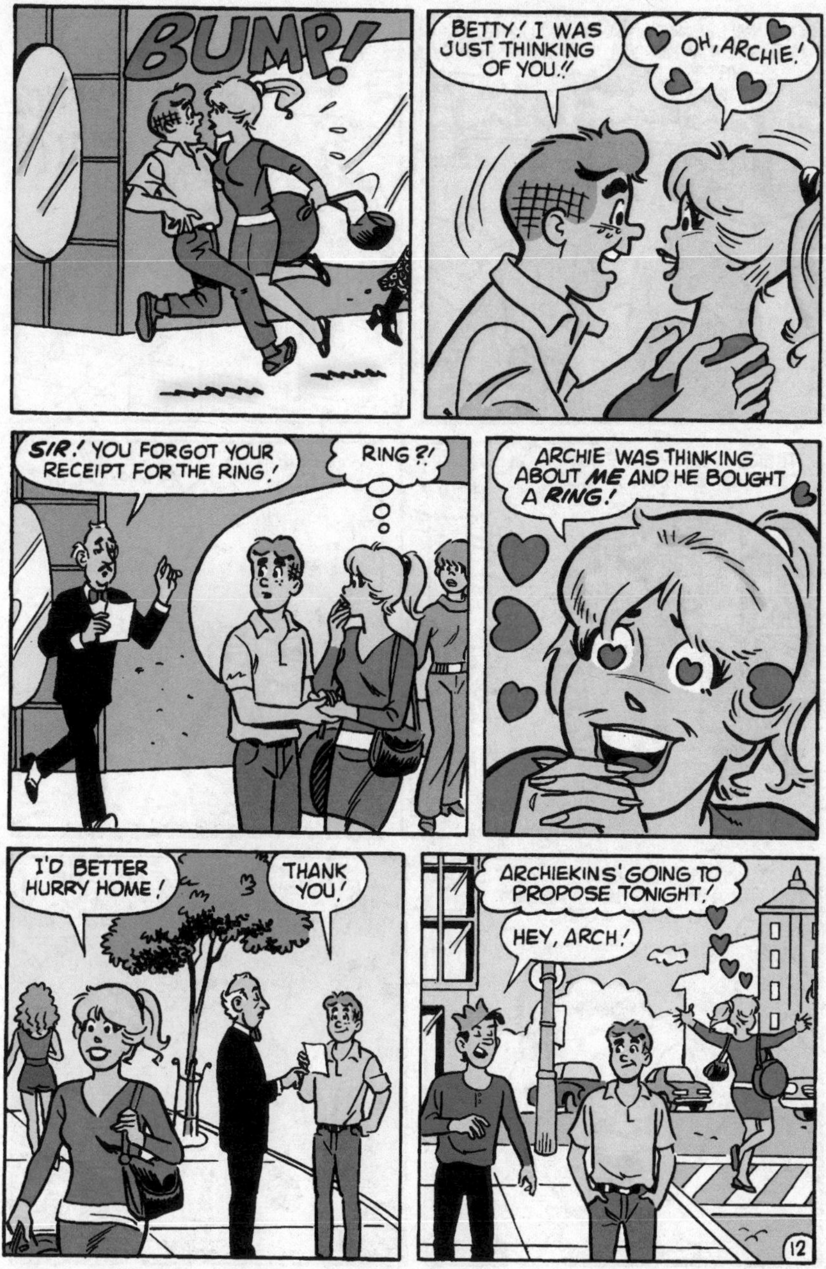

BUMP!
BETTY! I WAS JUST THINKING OF YOU!!
OH, ARCHIE!
SIR! YOU FORGOT YOUR RECEIPT FOR THE RING!
RING?!
ARCHIE WAS THINKING ABOUT ME AND HE BOUGHT A RING!
I'D BETTER HURRY HOME!
THANK YOU!
ARCHIEKINS' GOING TO PROPOSE TONIGHT!
HEY, ARCH!
12

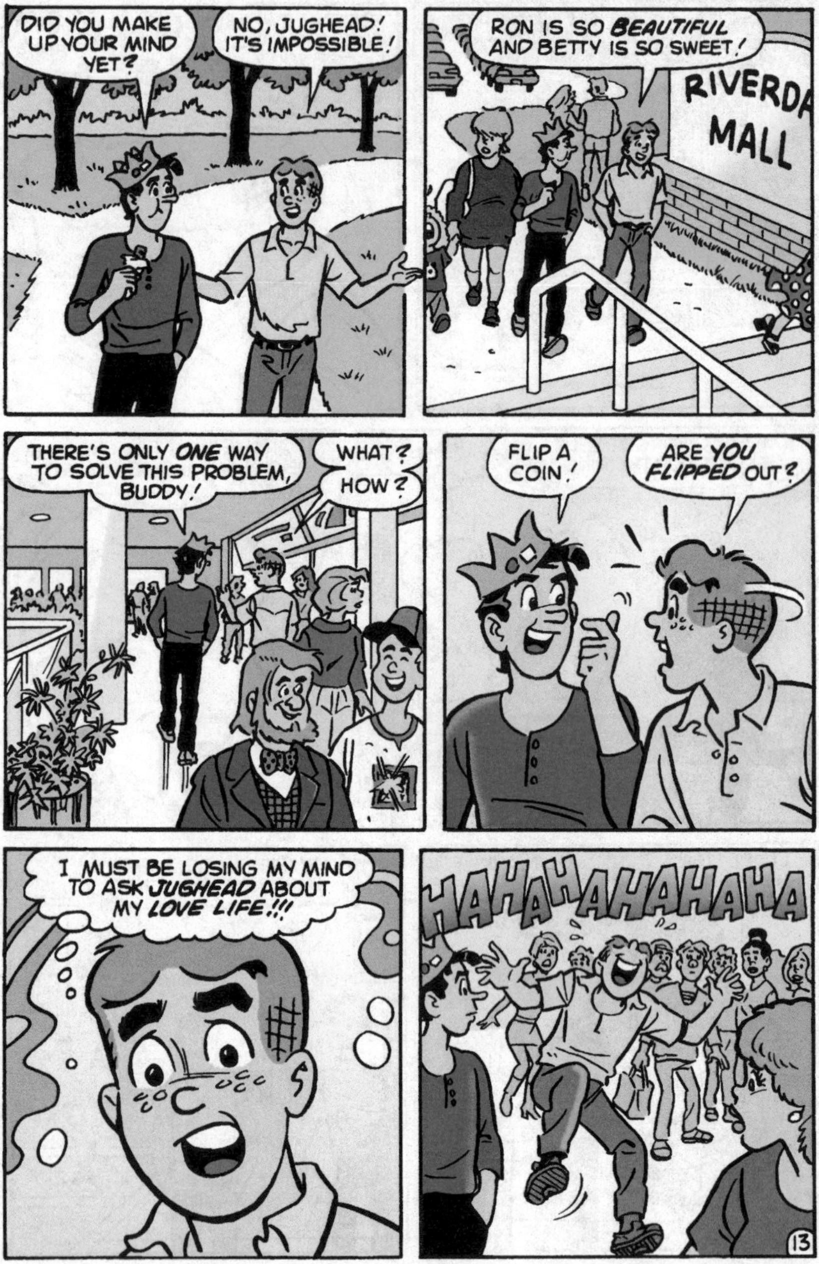
DID YOU MAKE UP YOUR MIND YET?
NO, JUGHEAD! IT'S IMPOSSIBLE!
RON IS SO BEAUTIFUL AND BETTY IS SO SWEET!
RIVERDA
MALL
THERE'S ONLY ONE WAY TO SOLVE THIS PROBLEM, BUDDY!
WHAT?
HOW?
FLIP A COIN!
ARE YOU FLIPPED OUT?
I MUST BE LOSING MY MIND TO ASK JUGHEAD ABOUT MY LOVE LIFE!!!
HAHAHAHAHAHAHAHA
13

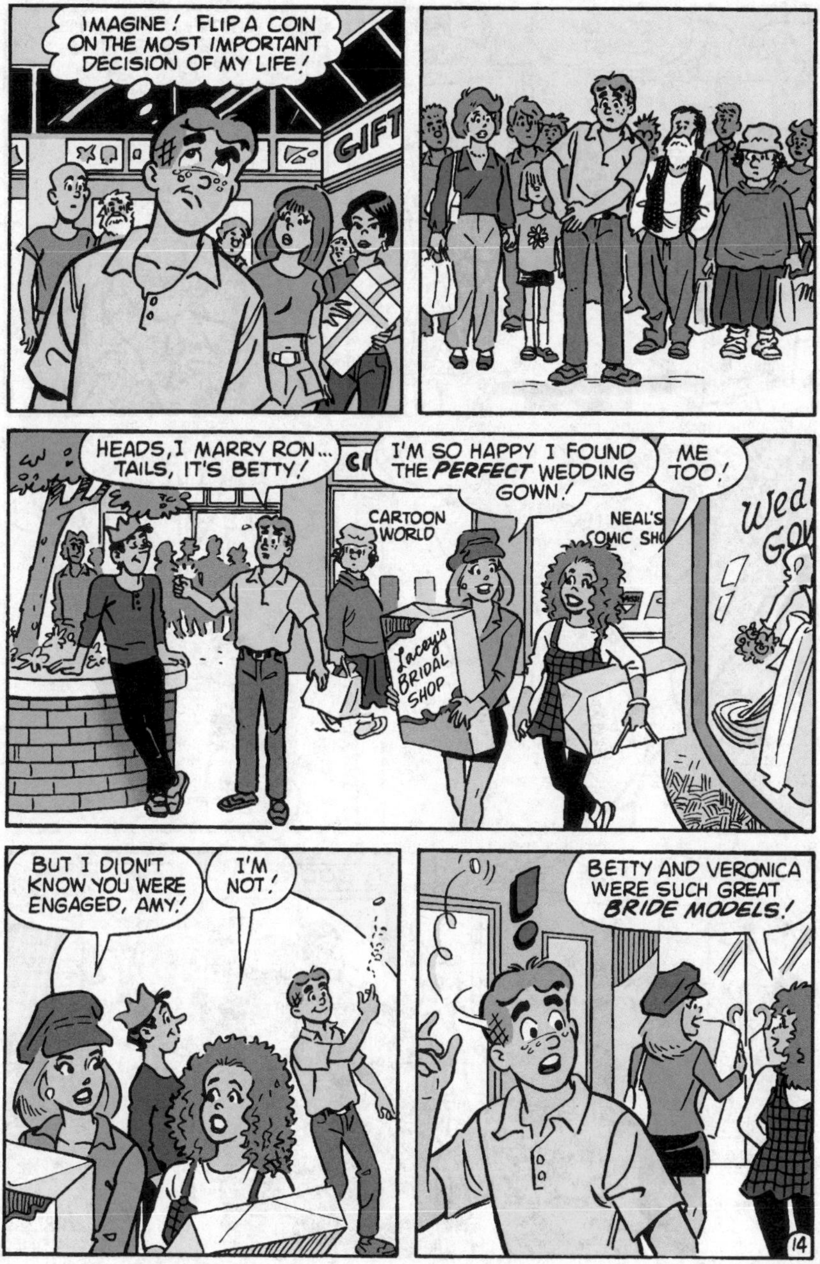

IMAGINE! FLIP A COIN ON THE MOST IMPORTANT DECISION OF MY LIFE!
GIFT
HEADS, I MARRY RON... TAILS, IT'S BETTY!
CARTOON WORLD
I'M SO HAPPY I FOUND THE *PERFECT* WEDDING GOWN!
ME TOO!
NEAL'S COMIC SHO
Lacey's BRIDAL SHOP
BUT I DIDN'T KNOW YOU WERE ENGAGED, AMY!
I'M NOT!
BETTY AND VERONICA WERE SUCH GREAT *BRIDE MODELS*!
14

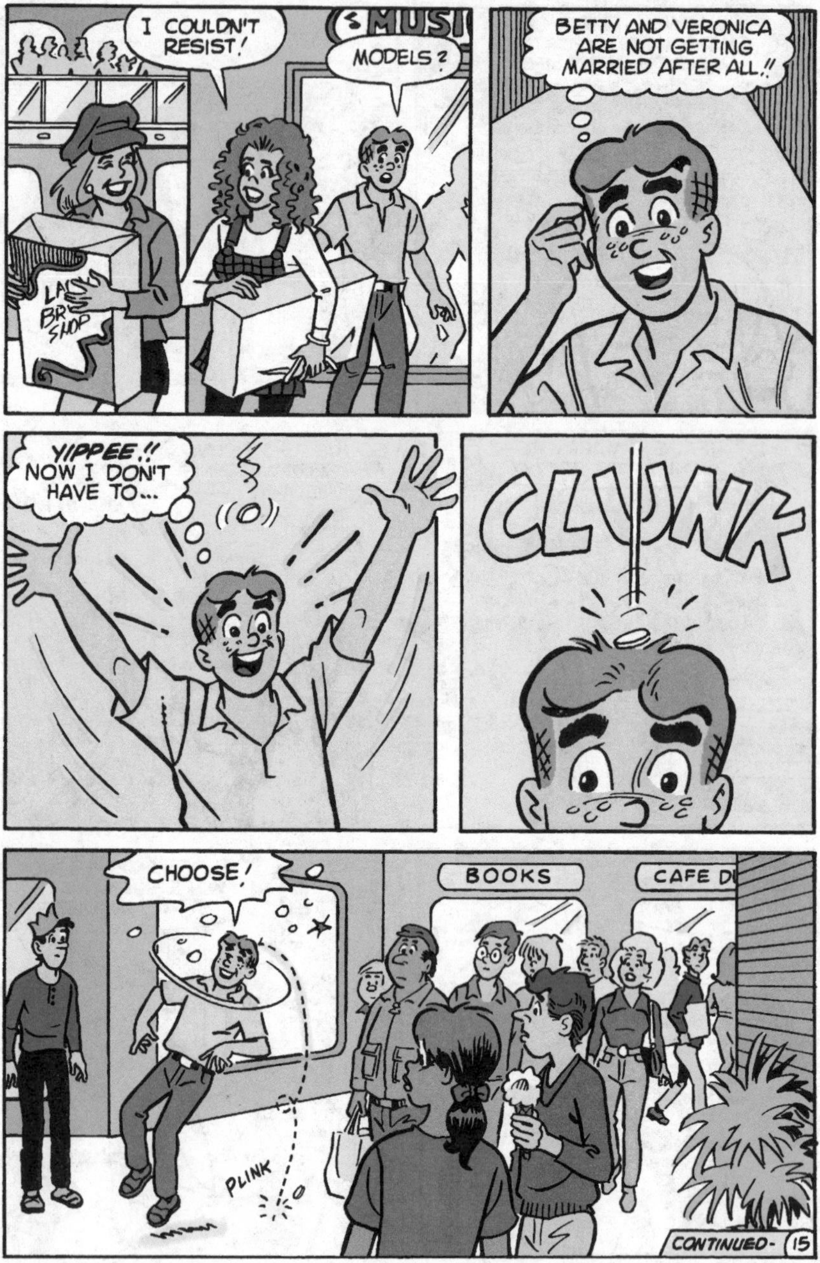
I COULDN'T RESIST!
MODELS?
BETTY AND VERONICA ARE NOT GETTING MARRIED AFTER ALL!!
YIPPEE!! NOW I DON'T HAVE TO...
CLUNK
CHOOSE!
BOOKS
PLINK
CONTINUED-

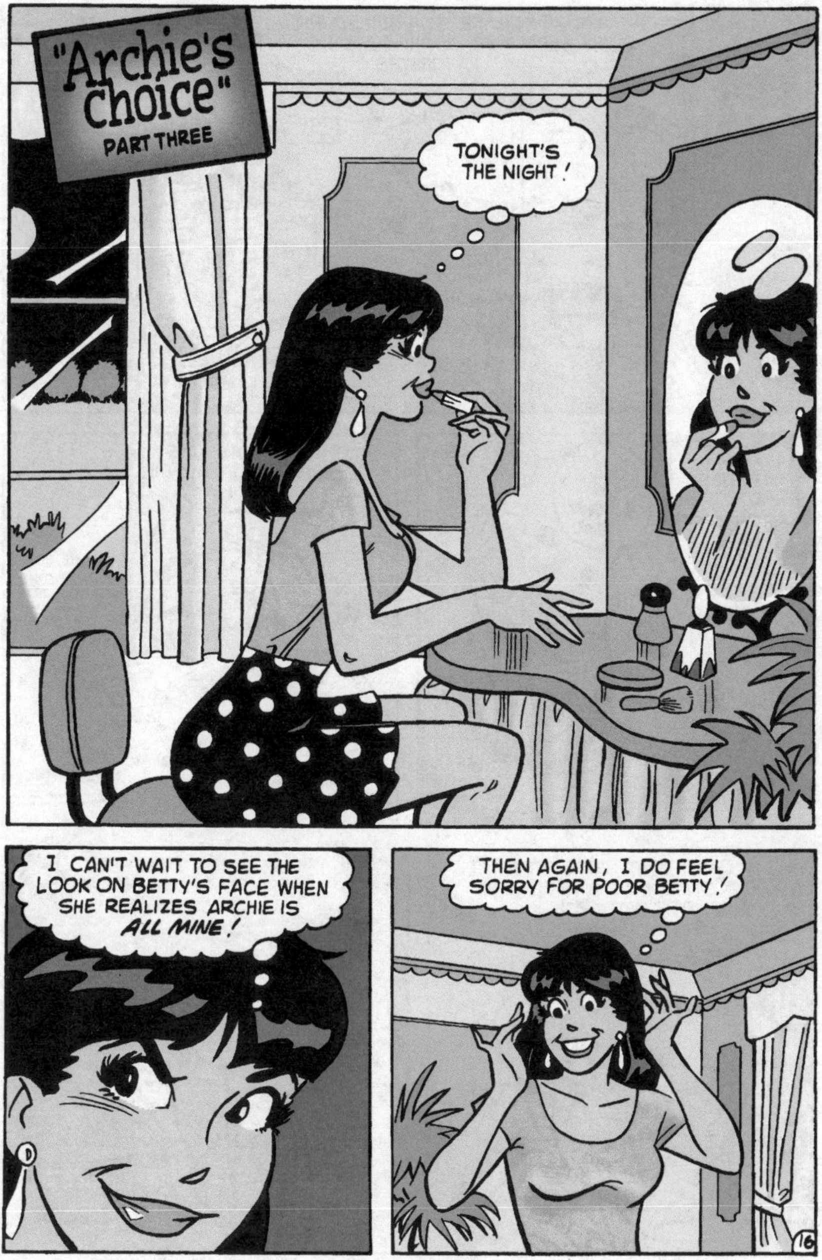
"Archie's Choice"
PART THREE
TONIGHT'S THE NIGHT!
I CAN'T WAIT TO SEE THE LOOK ON BETTY'S FACE WHEN SHE REALIZES ARCHIE IS ALL MINE!
THEN AGAIN, I DO FEEL SORRY FOR POOR BETTY!
16

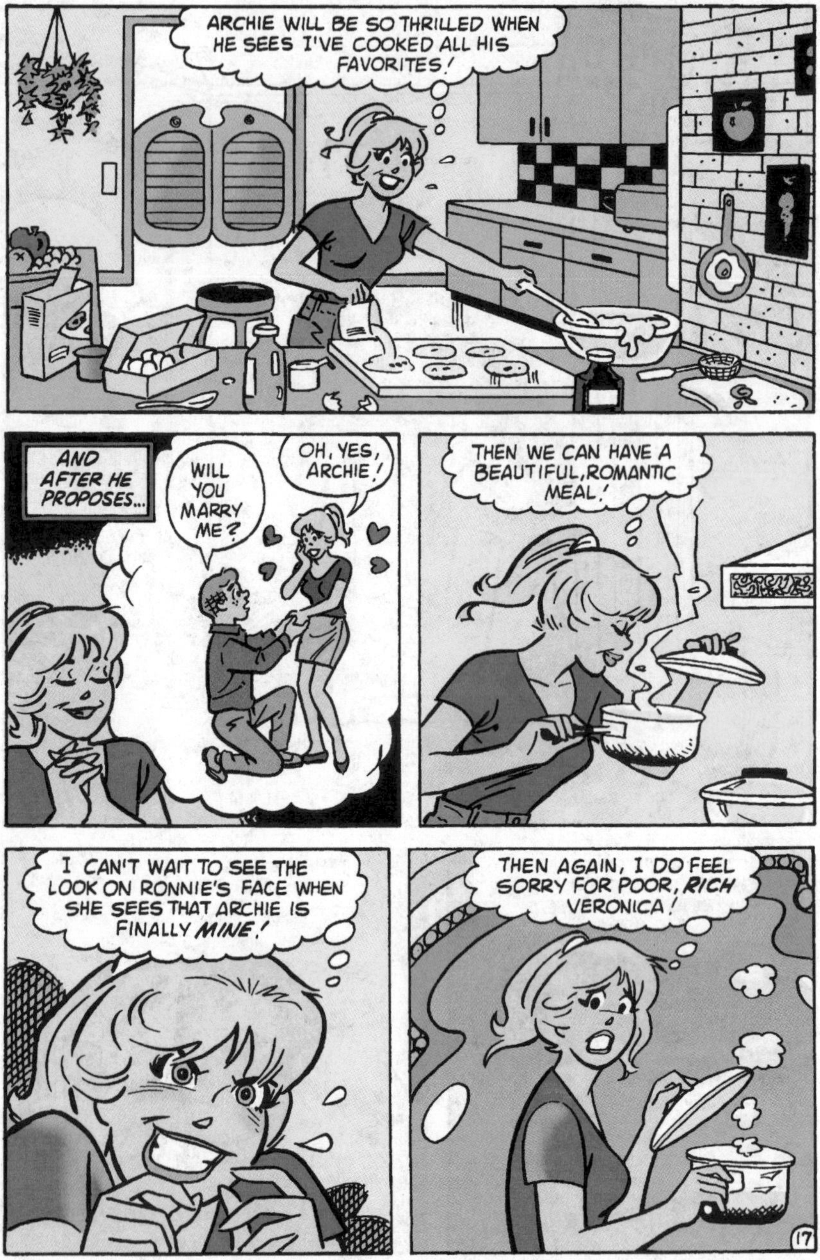
ARCHIE WILL BE SO THRILLED WHEN HE SEES I'VE COOKED ALL HIS FAVORITES!
AND AFTER HE PROPOSES...
WILL YOU MARRY ME?
OH, YES, ARCHIE!
THEN WE CAN HAVE A BEAUTIFUL, ROMANTIC MEAL!
I CAN'T WAIT TO SEE THE LOOK ON RONNIE'S FACE WHEN SHE SEES THAT ARCHIE IS FINALLY *MINE*!
THEN AGAIN, I DO FEEL SORRY FOR POOR, *RICH* VERONICA!
17

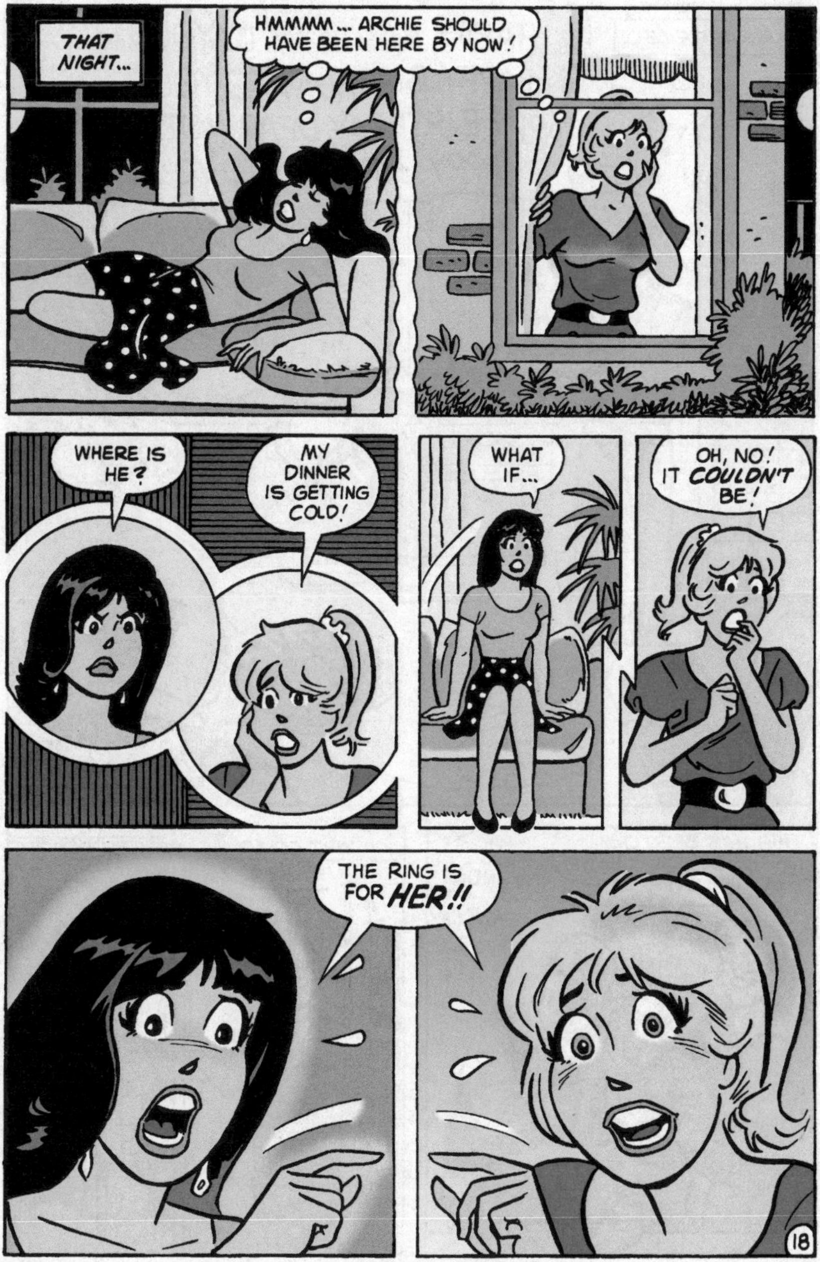
THAT NIGHT...
HMMMM... ARCHIE SHOULD HAVE BEEN HERE BY NOW!
WHERE IS HE?
MY DINNER IS GETTING COLD!
WHAT IF...
OH, NO! IT COULDN'T BE!
THE RING IS FOR HER!!
18

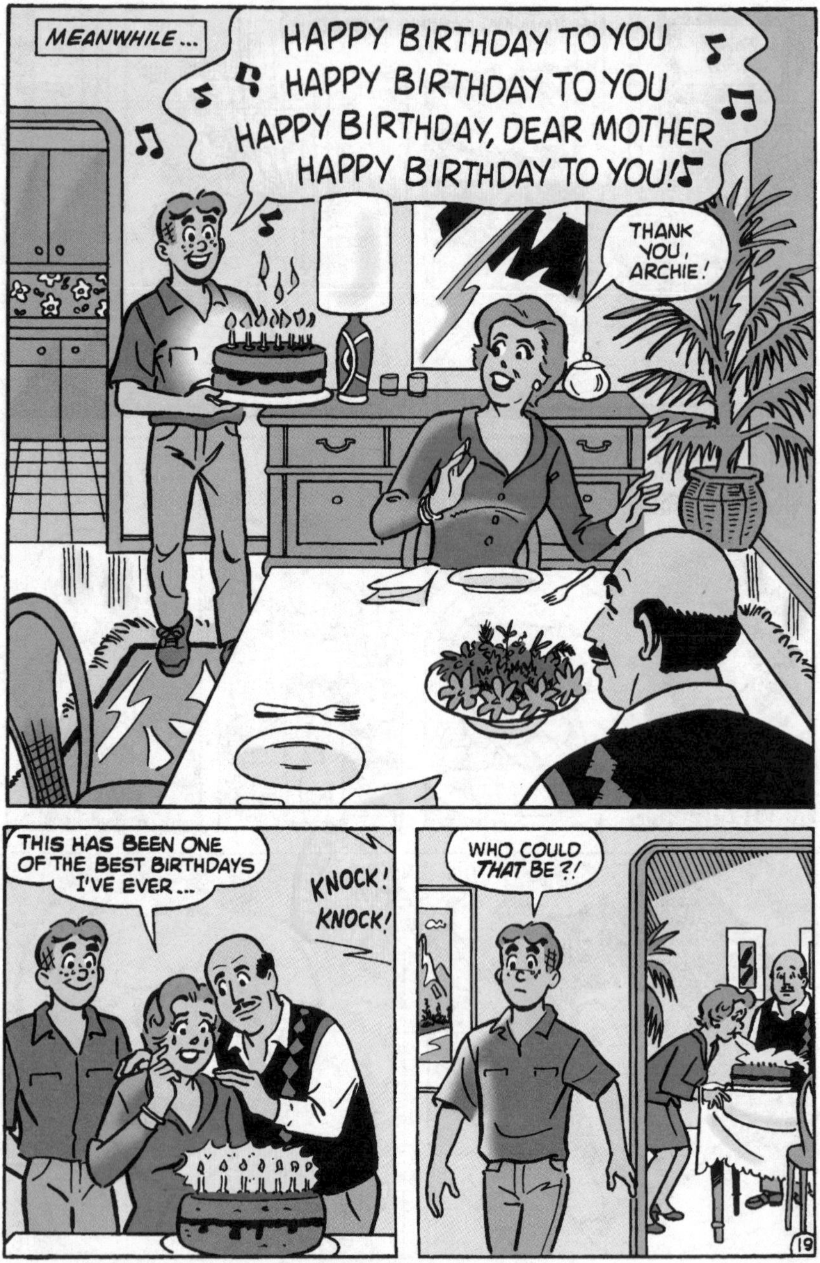

MEANWHILE...
HAPPY BIRTHDAY TO YOU
HAPPY BIRTHDAY TO YOU
HAPPY BIRTHDAY, DEAR MOTHER
HAPPY BIRTHDAY TO YOU!
THANK YOU, ARCHIE!
THIS HAS BEEN ONE OF THE BEST BIRTHDAYS I'VE EVER...
KNOCK! KNOCK!
WHO COULD *THAT* BE?!

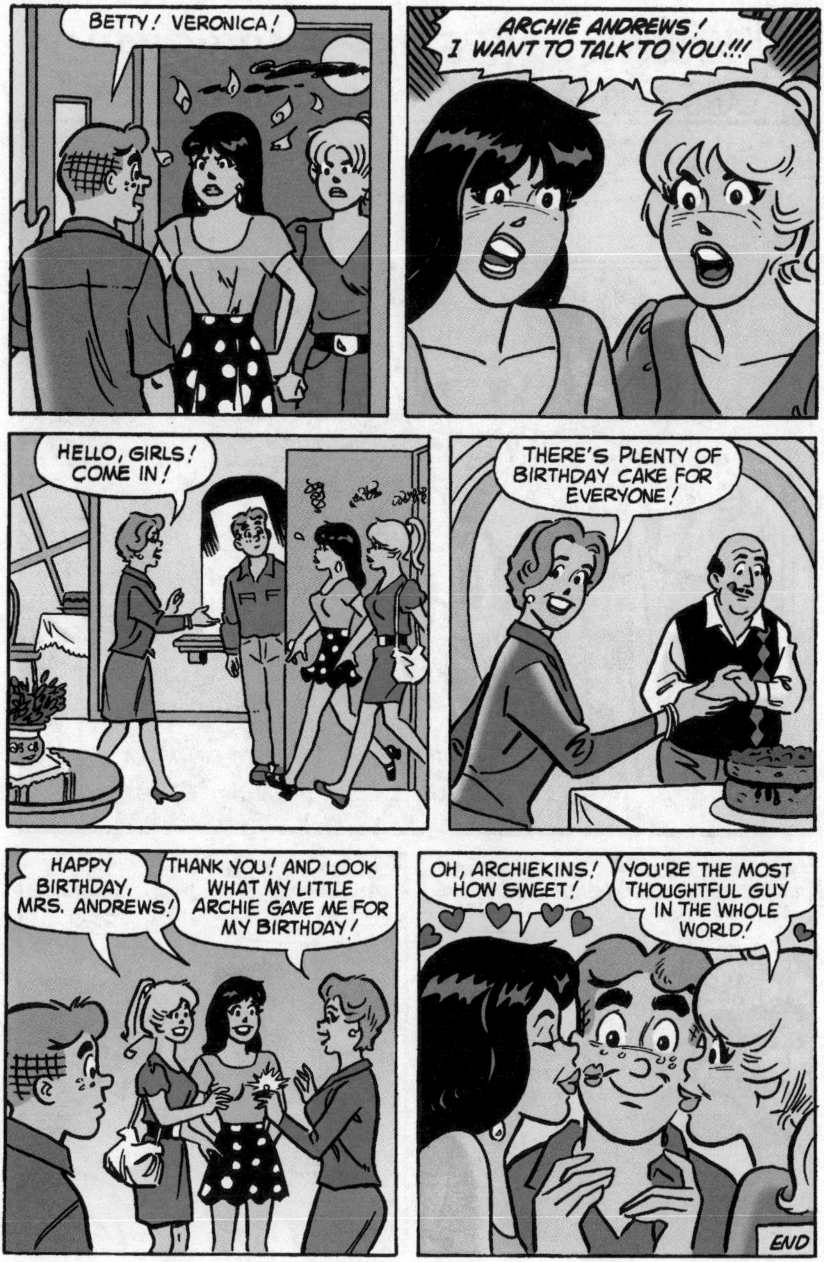
BETTY! VERONICA!
ARCHIE ANDREWS! I WANT TO TALK TO YOU!!!
HELLO, GIRLS! COME IN!
THERE'S PLENTY OF BIRTHDAY CAKE FOR EVERYONE!
HAPPY BIRTHDAY, MRS. ANDREWS!
THANK YOU! AND LOOK WHAT MY LITTLE ARCHIE GAVE ME FOR MY BIRTHDAY!
OH, ARCHIEKINS! HOW SWEET!
YOU'RE THE MOST THOUGHTFUL GUY IN THE WHOLE WORLD!
END

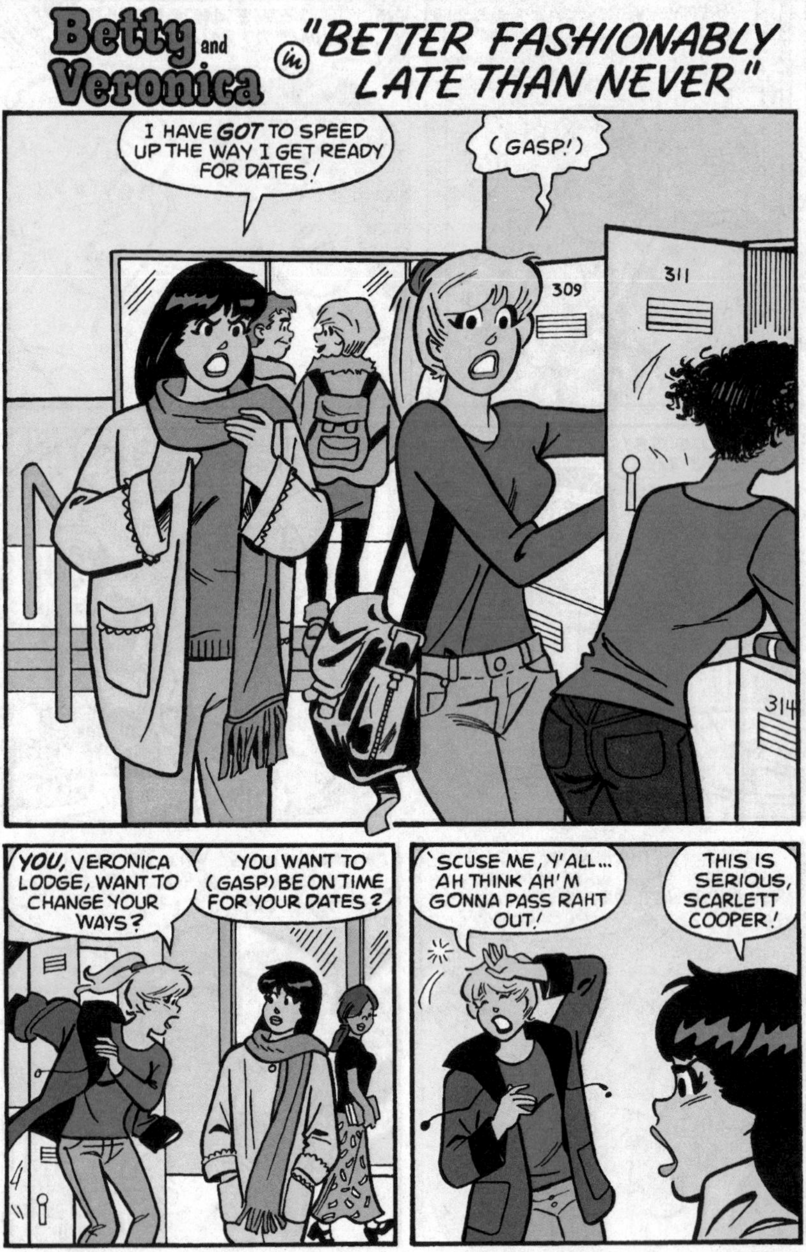

Betty and Veronica in "BETTER FASHIONABLY LATE THAN NEVER"
I HAVE GOT TO SPEED UP THE WAY I GET READY FOR DATES!
(GASP!)
309
311
314
YOU, VERONICA LODGE, WANT TO CHANGE YOUR WAYS?
YOU WANT TO (GASP) BE ON TIME FOR YOUR DATES?
`SCUSE ME, Y'ALL... AH THINK AH'M GONNA PASS RAHT OUT!
THIS IS SERIOUS, SCARLETT COOPER!

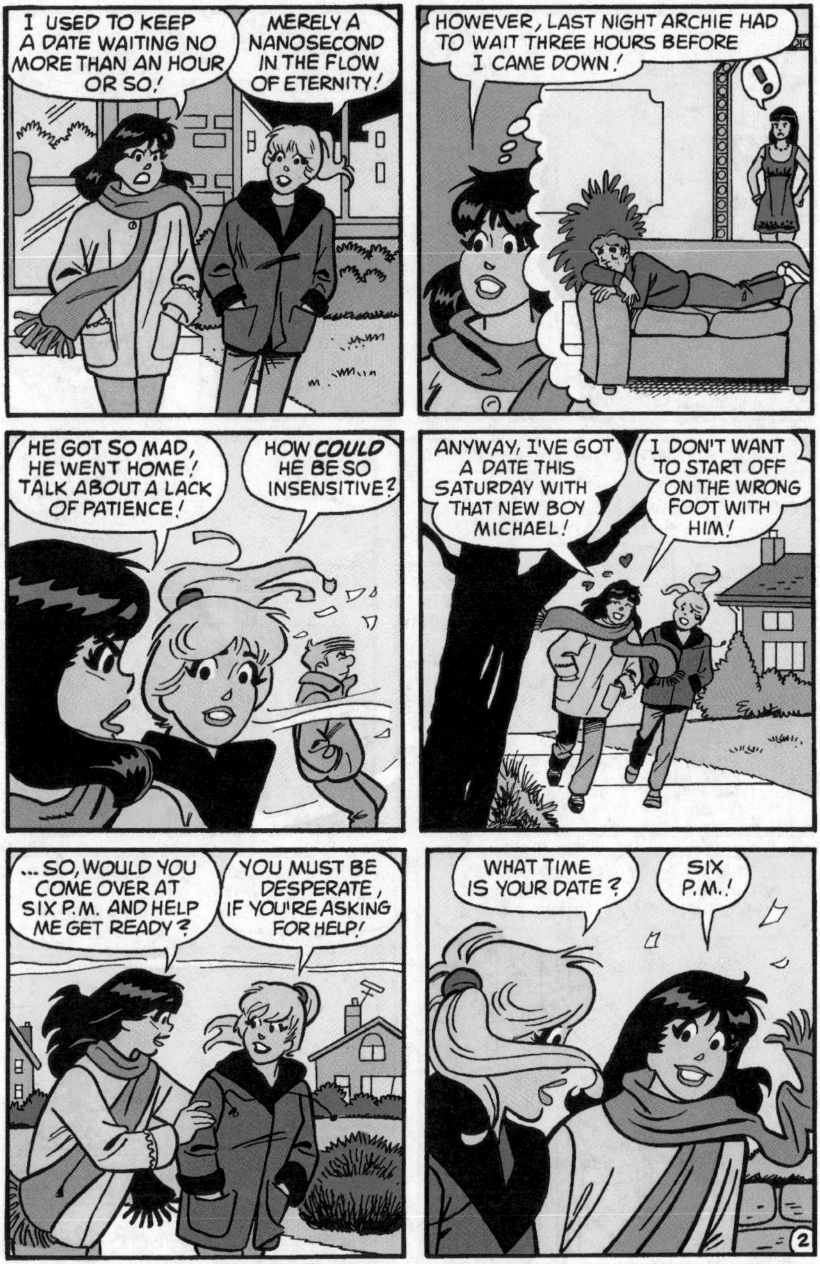
I USED TO KEEP A DATE WAITING NO MORE THAN AN HOUR OR SO!
MERELY A NANOSECOND IN THE FLOW OF ETERNITY!
HOWEVER, LAST NIGHT ARCHIE HAD TO WAIT THREE HOURS BEFORE I CAME DOWN!
!
HE GOT SO MAD, HE WENT HOME! TALK ABOUT A LACK OF PATIENCE!
HOW COULD HE BE SO INSENSITIVE?
ANYWAY, I'VE GOT A DATE THIS SATURDAY WITH THAT NEW BOY MICHAEL!
I DON'T WANT TO START OFF ON THE WRONG FOOT WITH HIM!
... SO, WOULD YOU COME OVER AT SIX P.M. AND HELP ME GET READY?
YOU MUST BE DESPERATE, IF YOU'RE ASKING FOR HELP!
WHAT TIME IS YOUR DATE?
SIX P.M.!
2

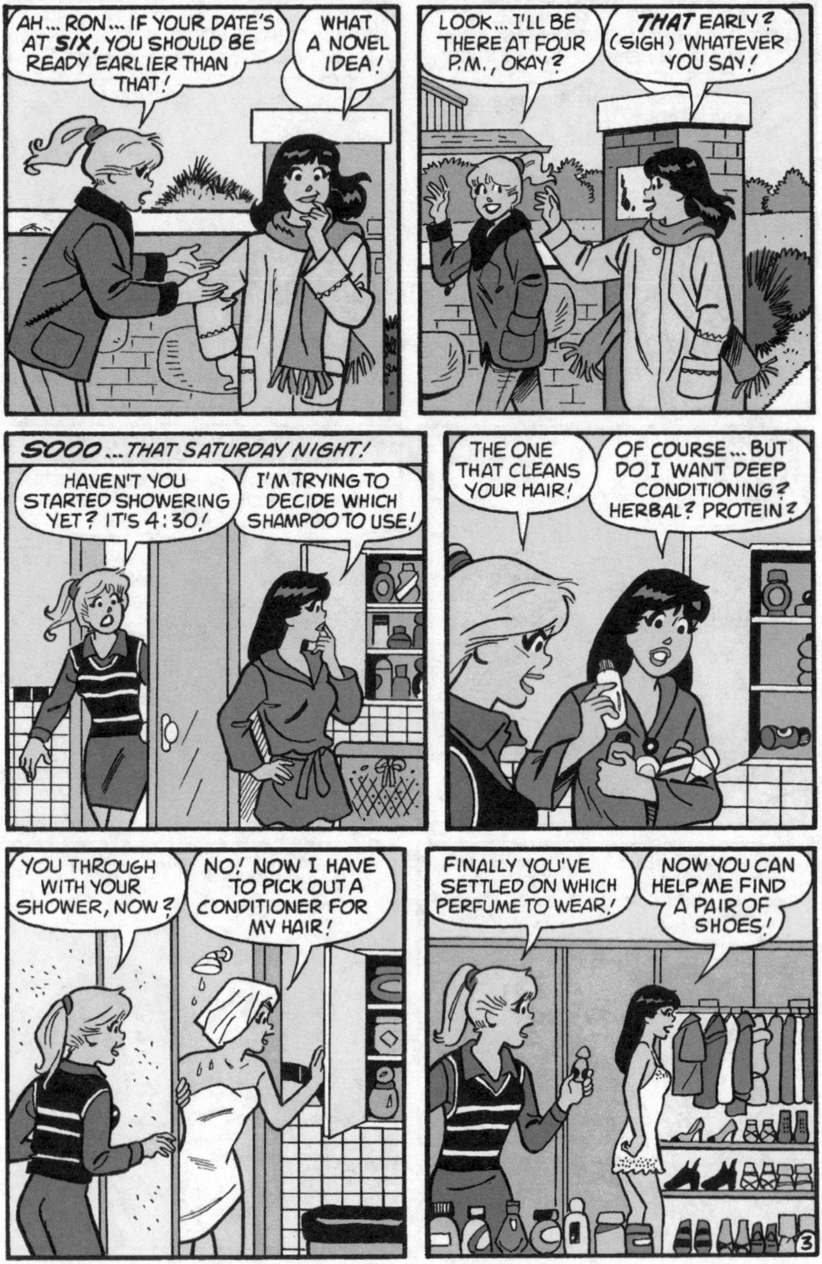

AH... RON... IF YOUR DATE'S AT SIX, YOU SHOULD BE READY EARLIER THAN THAT!
WHAT A NOVEL IDEA!
LOOK... I'LL BE THERE AT FOUR P.M., OKAY?
THAT EARLY? (SIGH) WHATEVER YOU SAY!
SOOO... THAT SATURDAY NIGHT!
HAVEN'T YOU STARTED SHOWERING YET? IT'S 4:30!
I'M TRYING TO DECIDE WHICH SHAMPOO TO USE!
THE ONE THAT CLEANS YOUR HAIR!
OF COURSE... BUT DO I WANT DEEP CONDITIONING? HERBAL? PROTEIN?
YOU THROUGH WITH YOUR SHOWER, NOW?
NO! NOW I HAVE TO PICK OUT A CONDITIONER FOR MY HAIR!
FINALLY YOU'VE SETTLED ON WHICH PERFUME TO WEAR!
NOW YOU CAN HELP ME FIND A PAIR OF SHOES!
3

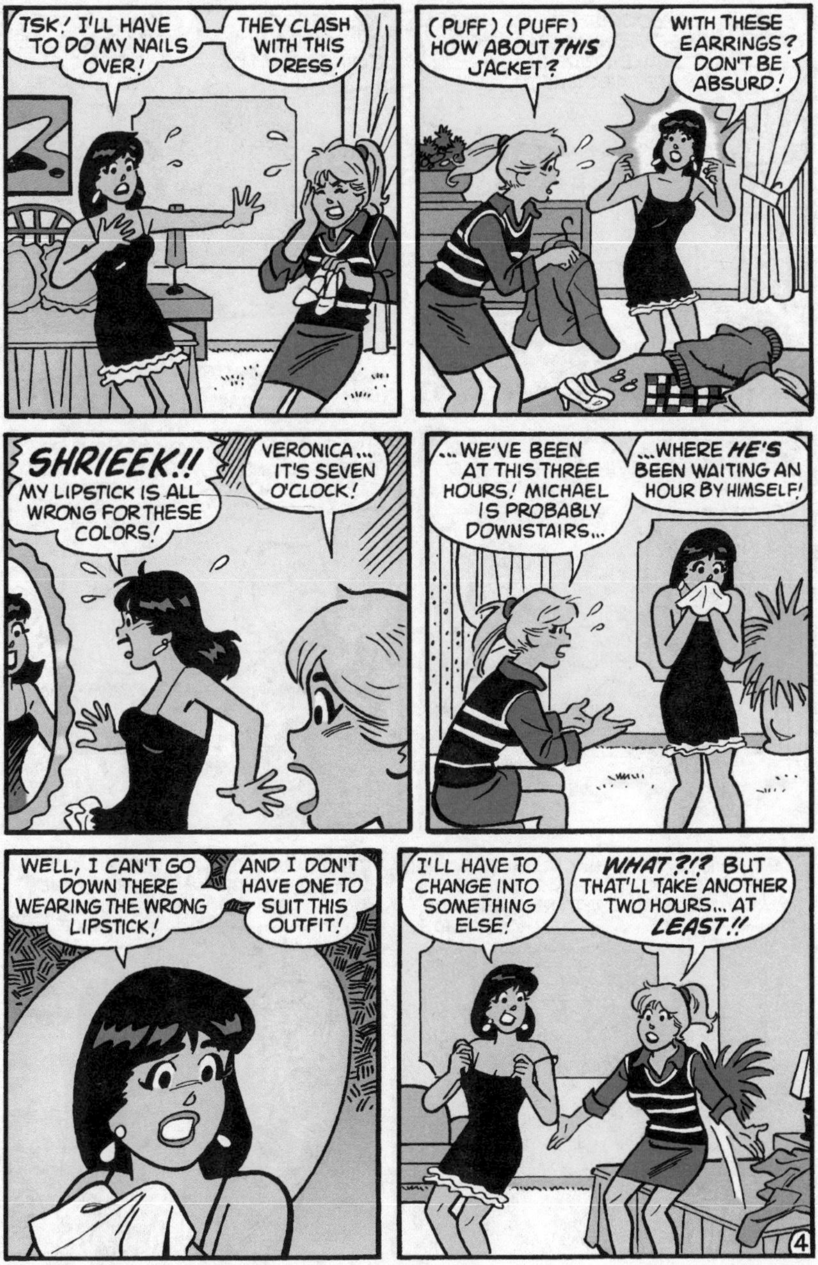
TSK! I'LL HAVE TO DO MY NAILS OVER!
THEY CLASH WITH THIS DRESS!
(PUFF) (PUFF) HOW ABOUT THIS JACKET?
WITH THESE EARRINGS? DON'T BE ABSURD!
SHRIEEK!! MY LIPSTICK IS ALL WRONG FOR THESE COLORS!
VERONICA... IT'S SEVEN O'CLOCK!
...WE'VE BEEN AT THIS THREE HOURS! MICHAEL IS PROBABLY DOWNSTAIRS...
...WHERE HE'S BEEN WAITING AN HOUR BY HIMSELF!
WELL, I CAN'T GO DOWN THERE WEARING THE WRONG LIPSTICK!
AND I DON'T HAVE ONE TO SUIT THIS OUTFIT!
I'LL HAVE TO CHANGE INTO SOMETHING ELSE!
WHAT?!? BUT THAT'LL TAKE ANOTHER TWO HOURS... AT LEAST!!
4

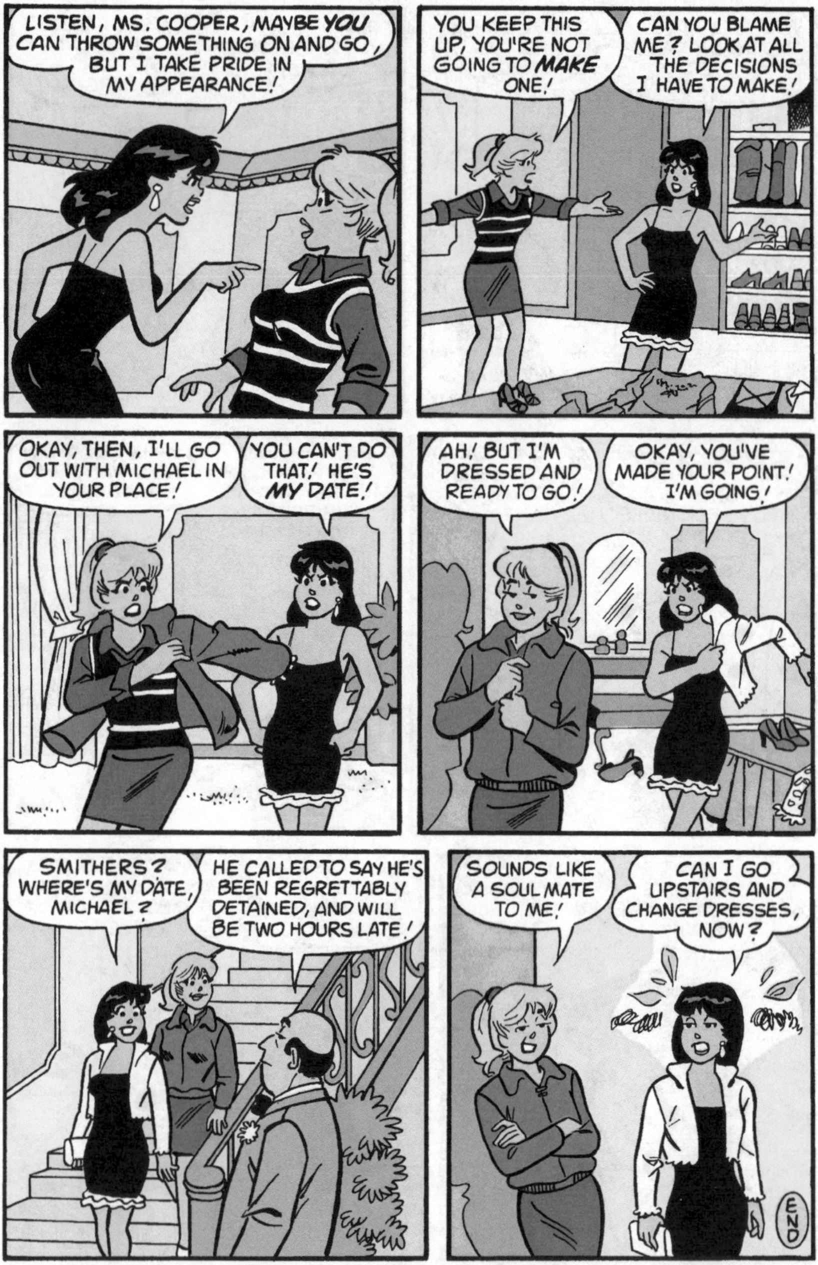
LISTEN, MS. COOPER, MAYBE YOU CAN THROW SOMETHING ON AND GO, BUT I TAKE PRIDE IN MY APPEARANCE!
YOU KEEP THIS UP, YOU'RE NOT GOING TO MAKE ONE!
CAN YOU BLAME ME? LOOK AT ALL THE DECISIONS I HAVE TO MAKE!
OKAY, THEN, I'LL GO OUT WITH MICHAEL IN YOUR PLACE!
YOU CAN'T DO THAT! HE'S MY DATE!
AH! BUT I'M DRESSED AND READY TO GO!
OKAY, YOU'VE MADE YOUR POINT! I'M GOING!
SMITHERS? WHERE'S MY DATE, MICHAEL?
HE CALLED TO SAY HE'S BEEN REGRETTABLY DETAINED, AND WILL BE TWO HOURS LATE!
SOUNDS LIKE A SOUL MATE TO ME!
CAN I GO UPSTAIRS AND CHANGE DRESSES, NOW?
END

THE BEST OF ARCHIE COMICS STARRING

BETTY & VERONICA

2000s

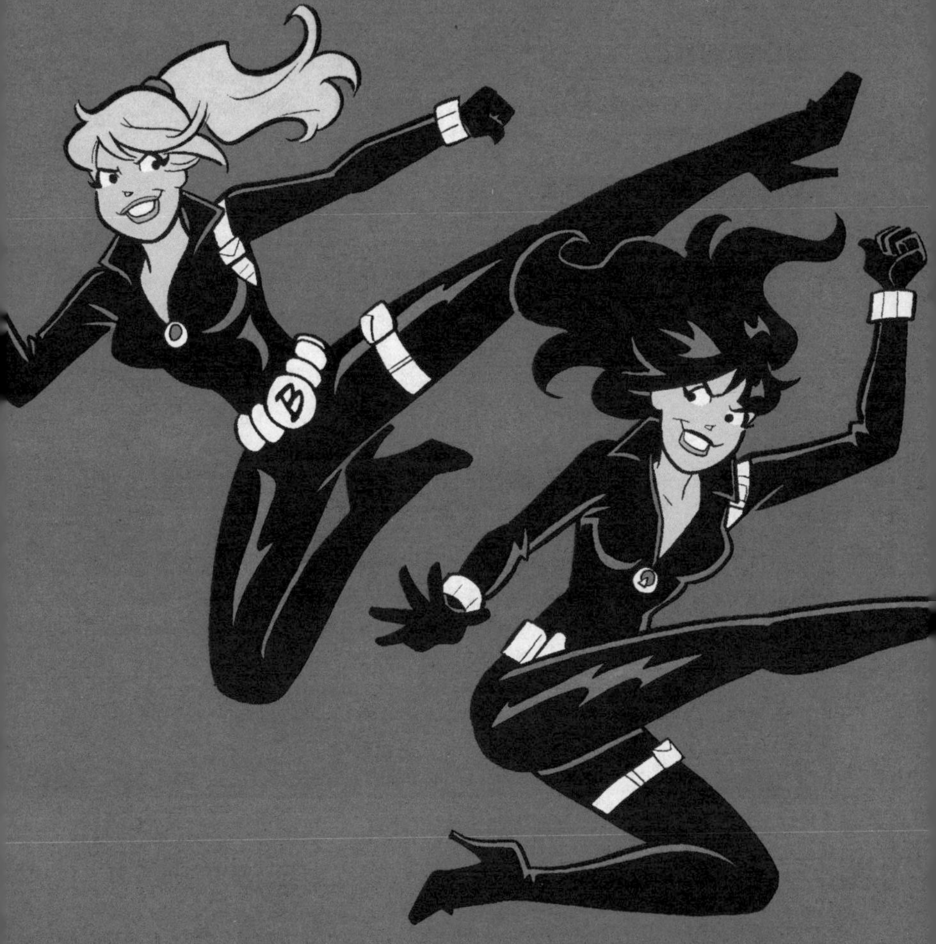

HOG WILD
BETTY & VERONICA VOL. 2 #148, 2000
Mike Pellowski, Dan DeCarlo, Henry Scarpelli, Bill Yoshida, Barry Grossman

UN-BULLY-VABLE
BETTY & VERONICA VOL. 2 #185, 2003
Angelo DeCesare, Jeff Shultz, Rudy Lapick, Bill Yoshida, Barry Grossman

I absolutely love the stories, themes, and narrative of these stories. I used to draw them all the time in different outfits, and even draw myself and my friends in this universe I love so much. They've always been there for me, inspiring me in my career and now I get to draw them being really cool, in their own motorcycle gang! I feel we have grown together like best friends. I love them so much!

- EVA CABRERA *Artist, Archie Comics*

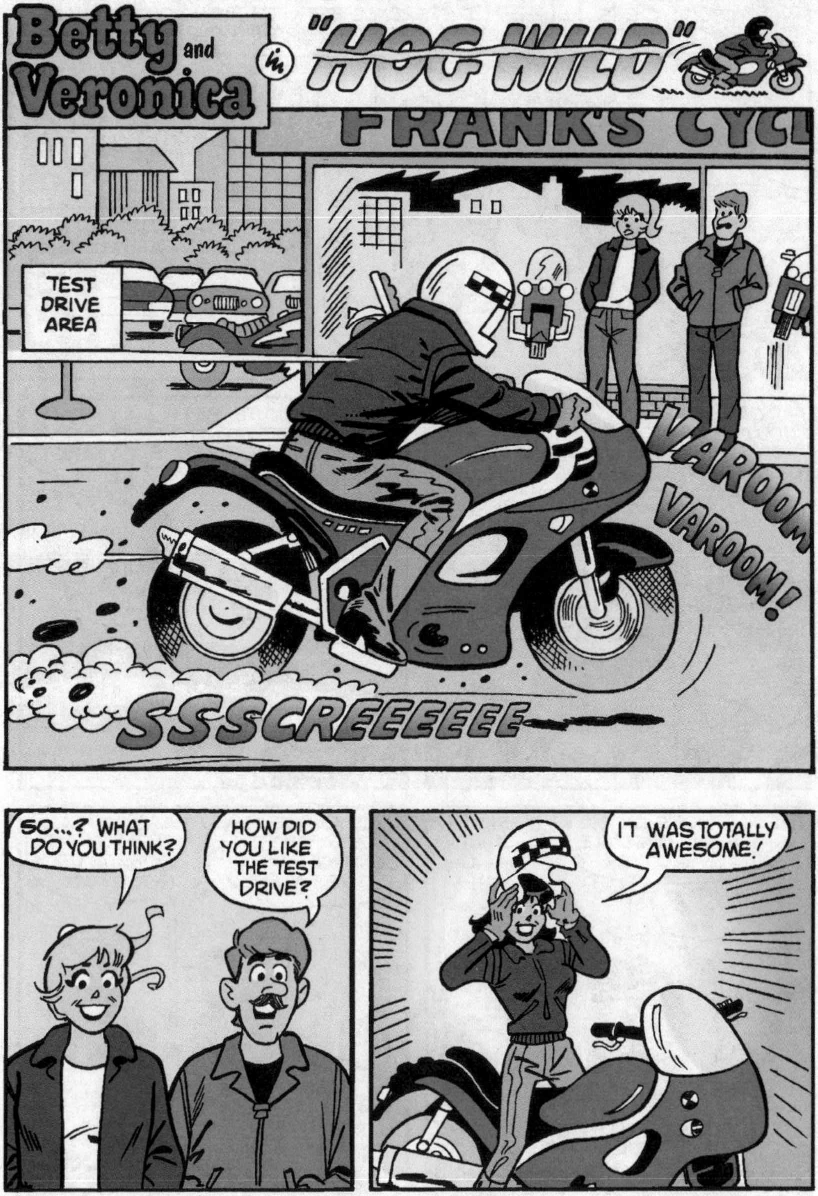
Betty and Veronica
in
"HOG WILD"
FRANK'S CYCL
TEST DRIVE AREA
VAROOM
VAROOM!
SSSCREEEEEEE
SO...? WHAT DO YOU THINK?
HOW DID YOU LIKE THE TEST DRIVE?
IT WAS TOTALLY AWESOME!

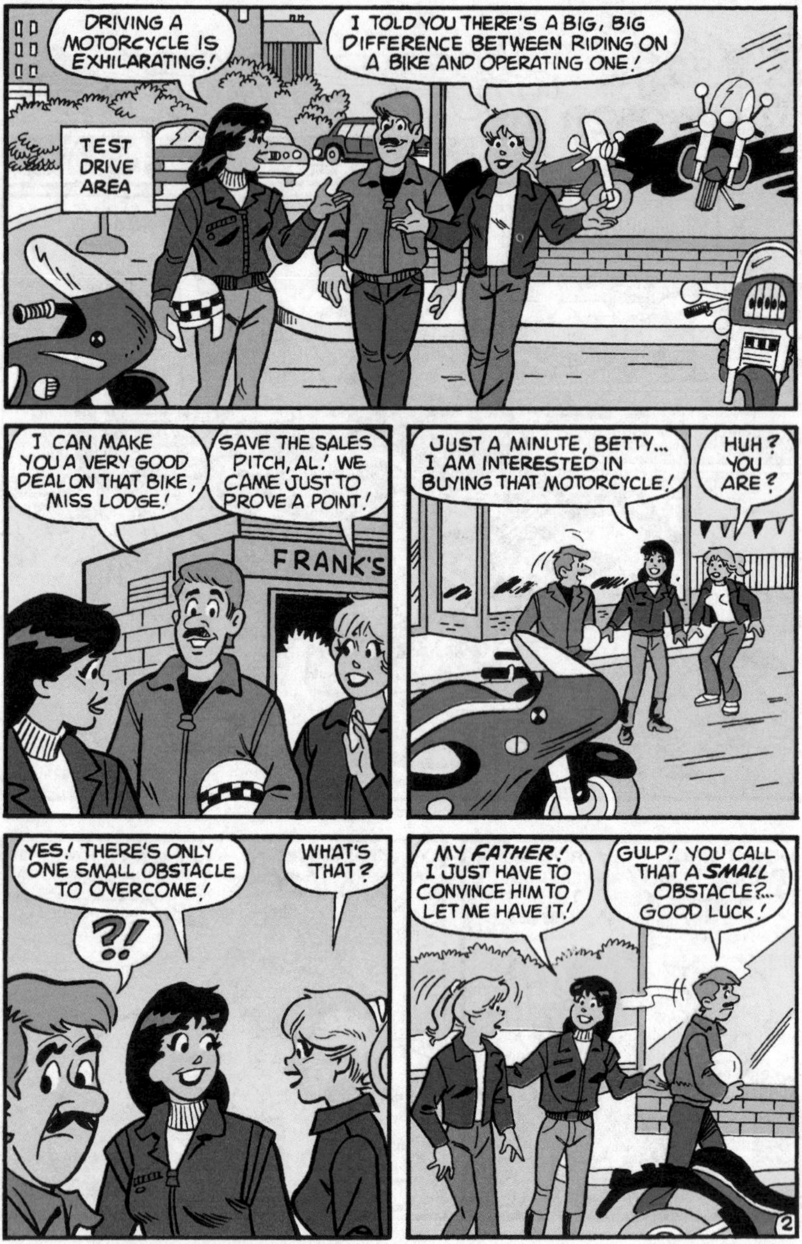
DRIVING A MOTORCYCLE IS EXHILARATING!
I TOLD YOU THERE'S A BIG, BIG DIFFERENCE BETWEEN RIDING ON A BIKE AND OPERATING ONE!
TEST DRIVE AREA
I CAN MAKE YOU A VERY GOOD DEAL ON THAT BIKE, MISS LODGE!
SAVE THE SALES PITCH, AL! WE CAME JUST TO PROVE A POINT!
FRANK'S
JUST A MINUTE, BETTY... I AM INTERESTED IN BUYING THAT MOTORCYCLE!
HUH? YOU ARE?
YES! THERE'S ONLY ONE SMALL OBSTACLE TO OVERCOME!
WHAT'S THAT?
?!
MY FATHER! I JUST HAVE TO CONVINCE HIM TO LET ME HAVE IT!
GULP! YOU CALL THAT A SMALL OBSTACLE?... GOOD LUCK!
2

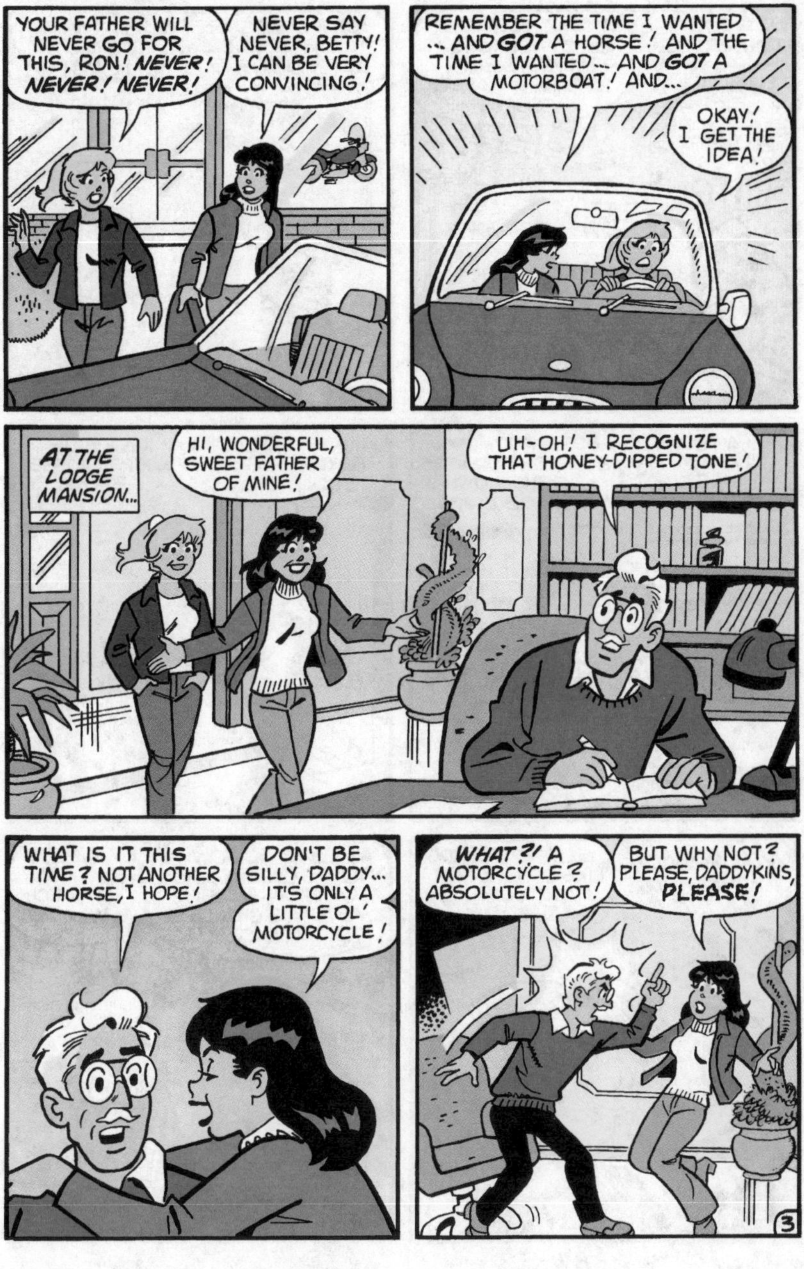
YOUR FATHER WILL NEVER GO FOR THIS, RON! NEVER! NEVER! NEVER!
NEVER SAY NEVER, BETTY! I CAN BE VERY CONVINCING!
REMEMBER THE TIME I WANTED ... AND GOT A HORSE! AND THE TIME I WANTED... AND GOT A MOTORBOAT! AND...
OKAY! I GET THE IDEA!
AT THE LODGE MANSION...
HI, WONDERFUL, SWEET FATHER OF MINE!
UH-OH! I RECOGNIZE THAT HONEY-DIPPED TONE!
WHAT IS IT THIS TIME? NOT ANOTHER HORSE, I HOPE!
DON'T BE SILLY, DADDY... IT'S ONLY A LITTLE OL' MOTORCYCLE!
WHAT?! A MOTORCYCLE? ABSOLUTELY NOT!
BUT WHY NOT? PLEASE, DADDYKINS, PLEASE!
3

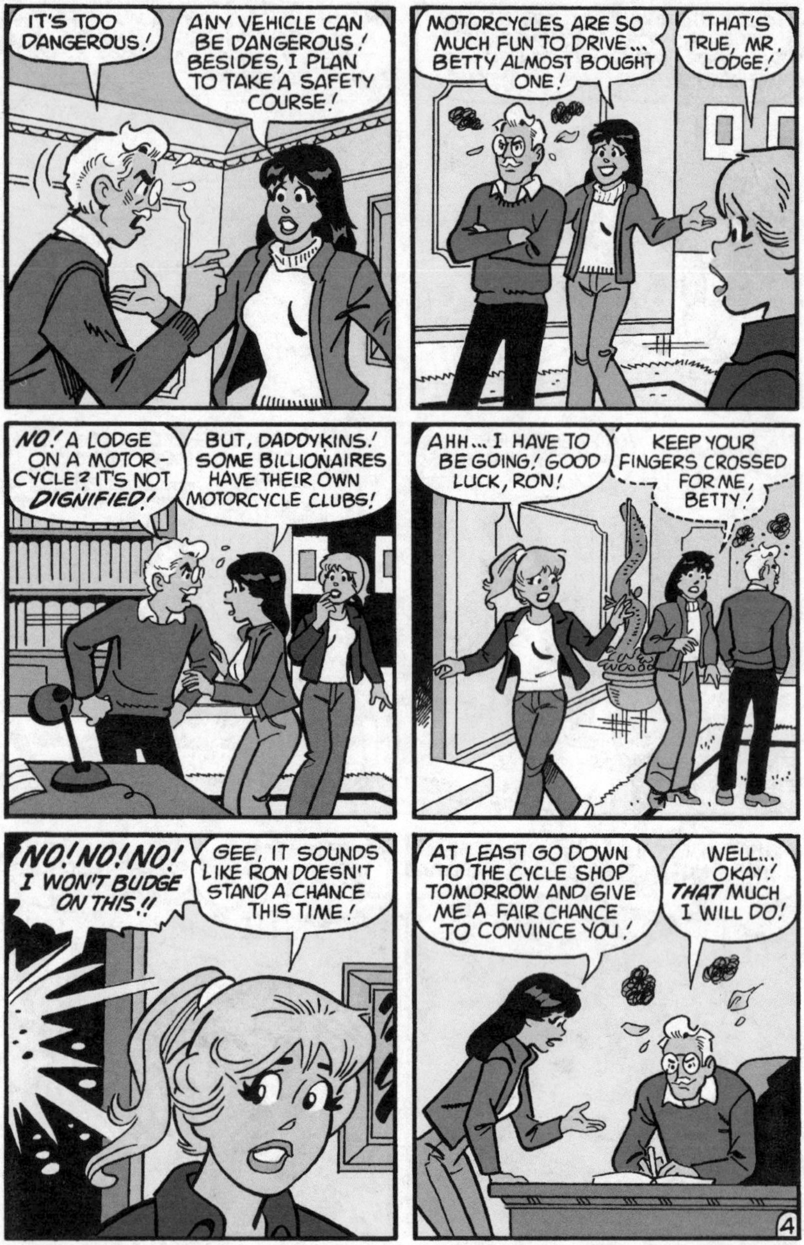
IT'S TOO DANGEROUS!
ANY VEHICLE CAN BE DANGEROUS! BESIDES, I PLAN TO TAKE A SAFETY COURSE!
MOTORCYCLES ARE SO MUCH FUN TO DRIVE... BETTY ALMOST BOUGHT ONE!
THAT'S TRUE, MR. LODGE!
NO! A LODGE ON A MOTORCYCLE? IT'S NOT DIGNIFIED!
BUT, DADDYKINS! SOME BILLIONAIRES HAVE THEIR OWN MOTORCYCLE CLUBS!
AHH... I HAVE TO BE GOING! GOOD LUCK, RON!
KEEP YOUR FINGERS CROSSED FOR ME, BETTY!
NO! NO! NO! I WON'T BUDGE ON THIS!!
GEE, IT SOUNDS LIKE RON DOESN'T STAND A CHANCE THIS TIME!
AT LEAST GO DOWN TO THE CYCLE SHOP TOMORROW AND GIVE ME A FAIR CHANCE TO CONVINCE YOU!
WELL... OKAY! THAT MUCH I WILL DO!
4

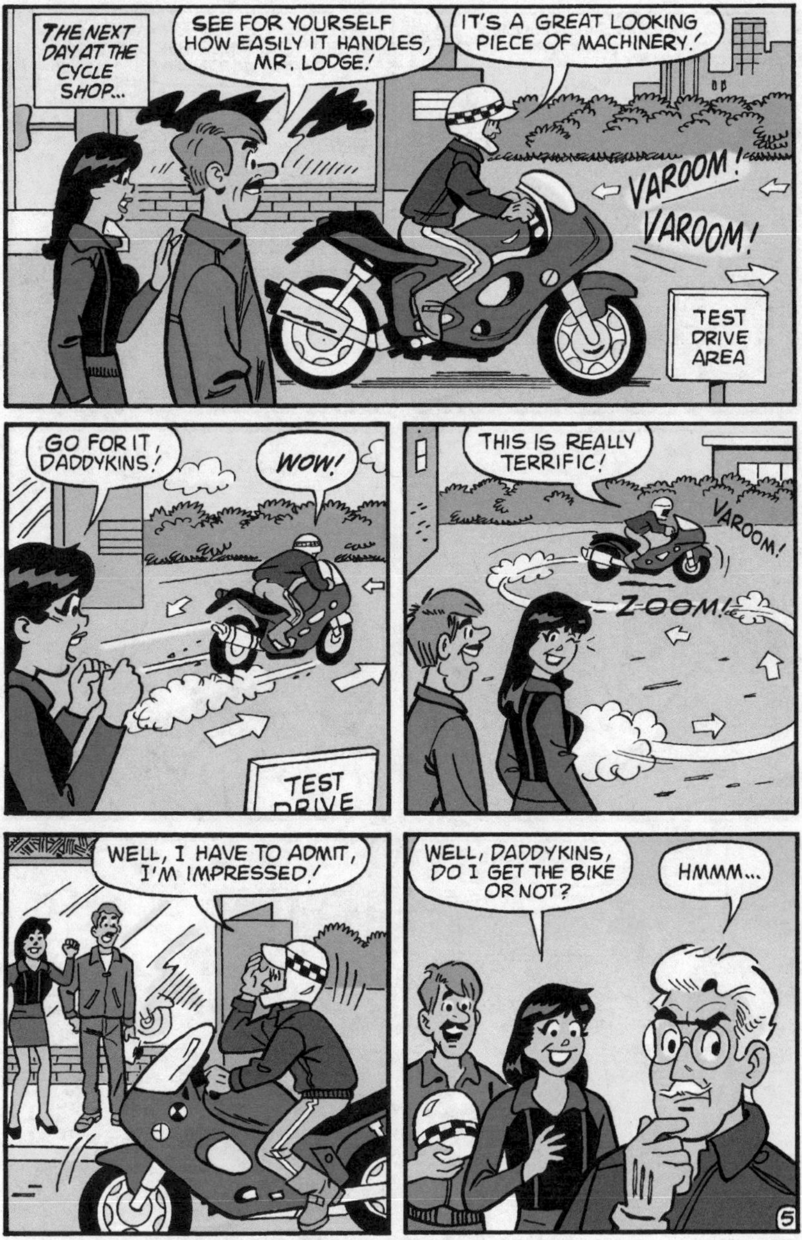

THE NEXT DAY AT THE CYCLE SHOP...
SEE FOR YOURSELF HOW EASILY IT HANDLES, MR. LODGE!
IT'S A GREAT LOOKING PIECE OF MACHINERY!
VAROOM!
VAROOM!
TEST DRIVE AREA
GO FOR IT, DADDYKINS!
WOW!
TEST DRIVE
THIS IS REALLY TERRIFIC!
VAROOM!
Z-OOM!
WELL, I HAVE TO ADMIT, I'M IMPRESSED!
WELL, DADDYKINS, DO I GET THE BIKE OR NOT?
HMMM...
5

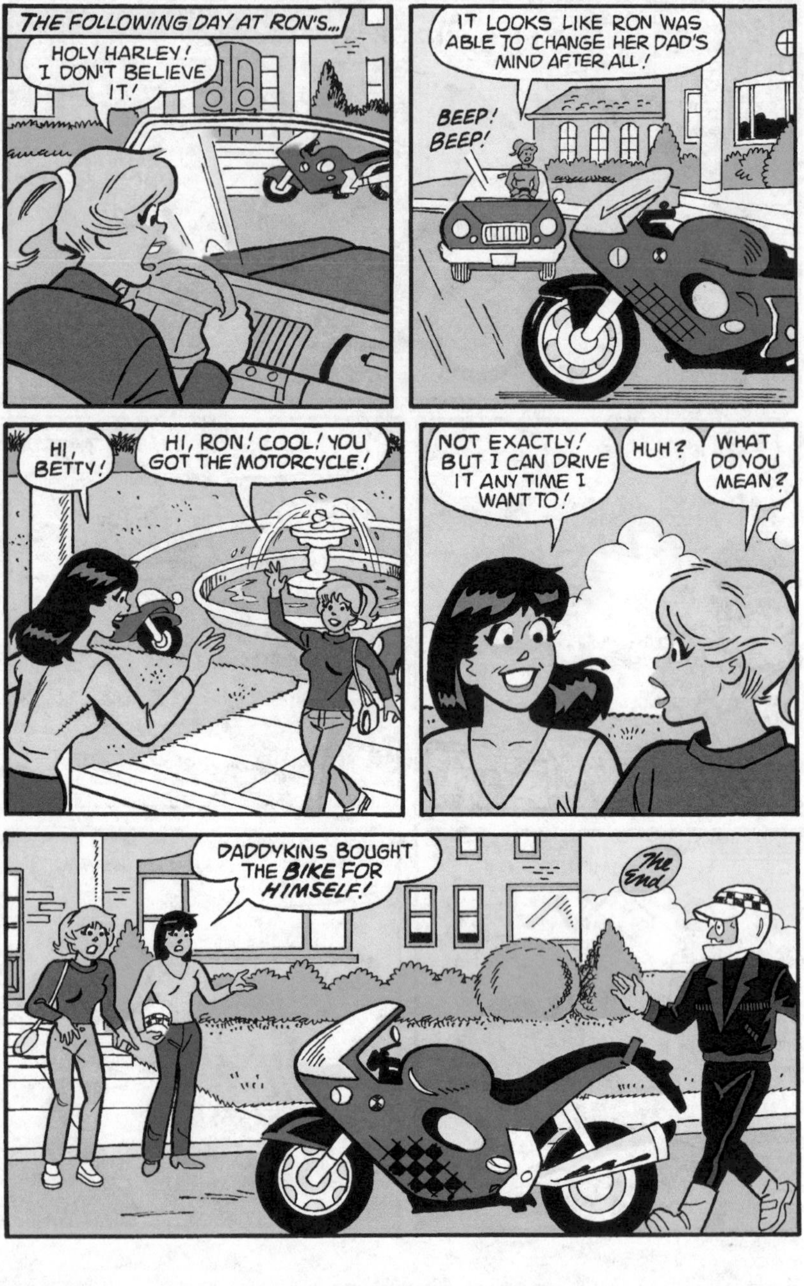
THE FOLLOWING DAY AT RON'S...
HOLY HARLEY! I DON'T BELIEVE IT!
IT LOOKS LIKE RON WAS ABLE TO CHANGE HER DAD'S MIND AFTER ALL!
BEEP! BEEP!
HI, BETTY!
HI, RON! COOL! YOU GOT THE MOTORCYCLE!
NOT EXACTLY! BUT I CAN DRIVE IT ANY TIME I WANT TO!
HUH?
WHAT DO YOU MEAN?
DADDYKINS BOUGHT THE BIKE FOR HIMSELF!
The End

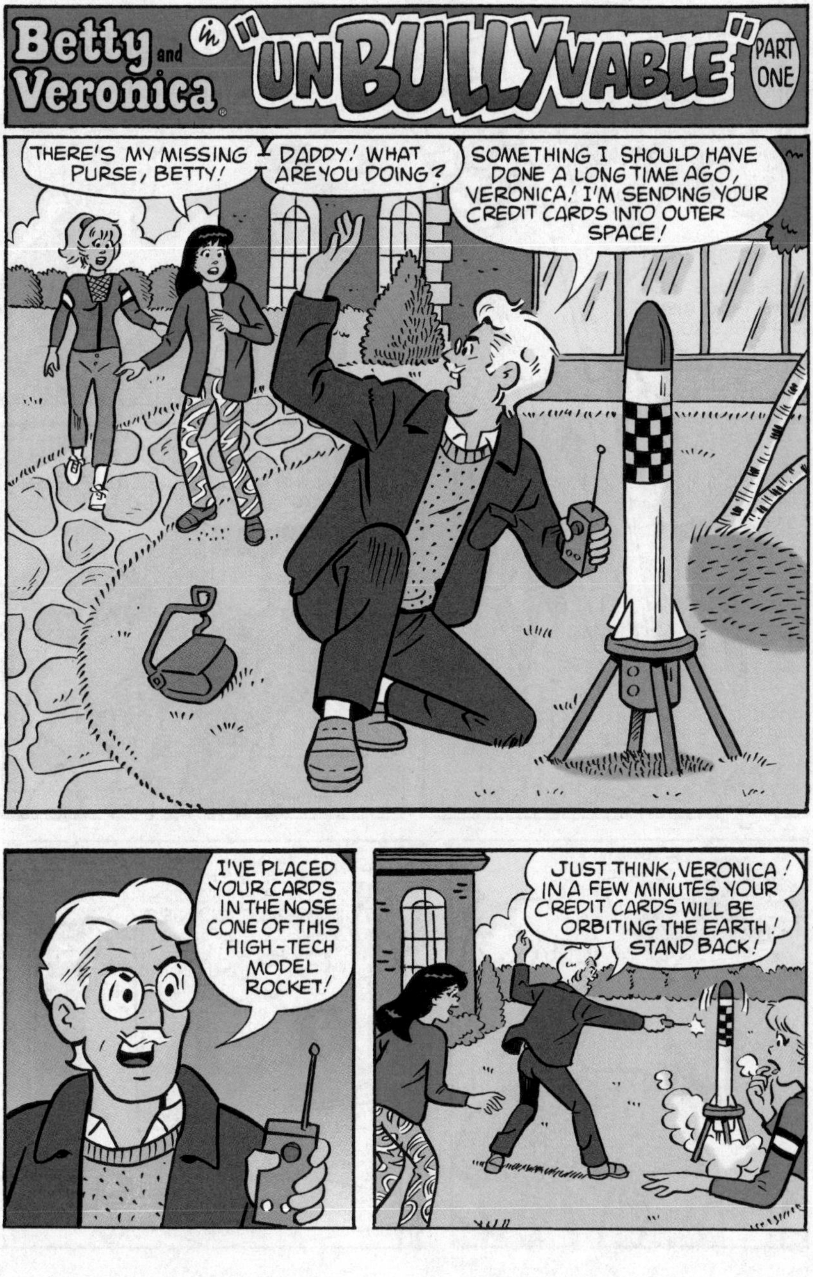
Betty and Veronica in "UNBULLYVABLE" PART ONE
THERE'S MY MISSING PURSE, BETTY!
DADDY! WHAT ARE YOU DOING?
SOMETHING I SHOULD HAVE DONE A LONG TIME AGO, VERONICA! I'M SENDING YOUR CREDIT CARDS INTO OUTER SPACE!
I'VE PLACED YOUR CARDS IN THE NOSE CONE OF THIS HIGH-TECH MODEL ROCKET!
JUST THINK, VERONICA! IN A FEW MINUTES YOUR CREDIT CARDS WILL BE ORBITING THE EARTH! STAND BACK!

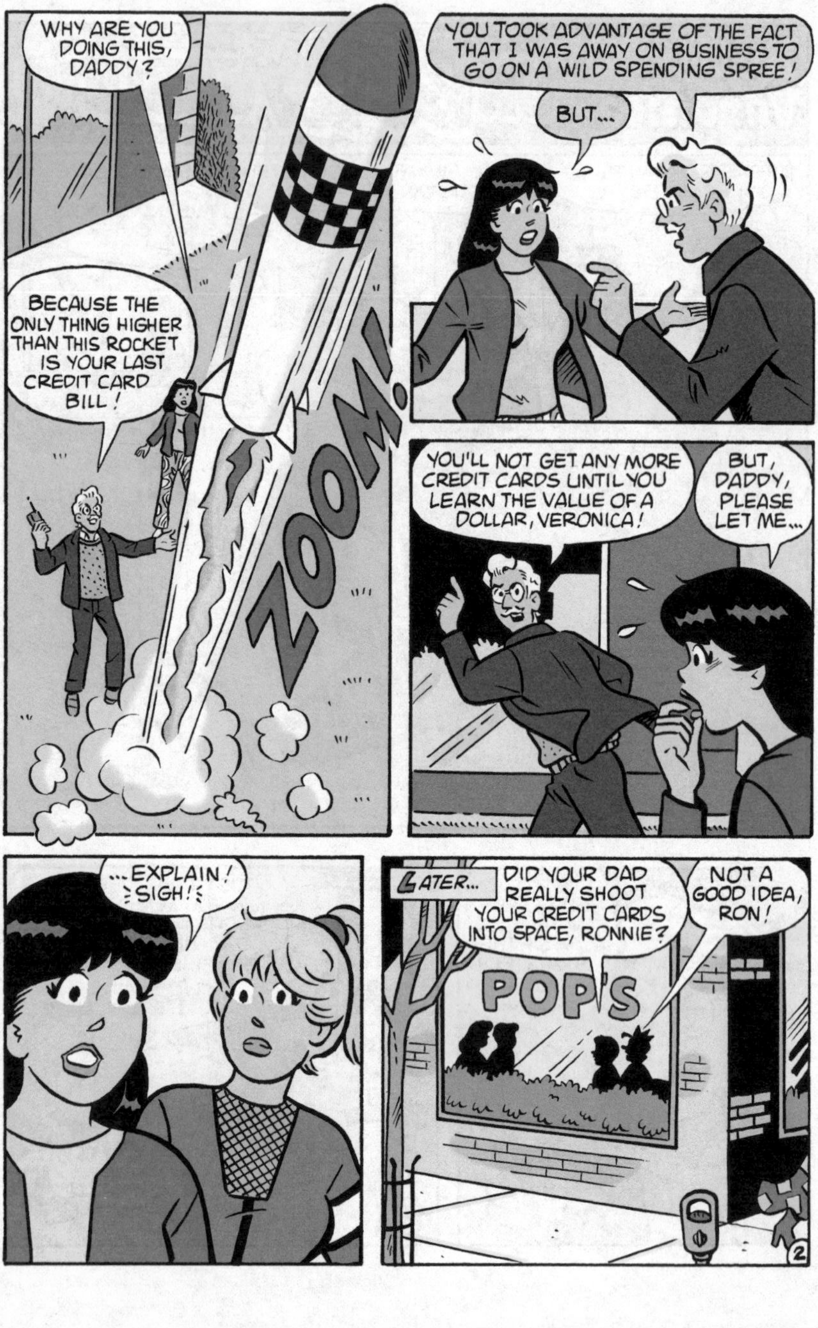
WHY ARE YOU DOING THIS, DADDY?
BECAUSE THE ONLY THING HIGHER THAN THIS ROCKET IS YOUR LAST CREDIT CARD BILL!
ZOOM!
YOU TOOK ADVANTAGE OF THE FACT THAT I WAS AWAY ON BUSINESS TO GO ON A WILD SPENDING SPREE!
BUT...
YOU'LL NOT GET ANY MORE CREDIT CARDS UNTIL YOU LEARN THE VALUE OF A DOLLAR, VERONICA!
BUT, DADDY, PLEASE LET ME...
...EXPLAIN! SIGH!
LATER...
DID YOUR DAD REALLY SHOOT YOUR CREDIT CARDS INTO SPACE, RONNIE?
NOT A GOOD IDEA, RON!
POP'S
2

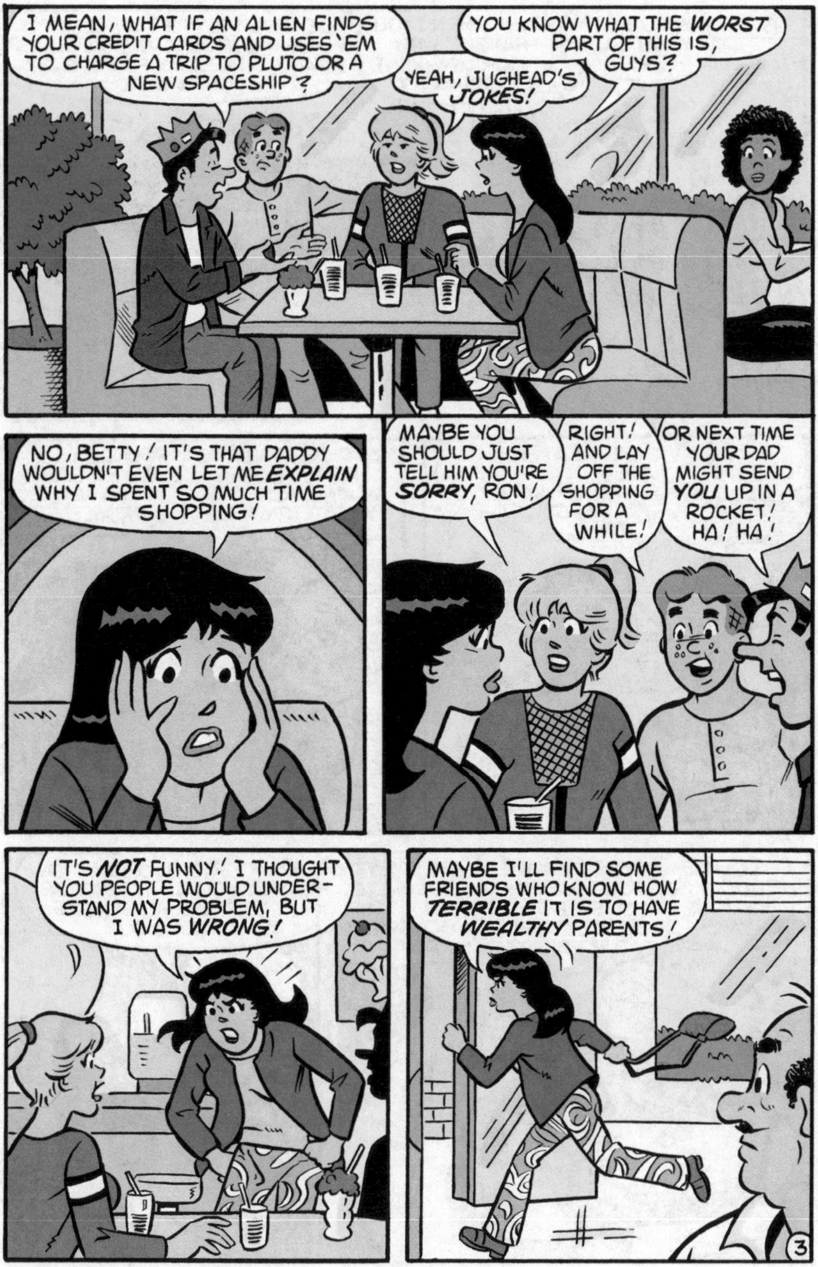
I MEAN, WHAT IF AN ALIEN FINDS YOUR CREDIT CARDS AND USES 'EM TO CHARGE A TRIP TO PLUTO OR A NEW SPACESHIP?
YEAH, JUGHEAD'S JOKES!
YOU KNOW WHAT THE WORST PART OF THIS IS, GUYS?
NO, BETTY! IT'S THAT DADDY WOULDN'T EVEN LET ME EXPLAIN WHY I SPENT SO MUCH TIME SHOPPING!
MAYBE YOU SHOULD JUST TELL HIM YOU'RE SORRY, RON!
RIGHT! AND LAY OFF THE SHOPPING FOR A WHILE!
OR NEXT TIME YOUR DAD MIGHT SEND YOU UP IN A ROCKET! HA! HA!
IT'S NOT FUNNY! I THOUGHT YOU PEOPLE WOULD UNDER-STAND MY PROBLEM, BUT I WAS WRONG!
MAYBE I'LL FIND SOME FRIENDS WHO KNOW HOW TERRIBLE IT IS TO HAVE WEALTHY PARENTS!

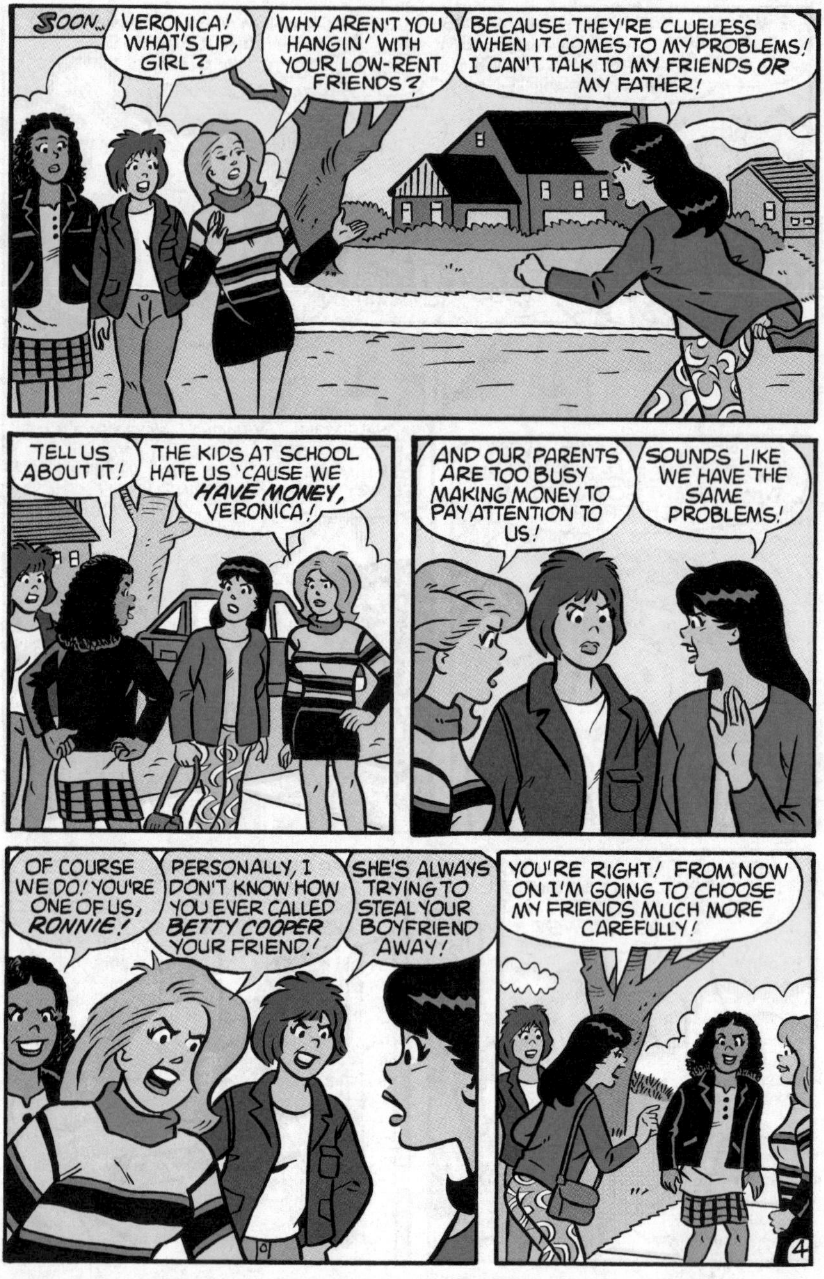
SOON...
VERONICA! WHAT'S UP, GIRL?
WHY AREN'T YOU HANGIN' WITH YOUR LOW-RENT FRIENDS?
BECAUSE THEY'RE CLUELESS WHEN IT COMES TO MY PROBLEMS! I CAN'T TALK TO MY FRIENDS OR MY FATHER!
TELL US ABOUT IT!
THE KIDS AT SCHOOL HATE US 'CAUSE WE HAVE MONEY, VERONICA!
AND OUR PARENTS ARE TOO BUSY MAKING MONEY TO PAY ATTENTION TO US!
SOUNDS LIKE WE HAVE THE SAME PROBLEMS!
OF COURSE WE DO! YOU'RE ONE OF US, RONNIE!
PERSONALLY, I DON'T KNOW HOW YOU EVER CALLED BETTY COOPER YOUR FRIEND!
SHE'S ALWAYS TRYING TO STEAL YOUR BOYFRIEND AWAY!
YOU'RE RIGHT! FROM NOW ON I'M GOING TO CHOOSE MY FRIENDS MUCH MORE CAREFULLY!
4

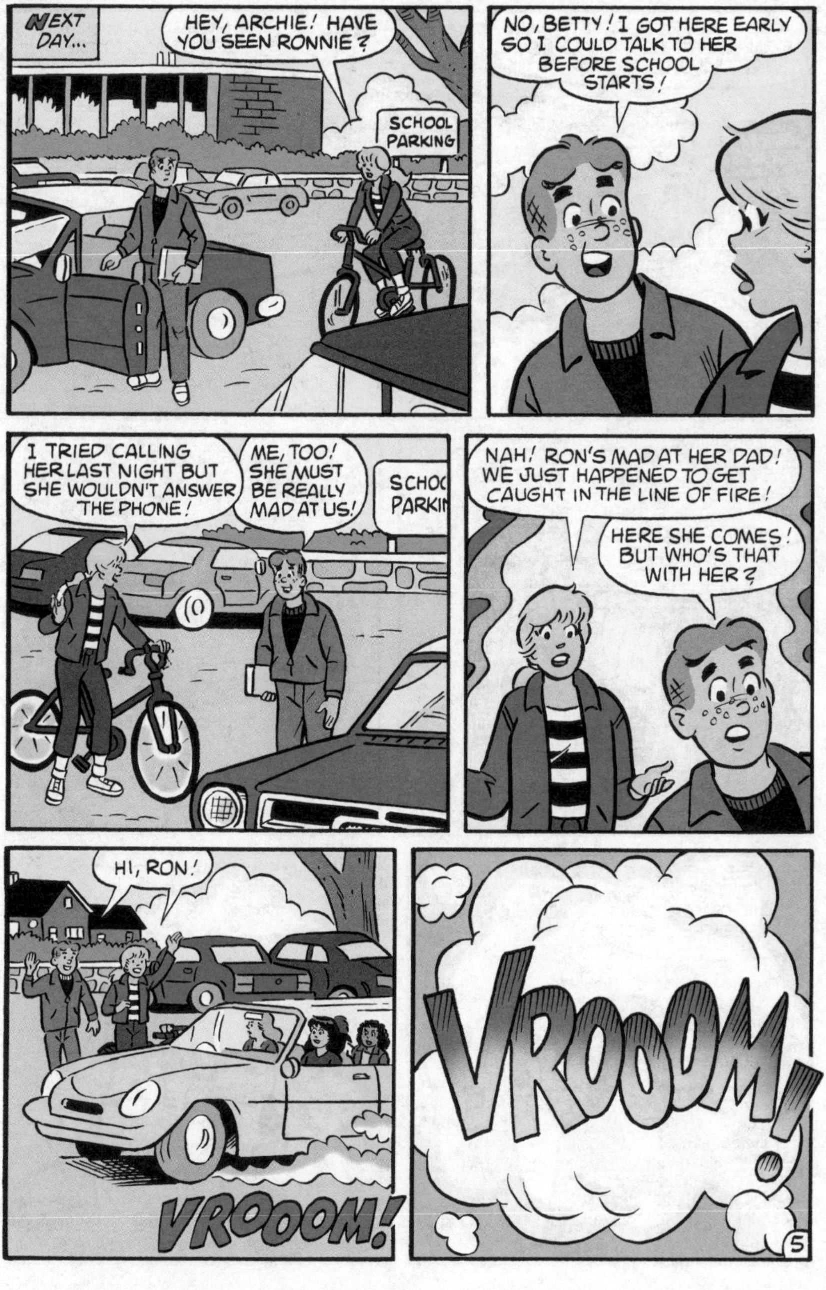
NEXT DAY...
HEY, ARCHIE! HAVE YOU SEEN RONNIE?
SCHOOL PARKING
NO, BETTY! I GOT HERE EARLY SO I COULD TALK TO HER BEFORE SCHOOL STARTS!
I TRIED CALLING HER LAST NIGHT BUT SHE WOULDN'T ANSWER THE PHONE!
ME, TOO! SHE MUST BE REALLY MAD AT US!
NAH! RON'S MAD AT HER DAD! WE JUST HAPPENED TO GET CAUGHT IN THE LINE OF FIRE!
HERE SHE COMES! BUT WHO'S THAT WITH HER?
HI, RON!
VROOOM!
VROOOM!
5

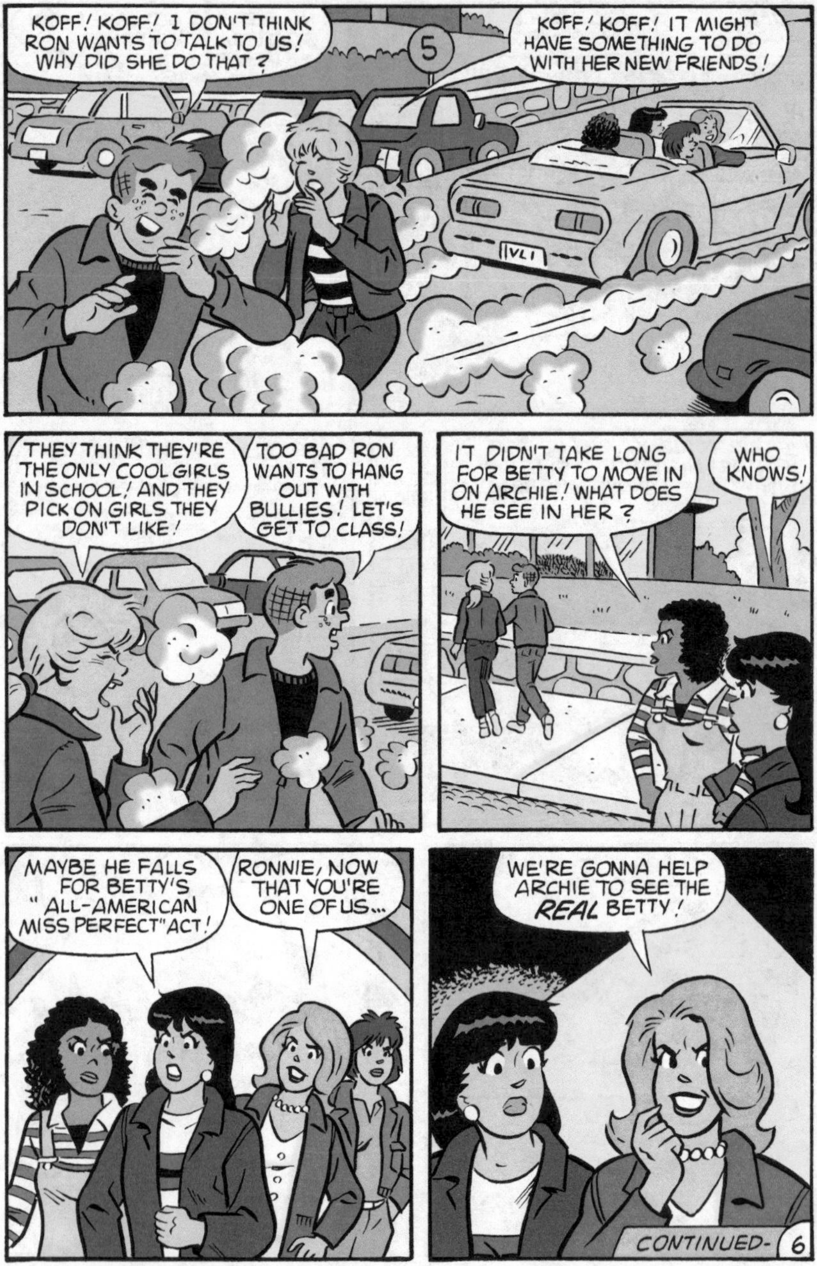
KOFF! KOFF! I DON'T THINK RON WANTS TO TALK TO US! WHY DID SHE DO THAT ?
KOFF! KOFF! IT MIGHT HAVE SOMETHING TO DO WITH HER NEW FRIENDS!
5
IVL I
THEY THINK THEY'RE THE ONLY COOL GIRLS IN SCHOOL! AND THEY PICK ON GIRLS THEY DON'T LIKE!
TOO BAD RON WANTS TO HANG OUT WITH BULLIES! LET'S GET TO CLASS!
IT DIDN'T TAKE LONG FOR BETTY TO MOVE IN ON ARCHIE! WHAT DOES HE SEE IN HER ?
WHO KNOWS!
MAYBE HE FALLS FOR BETTY'S "ALL-AMERICAN MISS PERFECT" ACT!
RONNIE, NOW THAT YOU'RE ONE OF US...
WE'RE GONNA HELP ARCHIE TO SEE THE REAL BETTY!
CONTINUED-
6

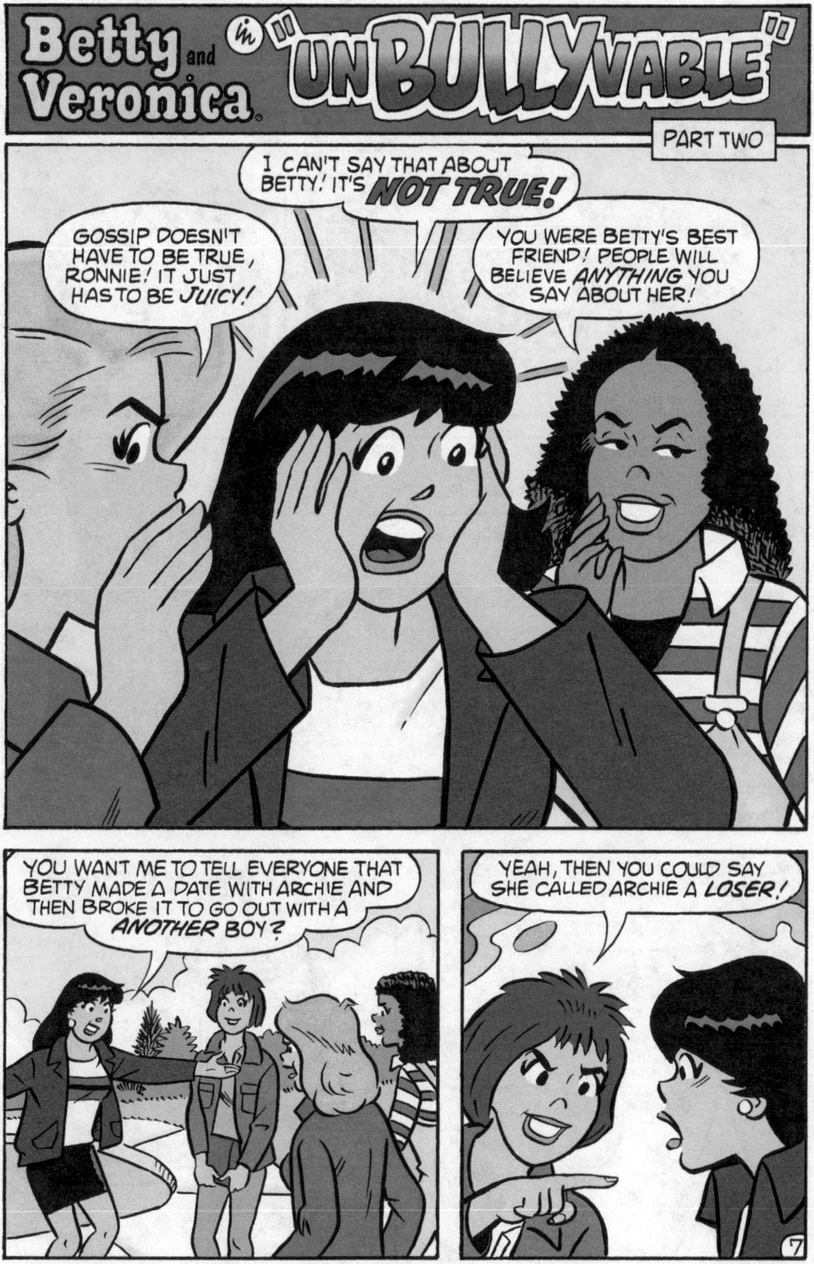
Betty and Veronica in "UNBULLYVABLE"
PART TWO
I CAN'T SAY THAT ABOUT BETTY! IT'S NOT TRUE!
GOSSIP DOESN'T HAVE TO BE TRUE, RONNIE! IT JUST HAS TO BE JUICY!
YOU WERE BETTY'S BEST FRIEND! PEOPLE WILL BELIEVE ANYTHING YOU SAY ABOUT HER!
YOU WANT ME TO TELL EVERYONE THAT BETTY MADE A DATE WITH ARCHIE AND THEN BROKE IT TO GO OUT WITH A ANOTHER BOY?
YEAH, THEN YOU COULD SAY SHE CALLED ARCHIE A LOSER!
7

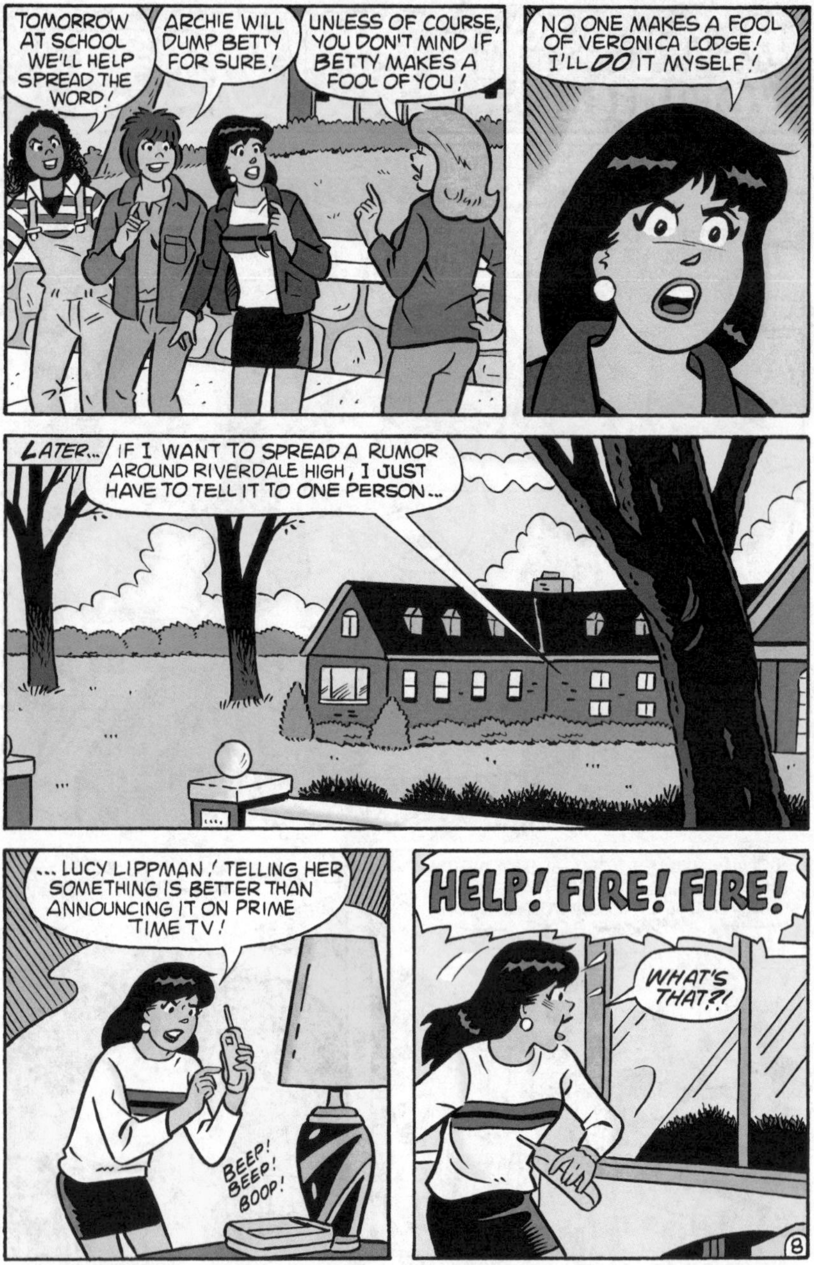
TOMORROW AT SCHOOL WE'LL HELP SPREAD THE WORD!
ARCHIE WILL DUMP BETTY FOR SURE!
UNLESS OF COURSE, YOU DON'T MIND IF BETTY MAKES A FOOL OF YOU!
NO ONE MAKES A FOOL OF VERONICA LODGE! I'LL DO IT MYSELF!
LATER...
IF I WANT TO SPREAD A RUMOR AROUND RIVERDALE HIGH, I JUST HAVE TO TELL IT TO ONE PERSON...
... LUCY LIPPMAN! TELLING HER SOMETHING IS BETTER THAN ANNOUNCING IT ON PRIME TIME TV!
BEEP! BEEP! BOOP!
HELP! FIRE! FIRE!
WHAT'S THAT?!
8

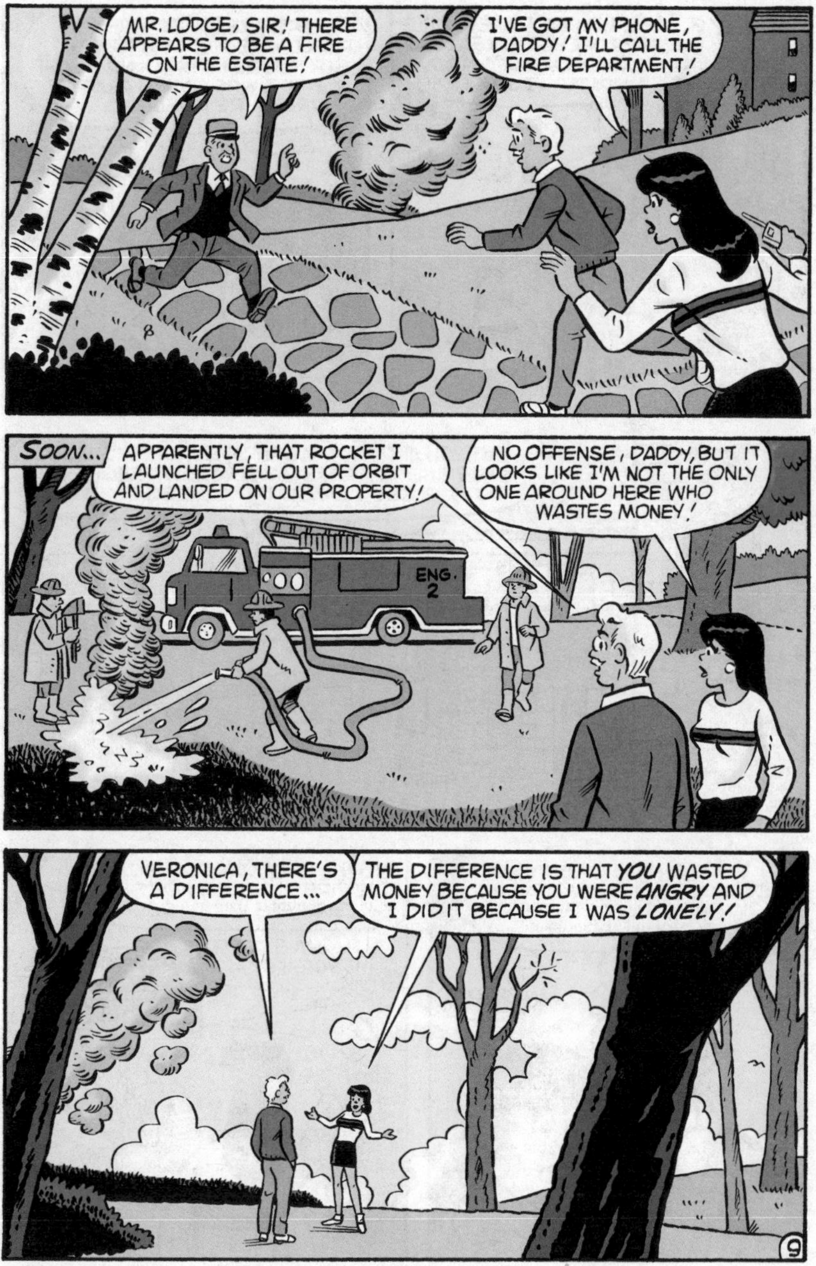
MR. LODGE, SIR! THERE APPEARS TO BE A FIRE ON THE ESTATE!
I'VE GOT MY PHONE, DADDY! I'LL CALL THE FIRE DEPARTMENT!
SOON...
APPARENTLY, THAT ROCKET I LAUNCHED FELL OUT OF ORBIT AND LANDED ON OUR PROPERTY!
NO OFFENSE, DADDY, BUT IT LOOKS LIKE I'M NOT THE ONLY ONE AROUND HERE WHO WASTES MONEY!
ENG. 2
VERONICA, THERE'S A DIFFERENCE...
THE DIFFERENCE IS THAT YOU WASTED MONEY BECAUSE YOU WERE ANGRY AND I DID IT BECAUSE I WAS LONELY!
9

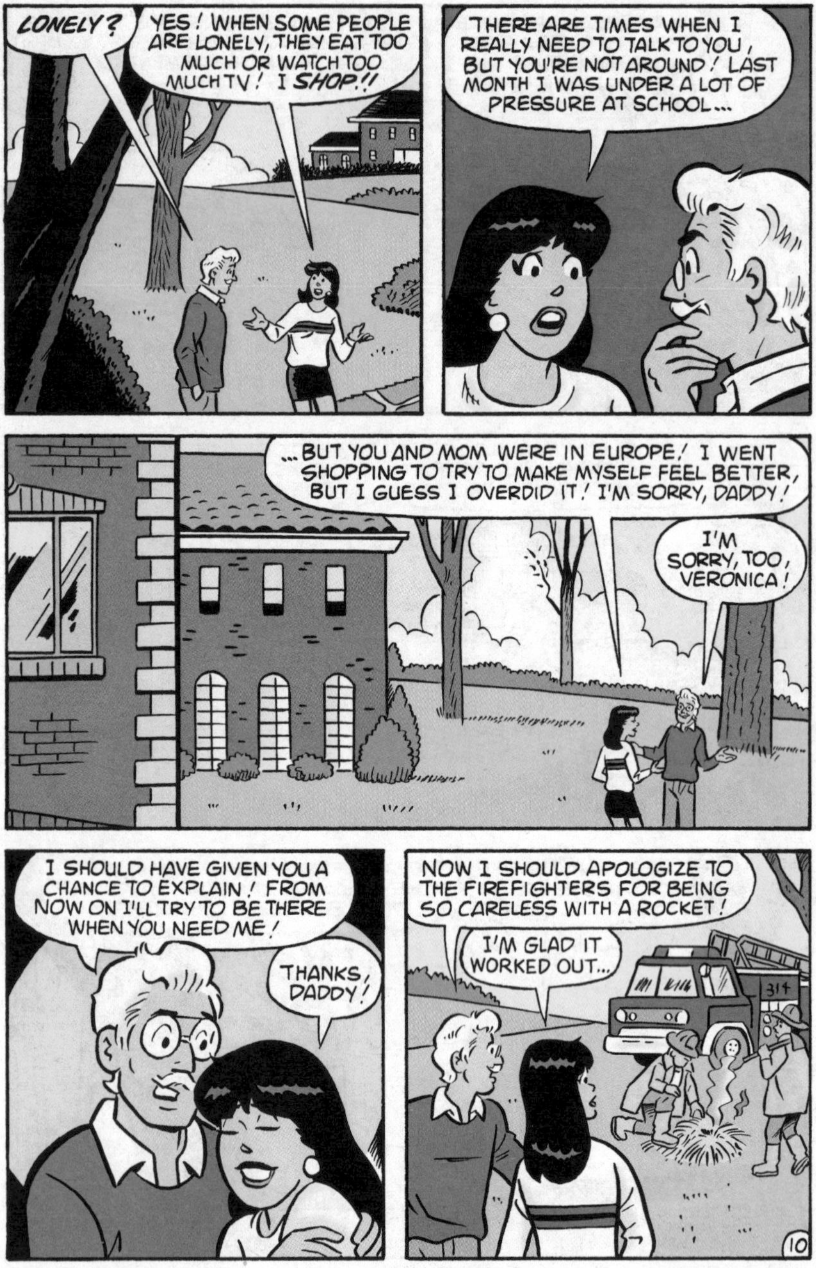
LONELY?
YES! WHEN SOME PEOPLE ARE LONELY, THEY EAT TOO MUCH OR WATCH TOO MUCH TV! I SHOP!!
THERE ARE TIMES WHEN I REALLY NEED TO TALK TO YOU, BUT YOU'RE NOT AROUND! LAST MONTH I WAS UNDER A LOT OF PRESSURE AT SCHOOL...
...BUT YOU AND MOM WERE IN EUROPE! I WENT SHOPPING TO TRY TO MAKE MYSELF FEEL BETTER, BUT I GUESS I OVERDID IT! I'M SORRY, DADDY!
I'M SORRY, TOO, VERONICA!
I SHOULD HAVE GIVEN YOU A CHANCE TO EXPLAIN! FROM NOW ON I'LL TRY TO BE THERE WHEN YOU NEED ME!
THANKS, DADDY!
NOW I SHOULD APOLOGIZE TO THE FIREFIGHTERS FOR BEING SO CARELESS WITH A ROCKET!
I'M GLAD IT WORKED OUT...
314
10

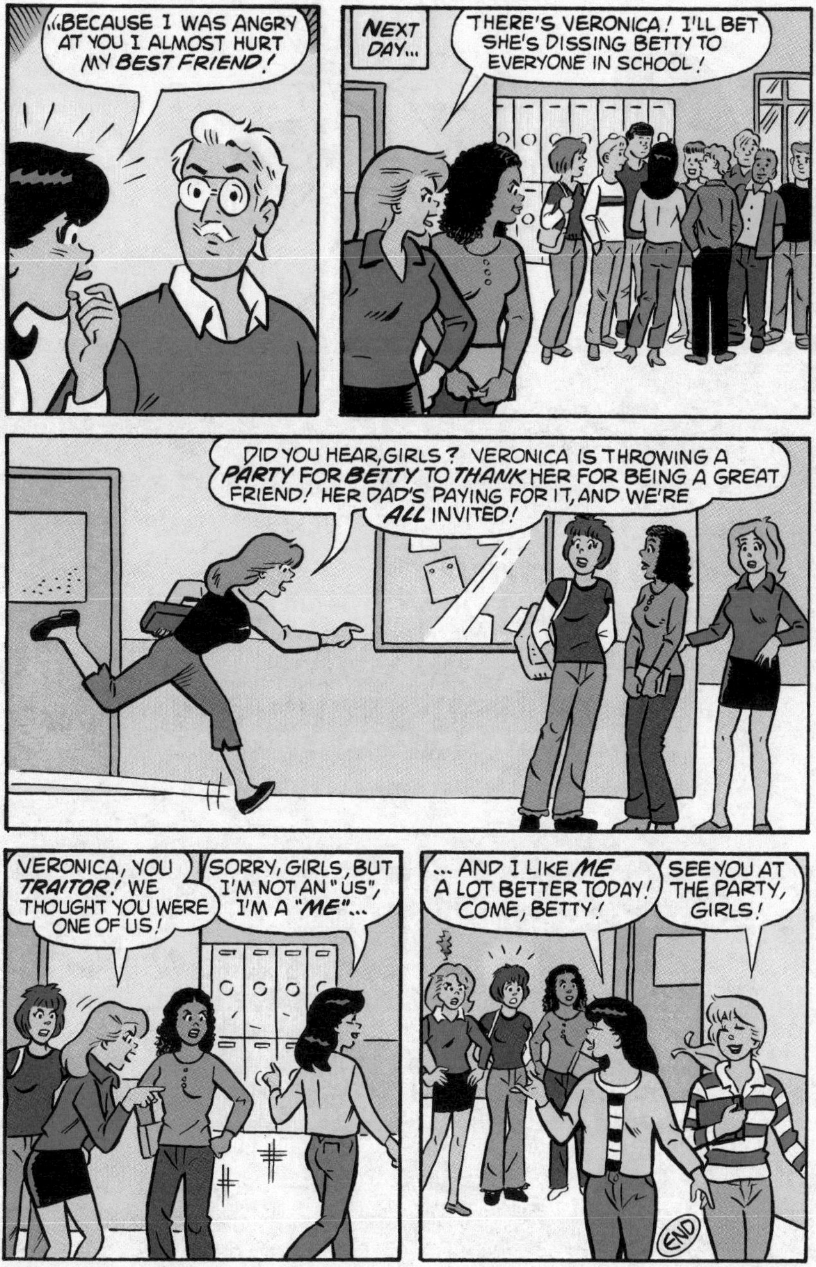
...BECAUSE I WAS ANGRY AT YOU I ALMOST HURT MY BEST FRIEND!
NEXT DAY...
THERE'S VERONICA! I'LL BET SHE'S DISSING BETTY TO EVERYONE IN SCHOOL!
DID YOU HEAR, GIRLS? VERONICA IS THROWING A PARTY FOR BETTY TO THANK HER FOR BEING A GREAT FRIEND! HER DAD'S PAYING FOR IT, AND WE'RE ALL INVITED!
VERONICA, YOU TRAITOR! WE THOUGHT YOU WERE ONE OF US!
SORRY, GIRLS, BUT I'M NOT AN "US", I'M A "ME"...
... AND I LIKE ME A LOT BETTER TODAY! COME, BETTY!
SEE YOU AT THE PARTY, GIRLS!
END

RABID RIVALS
BETTY & VERONICA VOL. 2 #189, 2003
George Gladir, Jeff Shultz, Henry Scarpelli, Barry Grossman, Bill Yoshida

SOOO SUPERFICIAL
BETTY & VERONICA VOL. 2 #211, 2005
Barbara Slate, Jeff Shultz, Al Milgrom, Barry Grossman, Vickie Williams

THE PAST WILL CATCH UP WITH YOU
BETTY & VERONICA DOUBLE DIGEST #196, 2009
Dan Parent, Rich Koslowski, Jack Morelli, Barry Grossman

A question that often comes up when discussing Betty and Veronica is the one of picking a side. Are you Team Betty or Team Veronica?

The rivalry gets a lot of talk but what's most important about these two iconic characters is their long-standing friendship. Any one of us would be extremely lucky to have a friendship like the one these two have shared for over 75 years. Whether it's holding a fundraiser to save Pop's or solving a mystery together, Betty & Veronica are at their best when they're Betty & Veronica—not Betty or Veronica.

- RON CACACE *Publicity Manager, Archie Comics*

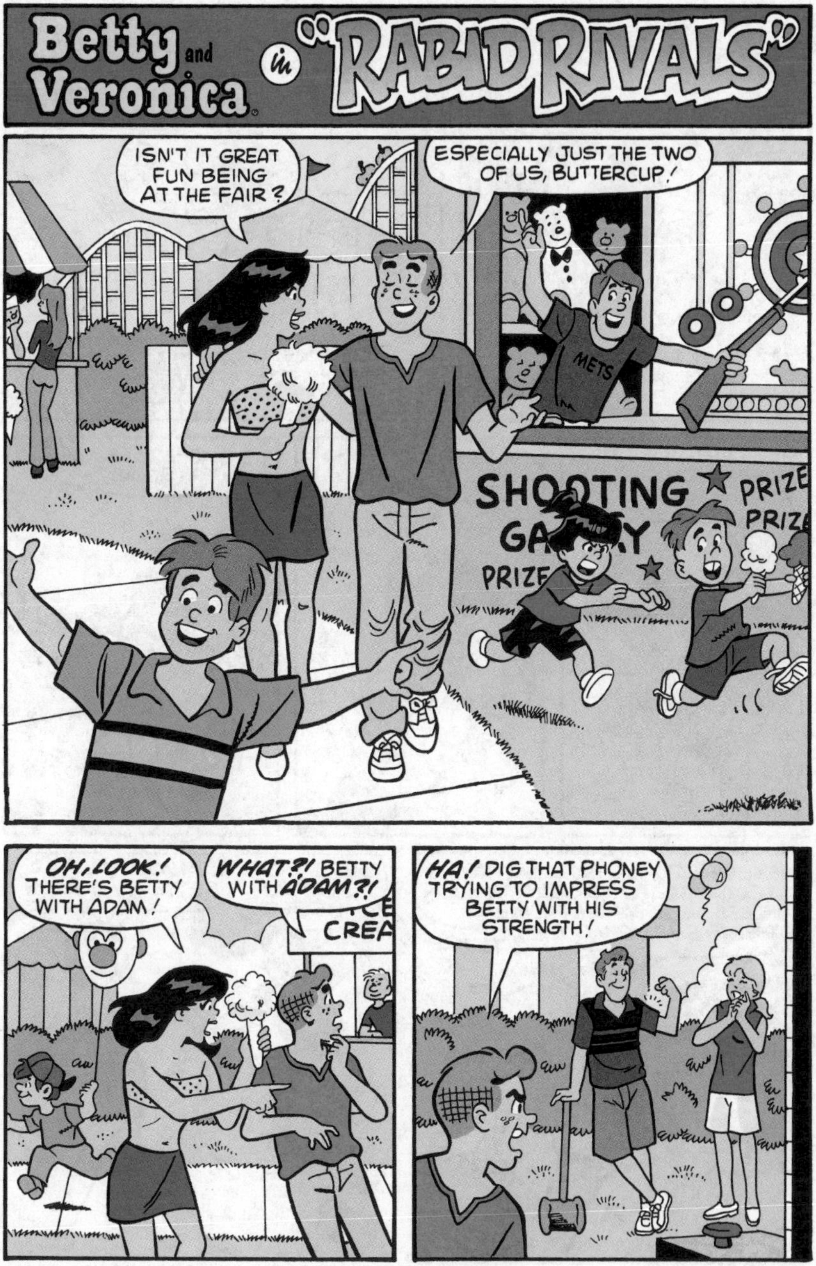
Betty and Veronica in "RABID RIVALS"
ISN'T IT GREAT FUN BEING AT THE FAIR?
ESPECIALLY JUST THE TWO OF US, BUTTERCUP!
METS
SHOOTING
PRIZE
PRIZE
PRIZE
OH, LOOK! THERE'S BETTY WITH ADAM!
WHAT?! BETTY WITH ADAM?!
ICE CREA
HA! DIG THAT PHONEY TRYING TO IMPRESS BETTY WITH HIS STRENGTH!

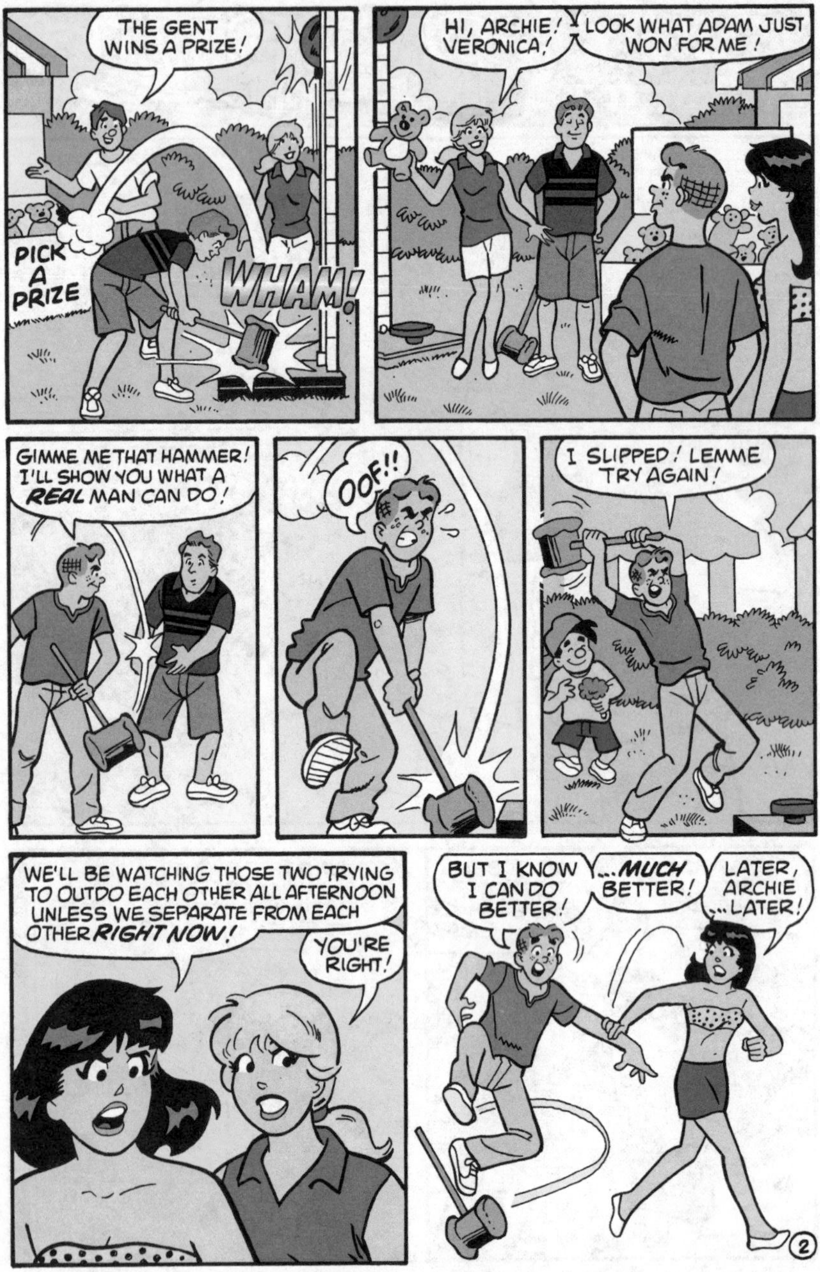
THE GENT WINS A PRIZE!
PICK A PRIZE
WHAM!
HI, ARCHIE! VERONICA!
LOOK WHAT ADAM JUST WON FOR ME!
GIMME ME THAT HAMMER! I'LL SHOW YOU WHAT A REAL MAN CAN DO!
OOF!!
I SLIPPED! LEMME TRY AGAIN!
WE'LL BE WATCHING THOSE TWO TRYING TO OUTDO EACH OTHER ALL AFTERNOON UNLESS WE SEPARATE FROM EACH OTHER RIGHT NOW!
YOU'RE RIGHT!
BUT I KNOW I CAN DO BETTER!
...MUCH BETTER!
LATER, ARCHIE ...LATER!
2

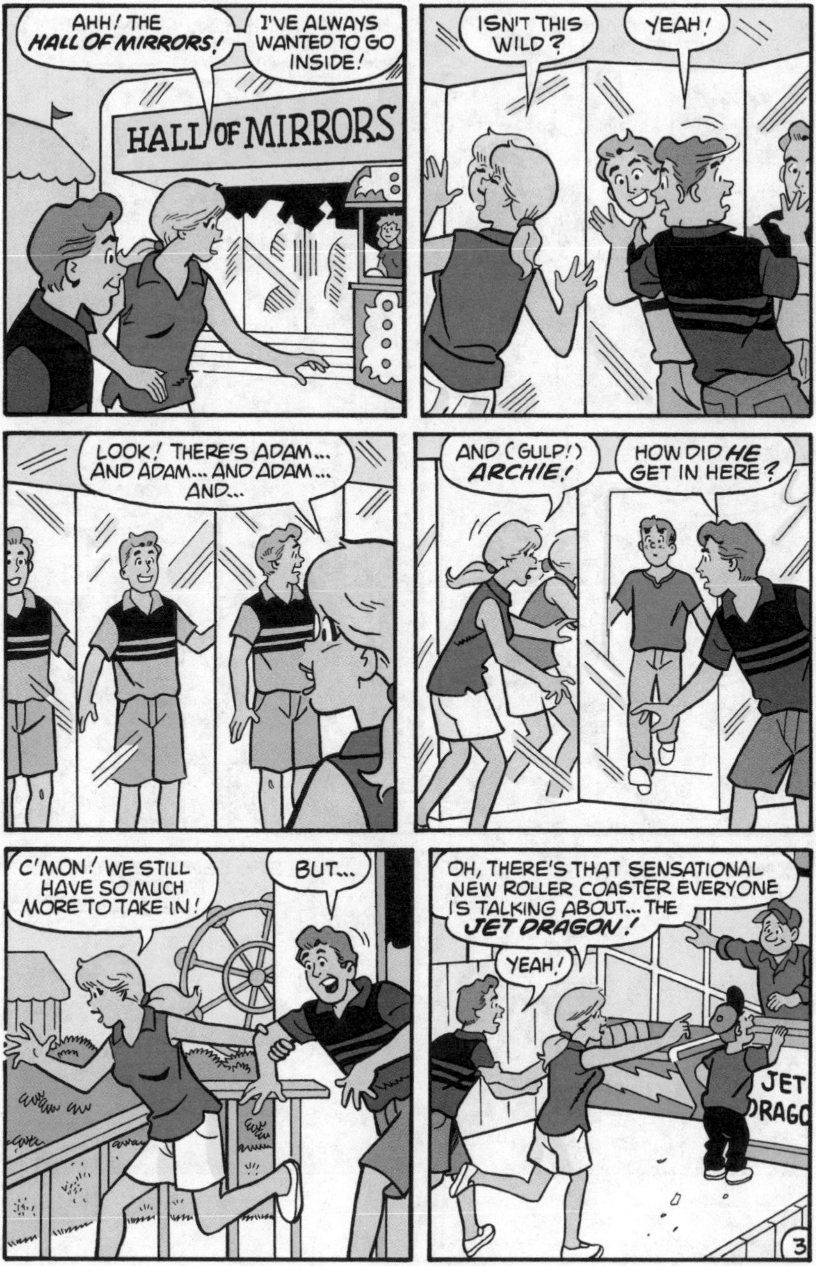
AHH! THE HALL OF MIRRORS!
I'VE ALWAYS WANTED TO GO INSIDE!
HALL OF MIRRORS
ISN'T THIS WILD?
YEAH!
LOOK! THERE'S ADAM... AND ADAM... AND ADAM... AND...
AND (GULP!) ARCHIE!
HOW DID HE GET IN HERE?
C'MON! WE STILL HAVE SO MUCH MORE TO TAKE IN!
BUT...
OH, THERE'S THAT SENSATIONAL NEW ROLLER COASTER EVERYONE IS TALKING ABOUT... THE JET DRAGON!
YEAH!
JET DRAGO

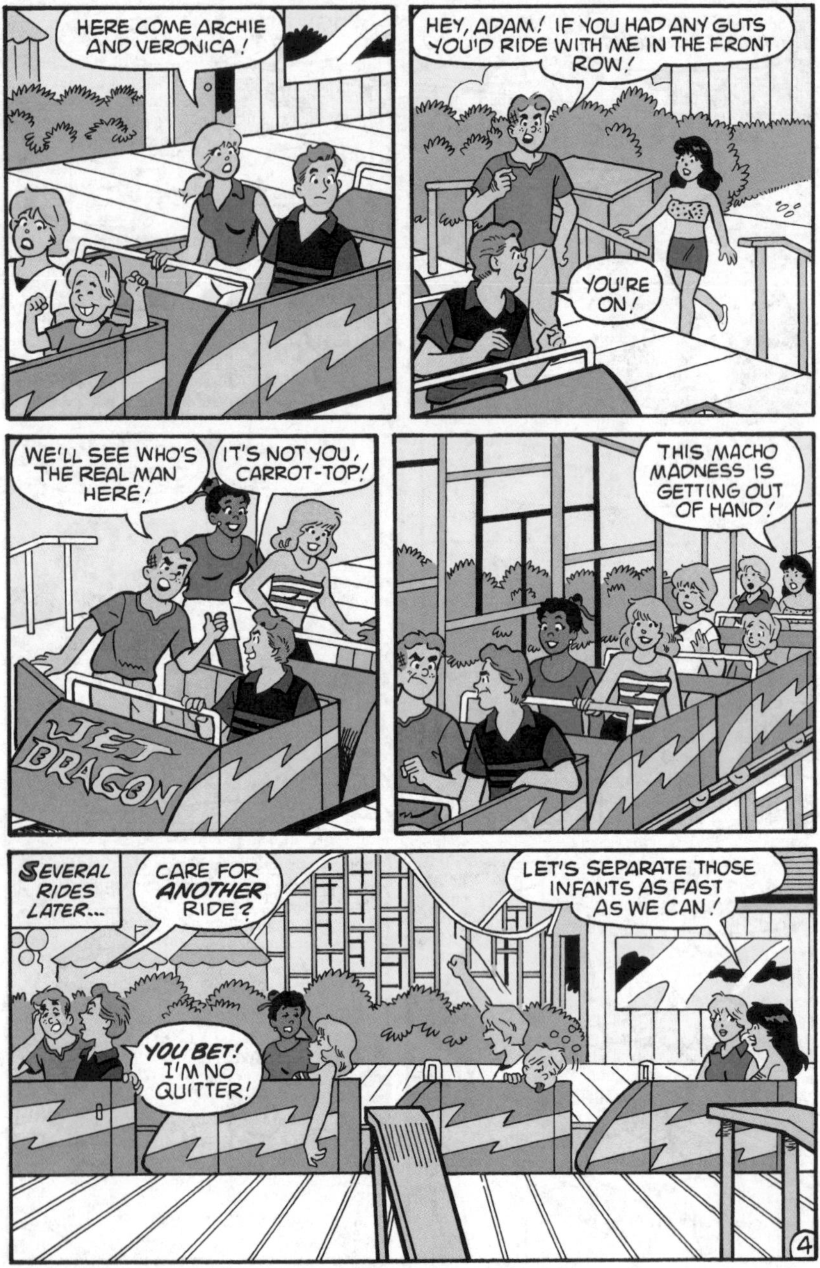
HERE COME ARCHIE AND VERONICA!
HEY, ADAM! IF YOU HAD ANY GUTS YOU'D RIDE WITH ME IN THE FRONT ROW!
YOU'RE ON!
WE'LL SEE WHO'S THE REAL MAN HERE!
IT'S NOT YOU, CARROT-TOP!
JET DRAGON
THIS MACHO MADNESS IS GETTING OUT OF HAND!
SEVERAL RIDES LATER...
CARE FOR ANOTHER RIDE?
YOU BET! I'M NO QUITTER!
LET'S SEPARATE THOSE INFANTS AS FAST AS WE CAN!
4

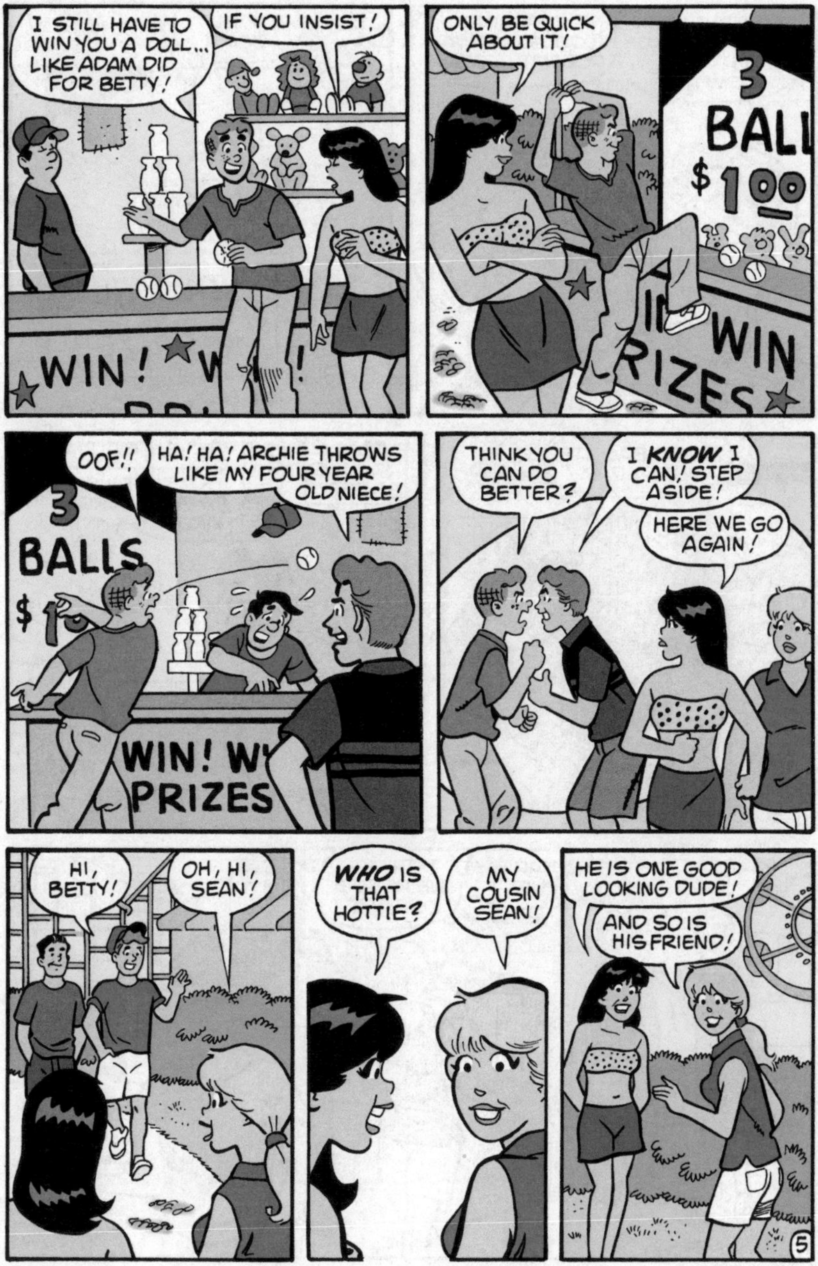

I STILL HAVE TO WIN YOU A DOLL... LIKE ADAM DID FOR BETTY!
IF YOU INSIST!
WIN!
ONLY BE QUICK ABOUT IT!
3 BALL
$1.00
WIN
RIZES
OOF!!
HA! HA! ARCHIE THROWS LIKE MY FOUR YEAR OLD NIECE!
3 BALLS
WIN! W
PRIZES
THINK YOU CAN DO BETTER?
I KNOW I CAN! STEP ASIDE!
HERE WE GO AGAIN!
HI, BETTY!
OH, HI, SEAN!
WHO IS THAT HOTTIE?
MY COUSIN SEAN!
HE IS ONE GOOD LOOKING DUDE!
AND SO IS HIS FRIEND!
5

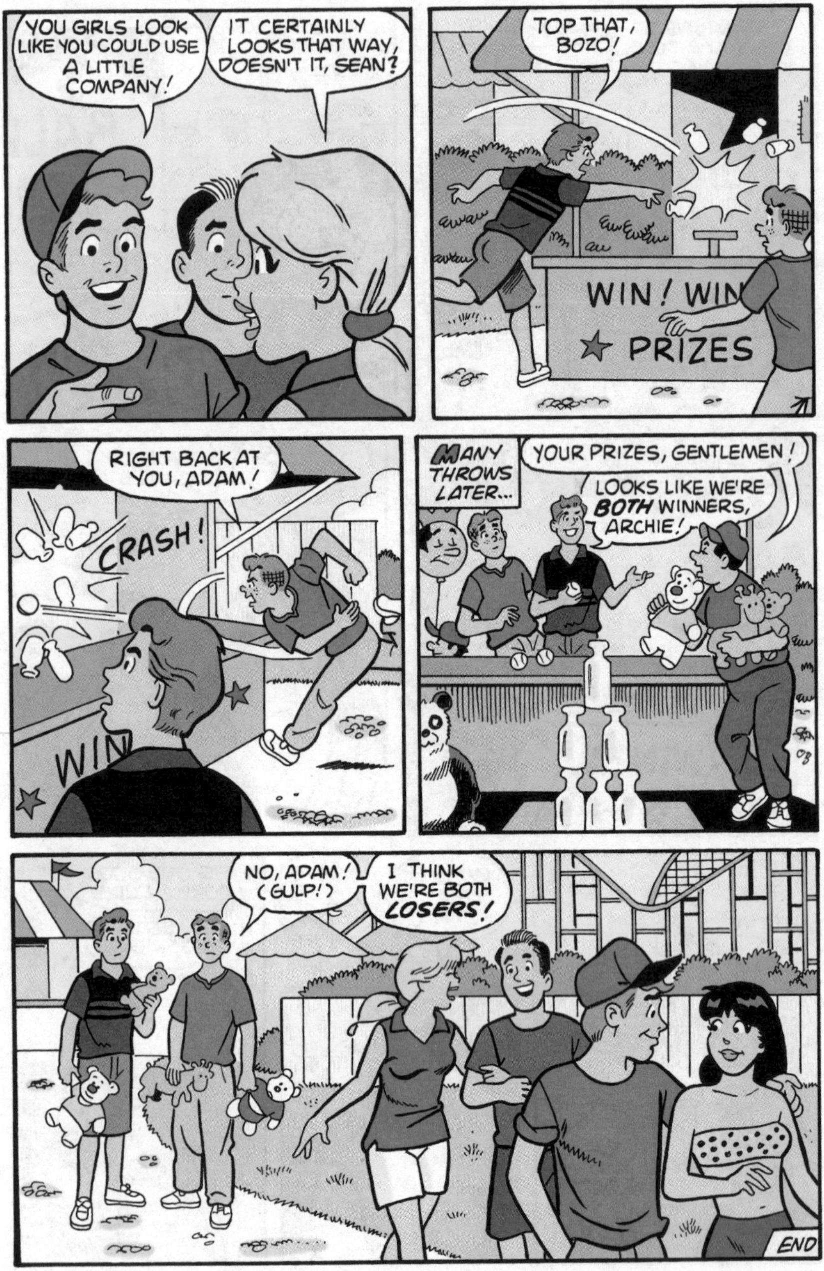
YOU GIRLS LOOK LIKE YOU COULD USE A LITTLE COMPANY!
IT CERTAINLY LOOKS THAT WAY, DOESN'T IT, SEAN?
TOP THAT, BOZO!
WIN! WIN
PRIZES
RIGHT BACK AT YOU, ADAM!
CRASH!
WIN
MANY THROWS LATER...
YOUR PRIZES, GENTLEMEN!
LOOKS LIKE WE'RE BOTH WINNERS, ARCHIE!
NO, ADAM! (GULP!)
I THINK WE'RE BOTH LOSERS!
END

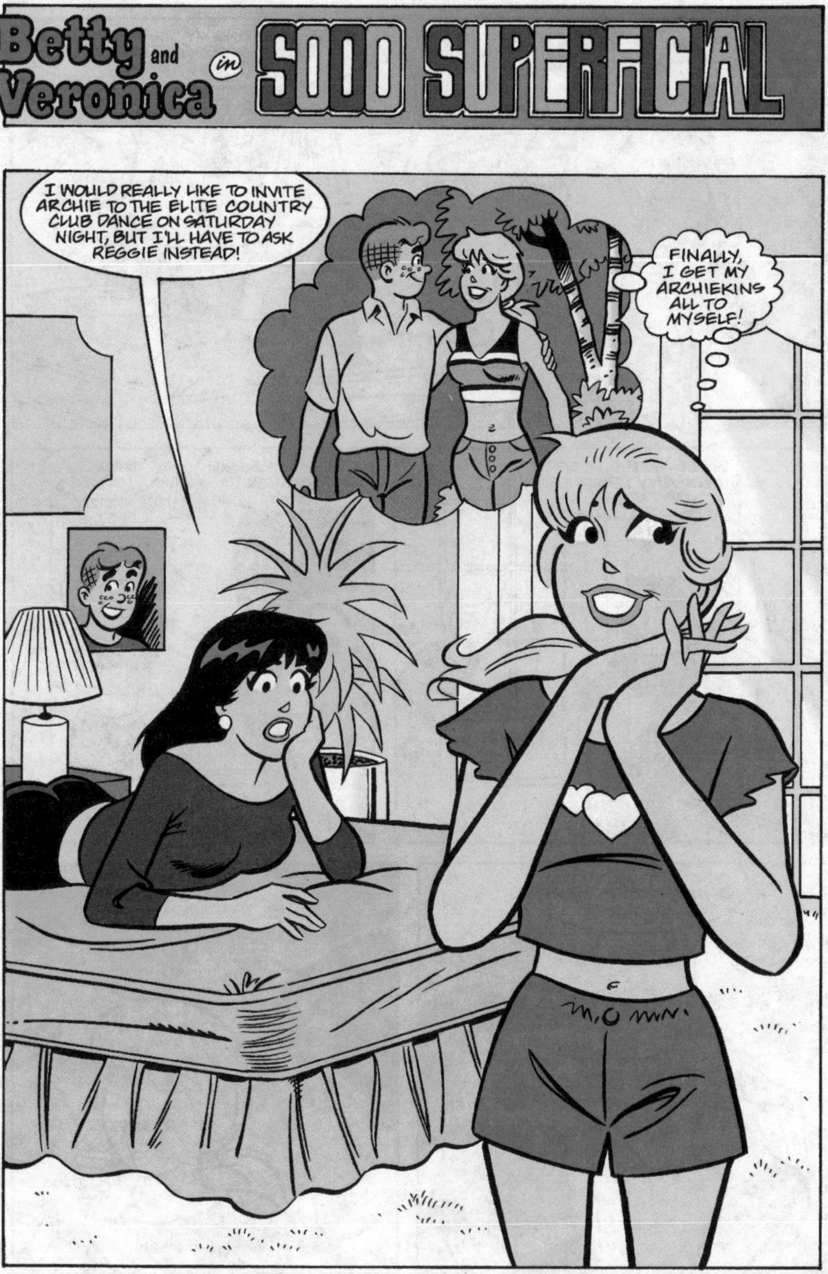
Betty and Veronica in SOOO SUPERFICIAL
I WOULD REALLY LIKE TO INVITE ARCHIE TO THE ELITE COUNTRY CLUB DANCE ON SATURDAY NIGHT, BUT I'LL HAVE TO ASK REGGIE INSTEAD!
FINALLY, I GET MY ARCHIEKINS ALL TO MYSELF!

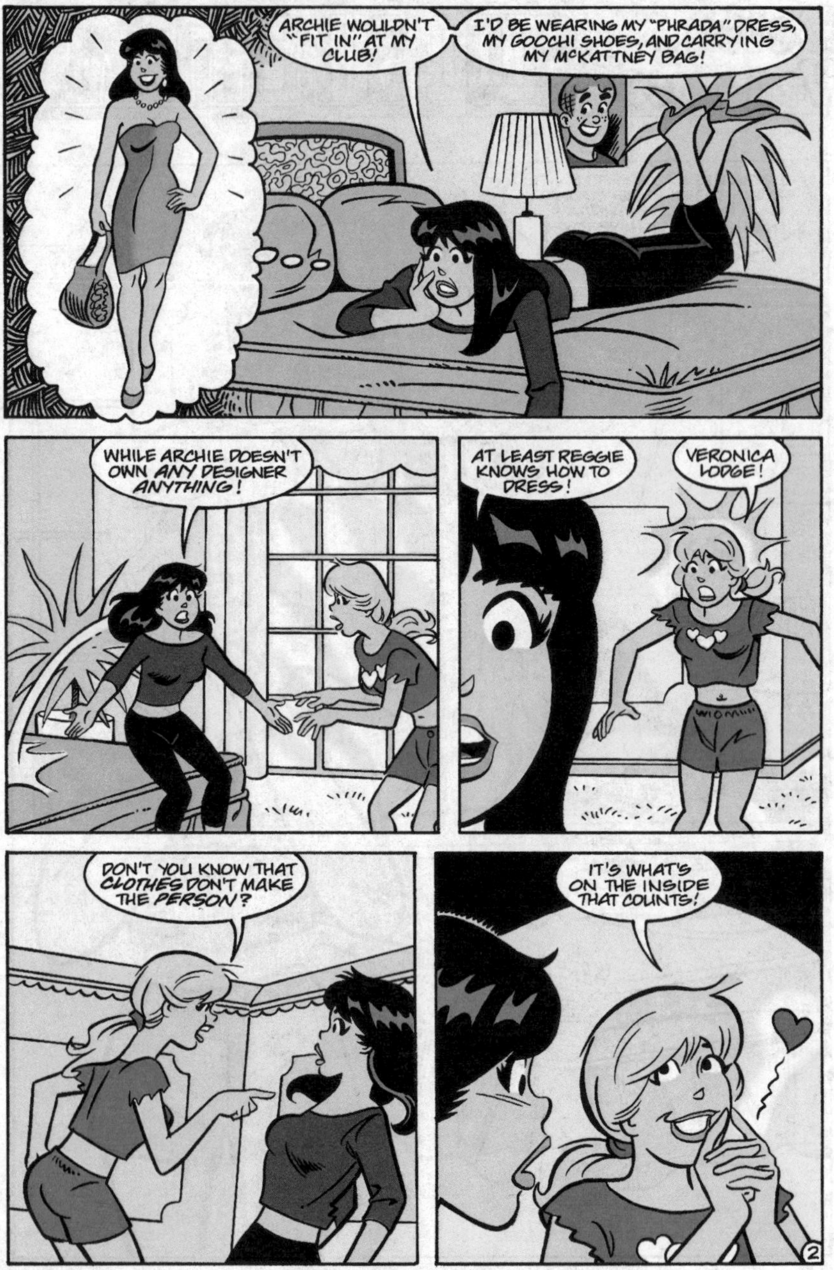
ARCHIE WOULDN'T "FIT IN" AT MY CLUB!
I'D BE WEARING MY "PHRADA" DRESS, MY GOOCHI SHOES, AND CARRYING MY McKATTNEY BAG!
WHILE ARCHIE DOESN'T OWN ANY DESIGNER ANYTHING!
AT LEAST REGGIE KNOWS HOW TO DRESS!
VERONICA LODGE!
DON'T YOU KNOW THAT CLOTHES DON'T MAKE THE PERSON?
IT'S WHAT'S ON THE INSIDE THAT COUNTS!
2

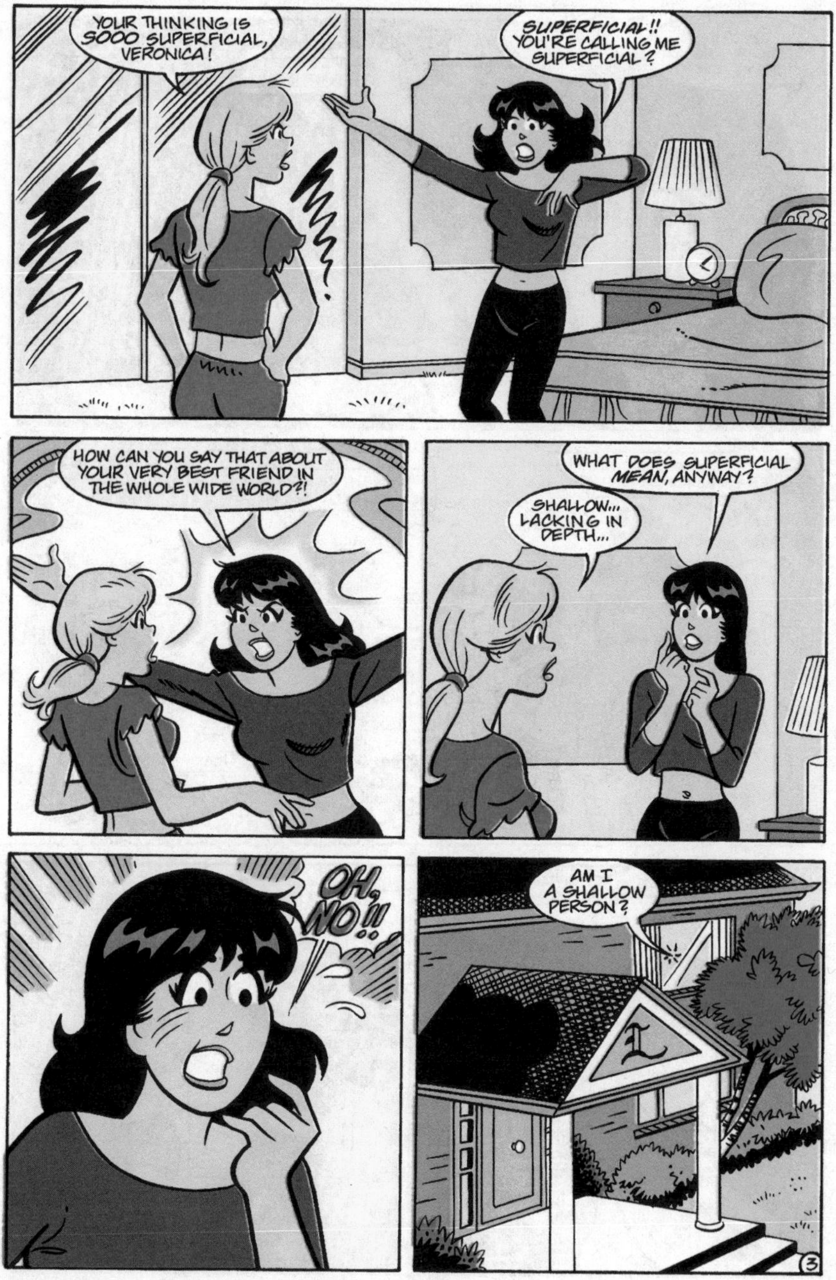
YOUR THINKING IS SOOO SUPERFICIAL, VERONICA!
SUPERFICIAL!! YOU'RE CALLING ME SUPERFICIAL?
HOW CAN YOU SAY THAT ABOUT YOUR VERY BEST FRIEND IN THE WHOLE WIDE WORLD?!
WHAT DOES SUPERFICIAL MEAN, ANYWAY?
SHALLOW... LACKING IN DEPTH...
OH, NO!!
AM I A SHALLOW PERSON?
3

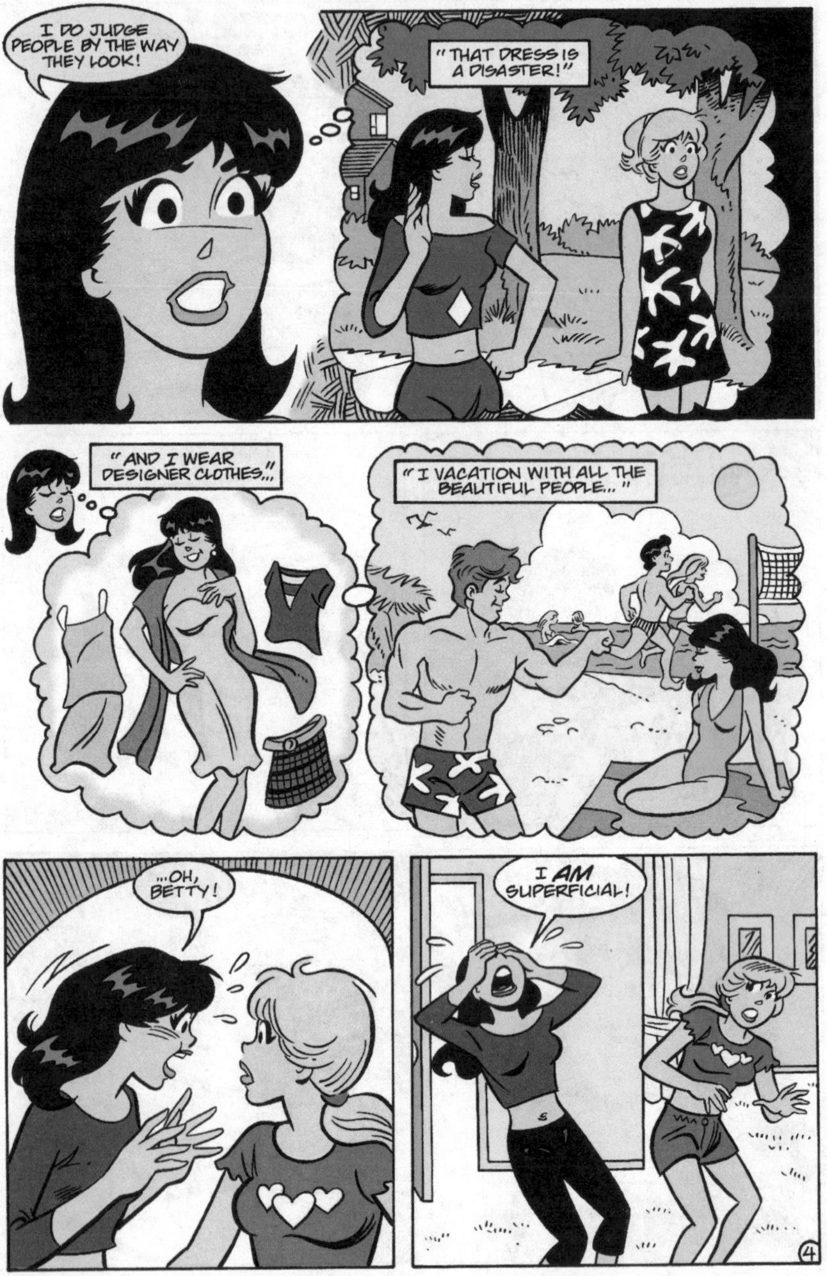
I DO JUDGE PEOPLE BY THE WAY THEY LOOK!
"THAT DRESS IS A DISASTER!"
"AND I WEAR DESIGNER CLOTHES..."
"I VACATION WITH ALL THE BEAUTIFUL PEOPLE..."
...OH, BETTY!
I AM SUPERFICIAL!

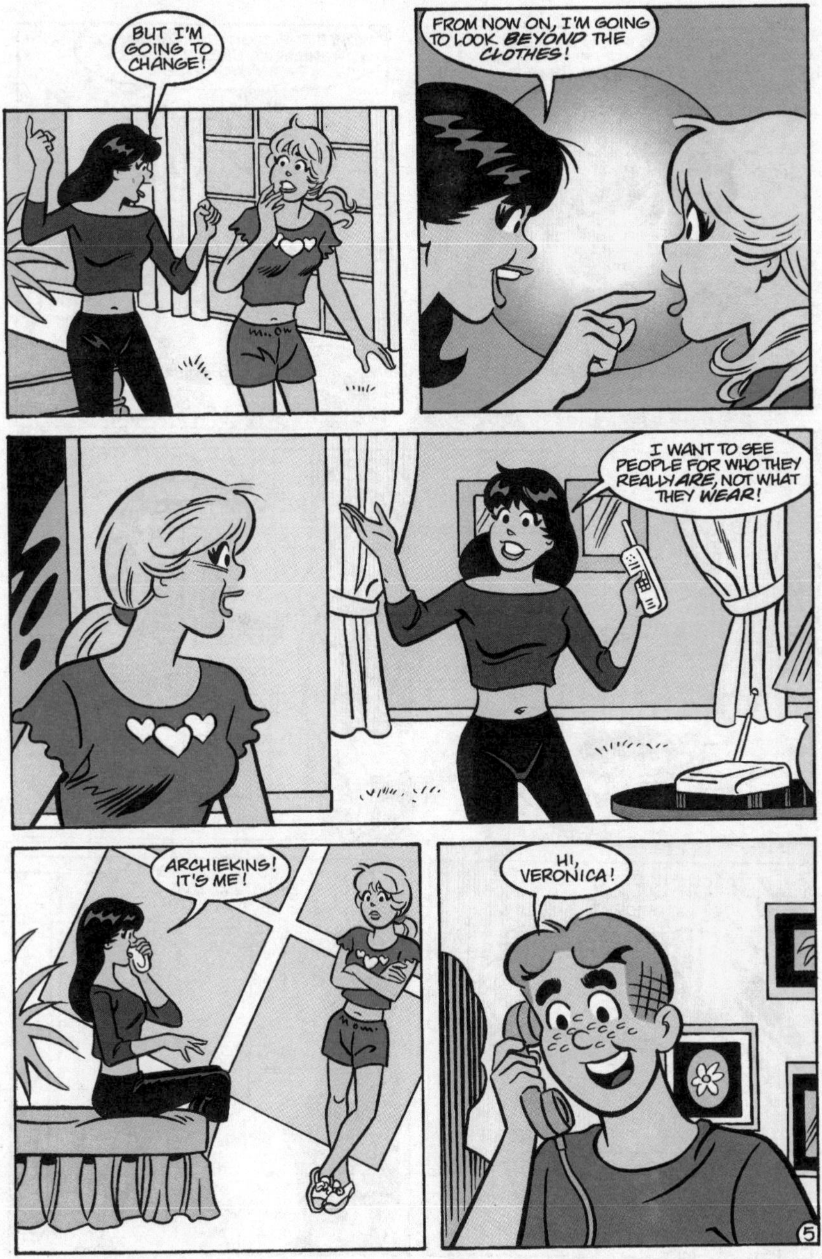
BUT I'M GOING TO CHANGE!
FROM NOW ON, I'M GOING TO LOOK BEYOND THE CLOTHES!
I WANT TO SEE PEOPLE FOR WHO THEY REALLY ARE, NOT WHAT THEY WEAR!
ARCHIEKINS! IT'S ME!
HI, VERONICA!
5

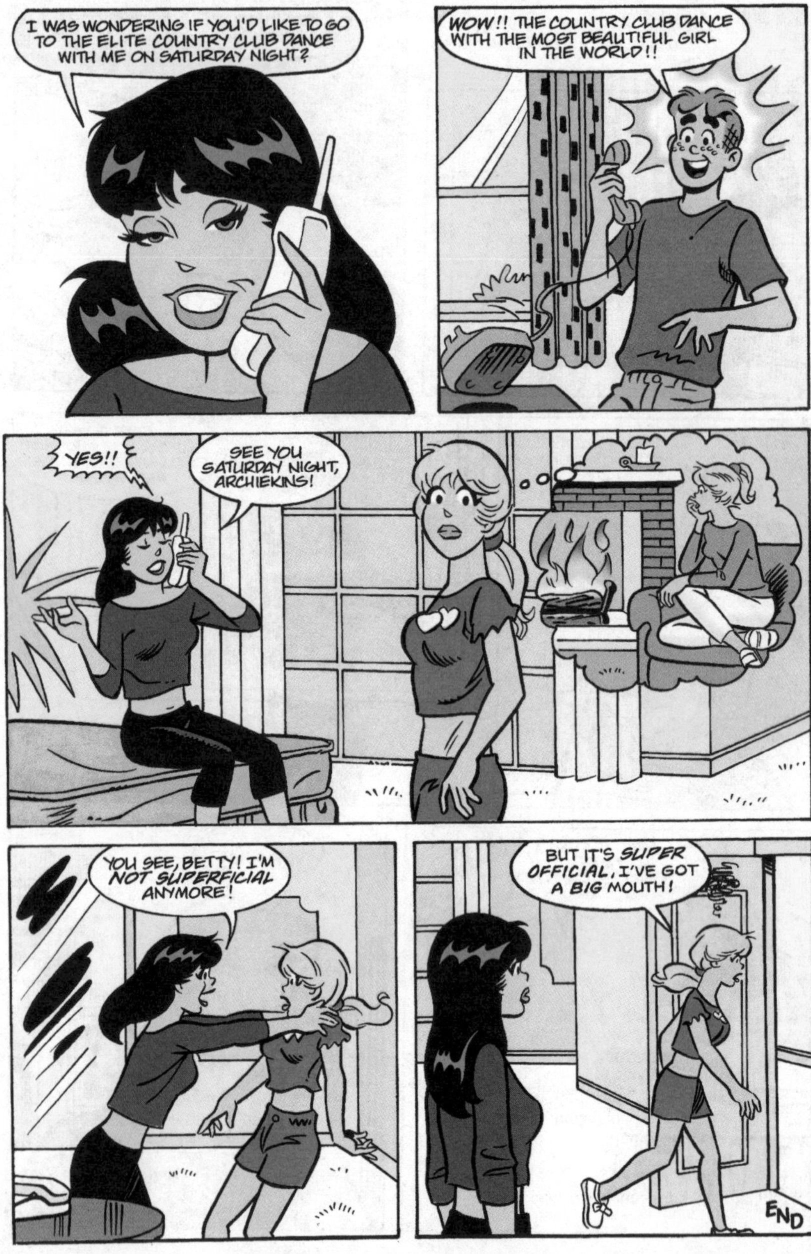
I WAS WONDERING IF YOU'D LIKE TO GO TO THE ELITE COUNTRY CLUB DANCE WITH ME ON SATURDAY NIGHT?
WOW!! THE COUNTRY CLUB DANCE WITH THE MOST BEAUTIFUL GIRL IN THE WORLD!!
YES!!
SEE YOU SATURDAY NIGHT, ARCHIEKINS!
YOU SEE, BETTY! I'M NOT SUPERFICIAL ANYMORE!
BUT IT'S SUPER OFFICIAL, I'VE GOT A BIG MOUTH!
END

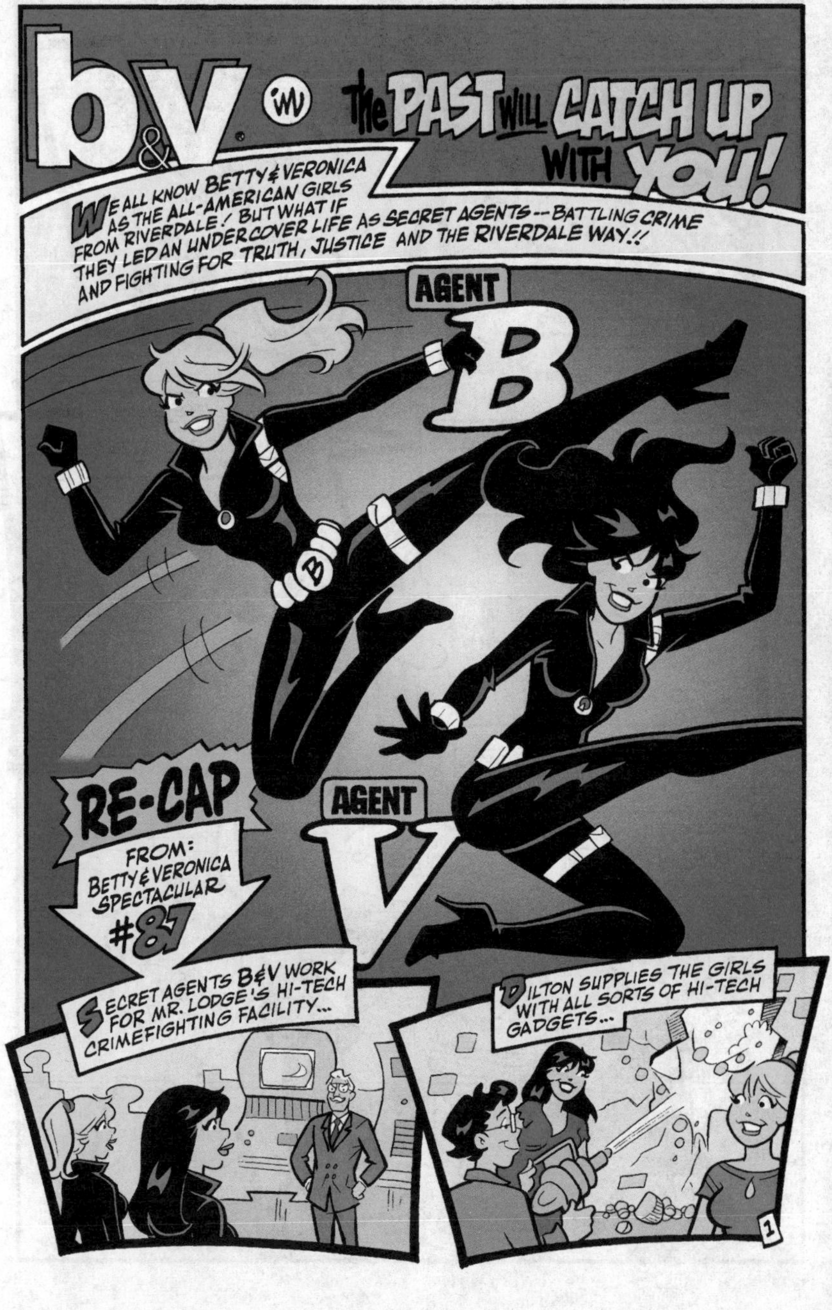
b&V
in
The PAST WILL CATCH UP WITH YOU!
WE ALL KNOW BETTY & VERONICA AS THE ALL-AMERICAN GIRLS FROM RIVERDALE! BUT WHAT IF THEY LED AN UNDERCOVER LIFE AS SECRET AGENTS -- BATTLING CRIME AND FIGHTING FOR TRUTH, JUSTICE AND THE RIVERDALE WAY!!
AGENT B
AGENT V
RE-CAP
FROM: BETTY & VERONICA SPECTACULAR #87
SECRET AGENTS B&V WORK FOR MR. LODGE'S HI-TECH CRIMEFIGHTING FACILITY...
DILTON SUPPLIES THE GIRLS WITH ALL SORTS OF HI-TECH GADGETS...
1

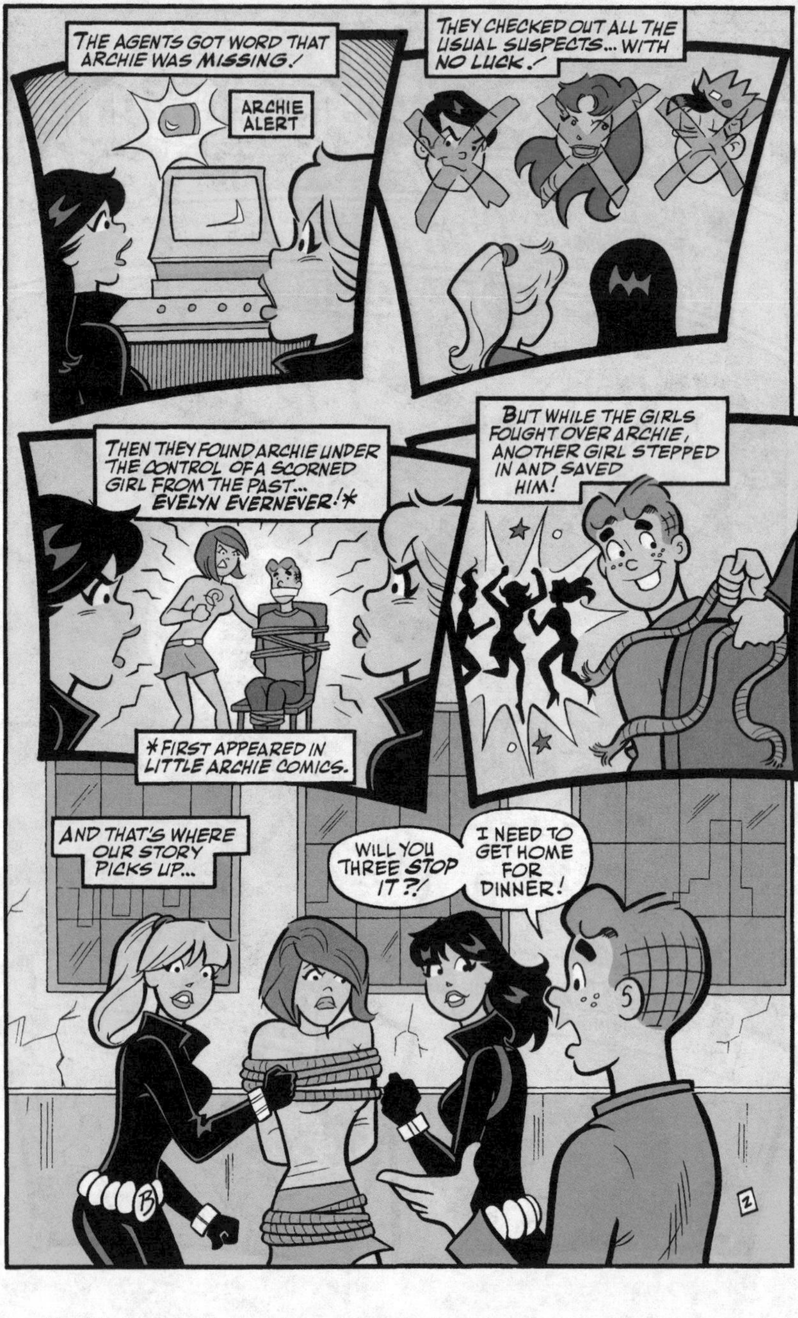
THE AGENTS GOT WORD THAT ARCHIE WAS MISSING!
ARCHIE ALERT
THEY CHECKED OUT ALL THE USUAL SUSPECTS... WITH NO LUCK!
THEN THEY FOUND ARCHIE UNDER THE CONTROL OF A SCORNED GIRL FROM THE PAST... EVELYN EVERNEVER!*
*FIRST APPEARED IN LITTLE ARCHIE COMICS.
BUT WHILE THE GIRLS FOUGHT OVER ARCHIE, ANOTHER GIRL STEPPED IN AND SAVED HIM!
AND THAT'S WHERE OUR STORY PICKS UP...
WILL YOU THREE STOP IT?!
I NEED TO GET HOME FOR DINNER!
B
2

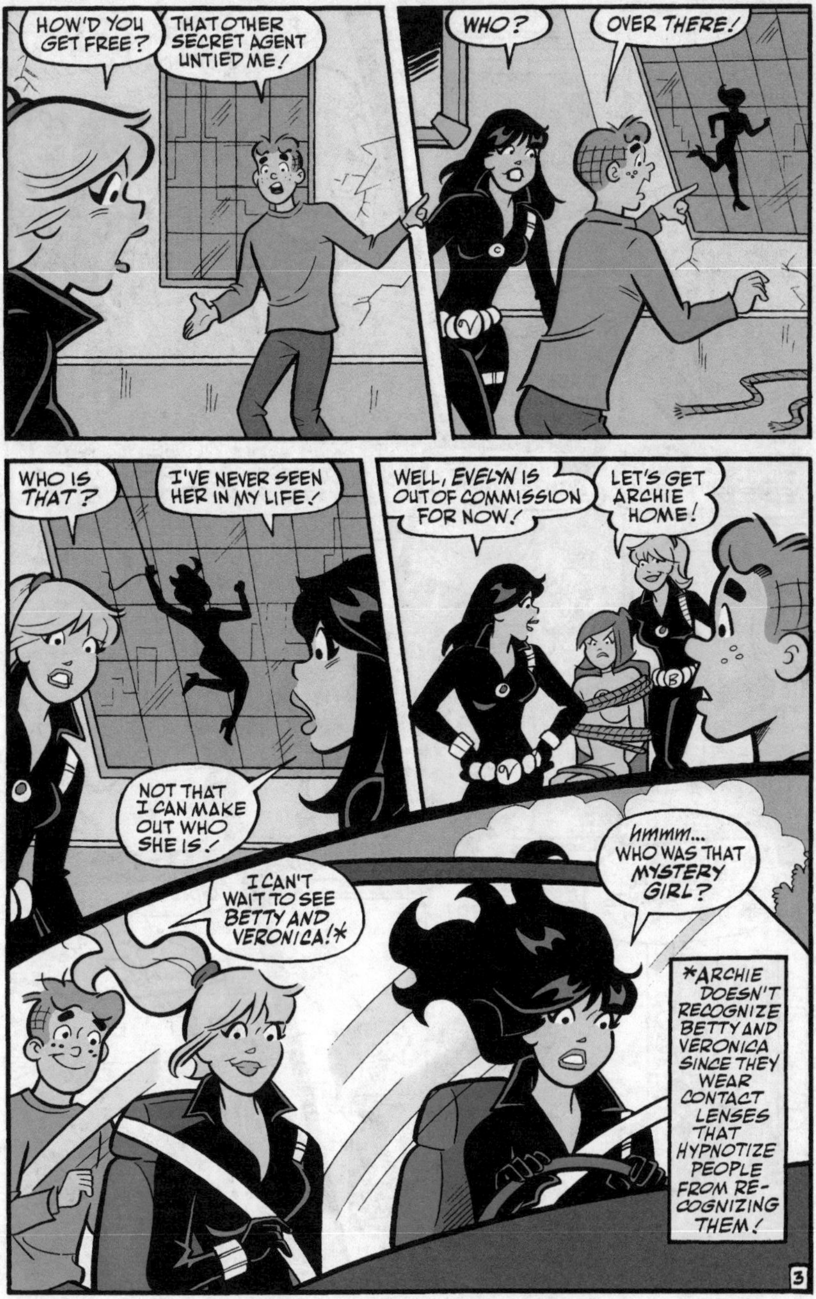

HOW'D YOU GET FREE?
THAT OTHER SECRET AGENT UNTIED ME!
WHO?
OVER THERE!
WHO IS THAT?
I'VE NEVER SEEN HER IN MY LIFE!
NOT THAT I CAN MAKE OUT WHO SHE IS!
WELL, EVELYN IS OUT OF COMMISSION FOR NOW!
LET'S GET ARCHIE HOME!
I CAN'T WAIT TO SEE BETTY AND VERONICA!*
hmmm... WHO WAS THAT MYSTERY GIRL?
*ARCHIE DOESN'T RECOGNIZE BETTY AND VERONICA SINCE THEY WEAR CONTACT LENSES THAT HYPNOTIZE PEOPLE FROM RE-COGNIZING THEM!
3

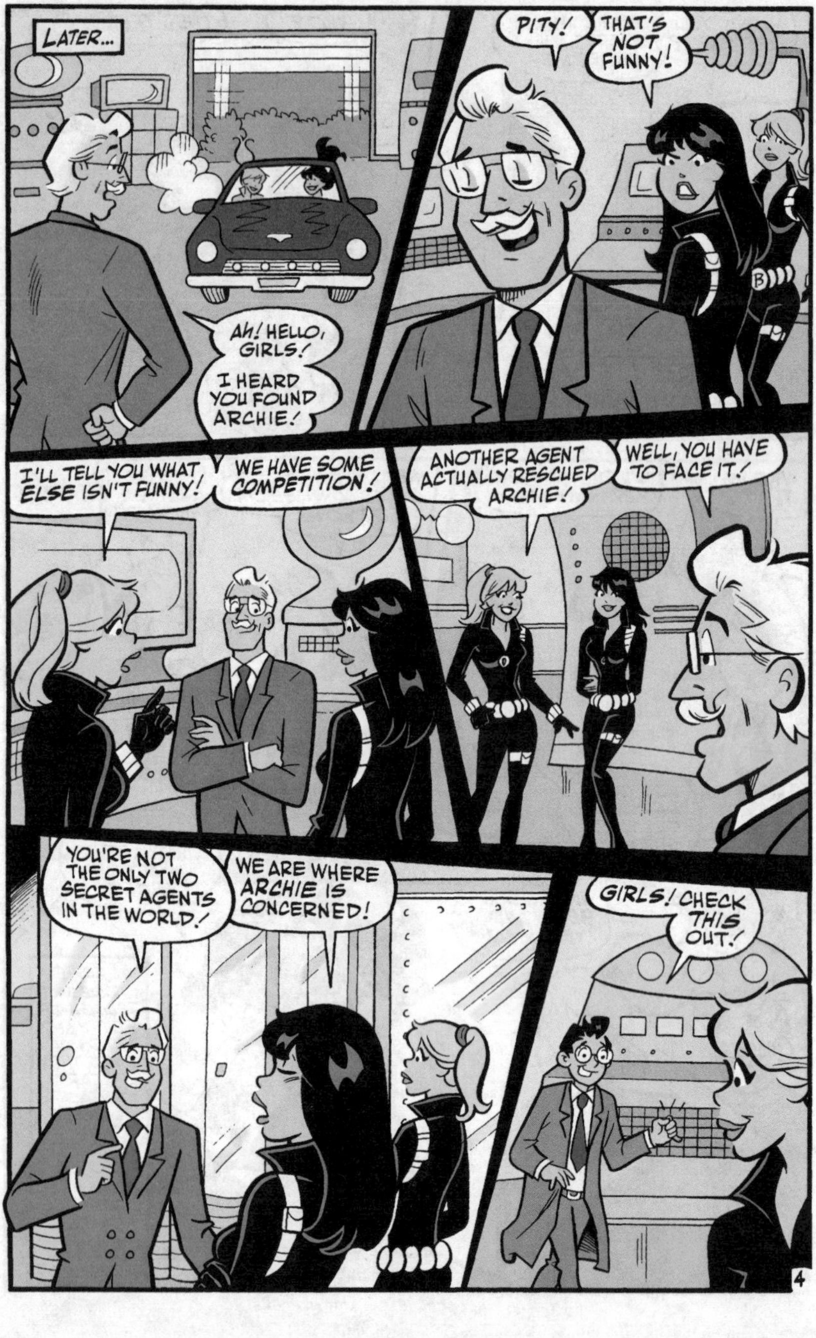
LATER...
Ah! HELLO, GIRLS!
I HEARD YOU FOUND ARCHIE!
PITY!
THAT'S NOT FUNNY!
B
I'LL TELL YOU WHAT ELSE ISN'T FUNNY!
WE HAVE SOME COMPETITION!
ANOTHER AGENT ACTUALLY RESCUED ARCHIE!
WELL, YOU HAVE TO FACE IT!
YOU'RE NOT THE ONLY TWO SECRET AGENTS IN THE WORLD!
WE ARE WHERE ARCHIE IS CONCERNED!
GIRLS! CHECK THIS OUT!
4

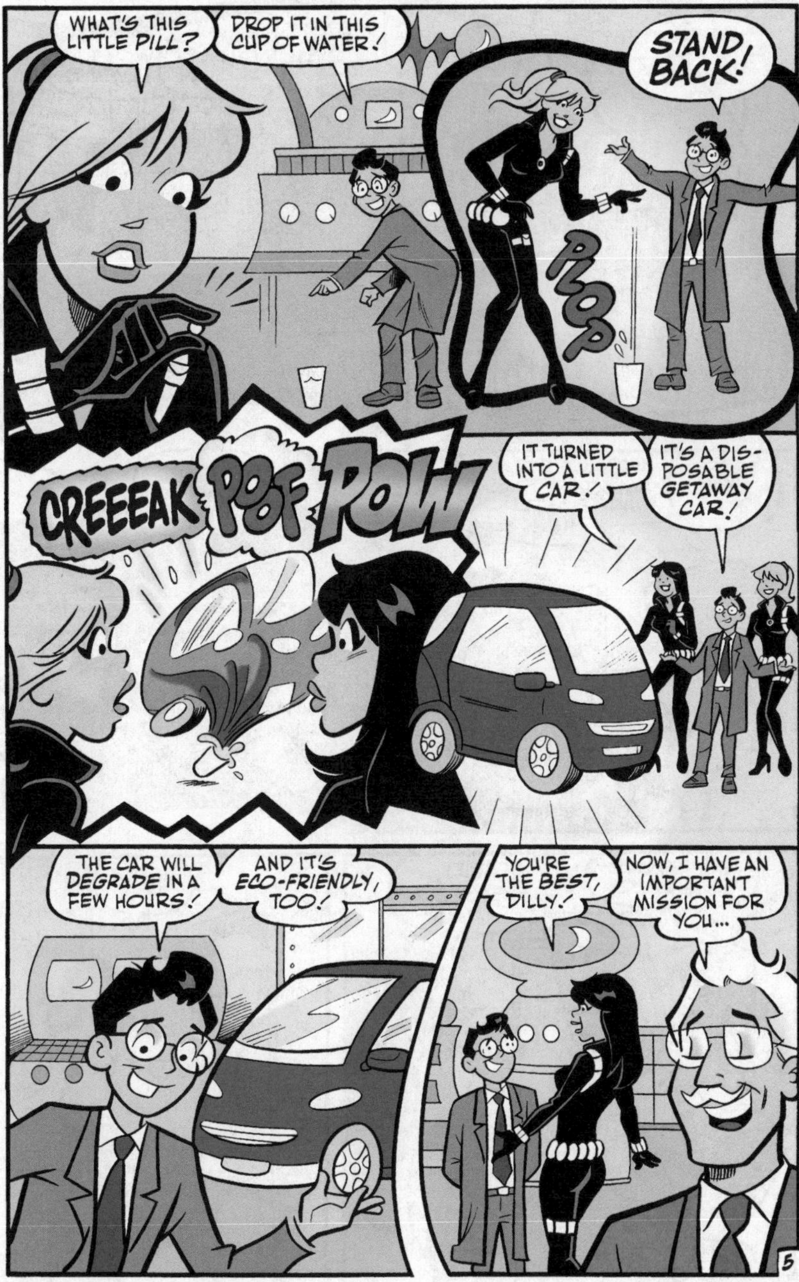
WHAT'S THIS LITTLE PILL?
DROP IT IN THIS CUP OF WATER!
STAND BACK!
PLOP
CREEEAK
POOF
POW
IT TURNED INTO A LITTLE CAR!
IT'S A DISPOSABLE GETAWAY CAR!
THE CAR WILL DEGRADE IN A FEW HOURS!
AND IT'S ECO-FRIENDLY, TOO!
YOU'RE THE BEST, DILLY!
NOW, I HAVE AN IMPORTANT MISSION FOR YOU...
5

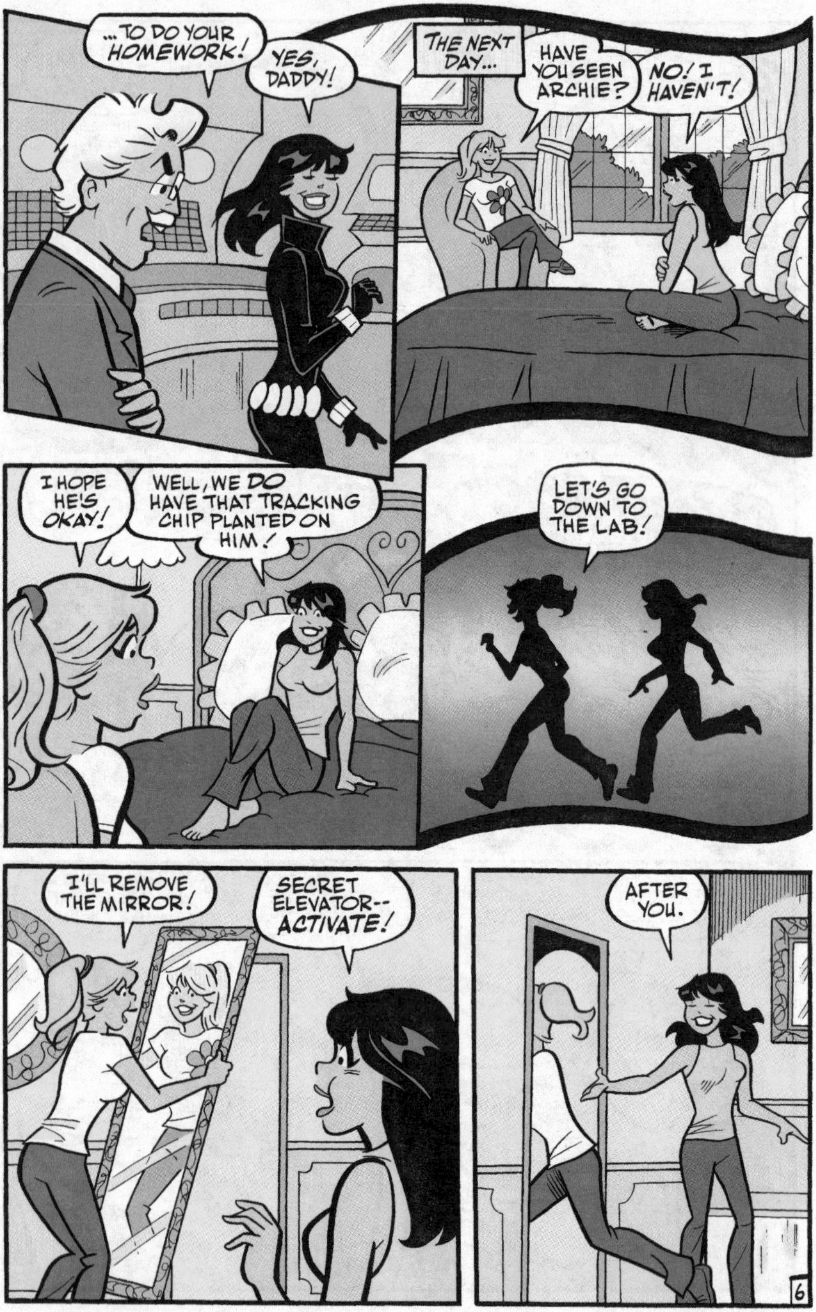
...TO DO YOUR HOMEWORK!
YES, DADDY!
THE NEXT DAY...
HAVE YOU SEEN ARCHIE?
NO! I HAVEN'T!
I HOPE HE'S OKAY!
WELL, WE DO HAVE THAT TRACKING CHIP PLANTED ON HIM!
LET'S GO DOWN TO THE LAB!
I'LL REMOVE THE MIRROR!
SECRET ELEVATOR-- ACTIVATE!
AFTER YOU.
6

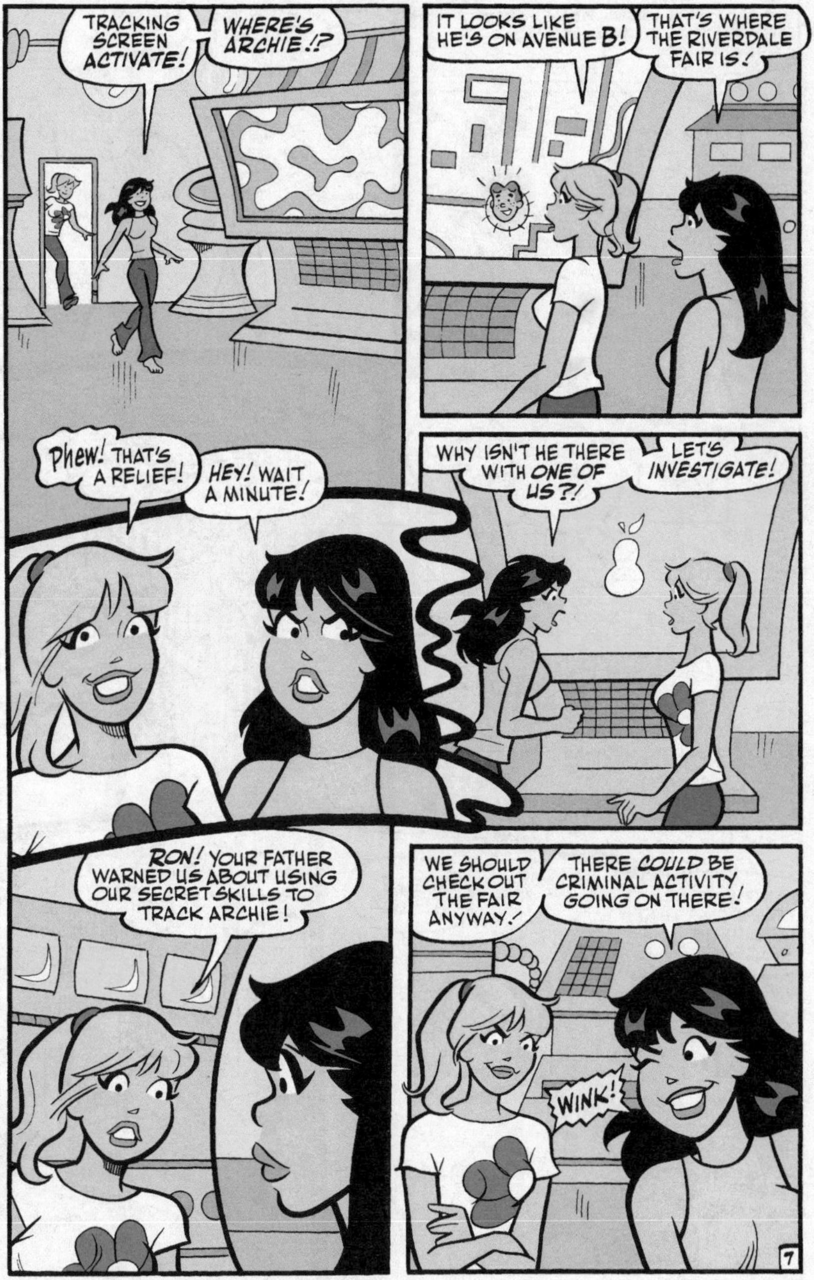
TRACKING SCREEN ACTIVATE!
WHERE'S ARCHIE!?
IT LOOKS LIKE HE'S ON AVENUE B!
THAT'S WHERE THE RIVERDALE FAIR IS!
Phew! THAT'S A RELIEF!
HEY! WAIT A MINUTE!
WHY ISN'T HE THERE WITH ONE OF US?!
LET'S INVESTIGATE!
RON! YOUR FATHER WARNED US ABOUT USING OUR SECRET SKILLS TO TRACK ARCHIE!
WE SHOULD CHECK OUT THE FAIR ANYWAY!
THERE COULD BE CRIMINAL ACTIVITY GOING ON THERE!
WINK!
7

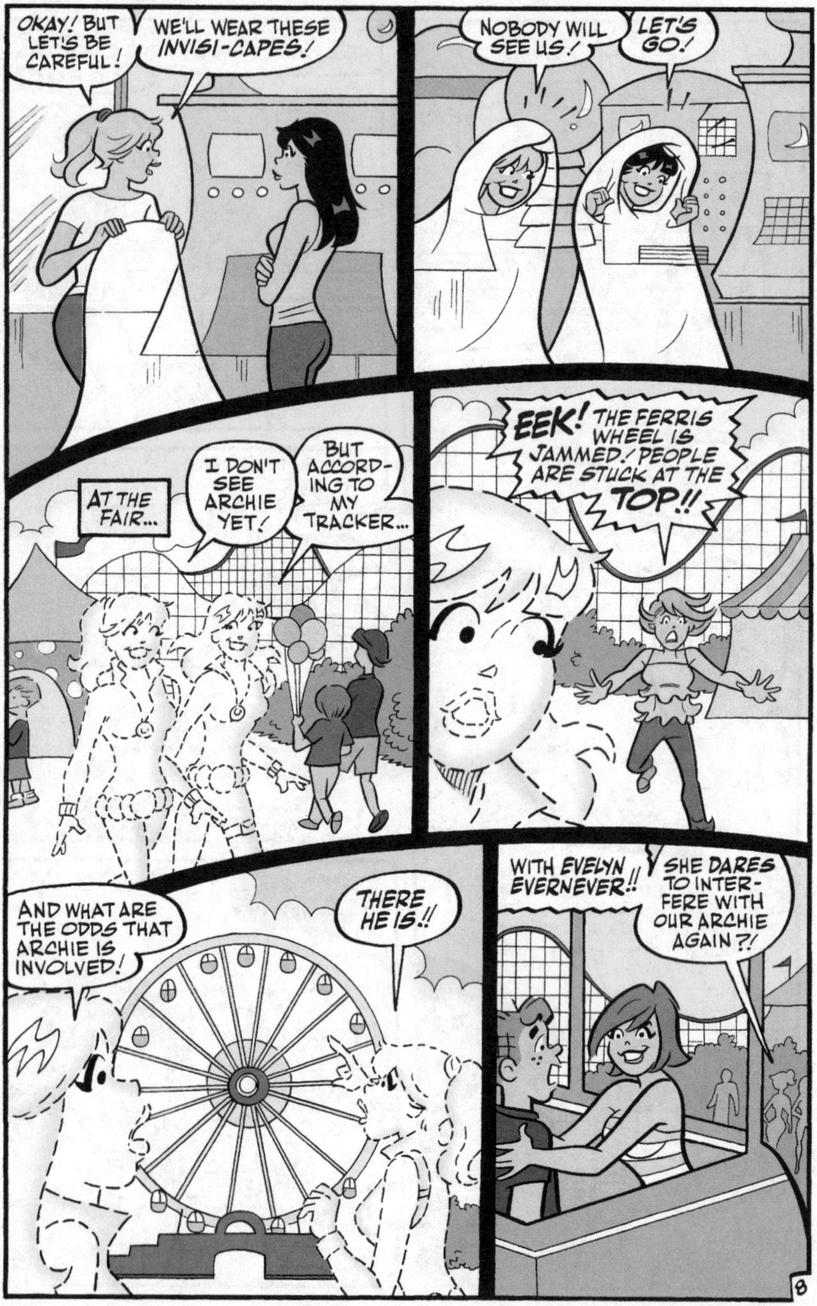
OKAY! BUT LET'S BE CAREFUL!
WE'LL WEAR THESE INVISI-CAPES!
NOBODY WILL SEE US!
LET'S GO!
AT THE FAIR...
I DON'T SEE ARCHIE YET!
BUT ACCORDING TO MY TRACKER...
EEK! THE FERRIS WHEEL IS JAMMED! PEOPLE ARE STUCK AT THE TOP!!
AND WHAT ARE THE ODDS THAT ARCHIE IS INVOLVED!
THERE HE IS!!
WITH EVELYN EVERNEVER!!
SHE DARES TO INTERFERE WITH OUR ARCHIE AGAIN?!

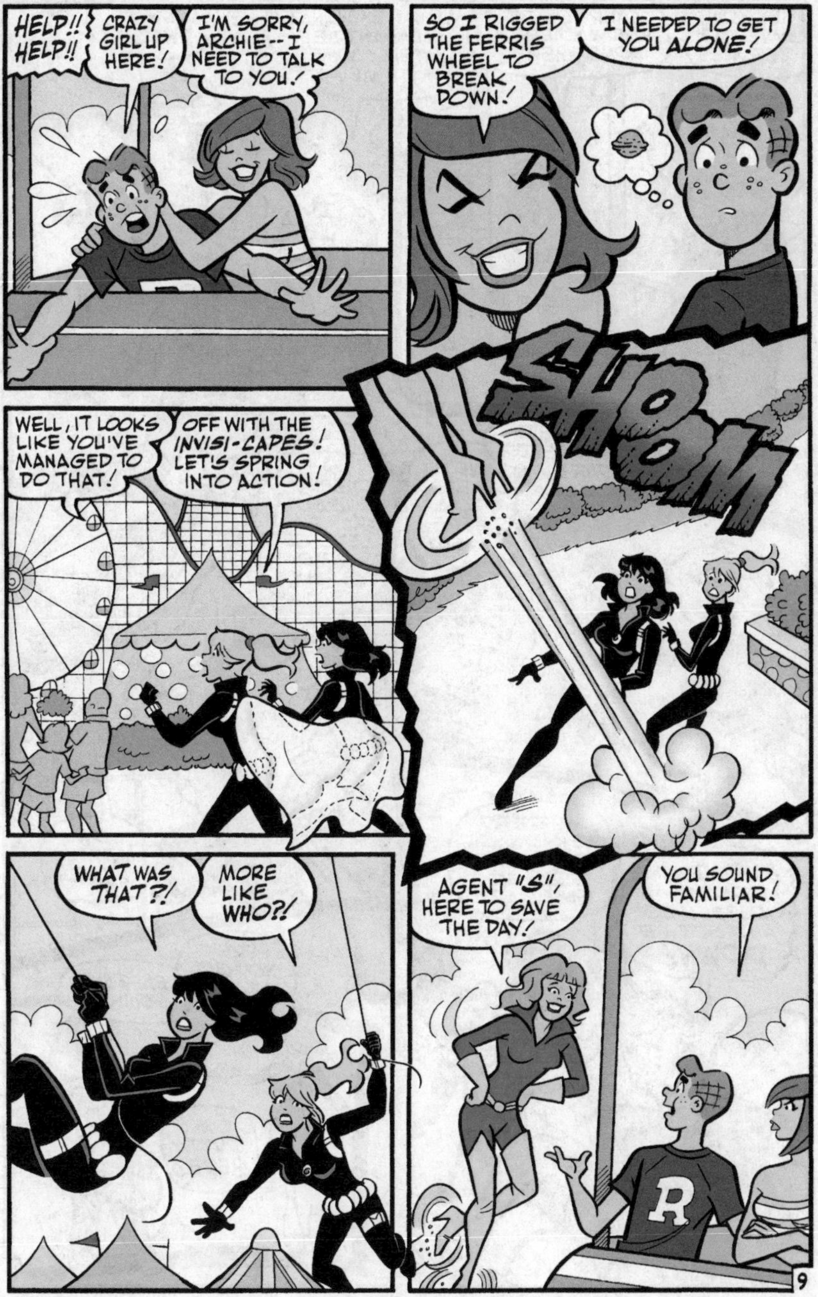
HELP!! HELP!!
CRAZY GIRL UP HERE!
I'M SORRY, ARCHIE-- I NEED TO TALK TO YOU!
SO I RIGGED THE FERRIS WHEEL TO BREAK DOWN!
I NEEDED TO GET YOU ALONE!
WELL, IT LOOKS LIKE YOU'VE MANAGED TO DO THAT!
OFF WITH THE INVISI-CAPES! LET'S SPRING INTO ACTION!
SHOOM
WHAT WAS THAT?!
MORE LIKE WHO?!
AGENT "S", HERE TO SAVE THE DAY!
YOU SOUND FAMILIAR!

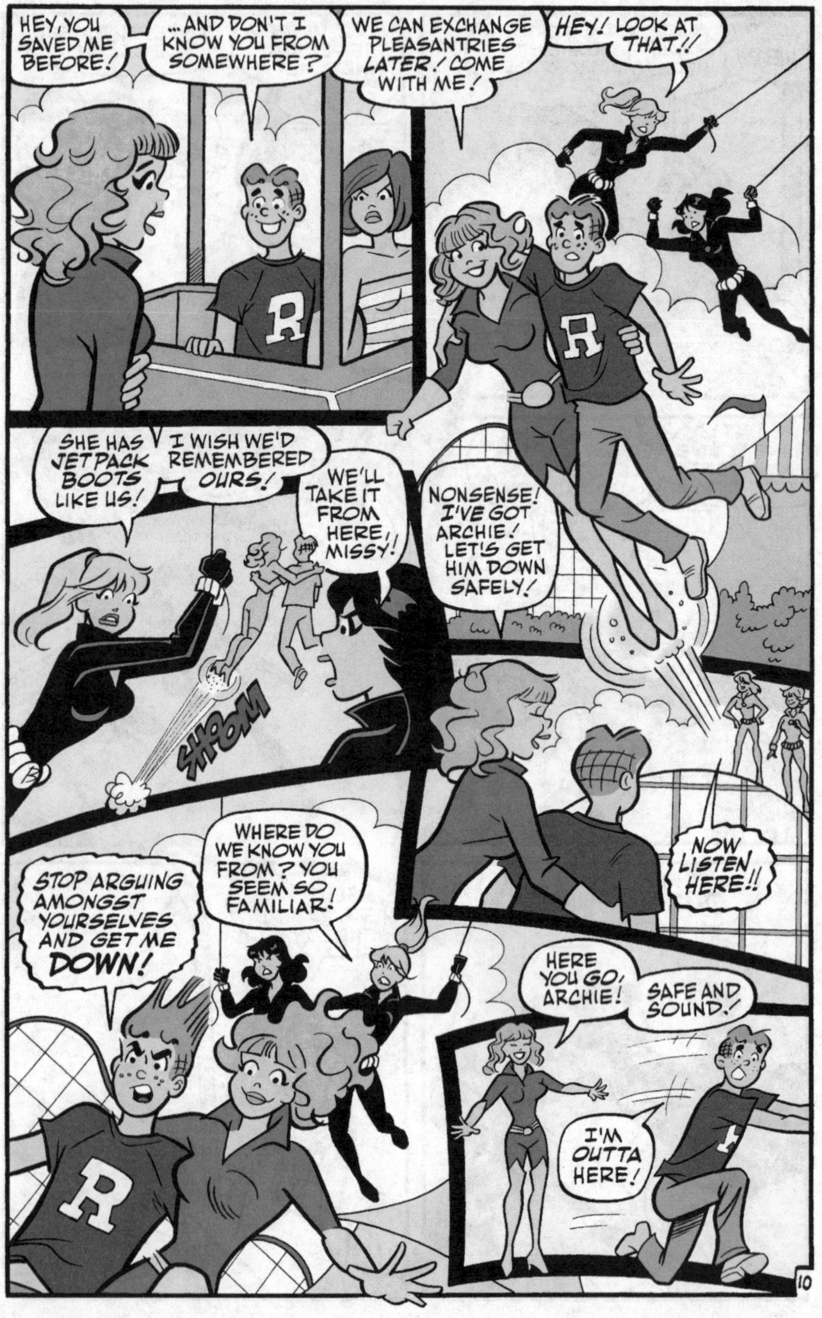
HEY, YOU SAVED ME BEFORE!
...AND DON'T I KNOW YOU FROM SOMEWHERE?
WE CAN EXCHANGE PLEASANTRIES LATER! COME WITH ME!
HEY! LOOK AT THAT!!
SHE HAS JETPACK BOOTS LIKE US!
I WISH WE'D REMEMBERED OURS!
WE'LL TAKE IT FROM HERE, MISSY!
SHOOM
NONSENSE! I'VE GOT ARCHIE! LET'S GET HIM DOWN SAFELY!
NOW LISTEN HERE!!
STOP ARGUING AMONGST YOURSELVES AND GET ME DOWN!
WHERE DO WE KNOW YOU FROM? YOU SEEM SO FAMILIAR!
HERE YOU GO, ARCHIE!
SAFE AND SOUND!
I'M OUTTA HERE!

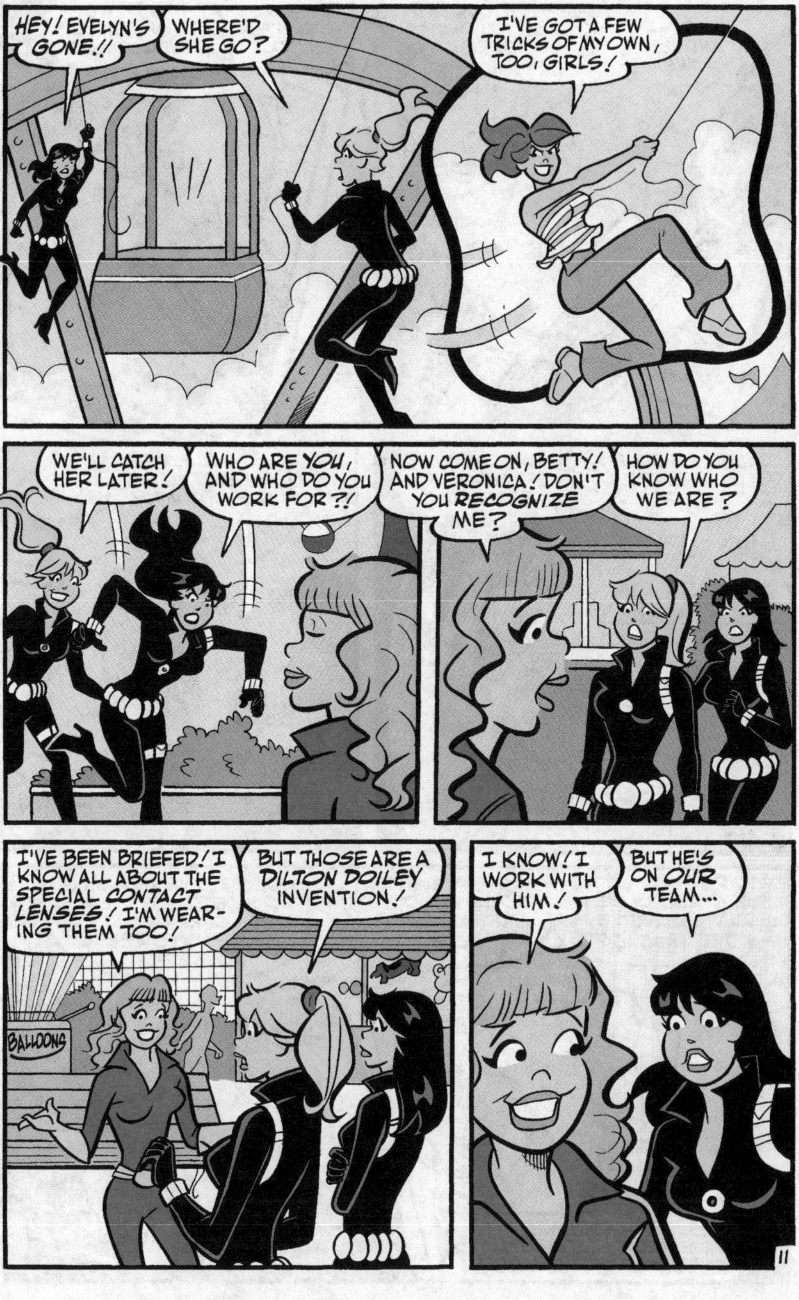
HEY! EVELYN'S GONE!!
WHERE'D SHE GO?
I'VE GOT A FEW TRICKS OF MY OWN, TOO, GIRLS!
WE'LL CATCH HER LATER!
WHO ARE YOU, AND WHO DO YOU WORK FOR?!
NOW COME ON, BETTY! AND VERONICA! DON'T YOU RECOGNIZE ME?
HOW DO YOU KNOW WHO WE ARE?
I'VE BEEN BRIEFED! I KNOW ALL ABOUT THE SPECIAL CONTACT LENSES! I'M WEARING THEM TOO!
BUT THOSE ARE A DILTON DOILEY INVENTION!
BALLOONS
I KNOW! I WORK WITH HIM!
BUT HE'S ON OUR TEAM...

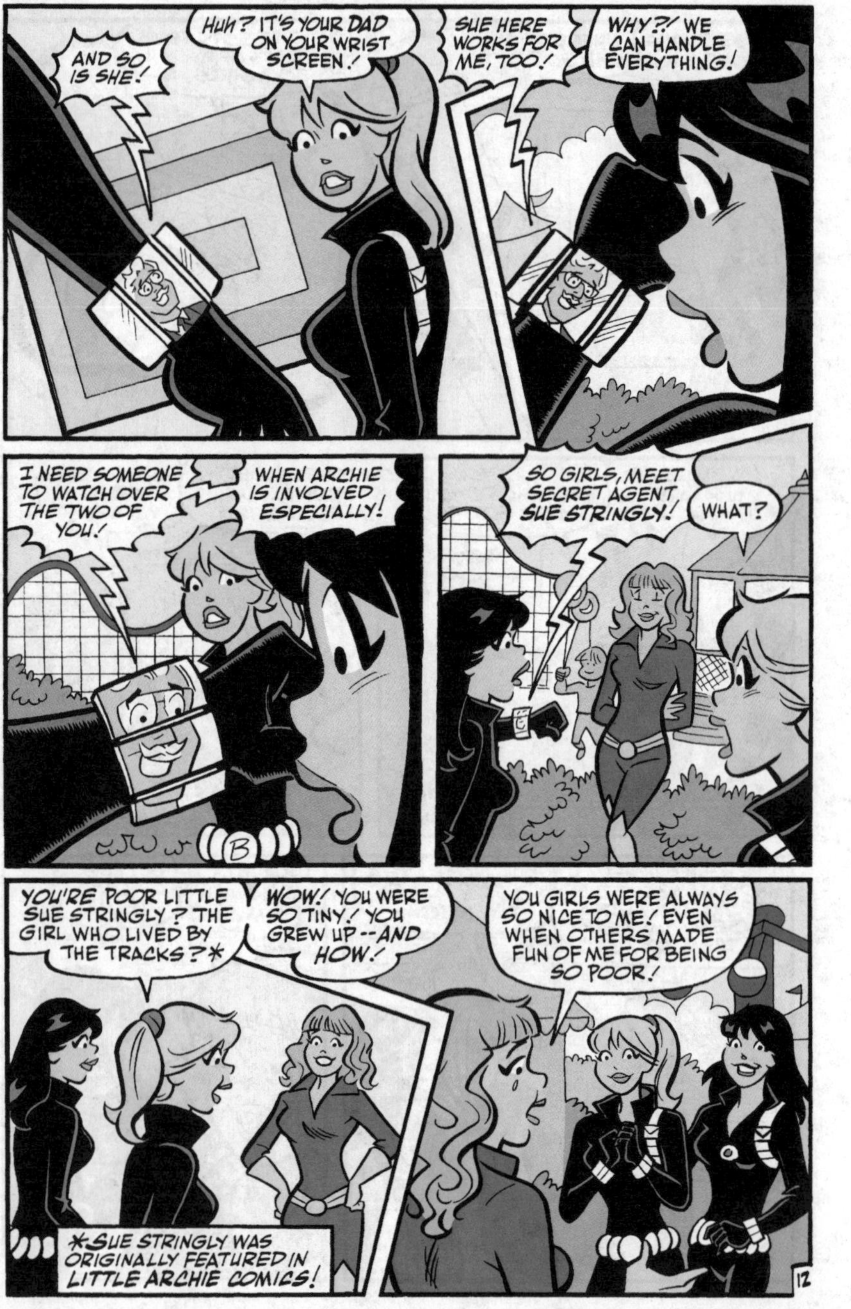
AND SO IS SHE!
HUH? IT'S YOUR DAD ON YOUR WRIST SCREEN!
SUE HERE WORKS FOR ME, TOO!
WHY?!! WE CAN HANDLE EVERYTHING!
I NEED SOMEONE TO WATCH OVER THE TWO OF YOU!
WHEN ARCHIE IS INVOLVED ESPECIALLY!
SO GIRLS, MEET SECRET AGENT SUE STRINGLY!
WHAT?
YOU'RE POOR LITTLE SUE STRINGLY? THE GIRL WHO LIVED BY THE TRACKS?*
WOW! YOU WERE SO TINY! YOU GREW UP -- AND HOW!
YOU GIRLS WERE ALWAYS SO NICE TO ME! EVEN WHEN OTHERS MADE FUN OF ME FOR BEING SO POOR!
*SUE STRINGLY WAS ORIGINALLY FEATURED IN LITTLE ARCHIE COMICS!

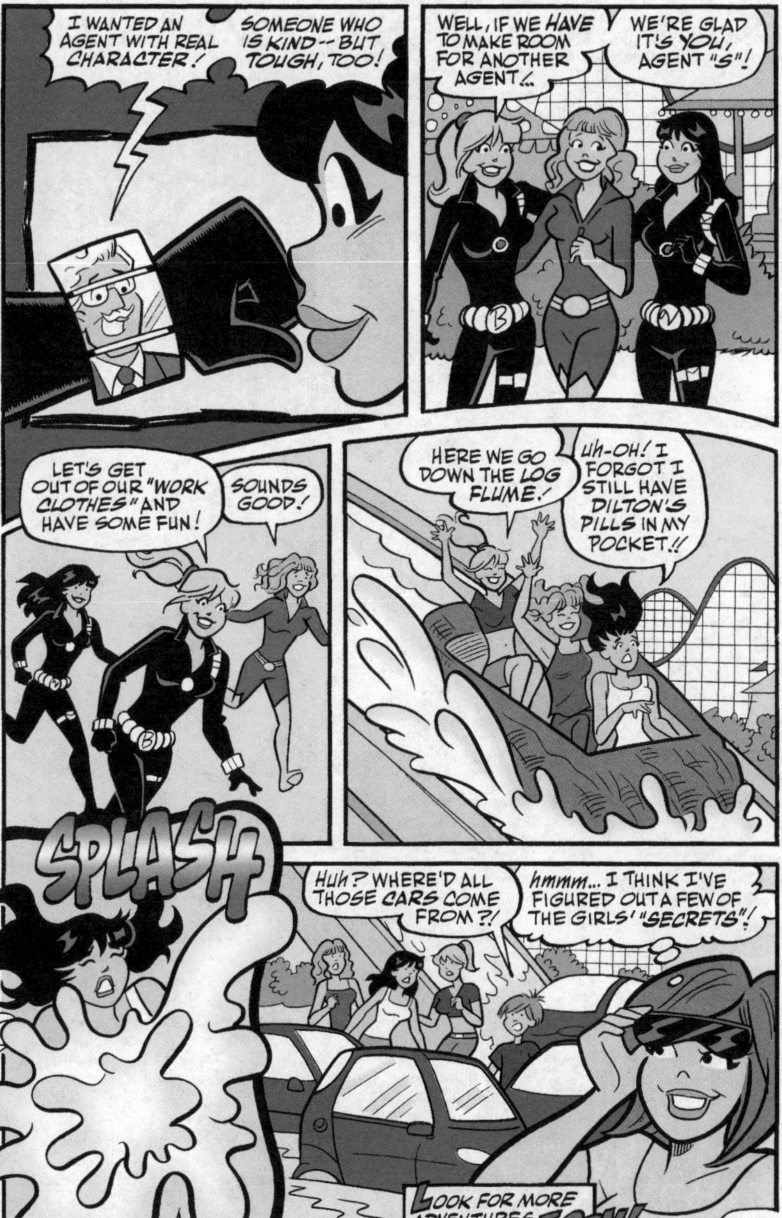
I WANTED AN AGENT WITH REAL CHARACTER!
SOMEONE WHO IS KIND-- BUT TOUGH, TOO!
WELL, IF WE HAVE TO MAKE ROOM FOR ANOTHER AGENT...
WE'RE GLAD IT'S YOU, AGENT "S"!
LET'S GET OUT OF OUR "WORK CLOTHES" AND HAVE SOME FUN!
SOUNDS GOOD!
HERE WE GO DOWN THE LOG FLUME!
UH-OH! I FORGOT I STILL HAVE DILTON'S PILLS IN MY POCKET!!
SPLASH
HUH? WHERE'D ALL THOSE CARS COME FROM?!
HMMM... I THINK I'VE FIGURED OUT A FEW OF THE GIRLS' "SECRETS"!
LOOK FOR MORE ADVENTURES SOON!
END

THE BEST OF ARCHIE COMICS STARRING

BETTY & VERONICA

2010s

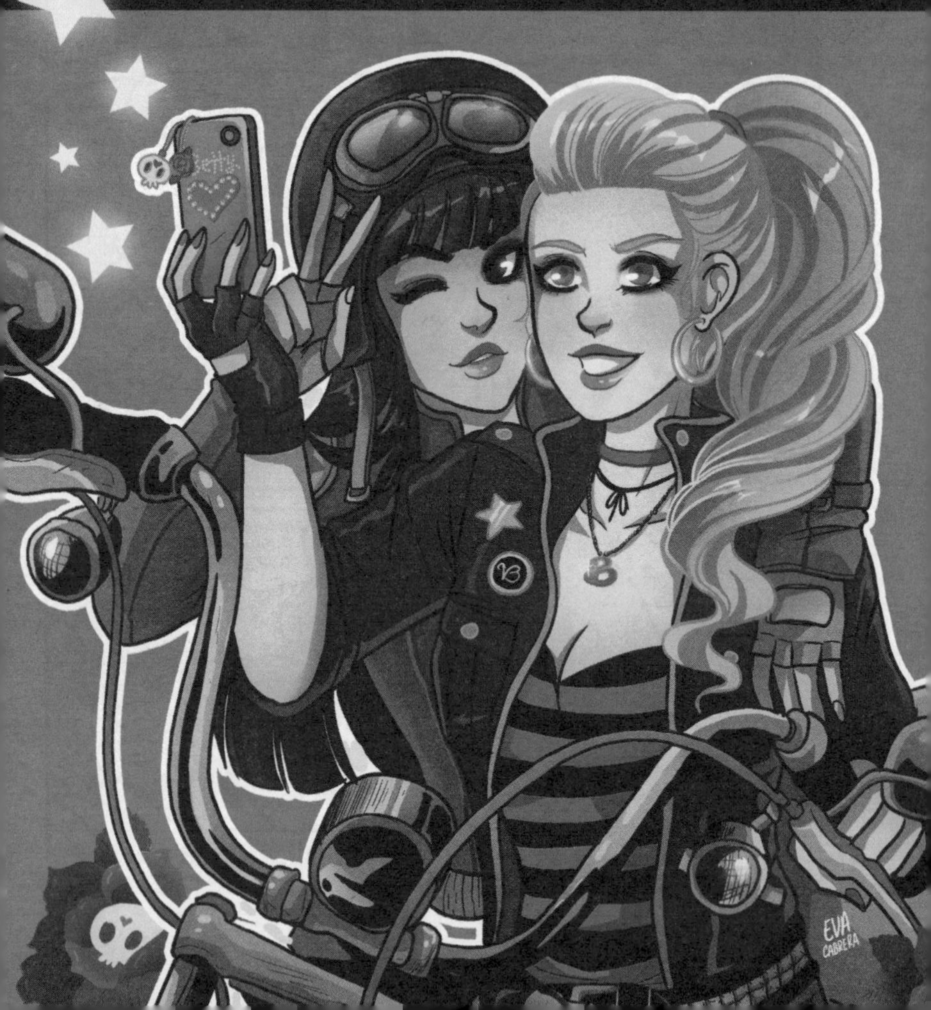
EVA CABRERA

BETTY & VERONICA #269 VARIANT COVER
BETTY & VERONICA VOL. 2 #269, 2014
Jeff Shultz, Rosario "Tito" Peña

JUST ANOTHER DAY!
BETTY & VERONICA VOL. 2 #269, 2014
Dan Parent, Jeff Shultz, Bob Smith, Glenn Whitmore, Jack Morelli

THE MINDS OF BETTY AND VERONICA
BETTY & VERONICA VOL. 2 #270, 2014
Angelo DeCesare, Jeff Shultz, Bob Smith, Glenn Whitmore, Jack Morelli

The power of Archie Comics has always been its strong connection to real world issues within the ficitonal world of Riverdale. As a society, we have come a long way in understanding the negative effects of physical and verbal bullying. If our created work can educate and inspire our readers to enact positive change in their daily lives, then we all win.

- JANICE CHIANG *Letterer, Archie Comics*

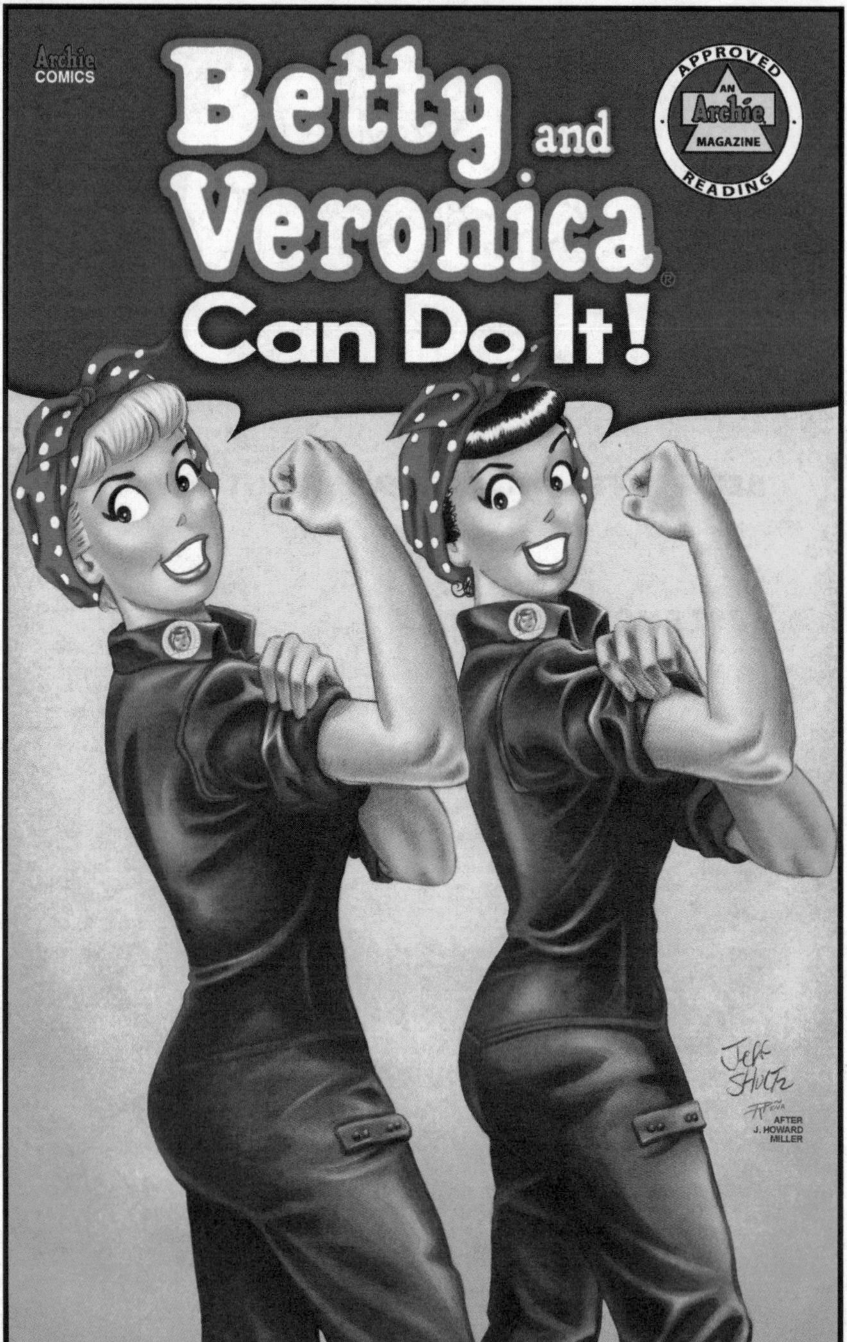
Archie COMICS
Betty and Veronica®
Can Do It!
APPROVED
AN Archie MAGAZINE
READING
AFTER
J. HOWARD
MILLER

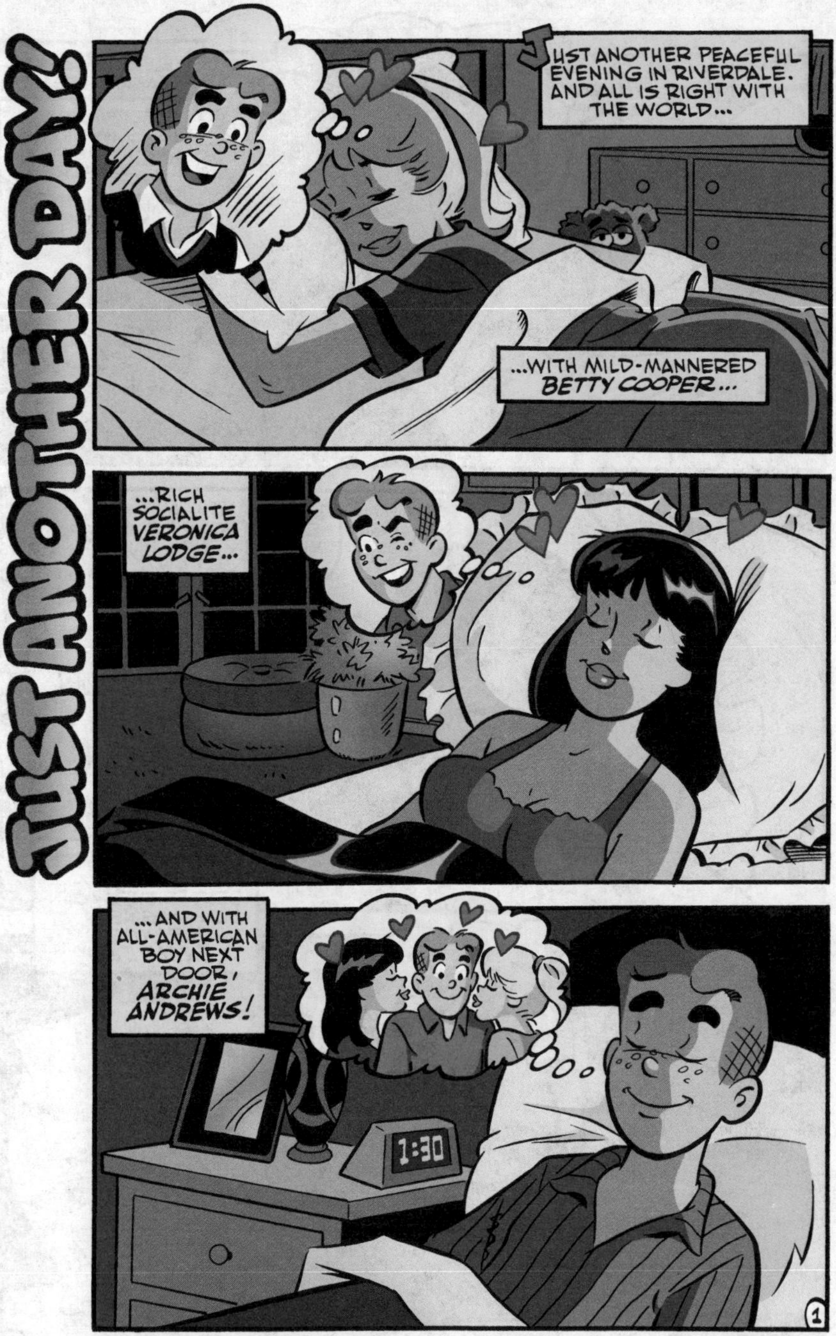
JUST ANOTHER DAY!
JUST ANOTHER PEACEFUL EVENING IN RIVERDALE. AND ALL IS RIGHT WITH THE WORLD...
...WITH MILD-MANNERED BETTY COOPER...
...RICH SOCIALITE VERONICA LODGE...
...AND WITH ALL-AMERICAN BOY NEXT DOOR, ARCHIE ANDREWS!
1:30

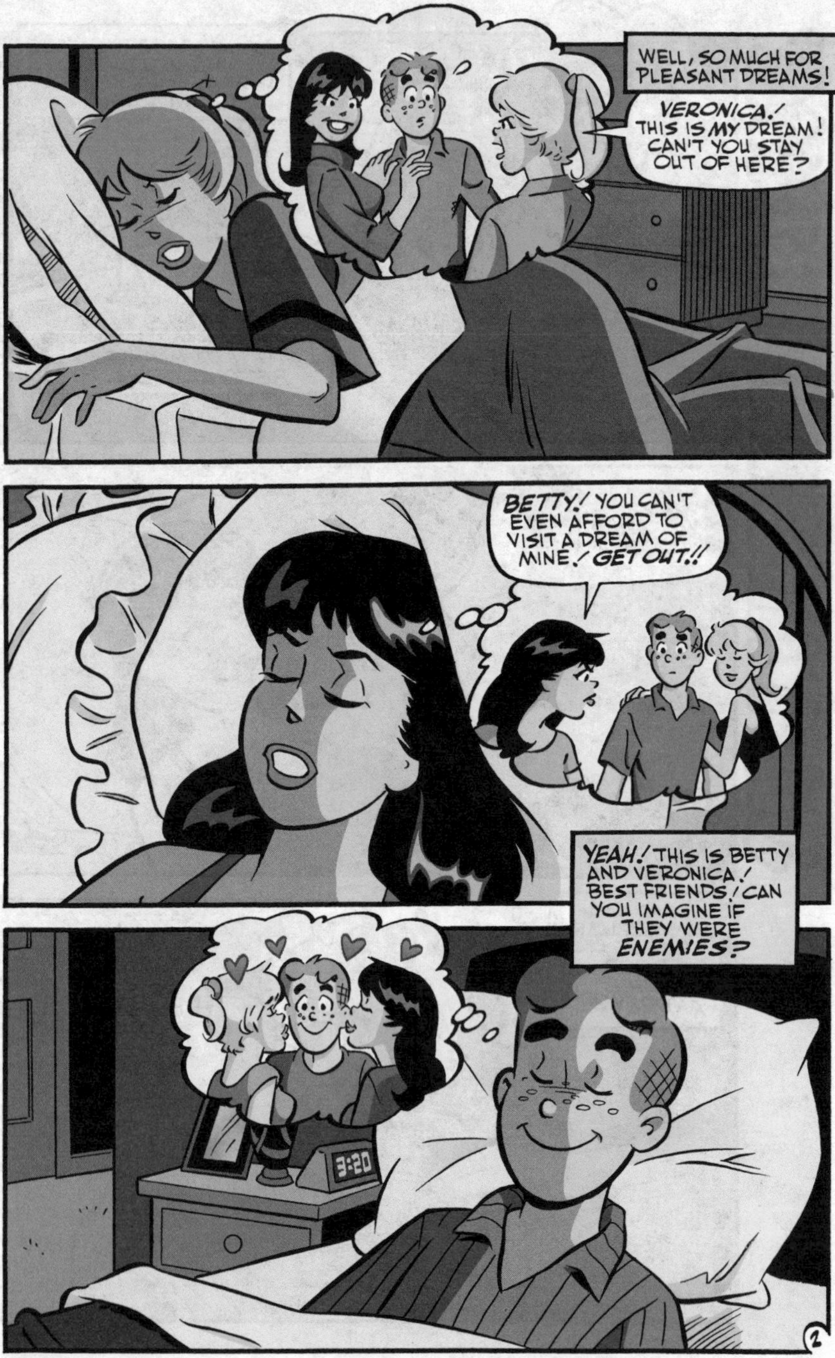
WELL, SO MUCH FOR PLEASANT DREAMS!
VERONICA! THIS IS MY DREAM! CAN'T YOU STAY OUT OF HERE?
BETTY! YOU CAN'T EVEN AFFORD TO VISIT A DREAM OF MINE! GET OUT!!
YEAH! THIS IS BETTY AND VERONICA! BEST FRIENDS! CAN YOU IMAGINE IF THEY WERE ENEMIES?
3:20
2

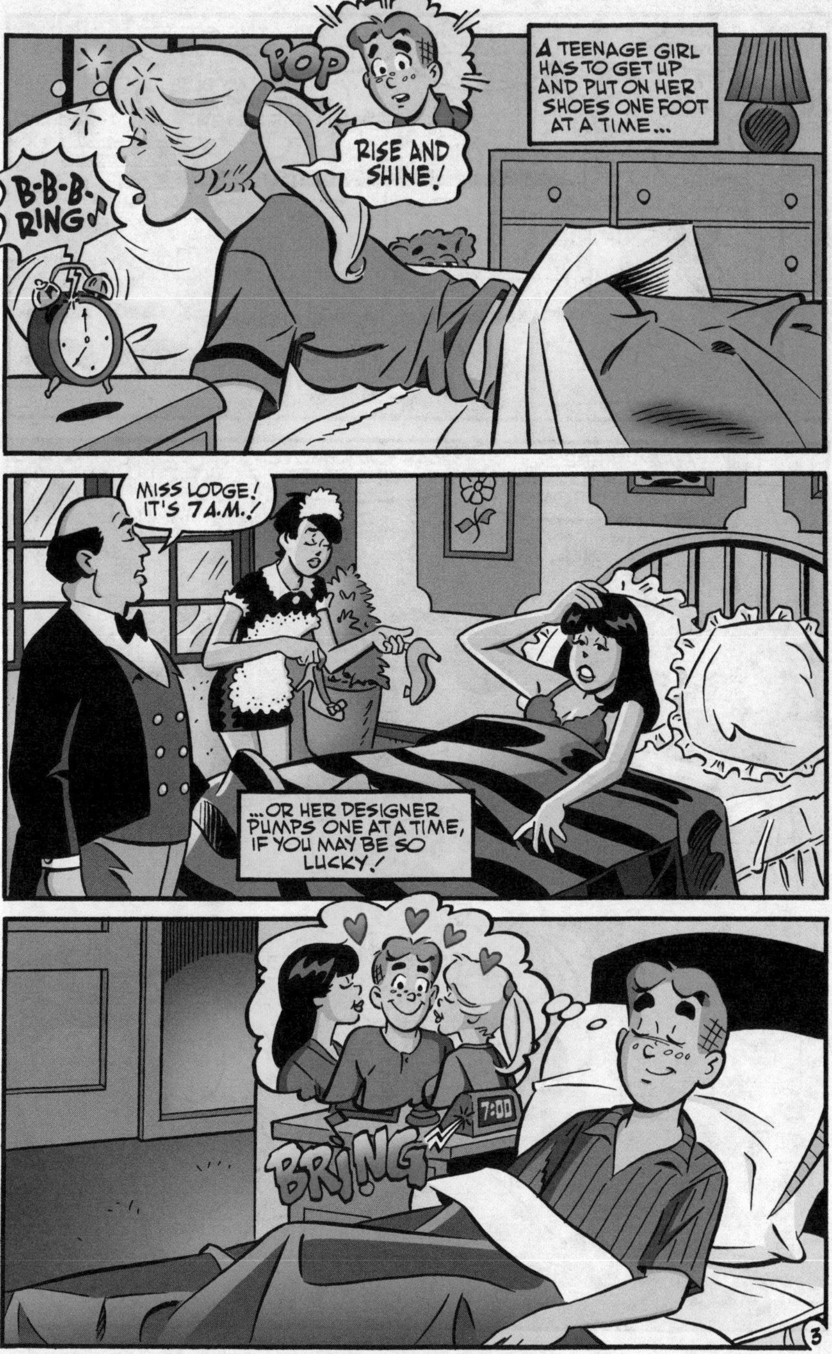
A TEENAGE GIRL HAS TO GET UP AND PUT ON HER SHOES ONE FOOT AT A TIME...
B-B-B-RING
POP
RISE AND SHINE!
MISS LODGE! IT'S 7 A.M.!
...OR HER DESIGNER PUMPS ONE AT A TIME, IF YOU MAY BE SO LUCKY!
7:00
BRING

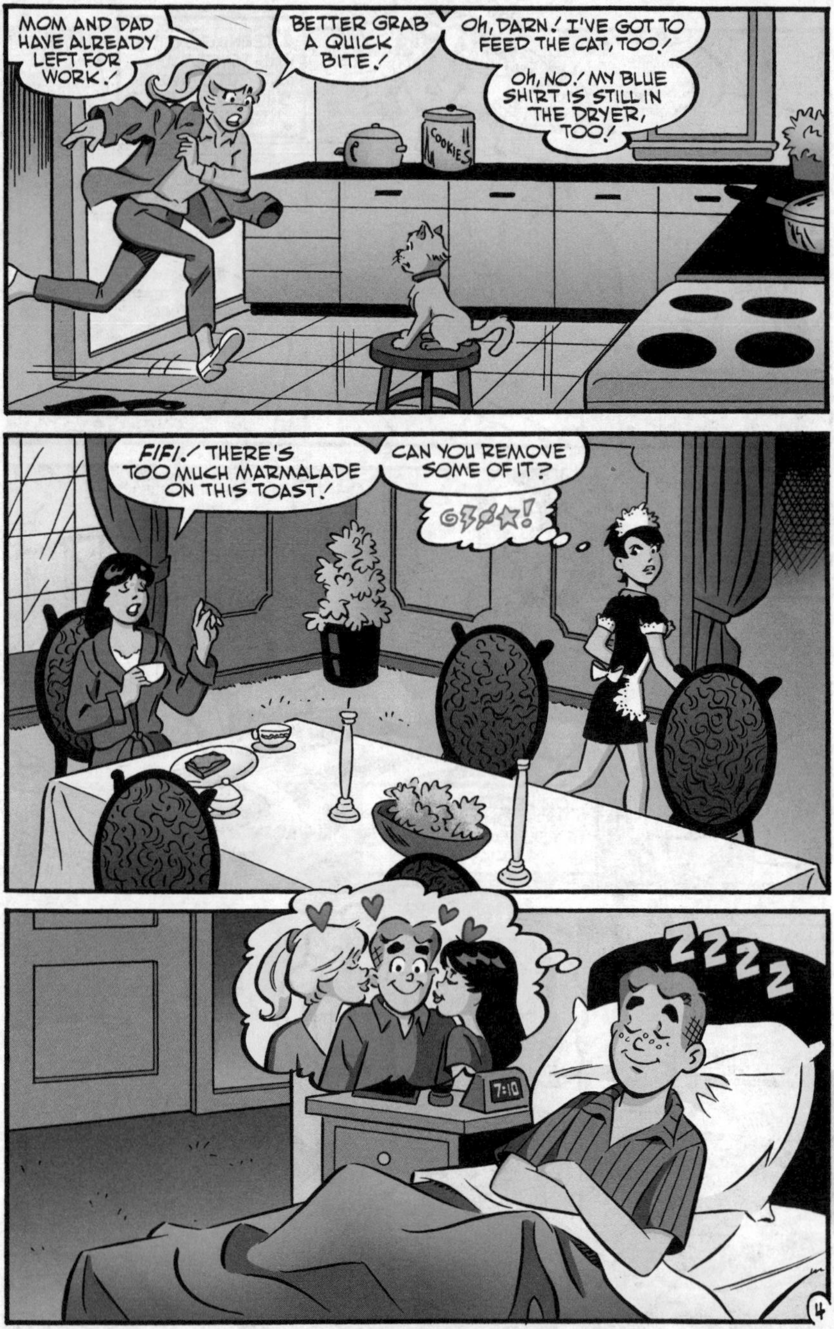
MOM AND DAD HAVE ALREADY LEFT FOR WORK!
BETTER GRAB A QUICK BITE!
Oh, DARN! I'VE GOT TO FEED THE CAT, TOO!
Oh, NO! MY BLUE SHIRT IS STILL IN THE DRYER, TOO!
COOKIES
FIFI! THERE'S TOO MUCH MARMALADE ON THIS TOAST!
CAN YOU REMOVE SOME OF IT?
7:10
ZZZZ

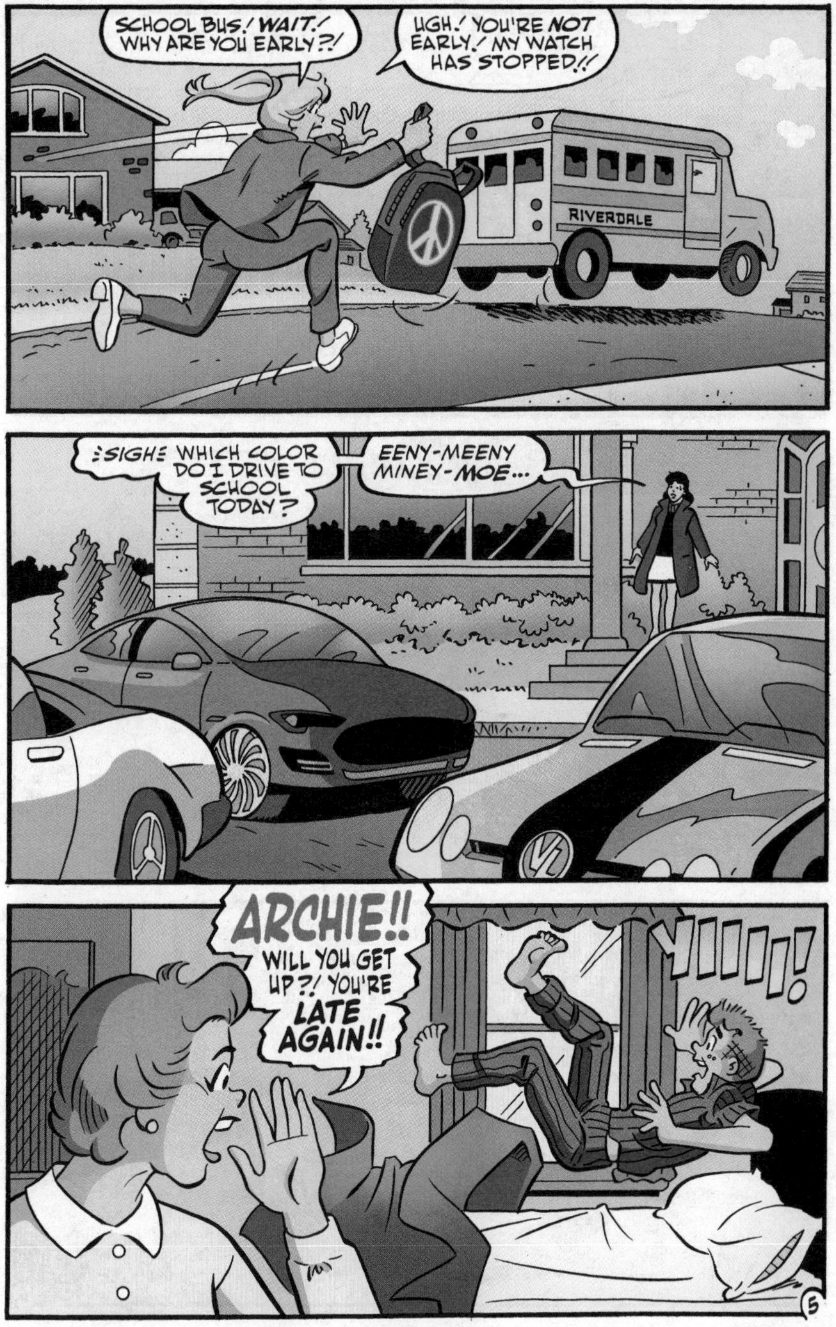

SCHOOL BUS! WAIT! WHY ARE YOU EARLY?!
UGH! YOU'RE NOT EARLY! MY WATCH HAS STOPPED!!
RIVERDALE
:SIGH: WHICH COLOR DO I DRIVE TO SCHOOL TODAY?
EENY-MEENY MINEY-MOE...
ARCHIE!! WILL YOU GET UP?! YOU'RE LATE AGAIN!!
YIIIII!

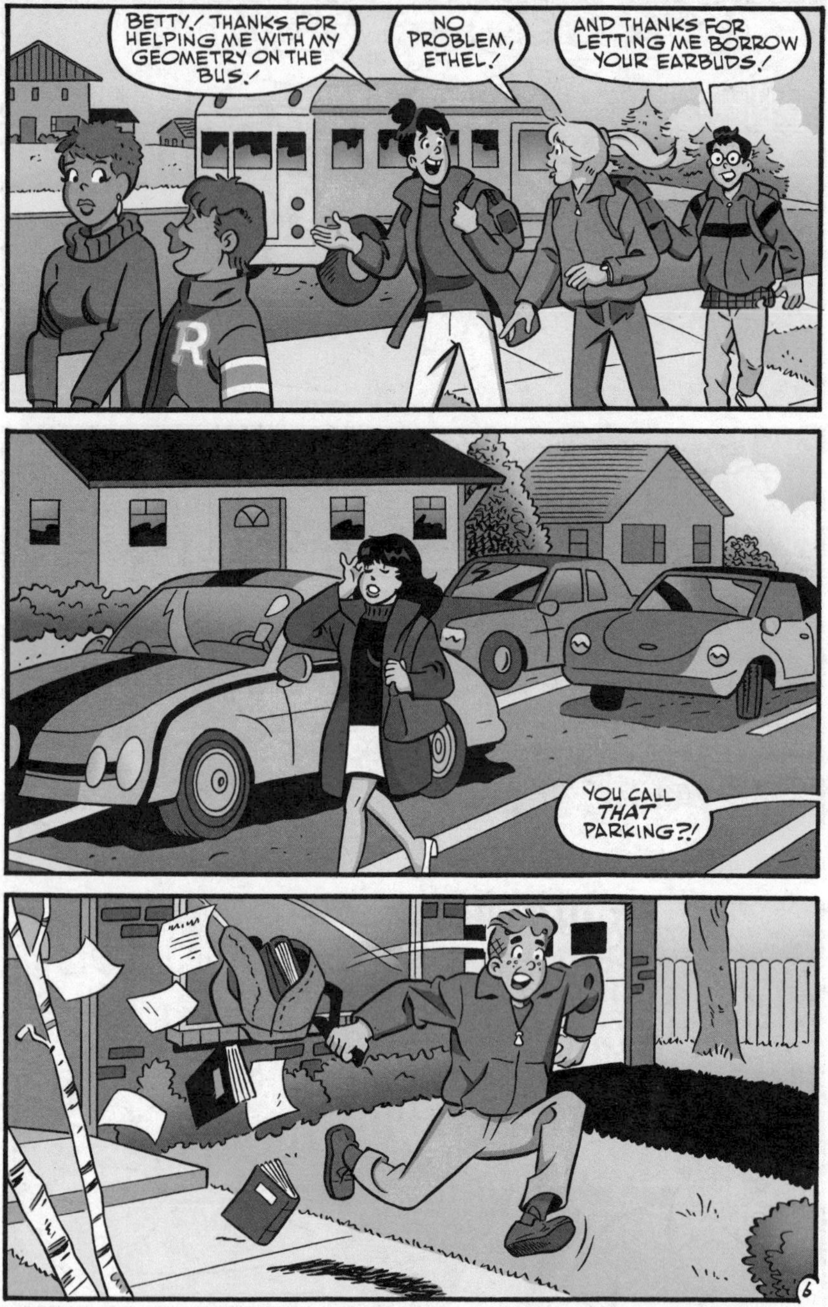

BETTY! THANKS FOR HELPING ME WITH MY GEOMETRY ON THE BUS!
NO PROBLEM, ETHEL!
AND THANKS FOR LETTING ME BORROW YOUR EARBUDS!
YOU CALL THAT PARKING?!

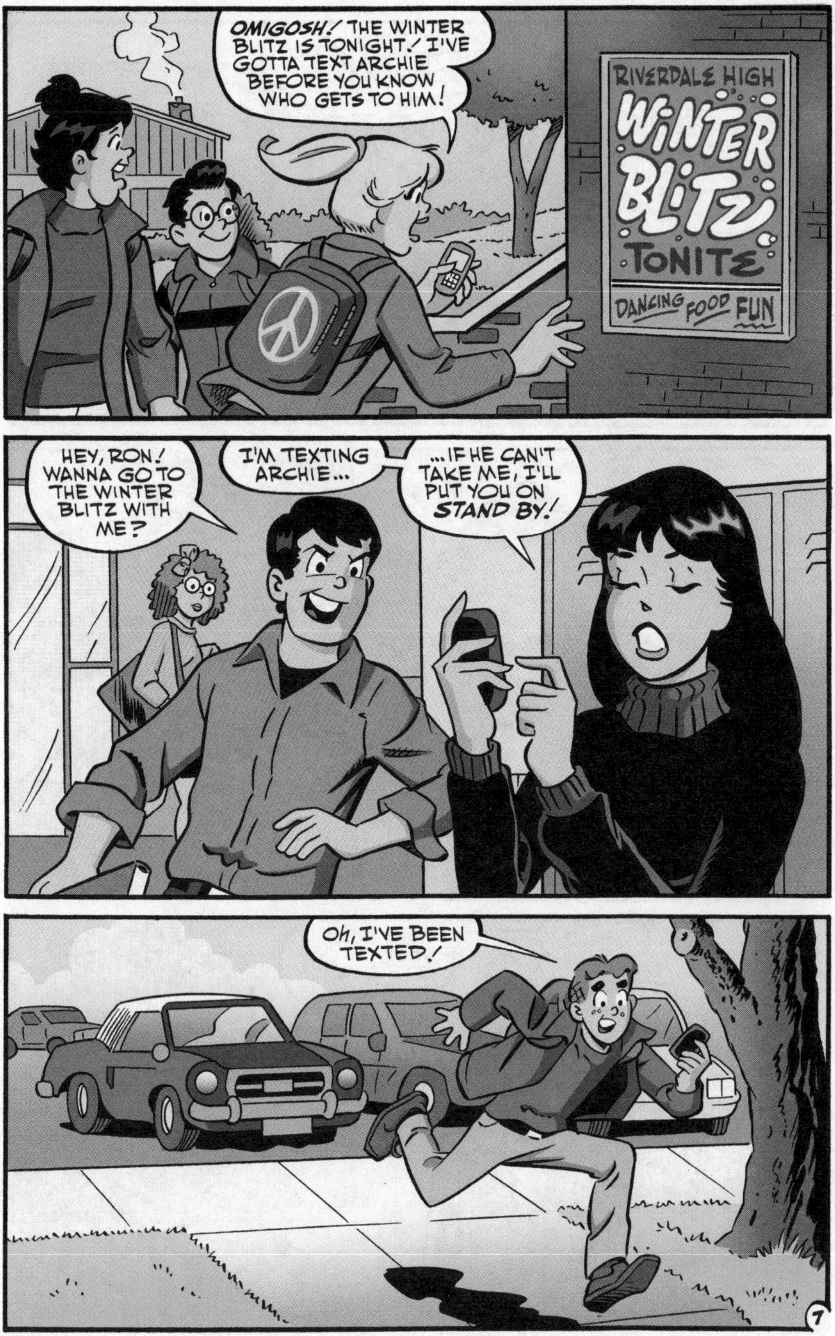
OMIGOSH! THE WINTER BLITZ IS TONIGHT! I'VE GOTTA TEXT ARCHIE BEFORE YOU KNOW WHO GETS TO HIM!
RIVERDALE HIGH
WINTER BLITZ TONITE
DANCING FOOD FUN
HEY, RON! WANNA GO TO THE WINTER BLITZ WITH ME?
I'M TEXTING ARCHIE...
...IF HE CAN'T TAKE ME, I'LL PUT YOU ON STAND BY!
Oh, I'VE BEEN TEXTED!
7

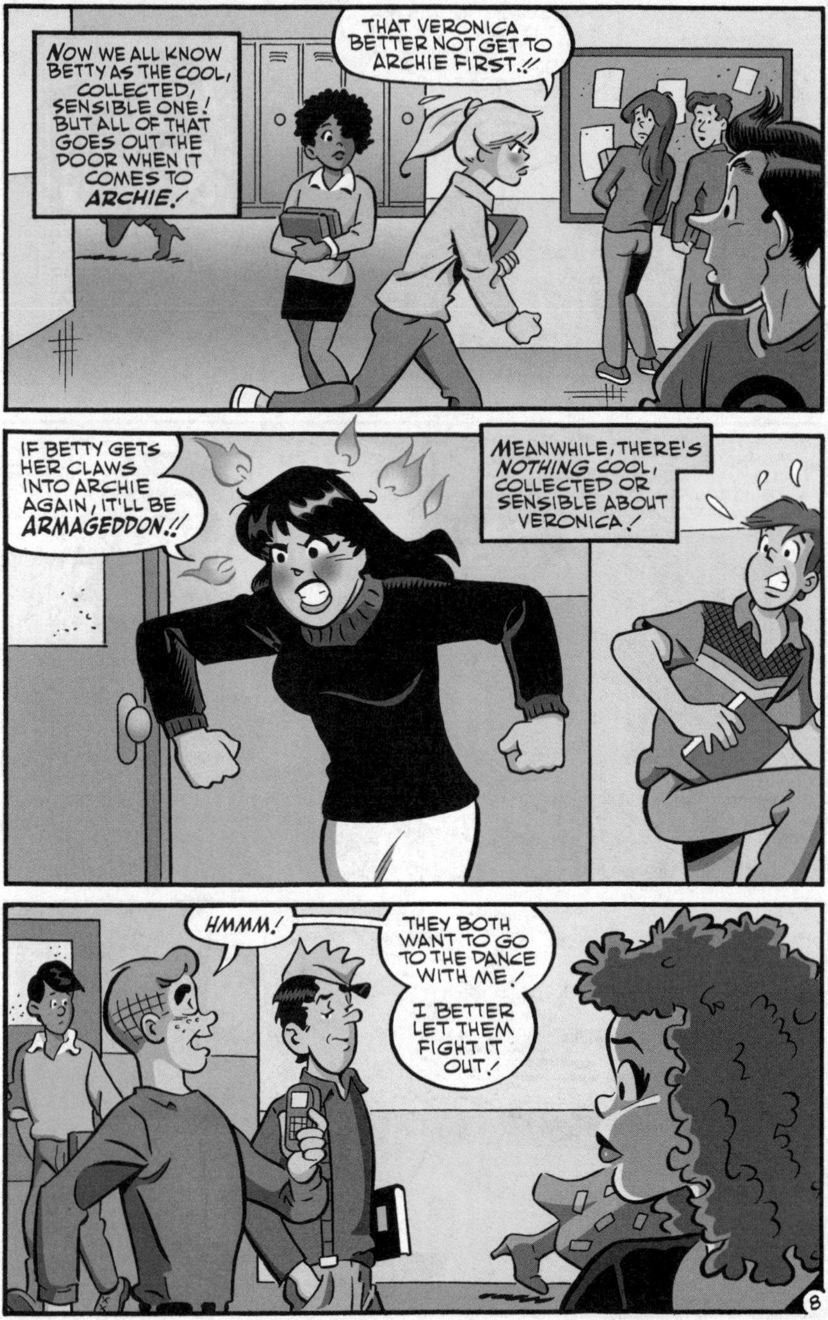
NOW WE ALL KNOW BETTY AS THE COOL, COLLECTED, SENSIBLE ONE! BUT ALL OF THAT GOES OUT THE DOOR WHEN IT COMES TO ARCHIE!
THAT VERONICA BETTER NOT GET TO ARCHIE FIRST.!!
IF BETTY GETS HER CLAWS INTO ARCHIE AGAIN, IT'LL BE ARMAGEDDON!!
MEANWHILE, THERE'S NOTHING COOL, COLLECTED OR SENSIBLE ABOUT VERONICA!
HMMM!
THEY BOTH WANT TO GO TO THE DANCE WITH ME!
I BETTER LET THEM FIGHT IT OUT!
8

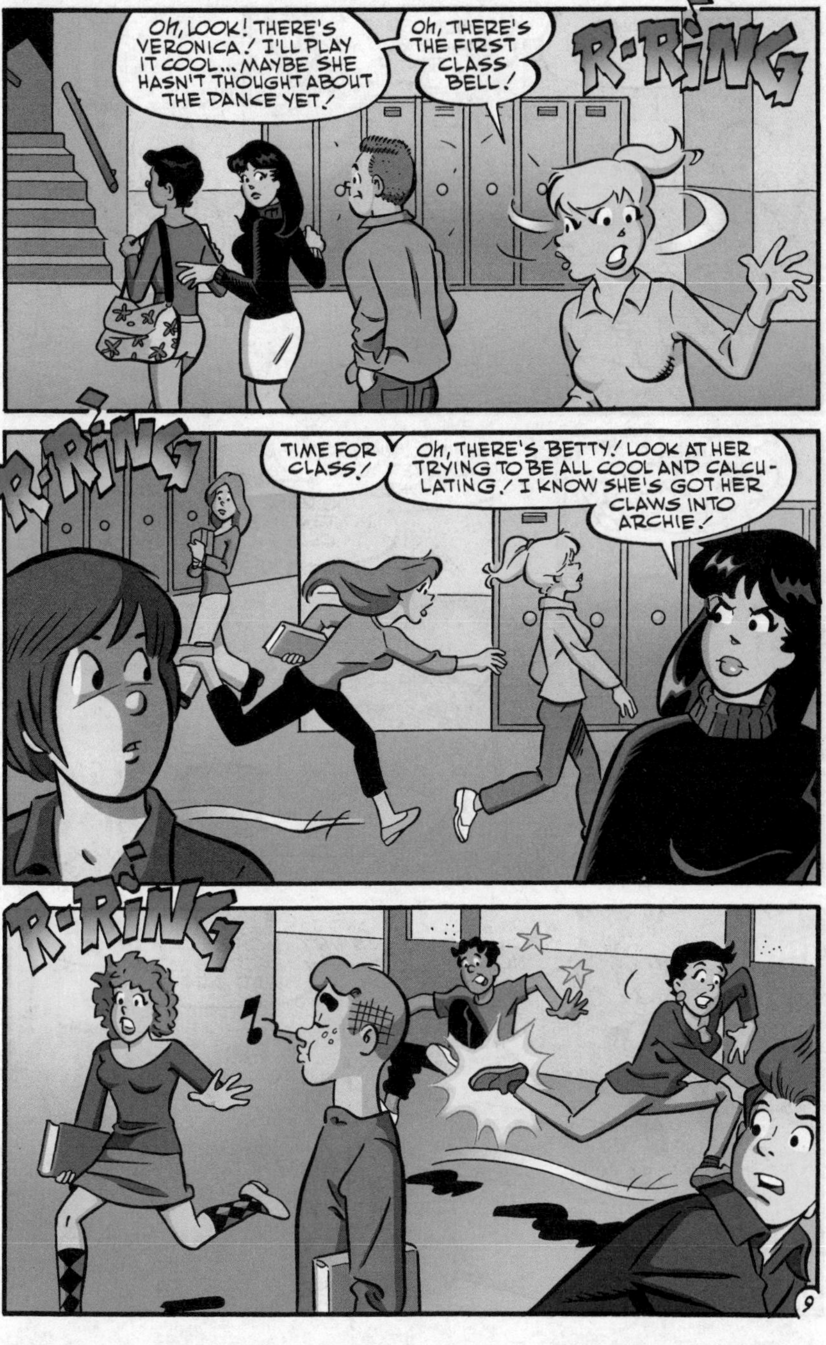
OH, LOOK! THERE'S VERONICA! I'LL PLAY IT COOL... MAYBE SHE HASN'T THOUGHT ABOUT THE DANCE YET!
OH, THERE'S THE FIRST CLASS BELL!
R-RING
R-RING
TIME FOR CLASS!
OH, THERE'S BETTY! LOOK AT HER TRYING TO BE ALL COOL AND CALCULATING! I KNOW SHE'S GOT HER CLAWS INTO ARCHIE!
R-RING

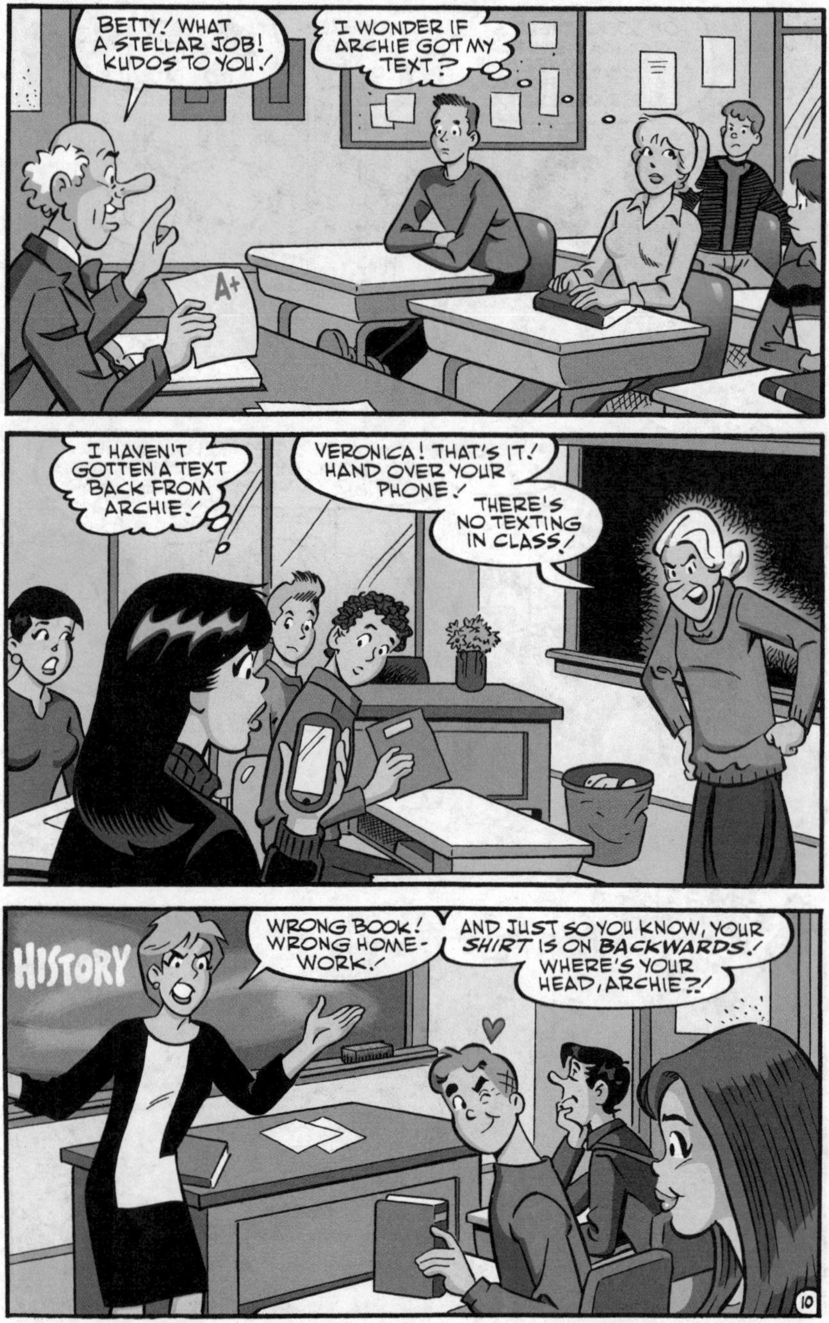
BETTY! WHAT A STELLAR JOB! KUDOS TO YOU!
I WONDER IF ARCHIE GOT MY TEXT?
A+
I HAVEN'T GOTTEN A TEXT BACK FROM ARCHIE!
VERONICA! THAT'S IT! HAND OVER YOUR PHONE!
THERE'S NO TEXTING IN CLASS!
HISTORY
WRONG BOOK! WRONG HOME-WORK!
AND JUST SO YOU KNOW, YOUR SHIRT IS ON BACKWARDS! WHERE'S YOUR HEAD, ARCHIE?!

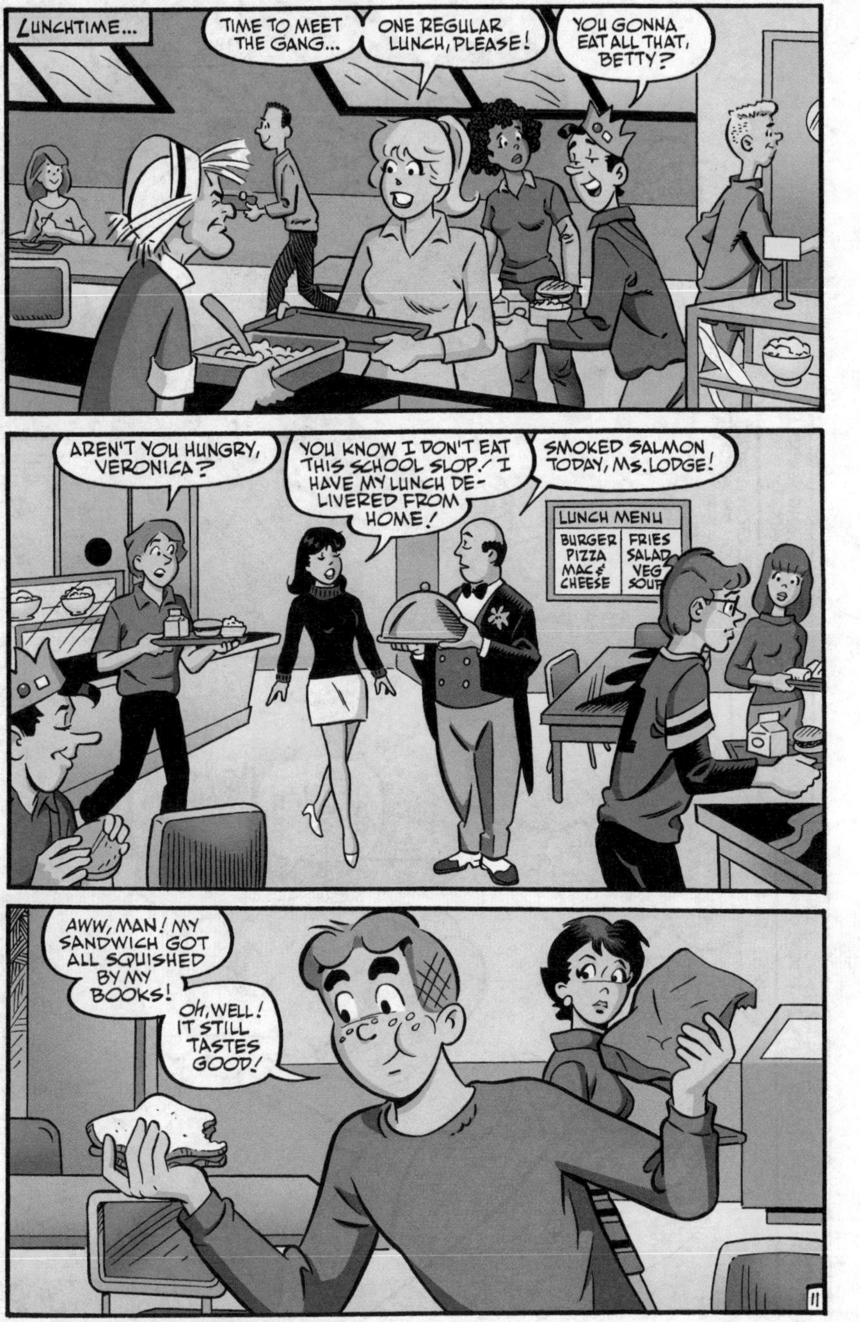

LUNCHTIME...
TIME TO MEET THE GANG...
ONE REGULAR LUNCH, PLEASE!
YOU GONNA EAT ALL THAT, BETTY?
AREN'T YOU HUNGRY, VERONICA?
YOU KNOW I DON'T EAT THIS SCHOOL SLOP! I HAVE MY LUNCH DE-LIVERED FROM HOME!
SMOKED SALMON TODAY, MS. LODGE!
LUNCH MENU
BURGER PIZZA MAC & CHEESE
FRIES SALAD VEG SOUP
AWW, MAN! MY SANDWICH GOT ALL SQUISHED BY MY BOOKS!
OH, WELL! IT STILL TASTES GOOD!
11

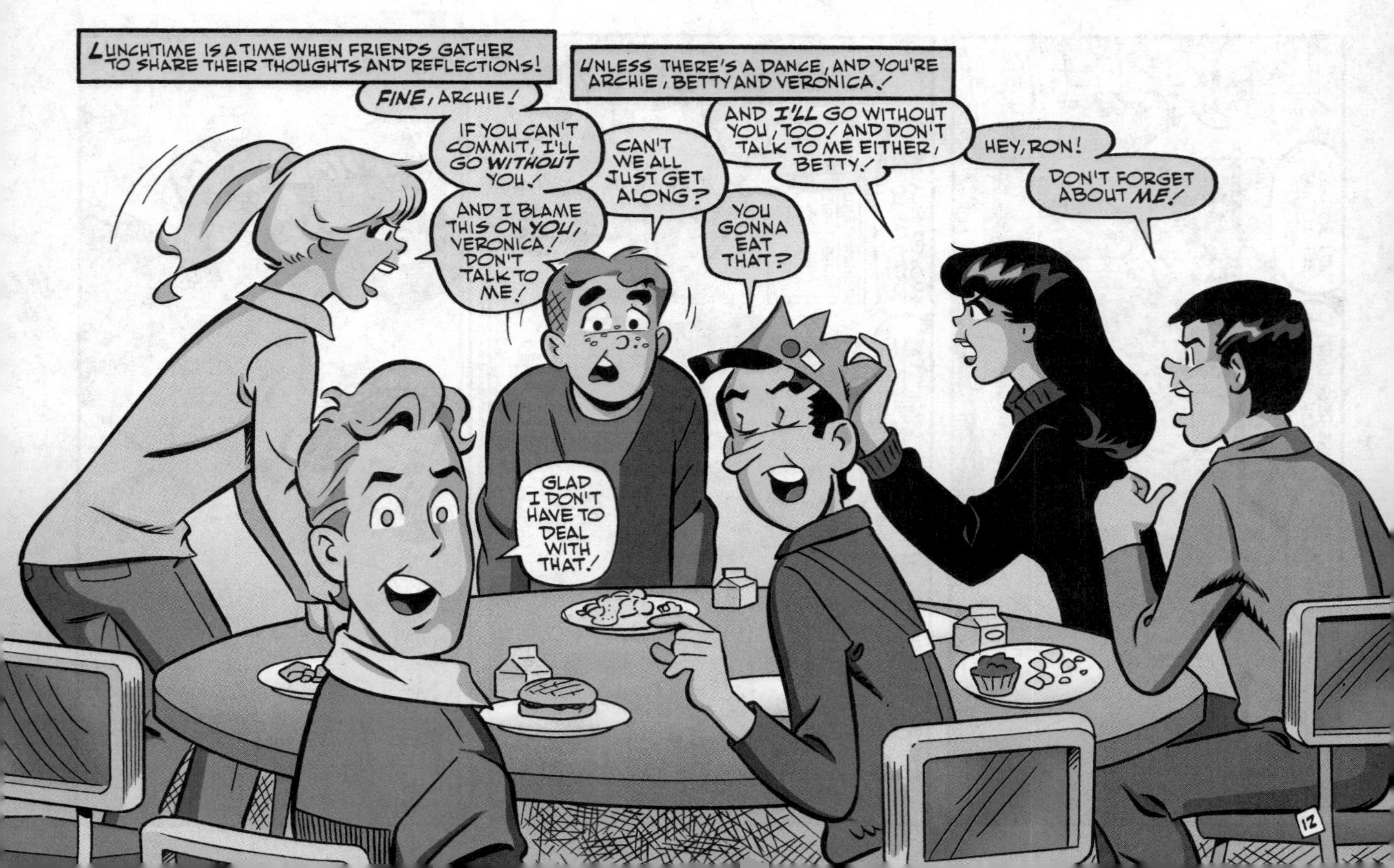

LUNCHTIME IS A TIME WHEN FRIENDS GATHER TO SHARE THEIR THOUGHTS AND REFLECTIONS!
UNLESS THERE'S A DANCE, AND YOU'RE ARCHIE, BETTY AND VERONICA!
FINE, ARCHIE!
IF YOU CAN'T COMMIT, I'LL GO WITHOUT YOU!
AND I BLAME THIS ON YOU, VERONICA! DON'T TALK TO ME!
CAN'T WE ALL JUST GET ALONG?
AND I'LL GO WITHOUT YOU, TOO! AND DON'T TALK TO ME EITHER, BETTY!
YOU GONNA EAT THAT?
HEY, RON!
DON'T FORGET ABOUT ME!
GLAD I DON'T HAVE TO DEAL WITH THAT!
12

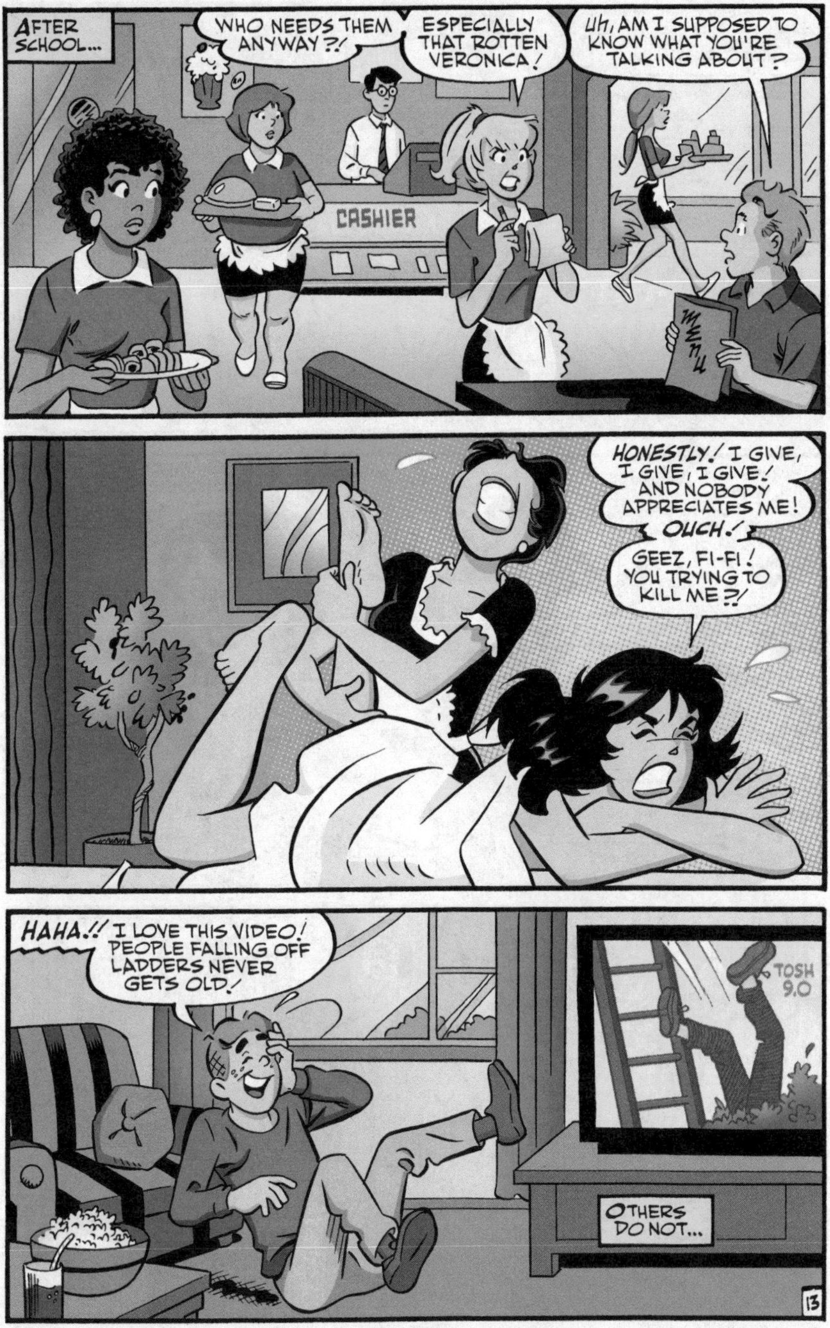

AFTER SCHOOL...
WHO NEEDS THEM ANYWAY ?!
ESPECIALLY THAT ROTTEN VERONICA!
UH, AM I SUPPOSED TO KNOW WHAT YOU'RE TALKING ABOUT?
CASHIER
MENU
HONESTLY! I GIVE, I GIVE, I GIVE! AND NOBODY APPRECIATES ME!
OUCH!
GEEZ, FI-FI! YOU TRYING TO KILL ME ?!
HAHA!!
I LOVE THIS VIDEO! PEOPLE FALLING OFF LADDERS NEVER GETS OLD!
TOSH 9.0
OTHERS DO NOT...
13

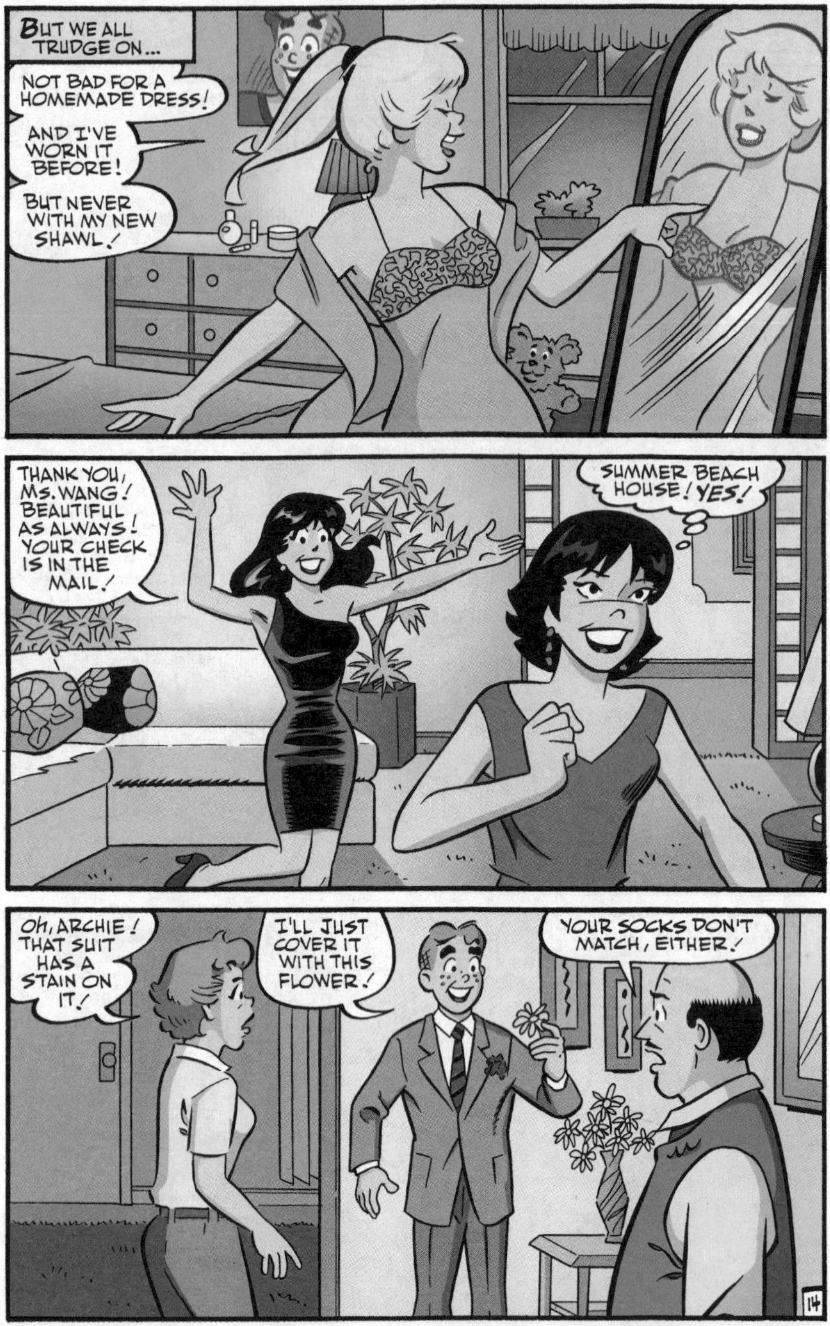

BUT WE ALL TRUDGE ON...
NOT BAD FOR A HOMEMADE DRESS!
AND I'VE WORN IT BEFORE!
BUT NEVER WITH MY NEW SHAWL!
THANK YOU, MS. WANG! BEAUTIFUL AS ALWAYS! YOUR CHECK IS IN THE MAIL!
SUMMER BEACH HOUSE! YES!
Oh, ARCHIE! THAT SUIT HAS A STAIN ON IT!
I'LL JUST COVER IT WITH THIS FLOWER!
YOUR SOCKS DON'T MATCH, EITHER!
14

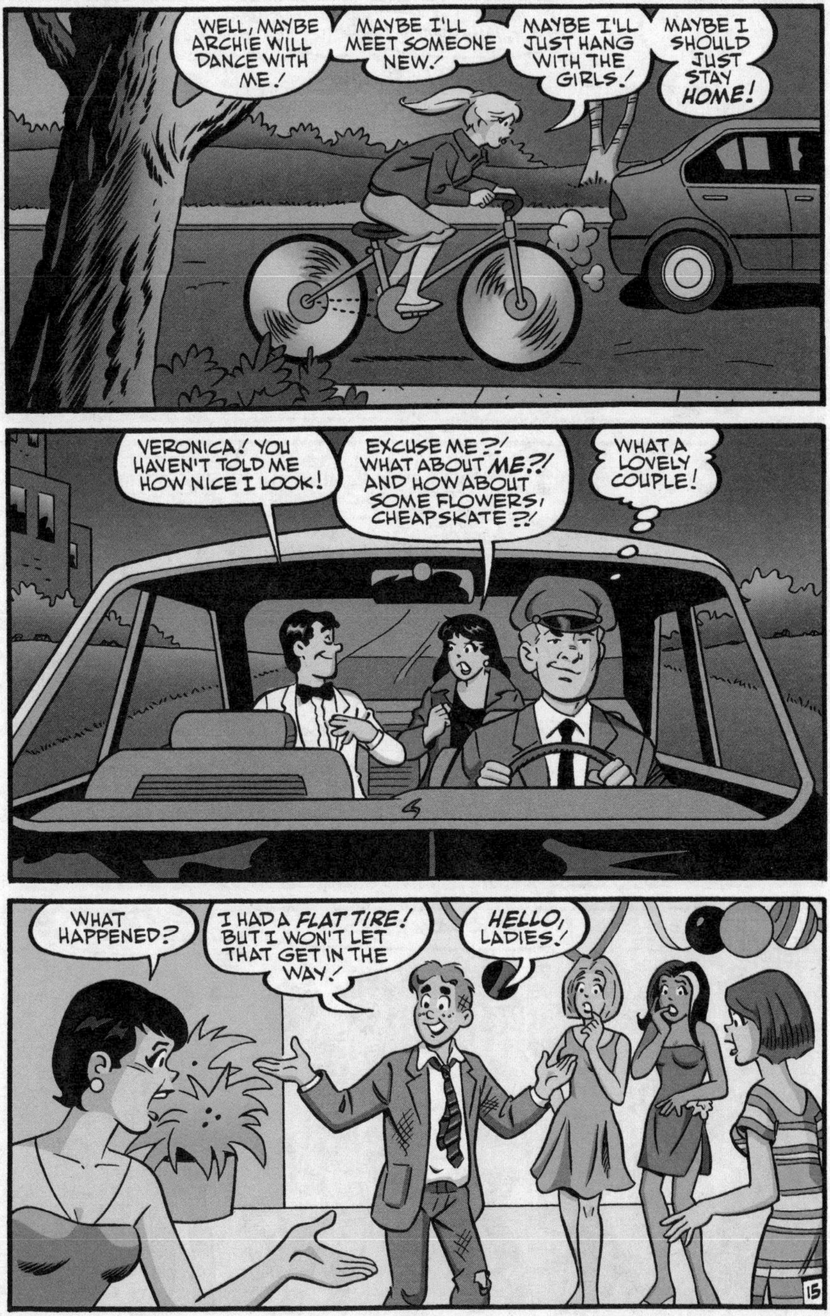
WELL, MAYBE ARCHIE WILL DANCE WITH ME!
MAYBE I'LL MEET SOMEONE NEW!
MAYBE I'LL JUST HANG WITH THE GIRLS!
MAYBE I SHOULD JUST STAY HOME!
VERONICA! YOU HAVEN'T TOLD ME HOW NICE I LOOK!
EXCUSE ME?! WHAT ABOUT ME?! AND HOW ABOUT SOME FLOWERS, CHEAPSKATE?!
WHAT A LOVELY COUPLE!
WHAT HAPPENED?
I HAD A FLAT TIRE! BUT I WON'T LET THAT GET IN THE WAY!
HELLO, LADIES!
15

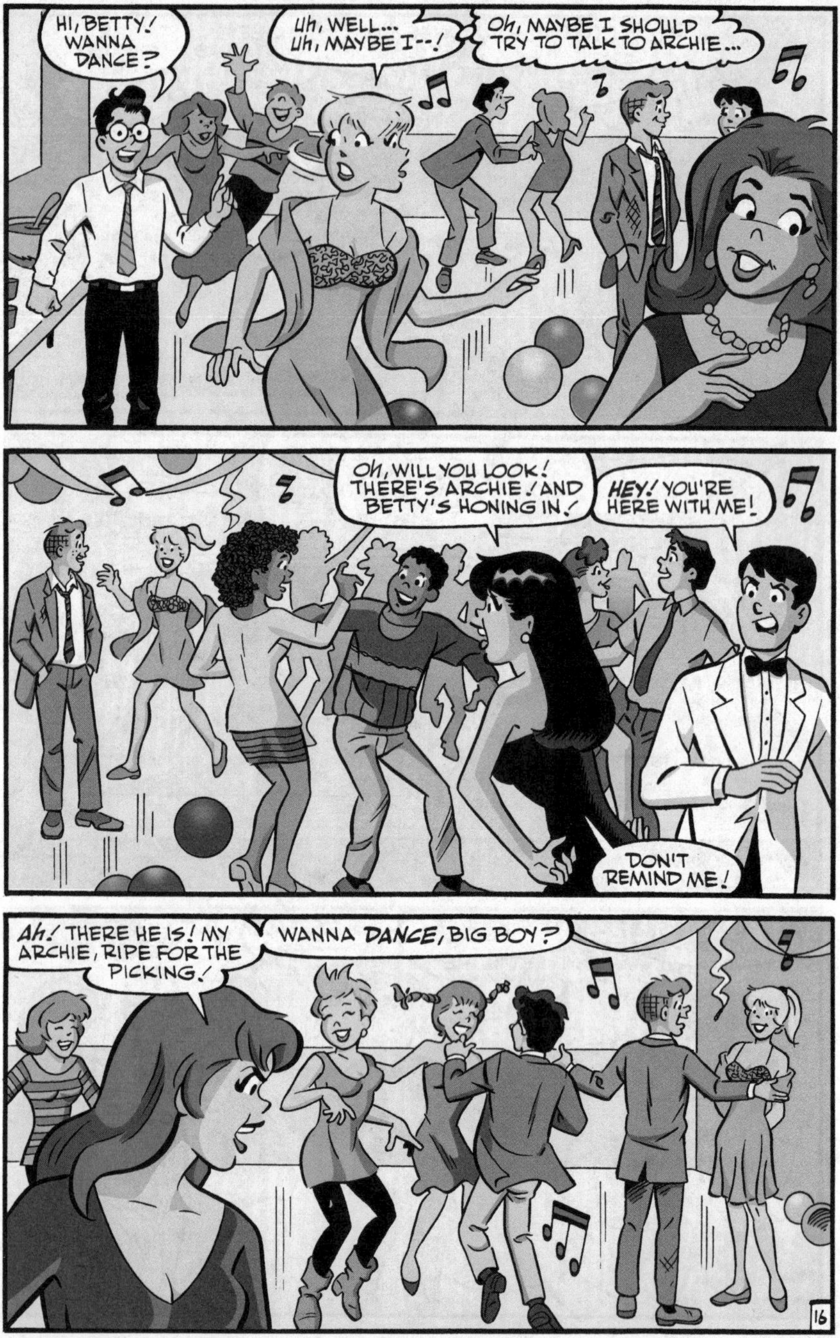

HI, BETTY! WANNA DANCE?
UH, WELL... UH, MAYBE I--!
OH, MAYBE I SHOULD TRY TO TALK TO ARCHIE...
OH, WILL YOU LOOK! THERE'S ARCHIE! AND BETTY'S HONING IN!
HEY! YOU'RE HERE WITH ME!
DON'T REMIND ME!
AH! THERE HE IS! MY ARCHIE, RIPE FOR THE PICKING!
WANNA DANCE, BIG BOY?
16

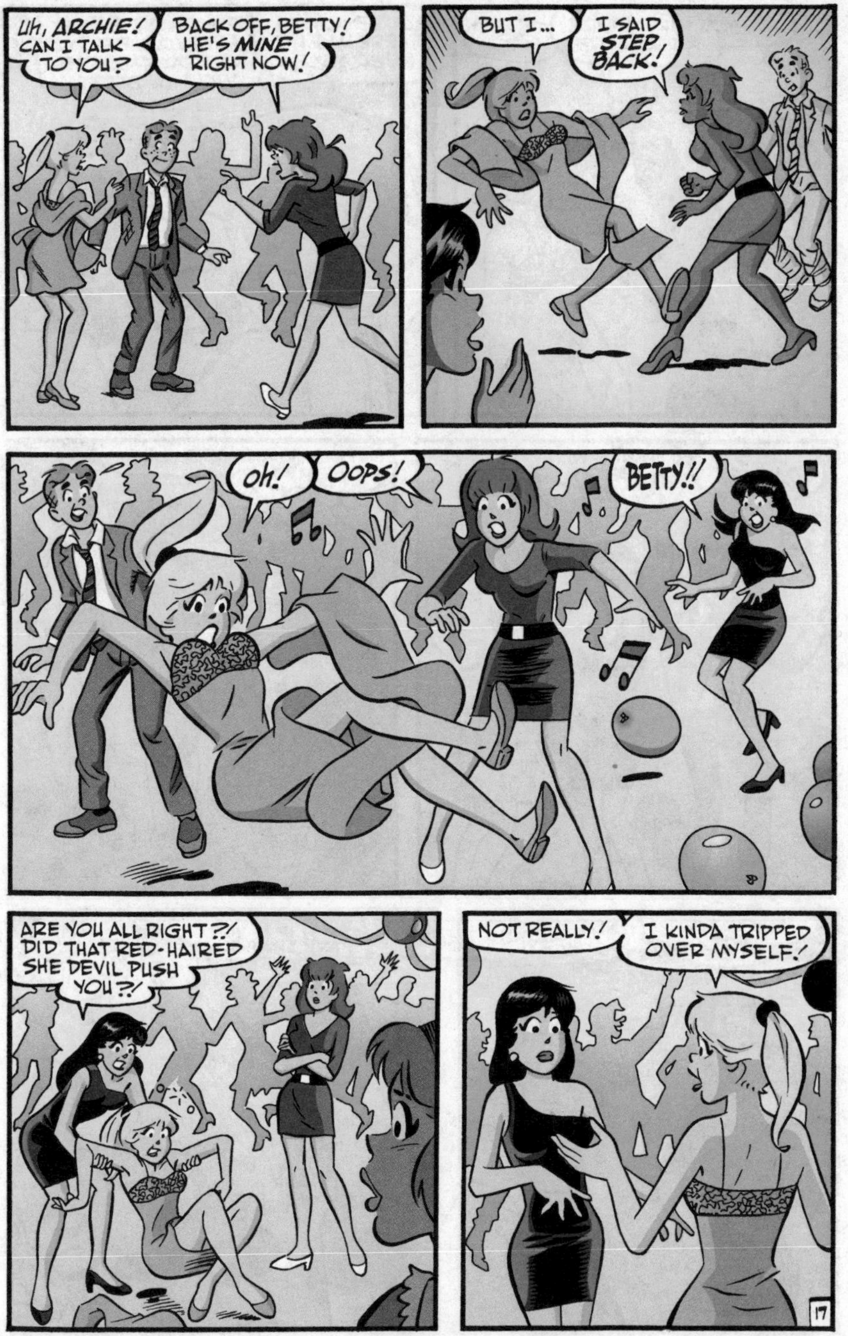

UH, ARCHIE! CAN I TALK TO YOU?
BACK OFF, BETTY! HE'S MINE RIGHT NOW!
BUT I...
I SAID STEP BACK!
OH!
OOPS!
BETTY!!
ARE YOU ALL RIGHT?! DID THAT RED-HAIRED SHE DEVIL PUSH YOU?!
NOT REALLY!
I KINDA TRIPPED OVER MYSELF!
17

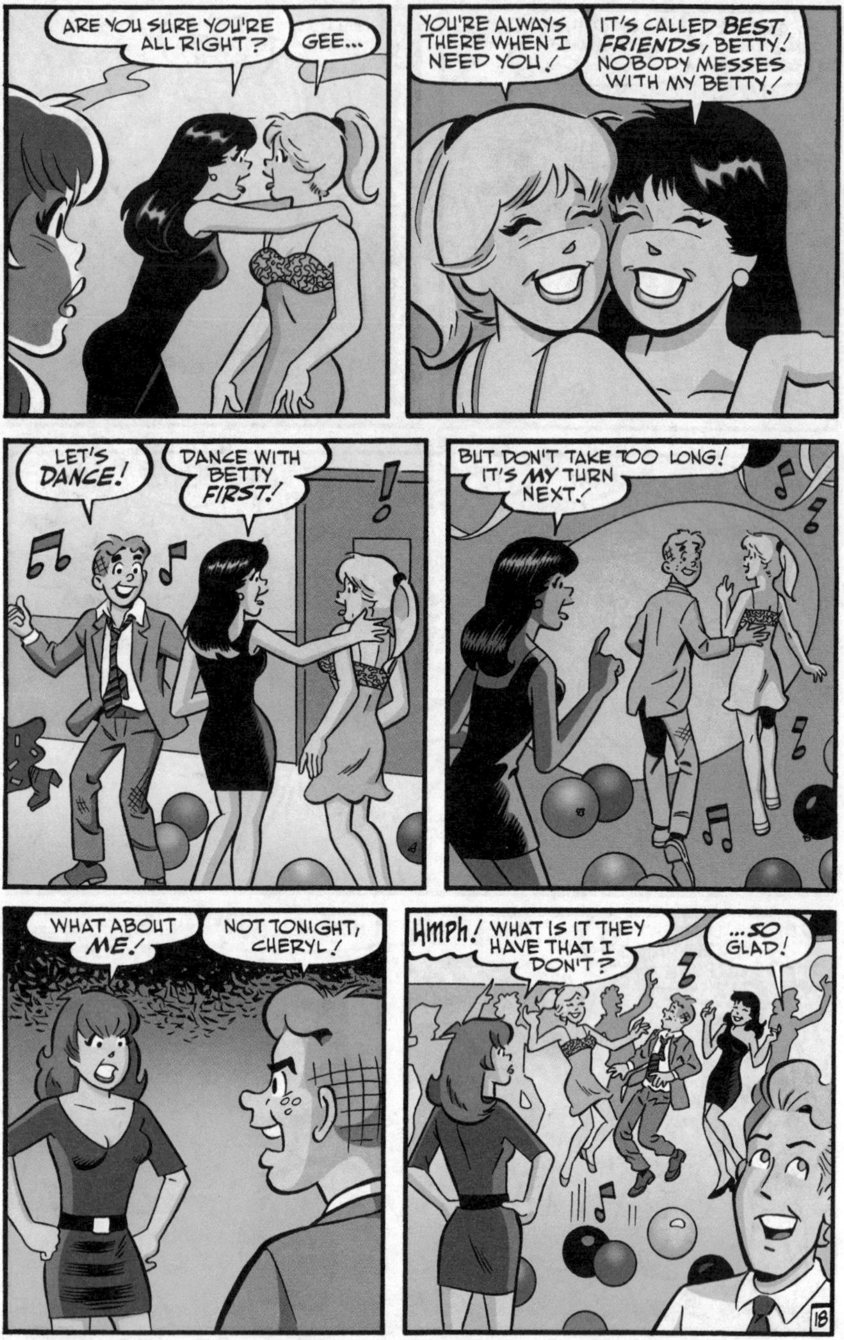
ARE YOU SURE YOU'RE ALL RIGHT?
GEE...
YOU'RE ALWAYS THERE WHEN I NEED YOU!
IT'S CALLED BEST FRIENDS, BETTY! NOBODY MESSES WITH MY BETTY!
LET'S DANCE!
DANCE WITH BETTY FIRST!
!
BUT DON'T TAKE TOO LONG! IT'S MY TURN NEXT!
WHAT ABOUT ME!
NOT TONIGHT, CHERYL!
Hmph! WHAT IS IT THEY HAVE THAT I DON'T?
...SO GLAD!
18

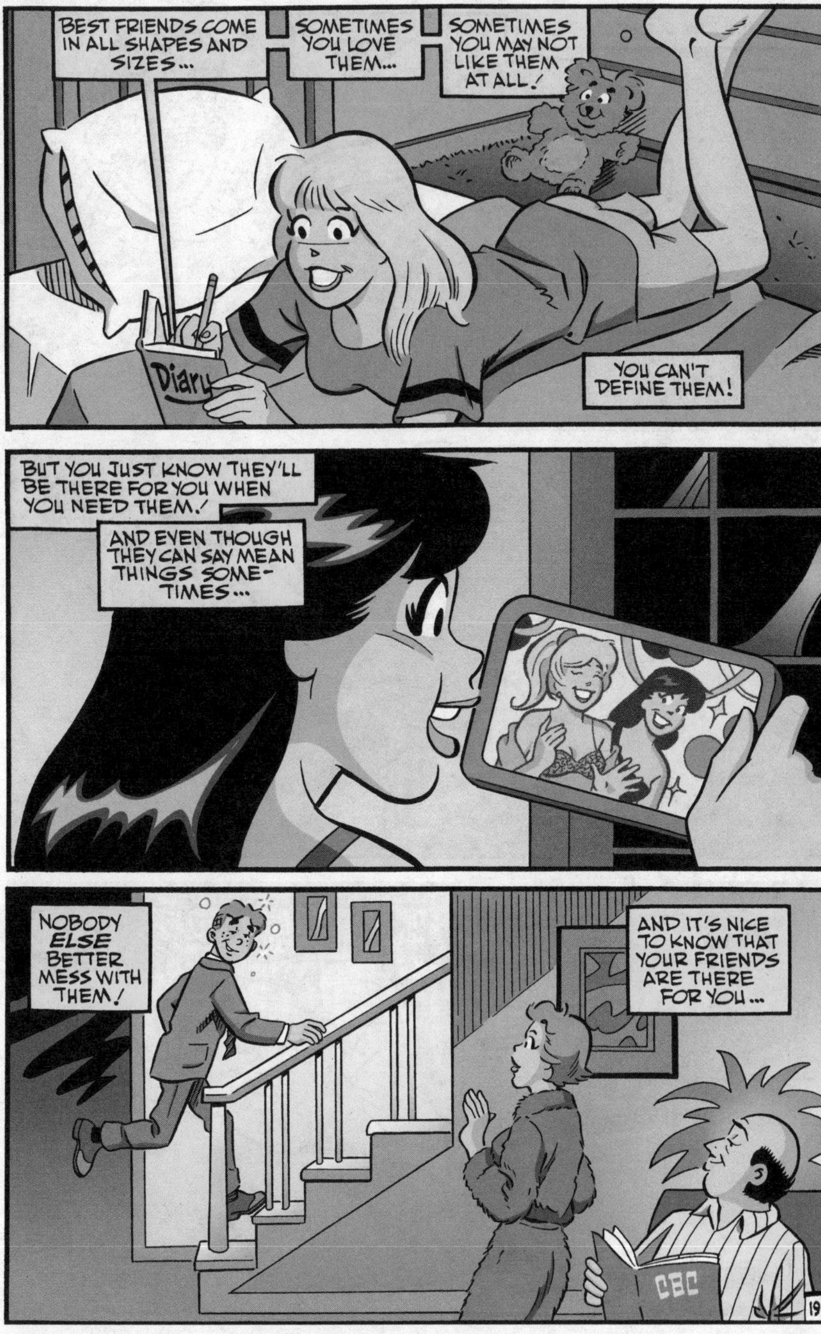
BEST FRIENDS COME IN ALL SHAPES AND SIZES...
SOMETIMES YOU LOVE THEM...
SOMETIMES YOU MAY NOT LIKE THEM AT ALL!
Diary
YOU CAN'T DEFINE THEM!
BUT YOU JUST KNOW THEY'LL BE THERE FOR YOU WHEN YOU NEED THEM!
AND EVEN THOUGH THEY CAN SAY MEAN THINGS SOME-TIMES...
NOBODY ELSE BETTER MESS WITH THEM!
AND IT'S NICE TO KNOW THAT YOUR FRIENDS ARE THERE FOR YOU...
CBC
19

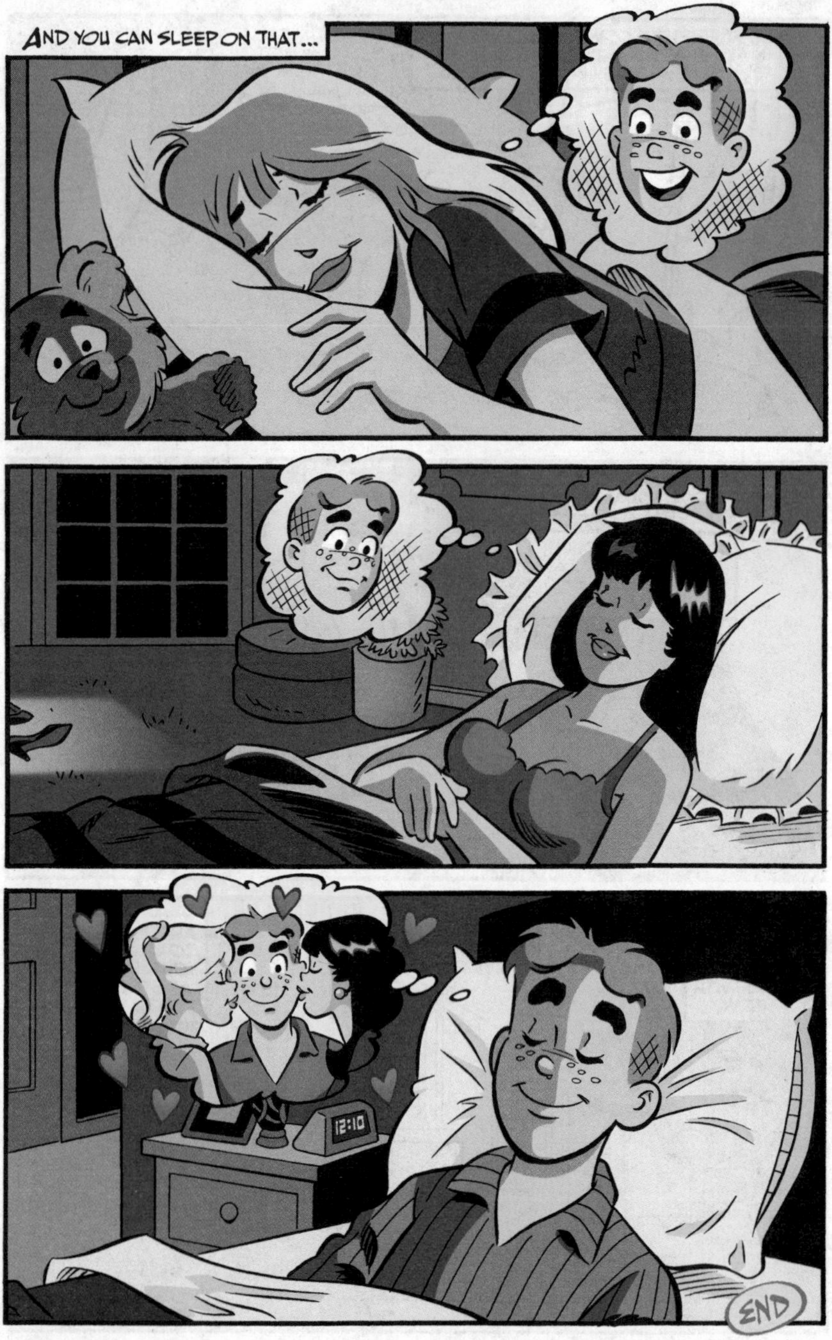
AND YOU CAN SLEEP ON THAT...
END

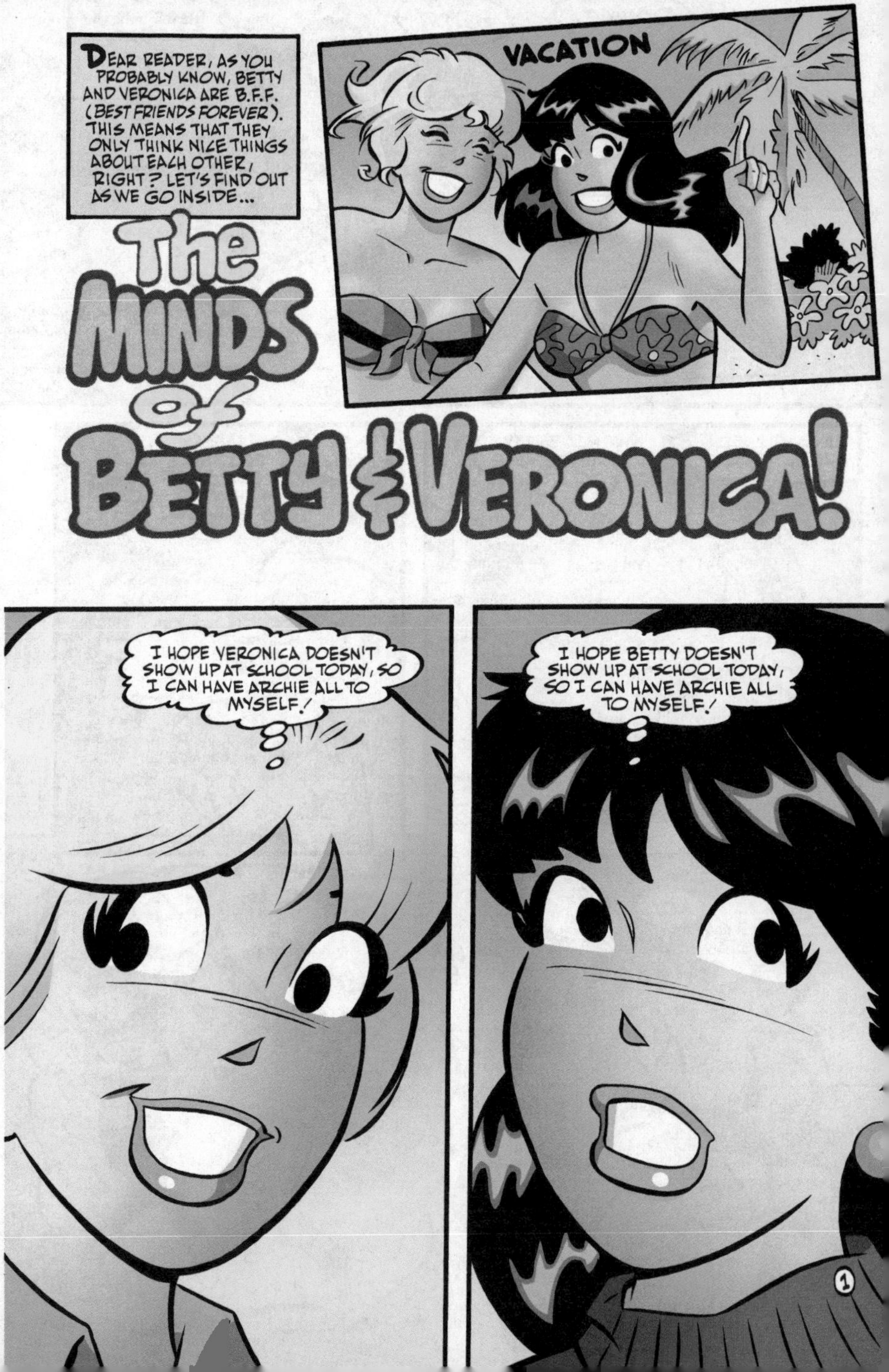
DEAR READER, AS YOU PROBABLY KNOW, BETTY AND VERONICA ARE B.F.F. (BEST FRIENDS FOREVER). THIS MEANS THAT THEY ONLY THINK NICE THINGS ABOUT EACH OTHER, RIGHT? LET'S FIND OUT AS WE GO INSIDE...
VACATION
The MINDS of BETTY & VERONICA!
I HOPE VERONICA DOESN'T SHOW UP AT SCHOOL TODAY, SO I CAN HAVE ARCHIE ALL TO MYSELF!
I HOPE BETTY DOESN'T SHOW UP AT SCHOOL TODAY, SO I CAN HAVE ARCHIE ALL TO MYSELF!
1

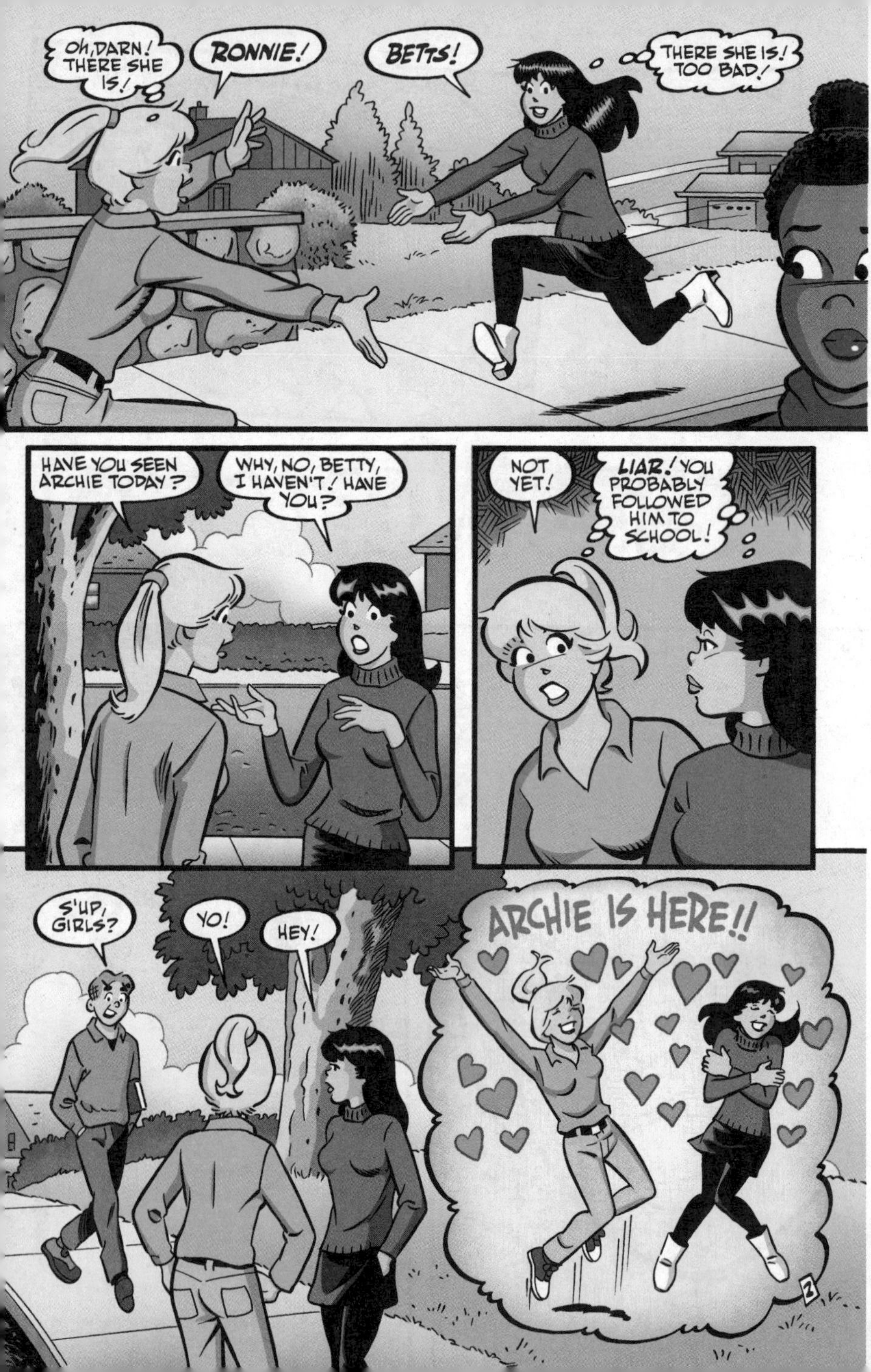

OH, DARN! THERE SHE IS!
RONNIE!
BETTS!
THERE SHE IS! TOO BAD!
HAVE YOU SEEN ARCHIE TODAY?
WHY, NO, BETTY, I HAVEN'T! HAVE YOU?
NOT YET!
LIAR! YOU PROBABLY FOLLOWED HIM TO SCHOOL!
S'UP, GIRLS?
YO!
HEY!
ARCHIE IS HERE!!
3

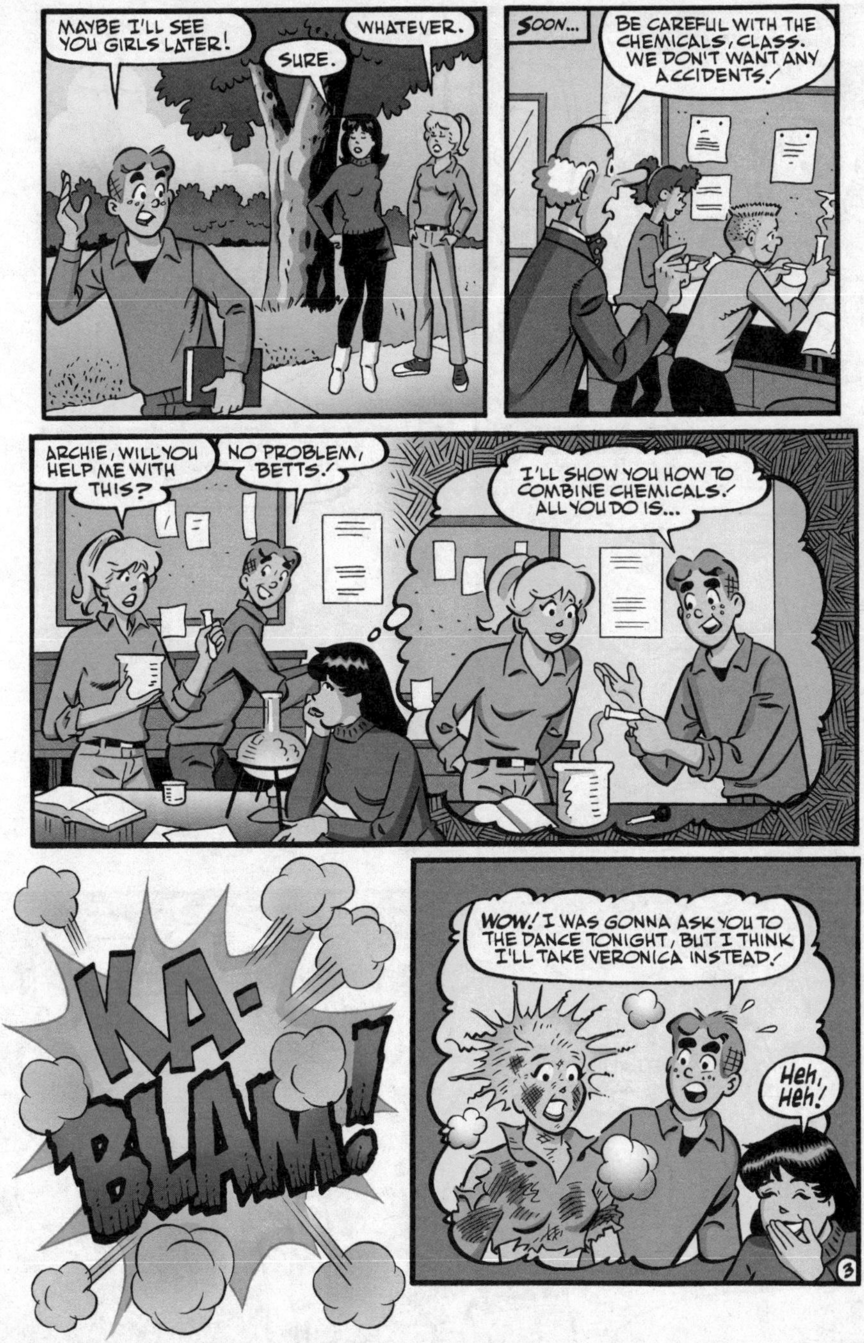
MAYBE I'LL SEE YOU GIRLS LATER!
SURE.
WHATEVER.
SOON...
BE CAREFUL WITH THE CHEMICALS, CLASS. WE DON'T WANT ANY ACCIDENTS!
ARCHIE, WILL YOU HELP ME WITH THIS?
NO PROBLEM, BETTS!
I'LL SHOW YOU HOW TO COMBINE CHEMICALS! ALL YOU DO IS...
KA-BLAM!
WOW! I WAS GONNA ASK YOU TO THE DANCE TONIGHT, BUT I THINK I'LL TAKE VERONICA INSTEAD!
Heh, Heh!
3

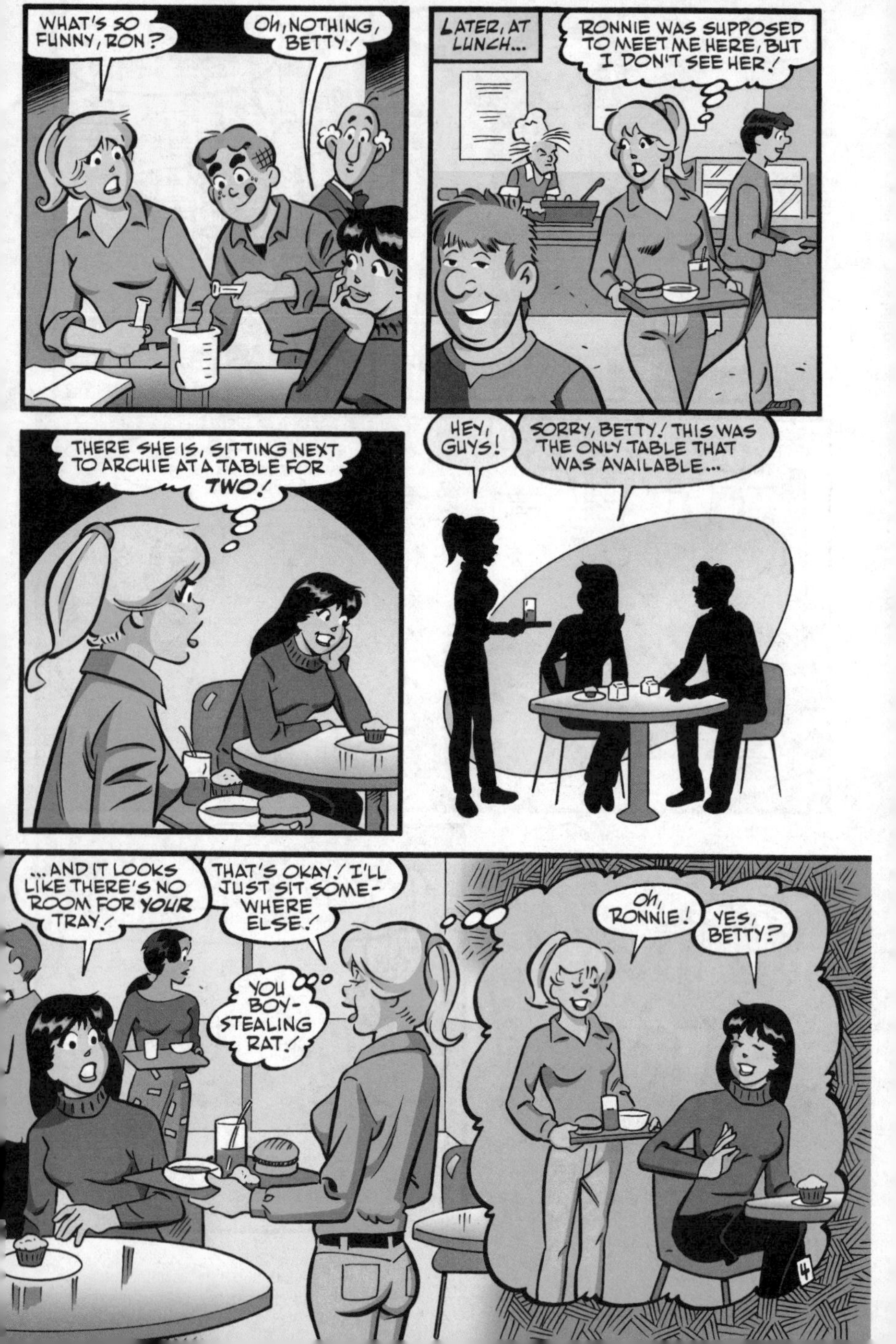

WHAT'S SO FUNNY, RON?
Oh, NOTHING, BETTY!
LATER, AT LUNCH...
RONNIE WAS SUPPOSED TO MEET ME HERE, BUT I DON'T SEE HER!
THERE SHE IS, SITTING NEXT TO ARCHIE AT A TABLE FOR TWO!
HEY, GUYS!
SORRY, BETTY! THIS WAS THE ONLY TABLE THAT WAS AVAILABLE...
...AND IT LOOKS LIKE THERE'S NO ROOM FOR YOUR TRAY!
THAT'S OKAY! I'LL JUST SIT SOME-WHERE ELSE!
YOU BOY-STEALING RAT!
Oh, RONNIE!
YES, BETTY?
4

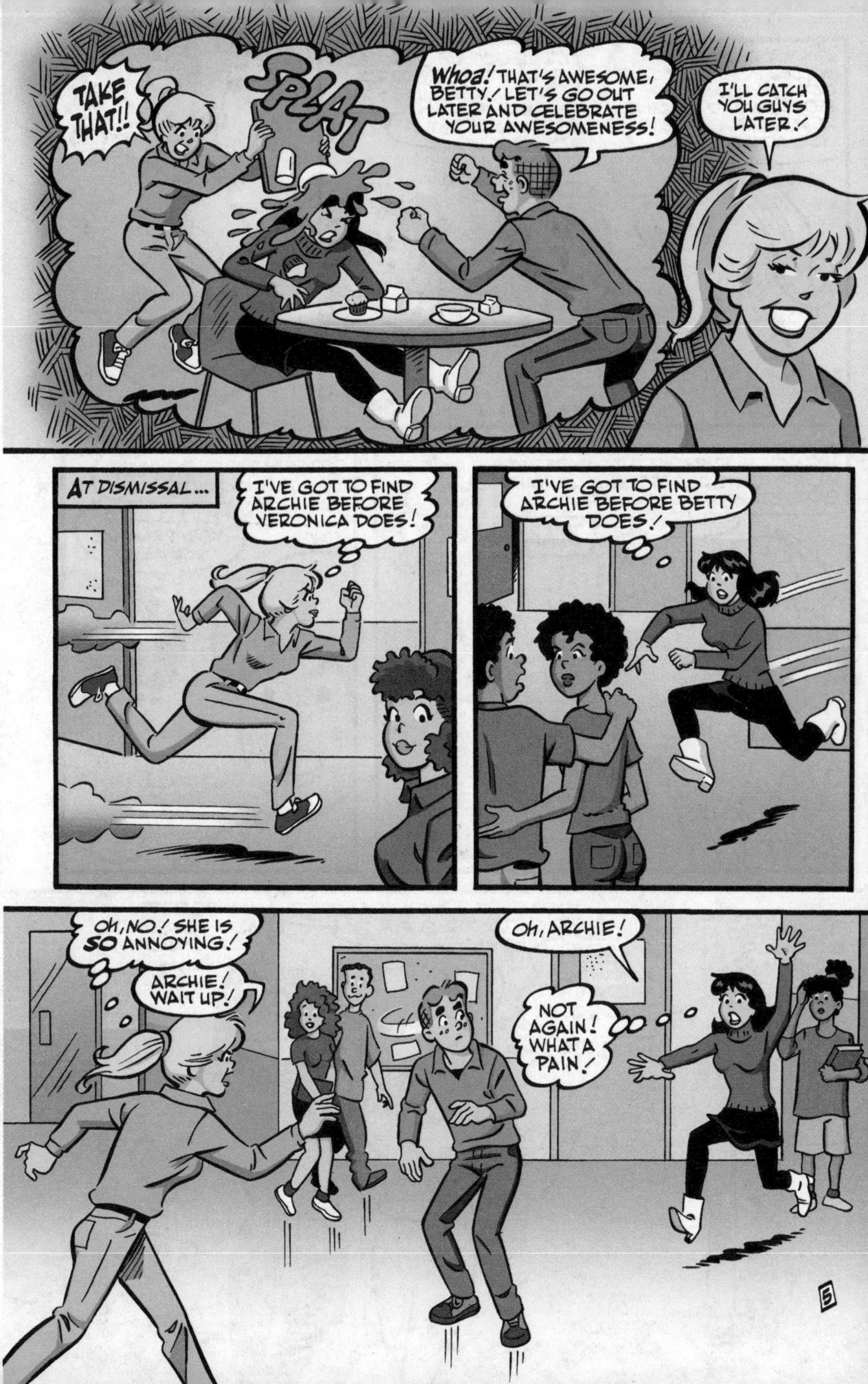

TAKE THAT!!
SPLAT
Whoa! THAT'S AWESOME, BETTY! LET'S GO OUT LATER AND CELEBRATE YOUR AWESOMENESS!
I'LL CATCH YOU GUYS LATER!
AT DISMISSAL...
I'VE GOT TO FIND ARCHIE BEFORE VERONICA DOES!
I'VE GOT TO FIND ARCHIE BEFORE BETTY DOES!
OH, NO! SHE IS SO ANNOYING!
ARCHIE! WAIT UP!
OH, ARCHIE!
NOT AGAIN! WHAT A PAIN!

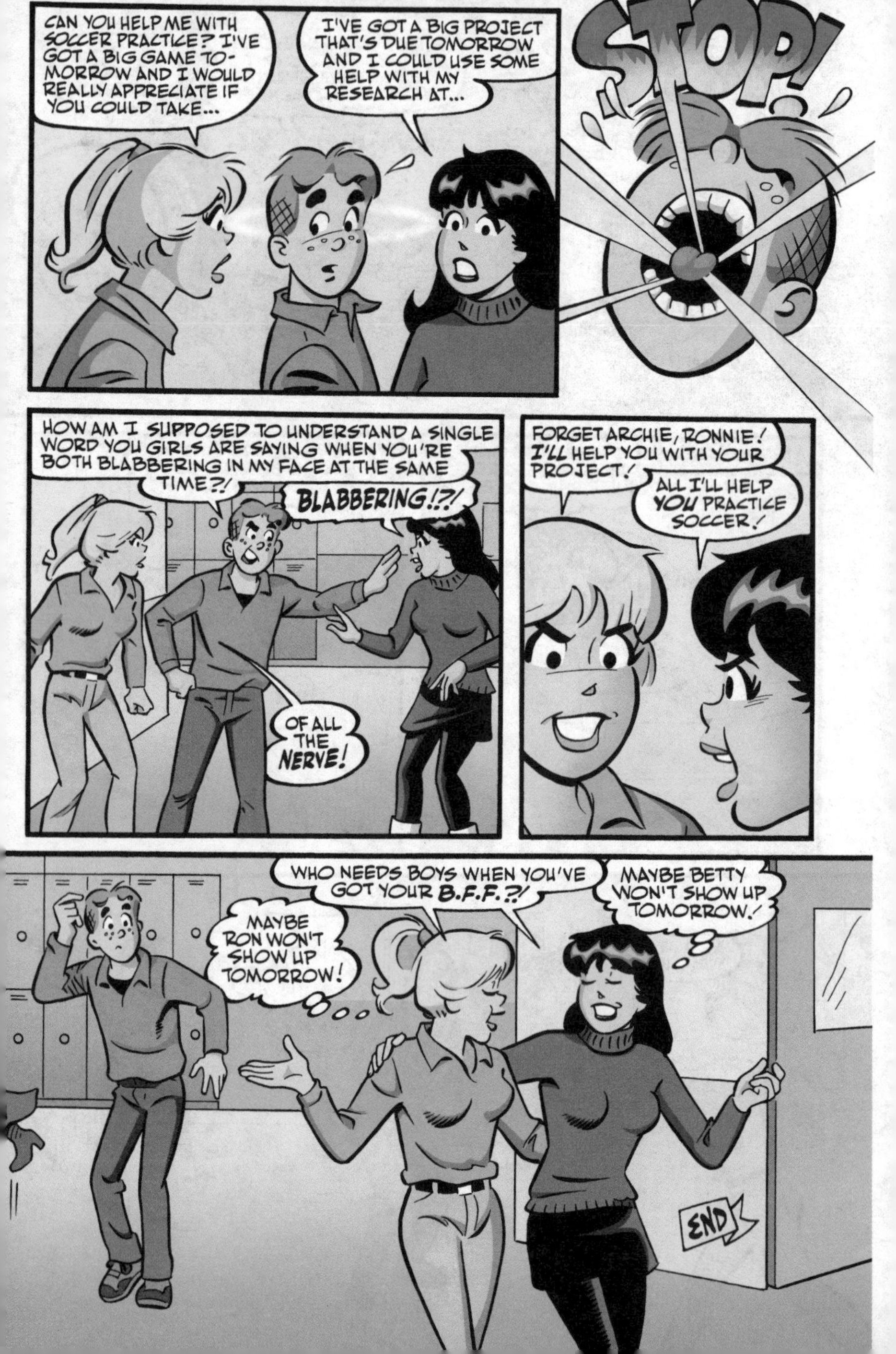
CAN YOU HELP ME WITH SOCCER PRACTICE? I'VE GOT A BIG GAME TO-MORROW AND I WOULD REALLY APPRECIATE IF YOU COULD TAKE...
I'VE GOT A BIG PROJECT THAT'S DUE TOMORROW AND I COULD USE SOME HELP WITH MY RESEARCH AT...
STOP!
HOW AM I SUPPOSED TO UNDERSTAND A SINGLE WORD YOU GIRLS ARE SAYING WHEN YOU'RE BOTH BLABBERING IN MY FACE AT THE SAME TIME?!
BLABBERING!?!
OF ALL THE NERVE!
FORGET ARCHIE, RONNIE! I'LL HELP YOU WITH YOUR PROJECT!
ALL I'LL HELP YOU PRACTICE SOCCER!
WHO NEEDS BOYS WHEN YOU'VE GOT YOUR B.F.F.?!
MAYBE RON WON'T SHOW UP TOMORROW!
MAYBE BETTY WON'T SHOW UP TOMORROW!
END

ARCHIE #2 COVER
ARCHIE #2, 2015
Fiona Staples

ARCHIE #3
ARCHIE #3, 2015
Mark Waid, Fiona Staples, Jack Morelli, Andre Szymanowicz, Jen Vaughn

The new Archie (Mark Waid, Fiona Staples) is my fave! Seeing Betty and Veronica as drawn by Fiona Staples took them from classic pop culture icons to girls I felt like I really KNEW. I'm a Veronica, for sure, but I love to befriend Betties!

- TINI HOWARD Writer

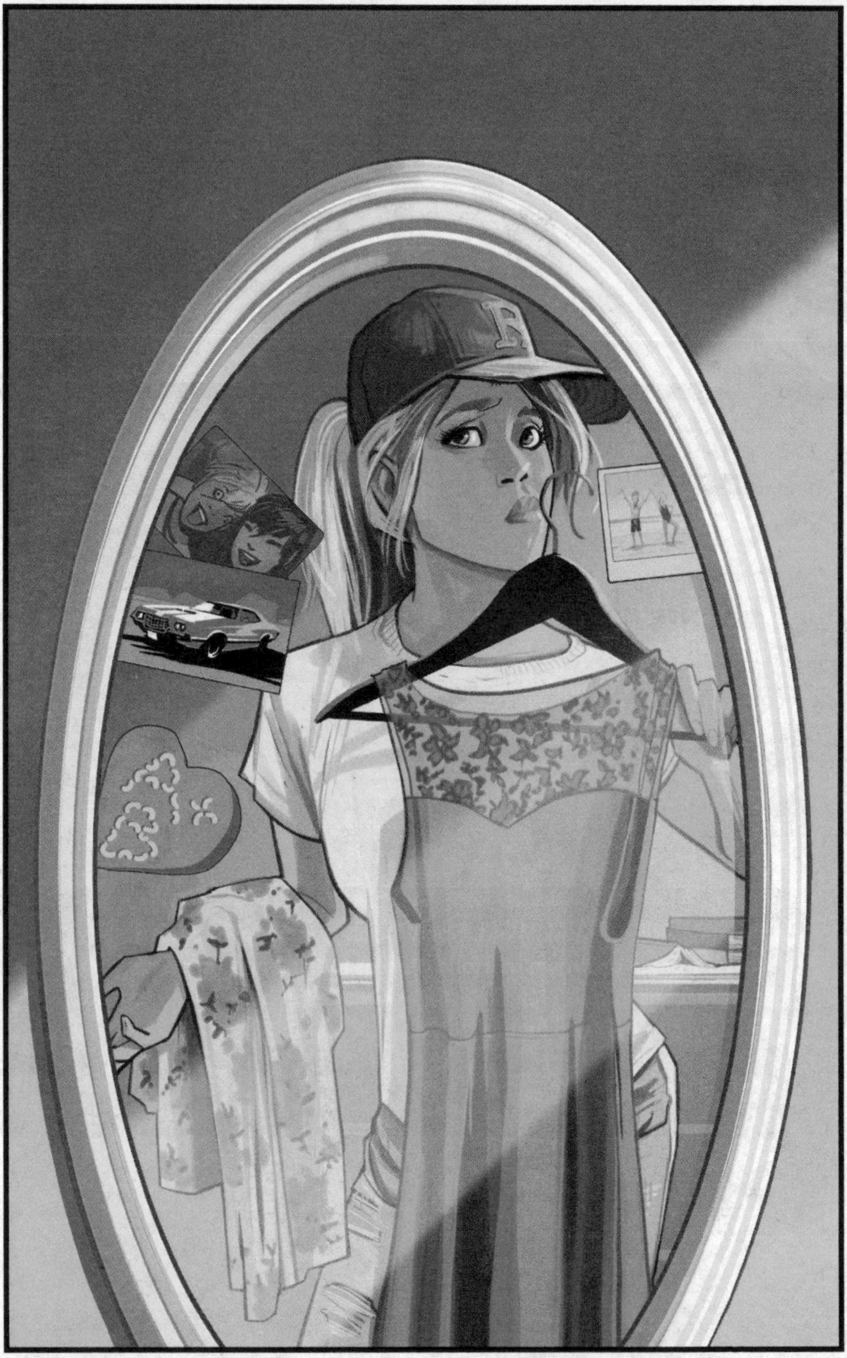

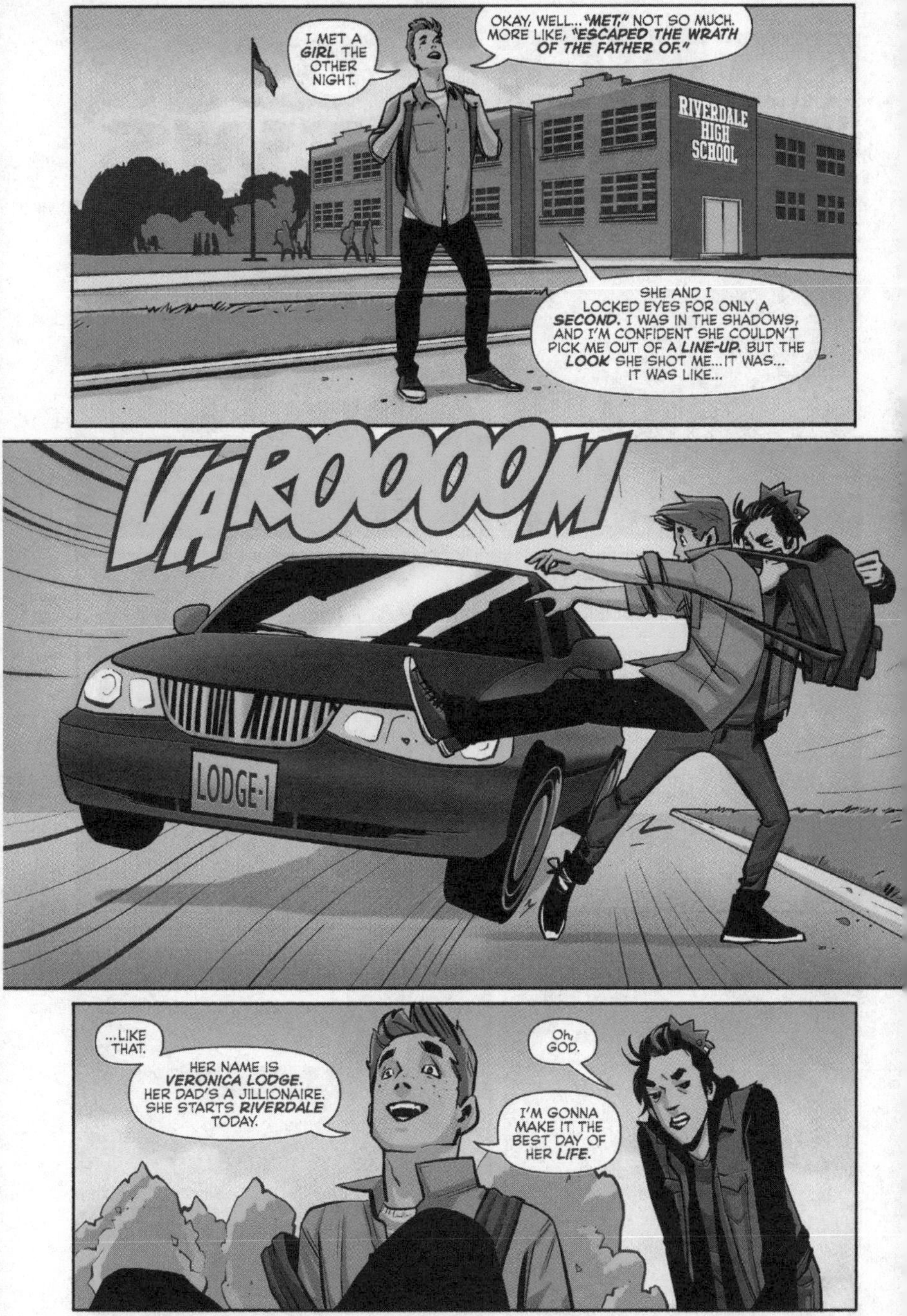
I MET A GIRL THE OTHER NIGHT.
OKAY, WELL... "MET," NOT SO MUCH. MORE LIKE, "ESCAPED THE WRATH OF THE FATHER OF."
RIVERDALE HIGH SCHOOL
SHE AND I LOCKED EYES FOR ONLY A SECOND. I WAS IN THE SHADOWS, AND I'M CONFIDENT SHE COULDN'T PICK ME OUT OF A LINE-UP. BUT THE LOOK SHE SHOT ME...IT WAS... IT WAS LIKE...
VAROOOOM
LODGE-1
...LIKE THAT.
HER NAME IS VERONICA LODGE. HER DAD'S A JILLIONAIRE. SHE STARTS RIVERDALE TODAY.
Oh, GOD.
I'M GONNA MAKE IT THE BEST DAY OF HER LIFE.

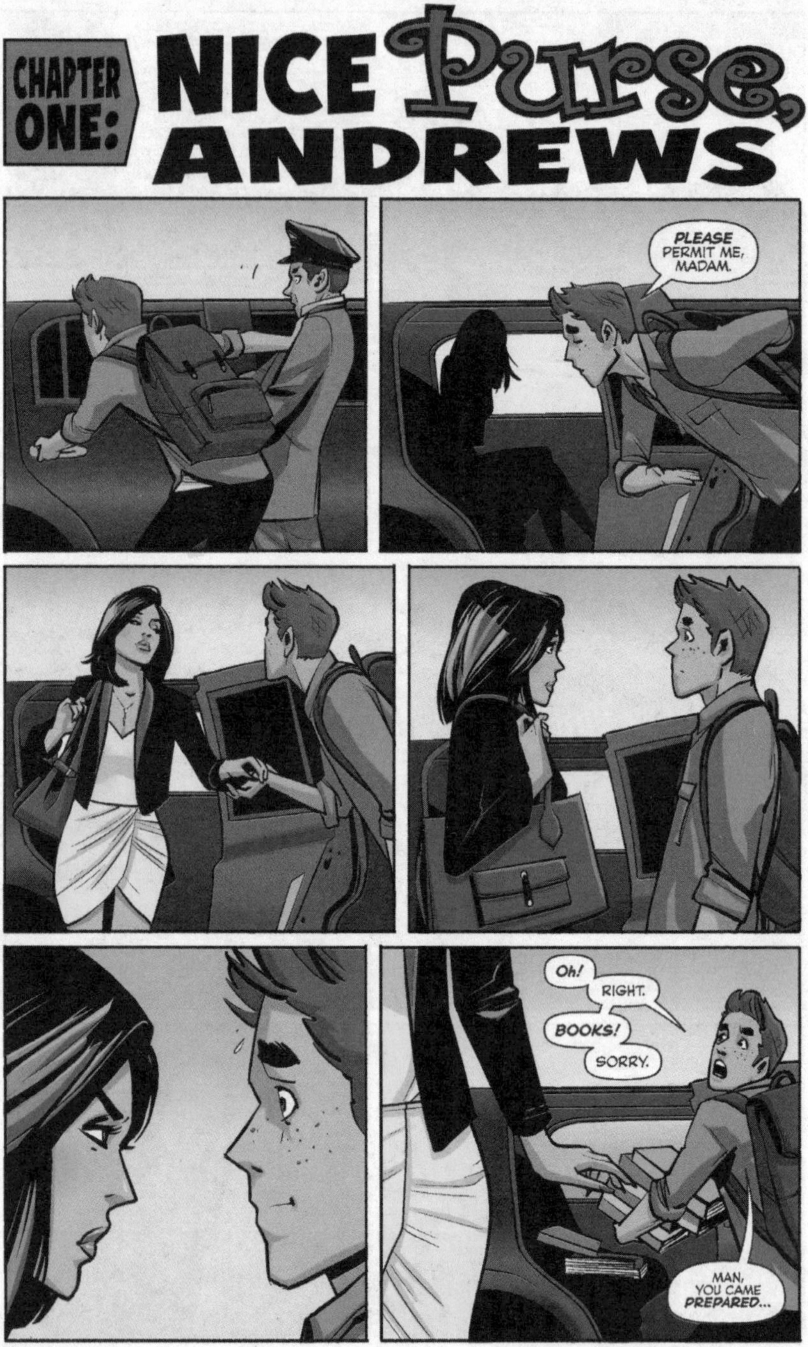
CHAPTER ONE:
NICE Purse, ANDREWS
PLEASE PERMIT ME, MADAM.
Oh!
RIGHT.
BOOKS!
SORRY.
MAN, YOU CAME PREPARED...

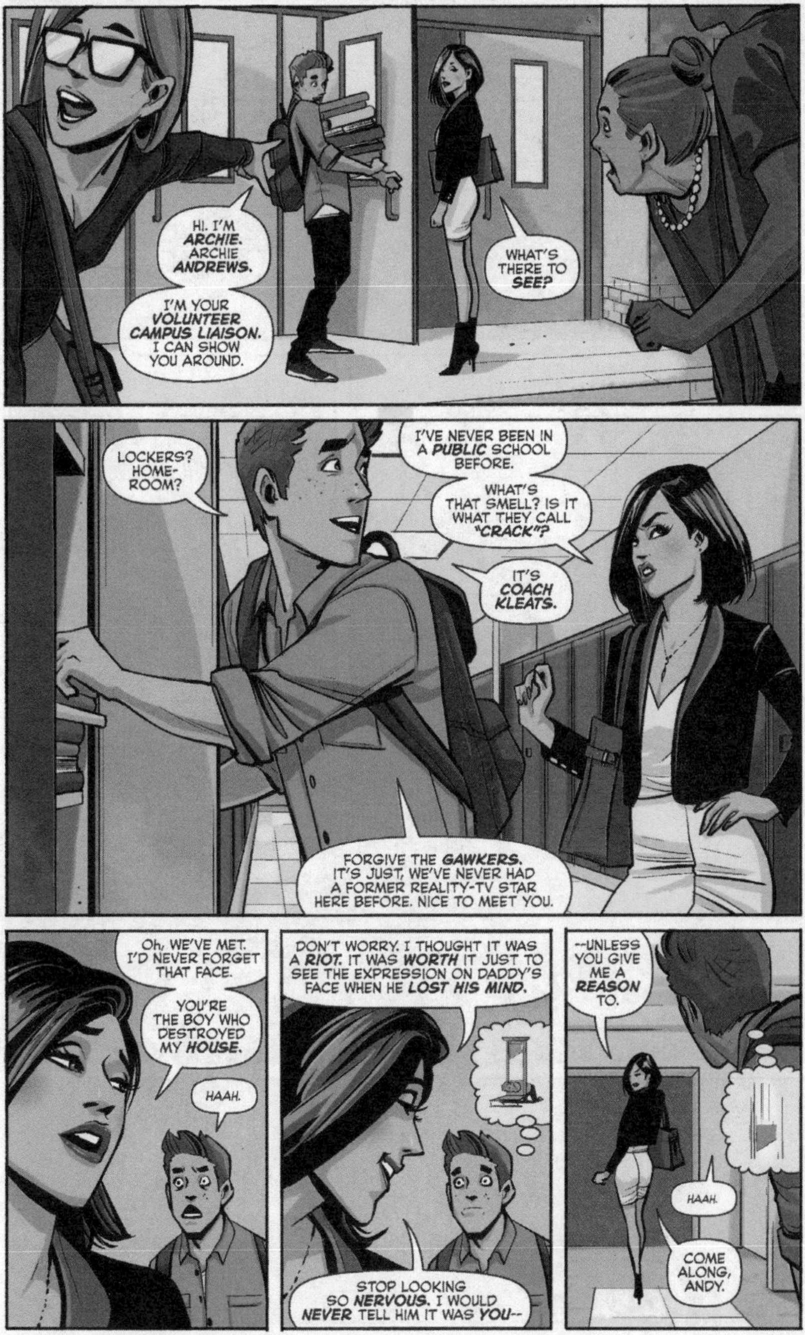
HI. I'M ARCHIE. ARCHIE ANDREWS.
I'M YOUR VOLUNTEER CAMPUS LIAISON. I CAN SHOW YOU AROUND.
WHAT'S THERE TO SEE?
LOCKERS? HOME-ROOM?
I'VE NEVER BEEN IN A PUBLIC SCHOOL BEFORE.
WHAT'S THAT SMELL? IS IT WHAT THEY CALL "CRACK"?
IT'S COACH KLEATS.
FORGIVE THE GAWKERS. IT'S JUST, WE'VE NEVER HAD A FORMER REALITY-TV STAR HERE BEFORE. NICE TO MEET YOU.
Oh, WE'VE MET. I'D NEVER FORGET THAT FACE.
YOU'RE THE BOY WHO DESTROYED MY HOUSE.
HAAH.
DON'T WORRY. I THOUGHT IT WAS A RIOT. IT WAS WORTH IT JUST TO SEE THE EXPRESSION ON DADDY'S FACE WHEN HE LOST HIS MIND.
STOP LOOKING SO NERVOUS. I WOULD NEVER TELL HIM IT WAS YOU--
--UNLESS YOU GIVE ME A REASON TO.
HAAH.
COME ALONG, ANDY.

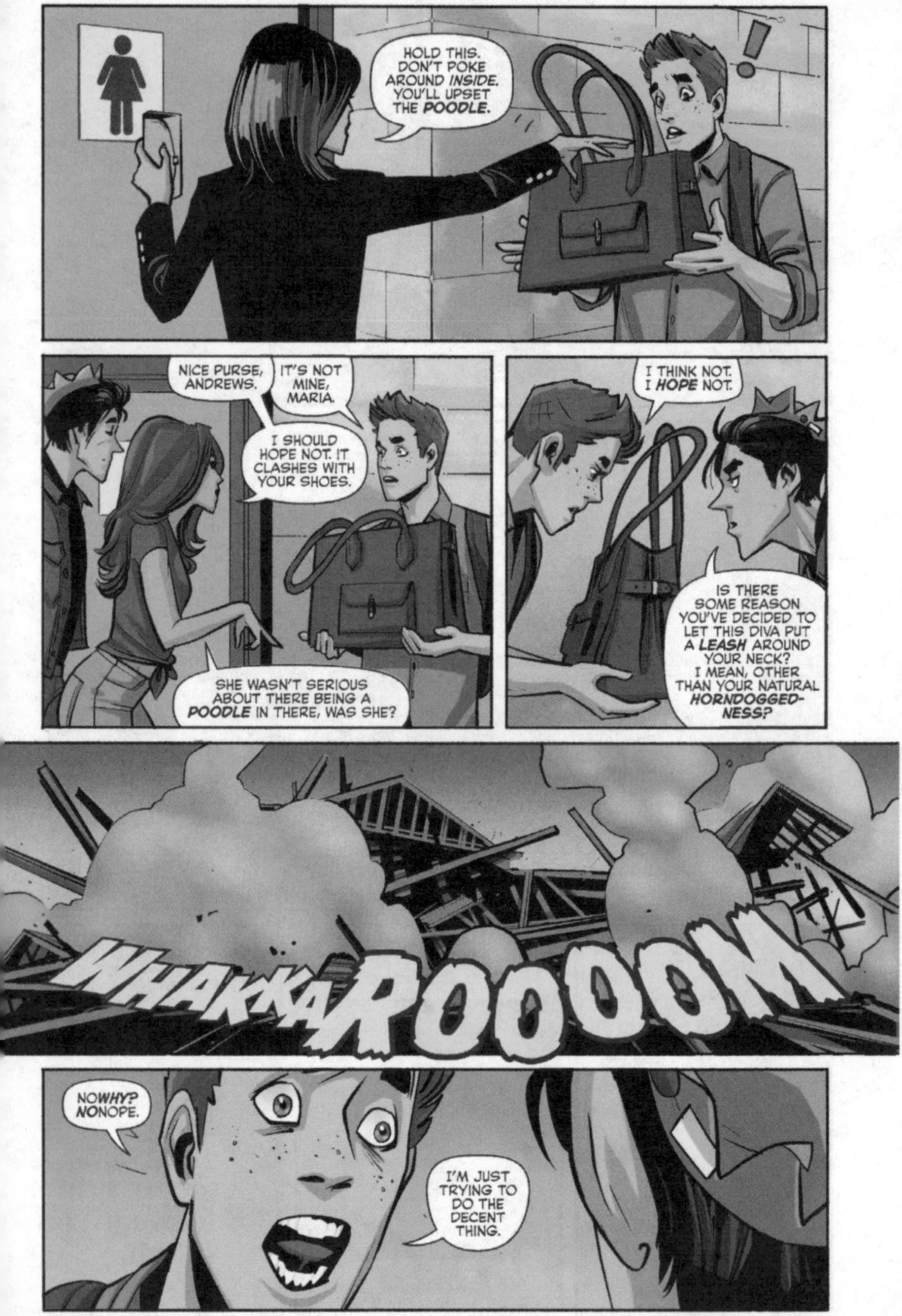
HOLD THIS. DON'T POKE AROUND *INSIDE*. YOU'LL UPSET THE *POODLE*.
!
NICE PURSE, ANDREWS.
IT'S NOT MINE, MARIA.
I SHOULD HOPE NOT. IT CLASHES WITH YOUR SHOES.
SHE WASN'T SERIOUS ABOUT THERE BEING A *POODLE* IN THERE, WAS SHE?
I THINK NOT. I *HOPE* NOT.
IS THERE SOME REASON YOU'VE DECIDED TO LET THIS DIVA PUT A *LEASH* AROUND YOUR NECK? I MEAN, OTHER THAN YOUR NATURAL *HORNDOGGEDNESS?*
WHAKKAROOOOM
NO*WHY?* *NO*NOPE.
I'M JUST TRYING TO DO THE DECENT THING.

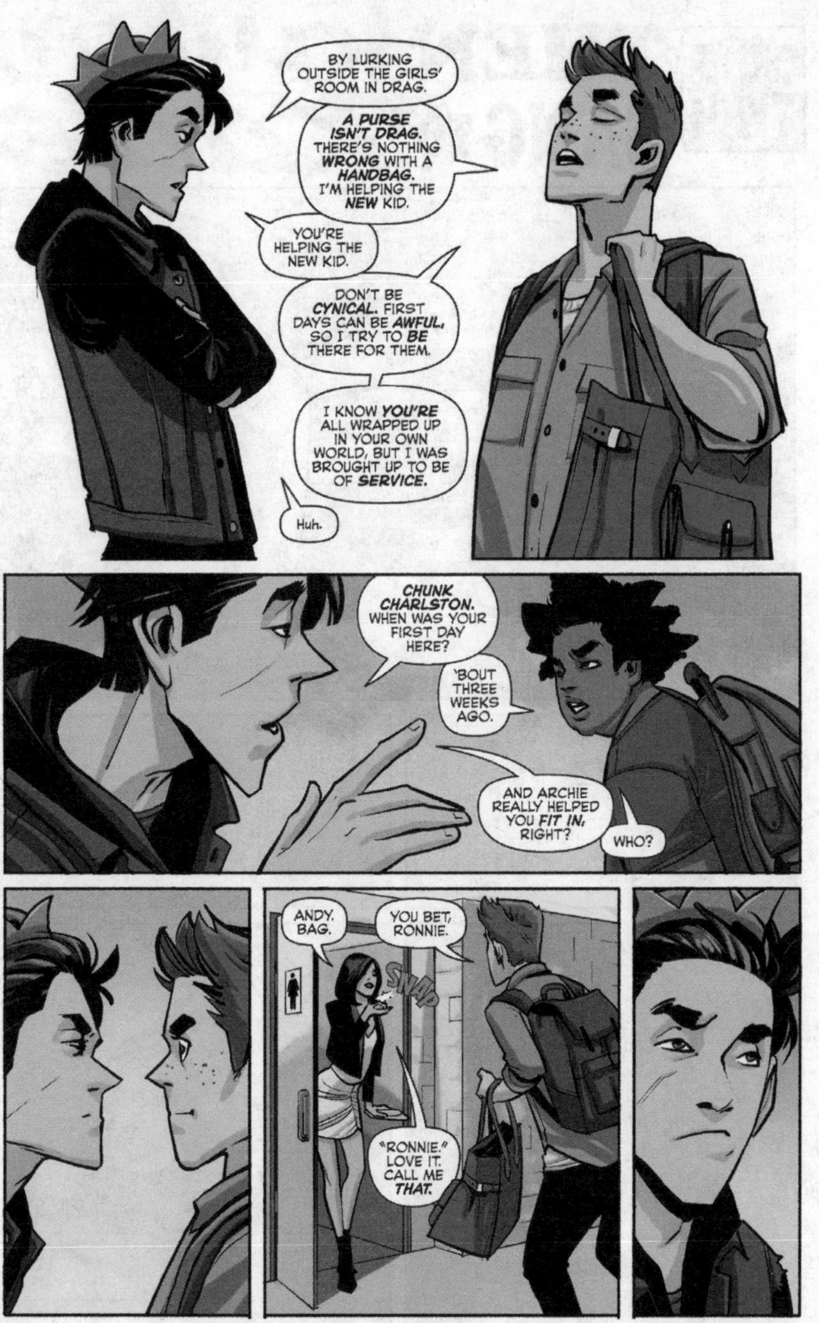
BY LURKING OUTSIDE THE GIRLS' ROOM IN DRAG.
A PURSE ISN'T DRAG. THERE'S NOTHING *WRONG* WITH A *HANDBAG.* I'M HELPING THE *NEW* KID.
YOU'RE HELPING THE NEW KID.
DON'T BE *CYNICAL.* FIRST DAYS CAN BE *AWFUL,* SO I TRY TO *BE* THERE FOR THEM.
I KNOW *YOU'RE* ALL WRAPPED UP IN YOUR OWN WORLD, BUT I WAS BROUGHT UP TO BE OF *SERVICE.*
Huh.
CHUNK CHARLSTON. WHEN WAS YOUR FIRST DAY HERE?
'BOUT THREE WEEKS AGO.
AND ARCHIE REALLY HELPED YOU *FIT IN,* RIGHT?
WHO?
ANDY. BAG.
YOU BET, RONNIE.
SNAP
"RONNIE." LOVE IT. CALL ME *THAT.*

CHAPTER TWO: THEN SANG TO Taylor Katie

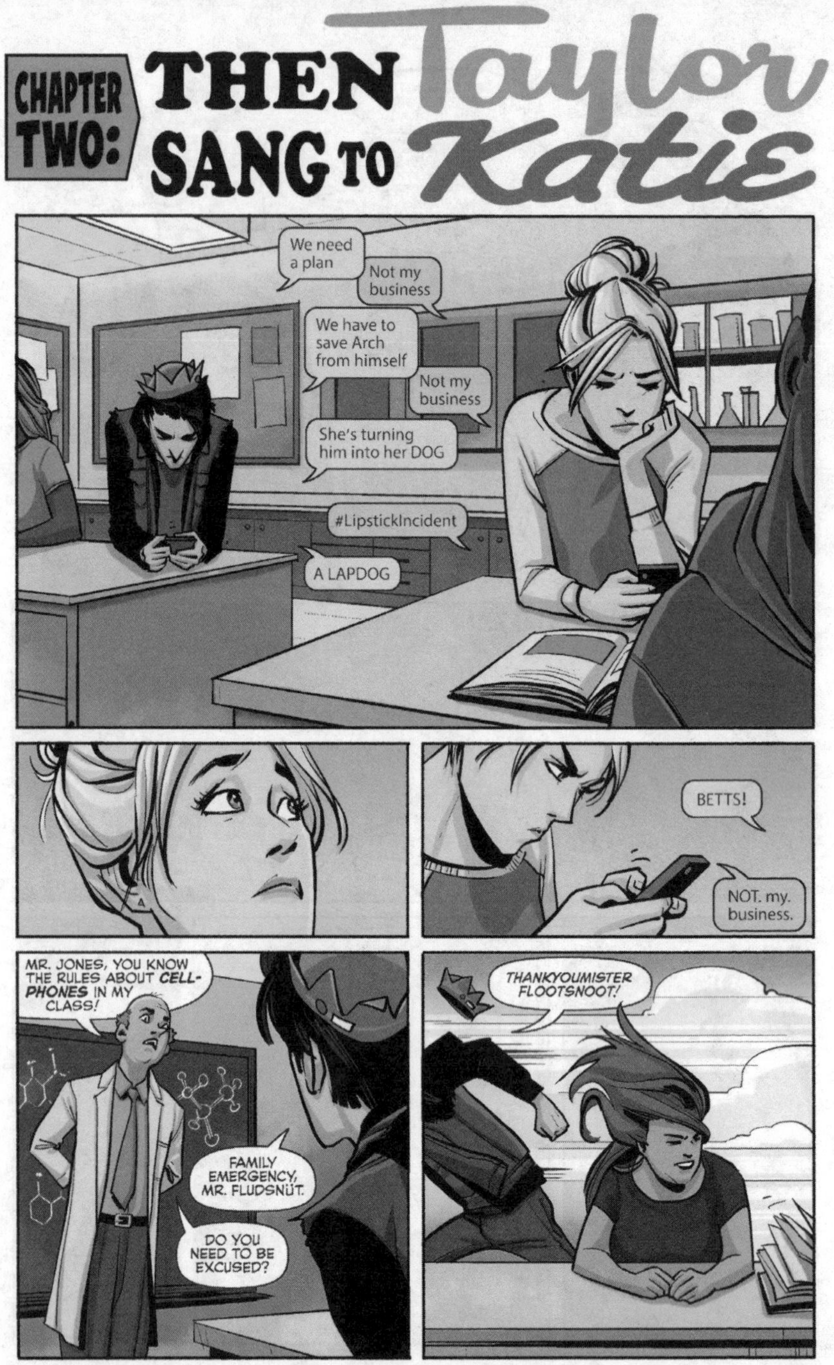
We need a plan
Not my business
We have to save Arch from himself
Not my business
She's turning him into her DOG
#LipstickIncident
A LAPDOG
BETTS!
NOT. my. business.
MR. JONES, YOU KNOW THE RULES ABOUT CELL-PHONES IN MY CLASS!
FAMILY EMERGENCY, MR. FLUDSNÜT.
DO YOU NEED TO BE EXCUSED?
THANKYOUMISTER FLOOTSNOOT!

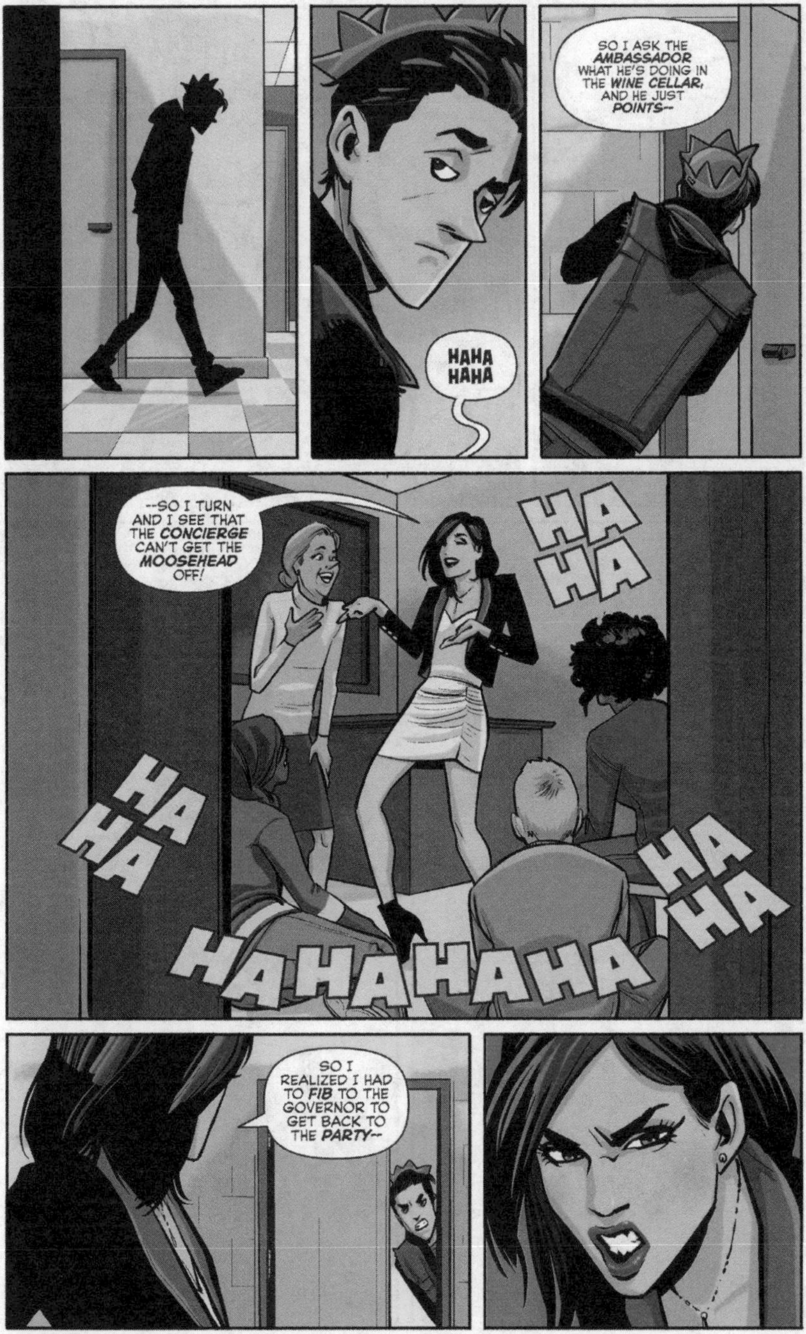
HAHA HAHA
SO I ASK THE AMBASSADOR WHAT HE'S DOING IN THE WINE CELLAR, AND HE JUST POINTS--
--SO I TURN AND I SEE THAT THE CONCIERGE CAN'T GET THE MOOSEHEAD OFF!
HA HA HA HA
HA HA HA
HA HA HA
HAHAHAHAHAHA
SO I REALIZED I HAD TO FIB TO THE GOVERNOR TO GET BACK TO THE PARTY--

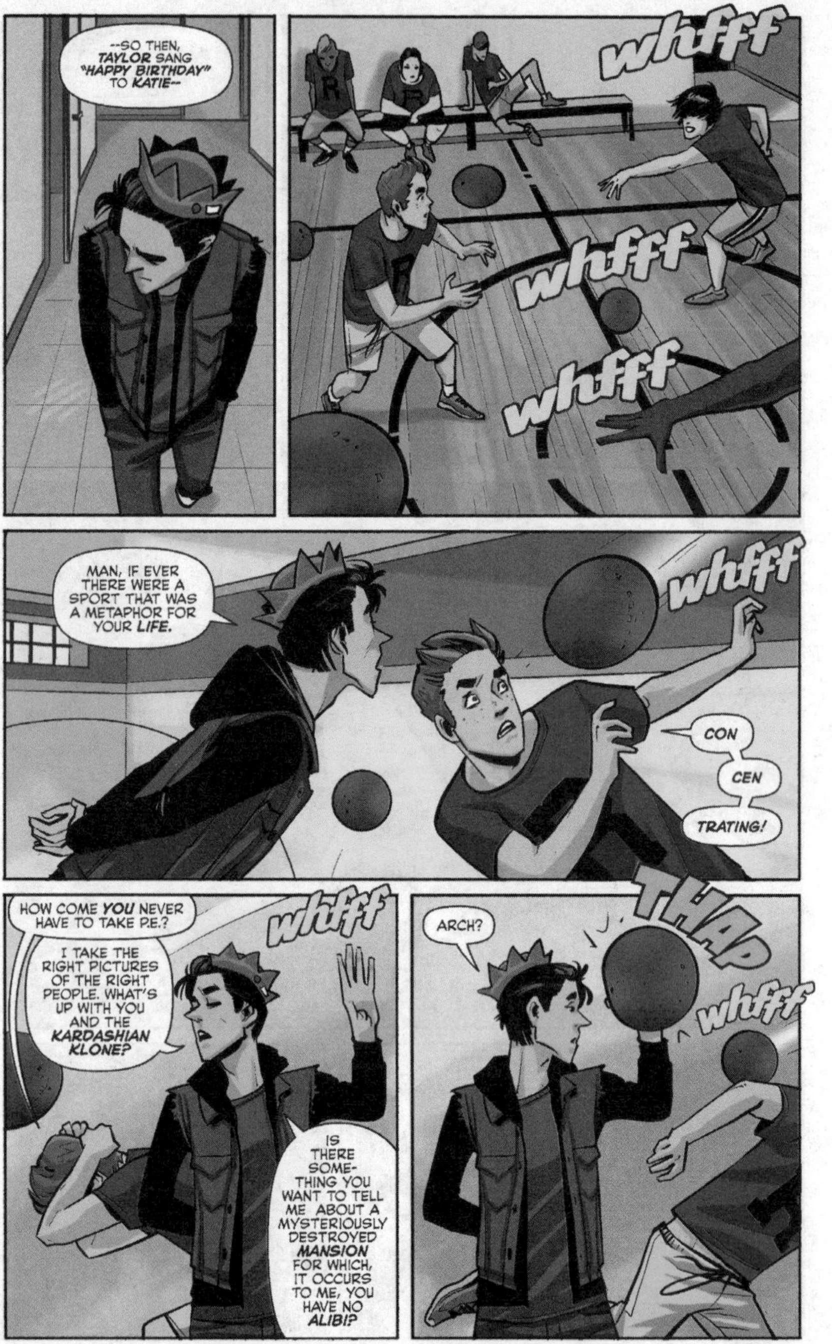
--SO THEN, TAYLOR SANG "HAPPY BIRTHDAY" TO KATIE--
whfff
whfff
whfff
MAN, IF EVER THERE WERE A SPORT THAT WAS A METAPHOR FOR YOUR LIFE.
whfff
CON
CEN
TRATING!
HOW COME YOU NEVER HAVE TO TAKE P.E.?
whfff
I TAKE THE RIGHT PICTURES OF THE RIGHT PEOPLE. WHAT'S UP WITH YOU AND THE KARDASHIAN KLONE?
IS THERE SOME-THING YOU WANT TO TELL ME ABOUT A MYSTERIOUSLY DESTROYED MANSION FOR WHICH, IT OCCURS TO ME, YOU HAVE NO ALIBI?
THAP
ARCH?
whfff

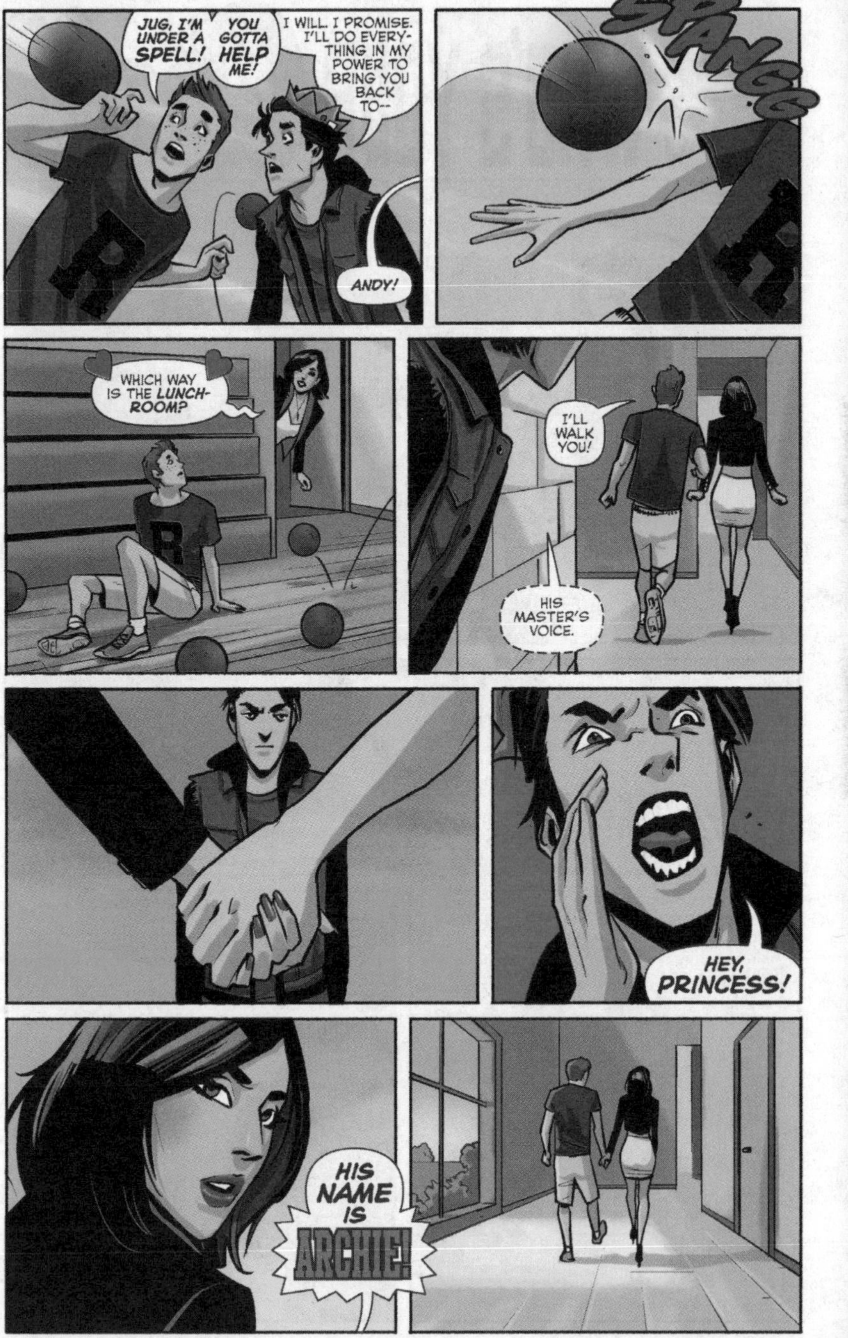
JUG, I'M UNDER A SPELL!
YOU GOTTA HELP ME!
I WILL. I PROMISE. I'LL DO EVERYTHING IN MY POWER TO BRING YOU BACK TO--
ANDY!
SPANGG
WHICH WAY IS THE LUNCHROOM?
I'LL WALK YOU!
HIS MASTER'S VOICE.
HEY, PRINCESS!
HIS NAME IS ARCHIE!

CHAPTER THREE: WHO'S YOUR Chef?

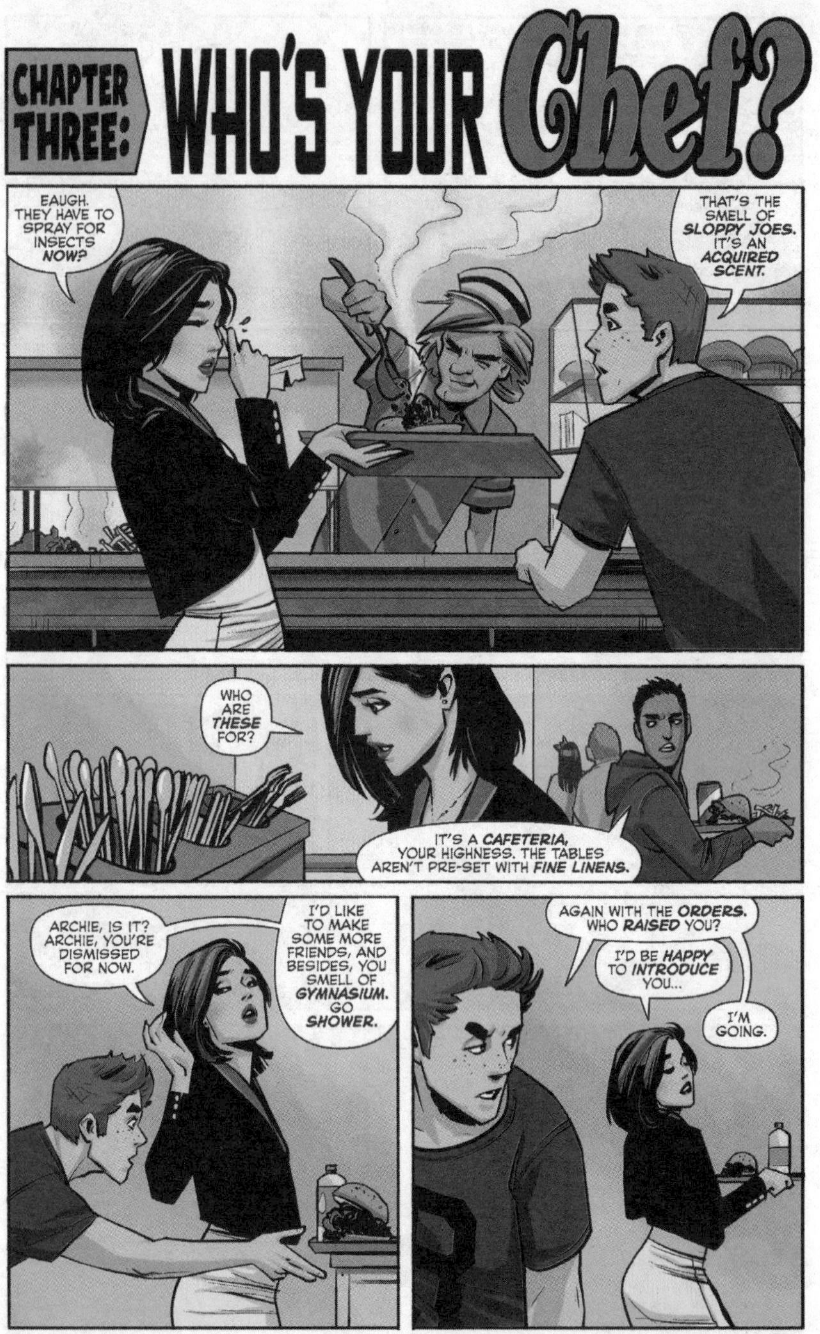
EAUGH. THEY HAVE TO SPRAY FOR INSECTS NOW?
THAT'S THE SMELL OF SLOPPY JOES. IT'S AN ACQUIRED SCENT.
WHO ARE THESE FOR?
IT'S A CAFETERIA, YOUR HIGHNESS. THE TABLES AREN'T PRE-SET WITH FINE LINENS.
ARCHIE, IS IT? ARCHIE, YOU'RE DISMISSED FOR NOW.
I'D LIKE TO MAKE SOME MORE FRIENDS, AND BESIDES, YOU SMELL OF GYMNASIUM. GO SHOWER.
AGAIN WITH THE ORDERS. WHO RAISED YOU?
I'D BE HAPPY TO INTRODUCE YOU...
I'M GOING.

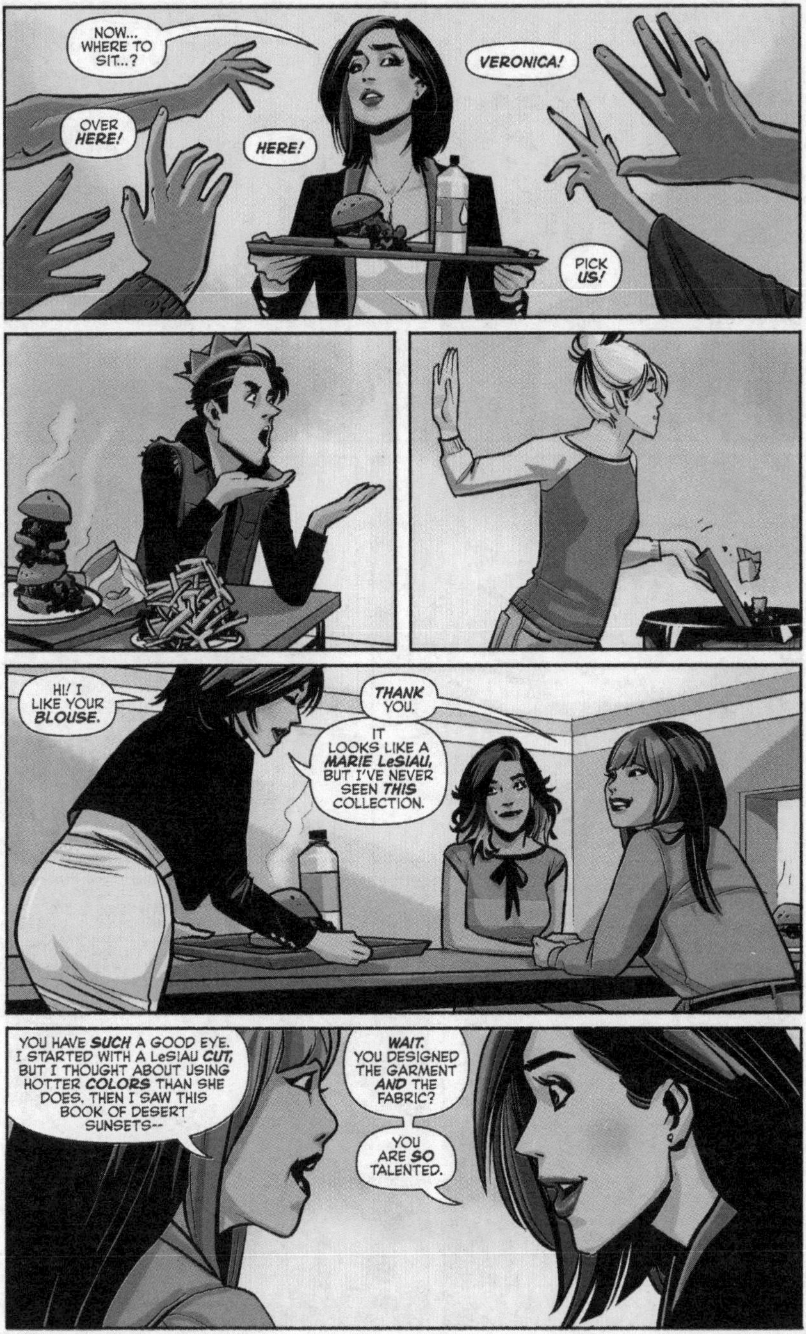
NOW... WHERE TO SIT...?
VERONICA!
OVER HERE!
HERE!
PICK US!
HI! I LIKE YOUR BLOUSE.
THANK YOU.
IT LOOKS LIKE A MARIE LeSIAU, BUT I'VE NEVER SEEN THIS COLLECTION.
YOU HAVE SUCH A GOOD EYE. I STARTED WITH A LeSIAU CUT, BUT I THOUGHT ABOUT USING HOTTER COLORS THAN SHE DOES. THEN I SAW THIS BOOK OF DESERT SUNSETS--
WAIT. YOU DESIGNED THE GARMENT AND THE FABRIC?
YOU ARE SO TALENTED.

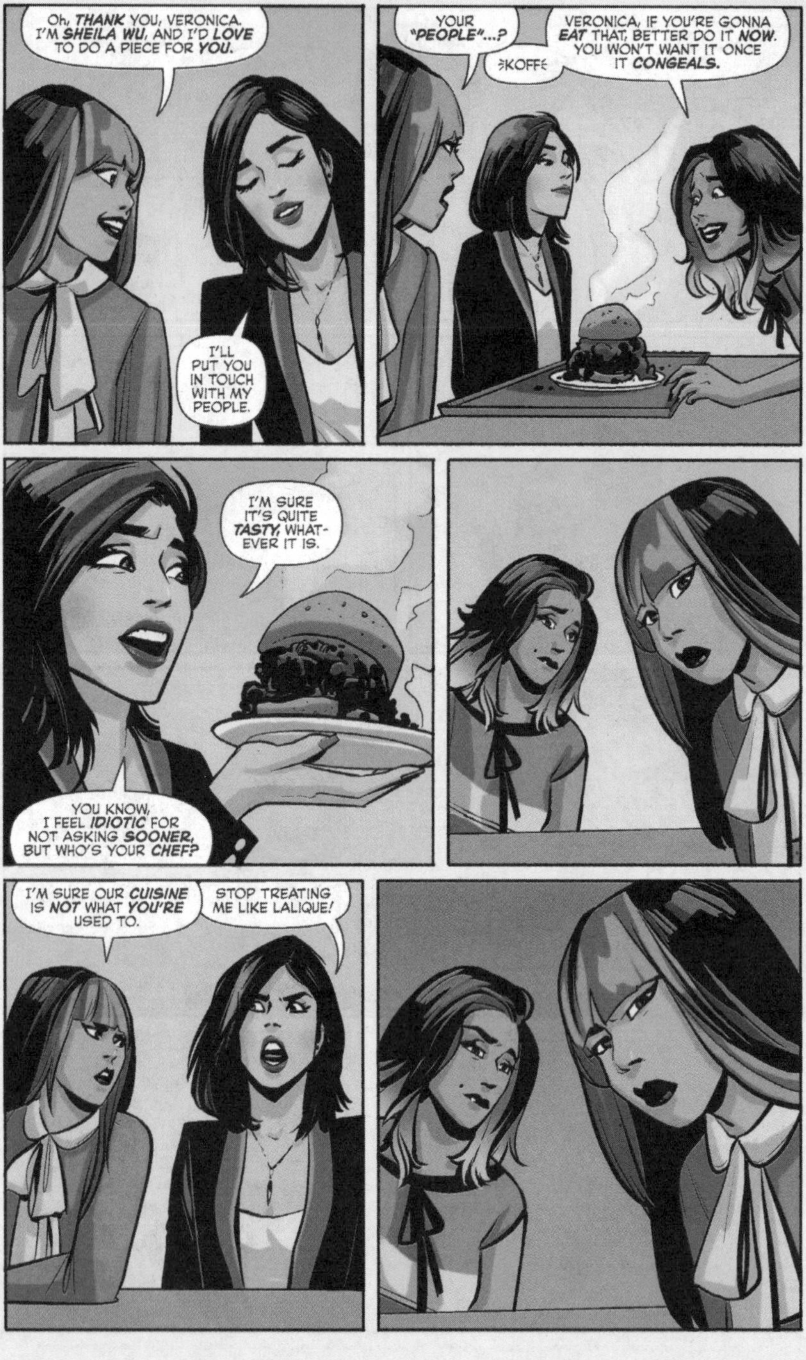
Oh, THANK YOU, VERONICA. I'M SHEILA WU, AND I'D LOVE TO DO A PIECE FOR YOU.
I'LL PUT YOU IN TOUCH WITH MY PEOPLE.
YOUR "PEOPLE"...?
KOFF
VERONICA, IF YOU'RE GONNA EAT THAT, BETTER DO IT NOW. YOU WON'T WANT IT ONCE IT CONGEALS.
I'M SURE IT'S QUITE TASTY, WHATEVER IT IS.
YOU KNOW, I FEEL IDIOTIC FOR NOT ASKING SOONER, BUT WHO'S YOUR CHEF?
I'M SURE OUR CUISINE IS NOT WHAT YOU'RE USED TO.
STOP TREATING ME LIKE LALIQUE!

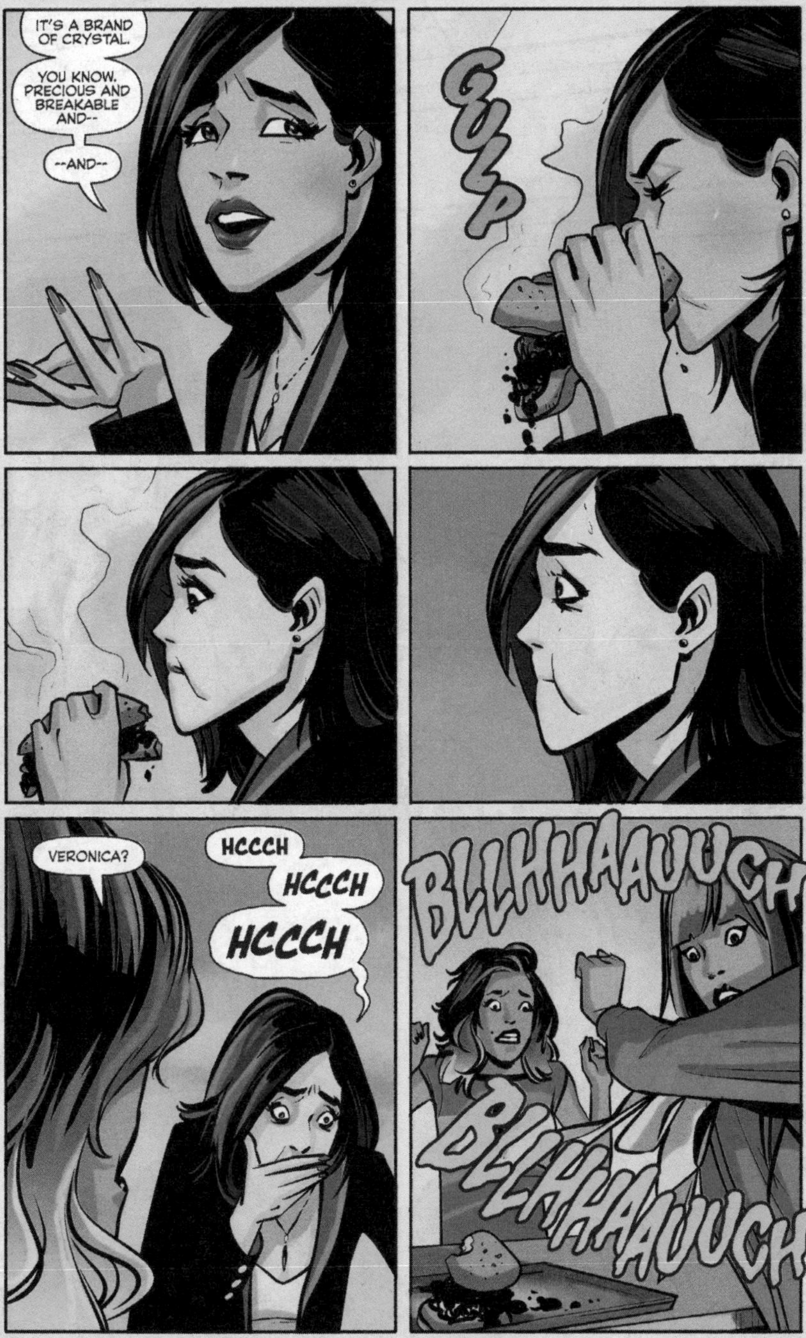
IT'S A BRAND OF CRYSTAL.
YOU KNOW. PRECIOUS AND BREAKABLE AND--
--AND--
GULP
VERONICA?
HCCCH
HCCCH
HCCCH
BLLHHAAUUCH
BLLHHAAUUCH

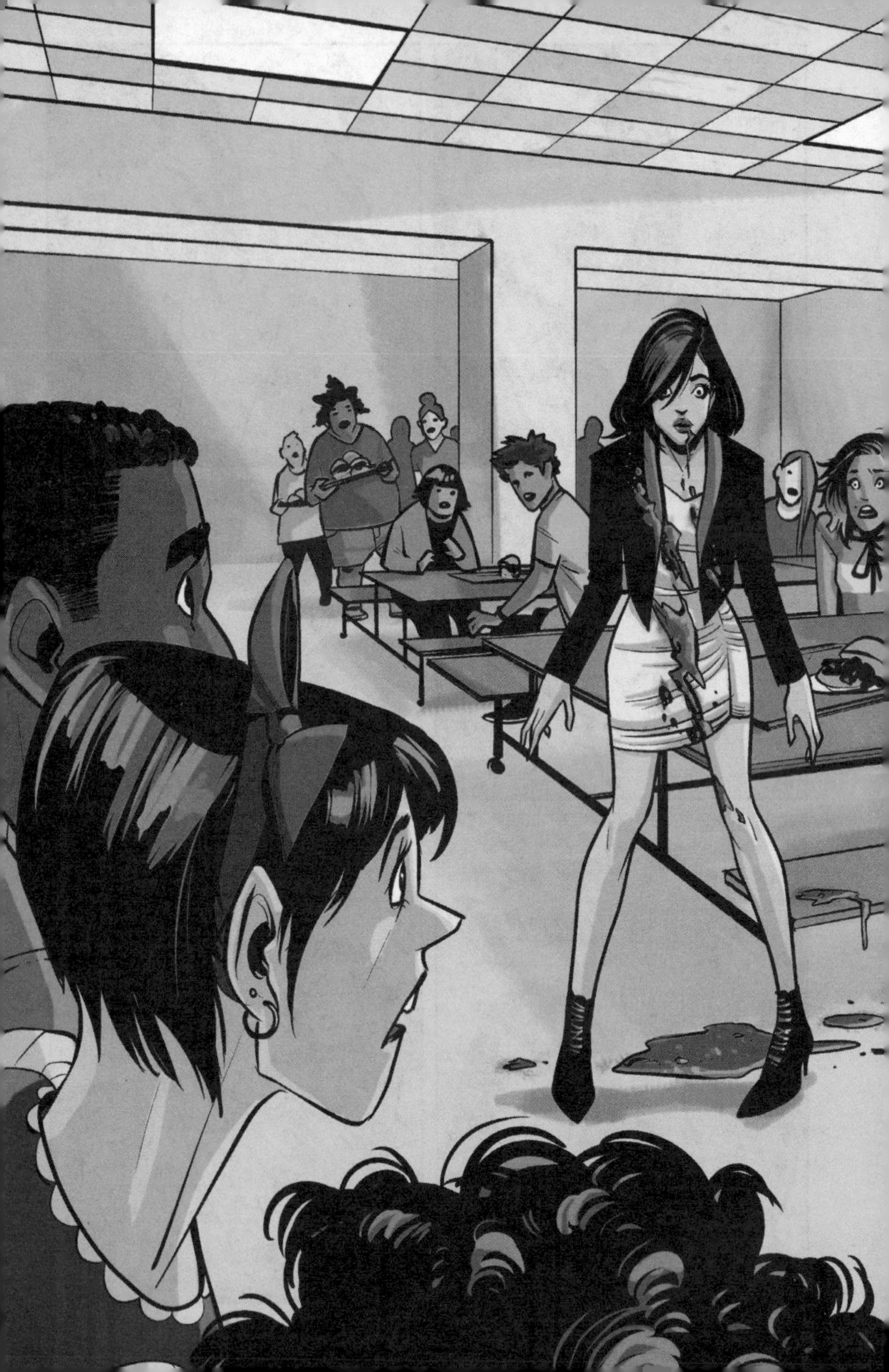

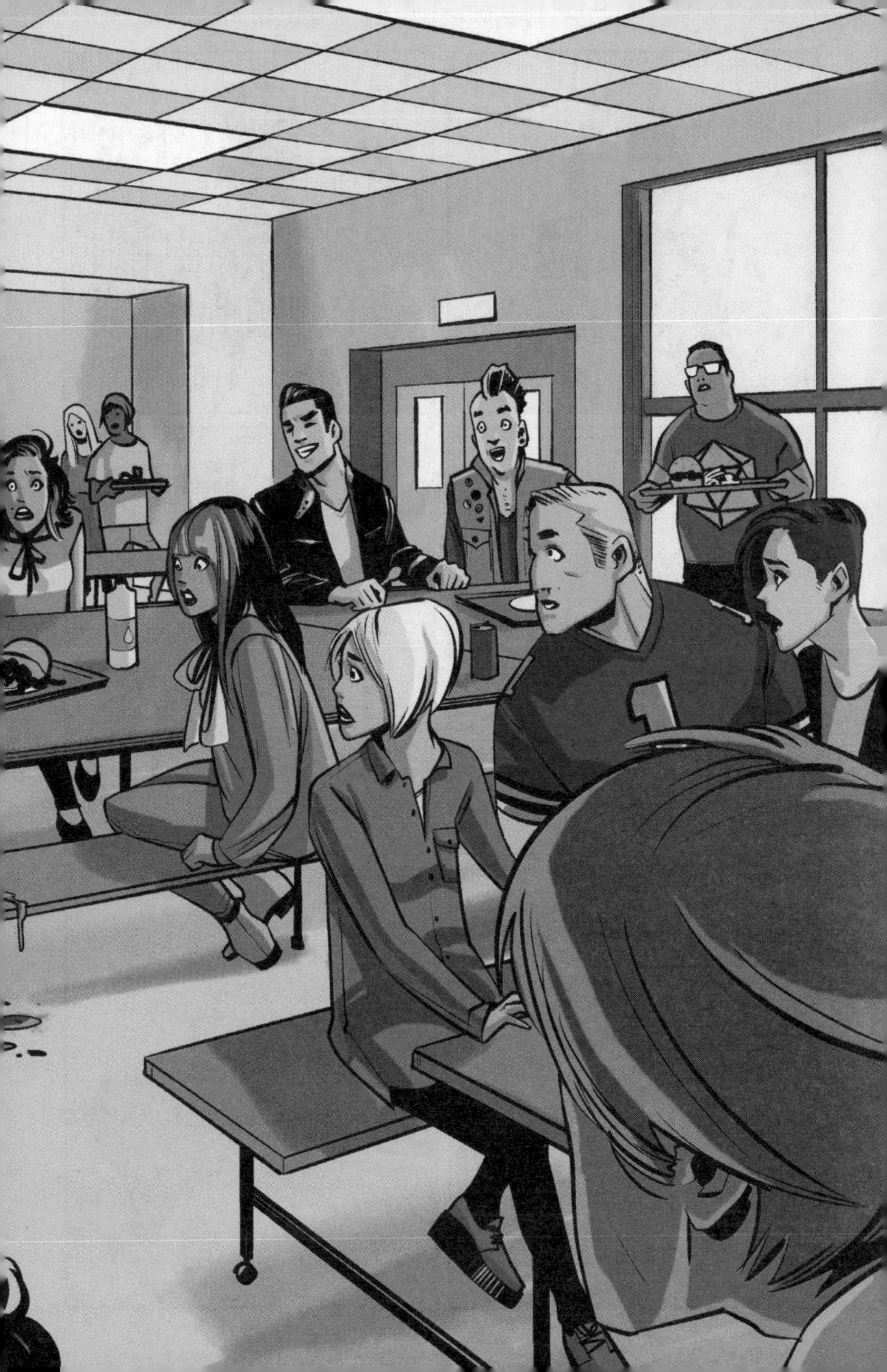

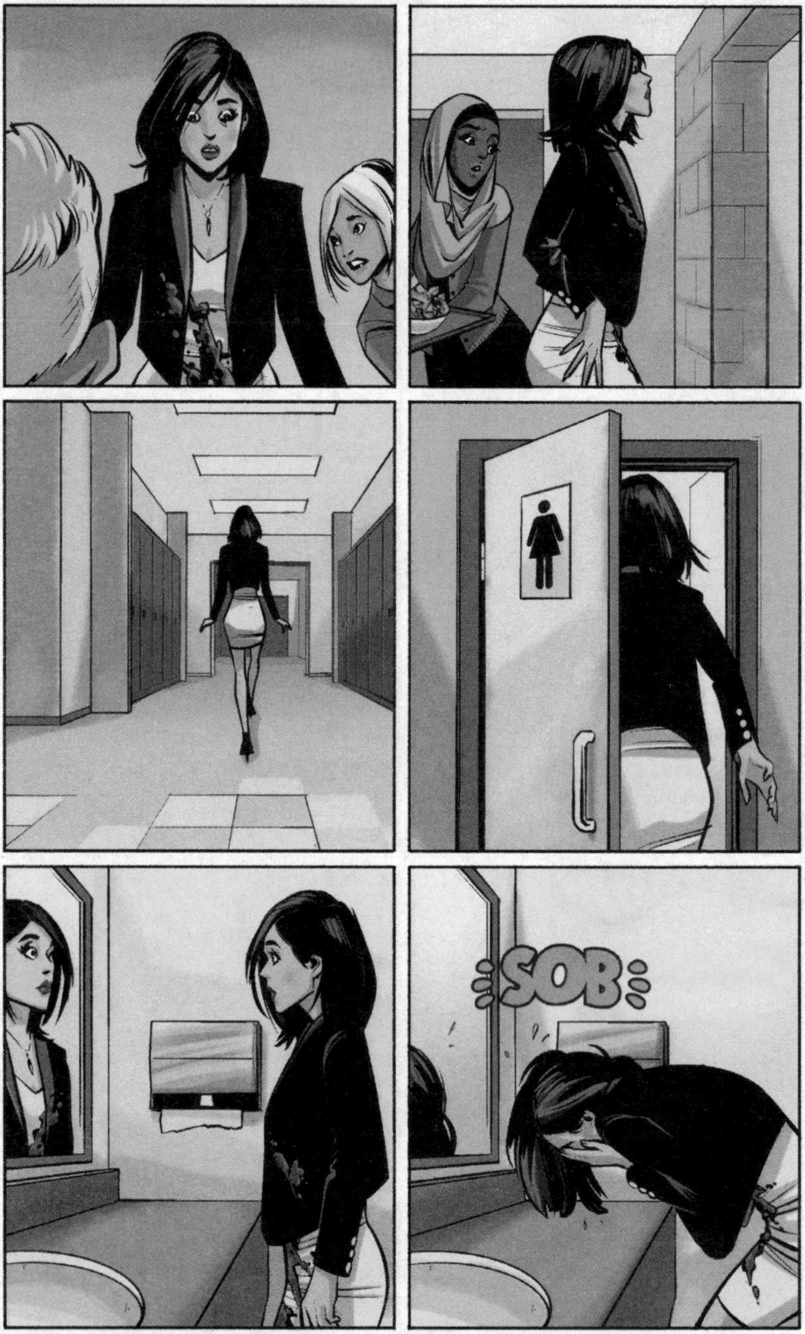
SOB

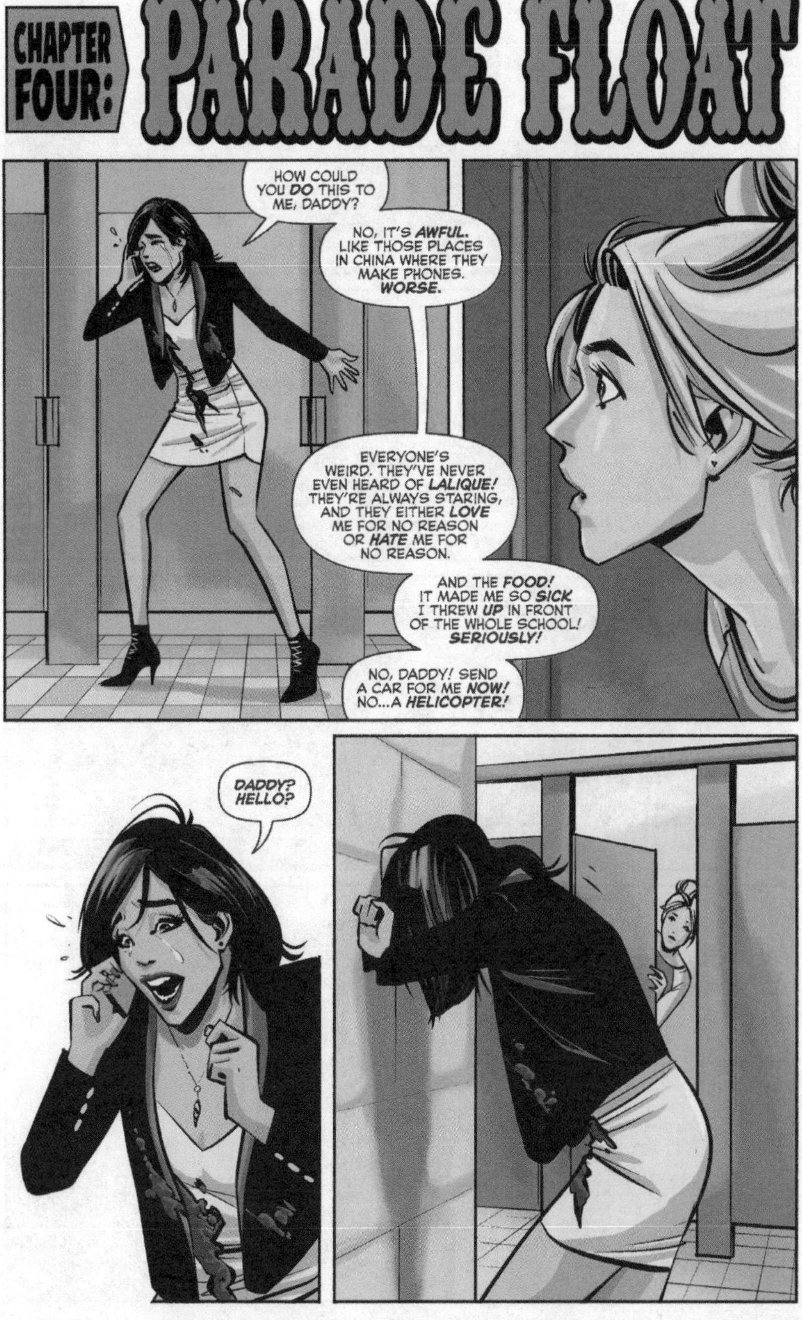

CHAPTER FOUR: PARADE FLOAT
HOW COULD YOU DO THIS TO ME, DADDY?
NO, IT'S AWFUL. LIKE THOSE PLACES IN CHINA WHERE THEY MAKE PHONES. WORSE.
EVERYONE'S WEIRD. THEY'VE NEVER EVEN HEARD OF LALIQUE! THEY'RE ALWAYS STARING, AND THEY EITHER LOVE ME FOR NO REASON OR HATE ME FOR NO REASON.
AND THE FOOD! IT MADE ME SO SICK I THREW UP IN FRONT OF THE WHOLE SCHOOL! SERIOUSLY!
NO, DADDY! SEND A CAR FOR ME NOW! NO...A HELICOPTER!
DADDY? HELLO?

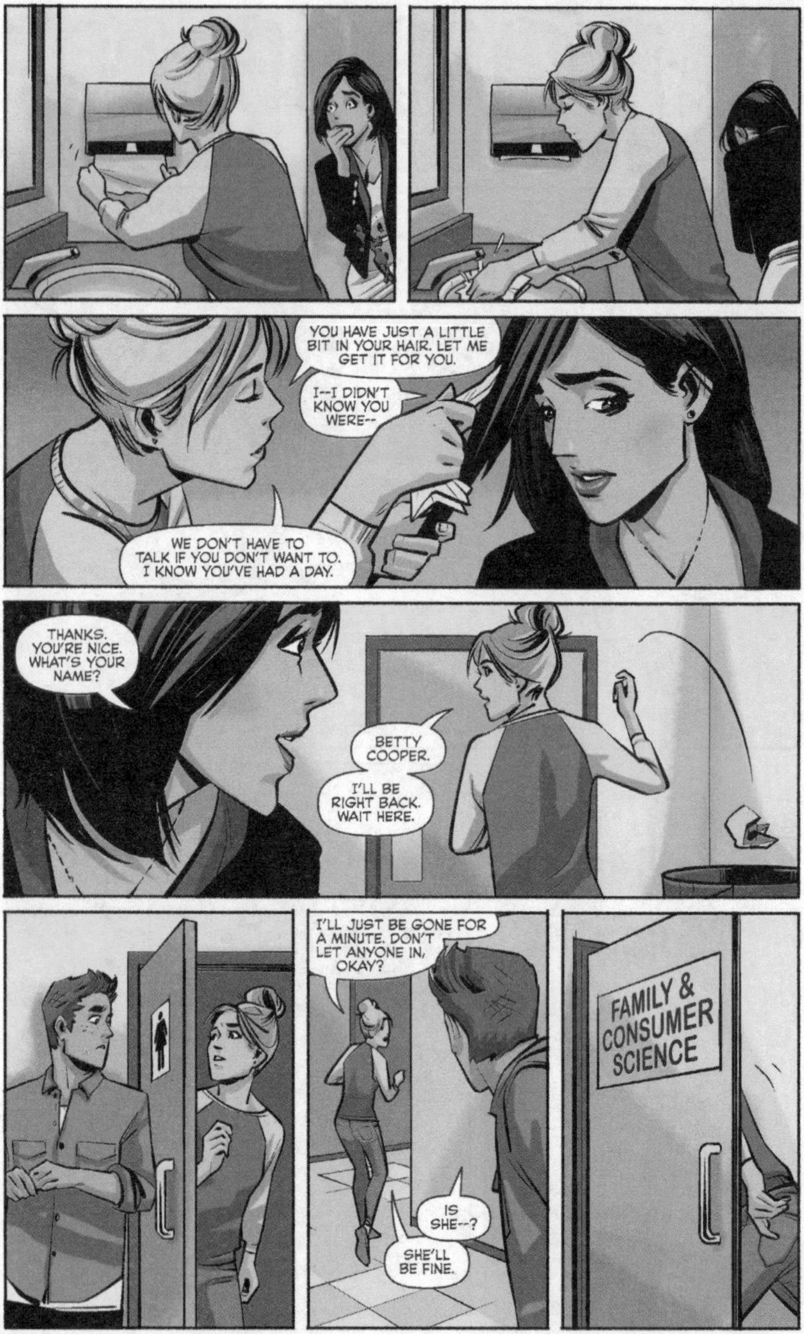
YOU HAVE JUST A LITTLE BIT IN YOUR HAIR. LET ME GET IT FOR YOU.
I--I DIDN'T KNOW YOU WERE--
WE DON'T HAVE TO TALK IF YOU DON'T WANT TO. I KNOW YOU'VE HAD A DAY.
THANKS. YOU'RE NICE. WHAT'S YOUR NAME?
BETTY COOPER.
I'LL BE RIGHT BACK. WAIT HERE.
I'LL JUST BE GONE FOR A MINUTE. DON'T LET ANYONE IN, OKAY?
IS SHE--?
SHE'LL BE FINE.
FAMILY & CONSUMER SCIENCE

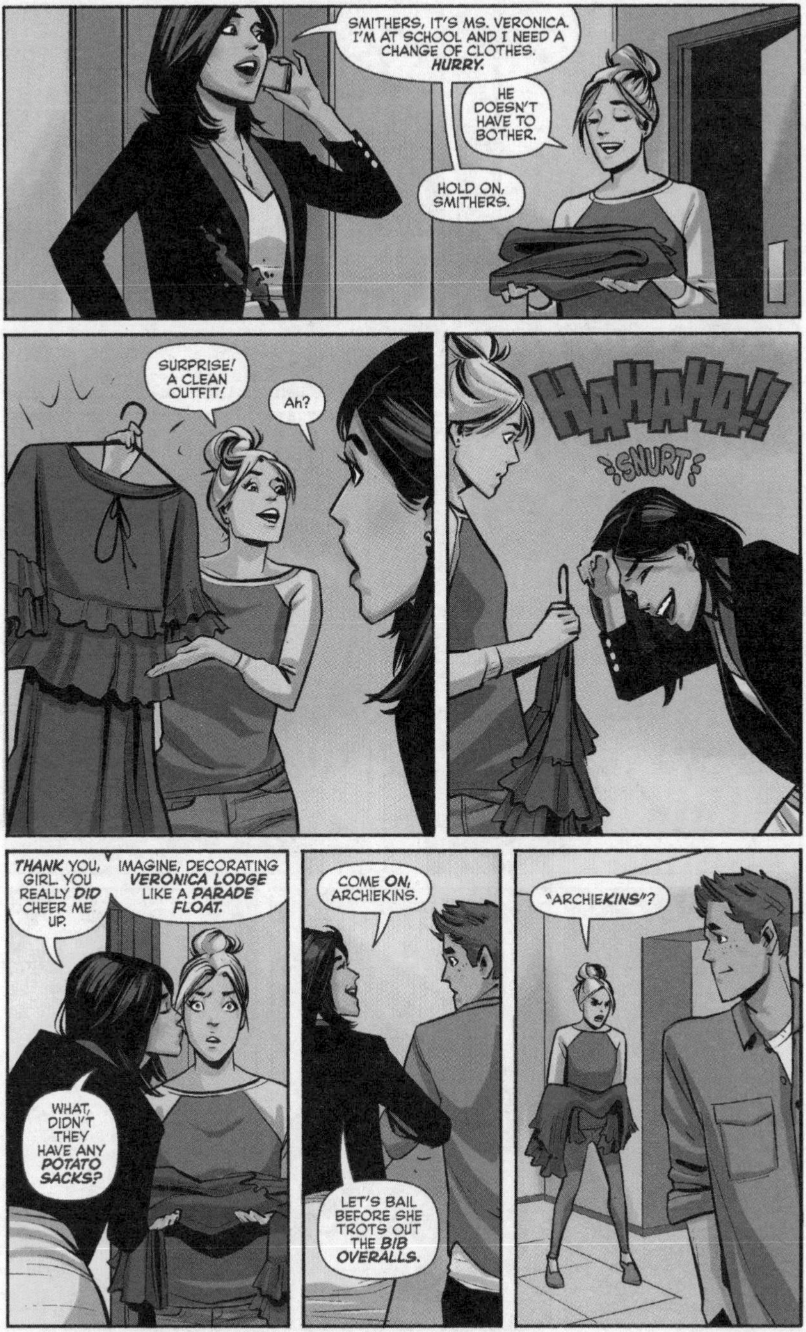
SMITHERS, IT'S MS. VERONICA. I'M AT SCHOOL AND I NEED A CHANGE OF CLOTHES. HURRY.
HE DOESN'T HAVE TO BOTHER.
HOLD ON, SMITHERS.
SURPRISE! A CLEAN OUTFIT!
Ah?
HAHAHA!!
SNURT
THANK YOU, GIRL. YOU REALLY DID CHEER ME UP.
IMAGINE, DECORATING VERONICA LODGE LIKE A PARADE FLOAT.
WHAT, DIDN'T THEY HAVE ANY POTATO SACKS?
COME ON, ARCHIEKINS.
LET'S BAIL BEFORE SHE TROTS OUT THE BIB OVERALLS.
"ARCHIEKINS"?

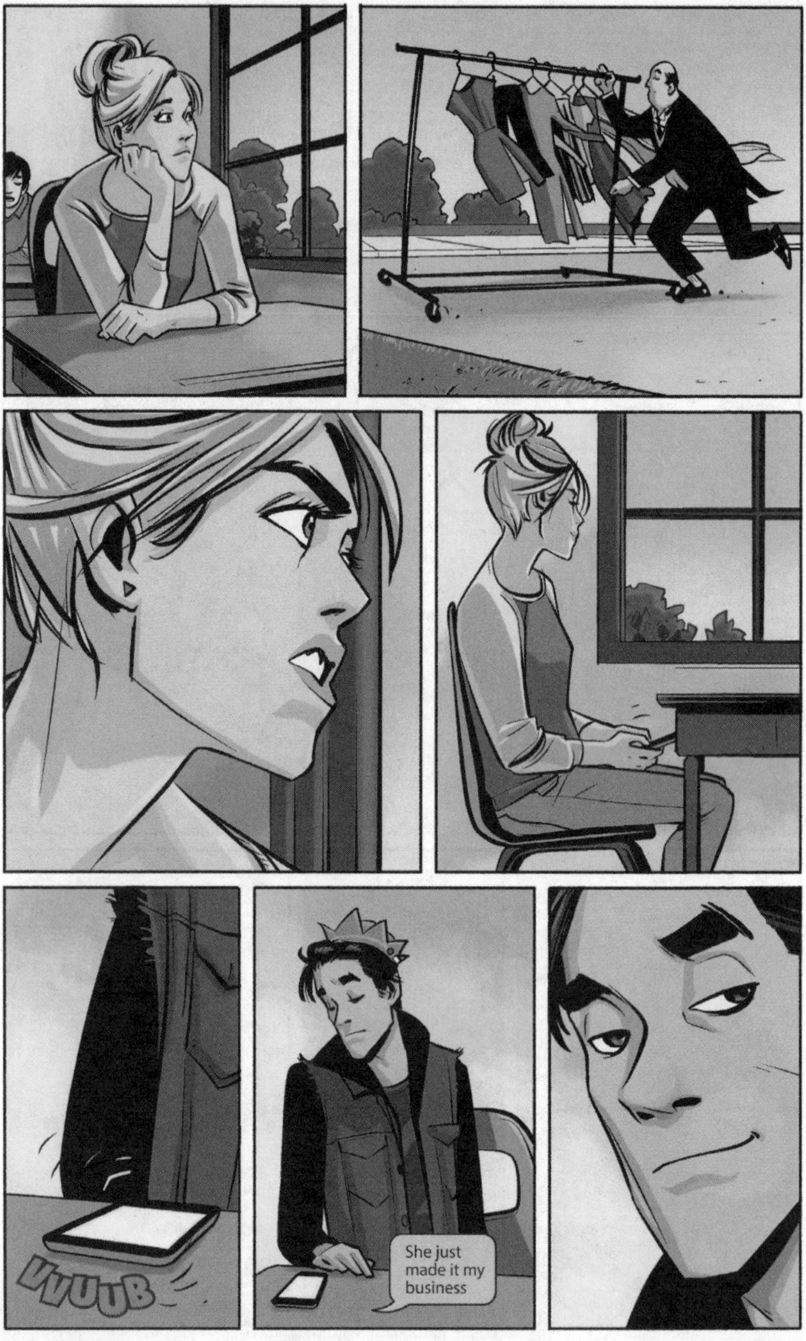
VVUUB
She just made it my business

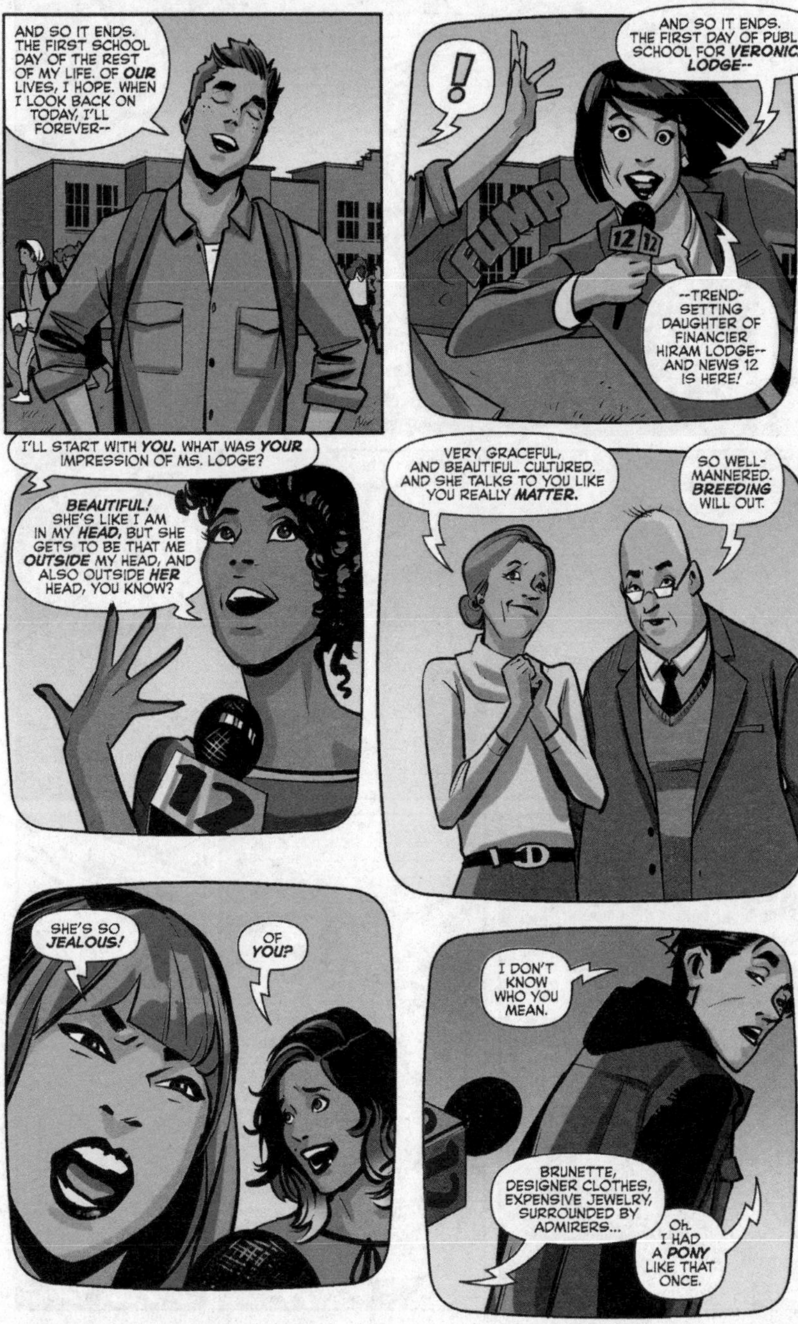
AND SO IT ENDS. THE FIRST SCHOOL DAY OF THE REST OF MY LIFE. OF OUR LIVES, I HOPE. WHEN I LOOK BACK ON TODAY, I'LL FOREVER--
!
AND SO IT ENDS. THE FIRST DAY OF PUBLIC SCHOOL FOR VERONICA LODGE--
FUMP
12 12
--TREND-SETTING DAUGHTER OF FINANCIER HIRAM LODGE-- AND NEWS 12 IS HERE!
I'LL START WITH YOU. WHAT WAS YOUR IMPRESSION OF MS. LODGE?
BEAUTIFUL! SHE'S LIKE I AM IN MY HEAD, BUT SHE GETS TO BE THAT ME OUTSIDE MY HEAD, AND ALSO OUTSIDE HER HEAD, YOU KNOW?
12
VERY GRACEFUL, AND BEAUTIFUL. CULTURED. AND SHE TALKS TO YOU LIKE YOU REALLY MATTER.
SO WELL-MANNERED. BREEDING WILL OUT.
SHE'S SO JEALOUS!
OF YOU?
I DON'T KNOW WHO YOU MEAN.
BRUNETTE, DESIGNER CLOTHES, EXPENSIVE JEWELRY, SURROUNDED BY ADMIRERS...
Oh. I HAD A PONY LIKE THAT ONCE.

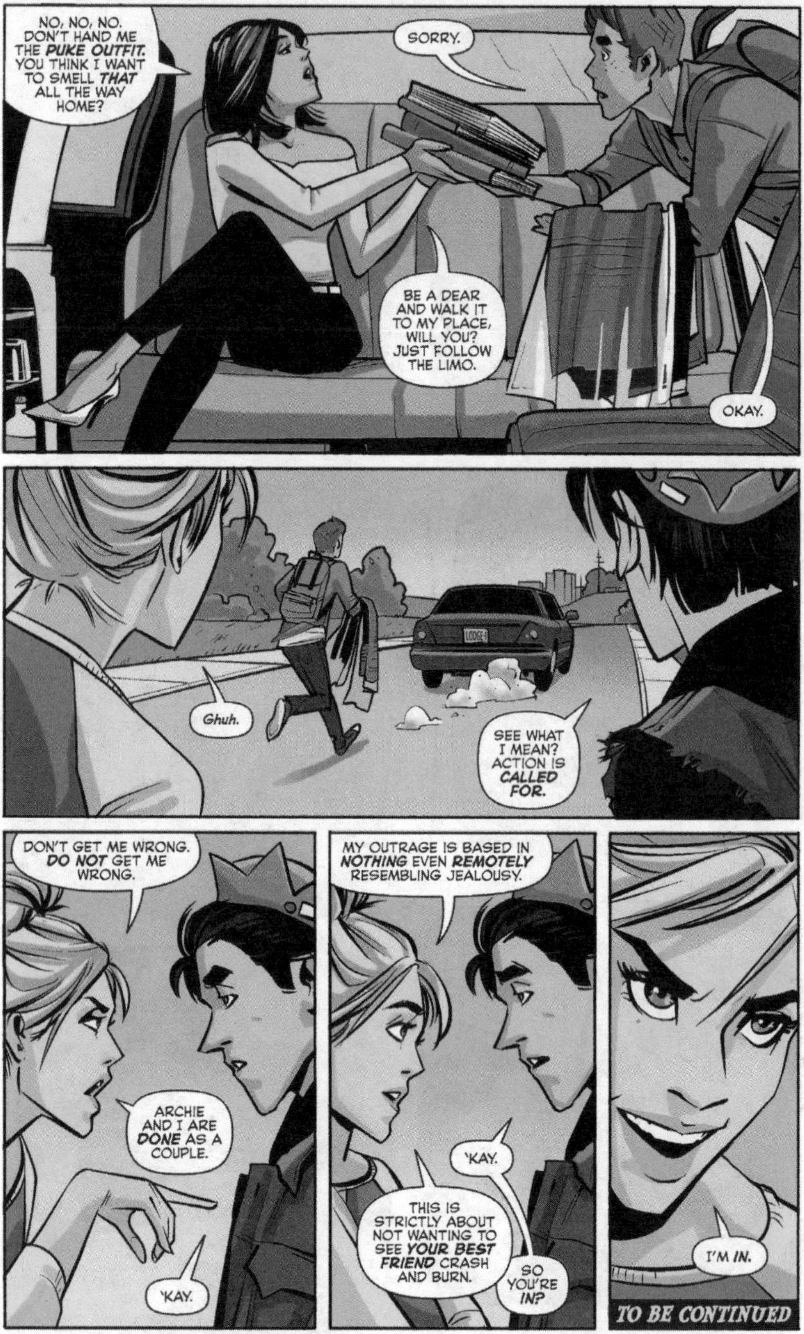

NO, NO, NO. DON'T HAND ME THE **PUKE OUTFIT.** YOU THINK I WANT TO SMELL **THAT** ALL THE WAY HOME?
SORRY.
BE A DEAR AND WALK IT TO MY PLACE, WILL YOU? JUST FOLLOW THE LIMO.
OKAY.
LODGE-1
Ghuh.
SEE WHAT I MEAN? ACTION IS ***CALLED FOR.***
DON'T GET ME WRONG. ***DO NOT*** GET ME WRONG.
ARCHIE AND I ARE ***DONE*** AS A COUPLE.
'KAY.
MY OUTRAGE IS BASED IN ***NOTHING*** EVEN ***REMOTELY*** RESEMBLING JEALOUSY.
'KAY.
THIS IS STRICTLY ABOUT NOT WANTING TO SEE ***YOUR BEST FRIEND*** CRASH AND BURN.
SO YOU'RE ***IN?***
I'M ***IN.***
TO BE CONTINUED

BETTY & VERONICA #2 COVER
BETTY & VERONICA VOL. 3 #2, 2016
Adam Hughes

BETTY & VERONICA #3
BETTY & VERONICA VOL. 3 #3, 2017
Adam Hughes, José Villarrubia, Jack Morelli

RIVERDALE VOLUME ONE COVER
RIVERDALE VOLUME ONE, 2017
Photo courtesy of The CW/Warner Bros.

BRING IT ON
RIVERDALE #1, 2017
Michael Grassi, Joe Eisma, Andre Szymanowicz, John Workman

In the new *Riverdale* series, I greatly enjoy the evolution of Betty and
Veronica. Partly due to the reversal of monetary fortunes of the Lodge
Family, Veronica must develop new skills to survive. In place of their
traditional rivalry, Betty and Veronica have a supportive friendship.
Their individual strengths come to the fore when there is a situation
which involves problem solving. This bond of unity ripples to family and
friends. In the life of Riverdale High, Betty and Veronica are important
to counteract the cynicism and narcissism of Cheryl and Reggie.

- JANICE CHIANG *Letterer, Archie Comics*

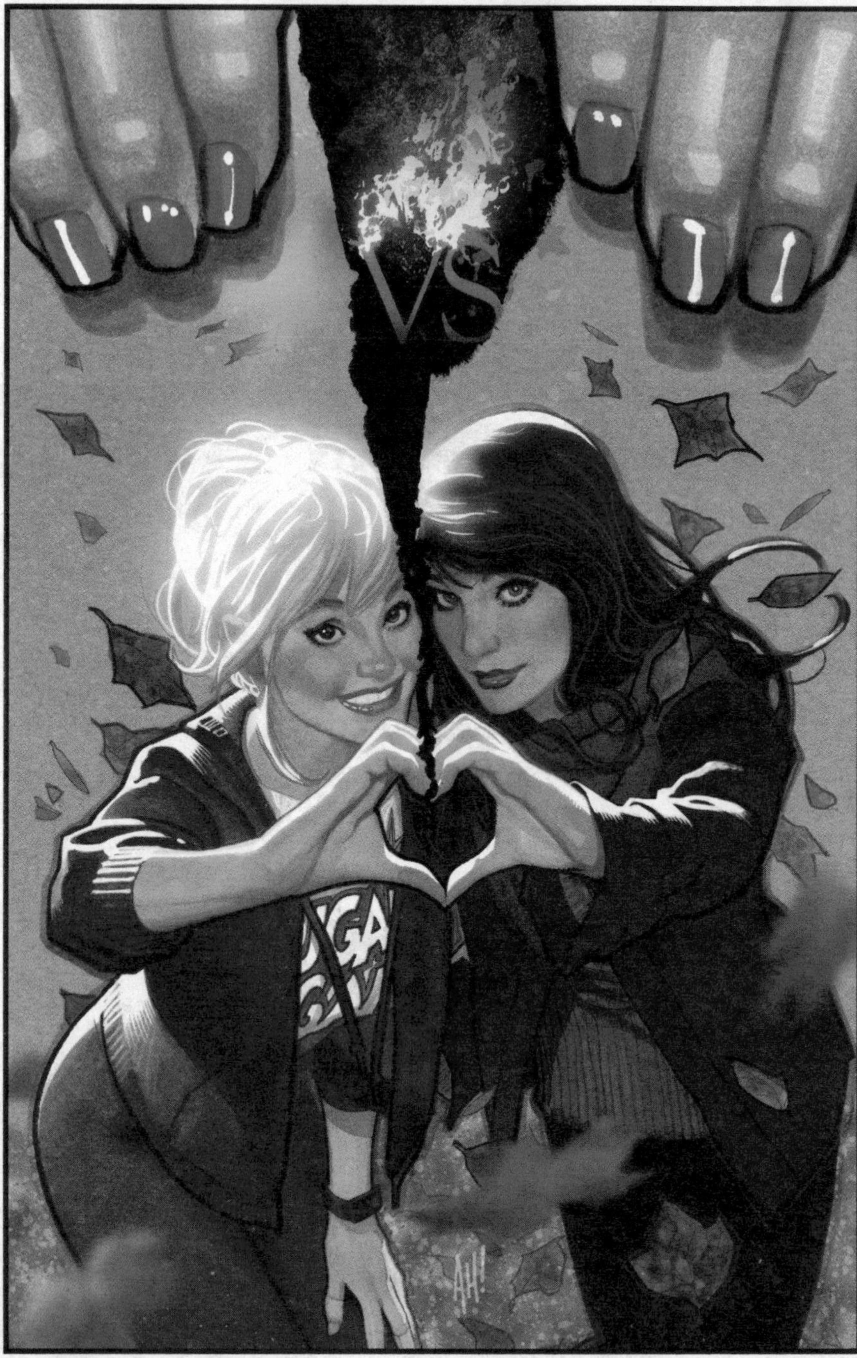
VS

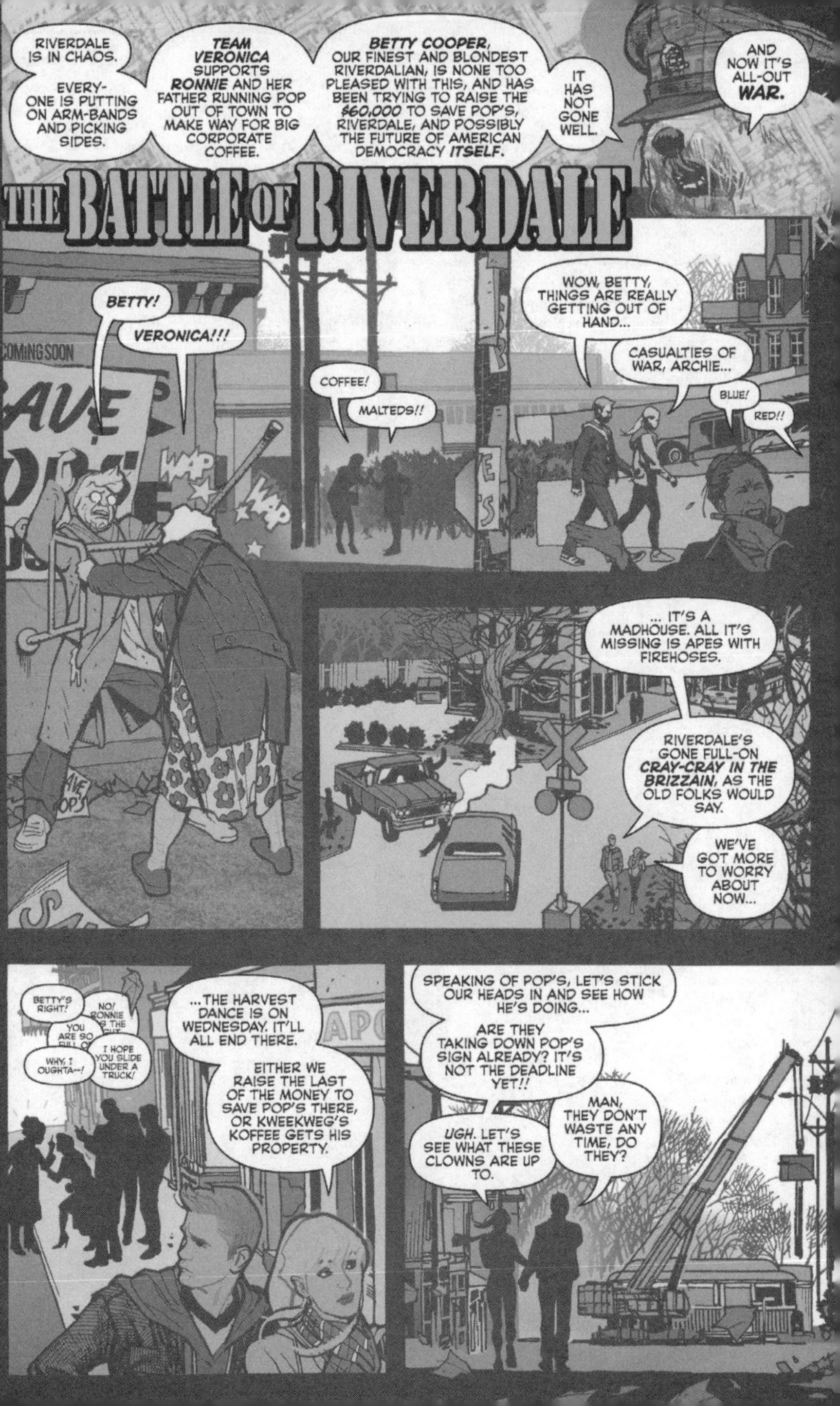

RIVERDALE IS IN CHAOS.
EVERY-ONE IS PUTTING ON ARM-BANDS AND PICKING SIDES.
TEAM VERONICA SUPPORTS RONNIE AND HER FATHER RUNNING POP OUT OF TOWN TO MAKE WAY FOR BIG CORPORATE COFFEE.
BETTY COOPER, OUR FINEST AND BLONDEST RIVERDALIAN, IS NONE TOO PLEASED WITH THIS, AND HAS BEEN TRYING TO RAISE THE $60,000 TO SAVE POP'S, RIVERDALE, AND POSSIBLY THE FUTURE OF AMERICAN DEMOCRACY ITSELF.
IT HAS NOT GONE WELL.
AND NOW IT'S ALL-OUT WAR.
THE BATTLE OF RIVERDALE
BETTY!
VERONICA!!!
COMING SOON
WAP
WAP
COFFEE!
MALTEDS!!
WOW, BETTY, THINGS ARE REALLY GETTING OUT OF HAND...
CASUALTIES OF WAR, ARCHIE...
BLUE!
RED!!
... IT'S A MADHOUSE. ALL IT'S MISSING IS APES WITH FIREHOSES.
RIVERDALE'S GONE FULL-ON CRAY-CRAY IN THE BRIZZAIN, AS THE OLD FOLKS WOULD SAY.
WE'VE GOT MORE TO WORRY ABOUT NOW...
BETTY'S RIGHT!
NO! RONNIE
YOU ARE SO
WHY, I OUGHTA--!
I HOPE YOU SLIDE UNDER A TRUCK!
...THE HARVEST DANCE IS ON WEDNESDAY. IT'LL ALL END THERE.
EITHER WE RAISE THE LAST OF THE MONEY TO SAVE POP'S THERE, OR KWEEKWEG'S KOFFEE GETS HIS PROPERTY.
SPEAKING OF POP'S, LET'S STICK OUR HEADS IN AND SEE HOW HE'S DOING...
ARE THEY TAKING DOWN POP'S SIGN ALREADY? IT'S NOT THE DEADLINE YET!!
MAN, THEY DON'T WASTE ANY TIME, DO THEY?
UGH. LET'S SEE WHAT THESE CLOWNS ARE UP TO.

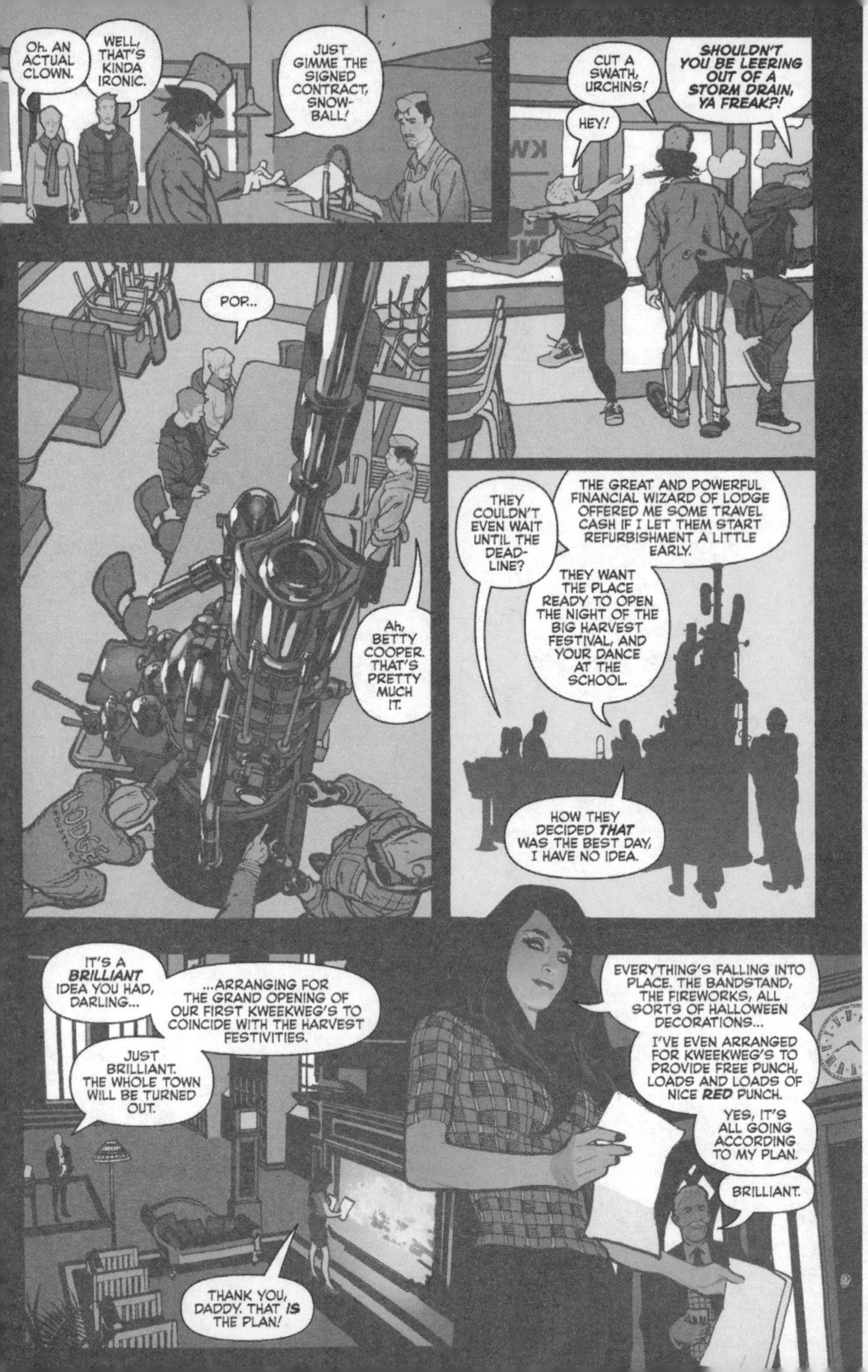
Oh. AN ACTUAL CLOWN.
WELL, THAT'S KINDA IRONIC.
JUST GIMME THE SIGNED CONTRACT, SNOW-BALL!
CUT A SWATH, URCHINS!
HEY!
SHOULDN'T YOU BE LEERING OUT OF A STORM DRAIN, YA FREAK?!
POP...
Ah, BETTY COOPER. THAT'S PRETTY MUCH IT.
THEY COULDN'T EVEN WAIT UNTIL THE DEAD-LINE?
THE GREAT AND POWERFUL FINANCIAL WIZARD OF LODGE OFFERED ME SOME TRAVEL CASH IF I LET THEM START REFURBISHMENT A LITTLE EARLY.
THEY WANT THE PLACE READY TO OPEN THE NIGHT OF THE BIG HARVEST FESTIVAL, AND YOUR DANCE AT THE SCHOOL.
HOW THEY DECIDED THAT WAS THE BEST DAY, I HAVE NO IDEA.
IT'S A BRILLIANT IDEA YOU HAD, DARLING...
...ARRANGING FOR THE GRAND OPENING OF OUR FIRST KWEEKWEG'S TO COINCIDE WITH THE HARVEST FESTIVITIES.
JUST BRILLIANT. THE WHOLE TOWN WILL BE TURNED OUT.
EVERYTHING'S FALLING INTO PLACE. THE BANDSTAND, THE FIREWORKS, ALL SORTS OF HALLOWEEN DECORATIONS...
I'VE EVEN ARRANGED FOR KWEEKWEG'S TO PROVIDE FREE PUNCH, LOADS AND LOADS OF NICE RED PUNCH.
YES, IT'S ALL GOING ACCORDING TO MY PLAN.
BRILLIANT.
THANK YOU, DADDY. THAT IS THE PLAN!

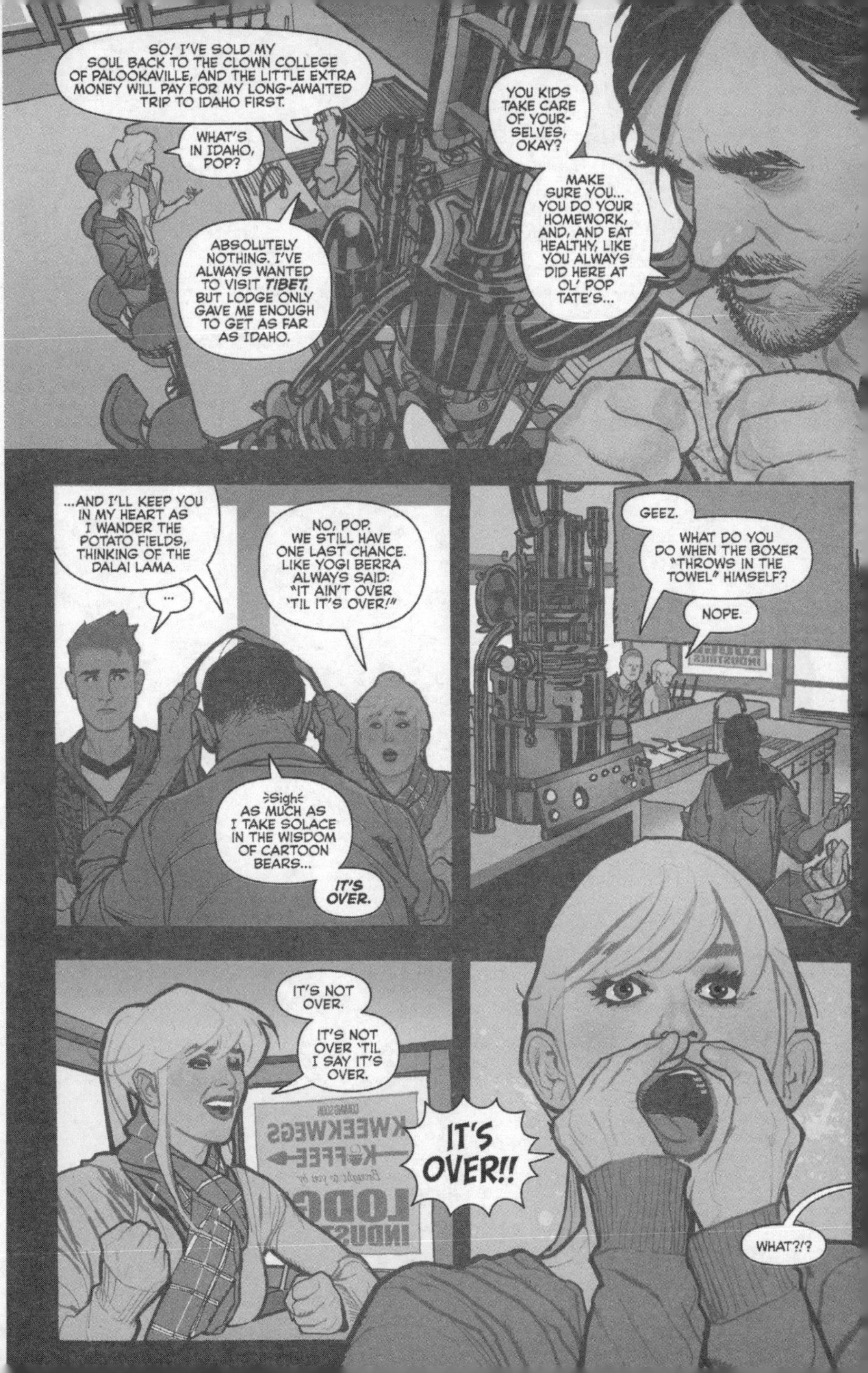
SO! I'VE SOLD MY SOUL BACK TO THE CLOWN COLLEGE OF PALOOKAVILLE, AND THE LITTLE EXTRA MONEY WILL PAY FOR MY LONG-AWAITED TRIP TO IDAHO FIRST.
WHAT'S IN IDAHO, POP?
ABSOLUTELY NOTHING. I'VE ALWAYS WANTED TO VISIT *TIBET*, BUT LODGE ONLY GAVE ME ENOUGH TO GET AS FAR AS IDAHO.
YOU KIDS TAKE CARE OF YOUR-SELVES, OKAY?
MAKE SURE YOU... YOU DO YOUR HOMEWORK, AND, AND EAT HEALTHY, LIKE YOU ALWAYS DID HERE AT OL' POP TATE'S...
...AND I'LL KEEP YOU IN MY HEART AS I WANDER THE POTATO FIELDS, THINKING OF THE DALAI LAMA.
...
NO, POP. WE STILL HAVE ONE LAST CHANCE. LIKE YOGI BERRA ALWAYS SAID: "IT AIN'T OVER 'TIL IT'S OVER!"
Sigh AS MUCH AS I TAKE SOLACE IN THE WISDOM OF CARTOON BEARS...
IT'S OVER.
GEEZ.
WHAT DO YOU DO WHEN THE BOXER "THROWS IN THE TOWEL" HIMSELF?
NOPE.
IT'S NOT OVER.
IT'S NOT OVER 'TIL I SAY IT'S OVER.
IT'S OVER!!
WHAT?!?

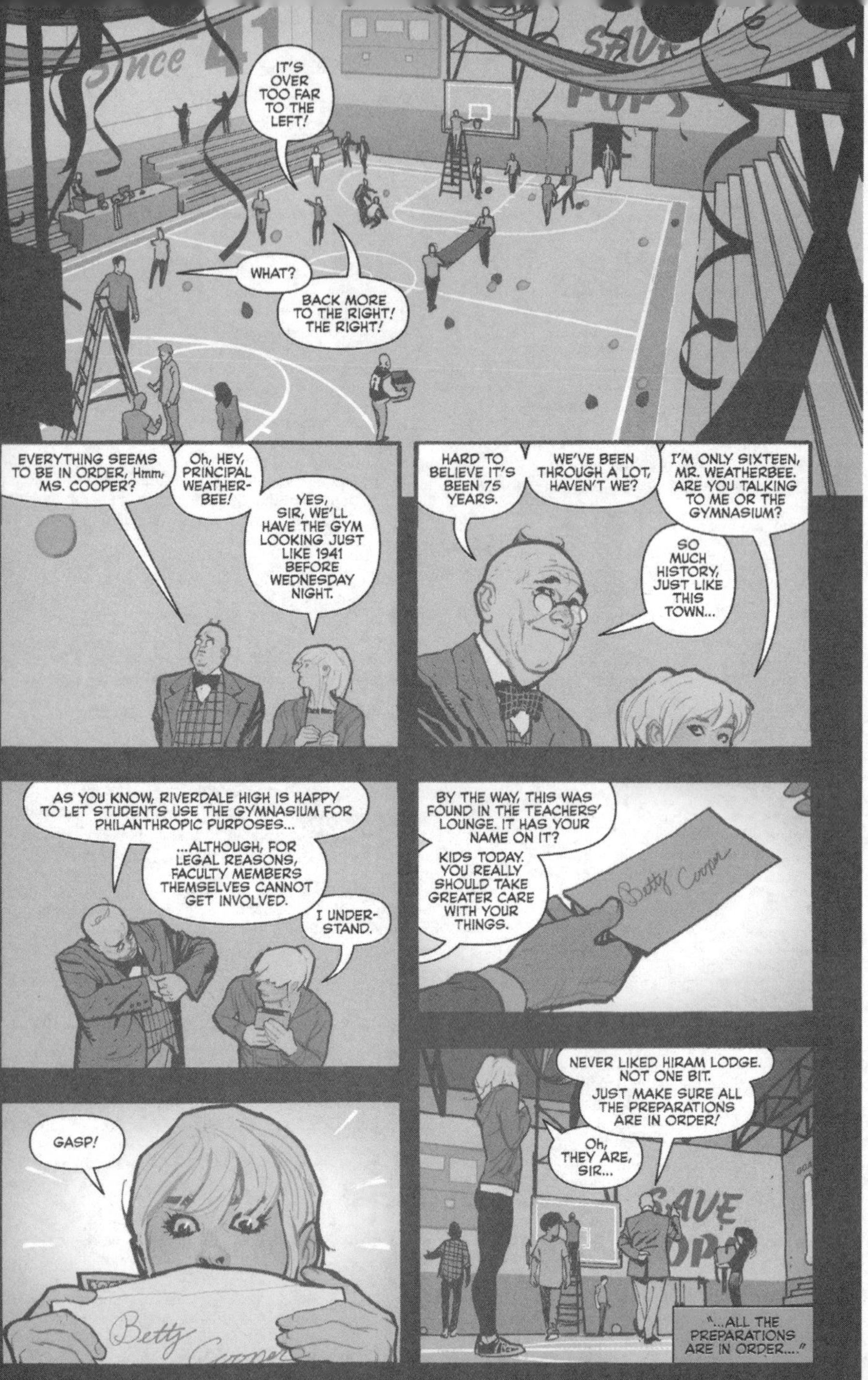
SINCE 41
SAVE POPS
IT'S OVER TOO FAR TO THE LEFT!
WHAT?
BACK MORE TO THE RIGHT! THE RIGHT!
EVERYTHING SEEMS TO BE IN ORDER, Hmm, MS. COOPER?
Oh, HEY, PRINCIPAL WEATHER-BEE!
YES, SIR, WE'LL HAVE THE GYM LOOKING JUST LIKE 1941 BEFORE WEDNESDAY NIGHT.
HARD TO BELIEVE IT'S BEEN 75 YEARS.
WE'VE BEEN THROUGH A LOT, HAVEN'T WE?
I'M ONLY SIXTEEN, MR. WEATHERBEE. ARE YOU TALKING TO ME OR THE GYMNASIUM?
SO MUCH HISTORY, JUST LIKE THIS TOWN...
AS YOU KNOW, RIVERDALE HIGH IS HAPPY TO LET STUDENTS USE THE GYMNASIUM FOR PHILANTHROPIC PURPOSES...
...ALTHOUGH, FOR LEGAL REASONS, FACULTY MEMBERS THEMSELVES CANNOT GET INVOLVED.
I UNDER-STAND.
BY THE WAY, THIS WAS FOUND IN THE TEACHERS' LOUNGE. IT HAS YOUR NAME ON IT?
KIDS TODAY. YOU REALLY SHOULD TAKE GREATER CARE WITH YOUR THINGS.
Betty Cooper
GASP!
Betty Cooper
NEVER LIKED HIRAM LODGE. NOT ONE BIT.
JUST MAKE SURE ALL THE PREPARATIONS ARE IN ORDER!
Oh, THEY ARE, SIR...
SAVE POPS
"...ALL THE PREPARATIONS ARE IN ORDER..."

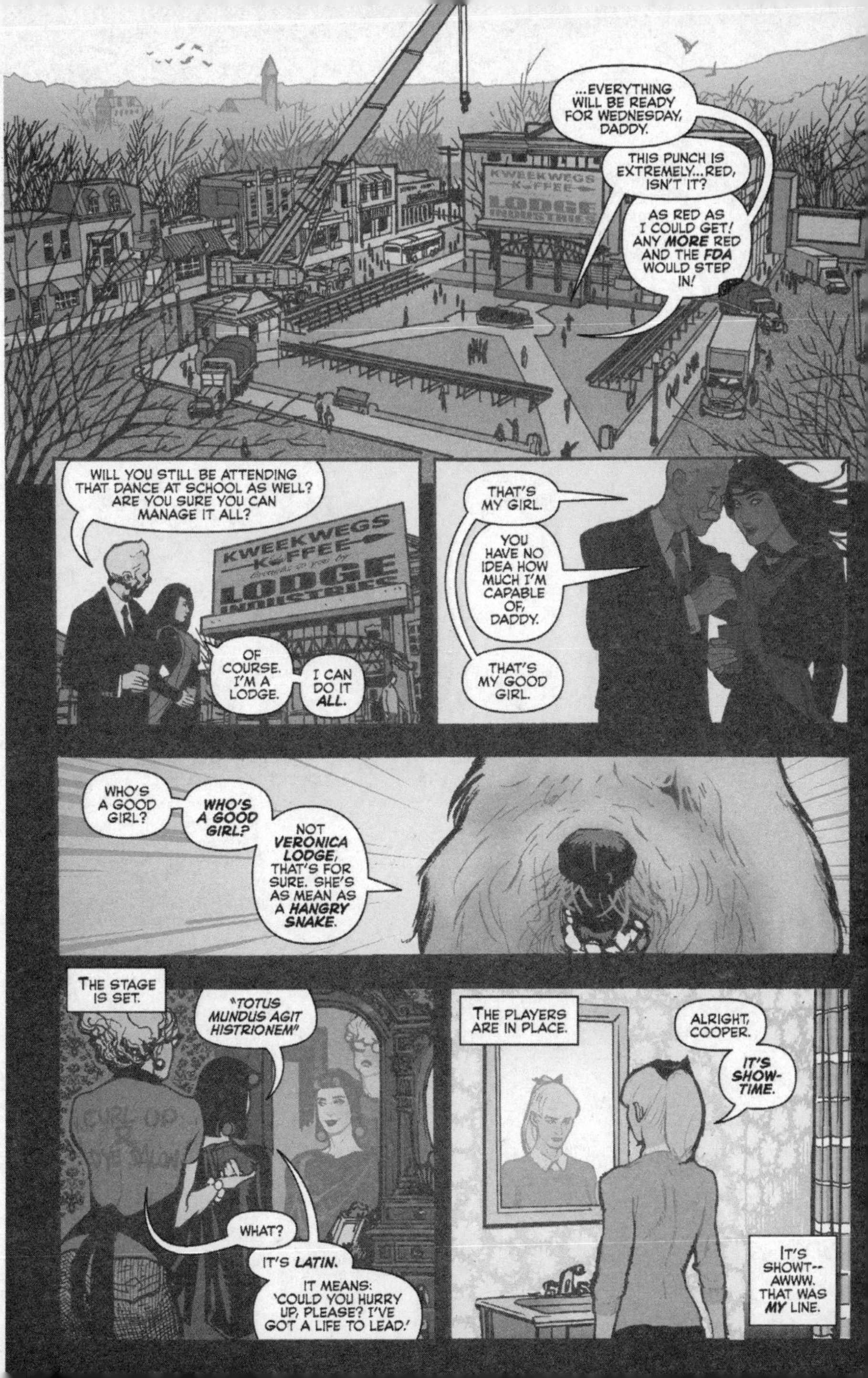
...EVERYTHING WILL BE READY FOR WEDNESDAY, DADDY.
THIS PUNCH IS EXTREMELY...RED, ISN'T IT?
AS RED AS I COULD GET! ANY *MORE* RED AND THE *FDA* WOULD STEP IN!
WILL YOU STILL BE ATTENDING THAT DANCE AT SCHOOL AS WELL? ARE YOU SURE YOU CAN MANAGE IT ALL?
KWEEKWEGS KOFFEE LODGE INDUSTRIES
OF COURSE. I'M A LODGE.
I CAN DO IT *ALL*.
THAT'S MY GIRL.
YOU HAVE NO IDEA HOW MUCH I'M CAPABLE OF, DADDY.
THAT'S MY GOOD GIRL.
WHO'S A GOOD GIRL?
WHO'S A GOOD GIRL?
NOT *VERONICA LODGE*, THAT'S FOR SURE. SHE'S AS MEAN AS A *HANGRY SNAKE*.
THE STAGE IS SET.
"TOTUS MUNDUS AGIT HISTRIONEM"
WHAT?
IT'S *LATIN*.
IT MEANS: 'COULD YOU HURRY UP, PLEASE? I'VE GOT A LIFE TO LEAD.'
THE PLAYERS ARE IN PLACE.
ALRIGHT, COOPER.
IT'S SHOW-TIME.
IT'S SHOWT--AWWW. THAT WAS *MY* LINE.

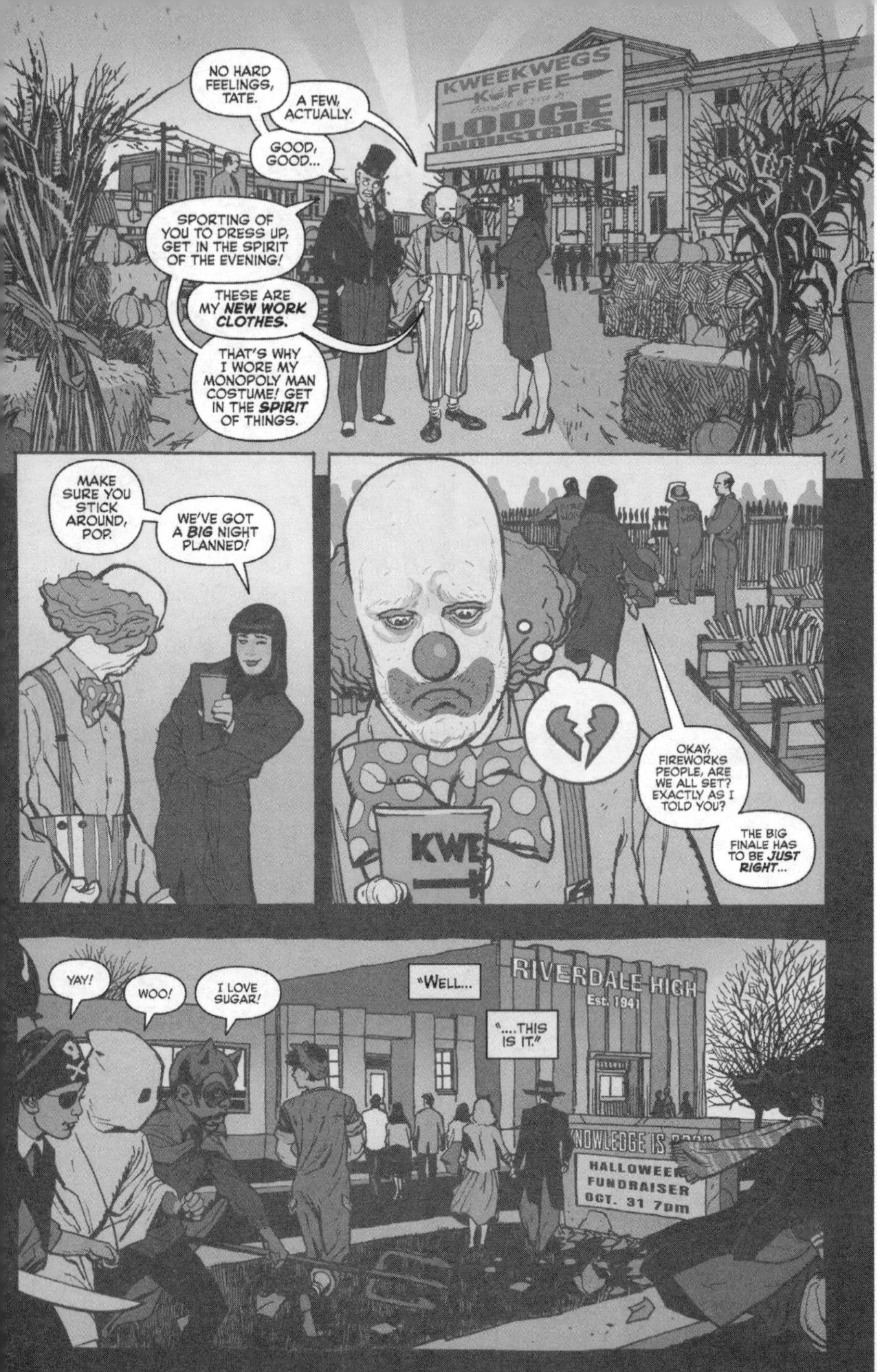

NO HARD FEELINGS, TATE.
A FEW, ACTUALLY.
GOOD, GOOD...
KWEEKWEGS KOFFEE
LODGE INDUSTRIES
SPORTING OF YOU TO DRESS UP, GET IN THE SPIRIT OF THE EVENING!
THESE ARE MY NEW WORK CLOTHES.
THAT'S WHY I WORE MY MONOPOLY MAN COSTUME! GET IN THE SPIRIT OF THINGS.
MAKE SURE YOU STICK AROUND, POP.
WE'VE GOT A BIG NIGHT PLANNED!
KWE
OKAY, FIREWORKS PEOPLE, ARE WE ALL SET? EXACTLY AS I TOLD YOU?
THE BIG FINALE HAS TO BE JUST RIGHT...
YAY!
WOO!
I LOVE SUGAR!
"WELL...
"....THIS IS IT."
RIVERDALE HIGH
Est. 1941
HALLOWEEN FUNDRAISER
OCT. 31 7pm

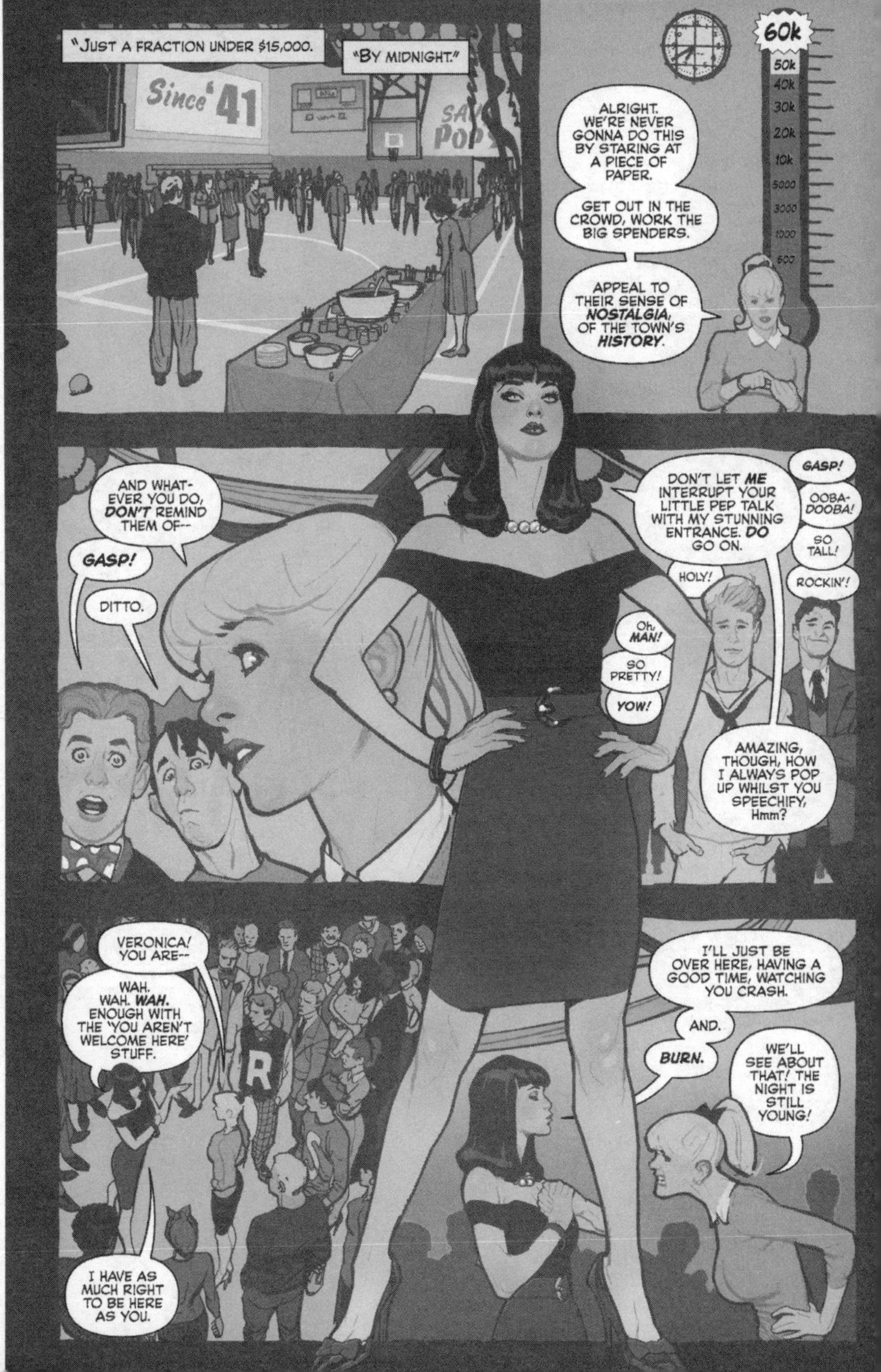

"JUST A FRACTION UNDER $15,000.
"BY MIDNIGHT."
Since '41
60k
50k
40k
30k
20k
10k
5000
3000
1000
500
ALRIGHT. WE'RE NEVER GONNA DO THIS BY STARING AT A PIECE OF PAPER.
GET OUT IN THE CROWD, WORK THE BIG SPENDERS.
APPEAL TO THEIR SENSE OF NOSTALGIA, OF THE TOWN'S HISTORY.
AND WHATEVER YOU DO, DON'T REMIND THEM OF--
GASP!
DITTO.
DON'T LET ME INTERRUPT YOUR LITTLE PEP TALK WITH MY STUNNING ENTRANCE. DO GO ON.
GASP!
OOBA-DOOBA!
SO TALL!
ROCKIN'!
HOLY!
Oh, MAN!
SO PRETTY!
YOW!
AMAZING, THOUGH, HOW I ALWAYS POP UP WHILST YOU SPEECHIFY, Hmm?
VERONICA! YOU ARE--
WAH. WAH. WAH. ENOUGH WITH THE 'YOU AREN'T WELCOME HERE' STUFF.
I HAVE AS MUCH RIGHT TO BE HERE AS YOU.
I'LL JUST BE OVER HERE, HAVING A GOOD TIME, WATCHING YOU CRASH.
AND.
BURN.
WE'LL SEE ABOUT THAT! THE NIGHT IS STILL YOUNG!

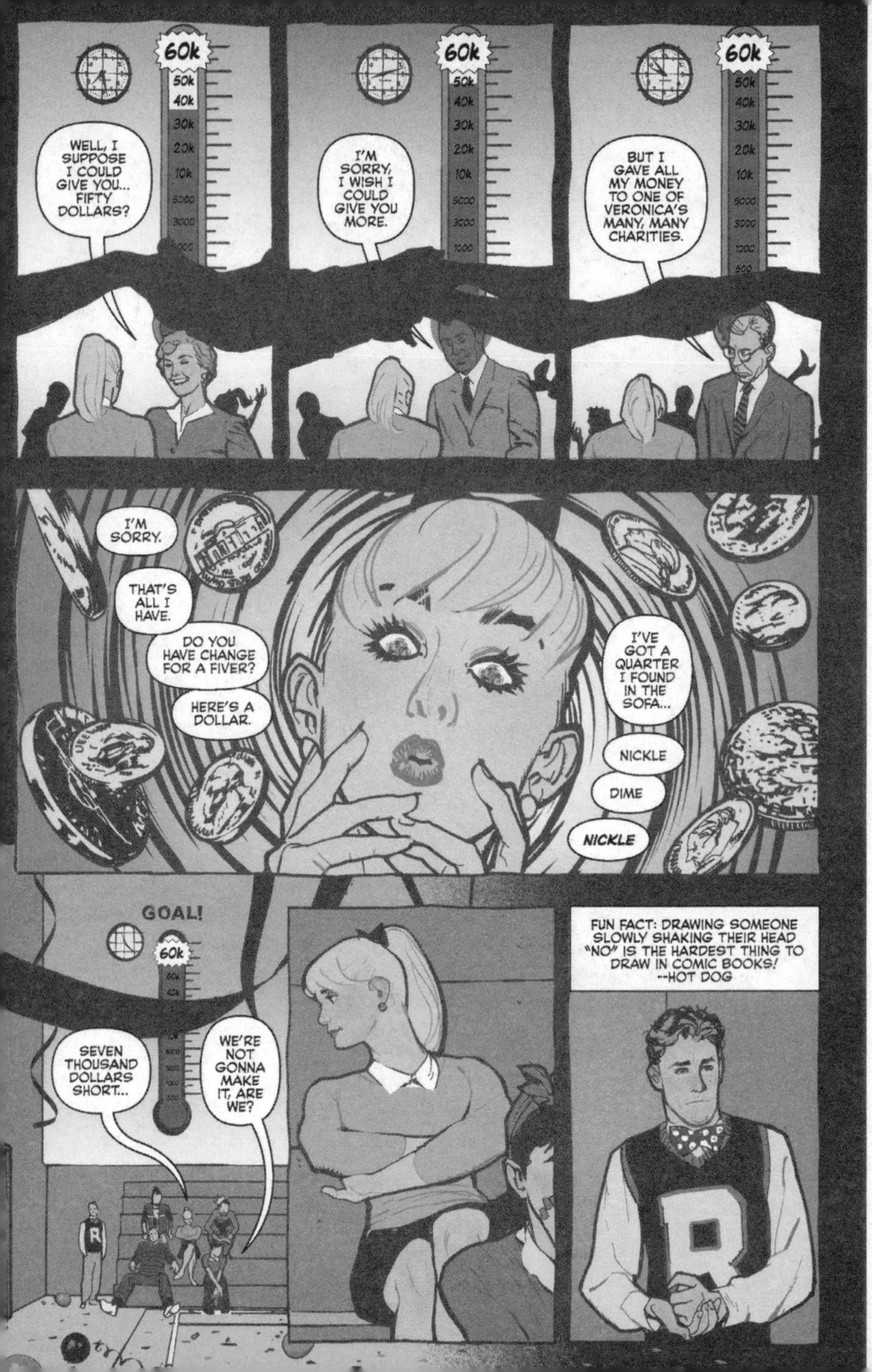

60k
50k
40k
30k
20k
10k
5000
3000
1000
WELL, I SUPPOSE I COULD GIVE YOU... FIFTY DOLLARS?
I'M SORRY, I WISH I COULD GIVE YOU MORE.
BUT I GAVE ALL MY MONEY TO ONE OF VERONICA'S MANY, MANY CHARITIES.
I'M SORRY.
THAT'S ALL I HAVE.
DO YOU HAVE CHANGE FOR A FIVER?
HERE'S A DOLLAR.
I'VE GOT A QUARTER I FOUND IN THE SOFA...
NICKLE
DIME
NICKLE
GOAL!
60k
SEVEN THOUSAND DOLLARS SHORT...
WE'RE NOT GONNA MAKE IT, ARE WE?
FUN FACT: DRAWING SOMEONE SLOWLY SHAKING THEIR HEAD "NO" IS THE HARDEST THING TO DRAW IN COMIC BOOKS! --HOT DOG

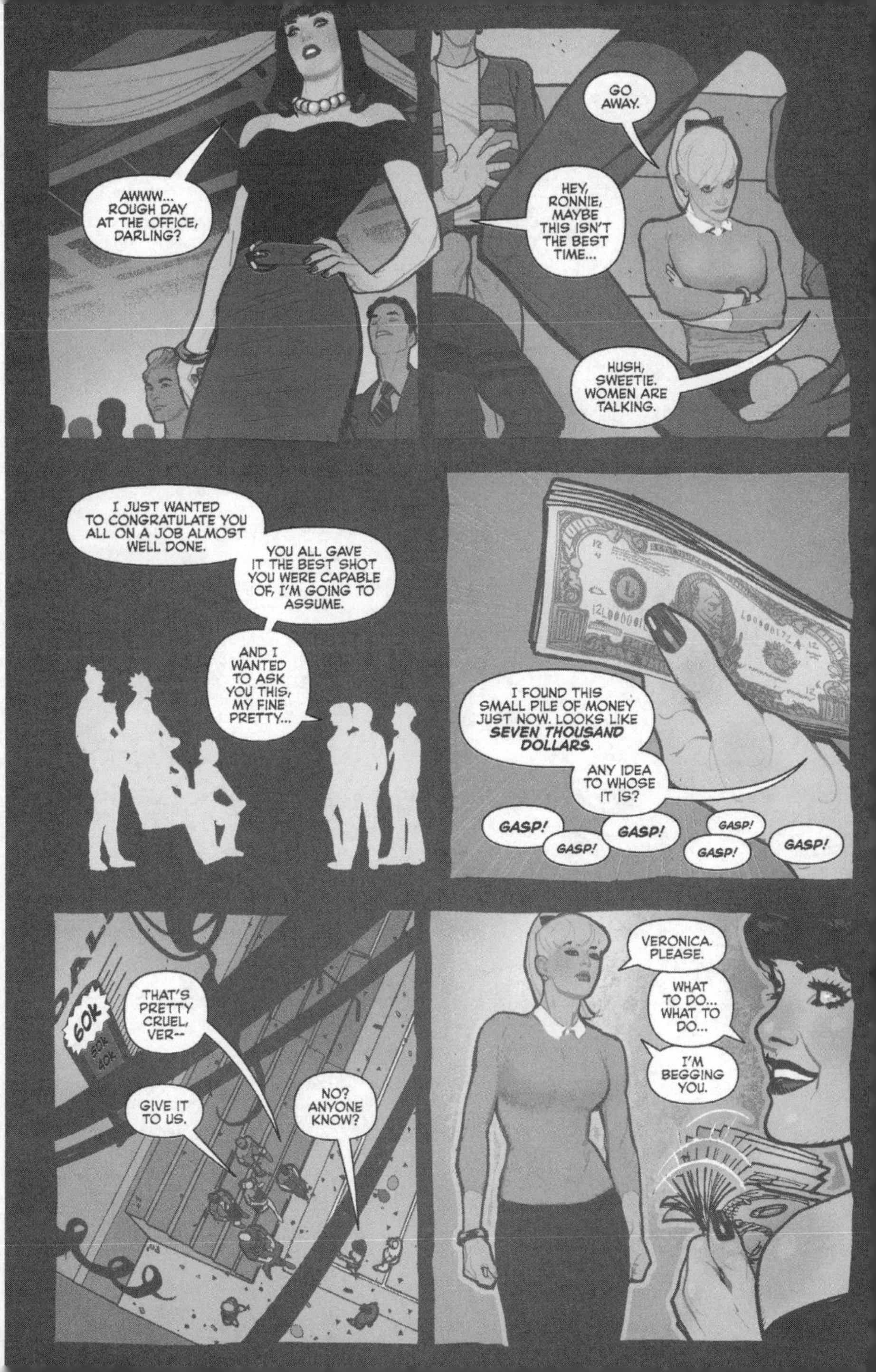
AWWW... ROUGH DAY AT THE OFFICE, DARLING?
GO AWAY.
HEY, RONNIE, MAYBE THIS ISN'T THE BEST TIME...
HUSH, SWEETIE. WOMEN ARE TALKING.
I JUST WANTED TO CONGRATULATE YOU ALL ON A JOB ALMOST WELL DONE.
YOU ALL GAVE IT THE BEST SHOT YOU WERE CAPABLE OF, I'M GOING TO ASSUME.
AND I WANTED TO ASK YOU THIS, MY FINE PRETTY...
I FOUND THIS SMALL PILE OF MONEY JUST NOW. LOOKS LIKE ***SEVEN THOUSAND DOLLARS***.
ANY IDEA TO WHOSE IT IS?
GASP!
GASP!
GASP!
GASP!
GASP!
GASP!
60K
50K
40K
THAT'S PRETTY CRUEL, VER--
GIVE IT TO US.
NO? ANYONE KNOW?
VERONICA. PLEASE.
WHAT TO DO... WHAT TO DO...
I'M BEGGING YOU.

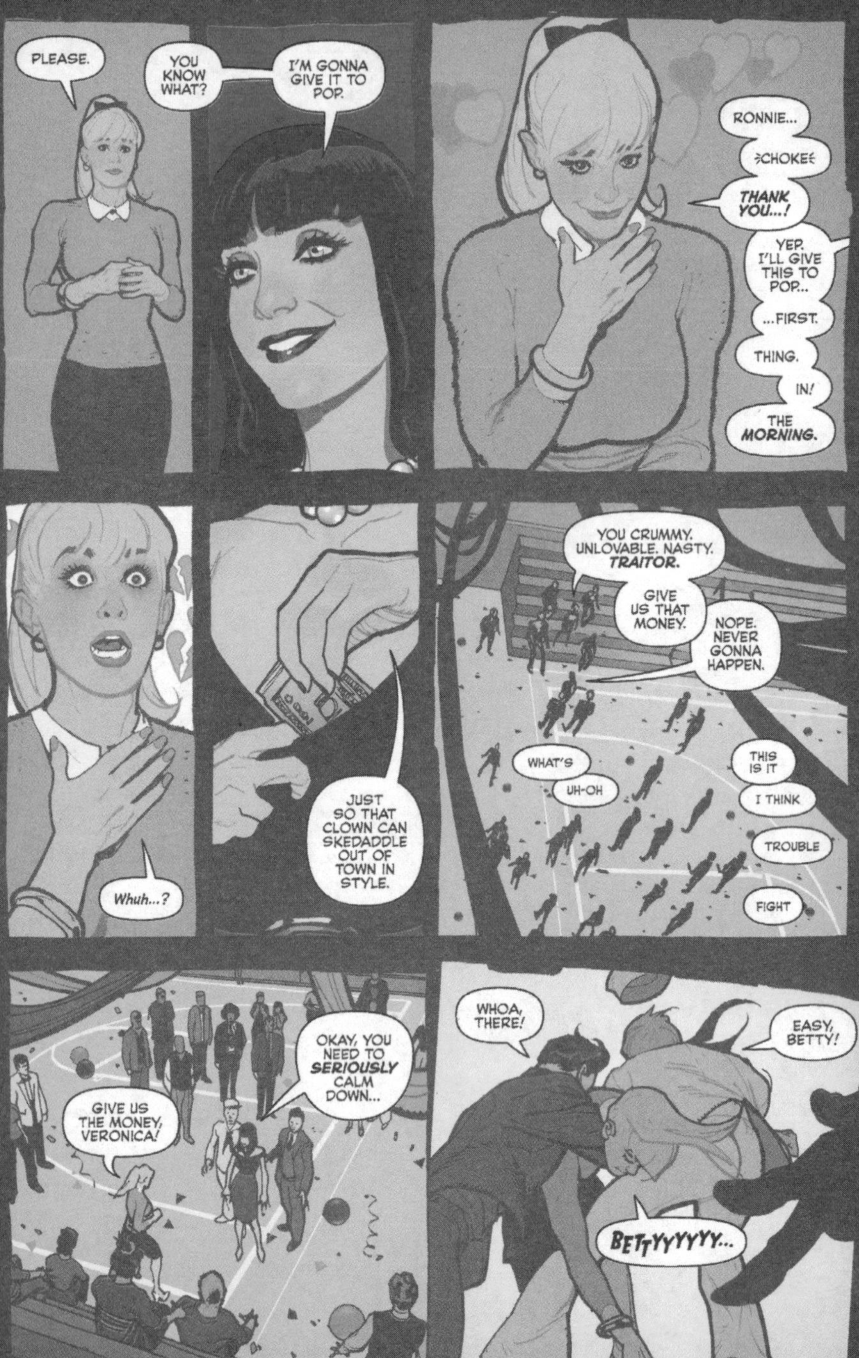
PLEASE.
YOU KNOW WHAT?
I'M GONNA GIVE IT TO POP.
RONNIE...
CHOKE
THANK YOU...!
YEP. I'LL GIVE THIS TO POP...
...FIRST.
THING.
IN!
THE MORNING.
Whuh...?
JUST SO THAT CLOWN CAN SKEDADDLE OUT OF TOWN IN STYLE.
YOU CRUMMY. UNLOVABLE. NASTY. TRAITOR.
GIVE US THAT MONEY.
NOPE. NEVER GONNA HAPPEN.
WHAT'S
UH-OH
THIS IS IT
I THINK
TROUBLE
FIGHT
OKAY, YOU NEED TO SERIOUSLY CALM DOWN...
GIVE US THE MONEY, VERONICA!
WHOA, THERE!
EASY, BETTY!
BETTYYYYYY...

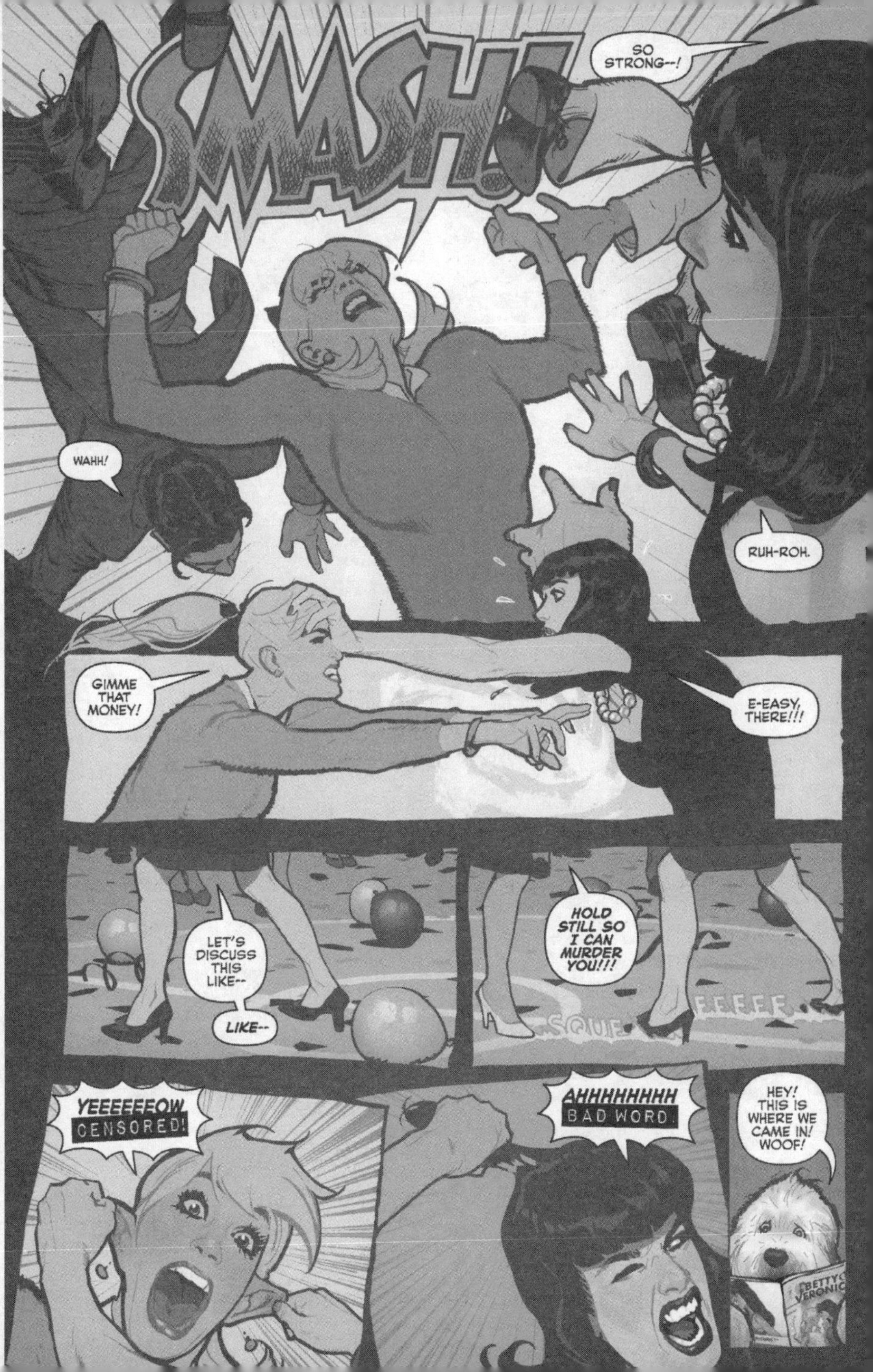
SMASH!
SO STRONG--!
WAHH!
RUH-ROH.
GIMME THAT MONEY!
E-EASY, THERE!!!
LET'S DISCUSS THIS LIKE--
LIKE--
HOLD STILL SO I CAN MURDER YOU!!!
SQUE
EEEEE
YEEEEEEOW
CENSORED!
AHHHHHHHH
BAD WORD.
HEY! THIS IS WHERE WE CAME IN! WOOF!

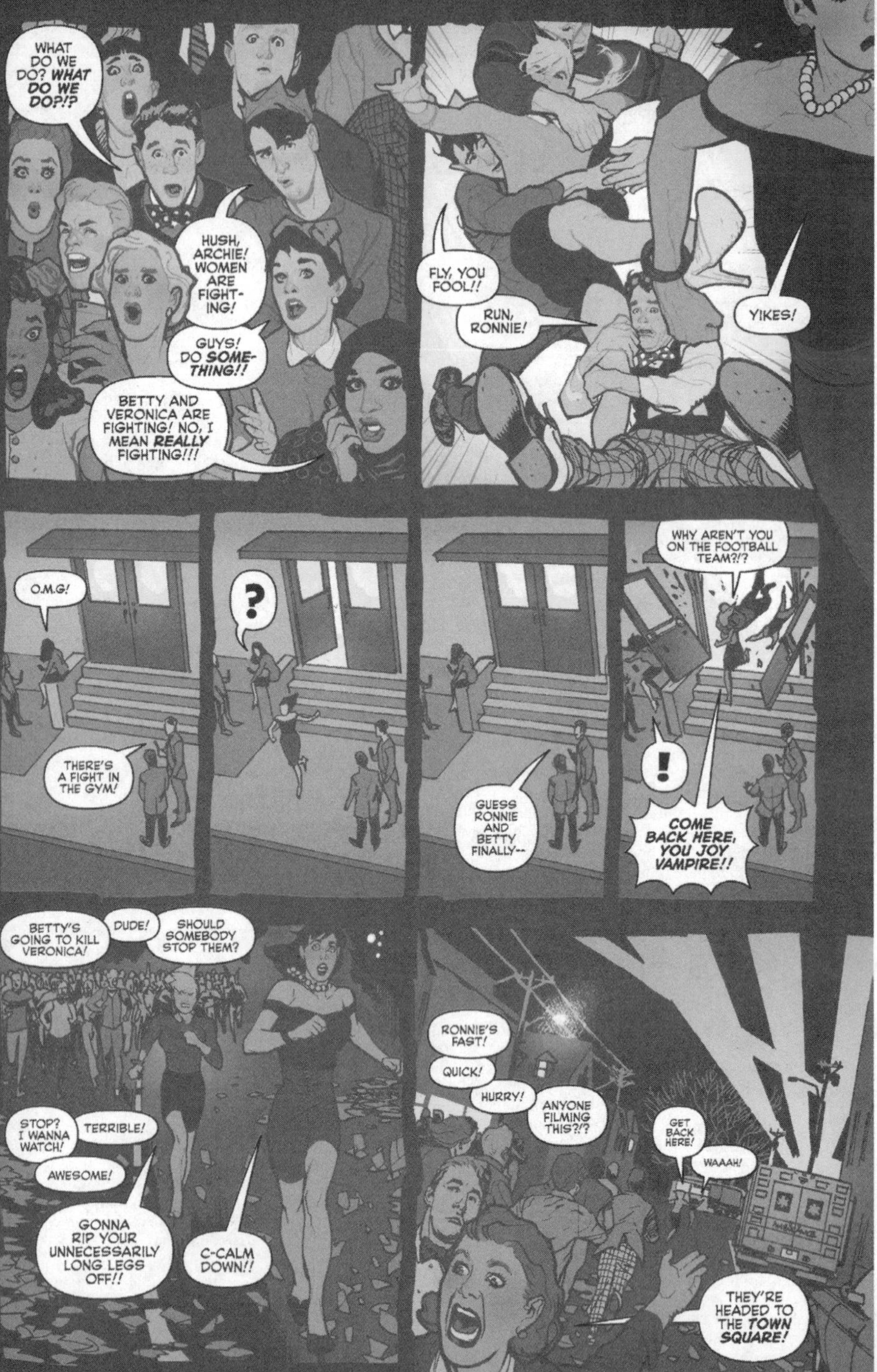
WHAT DO WE DO? WHAT DO WE DO?!?
HUSH, ARCHIE! WOMEN ARE FIGHT-ING!
GUYS! DO SOME-THING!!
BETTY AND VERONICA ARE FIGHTING! NO, I MEAN REALLY FIGHTING!!!
FLY, YOU FOOL!!
RUN, RONNIE!
YIKES!
O.M.G!
THERE'S A FIGHT IN THE GYM!
?
GUESS RONNIE AND BETTY FINALLY--
WHY AREN'T YOU ON THE FOOTBALL TEAM?!?
!
COME BACK HERE, YOU JOY VAMPIRE!!
BETTY'S GOING TO KILL VERONICA!
DUDE!
SHOULD SOMEBODY STOP THEM?
STOP? I WANNA WATCH!
TERRIBLE!
AWESOME!
GONNA RIP YOUR UNNECESSARILY LONG LEGS OFF!!
C-CALM DOWN!!
RONNIE'S FAST!
QUICK!
HURRY!
ANYONE FILMING THIS?!?
GET BACK HERE!
WAAAH!
THEY'RE HEADED TO THE TOWN SQUARE!

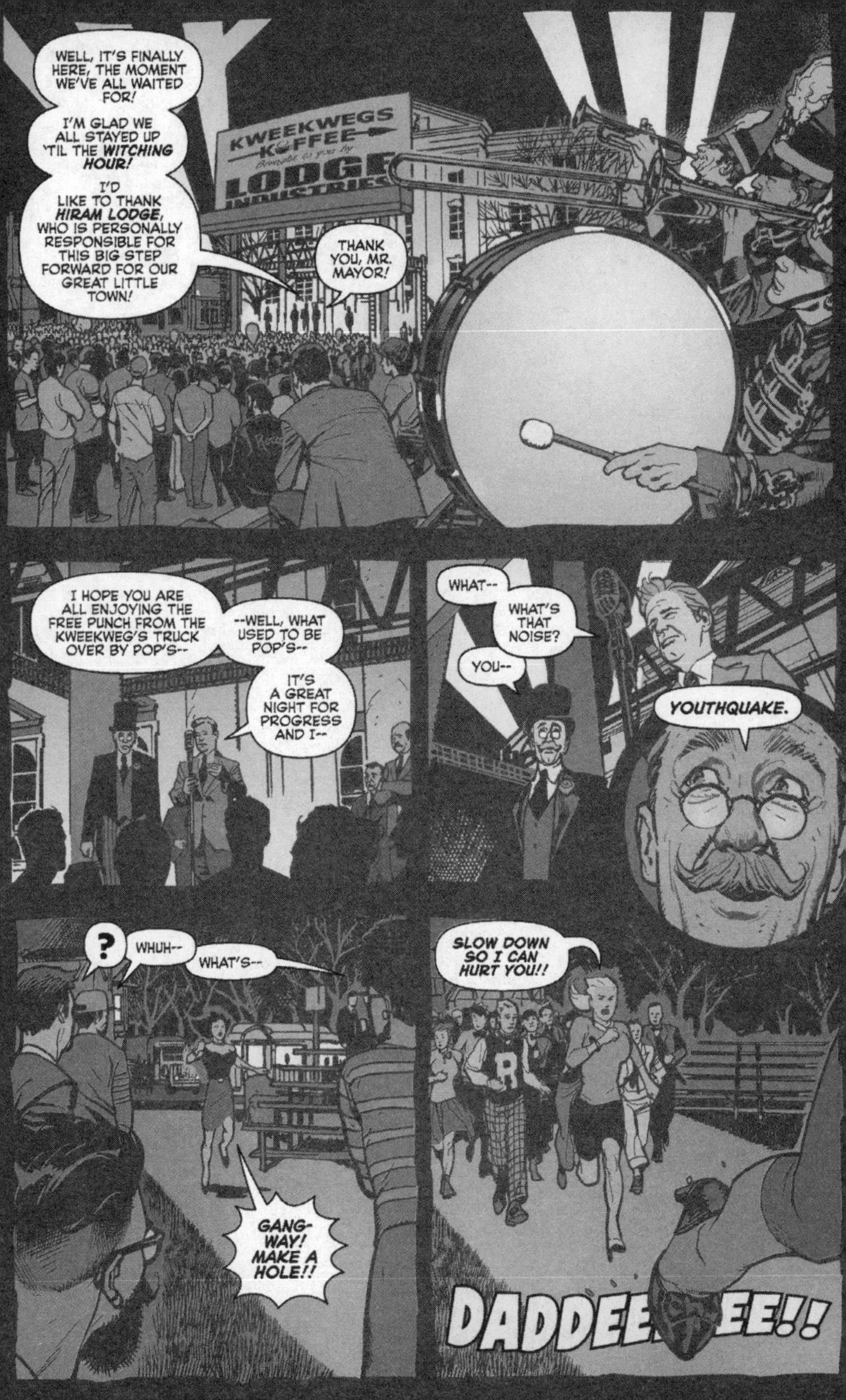
WELL, IT'S FINALLY HERE, THE MOMENT WE'VE ALL WAITED FOR!
I'M GLAD WE ALL STAYED UP 'TIL THE WITCHING HOUR!
I'D LIKE TO THANK HIRAM LODGE, WHO IS PERSONALLY RESPONSIBLE FOR THIS BIG STEP FORWARD FOR OUR GREAT LITTLE TOWN!
KWEEKWEGS KOFFEE
THANK YOU, MR. MAYOR!
I HOPE YOU ARE ALL ENJOYING THE FREE PUNCH FROM THE KWEEKWEG'S TRUCK OVER BY POP'S--
--WELL, WHAT USED TO BE POP'S--
IT'S A GREAT NIGHT FOR PROGRESS AND I--
WHAT--
WHAT'S THAT NOISE?
YOU--
YOUTHQUAKE.
?
WHUH--
WHAT'S--
GANG-WAY! MAKE A HOLE!!
SLOW DOWN SO I CAN HURT YOU!!
DADDEE EE!!

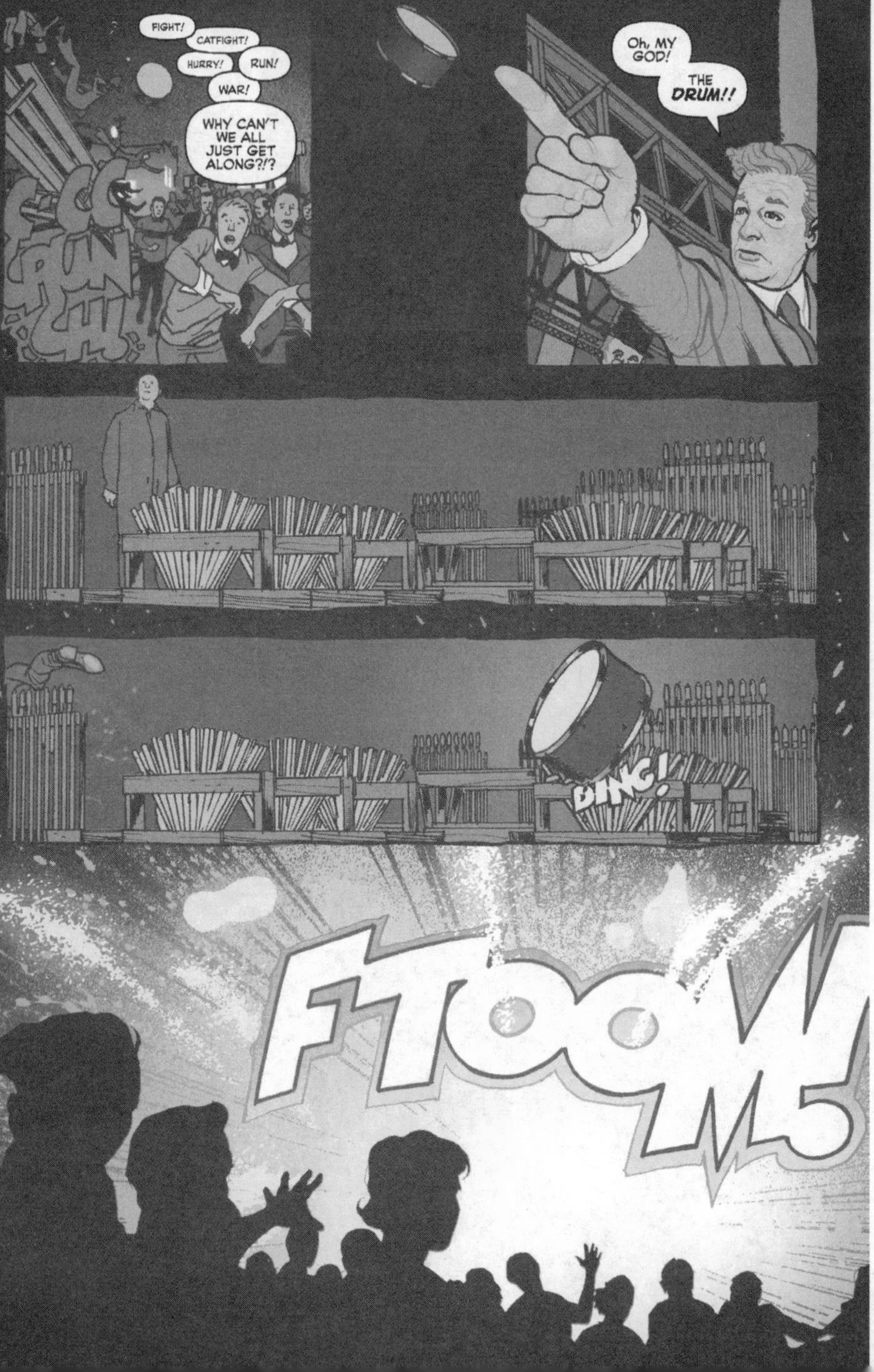
FIGHT!
CATFIGHT!
HURRY!
RUN!
WAR!
WHY CAN'T WE ALL JUST GET ALONG?!?
Oh, MY GOD!
THE **DRUM!!**
DING!
FTOOM

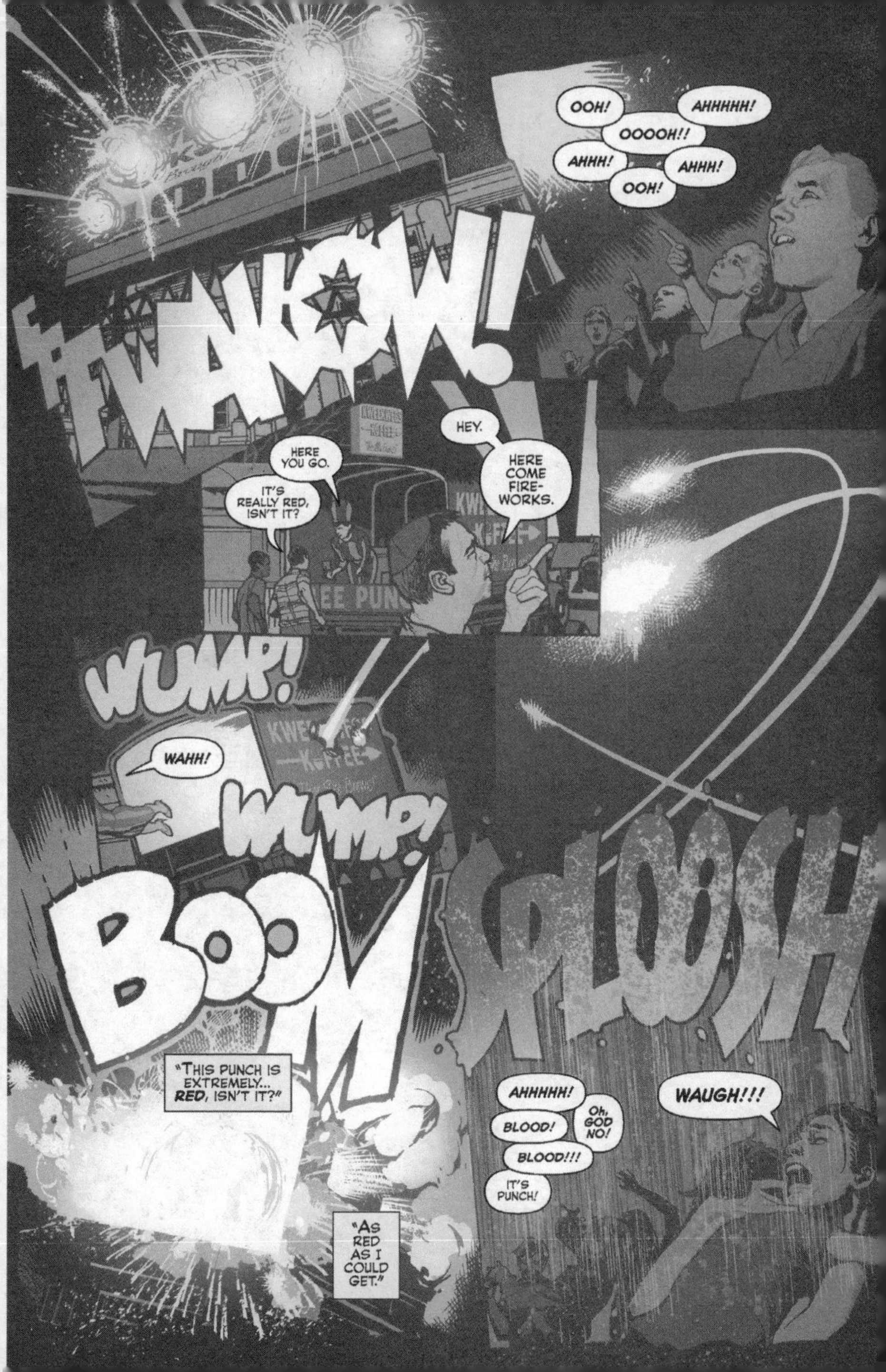

KWEEKWEG'S KOFFEE
OOH!
AHHHHH!
OOOOH!!
AHHH!
AHHH!
OOH!
FWOOM!
HEY.
HERE COME FIRE-WORKS.
HERE YOU GO.
IT'S REALLY RED, ISN'T IT?
KWEEKWEG'S KOFFEE
EE PUNC
WUMP!
WAHH!
WUMP!
BOOM
"THIS PUNCH IS EXTREMELY... RED, ISN'T IT?"
"AS RED AS I COULD GET."
SPLOOSH
AHHHHH!
BLOOD!
OH, GOD NO!
BLOOD!!!
IT'S PUNCH!
WAUGH!!!

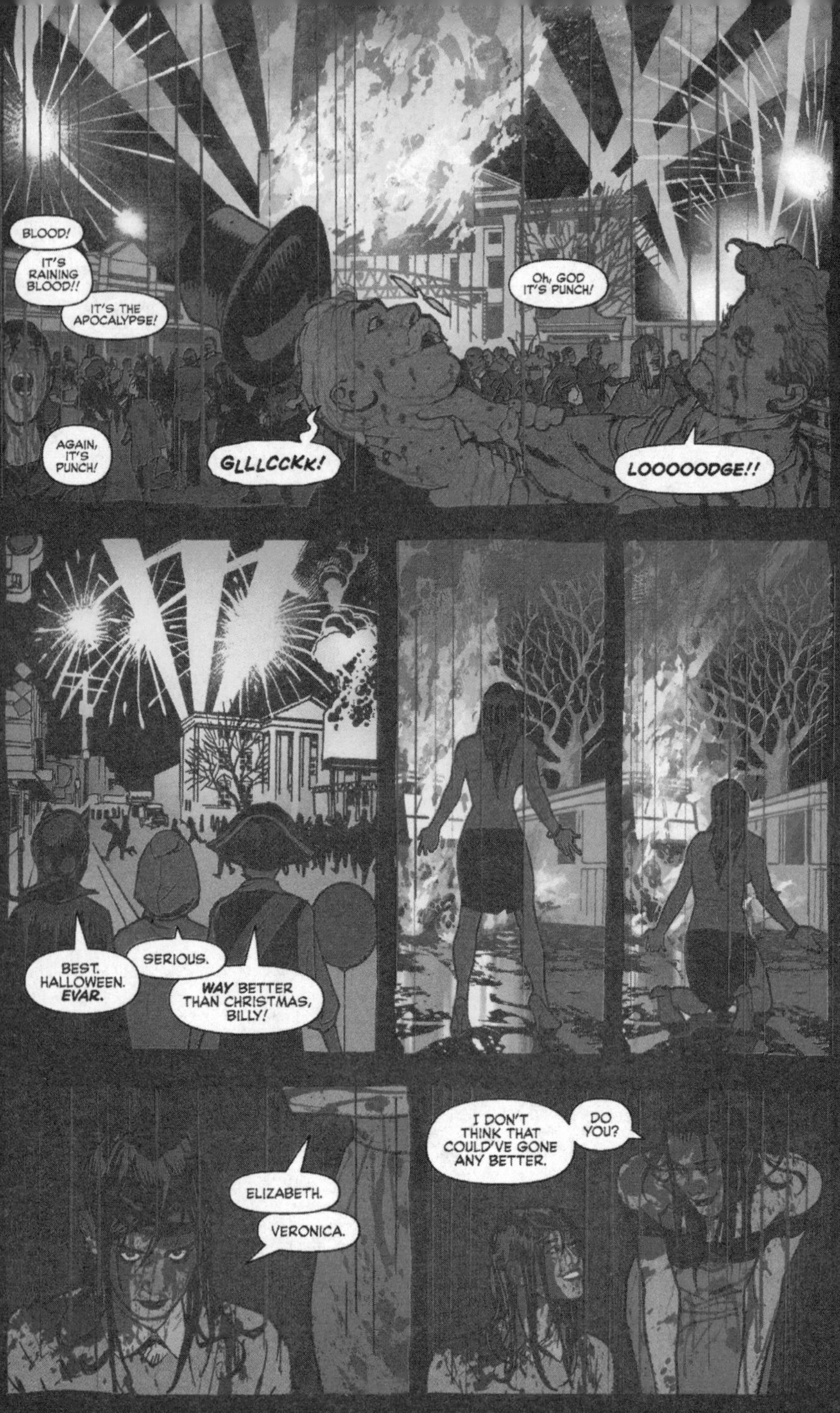
BLOOD!
IT'S RAINING BLOOD!!
IT'S THE APOCALYPSE!
Oh, GOD IT'S PUNCH!
AGAIN, IT'S PUNCH!
GLLLCCKK!
LOOOOODGE!!
BEST. HALLOWEEN. EVAR.
SERIOUS.
WAY BETTER THAN CHRISTMAS, BILLY!
ELIZABETH.
VERONICA.
I DON'T THINK THAT COULD'VE GONE ANY BETTER.
DO YOU?

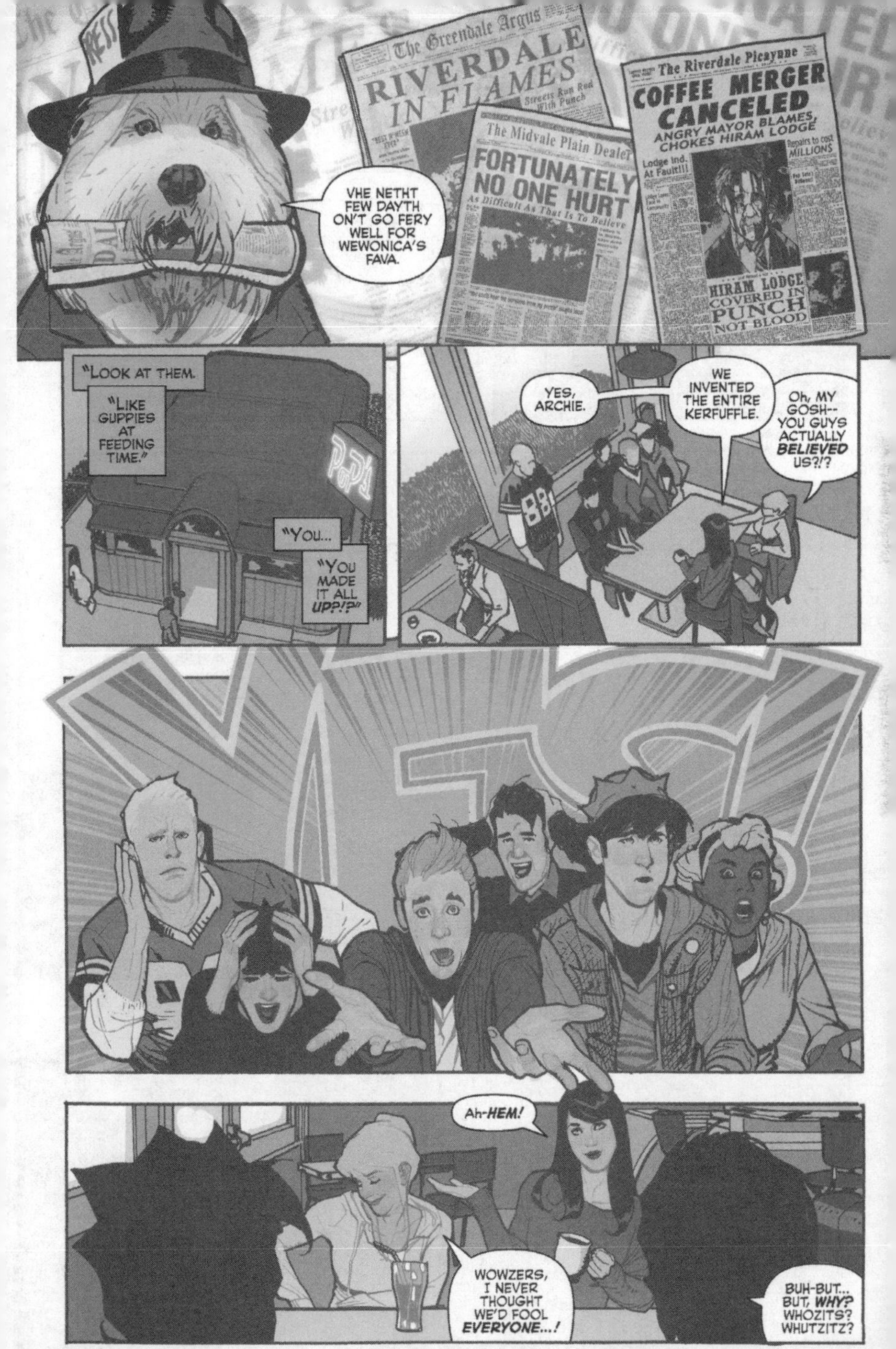
PRESS
The Greendale Argus
RIVERDALE IN FLAMES
Streets Run Red With Punch
The Midvale Plain Dealer
FORTUNATELY NO ONE HURT
As Difficult As That Is To Believe
The Riverdale Picayune
COFFEE MERGER CANCELED
ANGRY MAYOR BLAMES, CHOKES HIRAM LODGE
Repairs to cost MILLIONS
Lodge Ind. At Fault!!!
HIRAM LODGE COVERED IN PUNCH NOT BLOOD
VHE NETHT FEW DAYTH ON'T GO FERY WELL FOR WEWONICA'S FAVA.
"LOOK AT THEM.
"LIKE GUPPIES AT FEEDING TIME."
POP'S
"YOU...
"YOU MADE IT ALL UP?!?"
YES, ARCHIE.
WE INVENTED THE ENTIRE KERFUFFLE.
Oh, MY GOSH-- YOU GUYS ACTUALLY BELIEVED US?!?
Ah-HEM!
WOWZERS, I NEVER THOUGHT WE'D FOOL EVERYONE...!
BUH-BUT... BUT, WHY? WHOZITS? WHUTZITZ?

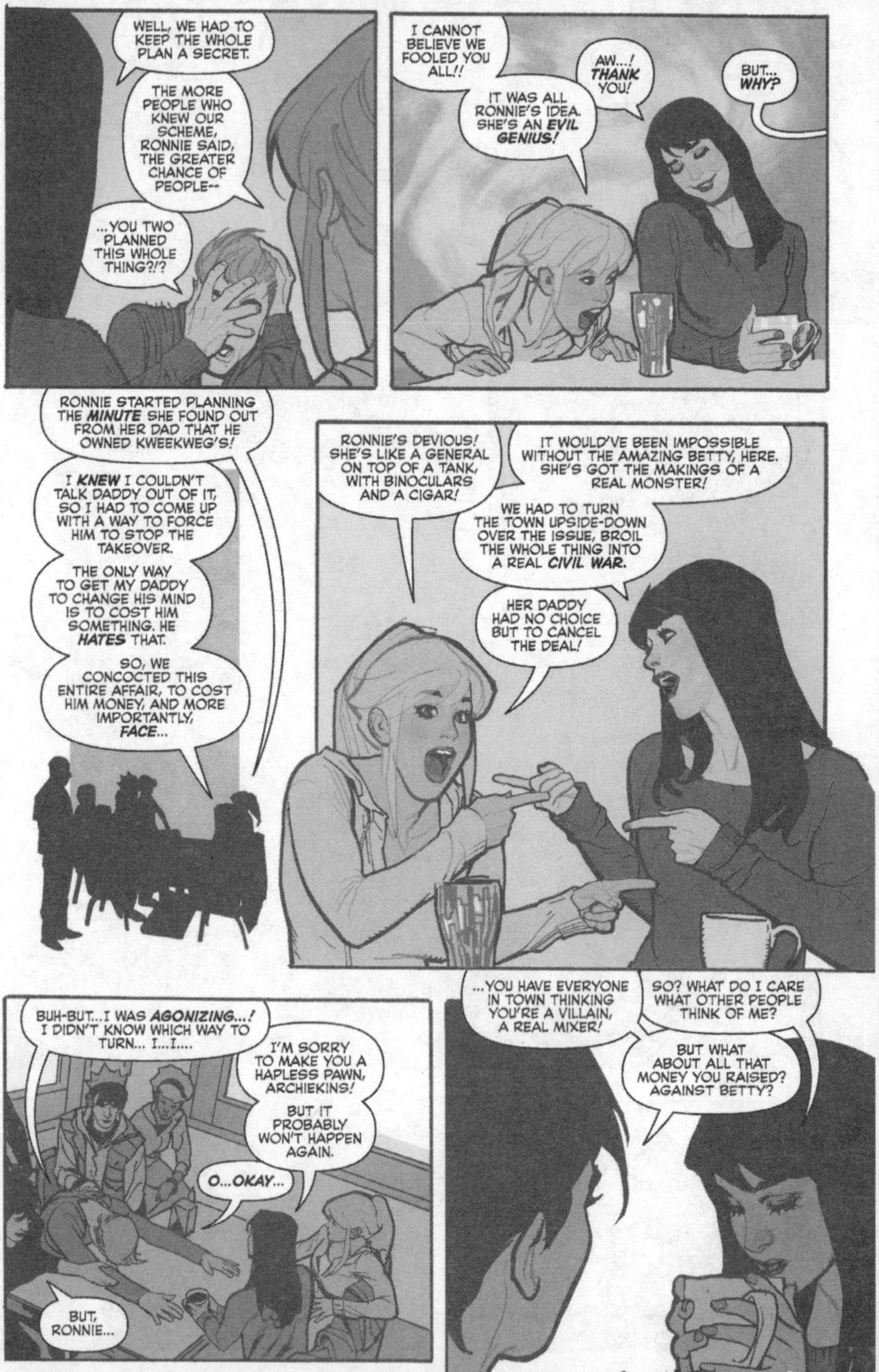
WELL, WE HAD TO KEEP THE WHOLE PLAN A SECRET.
THE MORE PEOPLE WHO KNEW OUR SCHEME, RONNIE SAID, THE GREATER CHANCE OF PEOPLE--
...YOU TWO PLANNED THIS WHOLE THING?!?
I CANNOT BELIEVE WE FOOLED YOU ALL!!
IT WAS ALL RONNIE'S IDEA. SHE'S AN EVIL GENIUS!
AW...! THANK YOU!
BUT... WHY?
RONNIE STARTED PLANNING THE MINUTE SHE FOUND OUT FROM HER DAD THAT HE OWNED KWEEKWEG'S!
I KNEW I COULDN'T TALK DADDY OUT OF IT, SO I HAD TO COME UP WITH A WAY TO FORCE HIM TO STOP THE TAKEOVER.
THE ONLY WAY TO GET MY DADDY TO CHANGE HIS MIND IS TO COST HIM SOMETHING. HE HATES THAT.
SO, WE CONCOCTED THIS ENTIRE AFFAIR, TO COST HIM MONEY, AND MORE IMPORTANTLY, FACE...
RONNIE'S DEVIOUS! SHE'S LIKE A GENERAL ON TOP OF A TANK, WITH BINOCULARS AND A CIGAR!
IT WOULD'VE BEEN IMPOSSIBLE WITHOUT THE AMAZING BETTY, HERE. SHE'S GOT THE MAKINGS OF A REAL MONSTER!
WE HAD TO TURN THE TOWN UPSIDE-DOWN OVER THE ISSUE, BROIL THE WHOLE THING INTO A REAL CIVIL WAR.
HER DADDY HAD NO CHOICE BUT TO CANCEL THE DEAL!
BUH-BUT...I WAS AGONIZING...! I DIDN'T KNOW WHICH WAY TO TURN... I...I....
I'M SORRY TO MAKE YOU A HAPLESS PAWN, ARCHIEKINS!
BUT IT PROBABLY WON'T HAPPEN AGAIN.
O...OKAY...
BUT, RONNIE...
...YOU HAVE EVERYONE IN TOWN THINKING YOU'RE A VILLAIN, A REAL MIXER!
SO? WHAT DO I CARE WHAT OTHER PEOPLE THINK OF ME?
BUT WHAT ABOUT ALL THAT MONEY YOU RAISED? AGAINST BETTY?

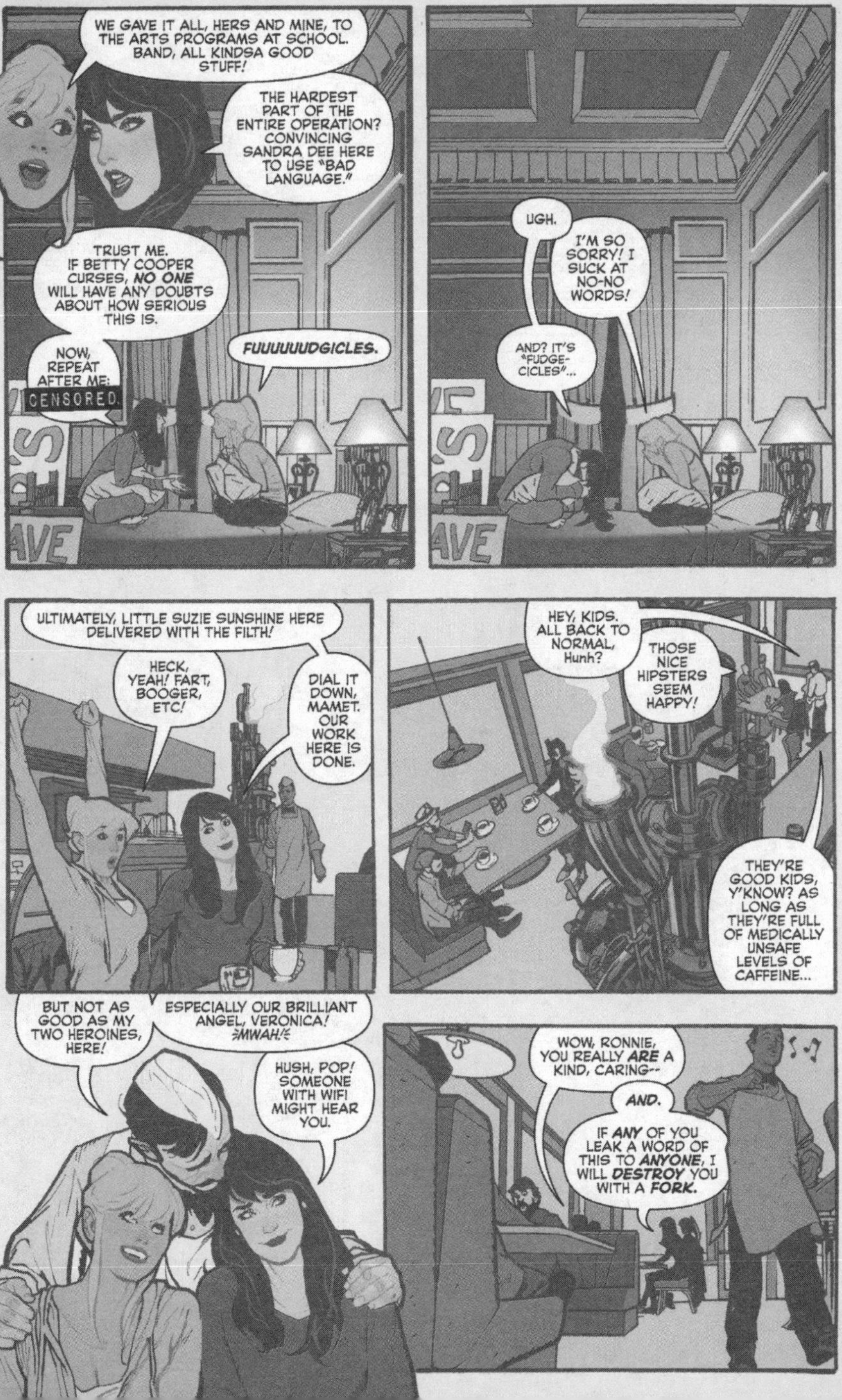

WE GAVE IT ALL, HERS AND MINE, TO THE ARTS PROGRAMS AT SCHOOL. BAND, ALL KINDSA GOOD STUFF!
THE HARDEST PART OF THE ENTIRE OPERATION? CONVINCING SANDRA DEE HERE TO USE "BAD LANGUAGE."
TRUST ME. IF BETTY COOPER CURSES, NO ONE WILL HAVE ANY DOUBTS ABOUT HOW SERIOUS THIS IS.
NOW, REPEAT AFTER ME: CENSORED.
FUUUUUUDGICLES.
UGH.
I'M SO SORRY! I SUCK AT NO-NO WORDS!
AND? IT'S "FUDGE-CICLES"...
ULTIMATELY, LITTLE SUZIE SUNSHINE HERE DELIVERED WITH THE FILTH!
HECK, YEAH! FART, BOOGER, ETC!
DIAL IT DOWN, MAMET. OUR WORK HERE IS DONE.
HEY, KIDS. ALL BACK TO NORMAL, Hunh?
THOSE NICE HIPSTERS SEEM HAPPY!
THEY'RE GOOD KIDS, Y'KNOW? AS LONG AS THEY'RE FULL OF MEDICALLY UNSAFE LEVELS OF CAFFEINE...
BUT NOT AS GOOD AS MY TWO HEROINES, HERE!
ESPECIALLY OUR BRILLIANT ANGEL, VERONICA! MWAH!
HUSH, POP! SOMEONE WITH WIFI MIGHT HEAR YOU.
WOW, RONNIE, YOU REALLY ARE A KIND, CARING--
AND.
IF ANY OF YOU LEAK A WORD OF THIS TO ANYONE, I WILL DESTROY YOU WITH A FORK.

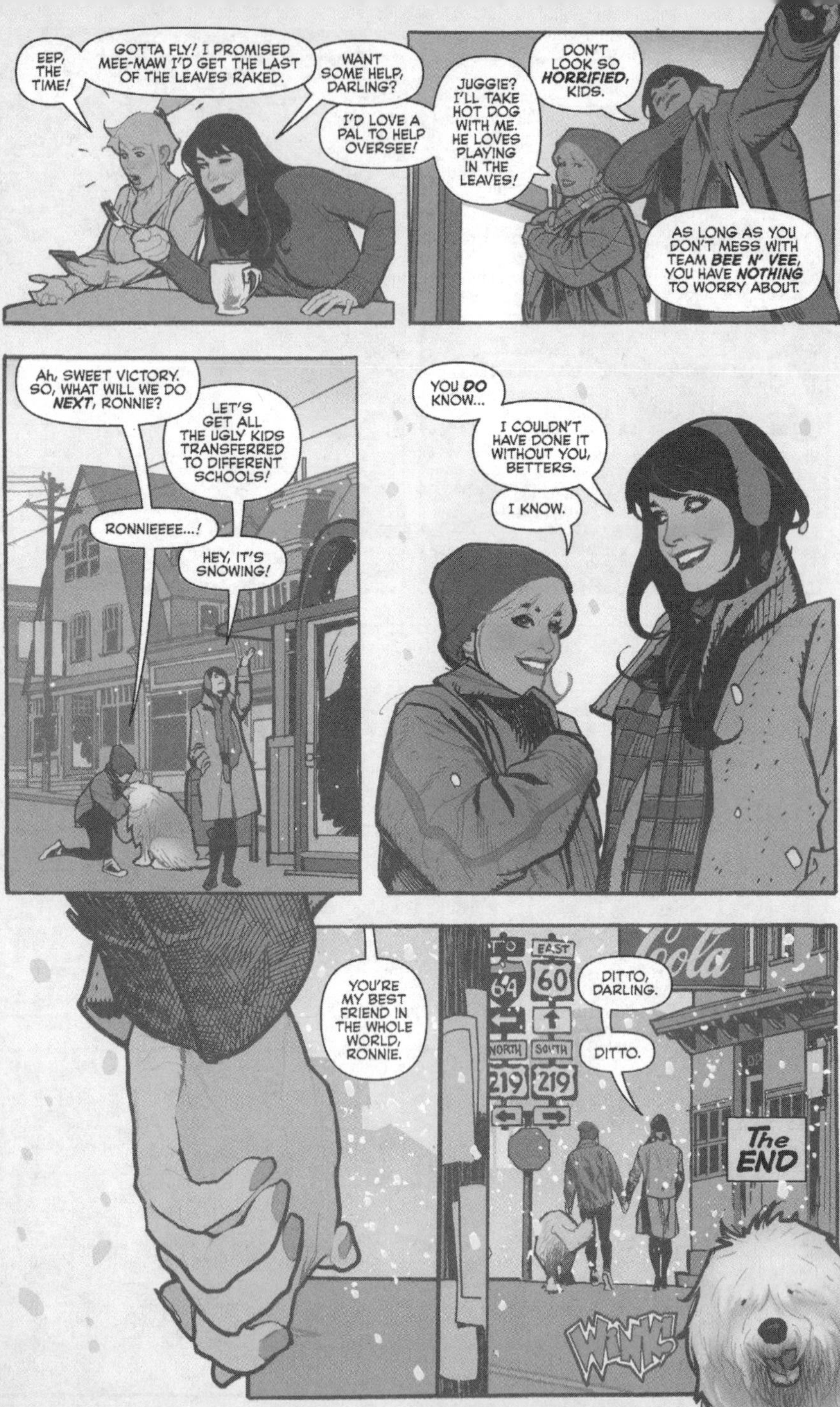
EEP, THE TIME!
GOTTA FLY! I PROMISED MEE-MAW I'D GET THE LAST OF THE LEAVES RAKED.
WANT SOME HELP, DARLING?
I'D LOVE A PAL TO HELP OVERSEE!
JUGGIE? I'LL TAKE HOT DOG WITH ME. HE LOVES PLAYING IN THE LEAVES!
DON'T LOOK SO HORRIFIED, KIDS.
AS LONG AS YOU DON'T MESS WITH TEAM BEE N' VEE, YOU HAVE NOTHING TO WORRY ABOUT.
Ah, SWEET VICTORY. SO, WHAT WILL WE DO NEXT, RONNIE?
LET'S GET ALL THE UGLY KIDS TRANSFERRED TO DIFFERENT SCHOOLS!
RONNIEEEE...!
HEY, IT'S SNOWING!
YOU DO KNOW...
I COULDN'T HAVE DONE IT WITHOUT YOU, BETTERS.
I KNOW.
YOU'RE MY BEST FRIEND IN THE WHOLE WORLD, RONNIE.
TO
EAST
64
60
NORTH
SOUTH
219
219
Cola
DITTO, DARLING.
DITTO.
The END
WINK!

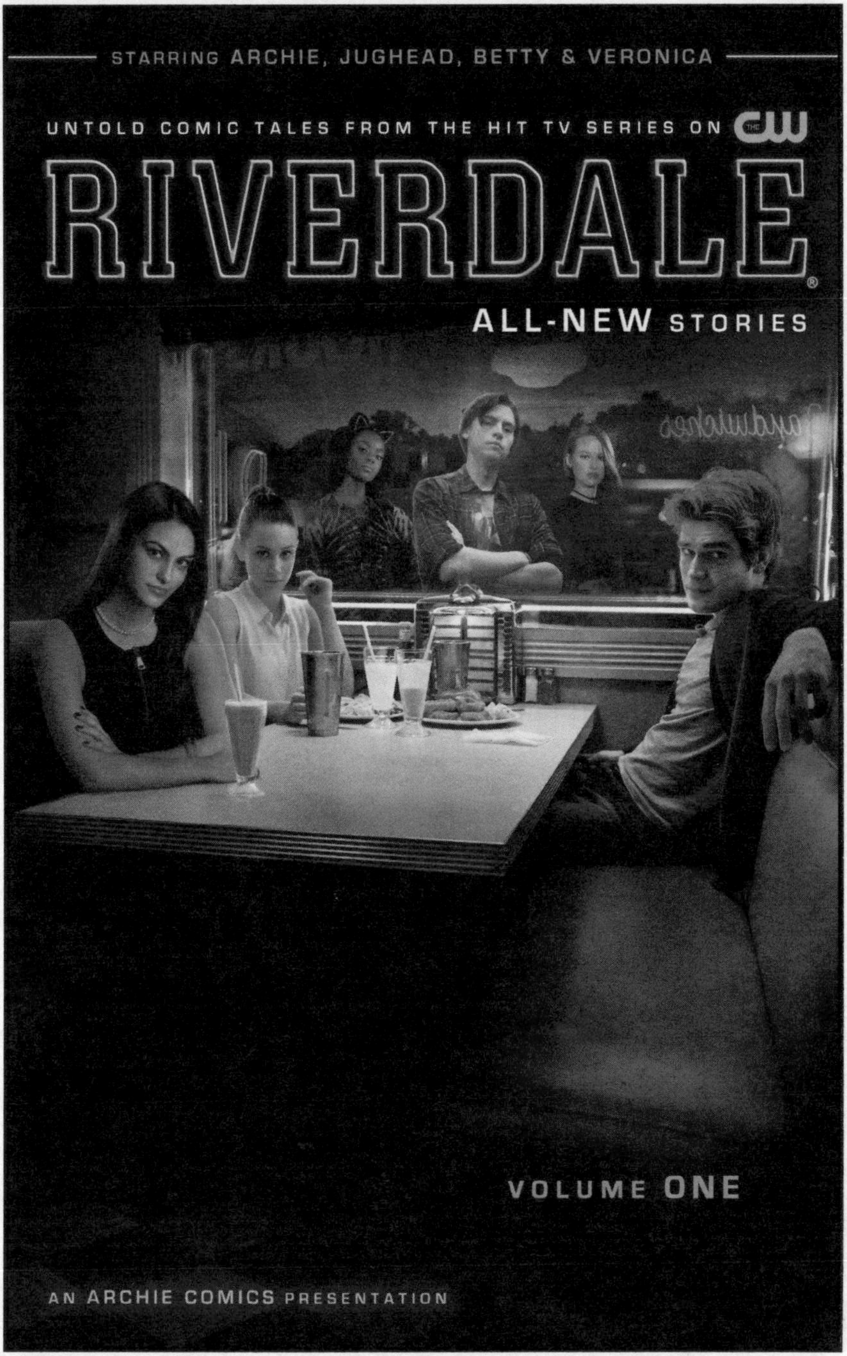
STARRING ARCHIE, JUGHEAD, BETTY & VERONICA
UNTOLD COMIC TALES FROM THE HIT TV SERIES ON
RIVERDALE®
ALL-NEW STORIES
VOLUME ONE
AN ARCHIE COMICS PRESENTATION

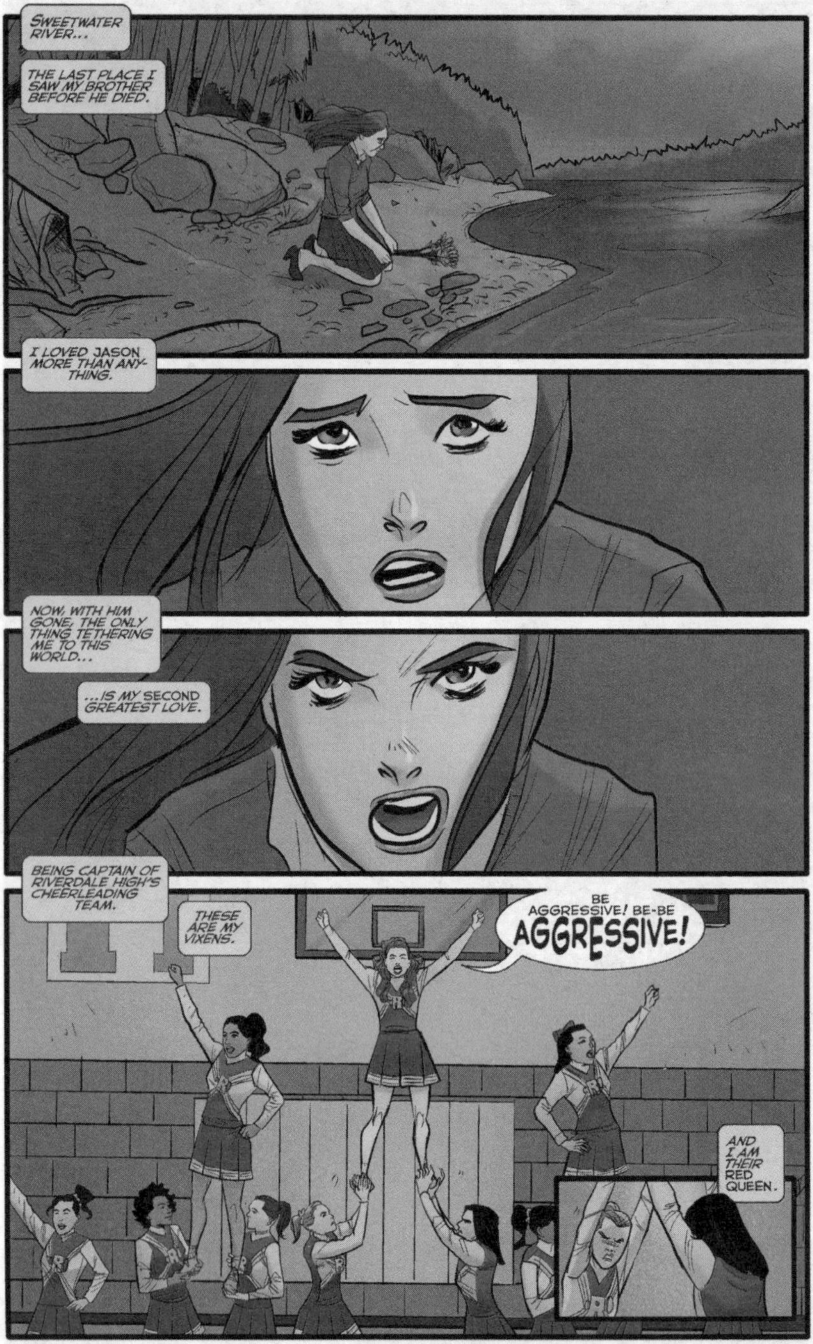

SWEETWATER RIVER...
THE LAST PLACE I SAW MY BROTHER BEFORE HE DIED.
I LOVED JASON MORE THAN ANY-THING.
NOW, WITH HIM GONE, THE ONLY THING TETHERING ME TO THIS WORLD...
...IS MY SECOND GREATEST LOVE.
BEING CAPTAIN OF RIVERDALE HIGH'S CHEERLEADING TEAM.
THESE ARE MY VIXENS.
BE AGGRESSIVE! BE-BE AGGRESSIVE!
AND I AM THEIR RED QUEEN.

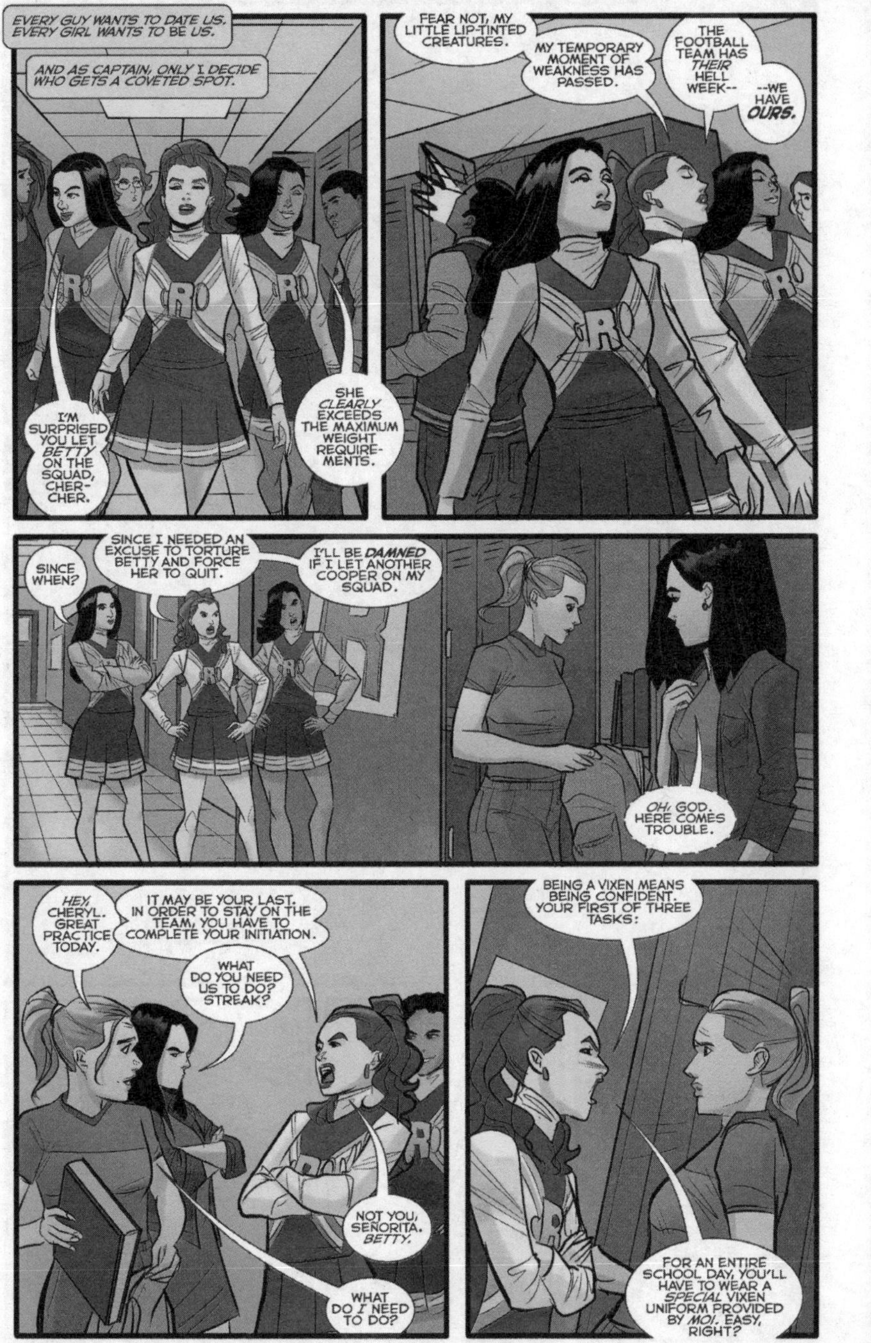
EVERY GUY WANTS TO DATE US. EVERY GIRL WANTS TO BE US.
AND AS CAPTAIN, ONLY I DECIDE WHO GETS A COVETED SPOT.
I'M SURPRISED YOU LET BETTY ON THE SQUAD, CHERCHER.
SHE CLEARLY EXCEEDS THE MAXIMUM WEIGHT REQUIREMENTS.
FEAR NOT, MY LITTLE LIP-TINTED CREATURES.
MY TEMPORARY MOMENT OF WEAKNESS HAS PASSED.
THE FOOTBALL TEAM HAS THEIR HELL WEEK--
--WE HAVE OURS.
SINCE WHEN?
SINCE I NEEDED AN EXCUSE TO TORTURE BETTY AND FORCE HER TO QUIT.
I'LL BE DAMNED IF I LET ANOTHER COOPER ON MY SQUAD.
OH, GOD. HERE COMES TROUBLE.
HEY, CHERYL. GREAT PRACTICE TODAY.
IT MAY BE YOUR LAST. IN ORDER TO STAY ON THE TEAM, YOU HAVE TO COMPLETE YOUR INITIATION.
WHAT DO YOU NEED US TO DO? STREAK?
NOT YOU, SEÑORITA. BETTY.
WHAT DO I NEED TO DO?
BEING A VIXEN MEANS BEING CONFIDENT. YOUR FIRST OF THREE TASKS:
FOR AN ENTIRE SCHOOL DAY, YOU'LL HAVE TO WEAR A SPECIAL VIXEN UNIFORM PROVIDED BY MOI. EASY, RIGHT?

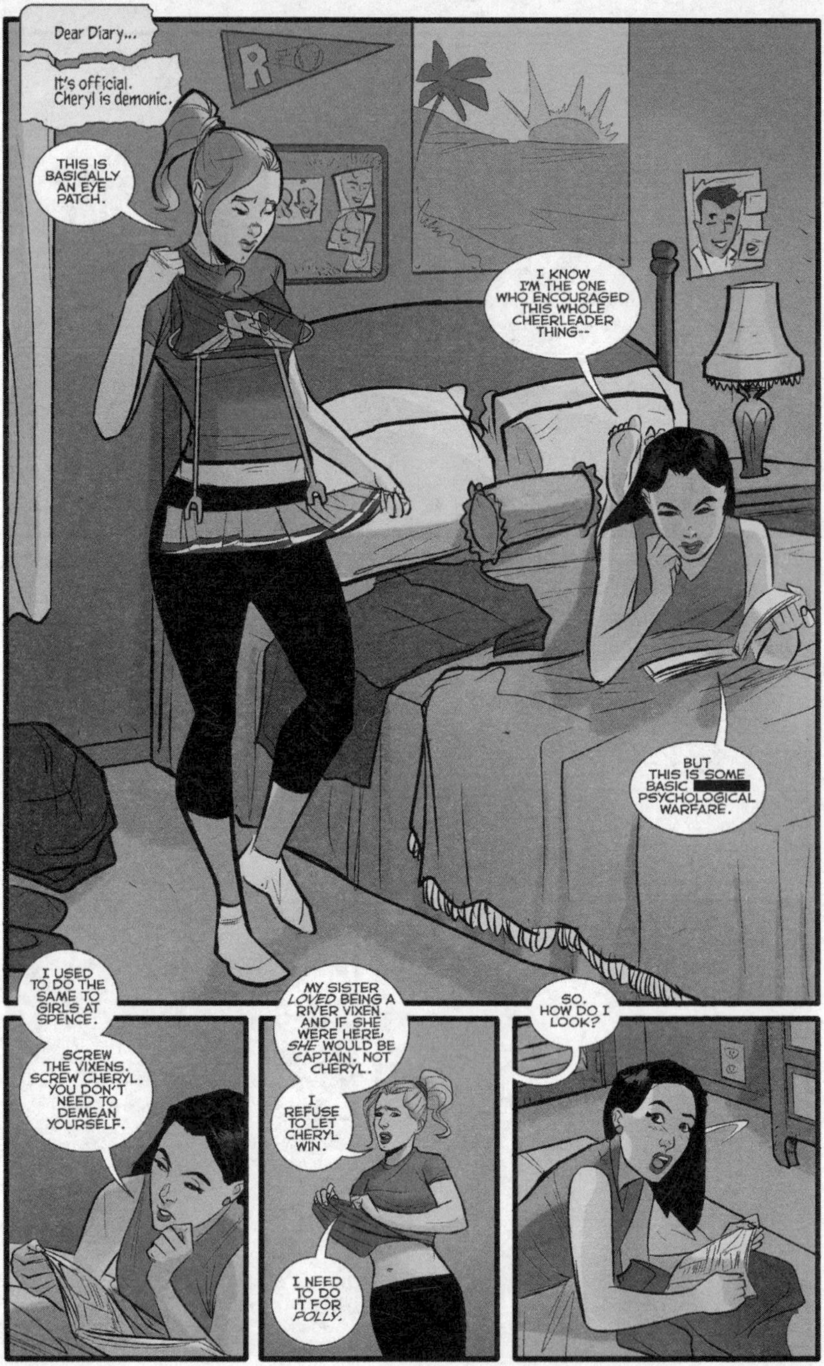
Dear Diary...
It's official. Cheryl is demonic.
THIS IS BASICALLY AN EYE PATCH.
I KNOW I'M THE ONE WHO ENCOURAGED THIS WHOLE CHEERLEADER THING--
BUT THIS IS SOME BASIC [redacted] PSYCHOLOGICAL WARFARE.
I USED TO DO THE SAME TO GIRLS AT SPENCE.
SCREW THE VIXENS. SCREW CHERYL. YOU DON'T NEED TO DEMEAN YOURSELF.
MY SISTER *LOVED* BEING A RIVER VIXEN. AND IF SHE WERE HERE, *SHE* WOULD BE CAPTAIN. NOT CHERYL.
I REFUSE TO LET CHERYL WIN.
I NEED TO DO IT FOR *POLLY*.
SO. HOW DO I LOOK?

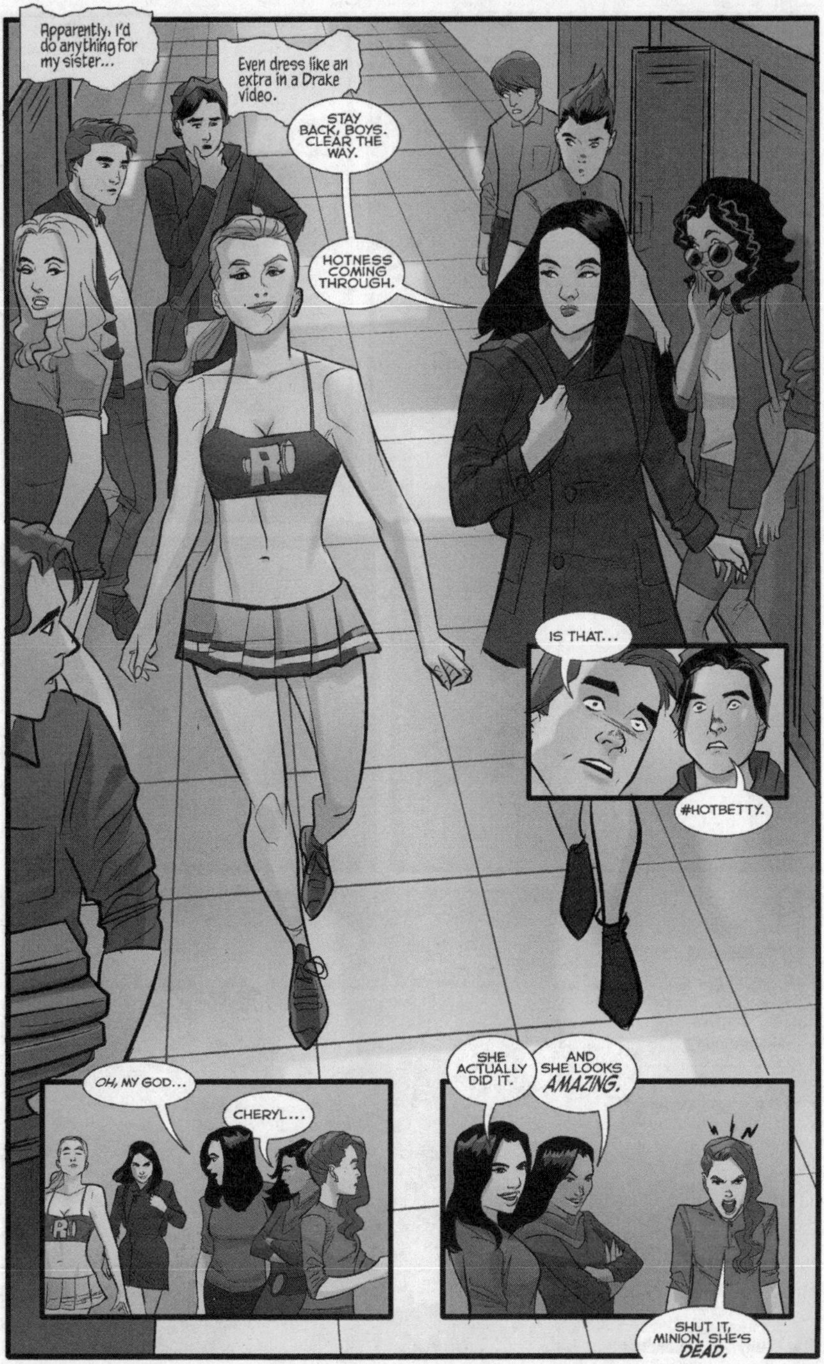
Apparently, I'd do anything for my sister...
Even dress like an extra in a Drake video.
STAY BACK, BOYS. CLEAR THE WAY.
HOTNESS COMING THROUGH.
IS THAT...
#HOTBETTY.
OH, MY GOD...
CHERYL...
SHE ACTUALLY DID IT.
AND SHE LOOKS AMAZING.
SHUT IT, MINION. SHE'S DEAD.

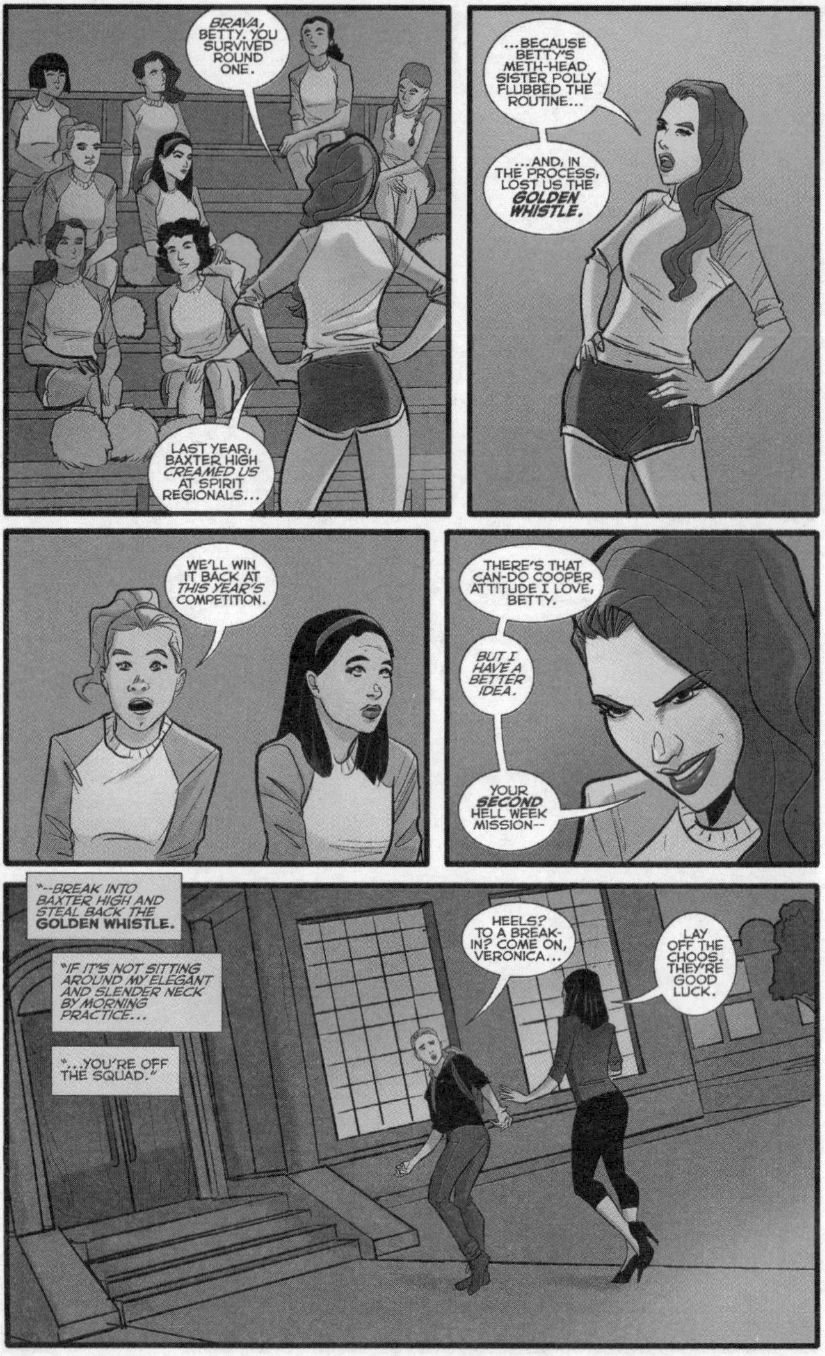
BRAVA, BETTY. YOU SURVIVED ROUND ONE.
LAST YEAR, BAXTER HIGH CREAMED US AT SPIRIT REGIONALS...
...BECAUSE BETTY'S METH-HEAD SISTER POLLY FLUBBED THE ROUTINE...
...AND, IN THE PROCESS, LOST US THE GOLDEN WHISTLE.
WE'LL WIN IT BACK AT THIS YEAR'S COMPETITION.
THERE'S THAT CAN-DO COOPER ATTITUDE I LOVE, BETTY.
BUT I HAVE A BETTER IDEA.
YOUR SECOND HELL WEEK MISSION--
"--BREAK INTO BAXTER HIGH AND STEAL BACK THE GOLDEN WHISTLE.
"IF IT'S NOT SITTING AROUND MY ELEGANT AND SLENDER NECK BY MORNING PRACTICE...
"...YOU'RE OFF THE SQUAD."
HEELS? TO A BREAK-IN? COME ON, VERONICA...
LAY OFF THE CHOOS. THEY'RE GOOD LUCK.

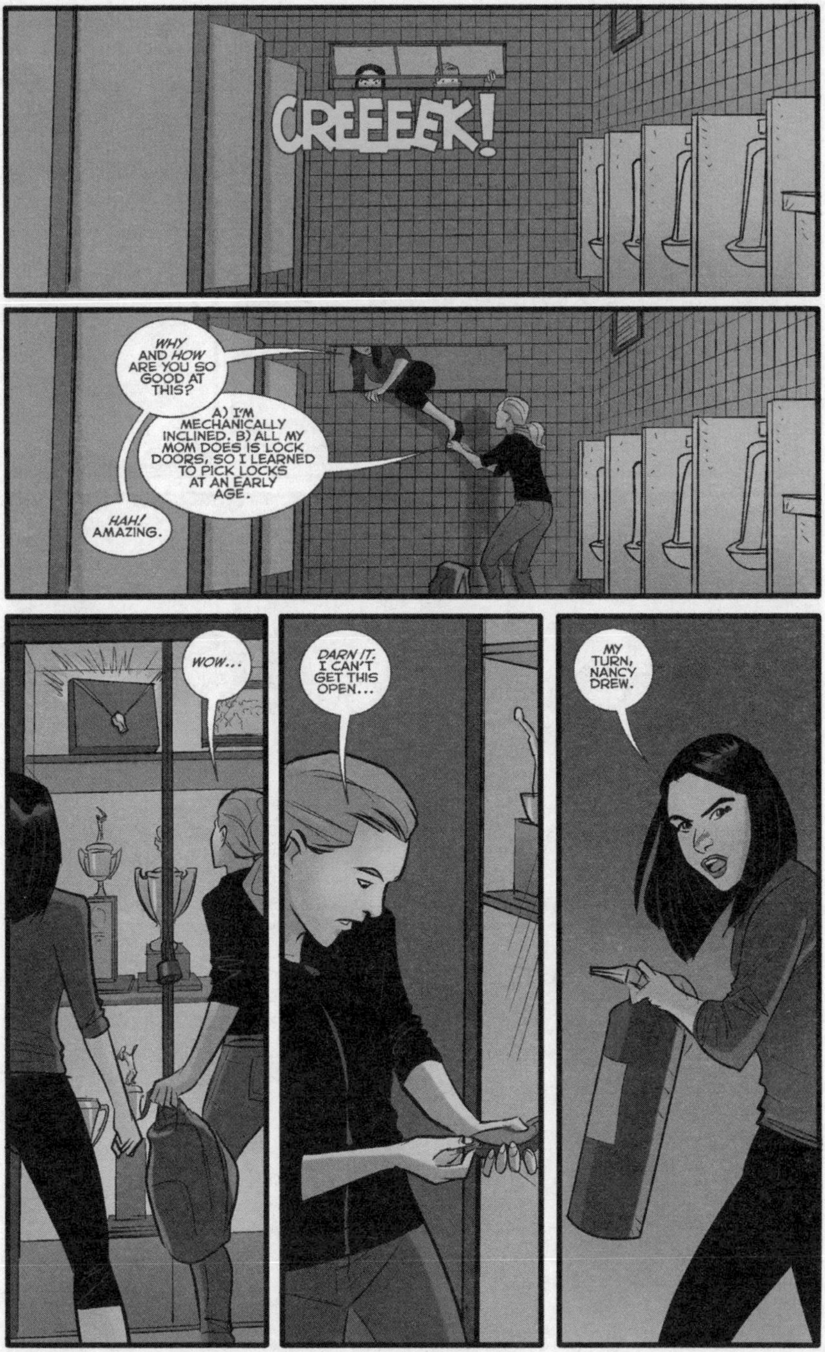
CREEEEK!
WHY AND HOW ARE YOU SO GOOD AT THIS?
A) I'M MECHANICALLY INCLINED. B) ALL MY MOM DOES IS LOCK DOORS, SO I LEARNED TO PICK LOCKS AT AN EARLY AGE.
HAH! AMAZING.
WOW...
DARN IT. I CAN'T GET THIS OPEN...
MY TURN, NANCY DREW.

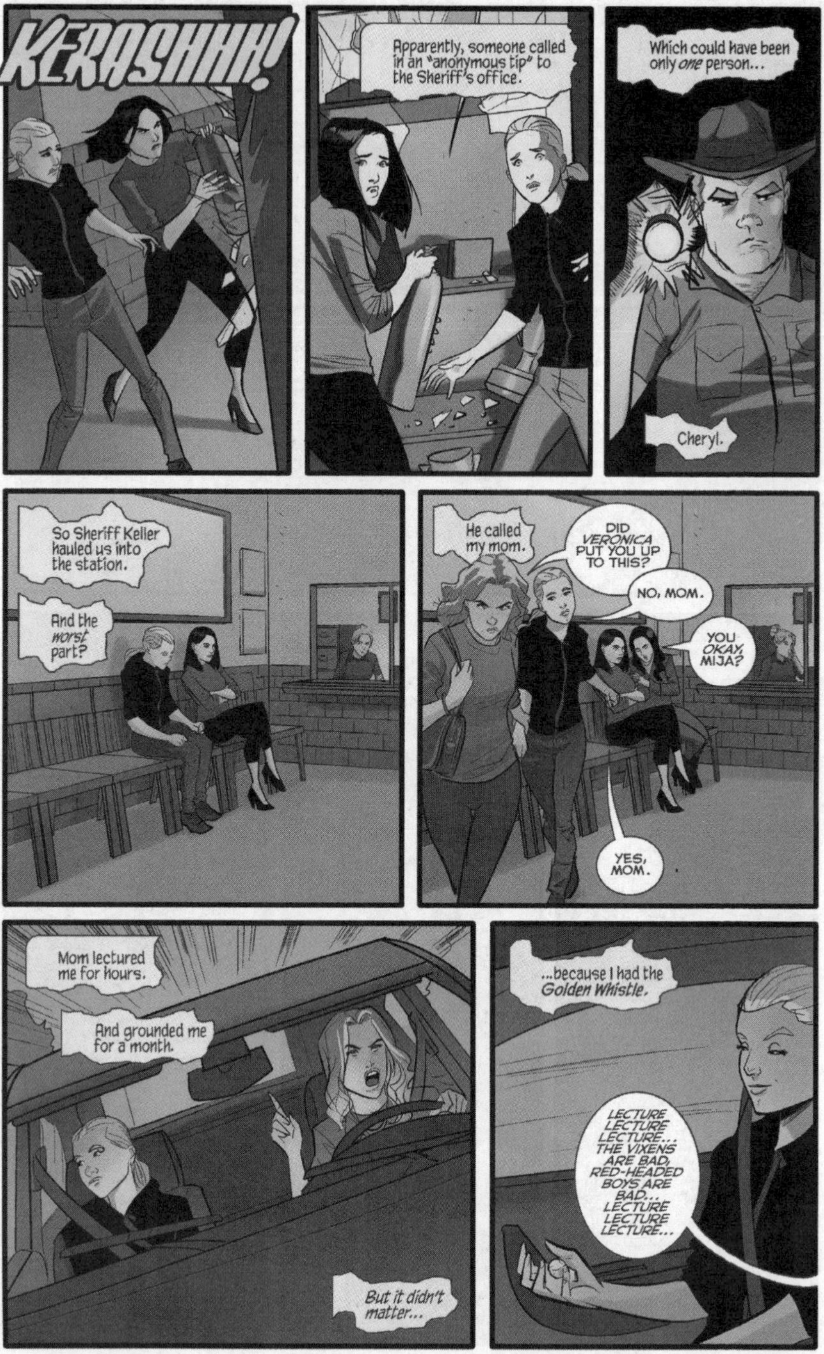
KERASHHH!
Apparently, someone called in an "anonymous tip" to the Sheriff's office.
Which could have been only *one* person...
Cheryl.
So Sheriff Keller hauled us into the station.
And the *worst* part?
He called my mom.
DID *VERONICA* PUT YOU UP TO THIS?
NO, MOM.
YOU *OKAY, MIJA?*
YES, MOM.
Mom lectured me for hours.
And grounded me for a month.
But it didn't matter...
...because I had the *Golden Whistle.*
LECTURE LECTURE LECTURE... THE VIXENS ARE BAD, RED-HEADED BOYS ARE BAD... LECTURE LECTURE LECTURE...

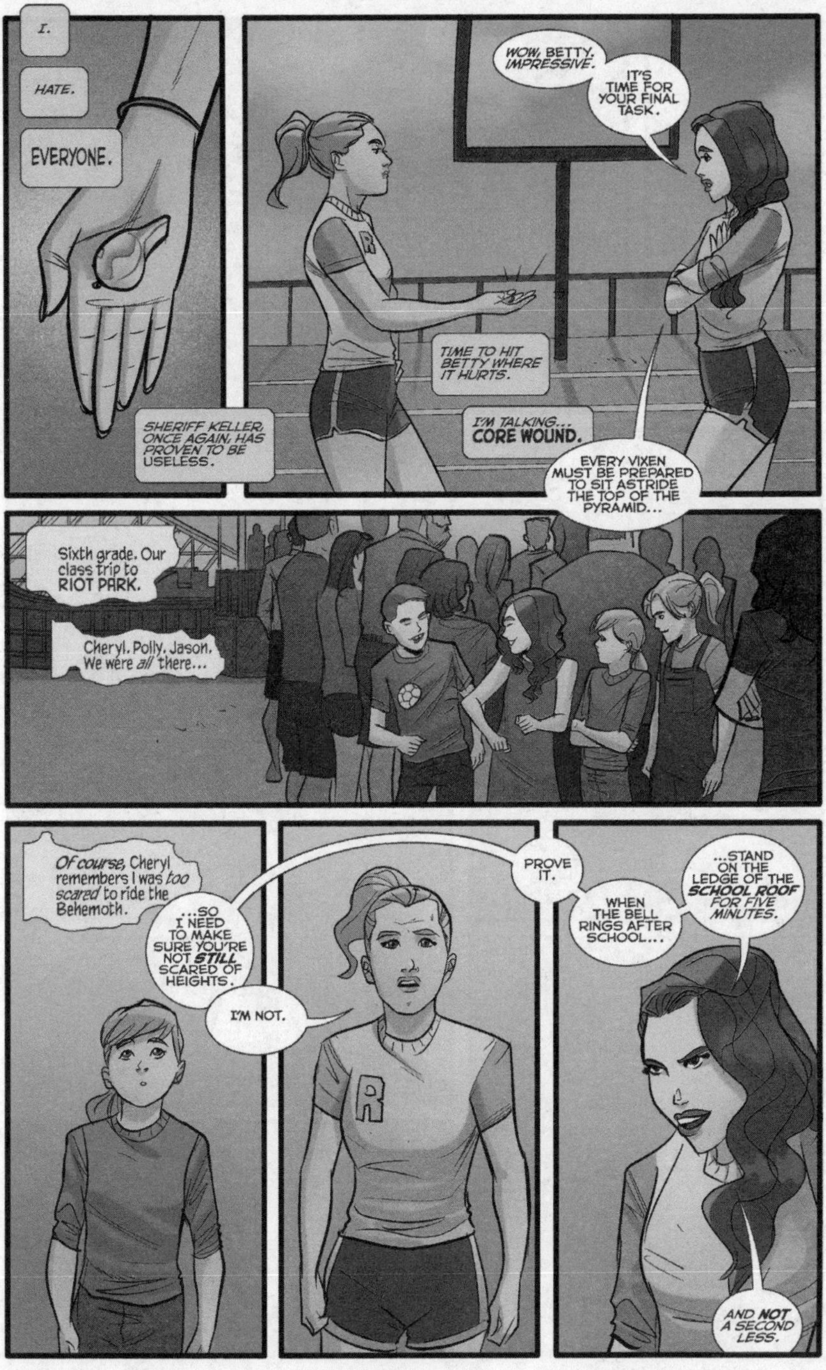
I.
HATE.
EVERYONE.
SHERIFF KELLER, ONCE AGAIN, HAS PROVEN TO BE USELESS.
WOW, BETTY. IMPRESSIVE.
IT'S TIME FOR YOUR FINAL TASK.
TIME TO HIT BETTY WHERE IT HURTS.
I'M TALKING... CORE WOUND.
EVERY VIXEN MUST BE PREPARED TO SIT ASTRIDE THE TOP OF THE PYRAMID...
Sixth grade. Our class trip to RIOT PARK.
Cheryl. Polly. Jason. We were all there...
Of course, Cheryl remembers I was too scared to ride the Behemoth.
...SO I NEED TO MAKE SURE YOU'RE NOT STILL SCARED OF HEIGHTS.
I'M NOT.
PROVE IT.
WHEN THE BELL RINGS AFTER SCHOOL...
...STAND ON THE LEDGE OF THE SCHOOL ROOF FOR FIVE MINUTES.
AND NOT A SECOND LESS.

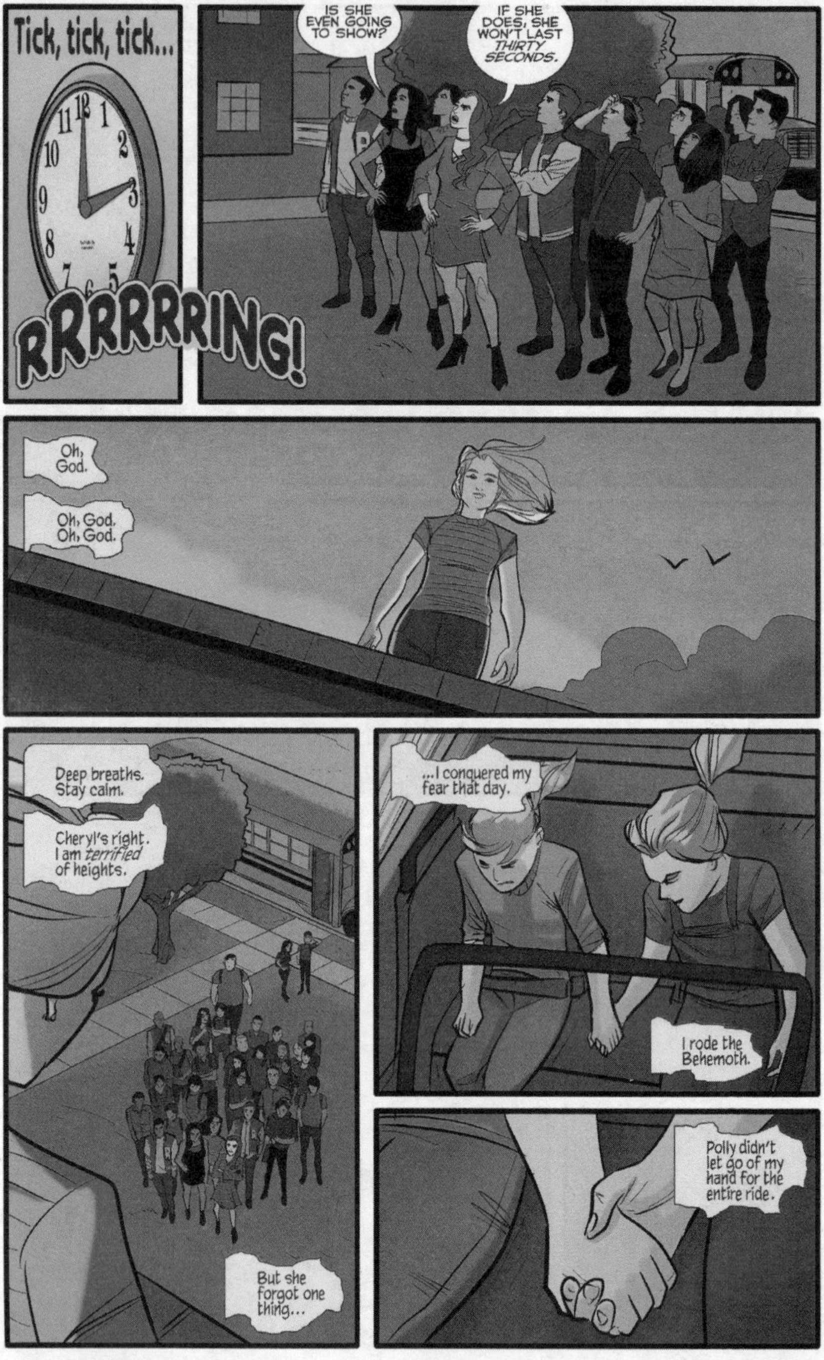
Tick, tick, tick...
RRRRRRING!
IS SHE EVEN GOING TO SHOW?
IF SHE DOES, SHE WON'T LAST THIRTY SECONDS.
Oh, God.
Oh, God. Oh, God.
Deep breaths. Stay calm.
Cheryl's right. I am terrified of heights.
But she forgot one thing...
...I conquered my fear that day.
I rode the Behemoth.
Polly didn't let go of my hand for the entire ride.

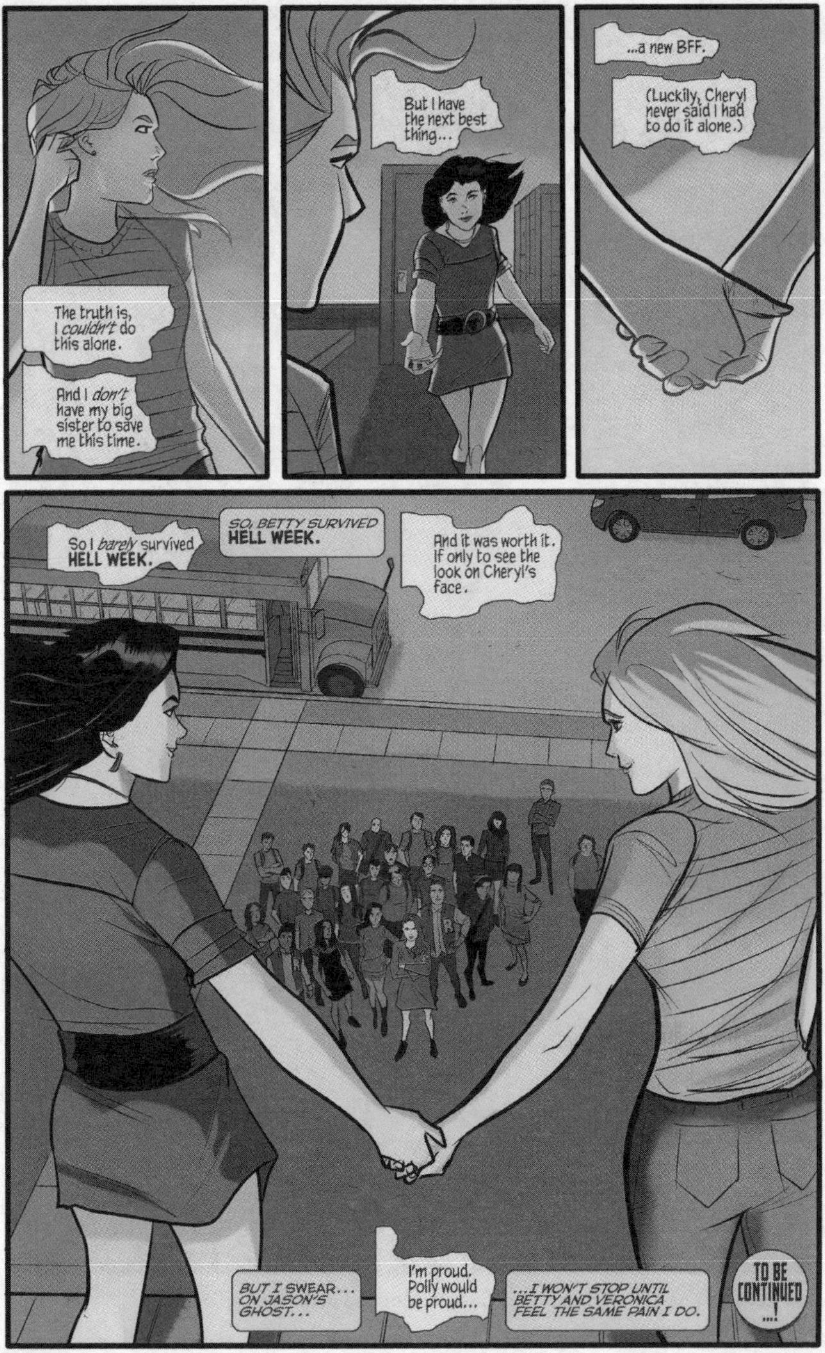
The truth is, I *couldn't* do this alone.
And I *don't* have my big sister to save me this time.
But I have the next best thing...
...a new BFF.
(Luckily, Cheryl never said I had to do it alone.)
So I *barely* survived **HELL WEEK.**
SO, BETTY SURVIVED **HELL WEEK.**
And it was worth it. If only to see the look on Cheryl's face.
BUT I SWEAR... ON JASON'S GHOST...
I'm proud. Polly would be proud...
...I WON'T STOP UNTIL BETTY AND VERONICA FEEL THE SAME PAIN I DO.
TO BE CONTINUED...!

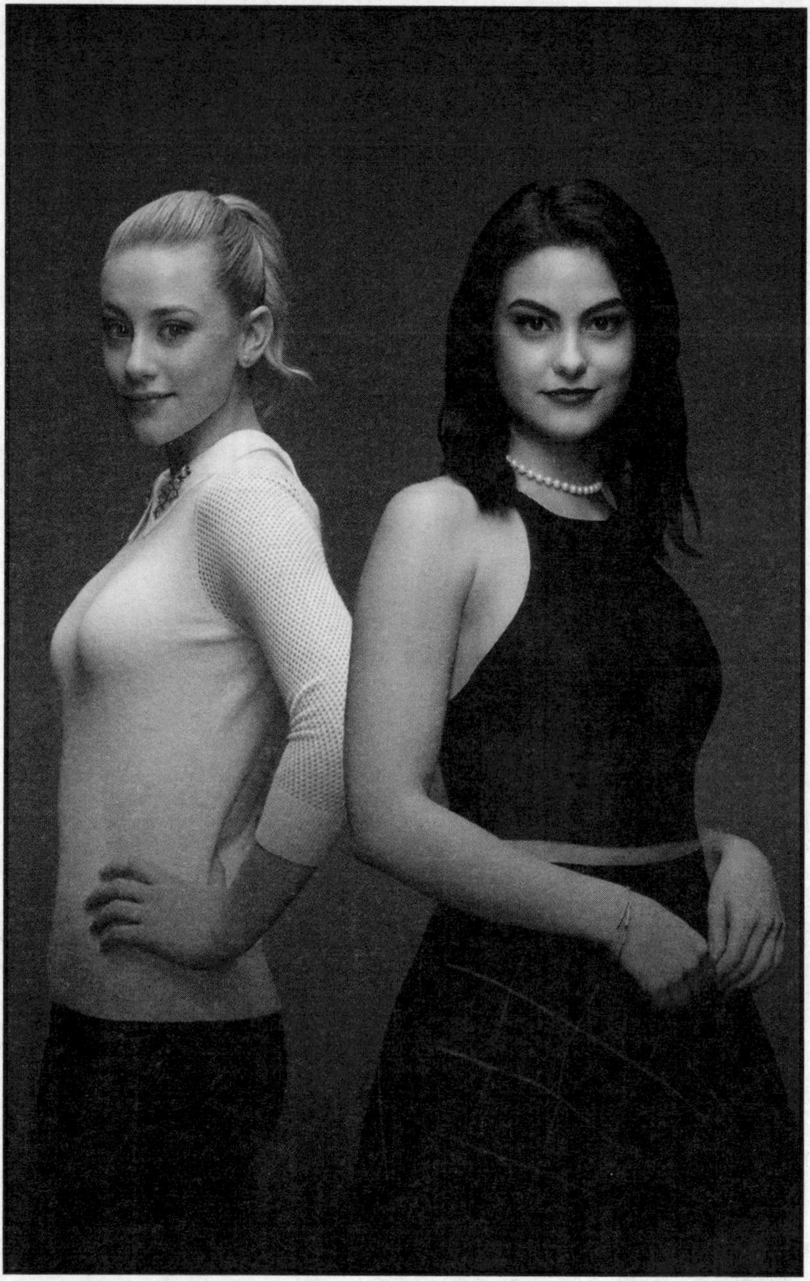

Lili Reinhart as Betty Cooper and **Camila Mendes** as Veronica Lodge on The CW's *Riverdale*.

BETTY & VERONICA: VIXENS #1 COVER
BETTY & VERONICA: VIXENS #1, 2017
Eva Cabrera

BETTY & VERONICA: VIXENS #1
BETTY & VERONICA: VIXENS #1, 2017
Jamie Lee Rotante, Eva Cabrera, Elaina Unger, Rachel Deering

Betty and Veronica were two of my earliest influences in terms of creativity—I loved every story featuring them and imagined them as my own two best friends. The possibilities for the characters were endless. I especially loved the stories where Archie was out of the picture and the two girls worked together in harmony. But never, ever in a million years did I imagine that one day would I not only be working at the publisher who created two of my favorite fictional female characters, but that I'd actually be writing them. And, just as it was when I was a kid, my favorite stories are always about Betty and Veronica—sorry, Archie!

- JAMIE LEE ROTANTE *Writer/Editor, Archie Comics*

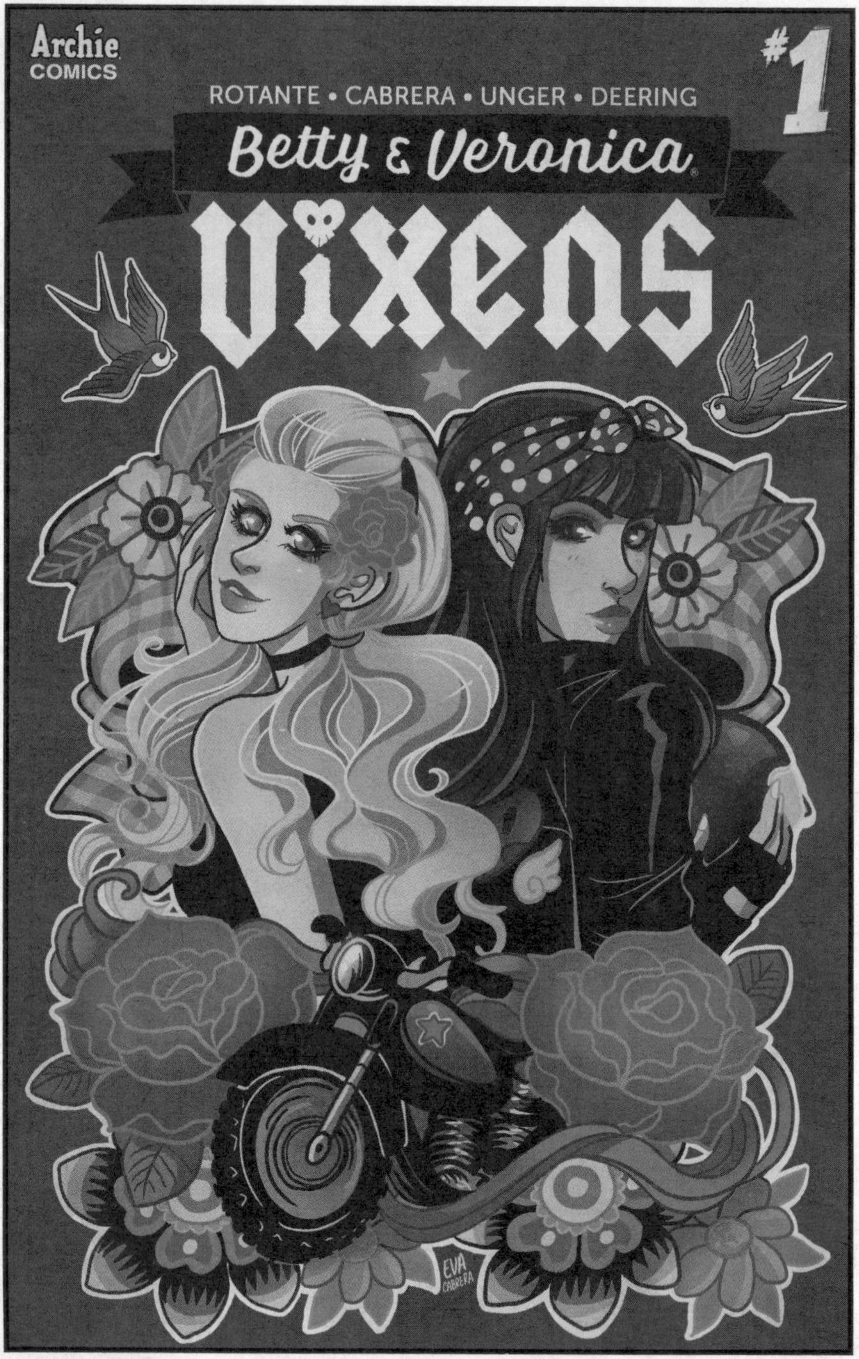
Archie COMICS
#1
ROTANTE • CABRERA • UNGER • DEERING
Betty & Veronica
VIXENS
EVA CABRERA

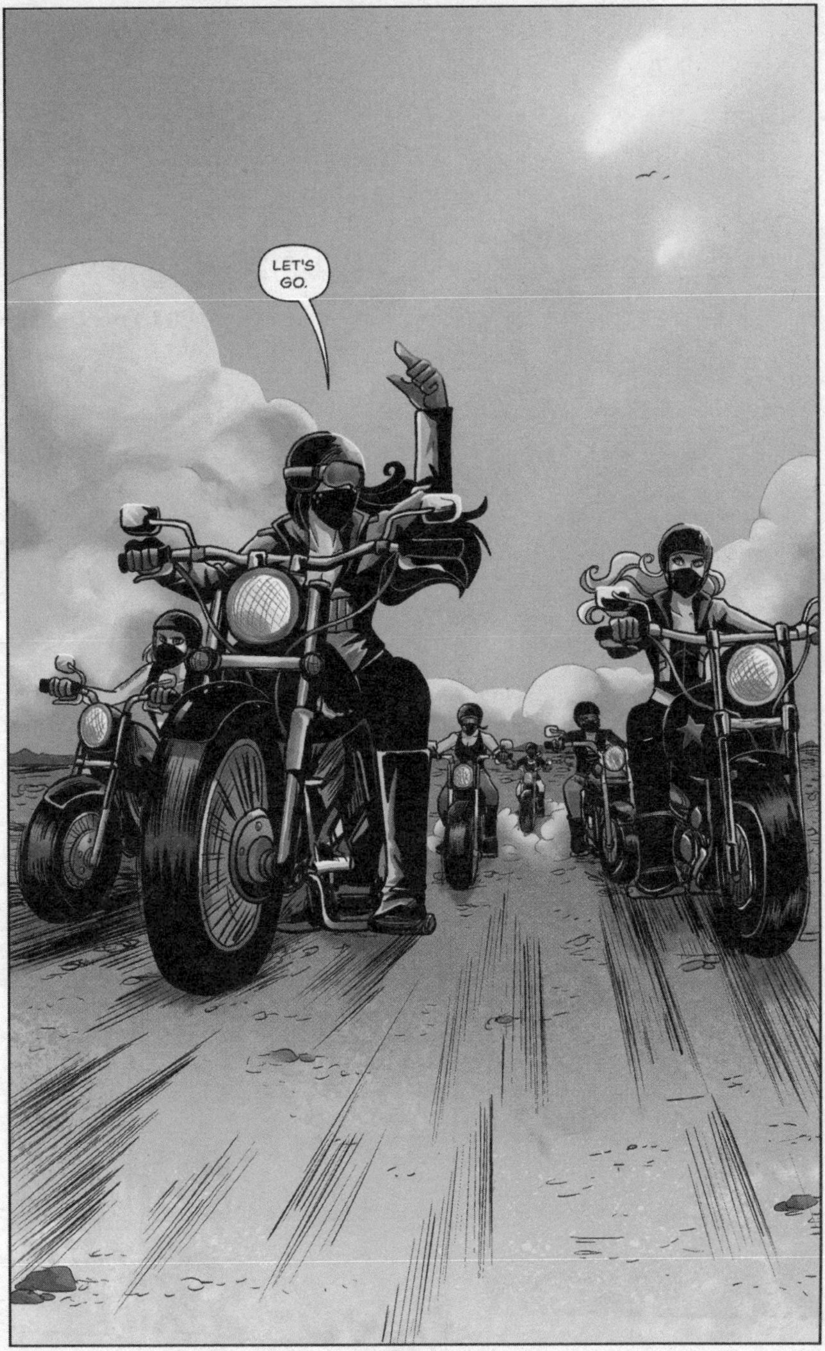
LET'S GO.

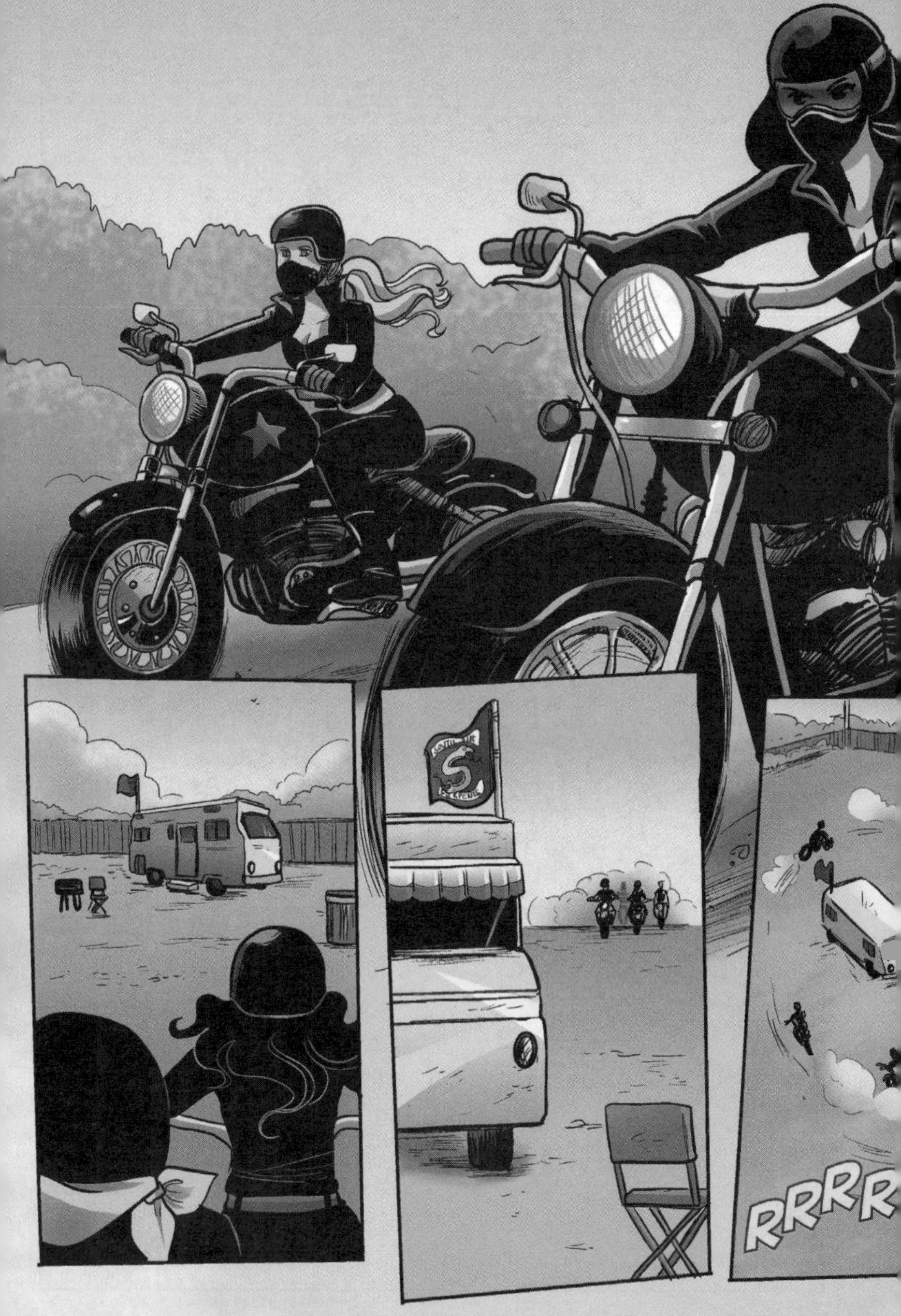
RRRR

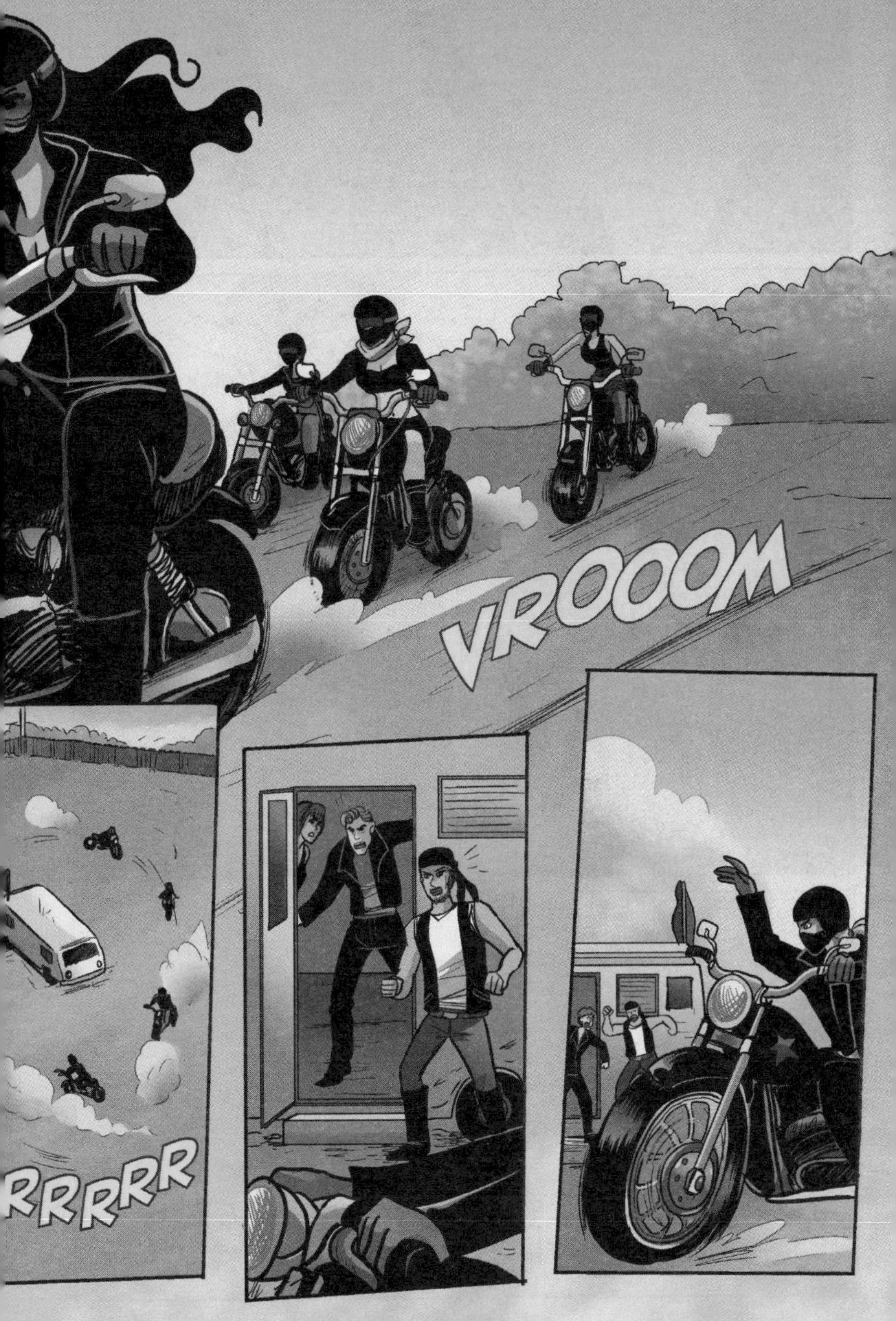
VROOOM
RRRRR

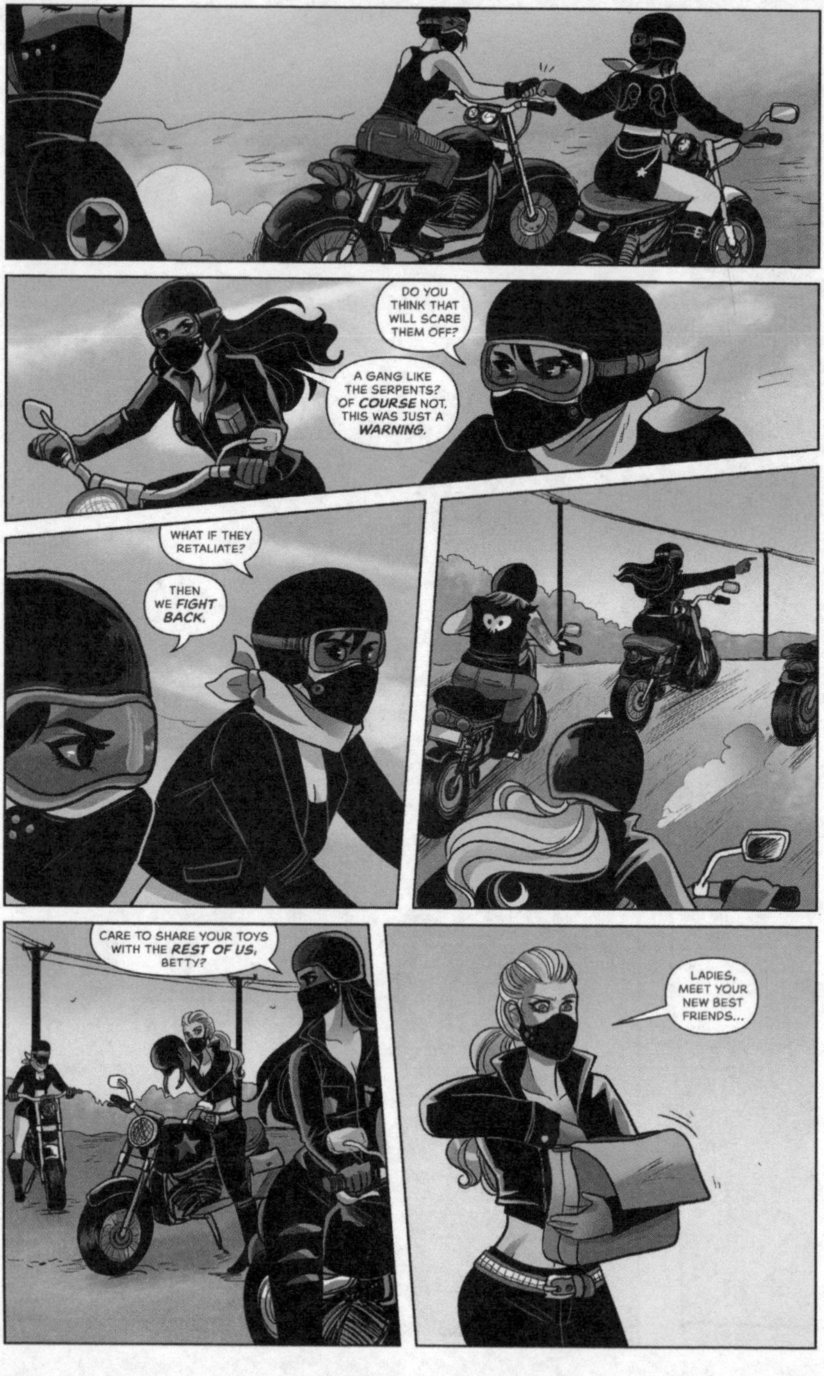
DO YOU THINK THAT WILL SCARE THEM OFF?
A GANG LIKE THE SERPENTS? OF COURSE NOT. THIS WAS JUST A WARNING.
WHAT IF THEY RETALIATE?
THEN WE FIGHT BACK.
CARE TO SHARE YOUR TOYS WITH THE REST OF US, BETTY?
LADIES, MEET YOUR NEW BEST FRIENDS...

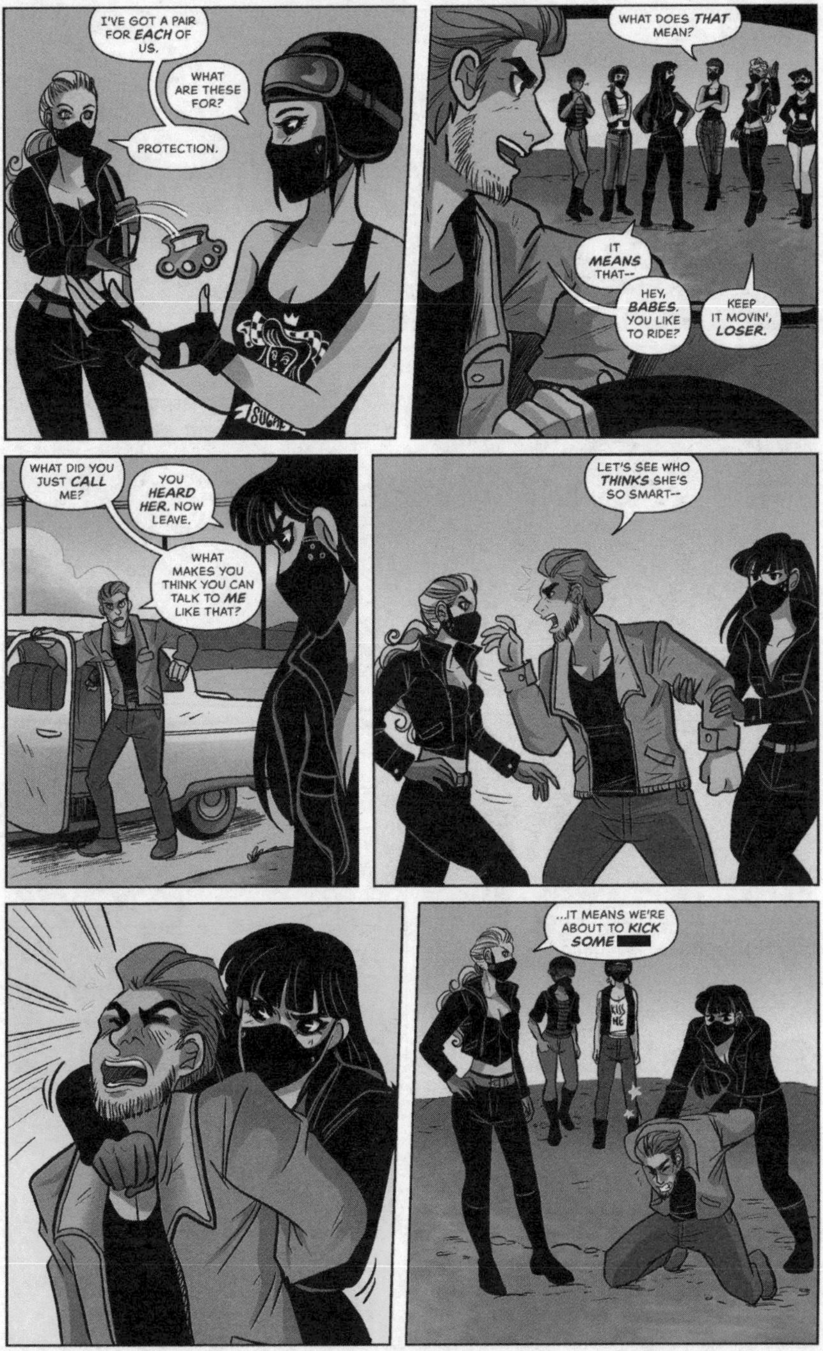
I'VE GOT A PAIR FOR EACH OF US.
WHAT ARE THESE FOR?
PROTECTION.
WHAT DOES THAT MEAN?
IT MEANS THAT--
HEY, BABES. YOU LIKE TO RIDE?
KEEP IT MOVIN', LOSER.
WHAT DID YOU JUST CALL ME?
YOU HEARD HER. NOW LEAVE.
WHAT MAKES YOU THINK YOU CAN TALK TO ME LIKE THAT?
LET'S SEE WHO THINKS SHE'S SO SMART--
...IT MEANS WE'RE ABOUT TO KICK SOME [redacted]
KISS ME

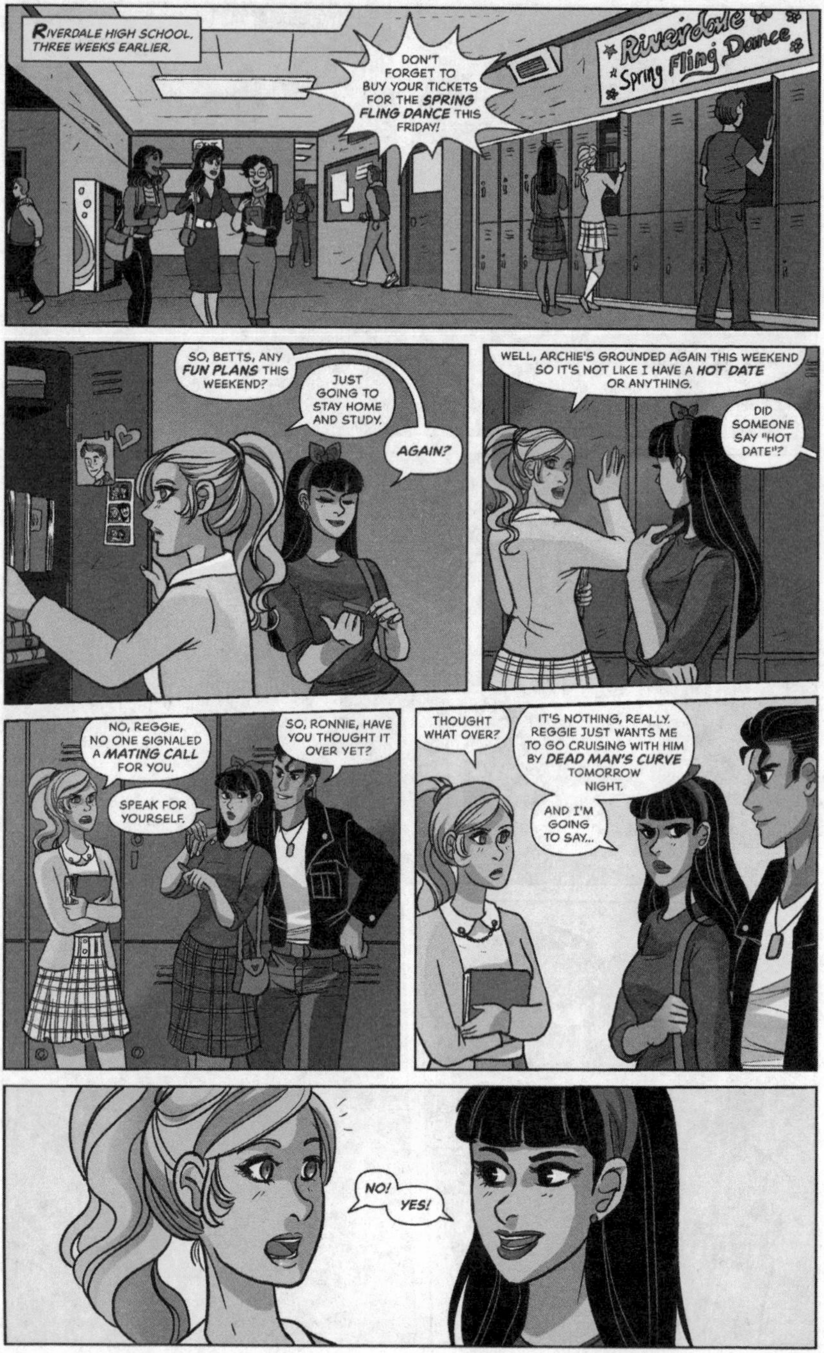

RIVERDALE HIGH SCHOOL. THREE WEEKS EARLIER.
DON'T FORGET TO BUY YOUR TICKETS FOR THE SPRING FLING DANCE THIS FRIDAY!
Riverdale Spring Fling Dance
SO, BETTS, ANY FUN PLANS THIS WEEKEND?
JUST GOING TO STAY HOME AND STUDY.
AGAIN?
WELL, ARCHIE'S GROUNDED AGAIN THIS WEEKEND SO IT'S NOT LIKE I HAVE A HOT DATE OR ANYTHING.
DID SOMEONE SAY "HOT DATE"?
NO, REGGIE, NO ONE SIGNALED A MATING CALL FOR YOU.
SPEAK FOR YOURSELF.
SO, RONNIE, HAVE YOU THOUGHT IT OVER YET?
THOUGHT WHAT OVER?
IT'S NOTHING, REALLY. REGGIE JUST WANTS ME TO GO CRUISING WITH HIM BY DEAD MAN'S CURVE TOMORROW NIGHT.
AND I'M GOING TO SAY...
NO!
YES!

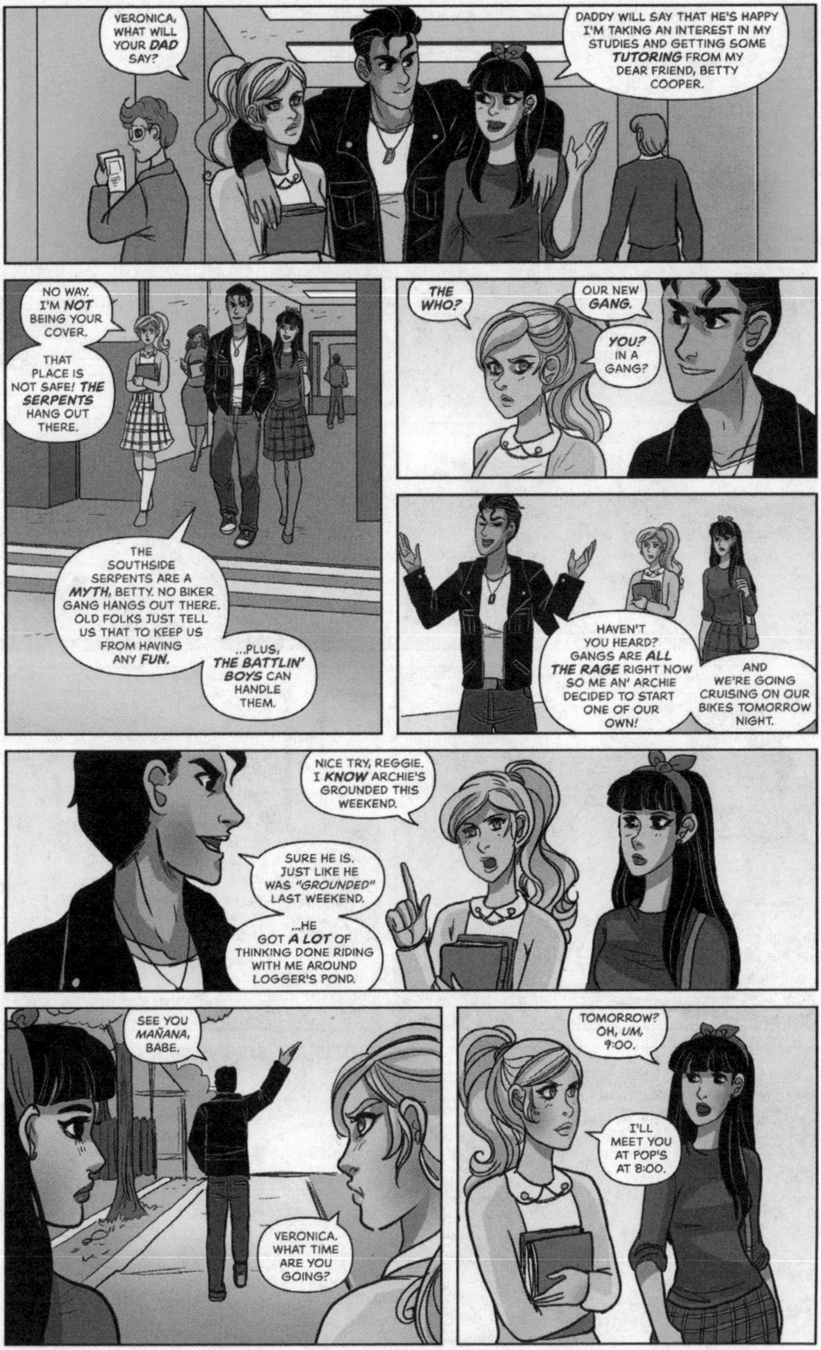
VERONICA, WHAT WILL YOUR **DAD** SAY?
DADDY WILL SAY THAT HE'S HAPPY I'M TAKING AN INTEREST IN MY STUDIES AND GETTING SOME **TUTORING** FROM MY DEAR FRIEND, BETTY COOPER.
NO WAY. I'M **NOT** BEING YOUR COVER.
THAT PLACE IS NOT SAFE! **THE SERPENTS** HANG OUT THERE.
THE SOUTHSIDE SERPENTS ARE A **MYTH**, BETTY. NO BIKER GANG HANGS OUT THERE. OLD FOLKS JUST TELL US THAT TO KEEP US FROM HAVING ANY **FUN**.
...PLUS, **THE BATTLIN' BOYS** CAN HANDLE THEM.
THE WHO?
OUR NEW **GANG**.
YOU? IN A GANG?
HAVEN'T YOU HEARD? GANGS ARE **ALL THE RAGE** RIGHT NOW SO ME AN' ARCHIE DECIDED TO START ONE OF OUR OWN!
AND WE'RE GOING CRUISING ON OUR BIKES TOMORROW NIGHT.
NICE TRY, REGGIE. I **KNOW** ARCHIE'S GROUNDED THIS WEEKEND.
SURE HE IS. JUST LIKE HE WAS *"GROUNDED"* LAST WEEKEND.
...HE GOT **A LOT** OF THINKING DONE RIDING WITH ME AROUND LOGGER'S POND.
SEE YOU *MAÑANA*, BABE.
VERONICA. WHAT TIME ARE YOU GOING?
TOMORROW? OH, *UM*, 9:00.
I'LL MEET YOU AT POP'S AT 8:00.

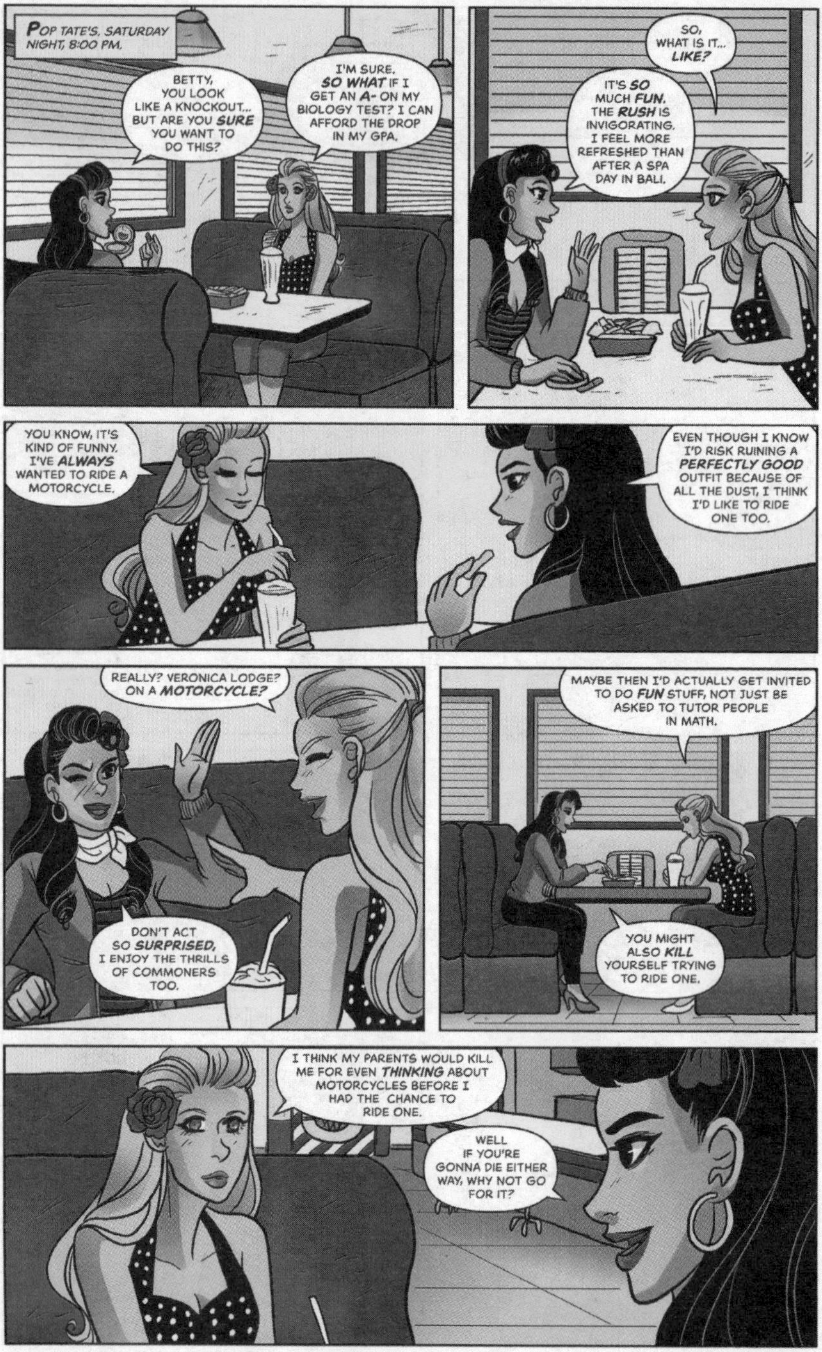
POP TATE'S, SATURDAY NIGHT, 8:00 PM.
BETTY, YOU LOOK LIKE A KNOCKOUT... BUT ARE YOU SURE YOU WANT TO DO THIS?
I'M SURE. SO WHAT IF I GET AN A- ON MY BIOLOGY TEST? I CAN AFFORD THE DROP IN MY GPA.
SO, WHAT IS IT... LIKE?
IT'S SO MUCH FUN. THE RUSH IS INVIGORATING. I FEEL MORE REFRESHED THAN AFTER A SPA DAY IN BALI.
YOU KNOW, IT'S KIND OF FUNNY. I'VE ALWAYS WANTED TO RIDE A MOTORCYCLE.
EVEN THOUGH I KNOW I'D RISK RUINING A PERFECTLY GOOD OUTFIT BECAUSE OF ALL THE DUST, I THINK I'D LIKE TO RIDE ONE TOO.
REALLY? VERONICA LODGE? ON A MOTORCYCLE?
DON'T ACT SO SURPRISED, I ENJOY THE THRILLS OF COMMONERS TOO.
MAYBE THEN I'D ACTUALLY GET INVITED TO DO FUN STUFF, NOT JUST BE ASKED TO TUTOR PEOPLE IN MATH.
YOU MIGHT ALSO KILL YOURSELF TRYING TO RIDE ONE.
I THINK MY PARENTS WOULD KILL ME FOR EVEN THINKING ABOUT MOTORCYCLES BEFORE I HAD THE CHANCE TO RIDE ONE.
WELL IF YOU'RE GONNA DIE EITHER WAY, WHY NOT GO FOR IT?

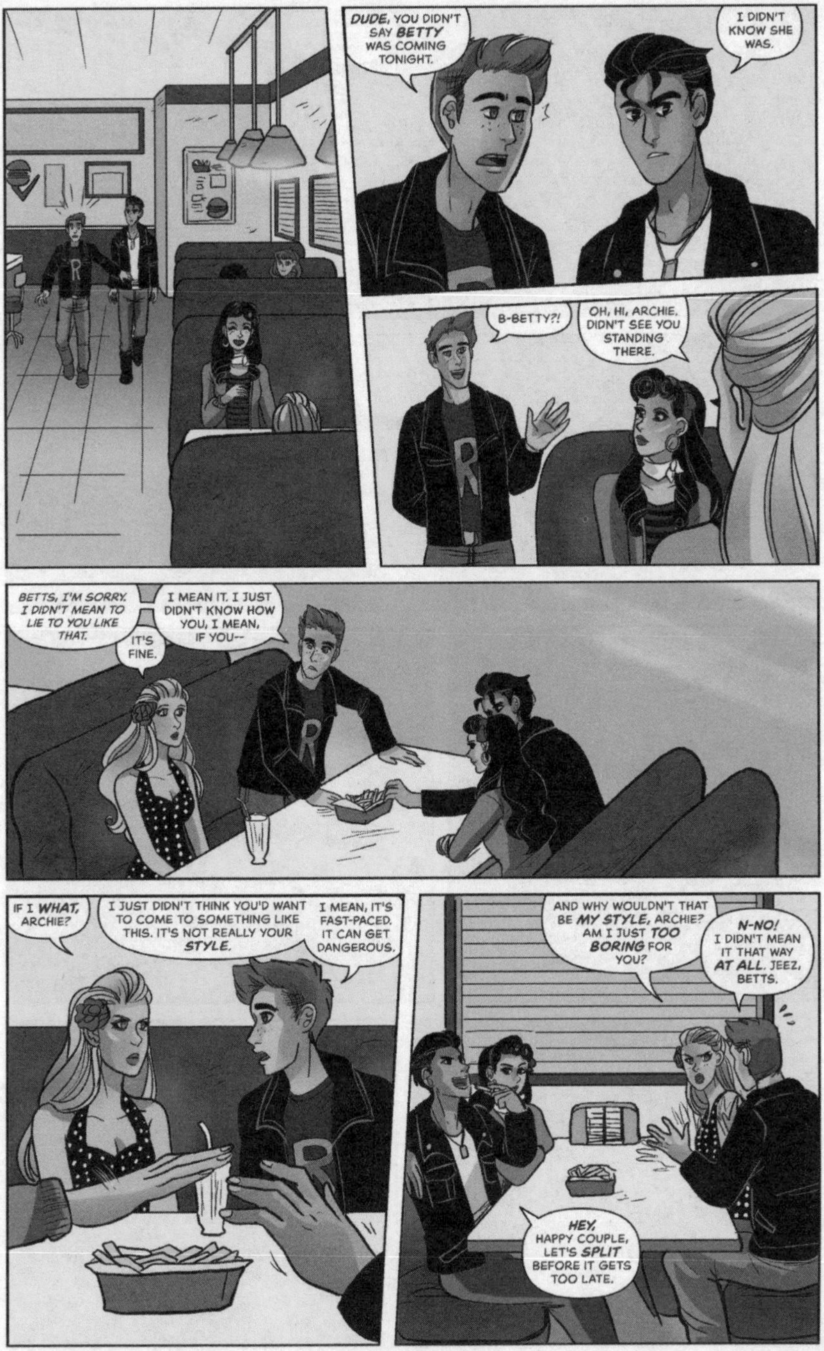
DUDE, YOU DIDN'T SAY BETTY WAS COMING TONIGHT.
I DIDN'T KNOW SHE WAS.
B-BETTY?!
OH, HI, ARCHIE. DIDN'T SEE YOU STANDING THERE.
BETTS, I'M SORRY. I DIDN'T MEAN TO LIE TO YOU LIKE THAT.
IT'S FINE.
I MEAN IT. I JUST DIDN'T KNOW HOW YOU, I MEAN, IF YOU--
IF I WHAT, ARCHIE?
I JUST DIDN'T THINK YOU'D WANT TO COME TO SOMETHING LIKE THIS. IT'S NOT REALLY YOUR STYLE.
I MEAN, IT'S FAST-PACED. IT CAN GET DANGEROUS.
AND WHY WOULDN'T THAT BE MY STYLE, ARCHIE? AM I JUST TOO BORING FOR YOU?
N-NO! I DIDN'T MEAN IT THAT WAY AT ALL. JEEZ, BETTS.
HEY, HAPPY COUPLE, LET'S SPLIT BEFORE IT GETS TOO LATE.

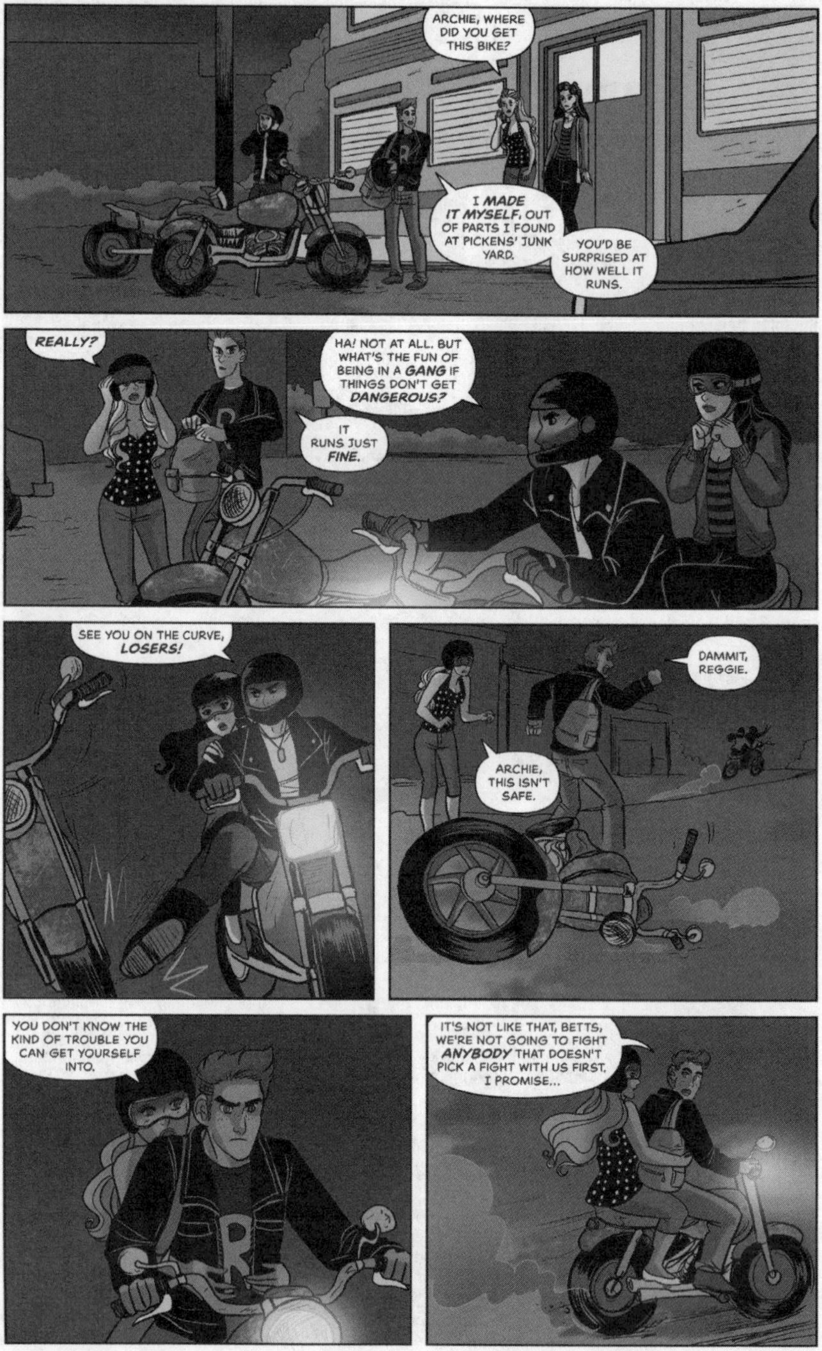
ARCHIE, WHERE DID YOU GET THIS BIKE?
I MADE IT MYSELF, OUT OF PARTS I FOUND AT PICKENS' JUNK YARD.
YOU'D BE SURPRISED AT HOW WELL IT RUNS.
REALLY?
HA! NOT AT ALL. BUT WHAT'S THE FUN OF BEING IN A GANG IF THINGS DON'T GET DANGEROUS?
IT RUNS JUST FINE.
SEE YOU ON THE CURVE, LOSERS!
DAMMIT, REGGIE.
ARCHIE, THIS ISN'T SAFE.
YOU DON'T KNOW THE KIND OF TROUBLE YOU CAN GET YOURSELF INTO.
IT'S NOT LIKE THAT, BETTS, WE'RE NOT GOING TO FIGHT ANYBODY THAT DOESN'T PICK A FIGHT WITH US FIRST. I PROMISE...

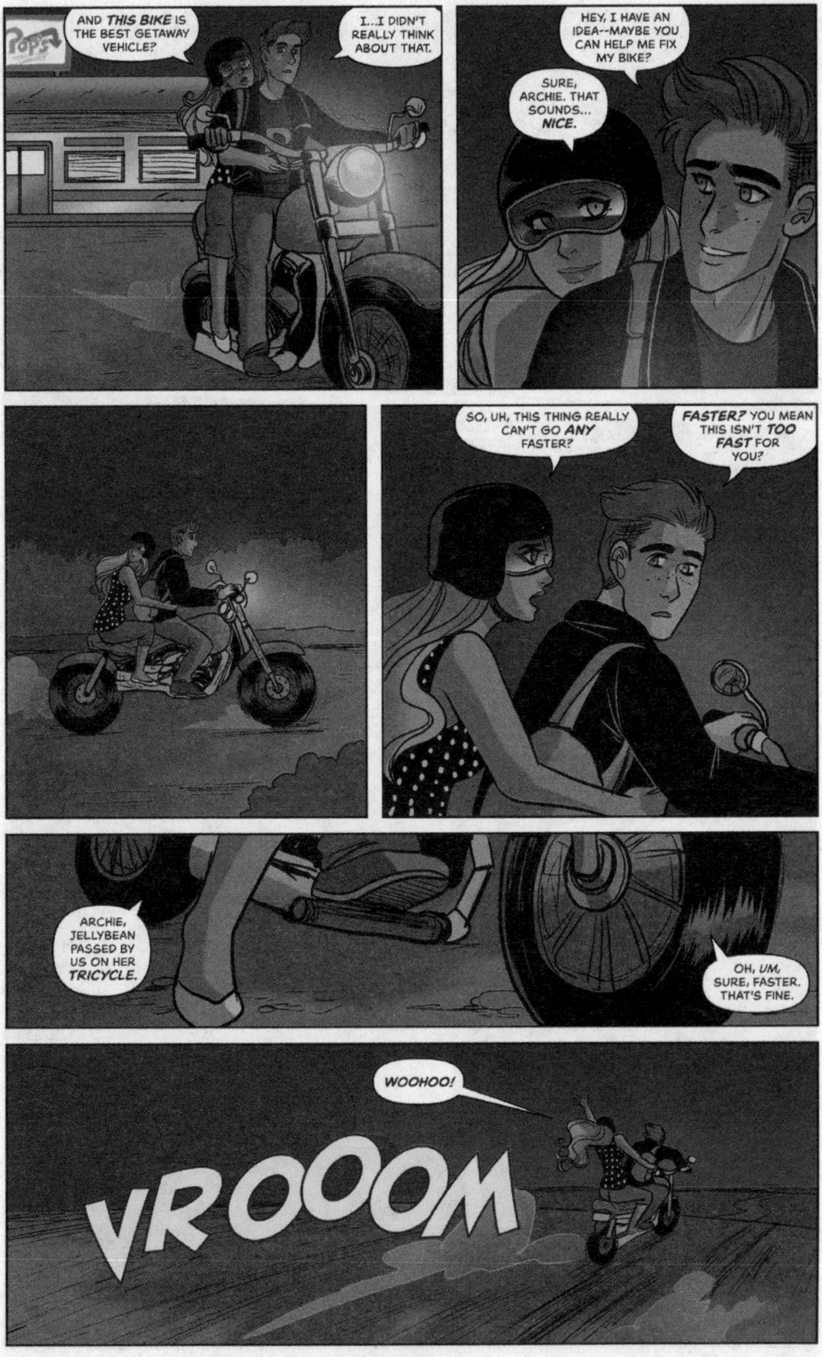
AND THIS BIKE IS THE BEST GETAWAY VEHICLE?
I...I DIDN'T REALLY THINK ABOUT THAT.
POP'S
HEY, I HAVE AN IDEA--MAYBE YOU CAN HELP ME FIX MY BIKE?
SURE, ARCHIE. THAT SOUNDS... NICE.
SO, UH, THIS THING REALLY CAN'T GO ANY FASTER?
FASTER? YOU MEAN THIS ISN'T TOO FAST FOR YOU?
ARCHIE, JELLYBEAN PASSED BY US ON HER TRICYCLE.
OH, UM, SURE, FASTER. THAT'S FINE.
WOOHOO!
VROOOM

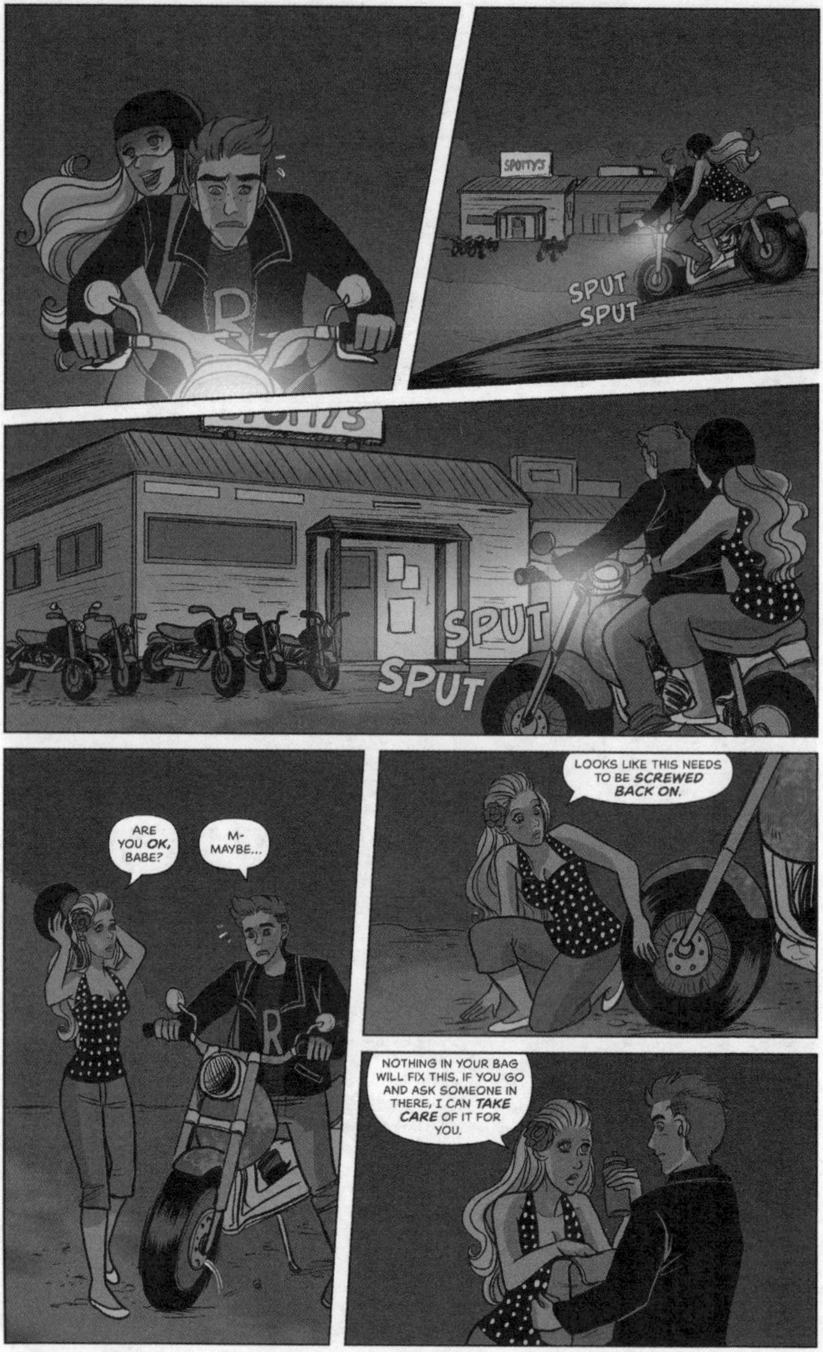
SPOTTY'S
SPUT
SPUT
SPUT
SPUT
ARE YOU OK, BABE?
M- MAYBE...
LOOKS LIKE THIS NEEDS TO BE SCREWED BACK ON.
NOTHING IN YOUR BAG WILL FIX THIS. IF YOU GO AND ASK SOMEONE IN THERE, I CAN TAKE CARE OF IT FOR YOU.

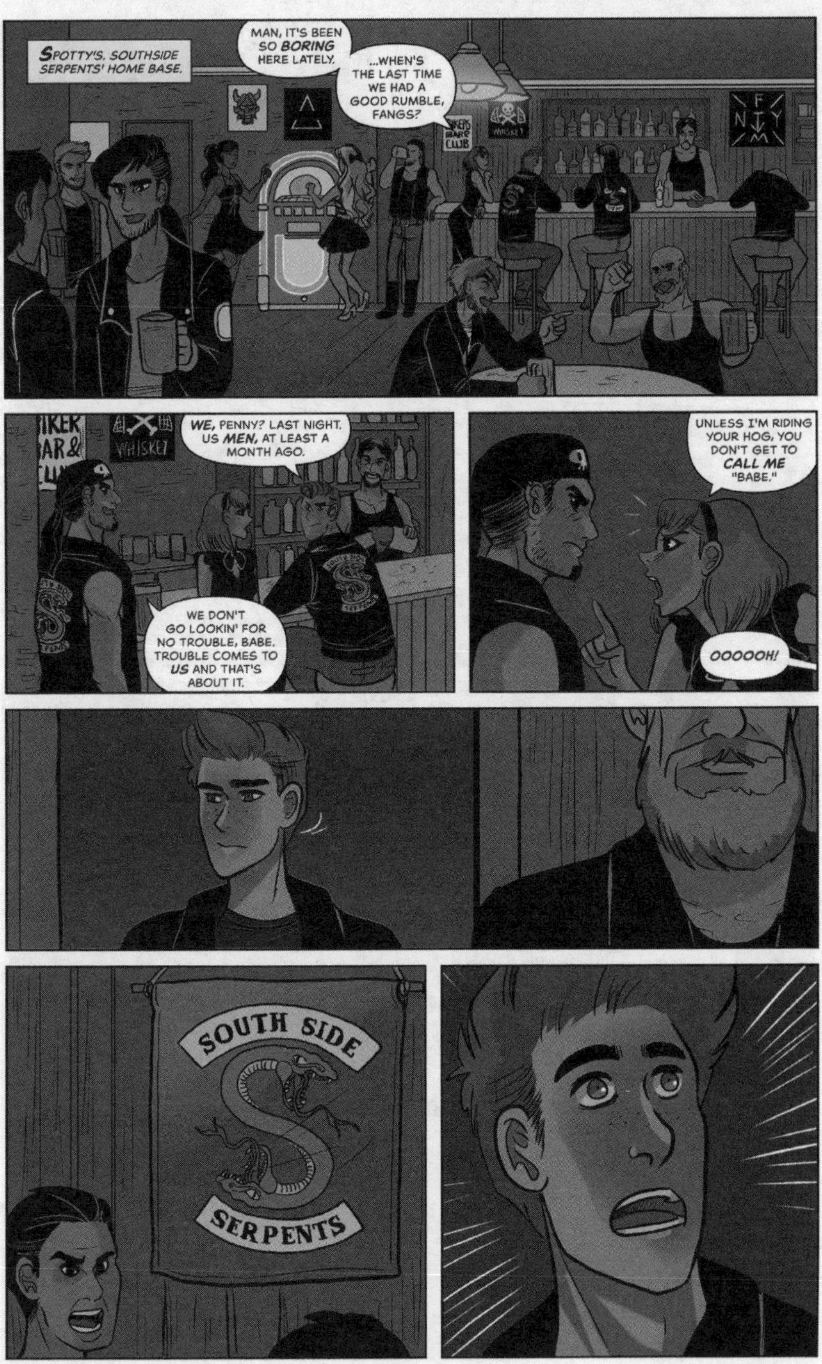
SPOTTY'S, SOUTHSIDE SERPENTS' HOME BASE.
MAN, IT'S BEEN SO BORING HERE LATELY.
...WHEN'S THE LAST TIME WE HAD A GOOD RUMBLE, FANGS?
WE, PENNY? LAST NIGHT. US MEN, AT LEAST A MONTH AGO.
WE DON'T GO LOOKIN' FOR NO TROUBLE, BABE. TROUBLE COMES TO US AND THAT'S ABOUT IT.
UNLESS I'M RIDING YOUR HOG, YOU DON'T GET TO CALL ME "BABE."
OOOOOH!
SOUTH SIDE
SERPENTS

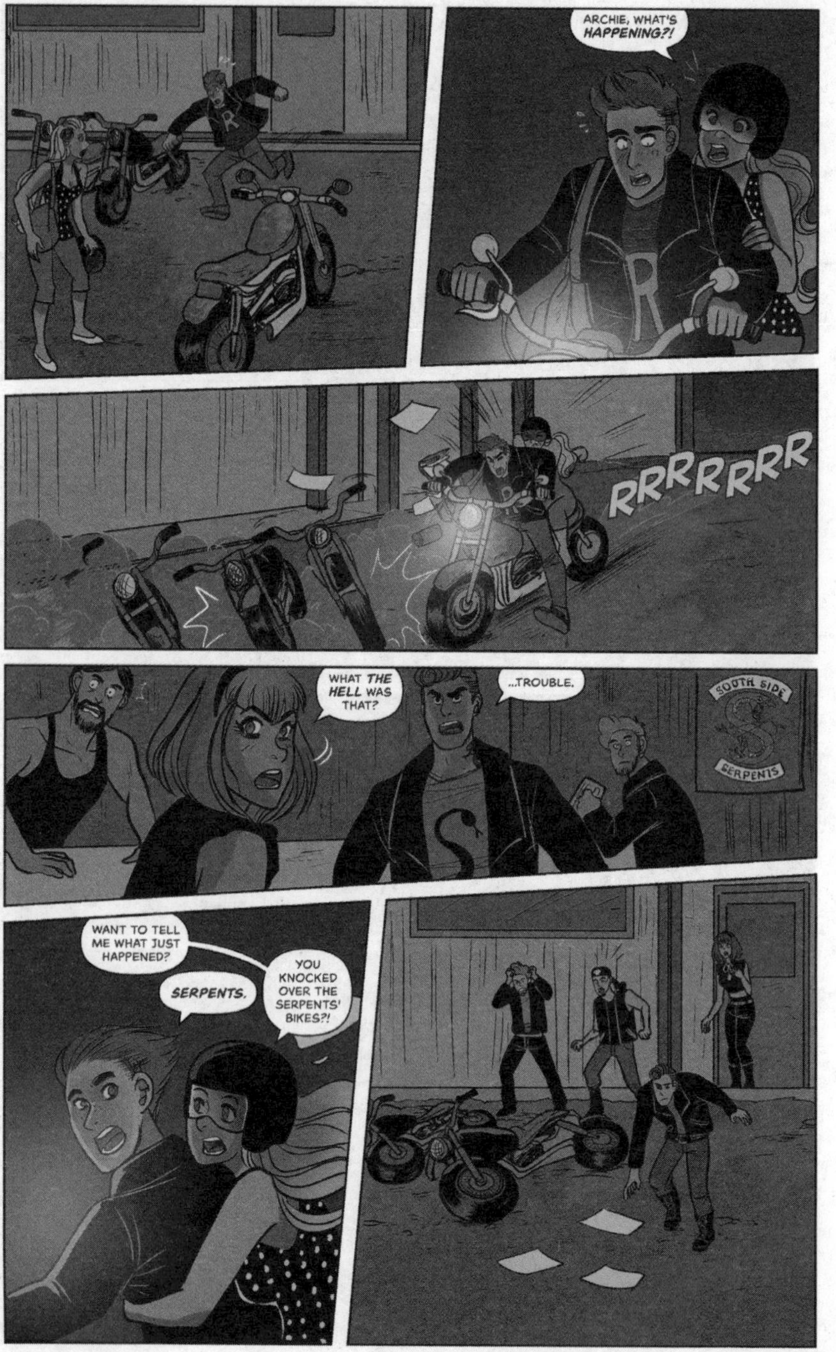

ARCHIE, WHAT'S HAPPENING?!
RRRRRRR
WHAT THE HELL WAS THAT?
...TROUBLE.
SOUTH SIDE
SERPENTS
WANT TO TELL ME WHAT JUST HAPPENED?
SERPENTS.
YOU KNOCKED OVER THE SERPENTS' BIKES?!

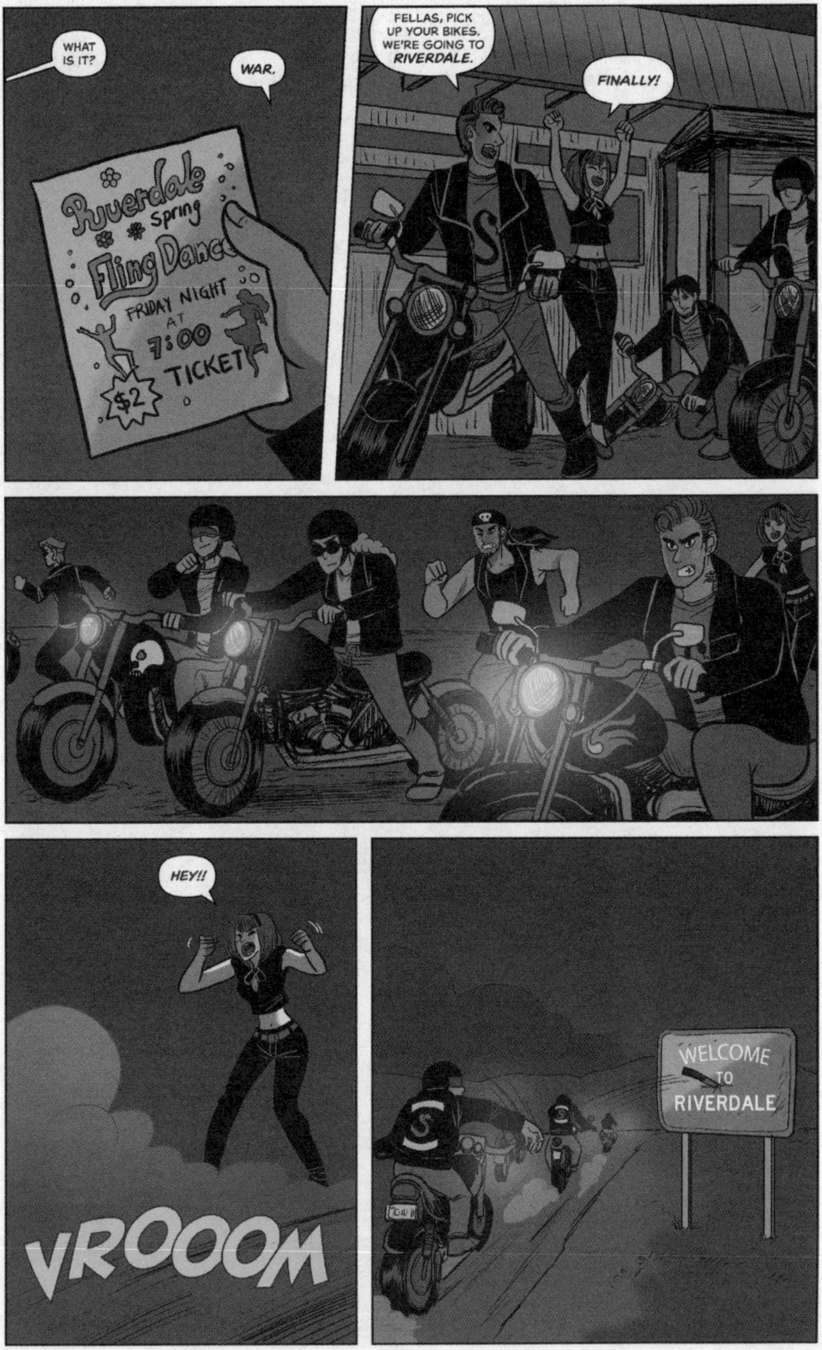
WHAT IS IT?
WAR.
Riverdale Spring Fling Dance
FRIDAY NIGHT AT 7:00
$2 TICKET
FELLAS, PICK UP YOUR BIKES. WE'RE GOING TO RIVERDALE.
FINALLY!
HEY!!
VROOOM
WELCOME TO RIVERDALE

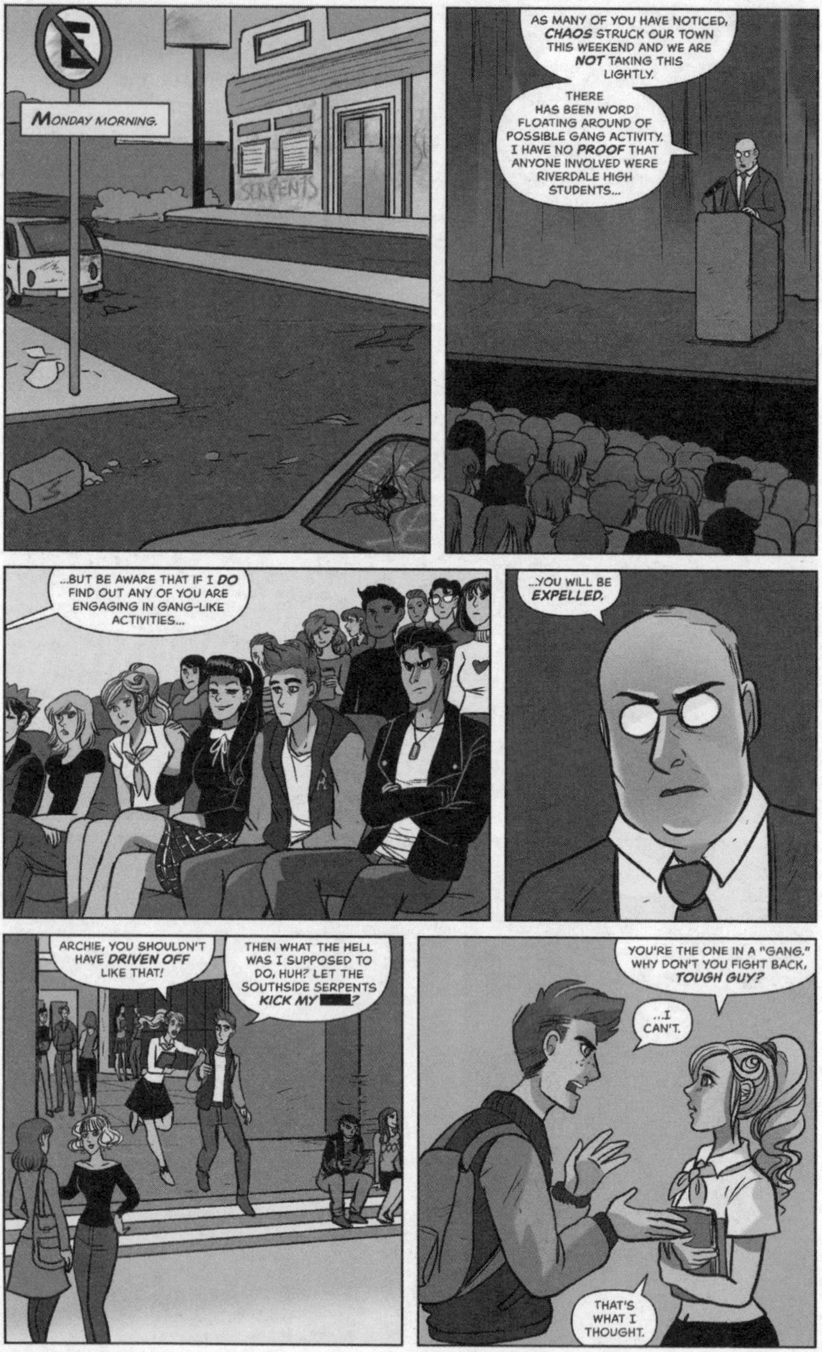
MONDAY MORNING.
SERPENTS
AS MANY OF YOU HAVE NOTICED, CHAOS STRUCK OUR TOWN THIS WEEKEND AND WE ARE NOT TAKING THIS LIGHTLY.
THERE HAS BEEN WORD FLOATING AROUND OF POSSIBLE GANG ACTIVITY. I HAVE NO PROOF THAT ANYONE INVOLVED WERE RIVERDALE HIGH STUDENTS...
...BUT BE AWARE THAT IF I DO FIND OUT ANY OF YOU ARE ENGAGING IN GANG-LIKE ACTIVITIES...
...YOU WILL BE EXPELLED.
ARCHIE, YOU SHOULDN'T HAVE DRIVEN OFF LIKE THAT!
THEN WHAT THE HELL WAS I SUPPOSED TO DO, HUH? LET THE SOUTHSIDE SERPENTS KICK MY [redacted]?
YOU'RE THE ONE IN A "GANG." WHY DON'T YOU FIGHT BACK, TOUGH GUY?
...I CAN'T.
THAT'S WHAT I THOUGHT.

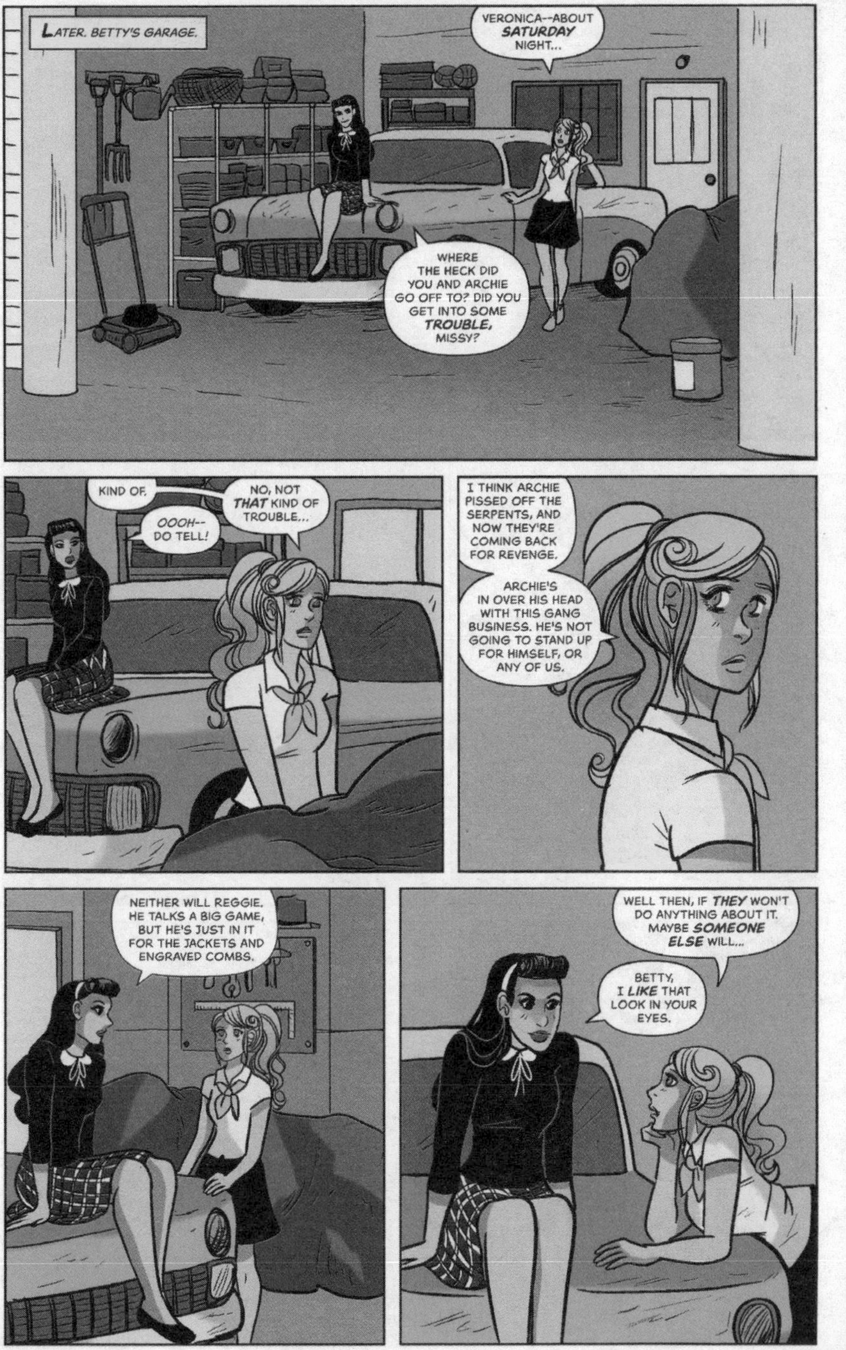
LATER. BETTY'S GARAGE.
VERONICA--ABOUT SATURDAY NIGHT...
WHERE THE HECK DID YOU AND ARCHIE GO OFF TO? DID YOU GET INTO SOME TROUBLE, MISSY?
KIND OF.
OOOH-- DO TELL!
NO, NOT THAT KIND OF TROUBLE...
I THINK ARCHIE PISSED OFF THE SERPENTS, AND NOW THEY'RE COMING BACK FOR REVENGE.
ARCHIE'S IN OVER HIS HEAD WITH THIS GANG BUSINESS. HE'S NOT GOING TO STAND UP FOR HIMSELF, OR ANY OF US.
NEITHER WILL REGGIE. HE TALKS A BIG GAME, BUT HE'S JUST IN IT FOR THE JACKETS AND ENGRAVED COMBS.
WELL THEN, IF THEY WON'T DO ANYTHING ABOUT IT, MAYBE SOMEONE ELSE WILL...
BETTY, I LIKE THAT LOOK IN YOUR EYES.

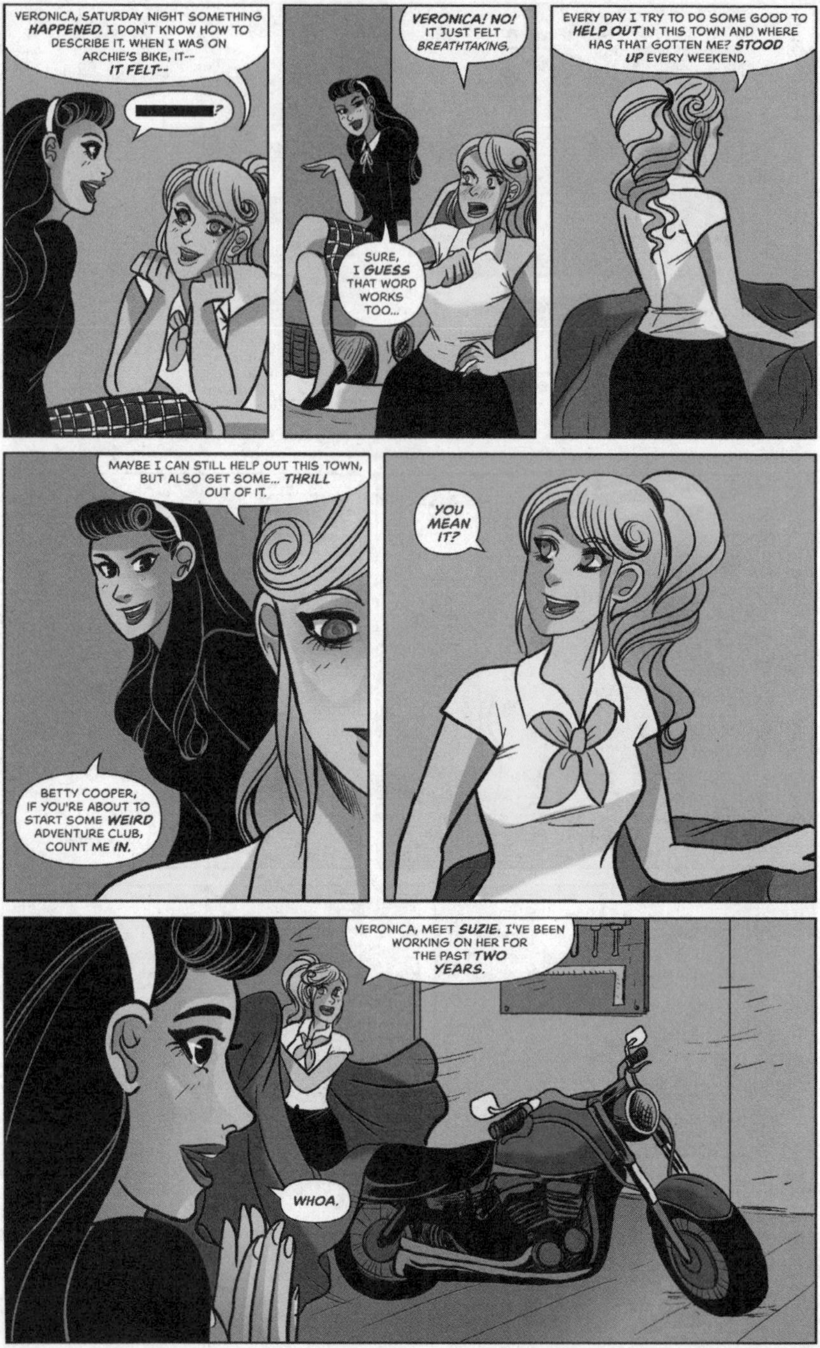
VERONICA, SATURDAY NIGHT SOMETHING HAPPENED. I DON'T KNOW HOW TO DESCRIBE IT. WHEN I WAS ON ARCHIE'S BIKE, IT-- IT FELT--
[redacted]?
VERONICA! NO! IT JUST FELT BREATHTAKING.
SURE, I GUESS THAT WORD WORKS TOO...
EVERY DAY I TRY TO DO SOME GOOD TO HELP OUT IN THIS TOWN AND WHERE HAS THAT GOTTEN ME? STOOD UP EVERY WEEKEND.
MAYBE I CAN STILL HELP OUT THIS TOWN, BUT ALSO GET SOME... THRILL OUT OF IT.
BETTY COOPER, IF YOU'RE ABOUT TO START SOME WEIRD ADVENTURE CLUB, COUNT ME IN.
YOU MEAN IT?
VERONICA, MEET SUZIE. I'VE BEEN WORKING ON HER FOR THE PAST TWO YEARS.
WHOA.

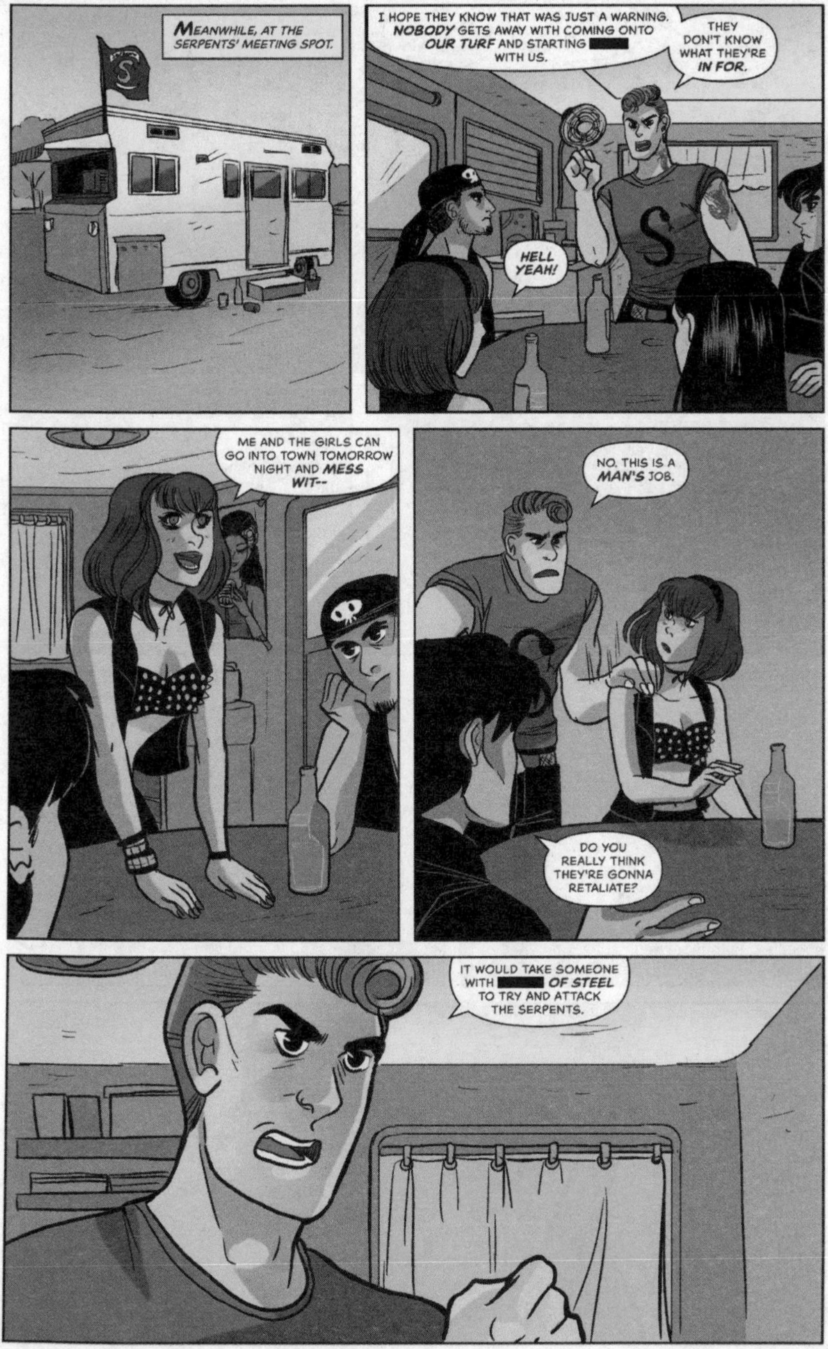
MEANWHILE, AT THE SERPENTS' MEETING SPOT.
I HOPE THEY KNOW THAT WAS JUST A WARNING. NOBODY GETS AWAY WITH COMING ONTO OUR TURF AND STARTING [redacted] WITH US.
THEY DON'T KNOW WHAT THEY'RE IN FOR.
HELL YEAH!
ME AND THE GIRLS CAN GO INTO TOWN TOMORROW NIGHT AND MESS WIT--
NO, THIS IS A MAN'S JOB.
DO YOU REALLY THINK THEY'RE GONNA RETALIATE?
IT WOULD TAKE SOMEONE WITH [redacted] OF STEEL TO TRY AND ATTACK THE SERPENTS.

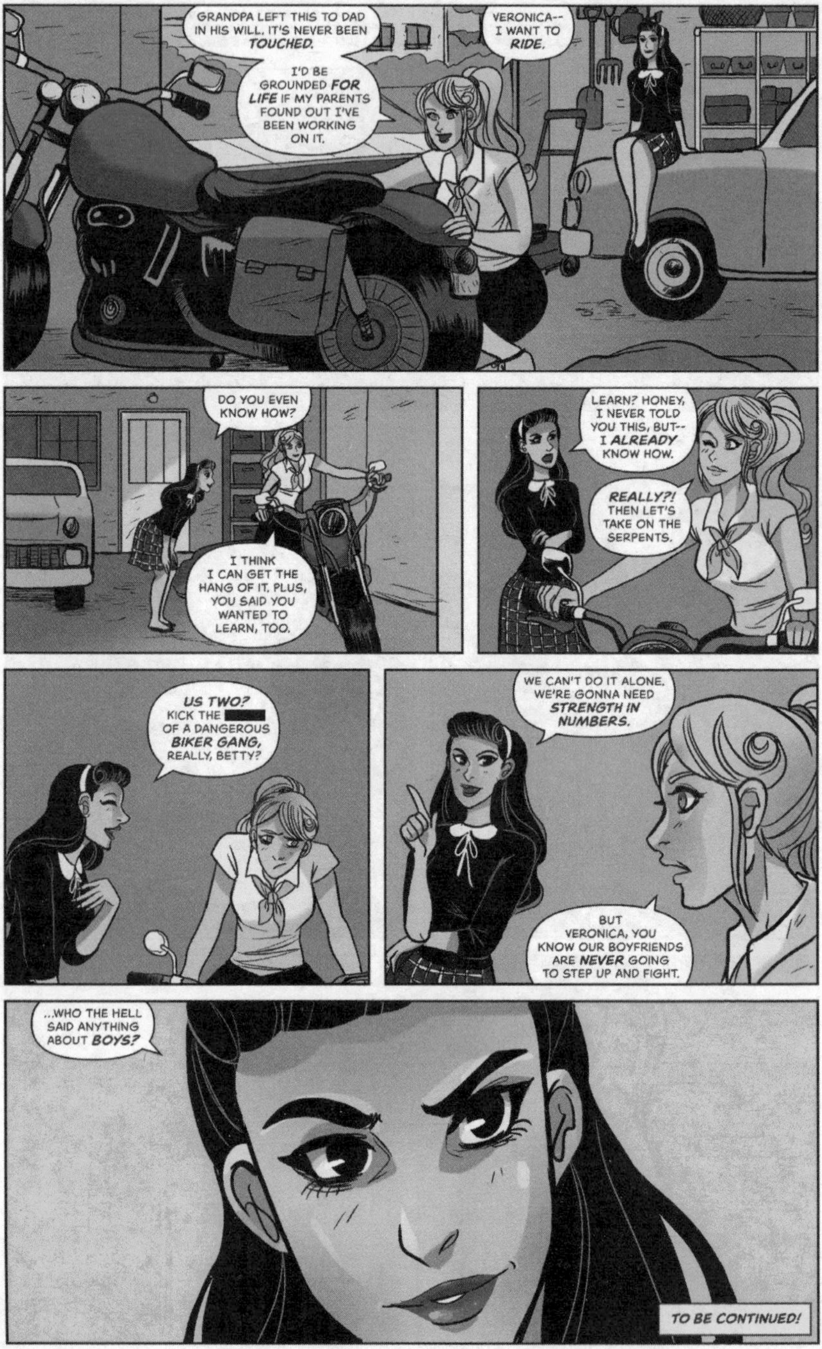
GRANDPA LEFT THIS TO DAD IN HIS WILL. IT'S NEVER BEEN TOUCHED.
I'D BE GROUNDED FOR LIFE IF MY PARENTS FOUND OUT I'VE BEEN WORKING ON IT.
VERONICA-- I WANT TO RIDE.
DO YOU EVEN KNOW HOW?
I THINK I CAN GET THE HANG OF IT. PLUS, YOU SAID YOU WANTED TO LEARN, TOO.
LEARN? HONEY, I NEVER TOLD YOU THIS, BUT-- I ALREADY KNOW HOW.
REALLY?! THEN LET'S TAKE ON THE SERPENTS.
US TWO? KICK THE [redacted] OF A DANGEROUS BIKER GANG, REALLY, BETTY?
WE CAN'T DO IT ALONE. WE'RE GONNA NEED STRENGTH IN NUMBERS.
BUT VERONICA, YOU KNOW OUR BOYFRIENDS ARE NEVER GOING TO STEP UP AND FIGHT.
...WHO THE HELL SAID ANYTHING ABOUT BOYS?
TO BE CONTINUED!